S0-BWV-692

Great Plains Publications
420 – 70 Arthur Street
Winnipeg, MB R3B 1G7
www.greatplains.mb.ca

Great Plains Publications gratefully acknowledges the financial support provided for its publishing program by the Government of Canada through the Book Publishing Industry Development Program (BPIDP); the Canada Council for the Arts; as well as the Manitoba Department of Culture, Heritage and Tourism; and the Manitoba Arts Council.

Design & Typography by Relish Design Studios Ltd.
Printed in Canada by Friesens

CANADIAN CATALOGUING IN PUBLICATION DATA

Main entry under title:
Silver, Alfred
A place out of time / Alf Silver
A novel.
ISBN 978-1-894283-74-8
I. Title

PS8587.127P53 2007 C813'.54 C2007-904013-6

A Place Out Of Time

Alfred Silver

PROLOGUE

On a bright summer day in 1896, a pair of swallows wheeled and darted above a crowd gathered in St. John's Anglican Cathedral Cemetery in the booming young city of Winnipeg, Manitoba, Dominion of Canada. The crowd had convened for the unveiling of the monument for a prominent citizen who'd recently deceased in Monterey, Mexico, where he had travelled in hopes of recovering his health.

On the back edge of the crowd stood Sheriff Colin Inkster. He'd rather have been fishing, or even catching up on his paperwork, but fifty years on the planet had taught him that if you're going to be paid out of the public purse you'd better show yourself at public functions. Especially if you'd been born halfbreed back before it was a dirty word. He was one of the few public functionaries who was of the Old Settlers, those who'd been living their lives at The Forks of the Red and Assiniboine Rivers for generations before the Coming of The Canadians. He could still remember the days when the latch-string was always on the outside of the door.

The monument ceremony today was a bit less uncomfortable for Colin Inkster than the great man's State Funeral in the spring. No hanging about unobtrusively at the back edge of the crowd then. As a public official, Sheriff Inkster had been expected to serve as an official pallbearer. Fortunately, that crowd had been much larger than today's, and all he'd really had to do was stand around and look solemn. And then, as today, most of the attention had been concentrated on the smallish, black-silked figure of the widow. At the moment, she was standing on a temporary platform and taking hold of a velvet cord hanging from the top of the drapery shrouding the monument. She pulled the cord and, through gravity and some artful slipknotting, the monument was unveiled.

It was quite impressive: a tall stone cross on a pedestal, with the wide Red River as a background. Below the cross was a stonecarved wreath of oak and maple leaves, and below the wreath a representation of a Lieutenant Governor's ceremonial headgear, sword and medals. Below the medals was a long inscription:

Sacred to the Memory of
Sir John C. Schultz K.C.M.G.

Sheriff Inkster's eyes travelled down to the second line of the inscription, then flicked back up again. There was something odd about the initials after the name, something missing. He would've thought 'M.D.' would be in there before the initials for one of the highest ranks of knighthood in the British Empire – after all, the departed was a Dr. before he was a Sir. Well, maybe all the other titles and accomplishments had crowded that out. Sheriff Inkster shrugged it off and carried on reading the words carved in stone:

Sir John C. Schultz K.C.M.G.
Jan. 1, 1840 - April 13, 1896
Lieut-Governor of Manitoba and Keewatin, 1888-95
Member of the Commons, 1871-82
And of the Senate, 1882-88
Banished for his Loyalty in the Rebellion of 1869-70
A Devoted Patriot, a Constant Friend, a Benefactor
Of the Indians, and an Ardent and Successful Worker
In the Best Interest of the Country – he was endeared
To all who knew him.

"Pity we *did* know him," popped out of Sheriff Inkster's mouth.

Something resembling a woman's laugh – more like an intake of breath – came from behind Sheriff Inkster. He hadn't thought there was anybody behind him, and he hadn't meant to mutter loud enough to be overheard, certainly not by Lady Schultz at the front of the crowd. In his time he'd dealt with mobs of drunken buffalo hunters, gangs of dangerously sober bank robbers, just about everything a frontier sheriff could expect to face. But he didn't fancy going toe-to-toe with Lady Schultz.

He turned to look behind him. Standing back as far as they could while still seeming part of the crowd, were the last two people he'd expected to see at the unveiling. But, there was undeniably the grey-crowned, deeply-etched face of Mrs. Janet Sutherland, and beside it the aged-cherub face of ex-Senator John Sutherland in its oval frame of white hair and beard.

Federal senators by nature didn't become ex, unless appointed to an even higher position, like Lieutenant Governor. People just didn't walk away from a position that guaranteed a handsome salary for life and highly elevated status. But John Sutherland had done just that. And Sheriff Inkster knew something else about John Sutherland that very few people knew – certainly no one had ever told Sir John Christian Schultz or Lady Schultz. Senator Schultz hadn't been the government's first choice for Lieutenant Governor of Manitoba; they'd offered it first to Senator John Sutherland. Senator Sutherland had respectfully declined.

The Sutherlands were of course standing arm-in-arm, with their off-hands clasped together over where their arms linked. Recently, someone had remarked to Sheriff Inkster how 'cute' and 'sweet' it was that the Sutherlands always had a hand on each other's shoulder, or sat close enough together that their knees were touching. He had refrained from telling that person there was nothing *cute* or *sweet* about it, and it wasn't a habit the Sutherlands had been in all their married life. Anyone who didn't know already would just twist the words of anyone who tried to explain it. And those who did know were just a trickle in the flood. Like when the Assiniboine River ran headlong into the wider Red, the Assiniboine was rolled under and drowned and what flowed on from The Forks was just the Red River.

Seeing the Sutherlands standing there threw Sheriff Colin Inkster back to a winter's morning twilight a quarter century before, out on that river so charmingly backgrounding the stone cross. There was blood on the snow, men running and yelling, a horse screaming in panic, and over all the other sounds the crowing rage of Dr. John Christian Schultz.

Sheriff Inkster blinked himself back to the present and discovered uncomfortably that he'd been baldly staring at John and Janet Sutherland. John Sutherland said softly: "You're right both ways, Colin – you do have to feel some pity for the man."

"No I don't!" As soon as that had burst unbidden out of Sheriff Inkster's mouth – seemed to be doing a lot of that today – Colin glanced around nervously, to see if it had come out loud enough to attract eavesdropping attention. There were opinions it wasn't healthy to express. Not socially healthy; not healthy for one's salary, and hence one's family.

"Oh, but you do," Janet Sutherland said, "needs must have some pity for him. You see – he never understood."

"Never understood what?"

"What's important."

John Sutherland nodded his head slowly and said: "Yes, he was a very important man."

Then the Sutherlands turned to go, but Colin Inkster said: "Senator...?"

The Sutherlands reversed and turned in tandem, like two arm-in-arm skaters who'd long been circling the same rink. John Sutherland said: "Yes, Sheriff?"

"How...?" The circumstances of the day, and the ripples around it, had ambushed Sheriff Inkster with a wave of perplexity. He hardly even knew how to say the question. "How could it've happened?"

Both Sutherlands went stony. Mrs. Sutherland said: "You know how that happened, Colin, as well as anybody."

"Oh, I didn't meant *that*... That was..." That was the last thing he meant to remind them of, as if they needed reminding. "What I meant was: How could it've lasted as long as it did?"

"Ah." John Sutherland's swan's-down eyebrows eased upward. "That is a question."

CHAPTER 1

On the same day the blue and the grey armies fought their first warm-up skirmish in Missouri, a ridiculous accident a thousand miles north-west started a chain of events that would settle the destiny of more square miles of North America than the American Civil War. The chunky paddlewheeler *The Pioneer*, steaming north from the Dakota Territory into Her British Majesty's vast Hudson's Bay Company territories, encountered a sandbar that hadn't been there on her last trip downstream.

The captain tried all the usual methods to work her free: reversing the sternwheel, fixing spars to the wheel to try and walk her over, sending a crew ashore to fix a rope to a stout tree and try to wind her over with the capstan. Finally he announced to the passengers that the only choice left was to gradually ferry the cargo ashore until *The Pioneer* was lightened enough to float free, then drift over the sandbar and load her up again. With luck it would only take two or three days.

One of the passengers didn't take it very patiently, but then he never took anything very patiently. He was a tremendously tall and broad young man, with red-gold hair, pale blue eyes and a ruddy complexion. He had been travelling west from civilization for six weeks – by rail and stagecoach and finally this ungainly tub of a riverboat – and had been told just that morning that they'd be at Fort Garry and the Red River Settlement by nightfall. Now that he was twenty-one and ready to make his own way in the world, he meant to do so quickly and not be held up by incompetence when he was in reach of the place where he could start effecting his ambitions.

He crossed his long arms tightly and turned to glare at the riverbank, away from the captain and his crew fumbling to unship the dinghy they'd been using to store firewood. The riverbank was a snaggle-toothed motley of shorn-off trees and tangled branches. Stories abounded of the Red River's demonically high spring flood this year, carrying a wall of jagged ice floes in front of it. No doubt the captain would claim that he couldn't've been expected to expect this sandbar because the water had been so high earlier in the year, but the man's business was to know the river, for God's sake.

Then a wondrous thing appeared on the crest of the riverbank above the shorn trees: a black-haired boy riding one horse and leading another, heading north. The boy slowed his horses to look curiously at the beached wooden whale. Despite the black hair, he wasn't dressed like an Indian, so maybe spoke English. The big passenger cupped his hands around his mouth and called: "Hallo! Is that the road to the Red River Settlement?"

The boy peered backward beyond the rump of the horse he was leading, then forward beyond the ears of the horse he was riding, then called across the water: "There ain't no road, but this is the way we go."

It seemed the boy was a bit dim-witted, but he did have two horses. The passenger called: "I'll give you a shilling if you'll let me ride one of your horses there."

A pause, then a shrug. "I don't mind."

The passenger picked up his valise, told the captain to deliver the rest of his luggage to Fort Garry and that he would expect a refund for the portion of the trip *The Pioneer* didn't carry him, and jumped boots-first into the muddy water. For most men, the depth of water and strength of the current over the sandbar would've been a debilitating wade, and the clay-mud slope strewn with broken trees a daunting climb, but for a healthy twenty-one-year-old who stood well over six feet tall…

The boy looked to be about thirteen years of age and was wearing sun-bleached homespun and no shoes. His clothes were clean enough, but loose and sloppy. He was riding bareback and neither horse had a bridle, only a rope halter tied around the nose. "What's your name, lad?"

"Hugh Sutherland. Well, John Hugh Sutherland to be proper, but… And you, Mister?"

"Doctor." He hadn't actually stayed on at Queen's University quite long enough to graduate, but was quite sure he knew more about modern medicine than anyone at Red River.

"Oh! Sorry, Doctor."

"Schultz. Dr. Schultz. Dr. John Christian Schultz." It seemed only thoughtful to be absolutely specific about it, so that fifty years later Hugh Sutherland would be able to definitively tell his grandchildren about the day he met Dr. John Christian Schultz. Schultz thumbed a shilling out of his waistcoat pocket and held it up to catch the sunlight. "Here's your shilling, Hugh – you'll get it when we reach my destination."

"I don't mind, me whatever." Hugh Sutherland slid down off his horse – the larger of the two, which wasn't saying much – and said: "You better ride mine – t'other one's a buffalo-runner and it ain't good for buffalo-runners to be rid except running buffalo. But I don't weigh much, me – she won't mind. You ever ride bareback, Dr. Schultz?"

"Not horses."

"Well, just hold on tight and don't worry about steering – he'll follow where I go. If you leave the halter slack and keep both your knees clamped even-like, he won't get confused."

Schultz didn't have to actually climb onto the pony, just lift one leg over and settle on with his boot toes scraping the ground. The Sutherland boy took the lead with the buffalo-runner – whatever the goddamn hell a buffalo-runner was – and the other horse fell in behind. Once Schultz became convinced that his horse would indeed follow along with no guidance, he let his gaze drift to the right to observe the country he was planning to call home. Away from the belt of broken trees along the riverbank there was a waving sea of waist-high grass with bursts of wildflowers here and there. There were a few islands of poplar groves dotted haphazardly, but other than them there was nothing to break a man's vision until the green sea met the base of the sky at a hazy horizon.

Hugh Sutherland had been right that there was no road, but there was a trail of sorts, with shorter grass and interlacing wheel ruts or possibly Indian travois. But the trail followed the bends and twists of the river, making them amble two miles for every mile of straight distance. Schultz said: "Wouldn't we make better time cutting straight north through the tall grass instead of following the trail?"

"Yup, but the musky-toes'd eat us alive. Blackfly season's almost over, but that means the musky-toes are coming on. This time of a hot, dusty day they're curled up asleep; better not to disturb'em. The Indians call us loony for bathing off the bug-pertection that builds up natural, but even the Indians don't go in the tall grass in the summer'less they have to."

Schultz didn't argue – there'd been a couple of times the steamboat had had to tie up to shore overnight, and the buzzing biting insects that swarmed out of the riverbank brush had made sleeping near impossible. Maybe importing mosquito netting would be a good business idea. He took his notebook and pencil out of an inside pocket and managed to scrawl that down without falling off his horse.

Another thing he wasn't going to dispute young Hugh Sutherland about was the 'hot day.' Away from the river, the sun drove down like a hammer and seemed to bounce back up from the baked-hard ground. It wasn't the cloying greenhouse heat Schultz knew from summers back home in Upper Canada, but being seared like a beefsteak was just as debilitating as being steamed like a Christmas pudding. He was glad for his wide-brimmed felt hat. Straw would've been even better, but he wouldn't have wanted to make his first appearance at Red River looking like a ploughman.

The sun didn't appear to bother Hugh Sutherland, though. He rode bareheaded and the nape of his neck showing between his blunt-cut hair and collarless shirt looked almost brown enough for an Indian, if it weren't that the hair was curly instead of Indian-straight. Well, not so much curly as leafy, as though the laurel wreath on a History text Caesar had grown together, but this specimen probably had no concept of what a Caesar might be.

The boy's blue-green eyes and black hair had put Schultz in mind of some varieties of Irish, or Highlander – which would fit with 'Sutherland' – but that usually meant a complexion that would freckle and peel instead of going gold brown. Maybe the freckles had all grown together. Or maybe the boy was one of the halfbreeds who were said to make up much of the population of the Red River Settlement. All sorts of unnatural sports were bound to appear when people started mixing races.

Hugh Sutherland said over his shoulder: "So you just come to Red River for a visit, Doctor…?"

Overhearing conversations on *The Pioneer* had educated Schultz to the fact that 'The Red River' meant the river; 'Red River' meant the settlement. He said: "No, I've come to live," he would've added 'and to make my fortune,' but it sounded too *Jack'n The Beanstalk*. "I have a half-brother, a Mr. McKenney, who asked me to come and help him with his business."

"Harry McKenney?"

"Yes," although it seemed a bit presumptuous for a peach-fuzzed boy to be referring to a grown man by his Christian name, much less the familiar 'Harry' instead of the christened 'Henry.' Schultz didn't quite know what attitude to take to Hugh Sutherland. The boy certainly wasn't rude – except in the sense of rustic – but he showed no trace of the bashful deference that should've overcome a barefoot youth encountering a deep-voiced, broadcloth-suited stranger who'd also revealed himself to be a Doctor. There was something a bit ridiculous about the easy-going chatter on adult matters coming out in a voice that was still changing. Well, it was to be expected that Red River people would have different manners. For half a century now, the Red River Settlement had been an island on the plains a thousand miles from the nearest civilization, founded by refugee Highlanders shipped to the middle of the continent through Hudson's Bay while the rest of white North America was still working its way west from the Atlantic seaboard.

After the horses had ambled on a little longer, Schultz said: "I could *walk* faster than these horses."

"Well, I was been running 'em for a while 'fore I saw the boat. Guess they's breathed out now."

Hugh Sutherland clucked his pony into a trot and Schultz's pony followed suit. It wasn't the smoothest trot Schultz had ever encountered, and with no stirrups to cock his long legs to control his bouncing on the saddle – no saddle, for that matter – it was a case of gripping the coarse mane with both hands and trying not to bounce so high he bounced off. He could've leaned forward and hugged his arms around the horse's neck, but that would've been admitting defeat and even less dignified than mane-clutching.

The pony began to shy and panic, and Schultz realized the cause was his valise banging against its neck. So he stuck out his valise-arm away from the horse and made do with a one-handed death grip in the shaggy mane. After what seemed like a long time – with Schultz oblivious to everything but his efforts to stay on the horse, and to keep intimate portions of his anatomy from getting crushed coming down from the latest bounce – Hugh Sutherland called back over his shoulder: "Guess it's time to wake'em again, if you don't mind."

Schultz was about to shout back: '*Wake who, blast it!*' when he saw that by 'wake' the boy meant 'walk,' as the horses mercifully slowed to a smoother gait. It seemed that Red

River's isolation had developed its own peculiar manner of speaking that would take some getting used to. 'Guess' was 'gace,' 'don't' was two syllables – 'doan't' – and 'dusty' was 'dooshty.' 'S' was often more like 'sh,' in the manner of Highland Scots or Shanty Irish. Schultz was half-Irish himself, but Protestant Orange Ulster Irish. Sober Irish. Not that he didn't take a drink from time to time, but hardly in the manner of those bog-trotting Papist hooligans.

The road that wasn't a road began to wind past scattered, squared-log huts with ragtag vegetable gardens and horse corrals. Dark-skinned, black-haired people in calico and leather loafed in the yards. Some waved at Hugh Sutherland, some stared at the stranger, some didn't look up.

Hugh Sutherland stopped the horses on the edge of a high bank where two muddy rivers joined. From studying maps, Schultz knew that the one flowing in from the west was the Assiniboine, and the wider Red would carry its waters north to Lake Winnipeg and eventually to Hudson's Bay.

To the right were two oversized, blackened, snaggle teeth that Schultz knew were the ruins of St. Boniface Cathedral – a corner item in an Upper Canadian newspaper had told of the disastrous fire last winter. Down on the river shore was a floating dock with several people whistling shrilly and shouting what sounded like: "Make dog!" And across the river was a sprawling, oblong, stone and timber fortress with bastions and gunports, and the roofs of tall buildings showing over the walls.

As impressive as Fort Garry was in the middle of all this wilderness prairie, it seemed to Schultz to be rather small for the continental headquarters of the world's biggest landlord next to the Russian Czars. Except for the tiny Atlantic Colonies and the narrow strips of Upper and Lower Canada along the St. Lawrence River, and the pocket colony of British Columbia clinging to a corner of the Pacific coast, all of North America north of the United States belonged to the Hudson's Bay Company.

Hugh Sutherland said: "Guess you might's well climb down off your horse, Doctor – not as it's much of a climb for you. McKenney's store and hotel's on t'other side, and me and the horses live on this side."

Schultz gratefully scissored his aching lower body off the pony. As Hugh Sutherland jumped down off the buffalo-runner and onto the other horse, Schultz said: "This side? Isn't this the French side?" Hugh Sutherland looked perplexed. Schultz continued: "My sister-in-law's letters told me that the east bank of the Red River is the French and Catholic side, and the west bank the English Protestant side."

"Oh, I wouldn't go calling my grandparents English was I you. Anyway, your sister's someways right, but it ain't so cut and dried. You go a few miles further up the east shore – what you called the French side – you'll find a parish called Little Britain. But I *was* born on the west shore, me – on Point Douglas. We don't live there no more, but we still got fields there and folks still call us the Point Douglas Sutherlands, to tell us from all the other Sutherlands around here. After the flood of '52 – much worse'n this year's – we come back from the high ground and found our house on Point Douglas was gone, washed away like most the others. Then my granny looks across the river and sees our house there on the other shore. It'd floated up against some big elm trees and settled down good as new. So'stead of building a new house, my Da just bought some yard-land around it from the Lagimodières and we boats across in summer to work our fields."

Schultz wasn't sure whether the boy was telling him tall tenderfoot tales. Hugh Sutherland looked down at the group shouting and whistling on the dock and said: "Looks like you're in luck, Doctor – sounds like MacDoog is back."

"MacDoog?"

"Old gentleman named MacDougall runs the ferry. But he likes a drink, so it's sometimes hard to roust him out, and he don't repair his boats, so it can get to be a leaky crossing. When The Company gets too many complaints, they takes away his ferry licence and gives it to someone else. The new fella makes the boats all shipshape and starts runnin' it business-like, so you don't get people backed up on the dock like you see now, shoutin' themselves hoarse to rouse the ferryman's attention."

Hugh Sutherland smiled as though he were letting the stranger in on something pleasant, and went on, "But, you see, MacDoog trusts people – if you ain't got a halfpenny for the fare, he'll say, 'Oh, pay me next time,' even if that's what you said the last time. And if you kill a couple chickens and bring him one, you can ride free all summer. But the new, business-like fella don't run his business that way, and after a few months getting yelled at by people expectin' credit, he gets disgusted and quits and The Company gives the licence back to MacDoog. The fixed-up boats are usually good for a year or two till they start springin' leaks again."

Schultz waited for the pleasant part of the information, but that appeared to be all there was to it. If both the boy's stories were true, then the Red River Settlement was an even more slipshod, ramshackle, inbred, stagnant backwater than Schultz had been led to believe – which *was* pleasant news for his prospects. He said: "So just how am I 'in luck' that MacDoog is back?"

"Oh, he's a nice old gentleman. Give you the shirt off his back, if you weren't partic'lar."

Hugh Sutherland turned to peer across the river, shading his eyes against the sun – this far north, the sun was still high on a June evening. "Yup, just foot passengers so they're sendin' out the dugout."

Schultz followed the boy's eyes to the dock on the other shore, where a long, crude, dugout canoe was pushing off. He said: "I'd best get down there, then," hefted his valise and stepped toward the path angling down the riverbank.

"Uh, Doctor…?"

"Yes, lad?"

"You said something about a shilling…?"

CHAPTER 2

With Dr. Schultz's shilling in his pocket, Hugh Sutherland reluctantly turned his horse's head toward the cart-trail that ran between the riverfront houses and the fields and pastures stretching out onto the prairie behind them. Hugh had two good reasons to not want to go down that cart-trail this evening: what was waiting for him at home and the stop he had to make along the way. But as his Gran always said, 'The longer you put off taking your medicine, the bitterer it will taste.'

He nudged his horse into a trot and held tight to the trailing buffalo-runner's halter in case she took it in mind to gallop ahead. After a half-mile or so he slowed them to a walk as the trail wound past a farmyard much the same as all the others: snug little whitewashed post-and-beam house and barn with chickens roaming the yard. There were no people in the yard, just as there hadn't been that morning, so maybe he just might get away with it.

Hugh turned the horses inland, into an unfenced pasture with a lone oak tree. Hanging from a lower limb, where he'd hung them that morning, were a pair of homemade, bull's hide and sheepskin hobbles. He reached them down and then slid off his horse, murmuring softly in Gaelic to the buffalo-runner in hopes she wouldn't bolt again. He knew she was more used to French, but his Gran always said that Gaelic was the best language for talking to animals.

Mercifully, the buffalo-runner seemed to have run herself out and just stood there meekly while Hugh knelt to buckle on the hobbles. Maybe, if he could get her hobbled and himself away before anyone noticed him, they'd think she'd just grazed her way into the poplar grove across the field and stayed in there through the heat of the day. Just one more buckle…

"Bonjour, Jean'ugh Sudderlan'!"

Hugh jumped. Coming across the cart-track toward him was a white-haired woman in a black dress. Hugh finished the last buckle and stood up with his cheeks flushing warm. He said in his roughcut Red River French: "Bonjour, Madame Lagimodière. I was just, um, I was…"

She said, in her Quebec convent-school French that fifty years in the wilderness couldn't muddy, "You were just bringing back the horse that you stole."

"I didn't steal her! I was just –"

Madame Lagimodière laughed. "I know. I saw you through the window this morning. My son-in-law and all his family went up to the lake for whitefish, so I'm alone here for a few days – plenty of time for gazing out of windows. I saw you come riding down the road and stop and stare at pretty Jouyeuse grazing in the meadow, and I could see you thinking: 'I wonder what it's like to ride a buffalo-runner?'"

Hugh couldn't say anything to that but, "Yes, ma'am." Not only had she read him right, he wasn't about to argue with the Widow Lagimodière about anything. Her voyageur fiancé hadn't been able to argue her out of coming west with him in the days when there wasn't another white woman within a thousand miles of Red River. "And I know buffalo-runners ain't s'posed to be rid except for runnin' buffalo, but... I thought just once around the pasture wouldn't do no harm, and I don't weigh much... But then..."

"Yes," Mme. Lagimodière nodded, "but then as soon as you had the hobbles unbuckled she kicked up her heels and galloped south. I saw. And I saw you jump on your horse and gallop after her. I was not too worried. I knew the grandson of Kate MacPherson would either bring Jouyeuse back safe or starve to death trying to catch her on the prairie."

"Do you have to, um... Do you have to tell your son-in-law what happened?"

She laughed. "No, I do not have to tell him – because everyone you passed by on your way back here will be asking him: 'Why was young John Hugh Sutherland leading around your new buffalo-runner?' Probably he will laugh about it. Probably. And now you had better be getting home before your mother and father think you've run away with the Indians."

"Yes, ma'am."

When Hugh turned his horse off the road and onto the Point Douglas Sutherlands' home place, he could see he was in even more trouble than he'd thought. There was no one in the yard, no one shooing the cows out of the barn after milking, no one splitting firewood or weeding the vegetable garden, no one tending the outdoor clay bake-oven. That meant they were all inside and had already started supper.

He put his horse into the fenced pasture with the others and turned toward the house. The house was bigger than Mme. Lagimodière's son-in-law's, but hadn't started out that way – new rooms had been added on to the sides and back and upper storey as the house grew with the family. As Hugh crossed the yard, the smells coming from the house reminded him that all he'd had to eat since breakfast was a stick of smoked sausage. He could smell roast beef and onions, fresh-baked bread, buttered peas. He could even smell boiled potatoes, and you had to be some hungry to smell boiled potatoes through an eight inch log wall and across a yard.

Hugh stopped at the door and washed his feet in the wooden tub by the doorstep. The water was muddy from his brothers and sisters, but Red River water was always muddy unless you let it stand overnight. He dried his feet with the least-wet of the rags hanging there, balancing himself on first his left leg and then his right, then turned to the door.

Like most Red River houses, the door to the Point Douglas Sutherlands' had a tacked-on entranceway, something like an inside-out closet, to help keep out the cold in the winter and the bugs in the summer. Hugh tugged the latchstring on the outer door and stepped inside. With the outer door closed behind him he was in semi-darkness. He could hear voices inside but was quite sure they hadn't heard him yet. He put his hand on the inner door, reminded himself to at least try and talk proper instead of the slangy way his friends learned from the buffalo hunters, took a deep breath and pushed open the door.

As he'd feared, they were all at the table and well into supper. His father and mother were at their places at either end of the table, and lined along both sides were Donald, Alexander, Morrison, Hector, Angus, Margaret, Catherine, William Robert and Christina – baby James didn't have a place at the table yet. At the midpoint of both lines of children, across the table from each other, were Hugh's grandmother and grandfather. The chair beside his grandfather's was empty.

The conversation stopped when Hugh shuffled inside and pushed the door shut with his hands clasped at the small of his back, but everybody pretended to keep on eating. All except his mother and father. Mum put down her fork and turned to look sadly and disappointedly at Hugh standing in the doorway. Da didn't have to turn, just fixed his stony blue eyes down the length of the table and over Mum's shoulder to pin Hugh against the door.

Da finished chewing his latest mouthful, swallowed and said: "John Hugh Sutherland."

"Yes, Father." It didn't seem the kind of circumstance for 'Da.'

"Come stand at your place."

"Yes, Father." Hugh walked forward slowly and stood behind his empty chair, not knowing what to expect. At the end of the last school year, Da told him he had now grown too much the man to be paddled like a child, but maybe today had put him back in the category of child.

Da said: "Do I recall correctly, John Hugh, that when you, um, *asked* this morning could you take one of the horses… to go have a look at how they're starting to rebuild St. Boniface cathedral, you… *promised* to be back by mid-afternoon to split firewood?"

"Yes, Father."

"Your mother has been worried sick that you might have taken a fall off your horse… and be, um, lying out on the prairie with a broken leg."

"I'm sorry, Mother."

"Obviously," Da went on, "both your legs are whole, and you did not *fall* in the river and drown…"

Hugh couldn't tell whether his father's emphasis of 'promised,' 'asked' and 'fall' were because Da was especially angry about those specific parts of the day's transgressions, or because of that other thing. Da had a kind of halting way of speaking, with lots of ums and uhs, and sometimes a blank pause, and then Da would bark out the next word that came after the gap. Maybe the halting awkwardness came from growing up in a home where English was a late add-on to Gaelic, but whatever the reason, it was just the way Da was. It could be confusing at times, but there was no confusing that right now Da was definitely angry, in his own measured way.

"So," Da came to the inevitable question, "why is it that you promised to be home by, um, mid-afternoon, and we are... *halfway* through supper before you come through the door?"

"Well, Father..." Hugh told them about the buffalo-runner and the long chase, slightly embroidering the parts where he'd almost had his hand on her and then she'd bolted again. Some of the younger children had to cover their mouths to pretend not to be giggling, and Hugh's grandfather was clucking his tongue and shaking his head, with something resembling a smile twisting his wiry beard.

When Hugh got to the end and the buffalo-runner back safe, Da said: "Well, John Hugh, you did the, um, responsible thing in chasing the lost horse until you caught her – but it was your own foolishness that... *caused* her to be lost. I hope this will teach you not to interfere with other people's animals without permission."

"Yes, Father."

"Now sit down and have your supper. And tomorrow you will clean out all the cow stalls."

"Yes, Father."

"Say a grace before you eat."

Hugh murmured: "Thank you, Lord, for what I am about to receive," adding silently: *And for me not receiving what I thought I was gonna get*, then reached for the beef and potatoes.

When he'd gobbled enough to slow down a little, Hugh took out Dr. Schultz's shilling and said: "I earned a shilling today anyways – I mean anyway. I wouldn't'a asked him for money, but he offered."

All eyes along the table were trained at the bright coin he was holding up. Coins weren't all that common at Red River; The Company printed paper money set at one pound sterling or five shillings. There were a fair number of American and English gold and silver coins about, but most small change was done in buffalo sinews – flat, wide, white strips that peeled apart into better sewing thread than money could buy.

Mum blinked from the coin to Hugh and said: "*Who* offered?"

Hugh told them of the stranded steamboat and of the big, blonde man who'd waded across the sandbar but wasn't much of a rider. "Said he plans to live here, too, at least a while. And he's a doctor, too."

Da said: "Well, we could do with another doctor. With poor Dr. Bunn, um, taking his heart attack in the flood, we've only got Dr. Bird and Dr. Cowan, and Dr. Cowan's... *first* duty's to The Company."

Mum said brightly: "No, we've got three doctors, counting Dr. Black. Do you remember what Sally Ross said about Dr. Black?"

Da nodded and allowed his lecture-set mouth to raise a little at one corner. Seven-year-old Margaret said: "*Granny* Ross?"

Mum nodded. Granny Sally Ross was no relation to the Point Douglas Sutherlands, but she was 'Granny' to everyone at Red River who didn't have their own grey hair. She was an Okanagan princess who'd married a fur trader who retired to Red River and got appointed Sheriff and Postmaster. Besides being a wife and mother, and mother-in-law to Dr. Black, she was a midwife and all-round medicine woman. Many early mornings when Hugh had been helping in the fields on Point Douglas, he'd seen old Sally Ross making her way back home from some neighbours' where she'd been up all night.

Mum explained to the rest of the table: "When the news came from Canada that the Reverend Mister Black had achieved his Doctor of Divinity and was now Dr. Black, Sally Ross clapped her hands and said 'Now he is a doctor and can make us all well!'"

Even those at the table too young to understand laughed. Donald, Hugh's only older brother, said as though putting the capper on it, "Ignorance is bliss." Poor Donald was always mis-stepping by figuring that being the oldest meant he had to pretend to be all grown up. And he read too much, so he could only see things in black and white.

Mum pursed her mouth, then said gently: "Donald, it is true that Mrs. Ross never went to school, but that doesn't mean she is ignorant. If you thought on it a little longer, it might occur to you that perhaps she was not being a joke, she was making a joke."

Hugh became aware that the only person at the table who hadn't laughed with everyone else was his grandmother. She was sitting rigidly, with her long back and wide shoulders even straighter than usual and her eyes fixed on him across the table. She said in almost a whisper, "You met a tall, golden-haired man by a river, and he offered you a silver coin… and you took it?"

Granda said: "Now, Catherine, someone who spends as much time in kirk as ye shouldnae be paying any heed to auld superstitions."

Usually Gran would've responded with something like: '*If there is any half-heathen in this family, Alexander Sutherland, it is not me,*' but she said nothing, just kept on staring at Hugh as though someone had stepped on her grave.

Hector said: "More potatoes, please."

CHAPTER 3

When young Dr. Schultz reached the top of the bank on the west side of the Red, he paused to gaze up at the top of the stone wall around Fort Garry – more than twice his height – and the huge flag floating high above it: a British Red Ensign with a large, white 'HBC.' The American traders said it stood for Here Before Christ. As per usual the Americans exaggerated, it had only been two hundred years since Charles II granted the company figureheaded by his cousin Prince Rupert absolute sovereignty over the northern half of North America, thenceforward known as Rupert's Land. John Christian Schultz and many of his friends back east believed that two hundred years was more than long enough for a pack of fur traders to rule that much of the world.

Schultz turned to his right and started striding north along the cart-track that was the last leg of his long journey. The knees of his trousers were wet from kneeling in the soggy straw that was the ferry dugout's nod to seating arrangements, but the hot, dry air was taking care of that. After some brisk walking, the stone wall passing by on his left became a wooden wall: stacked beams fixed tight together. Schultz guessed the wooden wall would be as thick as the stone wall, likely a log sandwich with a filling of earth. Impregnable. Or so it would seem to The Company's men in their oak-panelled counting rooms and silk-panelled drawing rooms.

The wooden wall was as long as the stone wall, but eventually Schultz was past it and out in the open. The evening birds were singing and although his destination was still almost a mile away there was nothing between him and it but grazed-down grass, so he could see it standing alone on the prairie: a two-storey, squared-log building with sheds around it. In the deceptive, clear air it seemed he could almost reach out his arm and touch it. But it looked like he would cut his hand if he did, since the clear air also meant the sunlight sharpened the edges of everything.

Halfway between Fort Garry and his destination, Schultz began to get an uncomfortable feeling, somewhat disorienting. He realized it was the sky. Up until now, his experience of the open prairie had been from a stagecoach, or a riverboat, or on horseback along the riverbank with a companion to distract him. When people had talked of the 'big sky' he'd thought it a poetic turn of phrase. But no, it was real: he felt like a microbe on a billiard table.

Soon he was close enough to the building to feel they were in the same picture, and the disoriented feeling went away. The red-lettered 'Royal Hotel & Dry Goods' sign above the front door couldn't've been painted more than a year ago, but was already weathered almost to grey-on-grey. He was raising his foot to the front step when he heard a familiar voice ringing in the open air. So he lowered his boot and loped around to the back. Outside the back door was his sister-in-law Lucille, with wisps of blonde hair escaping from her bun, and a folded bed sheet in her hands. She was brandishing the sheet at two dark-skinned women standing behind two filled laundry baskets, and saying to them loudly and forcefully: "Not clean! No clean!"

Schultz said: "Clean enough for baby brothers?"

Lucy shrieked: "Johnny!" dropped the sheet and flung her arms around his neck, which was quite a reach. Then she caught herself and stepped back, conscious of displays of affection in front of the servants. "But… I didn't even hear the steamboat whistle. Half the settlement charges down to the wharf to watch the boat come in – how could we have missed it?"

"Because it didn't come in. It's snagged on a sandbar downstream – I waded ashore and made my own way here."

"You would!" She reached up to pinch his cheek, then remembered the sheet, picked it up and dusted it off and muttered at it: "Well, I guess it'll have to do." She took a thin fold of paper shillings out of her skirt pocket, handed one to each of the two women and said loudly to get across the language barrier: "Next week, you understand? Next week again. *Compris?*"

One of the women nodded and the two of them turned and started walking inland across the prairie toward no human habitation Schultz could discern. Lucy picked up one of the laundry baskets, angling her eyes down for Schultz to take the other, and he followed her inside as she clucked: "They just don't understand *clean*. Not just the word, but the concept. Well, I guess they can only do so much with a boiling pot and lye soap, but *still…*"

The back room of the Royal Hotel was a cramped kitchen with a small table and a square woodstove. Sweating over a meaty-smelling pot was a fat, dark-skinned woman, with a blonde girl standing on tiptoe to see what the pot was doing. Schultz said to the girl: "You can't be Lu-Lu – she only comes up to my knees."

"Uncle John! How are you? Did you bring me anything from home?"

Lucy Sr. said: "Home is here, dear, for now and a while longer," and set her laundry basket on the table.

Schultz said: "You know, there just might be something labelled *Miss* Lucille McKenney in my trunk, if the steamboat ever gets here."

Lucy started sorting laundry and jogged her head toward the calico-curtained doorway out of the kitchen, saying: "Harry's in the Common Room – serve him right if you snuck up on him like you did me."

The Common Room of the Royal Hotel had a long, rough wooden table and chairs, and the evening sunlight through the windows filled the air with dancing gold dust. Hunched over a ledger on the table was a large man – though not quite as large as Schultz – with thick dark hair and beard, wearing a black vest and collarless shirt and his trousers tucked into his boots. The sight of Henry McKenney always made Schultz feel a little more sure of himself. Harry had already been twelve years old when Ludwig Schultz married the Widow McKenney, so was almost a man five years later when Ludwig Schultz took off to seek the fortune he never found. Wee Johnny had ended up being shuttled around between his mother and various aunts, and big Harry was the only constant male presence in his life. Even when Harry had to go far away at times, making his own way in the world, he always came back.

At the moment Harry had his back to the kitchen doorway and seemed throughly engrossed in his scratching pen. So Schultz took a couple of soft steps into the room and announced in a gravelly voice: "*Bailiff*, McKenney!"

Without turning his head, Harry said: "There's not a bailiff in the world's got feet that big," then swivelled his chair around. "Besides, I heard Lucy squealing your name outside."

Harry stood out of his chair so they could shake hands and slap each other's shoulders. "You've filled out a bit, Johnny, I'm glad to see – high time you started growing out as well as up. If I poured you a mug of beer would you drink it?"

"I wouldn't say no."

Harry took two tin cups from a cupboard – actually only a set of shelves with a sheet of sailcloth hanging in front – and went over to a barrel cradled on a pair of trellises in a corner. As he worked the tap, Harry said: "Last year a couple of enterprising locals put up an actual brewery – looks like three old barns glued end-to-end, but it's drinkable – down in Middlechurch, about halfway between here and The Stone Fort."

"The Stone Fort?"

"There's two forts in the Red River Settlement – the one at The Forks here you already seen, and another about twenty miles down the Red, just below St. Andrew's Rapids. Upper Fort Garry and Lower Fort Garry, but the locals call'em just Fort Garry and The Stone Fort. Don't see why – Fort Garry's almost as much stone as the Stone Fort – but that's what they call'em. Well, what do you think of Red River beer?"

Schultz took a tentative sip. Back home in Upper Canada there were a lot of different local breweries, each with their own taste. This one was a little thicker than some, a little thinner than others. He said: "Well, it's beer."

"That's what counts, Johnny. What's a hotel if the clientele can't have a mug of ale with their mutton chop? Royal Hotel's the first-ever legally licenced tavern in all Rupert's Land. Oh, there's no doubt been backwoods shanty-taverns since Moses was a pup, but we're the first full-out above-board commercial establishment. There's a Metis fella named Monchamps applied for a licence now, but we're still the first."

"Metis?"

"Metis, halfbreed, six of one half a dozen."

"Ah." Schultz looked around the empty common room. "Uh, there doesn't look to be much clientele, Harry – unless they've already had their supper and gone back to their rooms…?"

Harry scuffed his square boot toe on the floor, wiped foam off his mustache and said: "No, only just the one fella now, and he'll be heading back to St. Paul on the steamboat. It's the damn war."

"The war?"

"The American war." Harry started pacing around the room, boot-heels thumping. "Wait'll you get a look around the settlement in daylight, Johnny. Fat cattle and sheep grazing all around; thick crops that spring out of the ground as soon as the sun hits the seeds; and there's tens of thousands of acres of the same kind of land all around. But in the fifty years since this place became a settlement, there's been no immigration. Why?"

Schultz opened his mouth to venture an answer, but before he could Harry banged his fist on the table and went on, "Because the damned Here Before Christers don't want farms and towns mucking up the fur trade. Fifty years ago they brought in just enough colonists to grow food for The Company and make a cozy place for Company men to retire to, and then they slammed the door. And for fifty years the only way to get here was The Company's ships into Hudson Bay and The Company's boats from there – either that or take your chances with a thousand miles of wilderness and Indians."

McKenney paused to take a sip, burped, then carried on. "But now the American frontier's pushed this far west, and there's the paddle-wheeler and cart caravans north from there. All the good land in Upper Canada's taken up, and The Company can't stop British subjects from making their own way into British territory. They *will* come, Johnny – and when they do they'll stay at the Royal Hotel while they decide which parcel of land to buy from the lots we've staked out."

Schultz drained the last of his cup of beer and said: "You don't have to sell *me*, Harry. I didn't spend two months travelling here because I needed convincing," then clinked his empty cup against the table the way they used to tease Ma when the milk pitcher was empty.

Harry laughed and punched him on the shoulder and took their cups back to the beer keg. As he worked the tap, he said: "I guess I'm trying to keep *me* convinced – I expected a lot more business a lot sooner. But it's that damned American war – no one knows if it's just going to sputter or if the whole United States is going to go up in flames, or if all the troops in the Dakota forts are going to get pulled back east and leave the Sioux to collect customs duties. Till people got some idea how things are going to shake out, everybody's thinking twice about hauling their goods and chattels through American territory."

Harry handed Schultz his refilled cup and flopped onto a chair so emphatically a few drops sloshed out of his own. Schultz said: "*Sköl*."

"*Slainte*."

They both took a goodly swallow, then Schultz said: "Well, things will shake out in time."

"Yeah, *time*." Harry's bearded-hawk face tightened and his blue eyes focused at the far wall.

Schultz continued: "Well, the more time it takes, the more time we'll have to get set up before the customers come pouring in."

Harry laughed and slapped Schultz's knee. "That's my Johnny – take life's knocks as opportunities and never take no for an answer. I was planning the same way – figuring on putting up a bigger and better-stocked store next year with the proceeds from the hotel. Only there's no proceeds to speak of, and the letters of credit I brought from Canada all got used up on setting up this place, and a few little side-ventures that ain't paid off yet."

There was a small pause, then both of them said at the same time with different inflections: "Speaking of credit…"

Schultz unfastened the pin securing the inside pocket of his suitcoat, and drew out a slim packet of oilskin wrapped around an envelope. "As Junior Partner of McKenney & Co. I attended an appointment with Mr. Frederick E. Kew of London, England while he was in Toronto this spring." The envelope brought back a warming memory of a private luncheon at the King William Hotel, brandy and business cards, glove-leather wing chairs, and a City of London investment broker earnestly seeking the opinions of Dr. John Christian Schultz. "Mr. Kew agreed to serve as the London commission agent for McKenney & Co. and furnished me with a letter of credit for one thousand pounds sterling –"

"That's my Johnny!" Harry jumped out of his chair and walloped Schultz's shoulder so hard a smaller man would've been on the floor. "Lucy, get in here! A thousand pounds!"

Schultz shrugged, "That's more or less a down payment til he could get back to London and start beating the bushes."

Lucy came in from the kitchen wiping her hands on her apron and saying: "What's happened?"

"*This* is what's happened," Harry brandished the envelope at her. "Johnny closed the deal with Kew!"

"Oh, Johnny!" Lucy flew across the room and kissed Schultz on the cheek.

"Now we're in business," Harry crowed, heading back to the cupboard. "We'll build us a king-sized general store next year and stock it with all the goods The Company's too fat and lazy to import." He took down a dusty bottle and three small glasses from an upper shelf, then looked a mite confused as to how he was going to manage them and the envelope with only two hands. He settled on upending the glasses over three of his fingers and coming back to the table with the bottle in his other hand and the envelope clamped in his teeth.

Once Harry had removed the gag and started pouring, he could go back to spouting plans. "We'll put you in one of the upstairs rooms, John, and you can use one of the others for an office when you hang out your shingle. Might take awhile for you to get much in the way of patients, but in the meanwhile there's plenty to keep you busy around the hotel and the store – if you're not too proud to get your hands dirty, now as you're a doctor."

"I've never been too proud before, why start now?" In the summers between university terms, while his fellow students had been lounging about their parents' Toronto mansions and gentrified farms, Schultz had been working on the lake boats or in a country store to earn his board and tuition for the next term. He hadn't been ashamed of it – if anything, it made him proud to be out doing a man's work while the rest of his class were still overgrown schoolboys.

Harry handed him and Lucy filled glasses, raised his and proclaimed: "Lady and gentleman, I give you – McKenney & Company."

They clinked glasses and drank. It was some kind of aged whiskey that burned and soothed at the same time. Schultz caught his breath again and said: "It's even bigger than that, what we're doing..."

Schultz could feel his cheeks growing warm – not from the whiskey, but from the grandiosity of what he was trying to say. He assured himself it was the truth, and nothing to be embarrassed about, but nonetheless he found his mouth a little awkward. "This rough-planked Common Room out on the prairie is the same as the little, seaside shanty that grew into Johannesburg, the same as a hut in Bengal where a British merchant first did trade. We're not just building McKenney & Company, we're helping build The Empire. Lady and gentleman, I give you – The Queen."

Harry said: "I'd rather have one of her daughters."

Lucy scowled at him, but it was all in good fun – though Schultz was glad there was no one outside the family to hear the blasphemy. But then there was someone else there: a heavy-set, dark-skinned man with a thick mustache and stubbled cheeks, standing in the open doorway at the other end of the common room. Schultz glanced down and saw how such a heavy-set man could've come along the plank-floored hallway without footfalls preceding: moccasins.

Harry said jovially: "Bonjour, Isidor. Stopping in for a jar on your way home?"

The dark head nodded.

"My brother here – Dr. Schultz – will take care of you." As the moccasins padded toward a chair at the far end of the table, Harry added to Schultz in a confidential tone, "Beer's half-a-shilling the cup. Just mark it down, he'll be good for his chit when he gets back from the summer hunt."

Harry and Lucy went out the curtained doorway, leaving Schultz to rummage out another cup and try to figure out where he was supposed to mark it down. When Schultz set the filled cup down in front of the mixed-race gentleman, the greasy-haired head nodded again, but the rough-carved face remained impassive and only a grunt came out of the mustached mouth. Schultz went back to flip through Harry's ledger, trying to find a page of bar tabs, while the man at the other end of the table quietly proceeded to pack and light a pipe.

Bootsteps approached down the hall from the front door. Schultz looked up to see a red-bearded, freckle-cheeked man stop in the doorway and cock his fists on his hips. The man said: "If I'da known they was letting Papist squaw-droppings drink in here I woulda had second thoughts."

Isidor spoke. "'*Second* thoughts'?" and loudly sniffed the air. "If pasty-faced Protestants had even *first* thoughts they woulda thought to wipe the cowshit off their boots before they left the farm." Some of the words weren't in English, but Schultz had picked up a working grasp of French on the lake boats.

The red-bearded man walked slowly toward the table with his thick arms crossed, drawling: "Better cow-shit than buffalo shit."

The backs of Schultz's hands were tingling. He didn't know what to do. He was quite sure he was big enough to take both of them – although Isidor had an ugly-looking sheath knife in his belt – but he didn't fancy starting his career at Red River by breaking Harry's furniture, and he fancied even less calling for Harry to come tell him what to do.

Red-beard flopped into the chair across from Isidor's and said: "I thought the hunt woulda bin gone by now."

"Late start this year. Tomorrow morning. How's the wife?"

"Not so good. The fever broke –"

"That's a blessing."

"But she's pretty wore-down."

"I'll ask my wife to say a prayer for her, Marie's closer to le bon Dieu than me."

"Wouldn't be hard to be. But, merci, Isidor – I'm sure m'lady's on the mend, but a little extra help wouldn't hurt." Red-beard laid a five-shilling note on the table and turned to Schultz. "If you're serving, I'll have a cup of ale, please, and another for this buffalo-humper here."

"Better buffalo than cows."

"How would I know? Buffalo run faster'n cows."

Schultz rummaged out another cup, trying to keep his head from shaking too obviously. This was a very strange place he'd landed in.

Red-beard said to Isidor: "Hey, yesterday John Jems Corrigal and Willie Garge Linklater was out sootin' in the marsh and the canoe went appech-e-quannee and they both goes chimmuck. The water was sallow, whatefer, but Willie Garge kept bobbin' up and down callin' '*Lard save me.*' John Jems was on topside the canoe and he souted to Willie and sayed '*Never mind the Lard just now, Willie – grab fer the willas.*'"

Isidor and Red-beard both burst into laughter, and then glanced askance at the silent Schultz as though maybe he was deaf or unsociable or both.

CHAPTER 4

Hugh was torn awake by the screaming of the *ban shee*, the Fairy messenger of death his grandmother had told him of in her stories of the old country. It took him a moment to figure out where and when he was. Although he was shivering a bit, he was actually still snug in the feather bed he shared with Donald and Morrison; the pale hint of light in the parchment window meant it was barely dawn, which came very early at Red River in June. He seemed to be awake now, not dreaming, but the *ban shee* was still screaming.

A laugh snuffed out of his nose at his own foolishness. The *ban shee* was just the squealing of a Red River cart. The wooden wheel hubs and axles of ox carts couldn't be greased because the prairie dust would turn axle grease into concrete before you'd gone two miles. There were stories of old drovers stopping to shoot a prairie dog and smearing its guts on the axles just to get a few minutes' peace.

But finding an explanation for the *ban shee*'s wail didn't explain to Hugh why the sound would wake him. He'd heard the screeching of a Red River cart ten thousand times, and there must've been a thousand nights when a cart went by the house without disturbing his dreams.

Then he realized that the sound wasn't just one Red River cart, it was dozens, maybe hundreds. He climbed out quickly over Donald – who just put one arm over his head and kept on snoring – tugged his trousers on over his nightshirt, and felt his way downstairs and out the door; not the first time he'd snuck through the house and out in the dark.

The sky was just beginning to turn pink and gold, and the grass tickled Hugh's bare feet with dew. Now he could hear through the screeching the sounds of horses and human voices and the rumble of wooden wheels. He ran toward the sounds and stood by the side of the road to watch the parade pass by.

There were carts piled high with camp gear and women and children, and strings of empty carts – each pulled by a single horse or ox, and all made of a pair of dished-in, spoked wheels as tall as Hugh, and a wooden bed with a railed unroofed cage on top. There were men on shaggy ponies loping up and down the line. The people were mostly dark-skinned, but some were pale, and all were dressed in anything from frock coats to beaded buckskins and waist sashes. The one thing all the different styles of clothing had in common was the flares of colour – it seemed no coat or dress was complete without a yoke of prismic quillwork, or beaded flowers, or bands of ribbon. Brass earrings and silver necklaces flashed in the red light of the rising sun. Even the braided whips in the horsemen's hands had strands of colour woven into them, and the gunstocks had patterns of bright brass nailheads.

It was the mysteriously-appointed morning when the Red River Buffalo Hunt was heading south to rendezvous with the other hunters at Pembina, as they had every year since before the border survey put Fort Pembina into American territory. From there the whole well-armed caravan would strike west into Sioux territory, and come back with carts piled high with sacks of pemmican – dried buffalo meat preserved in rendered buffalo fat. Some years half the population of Red River would be gone for two or three months of the summer, and again for the fall hunt when the buffalos' coats were thick enough to make buffalo robes and the air cold enough to keep fresh meat fresh.

Hugh stood rooted to the ground watching the hunt pass by. Sometimes a horseman or one of the women on the carts would have an instant from the business at hand to notice him and call: "Bon matin." He would wave back shyly, but mostly he was just a pair of eyes focusing on fragments flickering past: a long knife in an embroidered sheath, sunlight glinting on a double-barrelled gun, a beaded butterfly on a velvet vest, bright eyes in dark faces, a mocassin with a toe-piece beaded in a pattern that looked like a crown...

Hugh's eyes held on the mocassin against the furry brown background of a horse's ribcage. It was on his left and approaching. Two things about the mocassin were strange. First, the beadwork design was unusual – definitely a copper-coloured crown, with a white and green border. The second thing was that the mocassin and the foot inside it were too small – a boy with a foot that small should have his legs ending halfway down the horse's side, not almost at the bottom. Hugh's eyes travelled up a smooth, slim-curved, golden brown leg to the embroidered hem of a blue skirt bunched just below the knee.

The mocassin was almost parallel to Hugh now. His eyes flicked up to the face that belonged to it. She looked to be about his own age and could be either Indian or Metis. Her face was in profile to him, like a cameo brooch – if they made cameos out of living copper and gold, with midnight sky for the eyes and hair. She started to turn her head toward him, as though she could feel his eyes. He quickly turned away, as though he'd just noticed something extremely interesting a little farther down the line. He could feel himself blushing.

Hugh waited a few long seconds, until he figured she was safely past him, then turned his head around. Her back view was trim shoulders in a puffy calico blouse, and long black hair hanging free. From the comfortable way her back rolled almost imperceptibly with the side-to-side motion of the walking horse, she could easily've been galloping up and down the line with the show-offs if she'd wanted. Watching that fluid, slight movement of her shoulders and back, Hugh could feel what her back would feel like against his fingertips. It was a strange notion and a strange sensation and he didn't know what shelf to put it on. It made him feel like he was standing naked by the roadside.

A high-piled cart with children perched on the summit came between him and the diminishing girl. The parade wasn't over yet, but Hugh hurried back into the farmyard to get his morning chores done before breakfast. As he rounded the house he saw the tail-end – the shirt-tails – of five brothers trooping down to the river, while wee Willy and the girls lined up at the outdoor washstand under Gran's watchful eye. Hugh followed down the river path where the boys-before-the-girls had disappeared into the leaves. In the Point Douglas Sutherland family, there were the boys before the girls – those born before Margaret and Catherine broke Mum's string of male progeny – and the boys after the girls. There were only two 'afters' so far, but Mum didn't look to be done yet.

When Hugh got to the bank, the rest of the boys before the girls were already crouched in a row along the water's edge, with careful Donald naturally beside eight-year-old Angus ready to throw out an arm if Angus lost his balance. Hugh crouched beside them for the summer morning ritual of sluicing river up over faces and hair, passing the wide-mouthed comb along the line and limbering sleep-stiff jaws with the loose language of Red River boys:

"Well if it ain't wanderin' Hugh. Where you been wanderin' to?"

"Watchin' the Buffalo Hunt go by."

"Snucked out in the night again, eh? You oughta get a cuff on the scruff."

"Aye, somebody give'im a cuff on the scruff."

"'Somebody' might could go swimmin'."

"I'd sluice that comb around'fore using it, Aleck. Looks like Morrison's got burrs in his hair."

"Worse'n burrs, I bet."

"Yeah, that cowlick's still standin' up. Better take a rock and beat it into submission."

"I'm near to starvin'."

"You know what Granda says," and they all choired their best imitations of: "'Ye must tae feed yer animals afore ye feed yerselves.'"

Not that there were all that many animals to feed. In the summer the cattle and sheep and most of the horses fed themselves. Hugh carried the kitchen slops out to the sow and her piglets, and by then his own stomach was growling.

Over a breakfast of thick slabs of their own bacon, and eggs fresh from the henhouse, Hugh's father said: "Would you, um, feel like taking a bit of a ride this morning?"

Little William chortled: "Purple *always* feel like a ride." 'Purple Hugh' had been a family nickname ever since a three-year-old Margaret had misinterpreted her grandfather singing the old song about Loch Lomond, '*Where in purple hue the highland hills we view...*'

Hugh swallowed his latest mouthful and said: "Where to, Da?"

"Your grandfather's, um, finished his book and would like another. I thought you might... *ride* down to the library for him."

"What kind of book would you like, Granda?"

"It doesna matter tae me. I was twice your age when your Gran taught me tae read, and it's only since I got too old tae be useful have I had the time to exercise it much. So any book's a novelty tae me. They'll have it writ down at the library which books I hae already read."

Hugh said tentatively: "Da…? Uh, are you going anywhere this morning?"

"Hm… it seems to me I've got a *Council* meeting to go to today."

Mum said: "That's next week."

"Oh. Well, then maybe today I should, um, ride up to Noel Parisien's and see when he wants me to bring around our bull."

"Bull!" said Gran. "Ye know flearin' well, Johnny, you're not going anywhere today, so stop torturing the poor lad and tell him he can take Montrose."

Da opened and closed his mouth a couple of times like a washed-up fish, then came out with: "Now as I've consulted my itinerary, John Hugh, it appears that I am not going anywhere this morning, so you may as well take Montrose," and the whole table laughed.

The Point Douglas Sutherlands had seven horses, six of them the common, scruffy, chunky, prairie ponies who could pull a plough or a cart in the summer and happily stand around outside through a February blizzard. But Montrose was a big black glossy gelding descended from the famous studhorse Fire-Away, who'd been brought to Red River by an officer of one of the British regiments that got posted there from time to time.

It would take more than the morning to ride to the library and back, even on Montrose, so Mum put together a roast beef sandwich and Hugh put it and the done-with book in his Cree-made shoulder pouch, and rode out of the yard on his father's saddle on his father's horse – after shortening the stirrups somewhat. He was only half aware that he was riding a fine, tall saddlehorse for only the ninth or tenth time in his life; he had other things on his mind.

He was just about sure the girl he'd seen in the Buffalo Hunt parade was about his same age – except that in the brief instant when their eyes touched, before he'd turned away, she'd seemed so much more sure of herself than he could imagine being. Her slant-cornered, shiny black eyes had had an unabashable directness to them, even a trace of regal amusement – or maybe he was just imagining that part because of the crowns on her moccasins. It seemed strange that even though he'd only caught a glimpse of her face he could remember it clearly: thin, straight, snub-ended nose, high, rounded cheekbones, wide mouth… And when he pictured her, he could smell roses.

Hugh looked at the passing roadside, laughed and shifted both reins into his right hand so his left could slap his face for being an idiot. Of course he could smell roses; it was June and there were wild roses blooming all along the road.

Idiot or not, he went back to thinking about the girl. Not that there was much to think about from just one glimpse and he didn't even know her name. It was more *imagining* about the girl – imagining her riding along beside him and Montrose; wondering what her voice sounded like and whether she would laugh at him for riding a horse too big for him…

He wondered if this was what people meant by 'falling in love.' It didn't seem likely that something as important as falling in love was supposed to be could happen just from standing by the roadside and seeing a stranger pass by. He'd lived all his life on a farm, so it was no big secret to him what males and females did together, but this wasn't about that. Although, when he remembered that long, smooth, bare leg disappearing up into her skirt, he felt a strange, achy tensing of tendons at the tops of his legs. But maybe that was just from a saddle he wasn't used to and a horse with a broader back than he usually rode.

What he wanted to do with the girl was talk to her, find out who she was and where she lived and what kind of songs she liked to sing, and maybe eventually brush his fingertips along her cheek to see what her skin felt like. The fact that she was Indian or Metis never made much never-mind at Red River – except to some of The Company's officers brought in fresh from England or Canada, and they usually got over it if they stayed long enough. Even the Reverend Dr. Black had married a woman who was half Indian, a daughter of the Okanagan medicine woman Granny Sally Ross, and nobody thought twice about it. Hugh's Gran had said that that was one of the reasons so many of The Company's senior men chose to retire at Red River instead of going home to civilization – because at Red River their brown-skinned wives and children were treated the same as everybody else. Hugh had taken Gran's word for it that that wasn't the case in the outside world, but it seemed like a dang silly way for supposedly-civilized people to carry on.

Hugh told himself he was getting pretty dang silly himself, letting thoughts that started with the girl wander into the territory of marriage and children and so on. They were both just children themselves and he didn't know if she'd even give him the time of day if they ever met. He clucked at Montrose, nudged him into a gallop, leaned forward into the flying mane and forgot about everything else awhile except the necessity for holding on.

The sun was high by the time Hugh could hear St. Andrew's Rapids up ahead, and see the flag of the Stone Fort above the trees on the other shore. He turned Montrose's head off the road and onto a farmstead that had only a one-room, thatched cabin and a cowshed and no other buildings. Angus LeBlanc was on his knees in the garden, hoeing with the short-handled hoe that was all he could handle with only one arm.

Angus Leblanc stood up to see who was coming into his yard. LeBlanc was about Hugh's father's age and although he'd only been a voyageur, not a Company officer, The Company had given him a retirement pension and a piece of land when he lost his right arm in an accident up along the Athabasca. He'd settled in at Red River with his young Metis wife, who soon after died giving birth to their stillborn first child. As Hugh's Gran put it, if it weren't for bad luck Angus LeBlanc would have no kind of luck at all.

"Good morning, Mr. LeBlanc. Might could I borrow me your boat to go across to the library?"

"I don't seem to be using it. You can hitch your horse to the side of the cowshed in the shade."

"Thank you, but I better water him first." Hugh climbed down off Montrose and led him down to the riverbank. LeBlanc came along for company. While Montrose drank,

Hugh said to. LeBlanc: "I, um, I guess you know a lot more people from St. Peters than we do up at the Upper Fort…?" St. Peters was the next parish down-river from St. Andrews and the Stone Fort, the farthest parish north in the Red River Settlement, butting into the south end of Lake Winnipeg. Most of the people of St. Peters were Saulteaux Ojibway, or mixtures of Saulteaux, Metis and white. Some were Swampy Cree, but let themselves be governed by the Saulteaux Chief – as much as anybody at Red River was governed by anybody.

"Guess I would. I don't know a lot of people, but I guess I'd see more from St. Peters nor you would."

"There was… I seen a girl riding by this morning with a funny pattern on her moccasins, never seen anything like it before."

"What kind of pattern?"

"Looked kind of like a crown – you know, kings and queens and that."

"Oh," Angus LeBlanc laughed. "That'd be one of Mr. King's granddaughters – there's a lot of 'em."

"Mr. King…?"

"Oh, I guess you wouldn't even been born when he got the name, and it didn't stick for long, except for legalisms and such. Old Chief Peguis, when he converted to a Christian, the missionary told him he'd have to take a more civilized name – since 'Peguis' means something like 'He Leaves The Houses of His Enemies in Ashes.' So Peguis says: 'Who's the most powerful man in a civilized country?' and the missionary says: 'The King.' And Peguis says: 'And who's the second most powerful?' and the missionary says: 'The Prince.' So Peguis says: 'Then I will be Mr. King and my sons will be Mr. Prince.' That's why there's Henry Prince and Tom Prince and all the rest of 'em."

"Um, you said, Mr. LeBlanc, that Chief Peguis has a *lot* of granddaughters…?"

"Yeah, and that's just the ones we know for sure of. How old would be the one you're wondering about?"

"Oh, about my age, I'd guess."

LeBlanc got a twisted smirk and said: "Yeah, I kinda figured so. Still don't narrow it down much. But wait a tic – you say she was riding a horse…?"

"Um-hm."

"Was she *riding* a horse or just sitting on it? I mean, did it look to you like she knew how to ride?"

Hugh shrugged, "I'd say so." She had looked to him like she could turn handsprings on the back of a galloping buffalo-runner, but he didn't want to sound too carried away.

"Wauh Oonae," Angus LeBlanc nodded. "Nancy Prince. Caused a bit of trouble in a horserace on last year's buffalo hunt, so they tell me. Some fellas from further west put their pony up against her father's and when he said she was going to jockey it they called it no fair 'cause a girl weighed less'n their boy. He asked them was they afraid to race against a female and they said:'Hell no, let's get to it, you'll be sorry.' She won hands-down."

"Wauh Oodae?" Like most people who lived at Red River, Hugh had a basic handle on the Cree language, but this didn't sound like Cree.

"Wauh Oo*n*ae," Angus LeBlanc corrected him. "Back when the Saulteaux moved in here from the east they had to learn Cree to get along with their new neighbours, but they're still Ojibway. And baptising Nancy Prince didn't stop her family from giving her an Indian name. Wauh Oonae means Whippoorwill." Mr. LeBlanc puffed up his chest and cupped his hands in front of it, in imitation of a nesting bird with a fluffed-out breast. "Nice, high little titties on her, too, bounce pretty when she rides, and she's still growing."

Hugh didn't know what to say to that. He'd sometimes traded dirty jokes with other boys in a corner of the schoolyard or out behind the barn, and thought nothing of it except it was fun and a little wicked. But to talk of tits and so on in relation to the specific, living and breathing girl he'd seen that morning seemed crude and rude and a little embarrassing. So he said nothing.

"Little Wauh Oonae Nancy Prince caught your fancy pretty hard, eh?"

"Well, no, I just... It was just, you know, I never seen moccasins like that before. Got me kind of... curious, and I thought maybe you might know, living close to St. Peters like you do, and now you did and now I know and now... I don't have to be curious anymore."

"Moccasins. Uh-huh."

"Well... I best be gettin' acrost to the library."

"I'll take your horse up and hitch him in the shade."

"Thank you."

Angus LeBlanc's boat was a dugout canoe bottom-up on the riverbank. When Hugh turned it over he found three paddles, one of them the short-hafted one that Mr. LeBlanc used for one-handing himself up and down the river amazingly adroitly. Hugh took one of the normal paddles and started across, angling left against the current; coming back would be much faster, as long as he didn't let the current carry him past Mr. LeBlanc's and have to fight his way back. A grebe in its wonderfully silly summer plumage of red vest, green collar and yellow-bristled ear tufts was paddling downstream into the angle he was paddling upstream. Instead of just altering course, the silly bird panicked, spread its wings and ran along the water with its webbed feet splashing and wings flapping until it got enough momentum to take flight. Hugh was sorry to disturb it, but appreciated the show.

The Red River Library was in the living room of a big, stone house in the part of the settlement called Little Britain, because most of its population was retired English or Scots officers of The Company. Janet Gunn opened the front door when Hugh plied the brass knocker. She was a year and a bit older than him and had wavy golden hair. He'd never noticed before the interesting, rounded way that the front of her dress bulged out. It seemed he was noticing a number of things today he couldn't remember noticing before. He put it down to the fact that it was a particularly bright sun today, so everything stood out more clearly. Nonetheless, he found it oddly difficult to say to Janet Gunn: "Um, me Granda, you see, he, um... finished his book and would like another."

"Father's in the library. Go on in."

Old Donald Gunn had a hawk nose and sharp cheekbones rising out of a snowdrift of beard. For a number of years he and Granny Sally Ross's husband had run a long, slow race – each writing his own book about the early days of the Red River Settlement, to be published in the wide world. Hugh figured it hadn't griped Mr. Gunn too much when he lost the race, since Alexander Ross had died the year his book was published. Better to be a live librarian than a dead author.

When Hugh had explained his errand, Donald Gunn took down a couple of ledgers from the packed bookshelves lining the room, noted down in one that *The Life of Sir Walter Raleigh* was back in the library, and in the other added it to the list of books taken out and returned by Alexander Sutherland P. D. – to distinguish Point Douglas Alexander Sutherland from the several other Alexander Sutherlands at Red River.

Mr. Gunn said: "Your grandfather's in luck, Hugh. One of the old hands from the Qu'Appelle is going home for a year's leave, and on his way through here donated his personal collection to the Red River Library – he'd probably read it all a dozen times anyway. *Rob Roy* by Sir Walter Scott should fit your grandfather like a glove. Oh, and there's an old number of *The London Illustrated News* has a historical item on the Spanish Peninsula war against Napoleon. That's where your grandfather got his gammy leg, isn't it?"

"Yes, sir – if I remembers the story aright." It was understood that when people spoke of Hugh's grandparents without attaching a surname, they were speaking of his father's parents. Since Hugh's father was an only child, it was only natural that when Da started a family of his own they would live in his parents' home on the land he would inherit. Hugh's MacBeth grandparents lived about as far north of Point Douglas as you could live and still be in Kildonan. The Point Douglas Sutherlands' relocation across the river put them even farther apart, so Hugh's family rarely saw them except Sundays at church, and christenings and Hogmanay and such. He wondered sometimes whether that bothered Mum more than it seemed to.

Mr. Gunn said: "And how about yourself, Hugh? Shall I pick you out a book to read?"

"Read? In the *summer?*"

CHAPTER 5

Schultz awoke to the sounds of demons in the lower depths. It was his half-brother and sister-in-law going at each other in the kitchen below his room: "How'm I supposed to put together a bloody picnic lunch when you don't tell me till half an hour before you want to go?"

"You did the last time, when we went to Bird's Hill."

"I had a cook then, and a kitchen maid! They've all gone on the bloody buffalo hunt! Why'd you think I've been doing our laundry myself for the last three weeks, or haven't you noticed?"

"Lulu can help you make lunch. How much bloody time can it take to hardboil some eggs and slap a few slices of beef between pieces of bread?"

"If you think that's all there is to it…!"

By the time Schultz got downstairs they'd yelled themselves out. Lucy was banging pots and pans around and Harry was slicing and buttering slabs of bread. Harry said: "You'll have to make your own breakfast, John, if you can get near the stove."

"I don't mind." Schultz maneuvered his way around Lucy to get a frying pan on the stove top, melt some fat to start a few thick rashers of bacon and break in half a dozen eggs. Red River might be far beyond the pale of civilization, but Schultz very much appreciated that farm produce here was cheap and plentiful enough that a large man with a large appetite could get a decent breakfast every morning for the first time in his life. He also appreciated how quickly the temperature went down when the sun went down. Back in Upper Canada summer nights could be just as hot and cloying as summer days. But here, no matter how blistering the day, by the time he went up to bed the air was cool and fresh for a good night's sleep.

While Schultz was busying himself at the stove, Harry said: "You'll want to put on your good suit when you've done breakfast. They're putting on a show at the Stone Fort today."

"A show?"

"The Company likes to inveigle The Imperial Government into posting troops out here – claiming there's some kind of threat from the Americans, or the Sioux, or whatever other excuse The Company can come up with. A few hundred soldiers can spread around a lot of ready money, and give second thoughts to anyone who don't want to abide by The Company's laws and rules. A few years ago The Crown shipped out The Royal Canadian Rifles – all the way around from The St. Lawrence into Hudson's Bay and then by York Boat here. But now it's pretty obvious the Americans are too busy fighting each other to come encroaching on British Territory, so The Royal Canadian Rifles are going home. They won't leave till mid-day, they'll want to have a good audience for parading down to the boats with flags flying and the band playing. But they won't wait much later'n that, so you better gobble your breakfast if we're going to catch the show."

Schultz took his plate upstairs and gobbled while changing into his black broadcloth suit and a blue bow tie, then they all squeezed into the family carriage, all except for Schultz's oldest nephew who was left behind to hold the fort. Lucy said: "You sit up front with Harry, John, so he can point out the sites. I thought Harry was being profligate when he said we should pay a fortune to have a proper carriage shipped out here with us, but for a change… A Red River cart's no pleasure vehicle, believe me."

Once the horse hit its trotting stride, Harry pointed his buggy whip at a wide, squat, thatched building standing alone on the riverbank, actually less like a single building than like several log cabins tacked end-to-end. "That's Andrew McDermot's store. He'll be our major competition when we open our general store. Wily old bugger's been in business here since even before The Company officially allowed private traders."

From the seat behind them, Lucy said: "He does have a clutch of pretty daughters, though, Johnny."

"More to the point," Harry said, "we'll be out of his clutches soon, thanks to you and Mr. Frederick E. Kew of London, England. Next quarter when the rent comes due I'll show old McDermot the letter of credit and tell him we'll buy the Royal Hotel outright."

"I thought McKenney & Company built and owns the Royal Hotel?"

"Just the add-ons. The original building still belongs to McDermot, but not much longer." Schultz had to wonder how many other little details of McKenney & Co's dealings hadn't been confided to the junior partner.

They passed by a tall windmill just like the one on the delftware soup tureen that was one of the few things Schultz's and Harry's mother had to prove there ever was a Ludwig Schultz. Then the river curved to the right but the road stayed straight. The scraggly prairie turned into a green wheatfield on the right and a rail-fenced pasture on the left where fat cattle were grazing. Schultz looked to right and left but could see nothing that looked like a house, only a couple of sheds. He said: "The farmers *live* in those sheds?"

"Hm? Oh, no, no – this is Point Douglas, where the river does a horseshoe. Owned by the Point Douglas Sutherlands – or most of it is – family of the boy you said borrowed you a horse the day you got here. Their house is on t'other side of the river. This is the biggest piece of private land near the crossroads of the north-south and east-west cart trails, the cart-trails that'll be highroads one of these days. Yep, when immigration starts pouring in and people start building up businesses and proper towns, whoever owns

Point Douglas is going to be sitting in the catbird seat." Looking at the green wheatfield, Schultz could envision it turning golden in a few months, and into gold in a few years.

The river curved back into sight and now the road was passing through farm after farm with no wild prairie in between; a constant repetition of thatched cabins and barns on the right and fenced fields and pastures on the left. Harry said: "We're in Kildonan now, the original Selkirk colony."

Lucy said over their shoulders: "You'll find no prospects here, Johnny. Oh, there's pretty girls enough, but Kildonan people stick to themselves. Even the ones whose parents were born here still speak some Gaelic. I think they have secret handshakes, like the Masons."

Schultz was finding Lucy a little annoying, and he certainly didn't appreciate people making jokes about The Ancient Order of Freemasons when they obviously knew nothing about it. He said lightly: "I'm not looking for 'prospects,' Lucy. I don't even have a bed of my own yet, just the one you lent me."

Harry pointed to the right with his buggy whip, at a couple of smallish, stone buildings behind some trees. "That's the Upper Church: Anglican Bishop's residence and St. John's Cathedral. Ain't much of a cathedral yet, but will be. There's basically five groups of people here, John – besides the Company hands in their forts, and the Indians that come and go. There's the Kildonan Scotch Presbyterians sent by Lord Selkirk in '14, the mostly French Catholic halfbreeds across the river who've been here a long time, the retired Company men and their families down past the Stone Fort at Little Britain – mostly Anglicans – and then Peguis's settled Indians at St. Peters, who're mostly Anglican, too. And there's a few people like us, and Andrew McDermot and such, who came here to do business – except McDermot's been here so long he's practically part of the landscape. Oh, everybody intermingles for things like New Year's or fighting prairie fires, but mainly there's those five groups."

Schultz nodded appreciatively at what Harry had told him. He liked knowing what groups to separate people into. He'd been only a baby when The Imperial Government combined French Catholic Lower Canada with British Protestant Upper Canada, and he'd grown up watching the disaster unfold. People belonged in the groups they belonged to, and forced marriages made for nothing but bickering and bad blood.

Having settled the segments of Red River in his mind, Schultz let it drift away into the pleasant compendium of sounds in the humming summer haze: the horse's hooves, the wind sighing through the tall grass, sun-drenched cattle lowing around their cud. Then a marvellous, fluting burst of song came from somewhere out on the prairie. "What was that – a bird?"

Lucy said: "A meadowlark. I had to be told what it was, too, when we first came here. The prairie may look empty, but it's full of life and it has its own music."

A larger and newer-looking house than the others they'd passed came into view between the river and the road; it had a high-peaked roof and large windows on either side of the front door. Harry said: "That's the Inksters' new house."

Lucy said: "They call it Seven Oaks."

The only trees around it were a few saplings that looked newly planted. Schultz laughed, "They should call it Seven Bushes."

"Oh, they don't call it that for their trees," Harry said. "This whole little meadow is called Seven Oaks – I guess there's bur oaks down by the stream there. This is where the Seven Oaks Massacre happened. About forty-five years ago a couple of dozen colony men men marched out here to teach some halfbreeds and Indians a lesson, and all but two or three of them got killed and scalped. The only white man still alive who was there that day is old Point Douglas Alexander Sutherland, and I'm told he don't talk about it. Stiff-backed old coot. And his wife's the tough one in the family."

"Kate MacPherson," Lucy called out.

Schultz looked around to see who in the landscape had set Lucy off on a tangent. He could see no one but a man and a boy fixing a fence. He said: "Who the devil's Kate MacPherson?"

"Old Alexander Sutherland's wife."

"Then why couldn't you just say 'Kate Sutherland'?"

"'Cause nobody else does," Harry said. "I don't know exactly what she did back in the old days when the colony was first getting started, but it must've made some impression, 'cause after fifty years married, the Kildonan people still call her by her maiden name. To look at her now you'd think she was just any old lady, but I got a feeling you still wouldn't want to cross her. Not that I've ever exchanged more'n two words with her, and that was just 'Good morning' as we drove past."

"You see, when we first came out here," Lucy extrapolated, "we used to take Sunday morning drives – to get a picture of the place we'd come to live – and we'd always pass this tall old woman walking along this road. I happened to mention it one time when I was in McDermot's store, and Mr. McDermot said: 'That'd be Kate MacPherson.'

"He told me there's two Sunday services at Kildonan church, and the Point Douglas Sutherlands always go to the second one – all except the grandmother, who goes to both. In the summer she gets one of her grandchildren to row her across from their home, which lands her near St. John's, but she walks right past the Anglican church and keeps on walking to Kildonan kirk. Mr. McDermot said he figured the Reverend Dr. Black'd fall down in a dead faint if Kate MacPherson wasn't waiting on the front steps when he came to church – rain or shine or snow. In the winter when the river's frozen she doesn't need to be rowed across. I asked Mr. McDermot the same thing you asked me, 'Why don't you call her Mrs. Sutherland?' And he said, 'Then who'd know I was talking about Kate MacPherson?'"

About twenty minutes later in trotting-horse time, Harry pointed out a rough-stone building with a steeple and arched windows and said: "That's Kildonan Church, where old Kate MacPherson walks to every Sunday morning."

Schultz thought back to how long the carriage had been trotting along since they passed by St. John's 'cathedral,' the vicinity of where Kate MacPherson apparently crossed the river every Sunday. "*How* old did you say she is?"

Lucy said: "Must be seventy-five if she's a day."

"Told you she was the tough one in the family. Not that her husband's any slouch. Quiet little fellow but gnarly as a blackthorn cane. All that generation, the first settlers, they've been through the Highland Clearances, the fur trade wars, massacres, floods, locusts, prairie fires, forty-below winters, and they're still here. Well, they're dying out now, but time's the only thing could kill'em. They may not be sophisticated, but don't ever underestimate them. I tell you, if somebody like old Kate MacPherson was to say: 'That Dr. John Schultz, I don't think he's much of a doctor,' everybody on both sides of the river'll be beating a path away from your examination room."

"They're not exactly beating the door down now."

"Oh, give'em time, don't let it get you down. People who've lived all their life in a backwater don't take easy to new currents."

The road entered a long stretch of woods and the cool shade was a pleasant relief from the sunblast on the open prairie. Unfortunately, the mosquitoes and blackflies seemed to think so, too. The woods ended at a mile-wide cleared space around a vast, pinkish stone-walled fort, with squat turrets at the corners and loopholes in the walls. Schultz didn't consider himself an expert on military design, but it looked to him that the way the loopholes slanted outward would be handier for attackers firing in than defenders firing out.

"That stone," Harry said, "what they built the Stone Fort with, and the stone half of Fort Garry, and the churches, and the big houses in Little Britain... There's a natural stone ridge quarry just a few miles north of here. *Lime*stone, so you can burn the tailings to make lime for mortar to hold the stones together. Yup, everything the human species needs to live in plenty – and plenty more human beings than are here now – is right around here. Even *salt*, fer gawdsakes, rendered out of the brine up at the lake."

There was already a crowd filling the open space between the face of the fort and the slope down to the riverbank. Well, not *filling* – they'd left a wide, open aisle down their middle from the front gates, but there were more than enough people to fill that in if allowed. There were Indians in paint and feathers and Indians in homespun farm clothes, Metis in bright shawls and sashes, Company gentry in frock coats and top hats or hoopskirts and bonnets, and children of all descriptions chasing each other around the forest of legs.

Harry sidled the carriage in at the back of the crowd so the family could use it as a grandstand. Schultz stood up on the driver's seat footboard and looked around. Down the bank at the river's edge were a couple of dozen boats, and boatmen in multicoloured, ribboned shirts smoking pipes and waiting. The boats were odd – about thirty feet long and tapered at both ends, something like a shrunken-down Viking ship without the dragonhead. Schultz had taken comfort in storybooks about Vikings when he was a boy. They reminded him that he wasn't descended from German potato farmers, but Norse seafarers. His father had been knighted by the King of Denmark for brave service in the Danish navy during the Napoleonic Wars. One of the few clear memories Schultz had of his father was Papa telling him that story.

Schultz pointed at the riverbank and said: “Is that what they call York Boats?”

Harry said: “Oh yeah, guess you ain’t seen one yet. Spring or fall you’d’ve seen dozens of’em up around Fort Garry. Those are The Company’s workhorses, hauling freight anywhere from the Rocky Mountains to Lake of the Woods to Hudson’s Bay. They can set a square sail in a good wind, but mostly it’s rowing – bloody killing work – and dragging the boats on wooden rollers across the portages from river to river. Most of the ones lined up there are to take the troops north across Lake Winnipeg and down the rivers to York Factory on the Bay, where their ship’s supposed to be waiting. But I’m told *one* of them boats is gonna split off and cut west to cause trouble for old Andrew McDermot.”

“McDermot the storekeeper?”

“Same fella. You see, Johnny, The Company’s monopoly on the fur trade ran out a couple of years ago – and I’m told even before that they’d given up enforcing it; not out of the goodness of their hearts, but ’cause the halfbreeds don’t like it and there’s thousands of halfbreeds and they all carry guns. So, anyone who has the capital can outfit a boat and crew with trade goods and send them north to the fur country. The Company can’t stop them. What The Company *can* do is try and find out where the independent trader is going, send out a loaded boat of their own and set up beside him and undercut him. No Indian’s gonna trade a fox fur pelt for one knife when he can get two knives for it next door. The Company can afford to take a loss; the little independent trader can’t. Couple of seasons like that and most independent traders go back to farming or hunting buffalo.”

Schultz said sourly: “Pretty slick.”

“That’s The Company’s way in most things, Johnny. You get to be an annoyance to them, they won’t come right out and knock you on the head, just gradually cut the ground away from under your feet. ’Cause they own the ground.” Harry chuckled, “Though I guess the Cree up north must get some entertainment from watching the white man’s boats play cat and mouse all up and down the lakes and rivers.”

From inside the fort a brass band squawked a couple of times and then launched into *Soldiers of The Queen.* Out of the gate came The Royal Canadian Rifles with flags flying, drums beating, and their pocket marching band out front. Schultz doffed his hat and put his hand over his heart in the civilian salute. It gave him a flush of pride to know that those proud soldiers of the Queen were *Canadian* troops, and no doubt a number of those smartly-uniformed, polished-weaponed, fierce-mustached men came from the same towns where he grew up and went to school. The crowd cheered, but Schultz could see there were tears as well, from some of the brown-skinned young women in the half of the crowd facing him.

It did seem a mite ridiculous that the regiment would have to travel four thousand miles – north, then east, then south, then west – when their destination was only one thousand miles east. But the only alternative would’ve been to travel through American territory. Schultz didn’t buy the Yankee brag that the reason their frontier had moved west so much faster than British North America's was they had more get up and go. The fact was that the Americans had only had to push west through forest and prairie, while the same longitudes north of the border latitudes were an impenetrable tangle of spruce bogs and twisted granite. As one of Schultz's professors had said to the class: "Geography *is* history." Not to mention the fact that there was little point hacking a road through that mess when all you'd find at the other end was more land that belonged to The Hudson's Bay Company.

The Royal Canadian rifles put on a good show of getting into the York Boats in an orderly fashion, and the boatmen put on an even better show of launching the boats in a clean line and setting off down-river with all oars in unison. Lucy said: "Well, there goes The Company's teeth."

Harry grunted: "Well, most of 'em, anyway."

Schultz said: "How's that?"

Harry said: "The Company rules here, right? By The Company's rules. They got their own court and hired judge, and the Imperial Government expects The Company to hold up British law. But the only law officer around to enforce it is the Sheriff of Red River. Oh, he can appoint Special Constables in an emergency, but there's nobody around here to appoint except farmers and buffalo hunters. So now..." Harry pointed his thick-bearded chin at the York Boats disappearing around a bend. "How's The Company gonna call out the troops when there's no troops to call out?"

Schultz found that very interesting.

CHAPTER 6

On the other side of the river from the Stone Fort, Kate MacPherson watched the dwindling of the last boat carrying the Royal Canadian Rifles away, then leaned back against the corner railing of the cart she was standing in. She would've liked to sit down instead of just leaning back, but squatting and standing weren't as easy operations as they once were, and she'd just have to stand up again in a minute once the cart started moving again – either that or have her bony bottom battered by all the jouncing and bouncing of the cart floor.

Hugh pointed across the river and said: "There's that doctor I told you about, Gran, that Dr. Schultz."

"Where?"

"Standing up in that carriage there. Oh, he's sat down now."

"How do you know it is him? Your eyes may be younger than mine, but it is still a long way."

"He took his hat off for a minute and the sun lit up his hair. Then once that caught my eye I knew it had to be him, 'cause he's so big. Bigger'n even Mr. Grant was, I bet."

"No one is bigger than Mr. Grant," but she said it teasingly. It was hard to be anything but affectionate with Hugh. Kate loved all her grandchildren and didn't like to play favourites, but there was no pretending there wasn't something different about Purple Hugh. He was her Christmas Boy – born with a caul on his head on Christmas Day the same year his mother's grandparents died. Kate felt more part of Janet's grandparents' generation than Janet's parents'. Old Alexander MacBeth had been a soldier like Alexander Sutherland, and Janet's father had been just a child through the brutal years when Janet's grandparents and John's parents were surviving together through the Highland Clearances, the brutal journey from Scotland to Red River and then the Fur Trade War. So when old age took ex-Sergeant MacBeth and his Christy in the same year, it had left a hole in Kate's life, and then along came her Christmas boy to fill it. But no, Kate couldn't say that would entirely explain her particular attachment to that particular grandson.

Sometimes Kate would try to tell herself it was just the fact that Hugh had black hair and blue-green eyes like her long-dead father, whom she'd last seen waving good-bye as she hiked through the Highlands to the ship that would carry her to North America

– odd that Hugh would have sea-green eyes when neither he nor his mother and father and sisters and brothers had ever seen the sea. But whenever Kate tried to explain it away that way, she ended up having to admit that it wasn't just Hugh's colouring, there was something else about his eyes. They were kitten eyes. Even at thirteen years old, his eyes still had that expression common to kittens and toddling children: wide to the world, comically curious and seriously intent on whatever never-before-seen was unfolding in front of them, be it sheet lightning in a roaring night sky or a tadpole in a puddle.

The cart lurched into motion, jarring Kate out of her ruminations but only for a moment. Hugh's mention of Mr. Grant brought back to her that there *was* something different about Hugh, not just her imagination and predilections and superstitions about a child born with a caul on his head. When Hugh and Donald were five and six years old, Kate and her husband had taken them on a day-long cart trip all the way to Grantown on the Assiniboine, so their grandsons could tell their grandchildren they'd shaken the hand of Mr. Grant. When that head-bandaged wreck of a man – with his rounded, Scots jaw and his black, Cree eyes – raised his massive hand off his deathbed, Donald had clung to his grandfather's leg in frozen terror. But Donald's little brother Hugh had marched straight forward and stuck his tiny hand into the hand that had killed or cold-cocked more men than a five year old's arithmetic could count.

Kate's husband's voice brought her back to the present again. Sandy was calling to the cart ahead of them carrying the other half of the family: "John, the children are getting peckish. What say ye we stop by the split willow and have our picnic there?"

Janet called back at her father-in-law: "Oh, *the children* are getting peckish, are they?"

John called over his shoulder and through his laughter: "Very well, Father, whatever's best for the *children*."

Kate watched Janet pat and stroke John's back, Janet using the slim possibility he might choke on his laughter as an excuse to caress her husband in public. Kate was aware that she was jealous of Janet at times. Jealousy came a distant second of the two major sins Kate now knew herself prone to – the first was pride, and it and jealousy went hand in hand. She hadn't been much aware of those sins for her first sixty years or so – there'd been too much to do – but nowadays she spent almost as much time staring out windows as being useful to other people.

The reason Kate had to be jealous of her daughter-in-law was that Janet had borne eleven children and would likely bear more – Janet showed no signs of being pregnant again yet, but it had only been seven months since James MacPherson Sutherland squalled hello to the cold world. Kate had only borne one child, and the midwife had said it was a miracle she'd had the one. On the other hand, Kate hadn't had to bear eleven children and counting.

The two family carts pulled up in the shade of the big willow tree that had been split by lightning and survived, where a bend in the river left a mossy crescent of shoreline relatively free of the biting bugs that swarmed in the tall grass. They laid out buffalo robes to sit on and, after Janet had said grace, plunged into the baskets of their own-made bread and cheese and smoked sausage and cold roast chicken and strips of fruit leather made from wild pincherries and saskatoon berries last fall.

Watching her grandchildren happily wolf down the bounty of their home and hands, Kate remembered times along this river when she would've traded her Bible for a loaf of bread, and times along the seacoast of County Sutherland when she probably would've sold her virtue for a meal if anybody'd been interested. Part of her wished that her son and daughter-in-law and grandchildren had gone through a little of that kind of experience, so they would know how truly precious were the gifts of God's grace they were thanking Him for. But most of her prayed they would never have to learn.

It occurred to Kate that maybe that's what it was about her Christmas Boy. Hugh seemed to know in his bones what none of the other children understood. How could they be expected to? They'd never lived in the outside world, and by the time they were born the blood price for the place they lived had already been paid. The fact was that despite deadly cold winters, spring floods, prairie fires, plagues of crop-eating insects, and all the other natural disasters lurking in this part of the world – partly *because* of them – the people who lived at Red River were the luckiest people on the face of the earth.

CHAPTER 7

Hugh's summer ended too early, as they always did. Except for a week off in late September to help with the harvest, he was back in jail five days a week in the little, stone schoolhouse on the grounds of Kildonan Kirk, and reminding himself to call the schoolteacher Mr. MacBeth instead of Uncle Hector. In what seemed no time at all, Hugh was able to walk across the river again – instead of squeezing into the dugout canoe with Donald and Aleck and Morrison and Hector and Angus and Margaret every schoolday morning – and Mr. MacBeth had to melt snow on the schoolhouse stove for their ink powder. Soon the year had grown old enough for the sun to be going down by the time the day's lessons were over.

On one of those darkening afternoons, the Point Douglas Sutherland schoolchildren were walking home in a pack as usual, crunching the snow double-time to try and keep some heat inside their duffle leggings and HBC blanket coats. This year Donald had graduated into a genuine coat, double-breasted buttons and all, that had been Da's until Da grew too 'stout.' Hugh hoped Donald wouldn't stouten up soon, because he actually preferred the coat Donald had hand-me-downed to him. It was a Metis style capote with a hood and held together with a couple of antler-point toggles and a ceinture flechée, an arrow sash. The multi-coloured pattern of interwoven arrowhead shapes was so strong that voyageurs could use their ceinture flechées as a tow rope for a laden York Boat. Not that Hugh had any plans to be towing any York Boats any time soon, but the capote and ceinture flechée made him feel like he could if he had to.

Halfway home from school, the Point Douglas Sutherlands caught up with Tim Matheson – who was a year older than Hugh but even dimmer at his books – and a couple of his friends. The reason Tim Matheson and his friends were catch-uppable was they were busy chucking chunks of snow crust at Norbert Parisien and driving him around in circles.

Norbert Parisien was a year or so younger than Hugh, and he didn't go to school. They'd tried him out for part of one year at one of the Catholic parish schools and decided it was a waste of time for him and the priests. He had a face that looked unfinished – thick, rubbery lips and nose and slanted, dark eyes – and at the moment he was crying, holding his mittened hands to the top of his head.

Hugh said loudly to Tim Matheson: "Stop that."

Tim laughed, "What?"

"Stop it! Leave him alone! What'd he ever do to you?"

Tim Matheson laughed again and stooped to break off another crust of snow. As Tim raised his arm to throw it at Norbert, Hugh went for Tim. Even though a year older than Hugh, Tim was a couple of inches shorter, but made up for it by being a good deal stockier. At the moment, though, Hugh wasn't thinking of odds or size or getting punched, or of anything except that he couldn't stand seeing harmless Norbert be tormented.

There was a flurry of arms and the next thing Hugh knew he had Tim Matheson's neck in the crook of his left arm pressed against his side, and Tim was bent over and struggling to get free. Hugh thought: 'That's handy,' and began driving his mittened right fist into Tim's trapped face.

After only three or four punches, Tim squealed: "That's enough! I give!" and Hugh let him go. Tim picked up his toque and marched back to his friends. For about an instant, Hugh was surprised that Tim's friends hadn't stepped in to pummel him while he was pummelling Tim. Then he remembered that Donald and Aleck and Morrison and the rest of the clan were standing behind him.

Hugh stepped over to Norbert, wiped the snow- and tear-smeared face with the palm of his mitten, and said: "You better be getting home, Norbert." Norbert nodded and headed along the path down river. Most of the Parisiens lived up river near The Forks, in St. Boniface or St. Norbert, but Norbert's family had a little farm somewhere down-river toward Chief Peguis's people at St. Peters.

As Hugh turned back to join his brothers and sisters, Donald said to them: "You are not to tell Mother and Father that Hugh has been fighting. Do you understand me?"

Angus said: "What about Granny and Granda?"

"Nor them. It is not a lie, it is just not saying."

Margaret said: "What if they ask us what happened in school today?"

"Then we will tell them what happened in school. Let's be getting home now." As they started off, Donald clapped Hugh on the shoulder and murmured: "Aye, Purple Hugh The Champion."

The next morning before school, all the boys stood stamping their feet or running about in the snowy schoolyard, hanging onto their last few minutes of freedom before Mr. MacBeth rang the bell. The girls were already inside the schoolhouse, warming their fingers by the squat, square, Carron stove. On days this cold Hugh sometimes wondered if the girls weren't more intelligent, but it wouldn't do for a boy to give up and go in before the bell rang.

One of the groups of boys dotted about the schoolyard was gathered around Tim Matheson. One of the older boys sauntered over from that group to the group Hugh was standing in, and said to Hugh, "Tim Matheson's telling everybody he beat you up good yesterday."

Aleck sputtered: "That's not true! Hugh walloped him till Tim said 'I give'!"

"Well, that's what you Sutherlands say. Tim says different, and no one else saw."

Hugh wanted to say: 'Ask his two friends, are they liars, too?' but that seemed like kind of a whiny way to go about it. It would've been even more foolish to say: 'Ask Norbert Parisien.'

"Tim's bragging," the older boy went on, "that he pounded you out and he'll do it again any time you ask for more."

Hugh could feel the eyes of the other boys on him. What had happened yesterday wasn't something he wanted to brag about, although he was pleased with himself the way it had turned out. It had never occurred to him that someone could make it completely different just by saying so. He said: "Matheson's lying."

"That's what you say."

Hugh chewed his lip. He could see only one way of proving it was a lie, and he'd handled Tim Matheson surprisingly easily yesterday. He said: "After school."

The older boy nodded and smiled and went back to the group around Tim Matheson, and then Mr. MacBeth stepped out the door swinging his handbell. Hugh spent the day trying not to look at Tim Matheson and telling himself to relax – today was going to happen just like yesterday. But at lunchtime he could only eat half of his bannock and cheese, and gave the rest to Hector and Angus.

After school, the Sutherlands and all the other pupils who lived up-river headed south along the side of the road as though it was a perfectly normal day. They were all aware that they had to get well away from the schoolyard, and as removed from the sight of other prying adult eyes as possible. There was a low spot on the bank where the Bannermans had been dragging logs across the frozen river, so the snow there was tramped down pretty good. And the naked bushes along the slopes on either side provided at least a little cover.

Hugh moved away from his brothers and sisters and turned around. Tim Matheson stepped towards him, and the other boys and even a few girls drifted into a wide, ragged ring around them. It looked to Hugh like half the school was there, even some whose homes were down-river.

The older boy who'd told Hugh about Tim's lie said: "First one to knock the other one down wins. Agreed?"

Hugh didn't know exactly what he was supposed to say, so he just nodded. Then he and Tim Matheson grappled with each other for a minute, trying to trip each other up, but neither of them could get a quick advantage so they broke away again. As Hugh stepped back, his high-topped, slick-soled winter moccasins hit a patch of ice. He flailed his arms to keep his balance, but his feet shot out from under him and he came down on his back hard. Tim Matheson was wearing boots with actual heels, so it was easier for him to keep his footing.

Hugh lay there for a moment catching his breath. Tim Matheson was shouting: "He's down, I win!" and other boys were yelling: "No, you didn't knock him down, he slipped!"

Hugh started to get up again. When he was up on one knee, he felt a strange, dull thump in the middle of his face and his eyes went blurry. When he was back on his feet, one of the other boys shouted: "Are you going to let him get away with that?"

Hugh said: "With what?"

"He kicked you in the head!"

"Oh." Hugh thought that if anything should do it, that should – bring back the surge of fury that had made him hurl himself at Tim Matheson yesterday. But it didn't come. He cocked his fists in what he guessed was an appropriate position and moved mechanically forward. They took a few swings at each other and landed one or two, then Hugh stepped back again.

There was a tree at one end of the ring of watchers. Hugh shifted sideways and put his back against it so he couldn't slip and fall. Tim Matheson said: "You quitting?" and Hugh cocked his fists again. Tim came on swinging and Hugh landed a hard punch on Tim's jaw that seemed to surprise him. Tim stepped back to reconsider and then came on again.

It went on like that for what seemed a long time – with Tim making an attack and then stepping back to recover, and Hugh keeping his back planted against the tree and fending him off. Although Tim was older and heavier-shouldered, Hugh's arms were longer and he was faster. Hugh knew he didn't know a thing about boxing, but it didn't take much science to react when a mittened fist was coming at your head. They only punched at each other's heads – it would've been pointless to punch at a body wearing a thick wool coat puffed with layers underneath.

Hugh's eyes weren't blurry anymore, but there was a strange numbness spreading outward from his nose. In fact, he felt a kind of disconnected numbness all over. He thought that if he kept getting charged and punched at for long enough, he was bound to eventually explode like he had yesterday. But he didn't. When Tim stepped back after being driven off yet again, Hugh heard someone say: "Nothing's gonna happen here," and out of the corner of his eye saw two of the older boys turn to walk away. The ring of watchers had already grown sparser.

Tim Matheson came on once again, and once again Hugh blocked most of his punches and drove his right fist into Tim's left cheek. But this time a screeching pain jolted from Hugh's hand all the way back up his arm. Hugh told himself to ignore it – it didn't hurt much when Tim Matheson punched him, why should it hurt when he punched Tim Matheson? But the next time he saw an opening and swung, his right arm stopped short of its own volition so it was barely a punch at all, and even that sent back another burst of pain.

Hugh threw up his open hands and gasped: "Wait!"

Tim Matheson stepped back and said: "Do you quit?"

"No, I... but I can't... I think I broke something in my hand."

"He quits! I win!"

Someone else muttered: "Only 'cause he broke his hand punching your stupid head."

Hugh looked down and saw there were spatters of blood down the front of his capote. He murmured: "When did that happen?"

Donald said: "When he kicked you in the head," and handed him an icicle. "Hold that against your nose."

Everybody else was already on their way back to the road, but Hugh's brothers and sister stood waiting, shivering from standing in the cold so long. Margaret and Angus were crying and Hector was trying not to. Donald said: "We'd best get walking before we all freeze to death," and added grimly, "There'll be no not-telling-tales this time."

On the walk home Hugh discovered an odd thing. Tim Matheson's punches, even his kick, hadn't really hurt. But now, some while after the fact, Hugh could feel a definite pain in his chin and a corner of his jaw and his puffed-up lower lip. And the numbness around the bridge of his nose had turned into a very distinct pain that seemed to hammer more sharply with every step. But all of that was nothing compared to the looming moment when he would have to walk through the door to his mother and father.

The first moment through the door was all horrified concern, with Da bustling him into a chair and Mum and Gran running to the pantry for water and cloths. The atmosphere changed when Da asked him what had happened and Hugh said: "I got in a fight." Mum and Gran kept on hurrying forward with a basin and pitcher, but their 'Poor dear's had evaporated.

Da turned to the other children standing by the door and said: "You're late for your after-school chores; best get them done before supper."

"Yes, Father," and they all went out again – except Margaret, who was too young yet to have winter chores.

"Margaret, take Catherine and William and Christina upstairs and read to them."

"Yes, Father."

Mum and Gran set the basin and pitcher on the table in front of Hugh, and Mum said: "Stand up so I can take your coat off. I don't know how I'm going to get it clean."

Gran said: "When the boys come in from their chores I will have them fetch me buckets of water, and start it soaking in a barrel."

As the sleeve slid over his right hand, Hugh winced and gritted his teeth. Mum and Gran looked at each other, but just took his coat, sat him back down and started dabbing at the dried blood on his face. On the other side of the table, Da turned an empty chair around, sat on it backwards with his arms crossed on the top and said: "All right, Hugh, tell us, um, how this came about."

It took awhile to get it out, what with a swollen lip and the wet cloths dabbing around his face, and the occasional wince when the cloths touched his nose too hard. He started by telling what had happened yesterday. When he finished that part of the story he paused, because now they knew he'd got himself into two fights, not just the one.

Da raised one eyebrow and looked at Mum. Mum put her hand on Hugh's arm and said: "That was a generous thing to do, Hugh – helping Norbert Parisien."

Gran said: "Brave lad."

Granda said: "Guid deeds have a habit of comin' back tae haunt ye."

Gran said: "Pay no attention to your grandfather."

Da scratched his beard and said: "When we, um, asked at supper yesterday what... happened at school, none of you said anything of this."

"Well, I... I knew you didn't like us fighting, except wrestling for fun, and it was only a scuffle, so... I asked them not to tell you about it. I told them it wouldn't really be lying, just not saying. And, well, I told 'em if you asked what happened at school they still wouldn't have to lie, 'cause the scuffle didn't happen at school."

"Um-hm. Speaking of lying, John Hugh... It is a kind impulse for you to try and um, take the blame on yourself, but... parsing fine points of law isn't your way of thinking. I will speak to Donald later. So, that was yesterday, what happened today?"

Hugh told them of Tim Matheson bragging around the school that he'd cleaned Hugh Sutherland's clock. "I was gonna just let yesterday be yesterday and forget about it, but I couldn't, um..." He didn't see a need to tell them much detail about the fight itself, just that it went on for a long time, that the blood happened when Tim kicked him in the head when he was down, and that it ended when Hugh couldn't punch anymore because of the pain in his hand.

Gran leaned over and lifted Hugh's right hand and gently felt along the back of it. When she touched the base of his little finger his head jerked back and his breath hissed in. She said: "I would say the bottom knuckle of his little finger is broken. So is his nose, at the top, but you cannot put a splint on a nose, and it looks as it will heal itself straight once the swelling comes down. But the finger must be re-set and bound. I could do it myself, or Sally Ross, but it would be better done by a doctor."

Mum said: "Dr. Cowan's still way north at Moose Factory, and Dr. Bird miles down-river at Bird's Hill if he's even home at all. There's that new doctor just across the river, Dr. Schultz."

Da went to the door and called out: "Donald, hitch a pony to the sled, please. Have Aleck lend you a hand."

The 'sled' was one of their Red River carts de-wheeled and set on wooden runners for the winter. As the sled bounced over the ruts worn in the wind-hardened snow on top of the river ice, Hugh held on to the rail with his left hand. He was swaddled in a too-big coat that smelled of pipe smoke and musty old-man smell. It wasn't much too big, though – his grandfather wasn't a large man, and had joked that in another year or two Hugh wouldn't be able to borrow his coat without splitting the seams.

The night was one of those crystalline, cruelly cold, clear winter nights when the sky was filled with stars – especially out on the river where there were no trees or buildings to hem the vision. The cold stabbed ice needles into the bridge of Hugh's nose, but he knew nobody would have reason to feel sorry for him if he complained. So he kept his mouth shut and looked up to find The Little Bear and the North Star. No one could get lost on a night like this.

Da didn't knock at the door of the Royal Hotel, just opened it and ushered Hugh in. There was a hallway that opened into a big room with a big table where the McKenneys were at supper, along with Dr. Schultz and another man in a checkered suitcoat. Harry McKenney stood up, wiping his beard with a napkin, and said: "Mr. Sutherland."

"Mr. McKenney. I'm sorry to intrude –"

"No intrusion – it's a Public House, after all."

"My son, you see, requires the services of a doctor. We could wait till you've done supper."

The copper-haired giant stood up – and up, and up – saying: "No need to wait – Doctors' hours are patients' hours. I'm Dr. Schultz."

"John Sutherland."

"I know – Councillor of Assiniboia and one of the finest farmers in the area."

"Well, the farming depends on, um, weather luck. And I'm not a... full-fledged Councillor, just a substitute – sort of an... apprentice councillor." Assiniboia was the thousands of square miles around The Forks originally granted to Lord Selkirk for his colony of displaced Highlanders, and was more or less governed by a council appointed by The Company. "I believe you've met my son, Hugh."

"I have. Spend your shilling yet?" Hugh nodded. Dr. Schultz turned back to Da. "What's wrong with the lad?" Hugh thought he might've asked him, but reminded himself he was in no position to get high-horsed about anything.

"We think he has a broken knuckle."

"Ah. Well, come on up to my examining room."

The examining room had a narrow bed, two chairs and a small table with a black leather doctor's bag on it. Dr. Schultz told Hugh to sit on the bed and unbutton his shirt, then took two wooden cylinders out of the satchel and fitted them together and screwed a sort of wooden saucer onto one end. There was a hole in the middle of the saucer. As the doctor leaned down to put the saucer against Hugh's chest, Da said: "It's his knuckle, not his lungs."

"Yes, yes – but we must make sure his heart is beating normally before we proceed with treatment." Dr. Schultz crouched down and put his ear to the other end of the cylinder, nodded and hmed, then stood back up and took the cylinder apart. "Perfectly normal. Now we can proceed. Which knuckle?"

Hugh pointed and then winced as the doctor took hold of his right hand. Hugh's whole hand barely covered Dr. Schultz's palm. "Hm, yes – fractured base of the digitus minor. Looks like a broken nose, too, but that will have to heal itself."

"That's what Gran said."

"This is going to hurt." Hugh clamped his jaw tight but still let out an embarrassing squeak when the doctor jerked his finger forward and then let it go again. "Well, that set it, but we'll have to keep it that way. Please excuse me for a moment. Keep your hand flat on your leg like that, Hugh."

The doctor stepped out and Hugh could hear his boots going down the stairs. Da sat down in the spare chair and looked at the wall. It was obvious he was thinking about something, and at times like that it was best to leave him alone and find out what he'd decided to say once he decided to say it.

The doctor came back with a short, thin slat of wood and proceeded to bandage it tightly to Hugh's finger. As he did so, he said breezily, "Been fighting then, Hugh?"

"Yes, sir."

"What's her name?"

"Um, whose name, sir?"

"The girl you were fighting over."

"Wasn't over a girl."

"Oh, a matter of honour, then. Well, he broke your nose, but you must've been pile-driving his head pretty good to break your hand."

Over Dr. Schultz's hunched-down shoulder, Hugh could see that his father didn't appreciate that line of talk. The doctor knotted the bandage and stood up saying: "Leave that on there for two weeks and you'll be good as new."

Da said: "What do I owe you, Doctor?"

"Oh, one of The Company's paper shillings if you happen to have one on you – that'll even us up for the pony ride last summer. By the way, Mr. Sutherland, would you be amenable to me stopping by your house some evening? I'd like to converse with you about a matter of business."

"What, um... variety of, uh, business?"

"Oh, you have other things on your mind just now, and it's liable to be a longish conversation."

Hugh appreciated the way Dr. Schultz didn't seem to notice Da's very noticeable, out-loud sort of nervous tic: all the ums and uhs and, worst of all, the sudden barking-out of a word for no reason after a blank pause. It was only a slight oddment at home with just the family around, but downright embarrassing in public. But then, John Hugh Sutherland wasn't exactly in a position to feel embarrassed about anybody else at the moment.

Da said to Dr. Schultz: "Well, um, any evening... except Sunday."

"Of course."

"We're, uh, on the other side of the river, by –"

"I know where you are. One of the first things Henry pointed out to me was the house of Councillor John Sutherland."

"Well... come along, Hugh. And thank the Doctor for letting us... interrupt his supper."

"Thanks."

"Oh, just part and parcel of the profession. Keep your thumb in tight next time and you won't break your knuckles."

On the way home, Da let the pony walk, even though the plates Mum would've saved for them from supper were waiting. Da kept thinking about something till they were out on the river, then said: "Hugh, yesterday you, um, leaped on Tim Matheson and had him... beaten in a minute. Today, you and Tim Matheson, um, punched at each other for a long time and you couldn't beat him down. Doesn't that seem strange?"

"Yeah, it... I dunno, I... I just couldn't get... Yesterday I didn't think about it, it just... happened."

"Why did you, uh, fight Tim Matheson yesterday?"

"'Cause – Well, no, I guess there's no excuse for fighting."

"No excuse, no, but... sometimes there's a reason. So, I'll, um... ask you again, what made you fight Tim Matheson yesterday?"

"It was the only way to make him stop! I don't... I just... Something just... blew up, exploded."

"And why did you fight Tim Matheson today?"

"Well, I told you – he was saying he beat me up yesterday, and that wasn't true."

"Did you hear him say that?"

"No, but people told me."

"Well... How do you know that the 'people' who told you, didn't just want to watch a fight, or, um... maybe wanted to see Tim Matheson or you get beaten up? So, they told you Tim Matheson was... bragging he beat you up, and maybe told Tim Matheson you were bragging about beating him up?"

"Well, they, um..." Hugh hadn't thought of that. "They wouldn't do that."

"Maybe not. In any case... why did you fight Tim Matheson today?"

"Well, he was lying about what happened yesterday, and other people believed him –"

"'Other people' again." As soon as that was out, Da closed his mouth again abruptly, as though kicking himself for asking a question and then interrupting the answer. But Hugh had lost whatever more he'd been trying to say, so after waiting a moment Da went on, "So, would it be fair to say that, um, yesterday you fought Tim Matheson because you had to, and today you fought Tim Matheson because you thought you should? Yesterday something just... welled-up inside you and exploded, and today was... 'a matter of honour'."

"Um... Yeah, I guess so, me whatever."

"You'll find that if you only... fight when you have no choice, when you've, um, done your damnedest to find any way you can to walk away, but it just bursts out of you, you'll be a tiger. But if you put your fists up because that's what you think you're supposed to do... well, your nose and your knuckle can tell you better than I can. If you can, um, learn that lesson now, you'll save yourself a lot of pain and humiliation. Took me a lot longer."

"You?"

"Oh, I wasn't always the, um, wise old man I am today. And the funny thing is, if you only fight when you... absolutely have to, you'll find you hardly ever have to fight at all."

Another funny thing, Hugh realised, was that Da's umming and uhing and all wasn't awkwardness, it was carefulness. Da was immensely careful about trying to say exactly what he meant to say. The blank pauses and barking were just pouncing on the right word when he found it. Since he was much more careful than most, maybe he should be listened to more carefully than most. At the moment, though, Hugh was mostly listening to his stomach telling him it had been a long and complicated time since he'd last fed it.

The next day at school, the left side of Tim Matheson's face was purple and yellow and puffed out in lumps, which made Hugh a little less embarrassed about his swollen nose and bandaged hand. But when Hugh eventually took the splint and bandage off, his little finger couldn't quite close up tight against its neighbour, and it never did again.

CHAPTER 8

Schultz waited a few weeks to pay his evening call on John Sutherland, so as not to seem too eager or unoccupied with other business. McKenney & Co did have other business plans besides this one, but none of them with near the potential payoff for what little it took to get one signature on a piece of paper.

On the morning of the day he'd decided enough time had elapsed to pay an evening call on Point Douglas John Sutherland, Schultz made his customary after-breakfast trek out to the Necessary shed set back behind the Royal Hotel. There was a substantial snowfall coming down, which he'd learned meant the day would be warmer than the clear winter days. He was only in the outhouse for a few minutes, but when he came back out again the world had changed. The snow wasn't falling now so much as pelting, driven almost horizontal by a wind that almost knocked him off his feet. The air was a white swirl so thick he couldn't even see the Royal Hotel.

But he knew the building hadn't blown away – at least he thought not – and was no more than thirty paces away. He could visualize the angle from the outhouse to the back door of the Royal Hotel, so he lined himself up in that direction, tightened his muffler around his throat and started marching. The battalions of snow pellets were striking his face so sharply that he slitted his eyes for fear they'd get needle-pierced. The wind sucked the air out of his lungs; he had to turn his head leeward to get a breath in.

Schultz became aware that he'd gone a good deal more than thirty paces and still hadn't fetched up against anything solid, and still couldn't see anything except the white maelstrom. He'd obviously got turned around and might be marching toward the Rocky Mountains for all he knew. It seemed ridiculously possible that all of John Christian Schultz's plans and prospects might end in a frozen heap out on the prairie, miles away from the path between the Royal Hotel and its outhouse. The wind was scouring tears out of his eyes and he could feel them freezing among the snow bullets driven into his cheeks.

"Johnny!" It was Harry's voice. Harry had a bellow on him that would put a bull elk to shame, but Schultz could barely hear him over the blizzard roar.

Schultz sucked in enough air to bellow back: "Harry!"

"Stay where you are! Don't move! And keep calling!"

Schultz stood with his back to the wind, feeling childish as he called out periodically, "Harry!... I'm here!... Harry!..." Then a dark shape appeared through the white and it was Henry McKenney, with a coil of rope in one hand and paying out the line behind him.

Harry barked: "Follow the rope to the hotel! When you get there, give the rope three tugs and go inside, then I'll find the outhouse and tie this end to it!"

"But... how will you find it?"

"I've walked this path more'n you have, and anyway I got the rope! No point standing here shouting in each others' faces, get along!"

Schultz got along, keeping one hand on the rope Harry was holding taut. After not very far, the big black bulk of the Royal Hotel loomed out of the whirling white cloud. The rope was tied to the hitching post beside the back door. Schultz gave the rope three tugs and went inside. He stood by the stove for a moment and then flopped onto a chair. After a few minutes Harry came in, stomping snow off his boots and unbuttoning his coat. He went to the stove and stood warming his fingers and catching his breath. He turned toward Schultz with one corner of his black mustache slightly lifted and said: "Welcome to Rupert's Land."

"I... We used to do that on the lake boats – string ropes across the deck in storms – but I never thought, on dry land..."

"We don't get all that many blows like this, but once in awhile... Even people who lived here all their lives've got caught by surprise, froze to death between the house and the barn, goin' around in circles. Sometimes they don't get found until the snowdrifts start to melt. Well, you won't be paying any calls on John Sutherland this evening. Even if this don't last long, everybody'll be busy digging out."

The next evening, Schultz bolted his supper and went up to change into his business suit. When he came back downstairs the table had been cleared, the children were up in their rooms or helping the halfbreed chore girl with the dishes, and Harry and Lucy had their heads together over the pencilled plans for the new store, bickering over whether it looked too big or too small. Schultz coughed to get their attention and said: "I'd best get going."

Lucy said: "Good luck, Johnny."

Harry said: "Don't press him too hard, John – just laying a foundation's good enough for now. And watch out for the old lady."

Before sitting down to supper Schultz had harnessed a horse to the cutter – the carriage body fitted onto runners – and hitched it to the lee side of the building. Out on the frozen river trotting into the wind, the cold bit through his new buffalo-pelt coat like it was cheesecloth. He kept the sleigh on the beaten track down the middle of the river until he got near the Sutherlands', then turned the horse to the right. When they got close to the riverbank, the horse swerved against the reins. Schultz started to curse it, then saw a black hole in the snow – probably the spot the Sutherlands kept clear of ice for their winter water supply. There was a path leading up the bank from the hole. Schultz hitched the horse to a broken tree and started up the path.

When he got up to the yard, several scruffy dogs spewed out of a hatch in the barn door and barrelled around his ankles, barking and growling. Schultz felt a twinge of fear but kept on walking – if any of them did any more than snarl he'd kick it over the barn. Before he reached the house, the door opened and a man with a gun stepped out, closing the door behind him. By the light coming out through the windows, the man was of only medium height, with yellow-white hair, and the gun was the versatile kind most favoured around Red River – a double-barrelled smooth-bore that could be loaded with either ball or shot.

Schultz stopped where he stood. The old man called out: "Quit yer fashin', lads. Shush. Here," and the dogs ran to him and sat in the snow glowering. Now that the dogs were quiet, Schultz could hear a strange, sharp, staccato knocking sound coming from the house.

Schultz said: "I'm Dr. John Schultz. Your son," guessing the old man to be Point Douglas Alexander Sutherland, "said I could drop by some evening for a business conversation."

"Well and good. Sorry about the welcome, we've had a weasel reconnoitring our henhouse – the dogs hae been able to scare him off but not to catch him. Come in."

Inside was a large room with a stone fireplace and a square little cast iron stove, both crackling away, and a long table with half a dozen boys of various sizes doing schoolwork or playing checkers. The knocking sound was coming from a wooden trough on the floor – sort of a midget dugout canoe – where two small girls were malleting the hulls off barley, under the supervision of a tall, grizzle-haired woman and a brown-haired woman who was in the midstage of pregnancy. The tall old woman's hair must've been red to begin with; now it looked like rusted iron.

John Sutherland got up from a chair by the fireplace, saying: "Oh, Dr. Schultz, um, come in, come in, let me take your coat. You've already… *met* my father, and he didn't shoot you. This is my mother, my wife Janet, my son Donald, Hugh you already know…"

With each name, the named came forward and shook Schultz's hand. When Hugh's turn came, Schultz said amiably: "I see the splint's off. How's your finger, Hugh?"

"Oh, it's all right, thank you."

The old lady said: "Just a wee bit… crooked."

John Sutherland and the procession went on: "… Alexander, Morrison, Hector, Angus, Catherine, wee William – and Christina and James are already… *abed.* Do sit down, Doctor – would you care for a cup of tea?"

"Thank you, but I don't want to put you to any bother."

"No bother," the younger Mrs. Sutherland said. "Milk and sugar?"

"Please," although he was quite sure that the 'sugar' would be the watery maple syrup the locals made.

Schultz sat down in the chair he was gestured to. He wasn't quite sure how to proceed. It was difficult enough trying to launch into a grown-up business conversation with a man twice his age without being surrounded by children and ancients overhearing. He thought maybe if he reminded John Sutherland that he'd come to talk about business, Sutherland would suggest they adjourn to another room. Schultz could see through an open doorway that there was another room, a small side parlour with a crackling fireplace of its own bookending the house with the kitchen fireplace. But before Schultz could start working around to the reason for his visit, John Sutherland came right out and said: "You said you wanted to talk to me about a... *business* proposition," and showed no sign of moving.

The girls and the old woman went back to the barley trough – one of the girls knocking with the mallet and the other turning the barley with a small paddle, which seemed appropriate for a midget dugout canoe. The boys at the table went back to their checkers or schoolwork, and the old man lit a pipe and went to whittling over a cloth on the floor to catch the shavings. The whittling looked of no useful purpose, just making an inch-thick, foot-long piece of branch gradually thinner. Several other like pieces of branch, with the bark still on, were stacked waiting on the table. Likely the younger Sutherlands collected branches and encouraged the old man to whittle toothpicks, keep him out of their hair.

Despite all the malleting and murmuring and checkers-talk, Schultz couldn't help but feel that every word he said was being listened to by all. He said: "Yes, um... Well, Mr. Sutherland, you no doubt surmise that my brother – Mr. McKenney – is planning to expand his business, putting up a general store next year and financing independent fur traders. Although we've settled on a location for the store, where the Portage la Prairie trail and the road to the Stone Fort cross –"

"*Where?*" John Sutherland interjected. "Oh, I, um, don't mean to interrupt, but – Did you say where the Portage trail crosses the main road to the Stone Fort?"

"Absolutely. Any land traveller going north or south passes by there, so does anyone going west, or coming back from the west."

"But it's... You'd be in a... *depression* of the flats; it floods there even in the, um, driest spring. And when it isn't flooded you're, um, a long haul from the river for drinking water. And the winds, man, there's no trees there or any kind of protection, and the wind... *howls* down from the North Pole. I've seen a shed out on the open prairie fly to pieces."

"Yes, I had an introduction to that kind of storm yesterday, and the Royal Hotel's still there."

"Some summer storms are worse, believe me."

"Well, just because nobody's tried building on that spot before doesn't mean it isn't doable. At any rate, that's my brother's plan and I'm just the junior partner. At any rate, although we've settled on a location for the store, we need a piece of good land close to the river to put up a house and gardens – several houses eventually, as the family grows – and to use as a staging area for the trading expeditions." He'd been particularly pleased, when mentally rehearsing his speech that afternoon, to come up with 'staging area.' "The only piece of good land on that side of the river that nobody's living on is Point Douglas."

John Sutherland said: "Are you saying you want to... *buy* Point Douglas?"

The hush that came over the room, and the sudden rattle from the saucered teacup Janet Sutherland was handing him, told Schultz this was going to be easier than he thought. They were obviously all dumfounded that anyone would be willing to pay good money for their little piece of farmland. Schultz thanked Mrs. Sutherland for the tea, and she turned in an apparent daze and wandered toward the barley trough, saying: "How are Catherine and Margaret doing?"

"Well enough and then some," said the old lady. "Come Saturday they can take a try at the big trough out back and see how lovely the wind does the winnowing for us."

"That's very good, girls, time for bed now. You, too, Hector and Angus. Kiss your father good-night and say good-night to our guest."

Schultz waited indulgently while the little ones bade their good-nights and started up the stairs, then said to their father: "We'd be willing to pay you a good deal more than the going rate for deeded farmland around here," *though not that much more, if I have anything to say about it.* "There's plenty of unused land behind you to the east that can be had at The Company's nominal land prices. You wouldn't have to cross the river to farm anymore, and from what I'm told, clearing virgin prairie land for farming isn't like clearing land where I come from.

"No, where I come from," Schultz shook his head with a companionably rueful smile, "clearing a few acres for farmland means years and years of chopping down trees as wide as you can stretch your arms, in a forest as old as Adam. Here on the prairies, all you have to do is burn off the grass and the land's bare for the plough."

"So it is," the old lady put in from where she was scooping hulled barley from the trough into a birchbark basket. "Bare, burnt earth, but just underneath the skin is a mass of tangled grass roots miles wide and deeper than you can dig. Try and put a plough through that and see how far you can get in a day, and how many horses you can kill."

John Sutherland said: "Point Douglas is farmland now, but it, um, didn't start that way. Oh, my parents tell me they could... *always* get some kind of crop off it, but not like the crops we get now, after three generations of tilling and manuring and... *fighting* the wild-grass roots."

"Well, all the more reason we should pay you handsomely for it. And since it's such good farmland, my brother and I might even take off a few crops of our own, if we end up having to wait a few years to build our houses there."

John Sutherland held his eyes on him and shook his head slowly, as though working out a puzzle, then said: "You're no farmer, Dr. Schultz, and neither is Mr. McKenney. And it, um, seems to me Point Douglas would be no better a… *'staging area'* for outfitting fur trade boats, than the riverbank nearest where you mean to put your store. As for, um, building houses – you seem comfortable enough in the Royal Hotel. And even if you plan to… *abandon* the Royal Hotel, I would guess you're planning to, um, relocate to living quarters above your new store. So… *why* do you want Point Douglas?"

Damn, Schultz thought, *fall back and re-group*. He knew that Harry only wanted him to lay out that first gambit and to leave it at that if John Sutherland didn't bite, just leave it as something for Sutherland to chew on. But Schultz decided that even though he was only the junior partner, Harry wasn't there and he was. He threw up his hands and forced a laugh that sounded natural. "Well, you're too sharp for me, Mr. Sutherland – but when it comes to business you can't blame a man for trying. The truth of it is, what McKenney & Company wants to do is take a gamble – just about everything we do is a gamble, only way to get a start in life when you're not born with a silver spoon.

"You see," Schultz leaned forward confidentially, "my brother and I aren't the only people from Upper Canada casting their eyes toward Red River, we're just the first to take the plunge. In a year or two, three or four at most, the dam is going to burst and thousands of people – *tens* of thousands – are going to come pouring into the west. Like I said, they' ll all have to pass by the crossroads of the Portage Trail and the north-south road. McKenney's store won't be the only business there, just the first. Pretty soon there'll be wagonwrights and farm implement dealers and banks and land offices… A thriving town spreading out from the crossroads. It won't take long for that town to spread as far as Point Douglas, and want to spread *onto* Point Douglas."

"But…" John Sutherland said again, this time confusedly, "Point Douglas is farmland."

"So was Yonge and Front Street once." John Sutherland looked even more confused. "Oh, the intersection of Yonge and Front Streets is the thrivingest business district in Toronto, and it once was somebody's cow pasture. That somebody could've been a very rich man if he'd had the right partners and advice."

Schultz paused to gaze around the room as though seeing it for the first time, hoping to draw the others' attention to what he was seeing: the rough-whitewashed, squared-log walls with only a square of needlework or bit of Indian quillworked leather for decoration, the homemade furniture whose adzed gouges still showed through years of smoothing wear, the blackened skillets hanging by the fireplace which was obviously the family's medieval cooking arrangement along with the crude little cube stove… "You have a fine and snug home here, Mr. Sutherland – much finer than the one I grew up in. But aren't there other people right here at Red River – the Company Factors in their forts, the retired officers in Little Britain – who have more than these simple necessities? Big stone houses with a fireplace in every bedroom, imported mahogany furniture, a piano in the parlour, dresses from Paris, boys sent to university in Canada or England… Point Douglas could buy that for you, once the immigration wave rolls in."

John Sutherland scratched his beard and said: "Well, what do you think of that, Mother?"

Schultz assumed that Sutherland was addressing his mother, but it was his wife who replied, "I've never had a yearning to wear corsets and hoopskirts."

John Sutherland said to Schultz: "If there will be a… *mass* of people coming from the east willing to, um, pay large sums of money for pieces of Point Douglas – then all I have to do is, um, sit and wait. I don't see why you and Mr. McKenney need be… *involved* at all."

Schultz was sweating, but trying to appear cool. Now that he'd gone and said more than he was supposed to, Harry would not be happy if he came home and said the game was blown completely. He said: "Everyone who speaks of you, Mr. Sutherland, says that you're a wise and careful man. But you're wise in the ways of the people of the west, where everything a man does stands out against the prairie sky, and the only cheating that goes on is a bit of exaggeration in a horse trade. Among the people coming from the east will be some who're used to telling any kind of lie to make a fast buck and then disappearing into the crowd. They'll come into your home and make you feel like they're part of your family while they're robbing you blind. You've had no experience with commercial real estate prices and what the market will bear.

"McKenney & Company could buy into Point Douglas now and share the profits with you when the time comes. We'll do all the finagling and haggling with the land-sharks, take care of all the contracts and sales, but your name's on the deed for Point Douglas so you've got us over a barrel, we got no choice but to cut you in for a fair share. If we're wrong and the immigration doesn't come through as fast and heavy as we're sure it will, you've got our down payment in your pocket and you still own Point Douglas. McKenney & Company takes the gamble and you can't lose."

The old man at the table set down his nonsensical whittling and said: "Save yer breath, laddie, ye're talking to the wrong man. The name on the deed for Point Douglas is *Alexander* Sutherland, and it's no' for sale as long as I'm on life."

CHAPTER 9

As her husband closed the door behind young Dr. Schultz, Janet Sutherland could feel a row coming on – or a 'discussion' at best. She said to the boys still at the table: "You'd best be getting to bed, too, or you'll be falling back asleep in the hay tomorrow morning instead of forking it down to the cows." Morrison, as the youngest of the four, got up and shrugged on his coat and went out to the necessary. Donald would be the last. Janet didn't know exactly how they'd come to that arrangement, but it was an arrangement and they didn't bicker about it so that was good enough for her. As for the overall habit of the children's bedtime trips to the necessary, Janet had years ago invented a rule that all children over the age of six had to empty their own chamberpots, and that had done wonders for the regulation of their bowels.

John got up to put a few more chunks of wood in the fireplace and stir the coals; his father went to the other corner to do the same to the Carron stove. John said over his shoulder, in that mild tone that meant he was thinking-over whether to use a hammer or an axe, "Could we have another pot of tea, Mother?"

Janet said: "Rose hip tea?" Not only was rose hip tea less likely to keep them awake, the rose hips they gathered and dried every autumn didn't cost them anything but time and trouble.

"That would be nice, thank you."

As Janet filled the small kettle from the bucket and set it on the square little stove, the silence behind her grew thicker. The only sounds were the snicking of her father-in-law's knife as he went back to whittling tree nails. Blacksmith-made iron nails were tremendously expensive, especially ones big enough for construction, and wooden pegs didn't rust. If you had a stock of tree nails on hand that were the right diameter and shaved smooth, you could just cut them to length as need arose. John's father had an eye for it, didn't even have to measure them against the auger.

Finally John said: "You know, Father, Dr. Schultz does have a point. If he and his, um, brother were to… *buy* into Point Douglas, we could use just a fraction of that money to buy an equal amount of the land out behind us from The Company. The new land wouldn't be as… *productive* for the first few years until we got it broken in, but all the land within a mile of the river is, um, four or five feet deep of good topsoil. You said yourself just last spring, when the flood was… *running* the river too fast to cross, that it was, um, ridiculous to be able to see our land ready for seeding and not be able to get to it."

"The Company does nae *sell* land!" Janet recalled that her grandfather's Scots burr had grown thicker as he grew older, especially when he was agitated. "It *rents* land!"

"Well, a nine hundred and ninety-nine year lease might as well be owning. And The Company practically… *gives* it away. Andrew Bannerman's rent is one peppercorn a year, and that hasn't been paid in, um, ten years. It's only a formality."

"Do ye no' understand the difference between ownin' and leasin'? Nine hundred ninety-nine years be damned – !" Janet's father-in-law sputtered to a halt, as though stymied to find words to explain the obvious.

Janet's mother-in-law had been sitting quietly looking down at her hands. Now she raised her head – steel-blue eyes framed by rusted-iron hair – and said: "There's no need to raise your voice to the lad."

"I was doin' him a favour – if I hadnae raised my voice you wouldhae raised yours, and that's enough tae wake the dead."

John's mother splayed her long fingers across the table rim, as though considering how to say what she had to say. Everyone waited, as all wise souls did when Kate MacPherson was endeavouring to find a way to speak her mind calmly. Janet and her mother-in-law had had their difficulties for the first few years – two women in one kitchen was a recipe for disaster – but they'd learned ways to get along passably well, and one of the ways Janet had learned was to allow her mother-in-law the opportunity to think before she spoke.

A hissing and sputtering sound from the stove reminded Janet that she was supposed to be doing something, not just watching and listening. She scooped crushed dried rose hips into the kettle, set it on a trivet on the table to steep and reached down four cups. Another couple of months and she wouldn't be doing much reaching for a while, but for now the baby was just a turnip-sized swelling.

As Janet set the cups beside the kettle, her mother-in-law said: "You well know the old story, John, but try to think of it as not just an *old* story. I grew up on a leasehold croft in County Sutherland – as did your father, on the other side the River Ulidh from me. Our families before us had lived on those crofts for maybe nine hundred and ninety-nine years, or maybe only five hundred and ninety nine, no one will ever know. But came the day when the Countess of Sutherland decided she would have more money if her lands were peopled with sheep for the wool trade, and so we had to go. Because we did not *own* the land."

John began: "But The Company would never –"

"Oh aye," his mother cut him off. "That's what we said: 'The Countess of Sutherland would never… ' And we had much more reason to believe it, because we were her *clanna*. And so like fools we stayed until the bailiffs and the soldiers came with clubs and guns and torches."

John's father said: "Ye've not seen law, Johnny, and what it can do. The only law you've ever had to live under is The Company's law, and that's a light hand – but it can change.

When the law goes against you, the machinery can crush you like a bug. But we have a freehold deed to Point Douglas signed to me and my heirs in perpetuity – signed by The Earl of Selkirk himself for land granted to him by The King and Parliament – and no law this side of God can take that away from us. No amount of money in your pocket will last forever, but the land will, and it will feed and house ye and your children till the crack o'doom."

John's mother said: "Why do you think we were so stupid as to keep coming back here after the North West Company drove us off after Seven Oaks and the time before? Because Point Douglas was the only land we'd ever owned and likely ever would own."

John didn't appear to have an immediate reply to that. Janet poured out the tea and the other three thanked her and sipped. She was hoping that a bit of warm, soothing rose hips might calm the atmosphere. Not that anyone was banging fists on the table, but she didn't like any whiff of discord between the adults in the house; with eleven-and-a-half children to care for she had enough daily agitation to deal with. She was raising her cup to her lips when she felt a sudden movement inside her, like a butterfly fluttering its wings. She jerked slightly and said: "Oh!"

Her mother-in-law leaned across the table and said: "What's wrong, lass?"

"Oh, nothing – nothing's wrong. I just, it just, he or she just moved for the first time – or the first time I could feel it. That's always the way, first just a little flutter after three or four months, and in another few months he or she will be kicking like a pony."

Her mother-in-law smiled and nodded, with a corner of reticence behind the smile. Janet felt like kicking her*self* for that airy 'always the way,' almost rubbing her mother-in-law's nose in the difference between them. Janet's mother-in-law could make all the lighthearted jokes she wanted about: *'A perfect arrangement – you have to bear them and I get to play with them,'* Janet knew that her heart wasn't entirely light.

John patted Janet's knee happily, then put his hand back on the table and said: "But you see, Da, if what Dr. Schultz and, um, Henry McKenney are saying – what a lot of people are saying – is true, then Point Douglas won't... *be* farmland much longer anyway. If... *immigrants* from Canada – or Britain or, um, the United States – start pouring into the west, this will be a crossroads and Point Douglas will be part of a town, maybe even a city someday."

"The Company would never let that happen. They dinna want Rupert's Land filled with settlers. Ye cannae trap furs in towns or farms, and furs are The Company's lifeblood – it's made a lot of powerful men in London wealthy and they mean to keep it that way. Except for a few odd folk drifting here betimes, The Company has allowed no immigration since our old Selkirk Colony – and that was a different time, and then The Company had its own reasons, as we found out to our regret."

"Well, maybe this is a different time than, um, the way times have been since then."

John's mother said: "Everything changes, Sandy, eventually. You know that as well as I."

"Well, one thing that doesna change is that a man who doesna own his own land is at the mercy of the winds. This tea's making me drowsy, I'm off to bed."

Janet's in-laws made their good-nights and went up the stairs. Janet put the tea cups in the pantry to do with the breakfast dishes instead of heating the big kettle twice. When she came back into the main room, John was still sitting at the table staring at the fire, and she could see he was unhappy that at forty years of age he was still his parents' 'wee Johnny' in some matters. She didn't know who was right and who was wrong in their disagreement about Point Douglas, but one thing she did know was that John's father wasn't going to listen to anything John had to say about it.

But John wasn't the kind to complain about a situation that couldn't be solved, just silently ponder whether there was a solution to be found. Some might call it brooding. Janet banked the fires in both fireplaces, put a round of wood into the stove and blew out all the candles except the one she picked up to light the way to bed. "John…?"

"Hm?"

"Bedtime."

"Hm? Oh. Oh, yes…"

Janet's husband was still brooding when Sunday rolled around. The Point Douglas Sutherlands' bought-and-deeded pew was back among the general congregation, not one of the six square pews flanking the pulpit that were owned by Company officers and such. Janet sat at the other end of the pew from her husband, with baby James in her lap and baby Mary Ann or Roderick in her belly. She and John hadn't sat side-by-side in church for some years now. The family sat in a row with parents and grandparents strategically placed to keep the children from fidgeting or whispering or not listening to the sermon.

But on this Sunday Janet felt like she was in need of an overseeing adult as much as any of the children. Kirk service was her only reliably calm and peaceful hour of the week, when there was nothing her hands should be doing and all eleven children were on their best behaviour, a time for drifting and dreaming. Not that she didn't listen to Dr. Black, but it was only one voice coming from one direction. Today, though, an odd, giddy mood had come over her that she couldn't push aside. It was just like getting the giggles in school, and it was just lucky there wasn't another giddy schoolgirl nearby to set her off. As it was, The Reverend Dr. Black's sonorous pronouncements became just the inconsequential, constant burbling of a stream she meandered down – a stream of past happenings that suddenly struck her as hilariously funny.

It started when she happened to catch sight of one of the young Pritchards in a pew three rows ahead. Old John Pritchard had been a fur trader who'd thrown his lot in with the Selkirk Colony and become the Earl of Selkirk's agent at Red River. As agent, he made good on a promise Lord Selkirk had made to his colonists: that the colony would be provided with an ordained minister. The minister Mr. Pritchard imported turned out to be Anglican; virtually all of Lord Selkirk's colonists were Auld Kirk Presbyterian. John Pritchard was Anglican. The funny part was that the Kildonan people had been willing to be part of an Anglican congregation if the minister allowed them to keep the customs of a Presbyterian kirk. Presbyterians stood to pray and sat to sing; Anglicans sat to pray and stood to sing. So for the first thirty years of Janet's life, Sunday services meant undulating waves as different portions of the congregation stood up as the others sat down and vice versa.

The event that eventually ended the wave-and-trough congregation unfortunately brought another giggley picture to Janet's memory: a picture of Point Douglas Alexander Sutherland looking like he'd just been hit on the back of the head with a meat mallet. When Sandy Sutherland stepped forward from the welcoming crowd and greeted the Reverend Mr. John Black in Gaelic, he'd got only a blank expression in reply. It had never occurred to anyone in Kildonan that there could be such a thing as an ordained kirk minister who didn't speak Gaelic.

The chain of funny pictures in Janet's mind circled back to the young Pritchard a few pews ahead of her, and the funniest part of all. Wily Old John Pritchard's plan had obviously been that if the children of Presbyterians grew up going to an Anglican church, they would naturally grow up to be Anglican. And indeed over the years John Pritchard's sons had married Kildonan girls in St. John's Anglican church. But when Kildonan kirk was finally built, they'd accompanied their wives and in-laws into the Reverend John Black's congregation. So the outcome of John Pritchard's clever plan was there were going to be a lot more stones chiselled 'Pritchard' in Kildonan kirkyard than in the cemetery of St. John's Cathedral.

Janet tried to distract her giggley self by following her eyes along the lines of stove pipe running overhead from the two Carron stoves and counting the little kettles hung under each join in the pipe to catch the sooty drip. When her eyes had counted back from the chimney to the squat cast iron boxes, she wondered if the clever Scotsman who'd invented the Carron stove had any idea how many times his unknown name had been blessed by the women of Red River. Up until his miraculous invention, the only available way of cooking or heating had been an open fireplace – except for The Company's officers and a few others who could afford the horrendous freight costs of importing a potbellied stove all the way across the ocean. But the Carron cube-stove could be broken down into six flat pieces, easy to transport and easy to assemble at the other end. Then again, being a Scotsman, the inventor probably cared less for uncountable blessings than the countable money his invention brought in. Unfortunately, that thought sprang another wellspring of giggles Janet had to suppress.

And then the service was blessedly over, and amid the bustle and murmuring Janet finally felt free to let out the loony laughter that had been stifling her. Heads turned toward her and she jogged James up and down on her knee, saying: "Oh you little muggins," as though the wee bairn had just done something hilariously wee-bairnish.

There was to be a meeting after the service, and many people who'd been at the early morning service came back and crowded into the aisles. John and the older boys stood up so a few of the older people coming in would have a place to sit. The Reverend Dr. Black, still in his black robe and white tab collar, said from the pulpit: "A suggestion has been put forward in light that the church coffers have built up a healthy surplus, and the steamboat from the United States now makes it possible to import articles that would've been devilish diffi – um, *very* difficult to bring here in the past. A catalogue from a company in Canada shows a very reasonably-priced and durable pump organ –"

The rest of what the Reverend Dr. Black meant to say was lost in the congregation's muttered arguments, and imprecations just barely fit for the inside of a church. People stood up in turn to express their opinions aloud. Opinion was divided – by and large the surviving generation of original settlers was dead set against it, while the younger generations couldn't see why a pump organ should cause any discord and might help to keep some of the all-congregation hymns in harmony.

Finally Hugh Polson creaked up from his seat on the Elders' bench and stood leaning on his cane and shaking. Janet wasn't sure whether his shaking was from anger or rheumatism – he'd grown so rheumatoid he hardly walked anywhere anymore but travelled in a sled or cart hitched to Old Bob, his almost equally ancient horse-of-all-trades.

Hugh Polson wheezed: "I thought it bad enough when we got a tutored choir – aye, wi' a pitch-pipe and choir master and all – instead o' just raising our voices in song from our hearts to the Lord. And now it's come to this. A *pump organ* – a caist o' whustles. What next? Gaudy stainglass in the windows to paint the Lord's pure sunlight all purple and green? I tell ye – if ye bring yon music-hall instrument into this kirk, I'll bring in Old Bob to drag the caist o' whustles out of the house of the Lord and dump it by the roadside."

Hugh Polson turned and stumped up the aisle and out. A fair number of the older generation, and a few younger ones, followed him. There was a silence, and then Janet's husband stood up. Janet knew full well he didn't like to put himself forward unless no one else seemed likely to. He said: "It seems to me, Dr. Black, um, that we have a, uh, a problem that will resolve it*self*… in the fullness of time. I personally see no harm in, um, bringing a pump organ into our church, but Mr. Polson does, obviously. And so do many others who were… *weaned* on the… *stark* traditions of the kirk in the Highlands. Even if a majority voted against Mr. Polson and his ilk, he would still feel it wrong. And *I* would feel it wrong to, um, turn any member of our congregation against the church. But I would also like my children to be able to feel Kildonan Kirk thrumming with the music of Jubal and David."

Janet nodded, and she could see other heads nodding as well, but not for exactly the same reason. She knew John didn't think he had much in the way of powers of persuasion, but he'd just managed to remind the congregation without saying so that some of the Patriarchs in the Bible were renowned for playing musical instruments.

"Hugh Polson is an old man and… *deserves* to have his wishes respected." John paused, not one of his blank and groping pauses, and then said again: "Hugh Polson is an old man. If we leave the issue of the pump organ lying fallow for a few years, Hugh Polson will be beyond feeling any offence, and my children will still be children when the caist o' whustles sings its first chords in Kildonan Kirk."

Janet's husband sat back down. There was a lot of head-nodding and murmurs of agreement. Dr. Black said: "Thank you, Mr. Sutherland, I believe the matter is resolved."

Janet could see that another matter had been resolved, too, but she doubted John would see it on his own. As the congregation rose and buttoned their coats, Janet jumped up quickly with Jamie in her arms and hurried down the aisle, to be sure she could meet up with her husband as he emerged from the other aisle. The older boys and their grandparents would herd the rest of the children along.

When Janet and her husband were walking side-by-side with the flow of the current out the church door, Janet glanced back to make sure John's parents were far enough back in the crowd to be out of earshot, then whispered to John: "Just as you said."

"Hm? I said... ?"

"The matter will resolve itself."

He looked confused for a moment, then his eyebrows went up and he nodded. But then his face pursed itself and he said: "It's not something to be wished for."

"No, but it will happen." She supposed she should think herself cold-blooded for being so matter-of-fact about it. But it was a fact, and she'd lived through it when it happened to her grandparents the year Hugh was born. Wishing had nothing to do with it.

CHAPTER 10

Spring bought Hugh almost two weeks off school, in two allotments – first when the river ice grew too thin to be walked across safely but still too thick to break a boat channel through; second when the breakup brought table-sized ice shards hurtling along the swollen current. The world turned from white and black to grey and brown, with soft pinpricks of silver along the riverbanks when the pussy willows bloomed. Veins of dark red and amber crept into the picture when the sap in the osiers – 'basket bushes' – began to flow again, then came a pale green haze as all the trees began to bud, and it seemed only the next day all the world was a thousand shades of green and always had been.

Come midsummer Hugh's father told him he was now old enough to swing a scythe in this year's hay race. On paper, the two miles back from the river behind every farm was that family's hay privilege. But the fact was that some farms had swampy land behind them, or alder thickets, so it had been long ago agreed that the 'hay privileges' were common land, and whatever area you carved a border around was yours for the summer. The Council of Assiniboia had long ago decreed that no haying could be done before the First of August, so no one could attack the prairie with a sickle or scythe before the last midnight in July. People scouted out their sites ahead of time and kept their eyes on who else was scouting out where.

In lush years it didn't much matter, and people ambled their carts out onto the prairie on the morning of August First. But this was a dry summer, and Hugh could see that his father was worried about whether they'd have enough hay to get their cattle through the winter – but then, Da was always worrying about something.

After supper on the Thirty-first of July, all of the family except the youngest children and Mum piled onto two carts loaded with blankets and buffalo robes and scythes and hay rakes and camp food and headed inland. It would've been a toss-up whether Mum or Gran stayed with the wee ones, except that it had been barely a week since Mum gave birth to Roderick Ross Sutherland. When she'd come due, all the children had been farmed out to neighbours for a couple of days, some across the river to Kildonan and some to their mostly French neighbours on the east bank. Hugh had stayed with the Riels – Madame Riel was a daughter of Gran's old friend Madame Lagimodière – who were generally nice people but sure did a lot of praying.

The carts jolted and squealed their way across the hummocks and bumps – unbroken prairie *looked* flat until you tried to cross it on wheels. They would've had smoother going on the land behind Point Douglas, but that would've meant all their hay would have to be ferried across the river. And there wouldn't be as much competition on this side, since a fair number of the Metis made their livings from the buffalo hunts and didn't keep much cattle. But Hugh could see a few dozen other carts heading out, and he could see something else. Up north towards the lake, the rim of the sky was a ragged band of charcoal with a sheer curtain of rain beneath it. It was still a good twenty miles off, but moving steadily toward them.

Hugh turned his attention closer, to the grasses they were passing through, some of them almost as tall as he stood in the cart. They tended to grow in drifts, and there were several different kinds. Hugh's favourite kind was the one topped with a silky silvery pale green-purply bearded fantail, but he didn't know whether cows and horses thought highly of it.

The sun had touched the horizon by the time Da and Granda stopped the carts. Da carefully pointed out the stretch of wild hay he'd judged to be the best: from the poplar grove up on the right, across to a slight rise in the ground, and back to where he'd stopped the carts. It seemed to Hugh that the grass *was* greener here than on the other side of the imaginary fence his father had drawn. He thought it might be just a trick of the light; the sun was low enough now to cast that light that slanted across the prairie instead of down on it, painting everything with a green-gold glow that seemed to grow from inside of whatever it touched. But then, that same light was on all the other grass, too. Hugh thought back over other summers when he might've ridden or walked by this spot, and seemed to remember a marshy patch that was devilish bad for mosquitoes. So this year the bad drainage made it just moist enough to grow better hay than the parched land around it –

"Hugh?"

"Hm?"

"Are you listening?"

"Oh, yes, Da."

Da went on laying out how they were going to cut a boundary around their winter's supply of hay: Hugh and his father and grandfather and older brother would each take a scythe to one side of it; the other boys and Gran would carry torches to light the way. Da took one last go at the scythe blades with the whetstone and said: "Now, Hugh, I know you've used a scythe before, but only for short stretches – keep alert. A man swinging a scythe and lets his mind wander can easily cut off his own leg. That's not a joke – it's true."

They took up their positions and waited into the night. As a pale sliver of moon poked up in the south-east, the northern half of the sky lit up with a white flare and a few seconds later came a crashing roar that seemed to split the earth. Gran muttered: "How many nights this summer have we prayed for rain – and it chooses to come this night. Whoever said the Good Lord doesn't have a sense of humour was never a farmer."

The thunder also meant they might not hear the cannons that would be set off in Fort Garry and the Stone Fort at the stroke of midnight. The family in the field next to them apparently had the same thought, for they called in French to ask Da if he had a pocket watch that kept true time. He called back that he did and there were only a few minutes left to go. And then the rain hit.

Fortunately it was only a medium rain; in an all-out prairie downpour they'd never have been able to keep the torches alight. But scything wet grass wasn't going to be easy. Gran said: "Well at least there's less chance of a dropped torch starting a prairie fire and burning us all alive."

Hugh pushed his soaked hair back out of his eyes – should've worn a hat – and took up a stance with the scythe blade propped on the ground, his left hand on the haft and his right hand on the peg fixed onto the haft. Between two claps of thunder he heard the cannons, sounding like pathetic little pops against the sky's artillery, and swung the scythe up over his right shoulder. He swept it down in an arc in front of him, hearing the blade slice through the grass, and then swung it back up again as he made a step to the right – putting his left foot where his right had been, as he'd been taught – and took the next cut.

As he worked his way along, it occurred to him that little Catherine hadn't been that far wrong to miscall a scythe a 'sigh.' The sound the blade made as it passed through the grass was very like a sigh. Or maybe it was the sound the grasses made when the blade passed through them –

"Hugh!"

"Yes, Gran?"

"Your mind is wandering. Remember what your father said."

"Yes, Gran." Hugh bore down to concentrate on step-and-swing. After a while the movement started to feel a bit more natural, but after a while longer his arms started to feel more wooden than the haft, and his rain-soaked hands couldn't hold a tight grip. He stopped for a moment to wipe his hands on his damp pants, and incidentally to lean on the scythe and rest his arms. Gran said: "Here, wipe them on this," and extended a corner of the thick plaid cloak draped over her head against the rain.

As Hugh wiped his hands, he looked around to see how the others were doing. His aged grandfather, on the opposite side of the field, had already cut a good deal farther than Hugh and was moving along with the scythe swinging in long, smooth arcs, like the scythe was his dancing partner.

Hugh caught a glimpse of a bobbing torch out on the prairie beyond their field. A flare of lightning showed a boy holding a torch for a large, black-bearded man scything along in a line that would intersect the line Hugh was cutting. If the man reached the intersection point before Hugh did, he could cut a good-sized chunk out of the Point Douglas Sutherlands' hayfield.

Hugh snatched up the scythe again and went at it as hard as he could. His brothers began to shout: "Go to it, Hugh, you can do it. Come on, Hugh," and from behind the man and boy came female voices shouting: "*Allez, allez*!"

A while longer and Hugh saw that the *Allezs* were going to carry the day – the other scythe was going to cross his path before he'd cut that far. The large man with the black beard had farther to go than Hugh did, but no matter how hard Hugh flailed, the gap was narrowing.

Gran's voice from behind him said briskly: "Hugh, stop!" Hugh did as he was told. Gran handed him her torch, "Hold this," and reached for the scythe. She'd thrown off her cloak, and her old blue dress was already darkening with the rain. "Stand well back, but give me light."

Then the scythe shot up over her shoulder so high it looked like it was going to take flight, and fly it did. She had the same smooth, apparently effortless swing as Granda, except her arms were longer and she was in more of a hurry. When she scythed past the intersection point, the large man was still a good five strides short of his goal. Gran scythed a few more steps for good measure, then stopped and stood leaning on the scythe and gasping for breath. She said to Hugh: "Another twenty, thirty years you'll get the rhythm of it."

Hugh said: "I'll fetch your cloak."

On his way back for the cloak, he passed by the large, black-bearded man standing leaning on his own scythe. The man looked around him and shrugged, "Oh well, I t'ink I got enough marked out for me already, me. So I just can cut up to your line and you save me the trouble of cutting a line around this side of my hay."

On his way back with the cloak, there was a double flash of lightning when Hugh's eyes happened to've wandered in the direction of the poplar grove. He stopped in his tracks. He was sure he'd seen what he saw. It had only been a glimpse, but it had been so clear… He asked his mind's eye to remember what he'd seen, and it showed him a Metis or Indian girl, black hair floating in the wind, sitting on her pony in the rain – bare leg against the horse's bareback side – and watching him. Wauh-Oonae. Whippoorwill. Nancy Prince. There was another flash of lightning. She was gone. Or maybe she'd never been there and he'd only seen wind-whipped leaf shadows playing tricks on his eyes.

"Hugh! Did you step in a bear trap?"

"I'm coming, Gran."

Hugh finished cutting his side of the border, with a little help from Da rounding the corner ahead of him. Now that their claim had been staked, there was no point trying to do anything more with their hay until the rain dried off, so no point camping out on wet ground or building up a fire to heat the pot of beef and barley soup Mum had packed up for them. They unhitched one of the carts and piled their tools under it, then all squeezed onto the other cart and headed for home with the other cart horse hitched behind.

Morrison and Aleck seemed asleep on their feet, but Hugh felt wide awake. He found himself standing next to Gran, gripping the same cart rail for balance, and found himself pondering on the contradictions in his grandmother. Although she was definitely a funny old thing who made the rest of the family shake their heads at times – like saving any leftover breakfast porridge to slice up cold for her dinner – she was still somehow someone people turned to in times of trouble and confusion. Hugh gave it up and shrugged it off; he knew that figuring out abstractions wasn't his strong suit. Besides, life probably wouldn't be as interesting if people could be all understood and put in neat boxes. But there was something else that was causing him some confusion, so he said: "Gran?"

"Aye?"

"Do you remember when Uncle Robert's barn burned down one fall, with all his winter's hay, and by next morning his neighbours had piled a hundred cartloads of hay in his yard? We had to do it at night, so he wouldn't know we were doing it…?"

"Oh, I have small doubt that even Robert MacBeth could hear scores of Red River carts coming and going just under his bedroom window. But if he and his family pretended to sleep through it, it would save everybody the embarrassment of thank-yous. Better he should just stand up in the kirk next Sunday and thank the Good Lord for putting generosity in the hearts of anonymous people hereabouts."

"So… if *we* didn't have enough hay to make it through the winter, our neighbours would help us out…?"

"Of course. They would even go short to help us, so long as they could keep their own animals alive on short rations."

"So then… why do we scythe away like crazy people through the night to make sure we've claimed plenty enough good hay to get us through the winter? If we run short, our neighbours will give us some of theirs."

"I swear, John Hugh, the questions you ask!"

Granda, who it seemed had been listening in, chortled: "I'm lookin' forward tae the answer."

"Well, Hugh, it's… We have to stand on our own two feet. That is, we can't look out for our neighbours if we can't look after ourselves. I mean to say… That is… Suffering saints, Hugh, it's just a plain fact! If you can feed and house and clothe yourself and your family with your own hands you don't have to bow your head to anybody!"

Granda said: "Sometimes an answer says more about the answerer than the question."

"Are you disputing what I said?"

"Not a bit of it. For me – I say it's no shame tae take help in need, provided ye've done all in your power to not need it."

"Did we answer your question, Hugh?"

"I guess so, me whatever. But… you're telling me 'why-nots,' not 'whys.'"

Hugh's grandparents looked at each other and inexplicably burst out laughing. Maybe that was another one of those rhythms he'd get in another twenty or thirty years.

"Oh!" came from Aleck, as though jerked fully awake by a revelation. Eyes and voices turned to Aleck with *What-is-it?*s and *What's wrong?*s. "Oh, I just stuck my hands in my pockets 'cause they were cold – my hands – and remembered I'd forgot I'd filled my pockets with buffalo jerky 'case I got hungry. Anybody want some?" Foolish question.

A week or so later, Hugh was pulling weeds in the vegetable garden when Norbert Parisien wandered into the yard. It wasn't unusual to see Norbert wandering anywhere in the community – up and down the riverbank or along the road – but he rarely wandered into people's yards. He stopped by the edge of the garden and said: "Hugh, you come with me, eh?"

Norbert had spoken in Bungee – the loose-skinned patois that had grown itself through the fur trade, made up of bits of Ojibway and English and Cree and French and Gaelic and a few improvised connectors – so Hugh replied in the same language: "With you where to, Norbert?"

"I got something to show you." Norbert's slanted, dark eyes – seemingly no irises between the whites and pupils – were gleaming with a secret, but he also seemed shy about whatever it was. Norbert was hard to read at the best of times, but even more so when he didn't have a hat on, because then your eyes were thrown off by trying to add together the black eyes with brassy blonde hair. What with all the mixing of races in Rupert's Land, Hugh had grown up used to contrarieties like a Cree chief with red hair and freckles, but impossibly metallic blonde hair on a black-eyed, sun-browned face took some getting used to.

Hugh shrugged, "I don't mind, me whatever. Just let me finish weeding this row."

Norbert offered to help, but when he reached for a fistful of carrot greens, Hugh said: "No! Don't… Oh, don't worry about it, Norbert – Mum won't skin me if I don't finish up till later. Let's just go, wherever it is we're going."

"You got a fish net?" Norbert made an upward motion with his fists, as though his hands were around an invisible handle, so he didn't mean the kind of net you dragged behind a boat.

Hugh said: "Sure," and went into the toolshed. Hanging from one corner rafter was the scoop-net Granda had made, with a willow hoop and handle and hand-knotted netting. It was handy for scooping out a fish hooked on a line, but didn't get used very often – angling wasn't the most efficient way to feed a family of sixteen.

Hugh followed Norbert out onto the road and turned north with him. Norbert seemed to have a hard time not breaking into a run and was almost wriggling with anticipation, though at the same time still seemed shy about revealing whatever the secret was. Whenever Hugh asked where they were going, Norbert just said: "You'll see! You'll see!"

There was a stream that the road crossed over on a rough-beam bridge. Norbert climbed down to the creek bed and along the rocky clay border between the brush and the feeble trickle the stream had shrunk to this summer. As they got near where the creek flowed into the river, there was a sort of ragged fence stretched across the streambed, only a couple of feet high, made of green poplar branches lashed together and planted securely in the clay. Its middle half was in water, where a bowl in the streambed made a pool. There was another fence like it a few feet farther along the pool, and a third one across the creekmouth. From the lines of pockmarks in the clay upstream of the first fence, Hugh figured it had either been moved a few times or there had been more.

Norbert scurried ahead to between the second and third fence and stood pointing down, biting his lip and holding his eyes on Hugh. When Hugh got there, Norbert nodded vociferously and kept jabbing his finger forward and down until Hugh looked where he was pointing.

The band of water between the two fences looked a little hazier and muddier than the rest of the pool. Then Hugh saw why. Swimming back and forth across the bottom was a very annoyed catfish. It wasn't a huge one, but not a small one, either – maybe a good ten pounds of meat anyway.

Hugh looked back up at Norbert. Norbert said, with more enthusiasm than his rubbery lips could manage smoothly, "You remember was a big rain, uh, couple days ago?"

"Last week."

"Uh-huh. Catfish like muddy water, eh? Not too deep, not too short, not too much current, eh?"

"Yeah."

"Well, I walk along here after the big rain, and I sees the pool here's got lots bigger from the rain and the…" Norbert fluttered one hand down on a slant, to show the stream flowing down with the run-off. "And in the pool is two big catfish come in from the riverbank. I says: 'Look at that, two big catfish – one for me and one for my friend. But how to get 'em?'

"Well, I know that pool gonna get back to just this size soon, couple days most'll be flowed into the river and so'll the catfishes. So I…" he pointed to a nearby poplar sapling and made knife-cutting motions, then weaving and tying motions. "And I puts one of these, um…"

"Fences?"

"Uh-huh. I puts it there," pointing at the one across the creekmouth. "And another one up there," pointing up the streambed, "where was the top of the pool when it was a big pool. Then I takes the other, um, fence, and I carries it into the water just down from the top, uh, fence, and I walks it forward a couple steps and plants it in before them catfishes come up and get past me. Then I waits till I sees the catfishes are down by the bottom fence, and I goes and takes out the top fence, lifts it over the new one, walk it a few steps in and plants it, and… like a slow sort of…"

"Leapfrog."

Norbert laughed. "Uh-huh, uh-huh – leapfrog! So, it weren't all one day – come back next morning and move it a bit smaller, and the pool getting smaller. One time, one of them catfishes got past me and I had to carry the… fence back out again and wait till he went back down." Norbert laughed again at that. "And today, I see them catfishes be like… like fish in a barrel!"

Hugh scratched his neck and shook his head. "Well, tie me to a tree. *You* did all that, and thought it up?"

"Uh-huh."

"Huh. Maybe you're not so... confused as people think. But, uh, Norbert, I can only see one catfish, maybe my eyes ain't –"

"I told you – 'One for me, one for my friend.' This morning I catched one and take him home, then I go get you."

"Oh, that ain't fittin', Norbert – after all the work you done, you should take 'em both."

"Don't you want him?"

"Well, sure, but –"

"You my friend."

Hugh had to clear his throat and look down. "Thank you, Norbert." Then he picked up his scoop net and said: "Well, I guess I better get 'im then."

Hugh stepped into the pool and Mr. Catfish headed for the other end of the alley of water. Hugh lowered his net to the bottom and took another step forward, then heard horse hooves walking down the streambed. He looked up. Ambling towards them was a saddle-less pony carrying a black-haired Metis or Indian girl wearing a calico blouse and dark skirt, the skirt bunched up so her bared legs caught the dappled sunlight coming through the trees. She looked to've grown a bit taller than when he'd watched her pass by in the Buffalo Hunt parade, and the chest of her blouse was belled-out a little farther than he remembered.

She stopped her horse a few feet short of Norbert on the bank. Norbert said: "Hello, Nancy."

"Hello, Norbert." Her voice sounded to Hugh like a flute – not the metallic sound in the Royal Canadian Rifles' band, but the woody tones he'd heard once at a regale in the Stone Fort, when a fur trader named O'Neill was asked to play.

Norbert turned to Hugh and said: "This my cousin Nancy – Wauh Oonae," and then didn't say any more.

Hugh coughed and started: "I'm –"

"I know Hugh you are." There was a hint of a twinkle in her dark eyes. Her eyes were slightly slanted, too, like Norbert's, but hers looked like they should be, while Norbert's looked like his maker's fingers had been clumsy with the clay. "You rescued my cousin Norbert and paid the price for it."

"Oh, no, I just..." He'd thought his voice had finished breaking. "Wasn't much to rescue him from."

She held her eyes on him, but didn't say anything. He became extremely conscious that he was standing up to his knees in muddy water, stupidly holding a fishing net. Then she turned to Norbert and said: "I'm heading home, Norbert, would you like a ride?"

"Uh-huh." Norbert went over to the horse, reached up his arm as she reached down hers, and half jumped, half was pulled up to perch behind her. He waved at Hugh, "Aur'voir."

"Aur'voir, Norbert. Thanks for the fat catfish."

Wauh-Oonae said: "Aur'voir, Hugh Sutherland."

"Aur'voir, Nancy Prince."

A flicker of something like puzzlement crossed her face, or maybe he'd only imagined it. Maybe she was trying to remember whether Norbert had said: 'My cousin Nancy Prince,' or just 'Nancy.' She turned her horse and headed back up to the road. Hugh turned back to netting Mr. Catfish. Tight-caged or no, it took some doing to get the slippery bugger bagged. It didn't help that Hugh's mind kept wandering back to the picture of Norbert's hands clasping Nancy Prince's waist to stay on the horse, and his own hands imagining what it felt like.

Hugh set off home with the net handle slung over his shoulder and the catfish flopping and thrashing in the net bag. It didn't flop for long. When he came into the yard it was obviously well past lunchtime – Mum and Angus, Catherine and Margaret were weeding and hoeing in the garden; the rest of the family would be across the river working the fields on Point Douglas, except Gran in the house with the youngest children. Mum glared across her hoe and said: "Where have you been this time? And what's that you've brought home with you?"

"Supper."

CHAPTER 11

Schultz just managed to grab the ink bottle before it bounced off the table. Although only September, Noah's Ark was already being buffeted and shaken by a wind roaring down from the north – not a steady wind, but gusting like a clever boxer who knows to throw a punch and wait, and then punch again just when his opponent thinks the attack is over. Noah's Ark was what the locals had christened the new McKenney & Co. Emporium And Lodging House. The nickname was partly because the building did look a bit like an ark floating on the prairie sea: squat and long and – except for the storefront – windows only on the second storey where the living quarters were, like a ship with no portholes on the lower decks. The other reason for 'Noah's Ark' was that the locals were sure that, come next spring, the melt-off was going to give this depressed plot of land the impression there'd been rain for forty days and forty nights.

Schultz refused to entertain the possibility that McKenney & Co. should've built elsewhere and differently. For future reasons, there was no better spot to be than the north-west corner of the crossroads of the north and west trails, and The Company had given in to the claim that Fort Garry's Reserve Land ended at the Portage Trail – or the Edmonton Trail, depending on whether a traveller only planned to go as far west as Portage la Prairie or all the way to the foothills of the Rocky Mountains. The Company didn't much care which piece of virgin land some private citizen wanted to build on, except for a mile-wide swath around its forts.

As for the actual construction on McKenney & Co's chosen site, the traditional Red River Style was post-and-beam: squared log upright posts grooved down their sides to fit the tongues carved onto squared log beams slotted between them to form the walls. But Schultz and the McKenneys had been in agreement that they wanted a proper building with a frame and clapboards. The frame was local rough-cut lumber and the clapboards imported by steamboat from a sawmill in St. Paul. The boards were clapping today.

Schultz dabbed his pen in the rescued ink bottle and went back to carefully forming loops and whorls into words on the page. He knew from schooldays experience that when he got worked up about something he would blot and botch his penmanship, unless he made a conscious effort to slow down. And he was certainly worked up about the subject of the moment, although it was hard to say how much of it was anger and how much elation.

He was writing a letter to the editor of *The Nor'Wester*, the local newspaper run by a pair of immigrant Canadians who'd carted an aged printing press all the way from St. Paul two years before Schultz arrived at Red River. The letter was about the new policies brought in by Governor Dallas, The Company's new Governor of Rupert's Land. Governor Dallas had decreed that The Company would no longer pay cash money for furs and pemmican and local farm produce and such, just credit at its own retail stores. And The Company would no longer sell wholesale bulk goods to independent storekeepers and traders.

Schultz was steaming mad that The Company could so easily make it more difficult for McKenney & Co. to attract cash customers to the store, or to outfit private fur trading expeditions. But part of him was a bit giddy with delight that The Company was making it so easy for him to take another step towards something even larger than McKenney & Co. and *The Nor'Wester* was the stepping stone. Most of the locals didn't seem to realize that *The Nor'Wester* was a good deal more than the neighbourhood gossip sheet and fish-wrap. Being the only newspaper in Rupert's Land it was the newspaper of record, and although it wasn't distributed widely in the east it was somewhat. A letter printed in *The Nor'Wester* complaining that the north western third of North America was groaning under a yoke of tyranny, would be gospel to any interested parties in Ottawa or Toronto or London or Washington.

Schultz wiped his pen and looked back over what he'd written so far. He'd just managed to formulate a thunderous closing sentence when *"Johnny!"* came from downstairs. "Come and help!" The screech in his sister-in-law's voice was just this side of panic. Schultz threw down the pen and hurried downstairs, barely remembering to duck his head under the lintel. Lucy was at the foot of the stairs. She pointed out the side door, shouting: "Harry can't lift it by himself! He – !" By then Schultz was out the door.

There was a lot of lumber piled on the prairie beside the store, some of it odds and ends left over from the basic construction, some in neat stacks for further work on the interior. Harry was trying to lift and drag an eight inch square beam that was at least twice as long as he was tall. The crookbacked old Metis man who was the only hired hand available with the fall Buffalo Hunt out on the plains was trying to help, but not succeeding. Schultz pushed him aside and hoisted one end of the beam easily onto his shoulder. Harry did the same with his end and headed around the corner of the building, calling over his shoulder to the old man: "Bring the fence maul."

The wind caught the side of the beam and almost knocked Schultz off his feet but not quite. A moment later they were safely around to the lee side of the building, but then Schultz could see why Lucy and Harry were in a panic. The second storey was actually buckling and leaning outward when the gusts hit the windward side – not much, but it wouldn't take much for the square joins of rafters and studs to get bent out of right angles, and a crooked skeleton wouldn't stand for long.

Harry plopped his end of the beam down by where one of the main studs ran up inside the wall – or at least Schultz thought that must be where the stud was, from as much as he could remember of when the building was just a frame. Schultz walked the beam upright, then leaned its top end into the wall and held it in place while Harry whanged it with the fatheaded fence maul to wedge it securely. They did that six more times, making a line of angled beams spaced every twenty feet or so along the wall. And then of course the wind died. Schultz and Harry stood breathing themselves out and looking back at their handiwork. Schultz said: "We should do that on the other side, too."

"Prob'ly no need. We don't get much wind from this direction."

"No, but I mean for the benefit of all those that call this Noah's Ark. Don't those beams look like long oars coming down from the upper deck? So we'll need some on the other side, too, or people'll think we're rowing around in circles."

Harry squinted at him, then said: "I don't recall Ma dropping you on your head, but I guess she must've."

Schultz glanced north along what people were starting to call just Main Road, toward Noah's Ark's nearest neighbour with its post-and-beam construction unperturbed by the wind. The Royal Hotel was now the Emmerling Hotel, and 'Dutch George' Emmerling was smoking a pipe on its front porch in a posture that somehow managed to convey amusement over more than a hundred yards. Schultz had been, and still was, suspicious of an American who'd suddenly decided to become proprietor of an establishment in British territory without showing any inclination of becoming a British subject. But Harry had said Dutch George's money was as good as anybody's, and since there wasn't anybody else offering theirs… And since old Andrew McDermot had agreed to let McKenney & Co gradually pay down their purchase of the original building, and Dutch George had paid them full-out cash, that gave McKenney & Co a good bit more operating capital.

"Hello," came from behind Schultz and Harry. Schultz turned around to see a horseman with grizzled muttonchop sidewhiskers, or 'sideburns' as the Americans were starting to call them, after their General Burnside of the Union Army. "I'm William Cowan, new physician at Fort Garry – well, not *new*, just the last few years The Company had me posted up at Moose Factory, but since poor Dr. Bunn took his heart attack in last year's flood they decided I should come back here. Amazing it only took them a year to make a decision. You'd be Dr. Schultz…?"

"I am."

Dr. Cowan leaned down from his horse to shake hands. "Pleased to meet you."

"And this is my brother, Henry McKenney."

"How do you do?"

"How do you do?"

Dr. Cowan said: "Once I'd got the wife and the progeny settled back in in our old quarters and all the unpacking done, I thought I should pay you a call. Professional courtesy and all."

Schultz felt a twinge of alarm, but just said: "That's very good of you."

Harry said: "Lucy's probably got tea on if you care to step in, Dr. Cowan."

"Why thank you, Mr. McKenney, I believe I will." Dr. Cowan stepped down and hitched his horse to one of the iron rings screwed into the bow of Noah's Ark. They went in through the front door, past the barrels of flour and chests of tea and bolts of cloth and the counter with the weigh scales. Dr. Cowan said companionably: "How's business?"

Harry said: "Well, we aren't been open long, and it's dang slow with half the settlement gone on the buffalo hunt. It'll pick up." Harry led the way up the stairs to the living quarters, where Lucy was in fact sitting in the kitchen with a cup of tea and two empty cups waiting by the pot. Introductions were made, Lucy reached down another cup and they all sat down to tea and biscuits.

Dr. Cowan said: "Yes, it isn't possible to have too many MDs around here. Oh, some days weeks will go by without a call, but there were times in my time here that Dr. Bunn and I were both run off our feet. Lucky for us some of the slack gets taken up by amateurs like Granny Sally Ross and her home remedies. You know, sometimes you'll see an Indian or a Metis walking along chewing on a willow twig. Ask 'em why and they'll say they've got a headache or a toothache. I tried it once when I had a slight toothache, and you know what? It works."

Lucy said interestedly: "Really?"

"Try it next time you feel a headache coming on. It has to be a fresh twig, though, with the green bark still on. Never taught me that in medical school. So where'd you take your degree, Dr. Schultz? I'm University of Glasgow, m'self."

Schultz had told the lie – or the slight exaggeration – many times by now, but never to an accredited Doctor of Medicine. "Queen's University, in Kingston, Upper Canada."

Dr. Cowan looked perplexed. "*Queens* at *King*ston?"

Schultz laughed, partly in relief that Dr. Cowan obviously didn't know anything about Queen's University or anyone there. "I think they chose the names to confuse American invaders."

"Ah. Never been to Canada, m'self. All my comings and goings to this part of the world were in and out of Hudson's Bay. Came here in '48 as physician to the Chelsea Pensioners Brigade when they got posted here. I fell in love with the country – well, fell in love with Harriet Sinclair, to tell the truth – and when the brigade went back to England I stayed on."

Schultz was a bit taken aback. 'Sinclair' in this part of the world was a halfbreed name. He could understand a lonely fur trader in a backwoods outpost taking a halfbreed woman to wife, but it seemed a bit strange for a physician who could obviously have had a life and career back in civilization. But at least the Sinclairs were mostly Protestant English halfbreeds, not priest-ridden French, so Schultz told himself to try and keep an open mind.

Dr. Cowan continued: "So, I don't know the first thing about Canadian geography. Is Kingston, or where your people are from, anywhere near Michilimackinac?"

"Not hardly. But I was there once, when I was working on the lake boats one summer between terms."

"Were you now?" Dr. Cowan set down his cup and leaned forward, with an almost religious light in his eyes. "Tell me, at Michilimackinac do they have any monument to Beaumont – a cairn or a plaque or such like?"

"Beaumont?"

"William Beaumont. 'Experiments and Observations on the Gastric Juice and the Physiology of Digestion.' It was at Michilimackinac where the French Canadian was shot."

Schultz quipped: "I imagine that over the years a lot of French Canadians were shot at Michilimackinac."

Harry laughed, but Dr. Cowan didn't – in fact, he was looking at Schultz rather oddly. "I mean the French Canadian with the stomach wound... The stomach wound that Dr. Beaumont healed, but amazingly the patient was left with a permanent gastric fistula that allowed Dr. Beaumont to study the actual workings of digestion...?"

"Oh, *that* Beaumont. No, I don't recall seeing a plaque or anything. Well, you know what they say about prophets in their own country."

"Huh. Yes, well, I suppose that's what they say. Well... I really mustn't take up any more of your time. Thank you very much for the tea, Mrs. McKenney. Dr. Schultz, before I go, maybe you'd indulge me by letting me have a peek at your examining room? Around here I don't get much chance to see how other members of the profession set themselves up."

"I'm afraid it isn't much, we only just got moved in."

"Of course, of course."

"Just down the hall here..."

In the examining room, Schultz stood watching Dr. Cowan glance around. A glance was about all it took; the entire contents were a cot, two wooden chairs and a small writing table sporting a mortar and pestle and three medical books, and his black bag stowed underneath it. Schultz gestured at the mortar and pestle and said: "I mean to be able to make a lot more use of that soon. Once the general store is making a profit I mean to use my share to build a free-standing pharmacy, so I can import supplies in bulk, both for the retail trade and my practice."

Dr. Cowan kept glancing around quizzically and finally said: "Dr. Schultz, modesty is a fine and rare trait in a young man, but it can be carried to extremes."

"Um, 'modesty'...?"

"You don't have your degree on the wall. Almost the first thing I unpack when we have to move somewhere is my degree, and find a prominent place on the wall for it."

"Oh, I would've done the same, but when I came to Red River the steamboat ran aground on a sandbar just a few miles from Fort Garry. The captain unloaded the cargo to float her free, and in the course of the operation some pieces of luggage ended up in the river. One of them was the trunk with my medical degree in it. Fortunately my medical books were in my other trunk." Schultz noticed Dr. Cowan's eyes flick at the three lonely texts on the table. "Although unfortunately some of them were in the trunk that went down."

"It would seem to me, Dr. Schultz, that Queen's University would be glad to furnish you with a duplicate degree, if you informed them of the circumstances."

"I'm sure they will, but these things take time. Especially at this distance."

"Hm. I suppose so. Well, I'd best be getting back to the fort."

Harry came out with Schultz to see Dr. Cowan off. As Dr. Cowan trotted away, Harry said: "Do you think he knows?"

"Knows what?" Schultz hadn't told Harry that he hadn't actually finished his medical degree. After all, it was just a formality and a piece of paper.

Harry said: "Huh," and looked at him with his hawk eyes hooded and tufted eyebrows taut, then looked away. "Well, I wonder how much his jaunt up here had to do with 'professional courtesy' anyways. Besides being a Doctor, he's a Chief Trader for The Company. Introducing himself to a brother medico could've just been a excuse to spy out the competition."

Schultz suddenly laughed. "Oh, I wouldn't worry too much about what Dr. Cowan might be thinking. Middle-aged muddlehead's been living in the backwoods too long. 'Willow bark' indeed." And the only other accredited medical practitioner at Red River, Dr. Bird, was entirely absorbed and obsessed with his dotty idea that public money should be used to provide free health care to the public. No, there was no reason for Dr. John Christian Schultz to worry at all.

CHAPTER 12

Point Douglas John Sutherland stepped out of his empty house, climbed onto Montrose and pointed his nose south along the cart road to the ferry to Fort Garry. It was unusual for a meeting of the Council of Assiniboia to be called during harvest time, but these were unusual circumstances. Terrible circumstances, in fact, if half the rumours from south of the border were true. So instead of paddling across to Point Douglas with the rest of the family as soon as the dew was off the ground, John was heading for a meeting with the Governor In Council.

There were two Governors at Fort Garry: Governor Dallas of all Rupert's Land, and Governor Mactavish of Assiniboia, the portion of Rupert's Land that was home to most of the farmers and buffalo hunters who supplied The Company with food for its employees. The dual-governor arrangement served to let the local populace more or less manage their own affairs and stay out of The Company's hair.

Not that The Company let 'manage their own affairs' go as far as elections. The Councillors were appointed by The Governor of Rupert's Land on the recommendation of the Governor of Assiniboia. But most people around Red River figured the appointed Councillors were the ones they would've elected themselves – although John had some doubts about that when it came to himself. But then, he wasn't an actual Councillor yet, and doubted he ever would be. He was only an apprentice substitute in case there weren't enough councillors for a quorum, which never seemed to be the case.

John stood in the stirrups to try and see through the leaves as Point Douglas passed by on the other side of the river. Through a gap in the trees he caught a glimpse of his family: some scything or sickling the wheat, oats and barley, some binding the felled stalks into standing sheaves, and the littlest Sutherlands hunting crayfish on the riverbank – except baby Roddy, who would be sleeping in a cradleboard hung from a tree, in the efficient way they'd learned from the Indians.

John sat back down on the saddle feeling a little guilty. He reminded himself that his father and mother could organise the work as well or better than he could, and that Donald and Hugh were big enough to do a man's work now, so his presence wasn't really necessary. *'There,'* he told himself, *'isn't that a mood-improver? Now instead of feeling guilty you can feel extraneous.'*

He shifted his mind to occupy itself with the ongoing task of trying to memorise the Laws of Assiniboia. He knew he had the four clauses of the first section, on controlling open-air fires, down pat, so he skipped his memory ahead to the next section, *Animals:*

V. If one or more animals be found in an enclosure where damage has been done, the said damage shall be paid for by the Owner of such animal as can prove to be generally known in his neighbourhood as fence breakers...

John worked his way down through the clauses on stallions and rams found roaming among the neighbours' mares and ewes, then got stumped partway through:

VIII. If between 31st March and 1st November any pig or pigs be found in any enclosed field without a yoke of one foot and a half wide and one foot and a half high...

Or was it one foot and three-quarters? But by then John was almost at The Forks, and could put the question away until he had a moment to check it against the printed copy. He left Montrose in the paddock of a Metis who lived near the ferry dock. It was one of those periods when MacDoug had had his ferry licence taken away, so the boat came smartly from the other shore and hardly needed baling. On the west bank, John climbed the well-beaten path angling up to the wide cart-road running beside the Red River wall of Fort Garry. He turned left and walked straight along it till he rounded the south-east corner, with its cone-topped, stone bastion like a turret out of King Arthur, except squatter and probably sturdier. In the centre of Fort Garry's Assiniboine River wall was the crenellated, stone gatehouse fit for any castle. The gates were standing open and people were coming and going as usual, but more anxious and agitated than usual. John didn't go through the gates, just threaded his way laterally through the comers and goers and kept on along the cart path that skirted the fort like a castle's moat.

When John rounded the south-west bastion, he could see his destination just ahead. Set back behind Fort Garry's west wall was a wide, long, wooden building with a shingled roof and a miniature version of itself snugged against its front; the entranceway had been added on after one too many snowstorms blew in with whoever came through the front door. A few saddlehorses and carts were tethered outside, and a couple of stragglers were disappearing through the entranceway. John followed them into the Courthouse and took a seat near the back. He'd attended a number of Council meetings by now, and none of them had had this air of grim nervousness. Greetings were subdued – as often as not just a nod instead of even a murmured 'hello' – and there was no pre-meeting joking about so-and-so's wandering hog or someone else's chokecherry wine.

Lanky, bristle-bearded Governor Mactavish occupied the judge's table up front, with the white-bearded Council Secretary at his left and Judge Black on his right. The Secretary was the executive officer of the Court of Rupert's Land, and the duties of his office were officially described as: *"to discharge all administrative functions as are not specially assigned to any other person."* Judge John Black wasn't technically a Judge, since he'd been appointed by The Company and not The Crown, so his official title was the Recorder of Rupert's Land.

The rest of the Council was made up of community representatives from each segment of the population – Kildonan, St. Norbert, St. Peters… – and prominent souls such as the Anglican Bishop of Rupert's Land, the Bishop of St. Boniface, Dr. Cowan and the Reverend Dr. Black. It was a little confusing having two John Blacks on the council. But a community containing a dozen Alexander Sutherlands and John MacBeths, and even more Mary Mathesons, quickly adjusted to differentiating between Dr. Black and Judge Black – even if he wasn't really a judge.

There were of course no women on the council, but John had small doubt that the female point of view on anything of import had already been expressed by each councillor's wife. Of course that didn't apply to Bishop Taché, but he had the Grey Nuns, who'd handily coped with matters at Red River through all the times he'd been away to Rome, or Montreal, or New York City, and would no doubt remind him of that in their humble, modest and obedient way.

Governor Mactavish called the meeting to order. The Councillor from St. Andrews immediately stood up and said: "Is it true?"

Governor Mactavish said: "Is what true?"

"The rumours. From Minnesota."

"There've been a lot of rumours. Tell me what you've heard and I'll tell you what's been confirmed."

"I heard that with so many American frontier garrisons sent east to fight in the war, the Sioux rose up and massacred a lot of farmers, took a lot of white women and children hostage, wiped out an Army column sent against them."

Governor Mactavish shook his head. "They didn't 'wipe out' an Army column – half of the soldiers made it back to their fort. All the rest is true."

John put his head in his hands. The rumours had been keeping him awake nights for weeks now, but it was worse to hear they weren't only rumours. Minnesota was only a few days up-river. Even the craziest War Chief wouldn't try conclusions against Fort Garry or the Stone Fort, but all the farms around them were naked to a surprise attack.

Someone muttered: "Bloody savages."

Someone else said: "'Savages' my arse – beggin' your pardon, Monseigneur. The way I heard it, the Sioux were starving to death on their reservation and one of the Indian Agents said, 'If they're all-that hungry they can eat grass, or their own dung.' After they killed that Indian Agent they stuffed his mouth with grass."

Governor Mactavish said: "No matter why the Minnesota uprising happened, it happened, and it's still happening. All the different bands of Sioux have come together under Little Crow and are still on the War Road."

The Reverend Dr. Black gaped at the Governor and said: "*Little Crow?*"

John would've voiced the same shock if he weren't keeping his teeth clamped together. The Sioux Chiefs weren't just names to the people of Red River. As far back as John could remember, the Sioux had been making periodic visits north to keep up friendly relations with 'the Hussen Bay men' at The Forks. The Sioux visits had always been a tense time for the people of Red River, given all the old vendettas between the Sioux and the local Crees, Ojibways and Metis. Years ago, the Sioux had signed a peace treaty with 'Mr. Grant, Chief of All The Halfbreeds,' pledging they'd never fight 'the wagonmen' again. But Mr. Grant wasn't around anymore. Little Crow was, though, and he'd proved to be a devoted smoother-over of confrontations and maker of peace. If Little Crow had now decided that the only road left open for the Sioux was The War Road, then now was a very dangerous and desperate time.

"Yes," Governor Mactavish nodded, "Little Crow. *And*, Little Crow also…" Governor Mactavish scratched his mustache, looked down at the table, breathed in and out, then reached into his pocket and pulled out a beaded buckskin pouch. "Little Crow sent me tobacco. The message that came with it was it's been too long since the Sioux and their white friends at The Forks have laid eyes on each other. He asks if we'd be amenable to them coming for a visit."

That ignited the room. John forgot his resolution to keep his teeth together, but it didn't matter, since all the councillors were spouting too loud to hear each other much less him. They were all saying essentially the same thing – even if Little Crow's proposed 'visit' were just to get The Company to give some food to his starving people, in the current climate it would only take one young man doing something impulsive and the whole place would explode.

Governor Mactavish thumped on the table for quiet, then said: "Under the circumstances, I don't think Little Crow would be too insulted if we asked him to postpone his visit a while. If I can put him off a couple of months, it'll be winter and they won't want to be travelling all the way up here in winter. In the spring, the ground's too soggy to move a mass of men on horseback. So that buys us till next summer."

A councillor put in: "By then the U.S. Army'll've sent troops to sort them out."

"I guess," Governor Mactavish shrugged. "But they can't kill the whole Sioux Nation. Even if they've killed Little Crow before next summer comes around, some other Sioux Chief will be bringing his people here for a visit. Summer's when Red River's the most vulnerable, when half our population is way out on the plains – and they're the half the Sioux least want to tangle with, the buffalo hunters.

"So what I suggest we do is circulate a petition through the settlement, a petition to the Imperial Government. The petition would explain that although we've always had good relations with the Indians of Rupert's Land, the Americans are doing a good job of making their Indians see all white men as enemies, and we're not far from the American border. If everybody in the settlement signed a petition that we need a garrison of Imperial troops here to protect thousands of British subjects from mortal danger… In the face of such a petition, the Imperial Government would pretty much have to send out troops."

A discreet cough drew John's and everybody else's attention to the youngest councillor. James Ross stood up and said to Governor Mactavish, with just the slightest hint of insinuation, "Was this your idea or Governor Dallas's?" James Ross had inherited his handsome high cheekbones and black hair from his mother, Granny Sally Ross, and the offices of Postmaster and Sheriff of Red River from his late father. Some people said the only reason The Company handed young James his father's appointments was it saved the trouble of actually making a decision, and of changing the old habit of referring to 'Postmaster Ross' and 'Sheriff Ross.' But John was of the opinion that The Company'd had better reasons than that. Young James had spent a few years getting a university education in Upper Canada, and when he came back the publishers of *The Nor'Wester* thought enough of his abilities to hire him on as editor.

Governor Mactavish replied: "Well, I *talked* to Governor Dallas about it, of course – he lives here now, too, in the same boat as the rest of us."

"Yeah, I bet you talked to him about it." James Ross ran one hand back through his elegant widow's peak to brush errant strands out of his eyes, and cocked his other fist on his hip like the copperplates of Prime Ministers addressing the Commons. John didn't think of it as striking poses; James Ross was just one of those people whose body naturally fell into classic postures. "The Company intends to use the Minnesota Massacre for its own ends, as it does everything. Any time Imperial Troops have been posted here, they've been seen not as Soldiers of The Queen, but Soldiers of The Company. Governor Dallas has already passed new orders to try and keep all trade and imports in the hands of The Company's stores; how much further will he go if he can use our Company-inflamed fears of the Sioux to get himself a garrison of troops?"

"Don't ye go bluidy imputin' tae *me*, laddy-buck!" Like John's father, Governor Mactavish's Scots came out stronger when he got agitated. "The Company pays my wages, but my job is to look out for the people of Assiniboia, and that's what I'm doing."

"As you say – The Company pays your wages."

Things got a little heated, but Bishop Taché and the Bishop of Rupert's Land managed to calm things down to a relatively civilized debate. After wrangling the question over for awhile, they broke for lunch in the officers' mess in Fort Garry, then went back to the courthouse and went back at it. Eventually the council came to the decision John had thought was obvious: to circulate the petition Governor Mactavish had proposed and see how many people would sign it. But then it became a question of how to word the petition, with twenty different individuals all wanting to put it in their own words. Finally Governor Mactavish suggested that the Secretary take away his notes and put them into a draft petition for approval, and by then everybody was too talked-out to argue. Except, of course, James Ross, who would've argued with God for eternity whether the sun should rise in the east or the west. But even James Ross could see that the rest of the men in the room were in no mood for further oratory.

By the time John emerged from the courthouse, his head numbed by democracy, the sun was painting the vast sky purple and orange. The blood-bubbling sounds of the Great Highland Pipes burst into the air. One of the articles Governor Dallas had brought with him to Red River was Mr. Piper McLellan, who at sunset marched the ramparts of Fort Garry in full kilted Highland regalia – which John's father said was a ridiculous costume got up by the British Army after the belted plaid had been outlawed for so long few Highlanders remembered. A few blanketed Indians stood at the foot of the walls staring up in stone-faced wonderment at the man in the checkered skirt making barbaric music. It actually did make for a relatively pleasant Vespers when the wind carried the piping as far as Kildonan, especially for the old people who'd grown up hearing that sound ringing off the hills and crags, but John wondered how pleasant it was going to be come next June when the sun didn't set till ten o'clock.

As Montrose trotted John into their homeyard, Hugh came out of the house carrying a candle in a worn-out old tin cup with one side cut out and said: "Mum's got a cold supper waiting for you. I'll take Montrose in and get him fed and bedded down."

John creaked down off the saddle, stiff from sitting all day, saying: "That's good of you, Hugh, thank you."

"Oh, I don't mind, me whatever."

John knew Hugh didn't mind, and neither would Montrose. He watched Montrose follow Hugh toward the barn without Hugh even taking hold of the reins. Montrose was tolerably friendly and obedient with John, but whenever Hugh came near he would've purred if he'd had paws instead of hooves. Donald and Aleck had the gifts Hugh lacked – the gifts of thinking in a straight line and shouldering a task through to its logical conclusion, while Hugh's attention could be distracted and rivetted by any bright or furry thing that crossed his path. But what made Hugh's lack its own sort of gift was that other creatures, human or otherwise, tended to respond to Hugh in kind. It could be infuriating when Hugh got sent out to fetch the cows and was found an hour later tossing sticks for the neighbours' dog in the cow pasture, but he was getting a little better at remembering his chores as he got older. John sometimes blasphemously wondered, though, whether Hugh's fanciful gift might get him through life better than Donald and Aleck's practical one.

"Well, wherever he got it," John muttered to himself, "it certainly didn't come from me," and went inside to his hearth and the rest of his family. John endeavoured to be a reasonably well-rounded human being, but he knew there was nothing fanciful about him, except that just now he fancied some supper.

John was glad to've successfully got through his civic duty so he could get back to less onerous things, like getting the wheat, oats and barley harvested and winnowed and the straw piled aside for winter bedding for the animals, like castrating the male calves to grow into beef steers and slaughtering the two year old steers once the weather got cold enough for the meat to keep, and making sausages and blood puddings out of the gristlier cuts and tanning the hides, like taking the older boys and the carts out to where the eastern woodlands met the prairie, for a few days of cutting firewood once the leaves were gone and the sap stopped running, like sawing and nailing new boards on the barn doors where the new cracks hadn't mattered through the summer…

September and October were always a well-occupied time, because if whatever needed doing to get ready for winter wasn't done before the first snow, it wasn't going to get done.

Since everybody else in the settlement was busy doing the same thing as the Point Douglas Sutherlands, and since anything that requires a few people to agree with each other takes time, John didn't expect the Petition For Troops to be ratified and circulated anytime soon, so forgot about it.

On the morning when the boys herded the five two-year-old steers into the holding pen – a different day than the pig-killing, because beef carcasses had to be skinned and hogs scalded and scraped – John pointed to the one with the spotted nose and said: "Not that one. Two beefs to sell and two to keep will get us through the winter. It's about time we had an ox again." He hoped he'd said it blandly; lying wasn't his strong suit. But then, as Janet had assured him, he wasn't lying, just not drawing the truth out to its furthest possible conclusion. He'd been keeping an eye on the steers all summer, to see which was the biggest and least skittish, and rehearsing what he was going to say when this day came.

John's father, leaning on the fence beside him, said: "D'ye think ye can teach this one tae be a stronger swimmer?" Their last ox had drowned the first year the Point Douglas Sutherlands lived across the river from Point Douglas. Old Samson had panicked mid-stream when they tried to raft him across for the spring ploughing. He had never been replaced, because the earth on Point Douglas was so well broken-in that even a scruffy pony could pull a plough through it, and getting a pony across the river was a lot less complicated than an ox. Which was exactly the train of thought John didn't want his father to follow through.

John said: "I won't try that again. What we can do is build a shed and a pen on Point Douglas, walk the ox across before spring break-up, and walk him back here once the river's frozen again. In the winter we can use him for hauling logs – the woods are getting farther away every year with so many people cutting back the edges. Slower going with an ox than a horse, but much heavier loads." All of which was true, as far as it went.

John's father said: "Well, it seems ye've thought it through without bothering tae discuss it. But that is reasonable of ye – planning years down the road is no longer a true concern tae me."

And that was it, over and done with. But not quite. John caught a glimpse of Hugh's green eyes looking quizzically from his grandfather to his father and back again, as though Hugh knew something more had just happened than seemed to but wasn't sure what. Then Hugh's head gave a little jerk as though the other shoe had just dropped on it, and he looked away towards the river. Hugh might not have his older and younger brothers' gift of thinking things through in a straight line, but he was better at seeing odd bits and pieces fall together naturally. John saw Hugh see that if Hugh's parents decided to sell Point Douglas after his grandparents were beyond caring, the Point Douglas Sutherlands would have an ox on hand to break new fields on the east side of the river.

John's father hefted his ancient, flintlock musket and said: "Well, let's get yon spotty-nosed one out the pen and get the deed done." They looped ropes around the four remaining steers' necks and reefed them up close to the fence, then John and his father and

Donald and Hugh lined up: four guns pointed between eight soft, brown eyes. Ex-private Sandy Sutherland said crisply: "Ready, aim, *fire*," and all four steers died without hearing their brothers go before them. Through the clearing, red-misted smoke, John saw two things. One was Aleck looking relieved that they hadn't needed five for the firing squad. The other was Hugh looking closed-in around the fact that living things had to die.

As in most years, there was snow on the ground by Hallowe'en, but this year there was also the Petition For Troops brought from house to house, for the householder to sign or not sign as he so chose. And then things got messier than John could've imagined from such a simple endeavour. John sourly told himself that he should've seen it coming, given all the givens.

Given that the only operational printing press close to hand was *The Nor'Wester* newspaper's, the Council of Assiniboia had logically commissioned *The Nor'Wester* to print the thousand copies of the petition that the council meant to distribute, and logically asked that the petition be published in the newspaper as well. Given that the proprietors of *The Nor'Wester* were recent immigrants from Upper Canada, it was no great secret that they believed the government of Upper Canada should be the proprietors of Rupert's Land. Given that their editor, James Ross, had been raised at Red River but educated in Upper Canada, he could logically be expected to have a divided opinion. Editor James Ross conferred with Sheriff James Ross and Postmaster James Ross to come up with a decision.

Given those givens, what *The Nor'Wester* logically decided to do with The Petition For Troops was print it as commissioned, with a few new clauses salted into the version published in the newspaper. Whoever signed that version of the petition would not only be asking the Imperial Government for troops, but also complaining against The Company's dictatorial rule that trampled on the sacred rights of British Subjects, etc. etc.

By the time the Council got wind of that, James Ross and others had already been going from door to door getting signatures on their petition. A lot of people at Red River weren't dab hands at reading, and a lot of the ones who were could think of better things to do than wade through all the Whereases and Therefores. They took James Ross's word for it that this was the petition prepared by the Council of Assiniboia – well it said so right at the top, didn't it? When councillors tried to convene public meetings in outlying parishes to get their petition signed, the befuddled parishioners said they'd already signed the damned thing two days ago – at a public meeting convened by James Ross and Dr. Schultz and others.

James Ross turned out to be fairly affable about allowing people to strike their names off his petition and sign the real one; he didn't have much choice when a few hundred aggravated people showed up at his front door. Governor Mactavish informed James Ross that he was no longer Postmaster, or Sheriff of Red River. Which some people thought was unfair but John thought perfectly reasonable – you don't keep paying a carpenter to fix your roof if he spends his off-hours digging holes in your foundations. But there was one part of the whole affair that utterly baffled John, and he voiced his bafflement one night after all the children had gone to bed, "He *lied.* James Ross went around and baldfaced *lied* to his neighbours."

John's wife said: "People do, John."

John's mother said: "He thought he was right, John. Some people, if they think they're in the right, will do anything."

The office of Postmaster and its ten pounds a year went to A.G.B. Bannatyne, who was an independent trader and storekeeper married to the Metis daughter of his friendly competitor, old Andrew McDermot. Mrs. Bannatyne also happened to be the sister of Governor Mactavish's wife. But if being related to somebody by blood or marriage disqualified you, nobody at Red River would be able to do anything.

That still left the question of who was going to be the new Sheriff.

CHAPTER 13

Schultz choked on his morning tea, coughed some of it up his nose, wiped his mouth with his sleeve and sputtered at Harry: "You wouldn't!"

"I would and I did."

"But… *why?*"

"Thirty pounds a year, for one thing. That's not enough to live on, but nothing to sneeze at. It's not a full-time job, I'm told most of the duties are serving writs for unpaid debts, and that don't happen a lot around here."

"But think about it, Harry – why would they want to appoint you Sheriff of Red River?"

Harry arched a tufted black eyebrow at him and said joshingly: "Think I'm not up to it?"

"Of course you are, but… Think about it, why you in particular?"

"Because I applied, I suppose, and not many else did – at least not many with much education who're hearty and active enough to not get scared off if somebody don't want to get served papers." Harry sluiced up some fried egg yoke with a corner of local cheese, popped it in his mouth and talked around his chewing. "Some people you'd think might be right for the job – like, say John Sutherland; he might like the idea of thirty pound a year, but he can't go dropping his hay fork and skipping off to the far ends of the settlement whenever the Recorder wants a writ served. Me, I can just leave you or Lucy in charge of the store and I'm on my horse. Even Lulu could mind the store on her own in a pinch."

"But, *think* about it, Harry. You and Bannatyne. Why did they pick Bannatyne for Postmaster?"

"Well, simple enough…" Harry slurped down the dregs of his cup and reached for the teapot. "Bannatyne's been around here a long time, knows everybody and everybody knows him. And he's already got a store he can put the post office in. Well, so do we, but we're just starting up."

"Uh-huh – Bannatyne's an *independent* businessman, no ties to The Company. And so are you…"

Harry just nodded blandly at the obvious, and obviously still didn't understand.

"Look, Harry…" Schultz put down his fork – he wasn't using it, anyway – to keep from jabbing his brother to get the point across. "If The Company can report to the

Imperial Government that the sheriff and postmaster here have no ties to The Company, then it looks like people here are being allowed their democratic rights as British citizens."

"Uh… but, Bannatyne and I *do* have no ties to The Company, so –"

"Can't you bloody understand!" Schultz had always found it infuriating when people willfully refused to see what was real. "You *will* have ties to The Company, as soon as you start taking their money."

"The Company don't pay the sheriff's wages, the Council of Assiniboia does."

"And where does the Council get the money to pay you? From The Company! The pittance of property taxes is barely enough to keep the roads in repair. The Governor and Council of Assiniboia, and Judge Black, and all their… their… *minions*, they live off the customs duties The Company deigns to pay on imports. He who pays the piper calls the tune!"

"For Christ's sake, John, if you think I can be bought for thirty pounds a year –"

"Thirty pieces of silver!"

"Don't you be pointing fingers at me! I used to help Ma change your diapers!"

"Hush!" came from the kitchen doorway. It was Lucy. "Can't you even say good morning to each other without hollering blue murder? You're scaring the children. And what if we had customers downstairs?"

Harry grunted: "Time I opened the store," and headed for the stairs, leaving Schultz staring at his congealing breakfast.

After that morning, McKenney & Co. settled into a kind of uneasy, armoured truce. At mealtimes, Schultz would talk to the children or Lucy, or the boarders when there were any in residence, and there usually were – Dutch George Emmerling's was a bit too rowdy or expensive for some travellers, and the few spare rooms tacked onto the family living quarters above the store brought in a bit of ready money. Schultz and Harry didn't talk to each other, except to ask where that ledger had got to or say the flour bin needed refilling, and occasionally one would mutter: "Looks like snow," and the other one would grunt a reply. Sometimes at supper Harry would mention to Lucy that he'd served a writ on some farmer or buffalo hunter, and Schultz would bite his tongue. Schultz took to spending a lot of his free time at the *Nor'Wester* office, talking politics and business, the sort of conversations he used to have with Harry.

One morning when Lucy was taking the children to school in the cutter and Schultz was opening the store, Harry came clumping down the stairs in his winter boots and buffalo coat and said: "You and Lucy'll have to hold the fort today – maybe tomorrow, too – and the kids might have to walk to school tomorrow morning, but it won't kill 'em. Soon's Lucy gets back I'm taking the cutter to Headingley."

Headingly was a 'village' about fifteen miles west along the Assiniboine; the usual cluster of scattered farms around a church. Schultz said: "Why?"

"Got to arrest and bring in a prisoner."

'Arrest' and 'prisoner' were unusual enough around Red River that Schultz broke his just-business rule and said: "Who?"

"The Reverend Griffith Owen Corbett."

"What? Why?"

"Oh, nothing serious," Harry said drily. "He just half-killed his servant girl – she might die yet."

"*What*?" Schultz set aside his broom and rubbed his forehead. What Harry was saying didn't make any sense, it felt like bees buzzing into his ears. He half-wondered if Harry weren't playing games with him. "That's crazy."

"That's one word for it. Seems as among his other accomplishments, the good Reverend fancies himself a bit of a medical man – being as how he once spent a few sessions loitering around King's Hospital in England." There seemed to be something particularly pointed about the way Harry said that last part. "A while ago, the Rev's pretty little halfbreed servant girl discovered she was pregnant. So the Reverend Mr. Corbett figured he'd help her out with an abortion, but it didn't take, so he tried again. He tried five times – *five times* – sometimes with instruments, sometimes with poison drugs.

"The Reverend Griffith Owen Corbett was very concerned, you see, that if she grew pregnant enough to show, people might ask her who the father was – people like the Reverend Mr. Corbett's wife and children. So now the girl's still pregnant but half-dead, and I'm going out to bring him in for trial."

The story was so impossible that Schultz just stared at his half-brother's dark and glowering face for a moment, then suddenly twigged and laughed half-loonily at the ridiculousness of it all.

"I don't see what's bloody funny about it."

"It's not funny, it's... Harry, don't you see what they're doing?"

"What who's doing?"

"The Company!"

"What the hell's The Company got to do with it?"

"Everything! The Reverend Corbett's always been a pain in The Company's neck. It was you told me that when he was in England a few years back he told a Parliamentary Committee that The Company shouldn't be allowed to keep playing Emperor here. And just lately he got a lot of people in his parish to sign James Ross's *Nor'Wester* petition.

"Well, The Company dealt with James Ross, as you well know – he'll be too busy scrabbling for a living now to do much agitating. So now it's the Reverend Griffith Owen Corbett's turn to get dealt with." As he said it, it occurred to Shultz that there was another local power besides The Company that didn't much care for the Reverend Mr. Corbett. Reverend Griffith Owen Corbett had often loudly declared – from his pulpit or anywhere else he could get an audience – that the Roman Catholic Church was a mediaeval sinkhole of superstition, incense and fancy dress. "And Bishop Taché and the Grey Nuns won't shed any tears if Reverend Corbett gets disgraced."

"Talk sense, Johnny." Harry's voice reverted to annoyingly big-brotherly. "Either the girl's pregnant or she isn't – The Company can't just make that up. And so far as I know there's only ever been one Immaculate Conception."

"The Company can't just make it up, but they could pick up a rumour – you know how rumours travel around here – that the Reverend Corbett's maid had gone and got herself pregnant, probably by some wandering buffalo hunter or… farmhand." Schultz wasn't used to sputtering for words. "Then The Company could give her a few hints that they suspect it must've been the Reverend Corbett – or maybe the girl made that up herself, so her parents would be angrier at him than her. Or maybe she has a grudge against her employer. It's been known to happen."

The more Schultz thought it out aloud, the more obvious it seemed, "The girl will never have to find another employer if she gets The Company beholden to her. So they keep building the lie bigger and bigger until it gets to be… this stinking pile of horse-shit. *Think* about it, Harry. The man's a clergyman – and not some wine-swilling priest, but a Presbyterian Minister. In his own *home*, with his wife and children in the next rooms? And then to torture the girl *five times* trying to abort her? It's a pack of lies."

"That'll get decided at the trial."

"In The Company's Court! And you're the tool they're using to arrest him and keep him in your jail. It's just like I said it would be when you said you were going to take this job. Why don't you tell The Company to find somebody else to do their dirty work?"

"For one thing, thirty pounds a year – prob'ly going up to sixty soon, I hear. If this bare beginnings of a store was our only source of income, we'd starve. And 'we' means you, too, John – your examining room ain't exactly flooded with patients."

"We've still got more than half the Letter of Credit from Kew – you don't have to do this."

"The Letter of Credit's for building the business – we don't touch our capital for living expenses unless we're starving. That's what we agreed. I'm trying to keep us from starving."

Harry stepped toward the door and Schultz stepped in front of him, saying: "Don't go." He seemed to remember standing between Harry and a door once long ago, and saying those same words. It was when Harry was going away to work in a lumber camp, and Schultz had been too young to understand that if Harry didn't go there'd be no money to feed Johnny and his mother and baby sister. Harry had promised he'd be coming back, but so had Johnny's father.

The difference between then and now was that Johnny had been barely as tall as Harry's midriff, and now Harry's hat brim was on a level with Schultz's nose. Either Ludwig Schultz had been a considerably bigger man than Henry McKenney Senior, or Henry Jr. had done a better job of feeding-up the young ones than Henry Sr. had.

Harry said: "Out of my way, John."

Schultz planted his back against the door and said desperately: "Don't you see what The Company's doing? They're also destroying McKenney & Co. before we hardly get started – by driving a wedge between you and me."

"You're the only one driving a wedge. Stand out of my way, John."

Schultz started to say something more to make Harry see, but Harry reached out both arms, grabbed two fistfuls of the bib of Schultz's shopkeeper's apron and the waistcoat underneath it, and heaved sideways. Schultz clutched a double handful of Harry's buffalo coat and heaved the other way. They careened about the store, cursing at each other and slamming into things.

A treble voice blared: "What in God's name are you doing?" Schultz and Harry stopped and looked, but still kept their grips. It was Lucy again, this time standing in the shop doorway with snow dusting her cloak and hat. "Have you two completely lost your bloody minds?"

Schultz and Harry let go and lowered their arms. Schultz looked around and saw that they'd knocked over the cracker barrel; there were chunks of hardtack crunching under his boots.

Harry straightened his hat and started for the door, saying: "Since you're back with the cutter, I best get going." Schultz lowered his head and looked at his hands.

As Harry went past her, Lucy said: "You'll be sure to look in on Maria Thomas?"

"I'll at least stop by the farm and ask how she's doing." Then he was gone.

Schultz could see nothing for it but to pick up his broom and start sweeping again. As Lucy came into the shop unfastening her fur-lined bonnet, he said: "Who's Maria Thomas?"

"She's the fifteen year old girl lying on a deathbed with her insides ripped up by the ministrations of the Reverend Griffith Owen Corbett."

CHAPTER 14

Hugh was passing Morrison the carrots when six year old Catherine said loudly: "What's a borshing?"

Mum said: "A what, dear?"

"A borshing. Betsy Bannerman said at school Rev'end Corbett got rested for giving Maria Thomas a borshing."

A silence descended, except for the clinking of forks and spoons, a few coughs, and a somewhat louder chewing and swallowing than perhaps strictly necessary, as most of the family affected to be focused entirely on their food. Hugh muttered to Aleck beside him: "Trust Her Royal Whyness," and Aleck had to stifle a laugh. 'Your Royal Whyness' was what Hugh had christened Catherine a few years back, since it often seemed that the first word she'd learned to speak must've been 'why?' The silly nickname gave him at least a little of his own back for getting christened Purple Hugh.

Finally Mum said: "Well, Catherine, do you remember a year or two ago, when you were little, and one of our cows was very sick and we were all very worried…?"

"I think so. It was Suzie…?"

"That's right, dear. Then we found out that why she was sick was because the calf she was carrying was dead. So we got Granny Ross to mix up a bucket of medicine that would make Suzie push the calf out early. That was an abortion. Not 'a borshing,' an abortion."

"Was Maria Thomas's calf dead?"

"Her baby. No. No, it wasn't."

"Then why'd the Rev'end Corbett give her… an a-bor-shun?"

A thicker silence than before descended. Then Gran said: "We don't know for surely that he did, Catherine." Gran had always seemed closer to Catherine than her other granddaughters, maybe just because they had the same first name. "That's why they will have a trial."

"Oh. And what'll they do there?"

Granda said: "I'll be able to tell you that as it unfolds. While I was out mending the milkhouse latch this morning, one of the Polson lads rode into the yard with an envelope for me from Judge Black. Seems it's my turn for Jury Duty."

There was a hubbub of surprise and *"Why didn't you tell us?"*

Granda just shrugged as if it was nothing worth mentioning if the subject hadn't happened to come up in conversation. "I dinna expect it to be much of a trial, at any boot. The poor scared girl just tried to hide in a lie, and then once she'd started down that path had to pile on more and more fancied tales with every step. I feel sorry for her when it all comes out at trial."

Mum said: "Sounds like you've already made up your verdict."

"Well what could her story be but fairy dust? The man's a Minister of the Kirk, for the Lord's sake. I could understand a kirk minister making a little slip – they're only human beings, too – but *this*. No, it's not possible."

Da changed the subject to his regular 'round the table of: "And what did you do in school today?"

Hugh expected that the trial would start in a few days, since the charge had already been laid and the jury given notice. But it turned out to be put off to the next regular Quarterly Session, partly because Maria Thomas couldn't very well be carted twenty miles to the courthouse when her baby was almost due, or soon after giving birth. Granda said that was more proof that her story was just a story: "It'd have tae be a miracle baby tae survive five tries to kill it."

On the first day of the trial, Hugh set off running as soon as school was out. The sky was bright blue, not the twilight it would've been only a month ago. But the days would have to get a lot longer before the sun had any effect on the snow and the cold. The sun did make the snow blaze, but not with warmth. Hugh took it in turns running at a steady lope, then slowing to a walk for awhile, then running again. He knew that horses' lungs froze more easily than people's, but people's could still freeze. He'd wrapped his woolen muffler around his mouth and nose, and pretty soon it was crusted with frozen breath and nose drip. By the time he reached Fort Garry the western sky was orange and his running stints were just a brisk walk. He figured that his breathing had slowed down enough now that he could safely pull down his muffler. The air tasted sweet without the flavour of damp wool.

The courthouse had three big windows on either side. People swaddled in wool and fur were clustered around the windows, stamping their feet to keep warm, so Hugh figured the inside must be jammed to the rafters. He went to the window with the smallest group around it and found a space between fur hats where he could peer over shoulders if he stood on tiptoe.

He picked out Granda easily, sitting in the front corner of the jury box nearest to the judge's platform. Judge Black was sitting behind an elevated table, with the white-bearded Secretary scribbling away at a lower table in front of him. In front of the benches for the audience were two tables facing the judge. The one on the left had to be the Defence, because one of the two men sitting behind it was Frank Larned Hunt. Mr. Frank Larned Hunt was unusual enough that people who didn't know him knew who he was: a big deal Detroit lawyer who'd chucked it all to move his family to Red River, which he called 'Britain's one utopia.' The first time Hugh had laid eyes on him, Frank

Larned Hunt had come to the Point Douglas Sutherlands' to buy some eggs. As Hugh helped Mum search through the henhouse for hidden nests, she'd said: "I don't mean to be nosy, Mr. Hunt, but they say you were a lawyer in the East...?"

"Guilty."

"Then why did you – oh, tell me it's none of my business and I won't be offended – what made you decide to move to Red River?"

"There are no lawyers at Red River. Ten thousand people and not one lawyer."

"Oh, so you thought it was an opportunity...?"

"Not that kind. You know what they say: 'This town's too small for one lawyer to make a living, but two could.'"

"Oh. But then, um, why did you want to come here?"

"As I said, Mrs. Sutherland: There are no lawyers at Red River."

The part of Assiniboia where Mr. Hunt had eventually settled with his family was the parish of Headingley, the Reverend Mr. Griffith Owen Corbett's parish. One of the many rumours swirling around in the weeks before the trial was that Frank Larned Hunt had been moved to take up lawyering one last time for the sake of his unjustly-accused pastor.

The other counsel at the he-didn't-do-it table, and the two at the he-did-it table, were just local men who'd read a few books and watched a few court sessions. That was the way of trials at Red River: the accused and the accuser asked a couple of well-spoken neighbours to do the talking for them. Except in this case the homegrown man sitting beside Frank Larned Hunt had read more than a few books: Granny Ross's universitied son James.

Hugh heard someone moving up beside him – moccasins squeaking the hard-packed snow – and the corner of his eye caught the white hood of an HBC blanket capote. But he kept his eyes trained through the window and strained his ears to hear. Sitting in the witness box was a dark-skinned girl maybe a year or so older than Hugh, her chin not much higher than the rail and – "Well, Hugh Sutherland, your grandfather's in the thick of it, ain't he?"

It startled him – straining to hear through the window and then suddenly a voice right beside him. He turned to look. Framed by the white hood of the blanket coat was an oval-shaped face with high cheekbones and dark slanted eyes and a few vines of black hair poking out around the edges. "Oh, um, hello Nancy Prince." It seemed her skin changed colour in the winter, less coppery and more creamy, with her cheeks brushed with pink by the cold, like a crabapple of the kind that ripens to an ivory flushed with rose. "Um, yeah, that's my Granda on the jury there."

"Not just *on* the jury – they elected him Foreman of the jury." Someone nearer to the window hissed back: *"Ssh."* Nancy Prince leaned closer to speak quieter, close enough that he could smell woodsmoke and tea and something else he couldn't identify. She whispered: "How'd you get here from your school?"

"I..." *'Ran'* sounded a little silly, "walked."

"Long way."

Hugh shrugged.

"I rode my pony. I'm going back that way, you can ride behind me if you want. This is just about done for today."

"I don't mind, me whatever."

He walked with her away from the huddle around the window and around to the lee side of the courthouse, where several hobbled ponies were pawing at the snow for crisp grass. He knew which one was hers – the buckskin with the spotted rump – and went toward it, saying: "What's his name?"

"Cheengwun."

Hugh knew just enough Ojibway to know Cheengwun meant Shooting Star. He said: "Hello, Cheengwun," pulled off one mitten, held his palm up to the pony's nose and then crouched to unbuckle the hobbles.

"Don't –"

"Don't what?" Hugh asked without interrupting his unbuckling.

She said: "Huh. 'Don't' nothing, I guess. Most strangers putting their hands on him get kicked at." She tightened the cinch on the homemade saddle and climbed aboard. Her skirt bunched up, but unfortunately she had sensible thick duffle leggings on underneath.

She reached one embroidered moosehide-mittened hand down toward him. Hugh was quite sure he was too heavy for her to hoist up like she had Norbert last summer, but he took hold of her hand anyway, then bent his knees and jumped. He just managed to clear his leg over Cheengwun's rump. But the rump proved too wide for him to straddle easily, so he edged forward until the puffed-out front of his capote just touched the back of Nancy Prince's. She clucked Cheengwun into a walk and said over her shoulder: "You better get a hold on me before I start him trotting."

Hugh would've liked nothing better than to wrap his arms around her waist and clasp her tightly, but instead he just took hold of the sides of her coat with his mittens. He said conversationally: "Well, so, Wauh Oonae –" Her head gave a little jerk, as though she would've looked back at him in surprise but the hood got in her way. He suddenly wondered whether her cousin Norbert had called her Whippoorwill when they'd met at the catfish stream last summer, or whether he'd only ever heard it from one-armed Angus LeBlanc two summers ago when he was casually asking Mr. LeBlanc about a girl with crowned moccasins. Well, too late to unsay it. "It seems to me… I mean… Why I come all the way up to the courthouse was to see my grandfather there in the jury. It's an even longer way for you." Damn, and now he'd admitted to finding out where she lived, more or less.

She said: "I came to see how they were treating my cousin."

"Your cousin?"

"Maria Thomas."

"Oh. Oh. Um, you sure got a whacking load of cousins. I mean –"

"I do. My grandfather had a lot of wives."

Was he supposed to know her grandfather was Chief Peguis…? "I guess. Um, so how are they treating your cousin?"

"She's holding up pretty good – even the people that call her a liar are starting to wonder how an ignorant little halfbreed girl could know so much about the ways an English doctor would go about making an abortion. The speakers for that pig-bastard Corbett try to trip her up, but can't."

Hugh decided to let 'pig-bastard' pass uncommented, since Wauh Oonae appeared to have strong opinions on the matter, and just said: "Even Frank Larned Hunt can't trip her up?"

"Frank Hunt ain't said much, just once in awhile asks a question or two. People figure he's saving himself up for the summa-whatchacallit, the last speech before it's all up to the jury."

"Oh." Hugh tried to think of something else to say, maybe some other subject that would get her to talk more in that voice that felt like warm breath on his ears. But before he could come up with something, she was slowing Cheengwun to a walk and they were almost at St. John's churchyard. The pony came to a stop and Hugh endeavoured to squirm his rump back onto the horse's, so he could bend one leg up and behind Nancy Prince to jump down. It would've been easier to shift backwards if he'd braced his hands on the back of her waist, but that seemed a bit forward. So instead he just pressed his hands against the back rim of her buffalo pelt-covered wooden saddle. But the piece of buffalo robe wasn't the only thing the saddle was covered with. He coughed to cover his embarrassment and slid off the horse.

With his feet on the ground, Hugh said: "Um, thank you, that was better'n walking."

"Are you coming back to the trial tomorrow after you done school?"

"I dunno, I, uh, hadn't thought."

"Well, if you do, Cheengwun and me can give you a ride back here again, if you want. Aur'voir."

She nudged the pony with her heels and Hugh watched her trot away into the gathering gloom. It was only after she disappeared around a bend in the road that it occurred to him to wonder how Nancy Prince knew that the south fence of St. John's churchyard was the Point Douglas Sutherlands' habitual crossing place to their home on the other shore. Probably she'd just guessed.

He turned and trotted down the riverbank, and moccasin-skated across the wide swath of ice that was the Sutherland and Inkster boys' unofficial duty to keep clear for a community skating rink. He did find it strange that he was suddenly noticing the cold again and hadn't for the last while. Maybe the sun going down had dropped the temperature. But that couldn't explain why the air seemed to be tingling with the music of silvery little bells.

The fairy sound of the bells got joined by the distinctly earthly sound of barking dogs. Hugh looked south toward the sounds and saw a distant dog team pulling a carriole

– basically a toboggan with a painted parchment leather housing, looking something like a giant Persian slipper Hugh had seen on a genie in a picture book. There didn't look to be anyone riding in this carriole, but a snowshoed driver was loping along behind, popping a long whip over the heads of his team and in front of the faces of farm dogs charging down the riverbank.

Hugh realised that the fairy music had been harness bells, and the carriole was the mail headed for A.G.B. Bannatyne's store instead of James Ross's house. As of just this year the mail came twice a week instead of once, since the U.S. Mail had extended beyond St. Paul to Fort Pembina. Hugh could remember, barely, the days when mail came only once a year from The Company's supply ships into Hudson's Bay.

Hugh waved at the mail driver, who probably couldn't see him, then hurried on home. He was a little late for supper, but that got forgiven and forgotten when he told them Granda was foreman of the jury. In all likelihood, given Granda's unique sense of the line between conversation and drawing attention, if Hugh hadn't brought the family the news they wouldn't've known until a neighbour happened to mention it in passing weeks later.

The younger children had gone to bed by the time Granda got home, gammy-legging his way up the riverbank from the cutter of another juror who lived farther downstream. Granda got sat down to a cold supper and responded to the storm of questions about the trial with: "I gied my oath to not say a word about the trial until it's over. But I will say this… There is something troubling about this trial, or around its edges. Maria Thomas is Metis Catholic, and the Reverend Mr. Corbett is… well, the Reverend Mr. Corbett. Some Catholics have already decided Maria Thomas must be telling the truth, and some Protestants that Maria Thomas must be lying and the Reverend Mr. Corbett innocent."

Gran said: "Is that not what you said at the outset?"

Granda shot her a look, then said: "That was for different reasons. Some people – not many yet, but some – are choosing up sides like a bat-and-ball game. It's a sickness, and a catching one. Were Mr. Grant still alive he'd cure it in jig time, but he's not, more's the pity."

Donald said confusedly: "But, Granda… wasn't it Mr. Grant led the Metis to kill all the white men at the Battle of Seven Oaks?" Donald was always trying to fit things in boxes.

Gran said: "Aye, and it was also Mr. Grant pitched his tent in front of the fort gates after the battle and the fort surrendered, like a watchdog guarding no harm would come to us inside."

Granda said bitterly: "That was no *battle*. I've been to battles. That was a slaughter. But it was that slaughter made us start to ken we weren't enemies – our enemies were the people who'd hae us believe we were enemies. Out here in this hard wilderness, so few people, a thousand miles from anywhere… Ye cannae be lookin' down on, or afraid of, a man of a different colour or religion after he's picked ye up out of a snowdrift in a blizzard. We're no *saints* here, but we learned to… We learned that… I mean tae say…"

Gran said: "If we couldn't learn to live together, we were all going to die together."

"Aye, Kate, ye were always the one tae untangle my tongue." Granda nodded and then kept on nodding, in a way that put Hugh in mind of a sick child rocking back and forth. "It's a rare and precious gift we hae here, and so easy broken. And now some people here are clamourin' that Maria Thomas or Griffith Owen Corbett are guilty or not guilty because o' the colour o' their skin or what church they go to."

Da said gently: "It's happened here before, old fella, and didn't last. Once the tempests in a teapot blew over, everything went back to normal."

"I suppose," Granda nodded. "I suppose I'm likely just a tired old man seeing bogles under the bed. I shouldnae hae let myself get spooked." But to Hugh it looked like the crevasses on the old man's face were still etched deeper than they had been yesterday, and there was something Granda wasn't saying.

The next afternoon, Hugh's running-and-walking progress to the courthouse was more running than it had been yesterday. The windows weren't as crowded as yesterday, and Maria Thomas wasn't in the witness box. Instead there was a flannel-shirted, middle-aged man whose hair looked like it wasn't used to being combed. Nancy Prince explained that he was Maria Thomas's father, and that the Reverend Corbett's defence team had run out of questions for Maria by mid-morning. Hugh noticed something odd through the window. Frank Larned Hunt was still in his chair not saying anything, but he'd moved his chair back from the defence table to the rail that separated the spectators from the playing field, and was leaned back with his arms and legs crossed, studying the ceiling.

Wauh Oonae said: "I gotta be getting home now. You want a ride, or – ?"

"Sure. Thanks."

Once Hugh was up behind her saddle, Nancy Prince said: "I gotta be home quicker'n yesterday, so I'll have to gallop him, so you better hold on tighter'n yesterday." Hugh tentatively reached his arms around her waist and clasped his hands in front of her. "You'll have to hold on tighter'n that or we'll both fall off."

Hugh obediently tightened his arms a little and snugged up closer, compressing the layers of baggy wool between her back and his front. Even through the layers, Hugh could feel that the bends of his elbows were at the indent between the bottom of her ribs and the top of her hips.

When she nudged Cheengwun into a gallop, Hugh tightened his grip just a little more – afraid he might hurt her if he pressed too tight – and held onto the horse with his knees and Wauh Oonae with his arms. When she leaned forward to balance herself with the surging momentum, he didn't consciously lean forward with her, just followed along with his body melded against hers. Happily, the wind blew her hood back so some of her hair escaped and whipped against his face. He didn't need to see, so he just closed his eyes and let her hair trail across his eyelids. Without sight, there was nothing in the world but the rolling drumbeat of the horse's hooves, Nancy Prince's steady, deep breathing through her teeth, the smell and feel of her hair against his face… He suddenly remembered someone telling him that you had to be careful about galloping a horse in winter, because snow can ball under its hooves and skate its legs out from under it at full tilt. He didn't care.

Too soon they were at the edge of St. John's churchyard, and the horse slowed to a halt. Nancy Prince stuck her right arm out to give him a balance rail as he maneuvered off Cheengwun; Hugh wondered if that was because she'd been offended by his mitts brushing against her backside when he'd pushed off from the back off the saddle yesterday. Once his feet were on the ground, she clucked her pony into a trot and went on her way. It seemed odd to Hugh that she'd been in such a hurry to get home they'd had to gallop to St. John's, but now was carrying on at just a trot. Maybe she'd wanted to shorten the time spent with him riding behind her. But she'd said 'Aur'voir' like she expected to see him tomorrow.

Hugh got home long enough before supper to help Donald and Aleck break the day's build-up of ice off the waterhole and ferry the night's and morning's water up to the house and barn. As Hugh was taking off his coat, Mum asked him what had happened at the trial today. When he'd told what little there was to tell, Gran said: "That's a long way to go to see so little." There seemed to be something slightly amused in her voice. Hugh just shrugged.

Da said: "And you made it back in jig-time, too. I'm… *surprised* you had enough breath left to help with the water, after, um, sprinting all the way from Fort Garry."

The girls and some of the younger boys giggled. Hugh felt himself blushing, and said he'd better wash up before supper.

When Hugh got to the courthouse the next day, there were more people outside than the days before, but they were gathered around a couple of tree trunk bonfires instead of looking through the windows. Hugh went to one of the windows, breathed- and rubbed-away the frost, and peered in. There was almost no one inside: a few people scattered around the spectators' benches, Judge Black and the Secretary looking over some papers at the judge's table, and the councils for the defence and prosecution at their own tables – except for Mr. Frank Larned Hunt, who'd moved his chair as far away from the defence table as it could go without leaving the fenced-in court area, and was leaned back with his hands in his pockets and his bootheels propped on a potbellied stove. The jury box was empty.

Nancy Prince said from behind Hugh: "The jury's deliverating."

Hugh turned around quickly. She was standing very close.

"Everybody had to come outside at noontime, when Judge Black cleared out the courtroom for the medical testimony. I guess some of it was pretty gruesome. Anyways, once that got done, most of the cleared-out people figured since they was out here anyways they might's well wait for the jury where they could stand around a warm fire and pass a bottle back and forth."

"They didn't go back in to hear Frank Larned Hunt's summation?"

"His what?"

"His summa-whatchacallit, like you said day before yesterday." Hugh wasn't precisely sure what 'summation' meant, just had a general notion. "His big speech to the jury before they went to... deliverate." He'd caught himself just before saying 'deliberate' and maybe sounding like he was correcting her.

"Hunt didn't make no big speech. Far's I hear he ain't said nothing all day – just sat there with his feet on the stove, whistling."

Someone called out the courthouse doorway: "They're coming in!" and there was a rush from the bonfires. Hugh and Nancy Prince stayed where they were and pretty soon there were other people pressing-in around and behind them, pushing Hugh's wool-padded shoulder tight against Wauh Oonae's. It occurred to him that he and she would take up less space and feel less crowded if he raised his arm and put it around her shoulders, but he wasn't that brave.

With so many people breathing on the window, the frost etchings melted away. A door at the back of the courtroom opened and Hugh's Granda led the rest of the jurors to their places. Through another doorway on the other side of Judge Black's table, the doorway to the jail cells, Sheriff McKenney escorted the Reverend Mister Griffith Owen Corbett to the prisoner's box.

When everyone was in their places, Granda stood up and unfolded a piece of paper. The paper fluttered in his hands – he looked to be trembling like the dog last winter who fell in the waterhole and managed to crawl back out onto the ice. Granda opened his mouth a couple of times, but no sound came out. He shook his head and handed the piece of paper to the Secretary. The Secretary started to hand it to Judge Black, but Judge Black shook his head – apparently the law was that the foreman of the jury had to speak the verdict aloud. The Secretary handed the piece of paper back to Granda, who looked down at it, blinked a few times, then rasped out: "Guilty, but..." the rest came out in a voice so bitter it made Hugh's throat constrict, "but with a recommendation for mercy because of his former good character."

Nancy Prince said flusteredly, as though she didn't really expect anybody around her to be able to answer, "What the hell did he say?"

Hugh realised this was one circumstance when he could hear what others couldn't; a voice he'd been hearing all his life was decipherable to him even in a hoarse whisper from the far side of a closed window. Hugh said: "Guilty, but –"

But he couldn't get out the rest of it, because Wauh Oonae was jumping up and down and shouting: "Guilty!" Answering shouts came from the crowds around the other windows, some joyous and some enraged. Hugh didn't really notice them, because Nancy Prince stopped bouncing up and down for long enough to throw her arms around him and kiss him on the cheek.

It happened so fast he could hardly be sure it had happened. She quickly jerked her arms away and stepped back, kind of like when he leaned in too close feeding the woodstove. But he could still feel the impression of her lips on his cheek. Her face was blazing with gladness. A light snow was sifting down and a few flakes sparkled in her hair.

She said: "Oh, Hugh, what kind of world would we be living in if they'd just said: 'He's a white, church minister so the little halfbreed girl must be lying?' Come on, I gotta tell my folks."

Hugh followed her around the corner to where Cheengwun and a few other horses were nosing at a small pile of hay on the lee side of the courthouse. On the way they passed by a knot of men shouting about "Injustice" and "The bloody Company"; the tallest and loudest was Dr. Schultz.

Wauh Oonae kicked Cheengwun into a gallop again, so Hugh had to hold on tight again. She kept bursting into trills of laughter and shouting out syllables that might've been Ojibway, as though whatever the trial verdict meant to her was too big for her body to contain. Her giddiness was contagious, and Hugh wondered if this was what it felt like to be drunk.

When they stopped at St. John's churchyard fence this time, she swivelled around on the saddle as far as her waist could twist, as though momentarily forgetting he was too heavy to lift down off the horse. Her face was within an inch of his; it seemed like the most natural thing in the world to put his mittened hands on her shoulders and kiss her. His eyes closed themselves as soon as their lips touched. He'd kissed women before – his mother and Gran, and aunts and cousins on New Year's Day – and when he was younger the boys and girls used to play kissing games behind the school. This was different. Her lips moved softly and firmly against his, and it was dizzy-making to feel there was only the thinnest of membranes between him and her. The skin of her cheek against the side of his nose felt like warm velvet. One of her hands came up to press against his back.

He didn't want to stop, but when it began to feel like both of them were going to suffocate he pulled back. He was afraid to look at her and was suddenly aware that it couldn't've been very comfortable for her to be twisted around in the saddle for so long. He pushed off against the horse's back and jumped down over its tail – not the smartest thing to do, but it got his feet on the ground fast, and he quickly skipped sideways in case Cheengwun got the urge to kick.

Hugh came to a halt up to his knees in snow and looked up at Nancy Prince. He took his toque off and said: "Well, um..." Her dark, slanted eyes were glistening and her lips looked redder than before – he wondered if he'd pressed too hard and bruised them.

Wauh Oonae's wide mouth twisted into something like a smile, which was strange considering that her eyes looked almost teary. She said huskily: "Aur'voir, Hugh Sutherland," and clucked her horse into a walk.

Hugh stood stupidly in the snow watching her go. It was encouraging that she'd said 'au revoir' instead of 'adieu,' but 'till I see you again' still left the unanswerable questions of when and how. He tugged his toque back on and got his feet onto the beaten path across the river.

By the time he got back home he'd remembered it was Friday, the day for cleaning out the cow stalls. Before he went to help the other boys, he figured he'd just stick his head in the house long enough to tell Mum and Da the verdict, but he heard voices coming from the milk shed so went there instead. Inside the milk shed door were wood-shored stairs cut into the earth, leading down to a cellar room that was below the ground frost in winter and cool in summer. Mum and Gran were down there with Margaret and Catherine, pouring the evening's milk into long, shallow pans to separate overnight. Mum paused in her pouring to look up at Hugh on the earthen staircase. Hugh said: "They got a verdict. Guilty, but with a, uh, recommending for mercy because of, uh… former good character."

Mum said: "Well, that's that," and went back to pouring.

Gran said: "How did your Granda take to that?"

"I don't know, I aren't talked to him. But his hands were shaking so fierce he could hardly read the verdict."

Gran clucked her tongue and pursed her mouth. Mum said: "The stalls will be almost done by the time you get to 'helping.'"

Hugh closed the milk shed door behind him and hurried through the kitty-corner door into the barn. The stalls *were* almost done, but the other boys didn't seem to mind, since he brought the news of how the trial had ended. Donald said: "That's too bad."

Hugh said: "'Too bad'? If he's guilty he's guilty."

"No I meant too bad you won't have an excuse to go courting – I mean, to the courthouse."

The other boys covered their mouths and chortled. Hugh said: "Hand me that scoop, Hector, you missed a pile in the corner."

Granda was home in time for supper but didn't eat much. Hugh figured that since the trial was over now Granda would be free to talk about it, but he didn't. At least not till after the younger children had gone to bed, and then Granda suddenly snarled from his chair by the fire: "Six months! Six whole months imprisonment for seducing a fifteen year old girl, almost killing her, and slandering her name to save his own. Six months, because the jury recommended mercy. It wasnae *my* recommendation, I can tell ye, but the others over-ruled me. 'Previous guid character…' It's rewarding the man for hypocrisy! Seems tae *me*, if a man represents himself as an upright citizen, a man of God and good works, someone an ignorant servant girl would look up to and trust and obey – that makes what he did *worse* . Ach, I'm going tae bed."

Sunday morning began as usual, with a breakfast built around the bannocks baked Saturday night so that no work that wasn't absolutely necessary would be done on the Sabbath Day. And as usual, while everyone else was still eating, Gran was already at the door tucking her Bible under her arm and her old blue cloak around her shoulders, saying: "I'll see you all at the afternoon service, my dears."

But then Granda said: "No." There was a pause. "Ye'll see the rest of the family, nae doubt, but ye'll no see me. I'll ne'er cross the threshold of a church again but the oncet, and ye know when that'll be."

For maybe the first time in his life, Hugh saw his grandmother absolutely at a loss for words. Mum and Da were looking from Gran to Granda to each other, but not saying anything. Gran was pointedly looking around at the children, as though that should convey something to Granda, but he just went on eating his breakfast. Finally Gran said: "Would you be good enough, Alexander Sutherland, to put on your coat and walk out to the barn with me?"

There was no question she didn't mean the thirteen year old Alexander Sutherland. Granda, still chewing his last mouthful, got up and shrugged his coat on and limped out the door after Gran. As soon as the door closed behind them, Her Royal Whyness said to Mum: "Why did Granda – ?"

"I don't know, dear, any more than you do. I imagine we'll be told in good time. Now eat your sausage."

Hugh pushed his plate back, stood up and said: "I think it's my turn to break the ice." Although enough water for the whole day had been carried up last night, it was still absolutely necessary work to clear the ice out of the waterhole on the Sabbath morn and evening, or it'd build up so thick it'd be hell to clear.

As Hugh toggled his capote on, Da said: "You're not planning to linger by the barn."

"No, sir."

He didn't have to linger, just not hurry – the voices were so loud he could hear them almost as soon as he stepped out the door. "For the Lord's sake, Sandy – Corbett is just one man, not the kirk!"

"Och aye, that's what ye told me over and over after the Highland Clearances, when our guid kirk ministers stood by the Improvers and told us to suffer the evictions meekly – and then took parts of the land for themselves. Ye inveigled me back into the kirk then; ye'll no do it again."

"But all the ministers in the Clearances weren't like that, some stood beside us. A kirk minister is still a human being, and humans come in all varieties. You're thinking like a child – that something has to be all good or all bad."

"Do you no understand, Kate? The kirk is there to teach us how to be better human beings. If a man who's spent his life steeped in those teachings, studying on the gospels and the beatitudes and Christian morals – if a man who's learned more than you and I will ever know of how the kirk says to be a good Christian, can do what the Reverend Mister Corbett did, then it's all paste and flummery."

Then Hugh was on his way down the riverbank and couldn't hear them anymore. At the edge of the riverside brush was a trimmed poplar pole and a breadpan-sized rock tied to a length of shagganappi rope – rope made from strips of buffalo hide braided together. When Hugh was a toddler he'd guessed that buffaloes must be as big as houses, because a strip of buffalo hide could be as long as the wide side of the house. Mum had laughingly explained to him – drawing in the dirt with a stick – that shagganappi was made by poking a knife through the middle of a buffalo hide and cutting outward in a spiral. When Hugh'd got old enough to wander outside the homeyard where most conversation was in proper English or Gaelic, he learned that 'shagganappi' could mean anything rough but reliable: a shagganappi pony, a shagganappi shack...

Hugh dropped the rock in the waterhole a few times to break the new ice, then stuck in the poplar pole and stirred the shards around to melt them. He was still stirring when Gran came down the riverbank path alone, with her back and shoulders stiff and her eyes fixed straight ahead. She didn't look at him or say anything, just kept on going across the river. Hugh watched her go: a tall old woman in a blue cloak striding through a world of white snow, black, leafless trees and grey sky.

When it came time for the rest of the family to climb onto the sleds for kirk, Granda said: "I'll get in a bit of reading and keep the fire fed – for a change the house will be toasty warm when you get back from kirk." Donald didn't seem at all disappointed that Granda staying home meant Donald would have to stand at the front of the second sled holding the reins.

The kirkyard before the service was always dotted with knots of parishioners exchanging the week's news and gossip, unless there was a blizzard or a thunderstorm. Hugh and Donald and Aleck and Morrison were standing with a group of other boys when the Reverend Dr. Black and Mrs. Black came out of the manse and walked toward the kirk. Mrs. Black – Granny Ross's half-Scots daughter – let go her husband's arm to come over to the Sutherland boys. She said: "I'm so sorry to hear about your grandfather, about his rheumatism."

Donald said: "Rheumatism?" Hugh would've spoken the same question, if it weren't the first son's place to speak first. Granda did have a touch of rheumatism, that's why he no longer played the fiddle much, but that was hardly news.

"Yes," Mrs. Black said, "your grandmother told us."

Donald said: "Uh, told you what, ma'am?"

"Why, about your grandfather's rheumatism – that it flared so bad he couldn't come to kirk." Hugh saw across the kirkyard his grandmother standing with a group of other women. The other women were gabbling away and laughing, but Gran was staring over their shoulders at the minister's wife talking to her grandsons. It seemed to Hugh that there was something uneasy in Gran's look. "I do hope your grandfather's well enough to come next Sunday."

Hugh said: "I wouldn't count on it, ma'am – bumping around on a cart-sled or hiking this far'd play hell with his knees, I mean, uh, make his rheumatism even worse."

Mrs. Black sighed, "What a cross to bear. But then, the Lord never sends us heavier burdens than we can carry. I'll ask my mother to make up some salve for your grandfather's knees."

"Thank you, ma'am." Then thankfully the church bell rang.

Sitting in church, Hugh found it all a bit confusing, wondering what was a lie and what was the proper thing. It got even more confusing when they got back home. After the supper dishes had been cleared away to the pantry to be washed on Monday morning, Granda happily took his turn at leading the younger children through the Shorter Catechism, and listening to the older children's interpretations of the Bible verse Da had given them last Sunday. But next Sunday Granda didn't go to church, nor any Sunday after.

The confusion didn't bother Hugh immensely. It was like wondering why a dog had to turn around three times before lying down – interesting to wonder, but don't expect to find an answer. Or, as he'd overheard an old voyageur say once: "Don't ask why the river decides to swerve this way, just keep on paddling."

CHAPTER 15

Schultz's life at McKenney & Co.'s General Store And Lodging House became even more unpleasant after the Corbett trial. It was patently obvious to Schultz that the Reverend Griffith Owen Corbett had been railroaded by The Company. Small coincidence that Dr. Cowan, who'd given the most damning medical evidence, was a Chief Trader in The Company's hierarchy. Yet Schultz was trapped living under the same roof as the Sheriff in charge of the jail cells where the Reverend Corbett was unjustly imprisoned. All of Schultz's meagre finances and his bright hopes for the future were tied up with McKenney & Co. He could either slink back to Upper Canada, where all the fortunes had already been made, and where society was peppered with alumni of Queen's University, or stay on as Henry McKenney's junior partner.

Schultz reached an unspoken agreement with Henry and Lucy that they wouldn't speak of anything except the weather and business. If Schultz wanted conversation in his off hours, there was always the *Nor'Wester* office, a log cabin in the small cluster of buildings on the Ross property, including the one that once had been the Post Office. Most of the men who frequented that informal club were staunch Protestants and as staunchly convinced as Schultz that the Reverend Corbett had been framed and hung on the wall.

One windblown April day Schultz dropped by the *Nor'Wester* office and found the editor and publisher scratching their heads over three densely handwritten sheets of paper laid out on a desk. The publisher, William Coldwell, was the sole remainder of the two ambitious young men who'd come west to found a newspaper. The two had seemed so much attuned they even combed their hair and trimmed their mustaches the same way. But one of the partners had given up, sold his share to James Ross and went back to Canada, while Coldwell stayed on and married James Ross's sister – the one not already married to Dr. Black. Schultz hoped the *Nor'Wester* was turning at least some profit, since that was the only income James Ross had left.

Schultz joined Ross and Coldwell looking down at the three sheets of paper. They turned out to be a letter to *The Nor'Wester* from The Reverend Griffith Owen Corbett. Which wasn't unusual in itself; the prisoner had been allowed the use of pen and paper and had been dispatching letters to anyone who might have any influence toward shortening his sentence: his Bishop, Governor Mactavish, Governor Dallas, the Councillors of Assiniboia…

This one was different. It was a long, rambling hallucination about meteors and railroads and constellations and an earthquake shaking the jail. It ended with: *"Peace – peace is the end of good government; advocate, then, the end of good government."*

Ross asked Schultz his opinion of the letter, and Schultz said: "Well, the diagnosis seems obvious – melancholic dementia. The poor man's gradually going insane from being locked up for so long."

The editor and publisher allowed as that's what it seemed like, and the three of them drew up and printed a petition then and there, urging the Governor of Assiniboia to have mercy on the prisoner's fragile mental state and release him before irreparable damage was done. Schultz found it illuminating and thrilling that he could suggest a few wording changes in the pencil stage, and then it was just a question of setting type and working the press and voila were his words in print as authoritative and official-looking as any statement from a Governor or a Member of Parliament.

Circulating-copies of the petition were handed out to anyone who passed through the *Nor'Wester* office, and within a few days there were a few hundred signatures to present to the Governor of Assiniboia. Governor Mactavish said the only person with the legal authority to alter the sentence was the Governor of Rupert's Land, and handed it on to Governor Dallas.

Governor Dallas's response was that if the prisoner truly had a predilection to mental instability, and wasn't just feigning for obvious motives, then the best thing his friends could do for him was leave him in peace and quiet and not agitate his delusions with false hopes of an early release. Governor Dallas also pointed out that although several hundred citizens of Assiniboia had signed the petition, several thousand hadn't.

The day after Governor Dallas's response came down, a number of angry men found their way to the *Nor'Wester* office, and Schultz was one of them. A schoolteacher named James Stewart from the Parish of St. James – about halfway between Fort Garry and Headingley – stood up on a chair and called out: "Gentlemen, gentlemen…!" to quiet the general hubbub. "It's obvious that The Company and its puppets aren't going to give the Reverend Corbett an early release, no matter how much damage the incarceration does him. So it looks like *we'll* have to!"

There was a pause, and then someone shouted: "Yes, by God!" and other voices joined in.

Stewart blared over them like a trumpet: "The Court is sitting its spring Quarterly Session tomorrow. The courthouse will be open to the public, and as usual there will be people coming in to sit and watch – just innocent spectators, nothing suspicious about that. I intend to be there, do you? Are you with me, lads?"

They shouted that they were and clapped each other on the back and passed the bottle around again. Even before the bottle came his way, Schultz felt all warm inside from the atmosphere of comradeship and common purpose. The only way to improve on it would've been if he'd been the one to call out: *"Are you with me, lads?"* and hear them shout back that they were. He wouldn't have needed to stand on a chair.

Not all of the men who'd been at the *Nor'Wester* office showed up at the courthouse the next morning. But about a dozen did, and brought a few like-minded friends with them. They were too wise to sit all in a clump, but salted themselves around the spectators' benches. Schultz sat in the back pretending to be mildly interested in cases of errant cattle and five shilling debts, pretending that his heart wasn't beating unnaturally quickly.

As usual, all the business of the quarterly session was done by early afternoon. Judge Black declared the court adjourned, and he and the Secretary tugged on their coats and hats and boots to head for home. A few of the spectators paused to gossip a few minutes on the way out, and the rescue party pretended to do the same. The last officer of the court to leave was Sheriff Henry McKenney, who glanced at Schultz oddly but kept on out the door to serve the couple of writs Judge Black had handed him during the session. As soon as Henry was gone, James Stewart looked around and said: "Let's do it!"

Schultz and the others followed Stewart through the doorway to the cells. The jailer on duty was a Metis about sixty years old and was just pouring himself a cup of tea when they came through the door. It wasn't hard to back him into a corner and keep him there. He shouted: "I don't give you my keys, me!"

Stewart said: "We don't need your damn keys," and produced a crowbar out of his overcoat. A couple of men stayed to guard the guard while the rest went with Stewart to the door of the Reverend Corbett's cell. The cell doors weren't anything as civilized as iron bars and case locks, just an ordinary, heavy wooden door with a Judas gate and clunky padlock. Stewart said: "Dr. Schultz, I'd say you have the brawniest shoulders among us. Would you do the honours?" and handed him the crowbar.

Schultz worked the crowbar in behind the padlock hasp and wrenched with all his strength, hoping to put up a good show. He did – with one heave the hasp popped loose, shooting squarehead nails out to ricochet off the coats of the men beside him. Laughing, they threw open the cell door to the Reverend Griffith Owen Corbett, who was standing smiling beatifically in his hat and greatcoat with his packed valise in his hand.

There were horses waiting outside the courthouse, two of them harnessed to carrioles. Reverend Corbett wedged himself into one carriole, Stewart the other, and they set off to the west with an escort of whooping outriders.

Some of the men whose homes were to the north in Little Britain had come in a cart sled, and they beckoned Schultz to climb on with them. It was a fine and jolly ride as far as Noah's Ark, and then Schultz was left alone. It had been one of the most exhilarating days of his life, and there was no one he could talk to about it.

Henry didn't get home until half past supper, and when he sat down at the table his dark hawklike face was even darker than usual. He said to Lucy: "Would you make me up a travelling lunch for tomorrow morning? Come first light I have to ride out to St. James."

"What for?"

"For a matter to do with a James who is nowise a saint." Henry shot a glance at Schultz. "I have to serve an arrest warrant on a schoolteacher named James Stewart."

By mid-afternoon the next day, James Stewart was lodged in the Reverend Corbett's old cell with a new lock on the door. The next morning, after Schultz had opened the store and stuck around long enough to be sure there wasn't going to be more business than Lucy could handle on her own, Schultz walked down to Fort Garry. The snow was decaying quickly, and if last spring was anything to go by, the ground he was walking on would soon be knee-deep, mucilaginous mud – what the locals called gumbo.

Between the fort gates and the riverbank were about eighty to a hundred men, many of them on horseback and many of them carrying guns. They looked to be clumped into two different groups, although the groups blended a little around the edges. In one group Schultz spotted a few of the men who'd helped free the Reverend Corbett, and went over to them. "Good afternoon, gentlemen."

"Dr. Schultz."

"What's the lay of the land?"

"Seems Governor Mactavish guessed we'd come calling to ask politely he should set Mr. Stewart free. First thing this morning, Mactavish swore in a few dozen Special Constables and they was waiting for us here. They allowed as how we could send in a delegation to talk to the governors and as many councillors as could be called in on short notice. So, we're waiting for our delegation to come back out."

Schultz drifted through the crowd to where the two groups blended together. Things were a lot louder there – men shouting at each other that Stewart should be set free or should be held to stand trial, men shaking guns and horsewhips in each others' faces. Then a sharper voice pierced the clamour, blaring: "MacGuigan!" Other voices picked it up, and arms were pointed at a horseman on the edge of the Special Constables group. The word *spy* joined the accusatory *MacGuigan*s, and from what Schultz could piece together it seemed that MacGuigan had been at an early morning gathering of some who wanted Stewart freed, and now had turned up as a Special Constable.

The front of the Free Stewart party surged forward and formed a ring of men on foot and horseback around MacGuigan, cutting him off from the rest of the Special Constables. The Special Constables and the men forming the ring pushed and shoved at each other, tentatively threatening with double-barrelled guns and pistols. MacGuigan had a double-barrelled gun of his own and was waving it at the bellowing men circling around him and scaring his horse.

Schultz pushed his way through the arc of the circle behind MacGuigan, grabbed the back of MacGuigan's blanket coat with both hands and lifted him down off his horse. Other hands tore the gun out of MacGuigan's hands, while others stripped the saddle and bridle off his horse and slapped it away. MacGuigan was hustled farther back into the Free Stewart crowd, while Schultz and the others up front turned shoulder-to-shoulder to face the Special Constables. There was no more blurring of the two groups' edges now, but a ten foot gap of trampled snow between them. Schultz noticed that two men who'd been standing by their horses filling their pipes from one tobacco pouch were now on either side of the gap and on their horses. The men standing next to Schultz's right shoulder were laughing at the Special Constables: "See? We can take prisoners, too!"; the men next to his left shoulder were standing stalwartly enough but silently casting sidelong, nervous glances at each other. Some of the Special Constables were standing in their stirrups to see that MacGuigan didn't get roughed up too much. Schultz could hear MacGuigan back behind him protesting he was no spy, had just come to the meeting that morning to see if they could convince him Stewart should be set free. And then someone farther back shouted: "There's another one!"

Schultz turned to see a horseman trotting towards the fort. The horseman quickly swerved and started galloping away across the prairie as half a dozen riders peeled off from the Stewart group and charged toward him. After a few minutes the riders came back with a disgruntled hostage. Schultz learned later there'd been an attempt to take a third prisoner, but this one had calmly turned his horse to face his pursuers, produced a 'horrible-ugly-looking' horse pistol and announced that the first man to lay a hand on his bridle would surely die, so they'd thought better of it.

The Special Constables yelled across the gap to let the hostages go; the men around Schultz yelled back to let Stewart go. Schultz's eyes and ears kept getting yanked from one sharply-defined fragment to another: the brass nailheads decorating the gunstock of the man directly across the gap from him, the blowing and stamping of the horse beside him, the beard-framed, brown teeth of the yelling man on his other side, the bowl of a broken clay pipe black against the snow where MacGuigan had been torn off his horse… All of those fragments were part of something larger than he could encompass, and so was he. For the moment he was no longer singular John Christian Schultz, but a functioning part of an entity that had its own will and being beyond any of its members. The feeling was intoxicating. And he'd noticed something else interesting: if one member yelled out something like *"A spy!"* or *"There's another one!"* the whole group would respond automatically and veer in the pointed direction.

The fort gates opened and out walked the delegation who'd been talking to the governors and councillors. All the men on both sides of the snowy gap hushed down as one of the delegates climbed up on his horse for a podium and announced: "They won't budge. They say Mr. Stewart's been arrested for jail-breaking a lawfully-confined prisoner and has to stand trial."

Some of the men around Schultz roared angrily, some just looked warily at the Special Constables. Something suddenly occurred to Schultz, and he bellowed without second thoughts: "To the courthouse!" then turned and jogged toward the south-west corner of the fort, bellowing it again as he went. He could hear other voices taking up the call behind him, and boots and hooves following him. They didn't all follow, some stayed behind to keep an eye on the Special Constables.

When Schultz rounded the south-west bastion, and the courthouse came in view, some of the horsemen who'd caught up to him swerved toward the courthouse door, then saw that wasn't where he was going. The idea had come to him all at once and fully formed: behind the jail cells at the back of the courthouse was a fenced-in yard where prisoners could get a bit of fresh air. The back wall of the fence couldn't be seen from the fort walls, because the courthouse was in the way.

The fence was made of upright, point-topped logs about nine feet high and too close together for a man to squeeze through. Schultz figured the pickets must be planted at least two feet deep, but although the ground wasn't yet gumbo it should be plenty soft and mushy under the mat of frozen grass. Schultz got his hands around one of the logs and started pushing it back and forth to loosen it. He could feel and hear the rail nailed behind it cracking. When the log seemed loose enough, he bent his knees, wrapped his arms around it and heaved upward with his arms and back and legs. The log came out of the ground all right but swayed crazily, threatening to balance him over and come down on top of him. He staggered around in a half-circle, let go of it and let it fall.

A laughing voice called: "Take a rest, Doctor, we'll get the next."

Schultz leaned back against the fence, gasping for breath. For a moment he could see nothing but a red haze, then his eyes cleared and he could see that two horsemen had looped shagganappi ropes around the top of the log next to the one he'd pulled out and were whipping up their ponies.

Two logs gone made a passable doorway. A number of men hurried through and came back a few minutes later with James Stewart. Someone lent Stewart a horse and he set off west with an escort of out-riders whooping and firing off their guns.

The ones who stayed behind laughed and passed a leather bottle around and clapped Schultz on the back. One of them said: "I better go tell the rest of the boys there's nothing left to argue about," and jumped on his horse. A few minutes later there was a crackle of gunfire from the front of the fort, but the cheers that accompanied it said it was only what the locals called feux de joie.

As far as Schultz could see, there was nothing left to do but go home, so he did. Henry came in just as supper was getting started, looking even less gruntled than suppertime the night before last. Schultz asked him lightly: "So, are you going to arrest James Stewart again?"

Henry chewed and swallowed, glowering at his plate, and bit out: "No."

"How about the Reverend Griffith Owen Corbett?"

"No."

Schultz laughed, "So much for The Mighty Company and its kangaroo court."

Henry's dark-browed eyes, now hard and cold as polished stones, came up off his plate to pierce across the table at Schultz. Henry shook his head and said: "I can't believe even a *half*-brother of mine could be such a bloody fool. Do you think those were a bunch of Upper Canada farmboys waving shovels at each other? Those men don't carry guns and knives for decoration. One gunshot and the whole mess could've exploded. Friends and cousins killing each other – all because you and your agitating cronies saw a way to embarrass The Company.

"And what about the Sioux just south of the border? Did you think of that? The American Army hanged a few dozen of them and shot a few hundred more, but there's still thousands left and they're more desperate-starving than ever. What do you think would cross their minds if they heard that we up here, with all our fat cattle and full larders, were busy fighting each other?

"The Governors and the Council could've got up on their high horse and said 'The law's the law and we'll enforce it,' – maybe they should've – but instead they decided to eat a little crow. They were thinking of all of us. I don't know what in the hell you and your friends were thinking of."

Schultz said stiffly: "Justice. We were thinking of justice."

"Balls! Yeah, that's what you were thinking of – balls."

Schultz got up and left the table. But in time he was gratified that events proved he'd been in the right and The Company'd been forced to admit it, inaction speaking louder than words. James Stewart was allowed to carry on with his life as though nothing had happened, and the same with the Reverend Griffith Owen Corbett. The Reverend Corbett lingered in Headingley awhile and then took himself back to England, leaving his wife and children to depend upon the charity of his ex-parishioners and on his promise to return someday. Some people thought that a callous move, but Schultz could see the worthier motive behind it. In England, the Reverend Corbett would have a much better chance of catching the Imperial Government's ear about how The Hudson's Bay Company was treating British subjects in Her Majesty's territory of Rupert's Land.

CHAPTER 16

A few weeks after the Red River jail breaks, as soon as the spring gumbo dried to ordinary mud, a train of Red River carts left for St. Paul and came back a month later loaded down with imports for The Company and the private traders. It also carried a family of British travellers from a long way away, somewhere down in the tropics. Well, a partial family: a middle aged man and his two full-grown but unmarried daughters.

The drovers weren't surprised that the older one was unmarried. She was gawky and brittle and colourless and unsociable. The younger one was another matter. She had thick hazel hair, a heart-shaped face, a bouyant-looking bosom for her size, and a willingness to smile at their jokes. Agnes Campbell Farquharson had lived all her life among negroes, mulattoes and Indians, so she didn't mind being companionable with men who had mahogany skin, India ink hair and high cheekbones – as long as they didn't forget she was white.

At an overnight camp that seemed no different from all the ones that had come before, Agnes noticed that the drovers were digging different clothes out of their travel sacks – bright calico shirts with satin ribbons sewn into them, leather vests covered with beadwork, buckskin jackets fringed and beaded – and draping them over the cart rails to wait for the morning. They were wrestling combs through each others' hair and sticking feathers in their hats.

Agnes went up to one whom she knew spoke passable English and asked what the occasion was. He said: "Tomorrow noon, ma'm'selle, we reach Red River. We do not want to roll in looking like dusty ragbags."

Agnes hurried back to her family's sleeping quarters – a couple of tilted-back carts with sailcloth awninged between them – and managed to cajole a little enthusiasm into Laura for the coming occasion. They delved into their steamer trunks and came out with dresses and corsets and shawls, and clean clothes for their father. As their father always said, as Agnes reminded her sister, *"You are what you look like to the eyes of the world."*

Partway through the next morning, the cart train began to pass scattered farms with thatched cabins and a ramshackle look to them. People in the farmyards waved and called to the drovers or fell in beside, easily keeping up with the plodding oxen. The carts ground to a halt where the Red met another river and swung off to the right. Agnes stood up precariously on the crates of freight that were her passenger seat and looked around. To her right was a huge stone cathedral surrounded by other buildings with crosses at their roofpeaks. Typical of Roman Catholics to build a lavish church while the churchgoers lived in shacks. Across the river was a sprawling, stone and timber fort under a red ensign with the Union Jack in one corner – the first clear sign that they were back on British soil. Agnes only looked around for curiosity, not to accustom herself, since the Farquharsons didn't intend to be at the Red River Settlement for long.

A flat-bottomed scow and a gaggle of wide boats with long oars, like water spiders, were already waiting to ferry freight across to the fort. The cart train and the riverbank became a frenzy of semi-organised activity – the drovers wouldn't be home until the last cart was unloaded. One of the drovers paused long enough to point Agnes's father toward a dugout boat, "That be the passenger ferry," and then point down-river at the first building beyond the fort, quite a ways beyond the fort, "and that be McKenney's lodging house."

On the other shore, Agnes paused to brush off the damp straw clinging to her skirt from kneeling in the dugout before climbing the bank to the flats in front of the fort. There was no evidence of any carriages for hire, so Agnes's father said: "It's not a far walk; they've promised to have our trunks delivered by the end of the day," and set off up the wide, dusty road. Agnes and her sister unfurled their parasols before proceeding – even this far north, the summer sun was bright enough to spoil the complexion.

McKenney's lodging house turned out to be a wooden building much longer than wide or tall; it put Agnes in mind of an overturned coal freighter. The front door opened into a general store dotted with barrels and crates and lined with shelves that could do with restocking. There was a pinch-faced woman behind the counter and a very tall, red-blonde man about Agnes's age sweeping the floor. The pinch-faced woman turned out to be Mrs. McKenney, who became much more friendly when Agnes's father explained they were looking for a few days' lodging, maybe a few weeks'.

It was arranged that the Farquharsons would rent two rooms – one for Agnes's father, one for her and her sister. Agnes's father added as an apparent afterthought: "Oh, and the freight captain promised to have our travelling trunks delivered here by sunset. If I happen to be upstairs resting, would you please tip the delivery men for me and add it to my account?"

Mrs. McKenney clucked, "Promise or no, you'd be lucky to see your trunks by next week. As soon as the freight's on the ground, the drovers'll be drinking and dancing till their money runs out. John, go fetch the Farquharsons' trunks."

'John' didn't reply, just sloped his broom against the wall, traded his shopkeeper's apron for a threadbare suitcoat and headed out the door. Agnes's father said: "It's very good of you, Mrs. McKenney, to send your hired man to –"

"Oh, he's not my hired man – that's my brother-in-law, Dr. Schultz. You'll meet him at supper."

It seemed to Agnes that Mrs. McKenney's curt ordering-about was a strange way to talk to a brother-in-law, much less a Doctor. Mrs. McKenney showed the Farquharsons up to their rooms, leaving the store untended, which made Agnes wonder whether the half-stocked shelves were because passersby loaded up their pockets when there was no one behind the counter. The room appointed for the young ladies had two beds in it, one against a blank wall and one by a window. Agnes sat down on the one by the window, taking possession, and beckoned Laura to come sit beside her to look out at the new landscape.

There wasn't much to see, just flat prairie, although wildflowers did dapple the grass prettily. The window faced south, so the picture also included the north face of the fort. Some trick of the flatness or the clear air made it look much closer than the mile Agnes knew she had walked. After awhile, a cart came up the road from the fort that was different from the other carts Agnes had watched coming and going – this one had a very tall driver with a fiery halo. The halo was the blazing prairie sunshine glinting on the red-gold hair of young Dr. Schultz. Agnes blinked a couple of times and he wasn't standing at the front rail of a rickety cart holding the reins of a scruffy pony, he was Lief the Lucky standing in the prow of a Viking ship bearing down on the New World.

Agnes watched Dr. Schultz stop the cart below her window, step down and reach back to start lifting out the four steamer trunks stacked inside. Most men would've heaved out just one and settled it on his shoulder; Dr. Schultz took hold of the handles of two and carried them toward the store's front door as though they were slightly over-sized valises.

The trunks in question, and in Dr. Schultz's hands, were the blue one and black one packed with Agnes's father's things. Agnes pinched her cheeks to bring out a hint of rose, fluffed and patted her hair and went and stood by the open doorway of her and her sister's room – behind the door, so she couldn't be seen from the corridor. She waited until she heard heavy footsteps coming down the hall, and then her father's voice saying: "Oh, in here, please."

Agnes moved out from behind the door and across the hall, saying: "Father, dear, I was just wondering whether – Oh!" She affected to be surprised to find a stranger in her father's room, then stepped toward the stranger with her hand held out. "Agnes Campbell Farquharson."

"Dr. John Christian Schultz. How do you do."

"How do you do." The hand that enveloped hers for an instant's courteous pressure wasn't as soft as she expected a doctor's hands to be, but callused like a workman's.

Dr. Schultz said: "Um, well, I'll just fetch in the rest of the trunks…"

Agnes's father said: "I'd lend you a hand, but my back…"

Dr. Schultz nodded sympathetically, "Sacroiliant conditions mustn't be aggravated."

Once Dr. Schultz had left the room, Agnes's father said: "Wouldn't be right to tip a doctor, would it? He'd take it as an insult." His question wasn't really a question, and he didn't ask her what she'd been 'just wondering,' and Agnes didn't expect him to. Her father knew what she was just wondering.

When Dr. Schultz brought the girls' trunks into their room, Laura of course didn't introduce herself and Agnes didn't offer. So there was no question who Dr. Schultz was addressing with: "Well, I expect I'll see you at supper, Miss Farquharson."

Agnes gave him a little smile, "I expect so, Dr. Schultz." But she was a little disappointed that an educated man of British heritage should fall into the American usage of 'supper' as the evening meal, instead of 'tea' being the main meal of the day and 'supper' a late night repast after an evening of music or cards.

At supper, the long trestle table in the Common Room – common indeed – wasn't particularly crowded by the McKenney family, the Farquharson family, Dr. Schultz, and an older gentleman in a buckskin coat who appeared to be the only other lodger at McKenney's Lodging House. The meat was stewed mutton, which Agnes found a pleasant change from the pemmican stew that was the staple on the cart train. But she only picked at it delicately as a lady should.

Mr. McKenney said as he chewed: "Well, Mr. Farquharson, the wife tells me you hail from the tropics. These parts'll be a cold change for you."

"Not so much for myself, more so for the girls. I grew up in Scotland and immigrated to Newfoundland, where I met my dear, departed wife. You see, I'm a housepainter by trade –"

Agnes forebore to interject: *"Among other things."*

" – and when I ran out of houses to paint in Newfoundland, I heard there was more work in British Guiana, so we immigrated there."

Agnes had only been a pregnancy when her family performed that immigration, but she strongly suspected that they'd left Newfoundland the same way they left British Guiana – sneaking onto a ship in the dead of night without saying good-bye to anyone, especially her father's creditors.

"We had a reasonably comfortable life in British Guiana," her father went on, "but I'm not an old man yet, and 'reasonably comfortable' isn't how I want to end my days, or pass on to my progeny. So, a year-and-a-half ago I became inspired by the news of a gold rush from all corners of the Empire to the mountains of British Columbia." Agnes suspected that he'd also been inspired by having tapped out every Peter in British Guiana to pay Paul. "Well, 'there comes a tide in the affairs of men,' as The Bard says. So as soon as I could wind up my affairs in British Guiana, we took ship to New York and then overland by rail and stagecoach to St. Paul."

"Oh dear," Mrs. McKenney interjected, "with the war on down there? And travelling with young ladies?"

"No fear, Mrs. McKenney," Agnes's father waved his fork assuringly. "The war is so far south of where we were travelling, we hardly noticed any difference from a country at peace."

Agnes had noticed a difference – a drastic shortage of able-bodied young men, and most of the ones she'd seen from the stagecoach or railcoach windows had been wearing blue and marching south.

Dr. Schultz said: "Any news of how the war is going now, then?" It was the first he'd spoken since they all sat down to dine. Agnes had been surreptitiously glancing in his direction, and in all that time he'd barely raised his eyes off his plate, as though it were best for him to keep his head down.

"Well," Agnes's father said, "they talk of little else in St. Paul, but they've little to say. It seems there's an extravagant battle going on at a place called Vicksburg, way down the Mississippi. Been going on for months."

Mr. McKenney said: "For Christ's sake, John, he wouldn't know any more about the war than we do. St. Paul may be in the United States, but it's almost as far from the fighting as we are."

Dr. Schultz's face grew a little red, and it looked to Agnes like he wanted to reply in kind to Mr. McKenney's derision. But instead he just lowered his eyes to his plate again, surgically bisected a more-than-bite-sized chunk of mutton, and loaded up his fork with potatoes and gravy. Agnes didn't understand it – Mr. McKenney was a large, dark, fearsome-looking man, but Dr. Schultz was considerably larger.

"So, as 'twas," Agnes's father went on blithely, "the Civil War in the United States didn't interfere with our travels, but when we reached St. Paul, another kind of war got in the way."

"The Minnesota Massacre," came from the old man at the other end of the table.

"Exactly. My plan had been to carry on by steamboat to the Red River Settlement, where we could join up with one of the many overland expeditions I heard were trekking from here to the goldfields. But nothing would move between St. Paul and Fort Garry until the Red Indian uprising had been put down. So we had to languish in St. Paul until that was accomplished, and by then it was winter and we had to wait until the ice was off the Red River."

Agnes smiled to herself at some of the memories brought back by talk of last winter. She hadn't minded languishing; snow was exotic to her, and there were plenty of sleigh rides and dances, given that the Sioux war meant there were a lot more handsome young military officers in St. Paul than there would've been otherwise. She was aware that at twenty-four most women were already wives and mothers, unless they were ugly and graceless and she knew she was neither. There'd been young men come calling in British Guiana, but the ones of any substance soon got tired of her father cadging money off them, and the ones who were fool enough to let her father bully them weren't of any interest to her. She'd regarded her winter in St. Paul as her last fling of girlish gadding about, and then it would be time to get serious. The goldfields of British Columbia seemed to be just the place to find an ambitious young man.

"And then," Agnes's father sighed, "when spring finally came to Minnesota..."

"You don't need to tell *us*," Mr. McKenney said. "That's why our store shelves is half empty. Damn fool captain of the *Pioneer* got her trapped and crushed in the ice last spring, and the new *International* snugged up to Fort Abercrombie at the first Sioux war whoop and refuses to budge. No steamboats plying the Red."

"But," Agnes's father smiled, "there's always a way, if you trust in fate. It seems the half-breeds' cart-trail from here to St. Paul skirts Sioux territory –"

"The Crow Wing Trail," Dr. Schultz said brightly, then lowered his head again as if he should've known better than to raise it.

"So here we are – a little later than we planned, but here nonetheless."

"Later'n you think," said Mr. McKenney. "This time last year was three expeditions come through here on their way west to the goldfields, and you could've joined up with any of them. This year there's none, and don't look to be."

Agnes's sister dropped her fork on her plate with a clang and looked at the ceiling. Agnes's father said: "Oh. Oh, well then, it looks like we'll be lodging here a little longer than we planned, Mr. McKenney."

"*Sheriff* McKenney," Mrs. McKenney put in sweetly and proudly. "My husband is the Sheriff of Red River."

"Oh. Um... *Sheriff*, you say. Well, um... congratulations."

For the next few days, Agnes's father was gone from morning till evening and sometimes longer, nosing around Fort Garry and the *Nor'wester* newspaper office, anywhere a few of the locals might be gathered for a bit of idle conversation. On Sunday the family attended morning services at St. John's Anglican, which the locals called the Upper Church, and afternoon services at St. Paul's, the Middle Church, a few miles down river. Agnes was quite sure they would've carried on to evening services at St. Andrew's, the Lower Church, except that it was more than a few miles farther. She was more than quite sure that all this religious activity had nothing to do with her father suffering a sudden attack of piety.

The upshot of all those conversations in churchyards and over cracker barrels was, as usual, Agnes's father scrounging up opportunities where none seemed to be. There were a number of well-to-do retired fur traders around Lower Fort Garry in a segment of the settlement called Little Britain, and their wives vied with each other to have their parlours repainted by a genuine professional housepainter who knew the secrets of mixing oil and paint powder and plaster. A gentleman in Middlechurch had an abandoned cabin on his property that he was willing to rent for a nominal fee, especially to fellow Church of Englanders stranded by circumstances. Agnes's father informed Sheriff McKenney that they'd be moving out as soon as the cabin was made liveable, and that he would of course settle up the bill for their lodging as soon as his new income started coming in.

As those events progressed, Agnes puzzled at the contradictions in Dr. John Christian Schultz. When he was away from the McKenneys, such as when he drove the Farquharsons to church in the McKenneys' carriage before doubling back to fetch the McKenneys, he was a changed man: laughing and joking and filled with authoritative information about the community Agnes and her semi-family had washed up in. But around the McKenneys' table or in their store he was a shambling shadow who seemed reluctant to speak, and when he did voice an opinion Sheriff McKenney would invariably dismiss it with some sarcasm and Dr. Schultz would make no reply. Agnes couldn't fathom it. Here was a tall, strong, handsome young man – and not so young as to still have the uncertainties of a boy turning into a man – who had a medical school education and experience in the world of business. Why would he hide his light under a bushel and allow himself to be bullied by his older-but-no-wiser half-brother?

A couple of days before the Farquharsons were due to move to their new abode, Agnes decided that she was never going to be able to explain it to herself, and there was only one way to get someone else to explain it to her. When she woke up the next morning, instead of getting out of bed she took in a deep breath, held it and pushed with her stomach muscles as though driving the air back out, but keeping her lips clamped shut and tightening the soft tissue at the roof of her mouth to close off her nose. She could feel the pressure building up in the back cavities of her nose, but also felt herself growing dizzy, so she exhaled, breathed in again and repeated the exercise. After the third time, she felt a trickle at the back of her throat and tasted blood. She spat into her hand and the spittle came out red. She called plaintively to Laura to please fetch her a handkerchief, and delicately spat droplets of blood onto it. Sallow-faced Laura looked down at the handkerchief, then at Agnes, then marched out to the hallway calling: "Papa, Aggie's sick again!"

When her father came into the room, Agnes held up the blood-speckled handkerchief and tried to look wan. Her father said: "Oh dear, oh dear. Luckily, there'll be a doctor just downstairs at the breakfast table. Come along, Laura."

Laura followed their father out the door, saying over her shoulder: "Yes, we'll go fetch the doctor." Agnes detected a certain archness in her sister's voice.

A few moments later, Agnes heard heavy footsteps coming briskly down the hall. She quickly fluffed her hair, undid the top button of her nightgown and let out a few weak little coughs. Dr. Schultz came into her room carrying a black leather doctor's bag, closed the door behind him and pulled a chair over next to her bed. "Well, Miss Farquharson, this has happened before, hasn't it?"

"Mm-hm."

He put his hand on her forehead, then said: "Hm, doesn't seem to be any fever. I'd best have a listen to your lungs." He opened his satchel and assembled a wooden stethoscope much like the one her doctor in Guiana had used. She furled down the bedclothes far enough that her left breast was exposed – still covered by her thin, summer nightgown, but that was all. She raised her left arm back behind her head to give him access to the side of her ribcage, which incidentally pushed her left breast up against the tropic-weight cotton.

Dr. Schultz knelt down and fumbled to place the belled end of the listening tube against her side without actually touching her with his fingers. He cupped one hand around his ear at the other end of the cylinder, and asked her to breathe in and out slowly. After she'd done that a few times, he sat back up into the chair and disassembled the stethoscope, saying: "Well, I hear no congestion or wheezing. How often has this happened previous?"

She didn't say *'previously'*, but he obviously needed someone to take him in hand about the finer elements of The Queen's English. She said: "I'll answer your question, and tell you a secret – a secret I've never told anyone – if you'll answer *me* a question."

"What kind of question?"

She shook her head and felt a mischievous smile tingling her lips. "I'll ask you after I've answered your question, but you must agree first – a secret for a secret."

He looked perplexed and vexed, but shrugged, "All right."

"You asked me how often this has happened previously." She was quite pleased with the way she'd snuck in the correction without correcting him. "The answer, and the secret is: whenever it's useful."

"Pardon me?"

"It's something I found out quite by accident when I was a little girl, throwing a tantrum over something-or-other. I can't explain it scientifically, but I think it has something to do with the little veins at the back of my nose –"

"Capillaries."

"They're weak, or somehow not as sturdy as other people's. If I hold my breath and push, eventually I get a little blood trickling down into my mouth. It looks alarming, spitting blood, but that's all there is to it. I've never told a living soul, though I think my sister suspects. I don't use it very often – the boy who cried wolf and all – only when it's useful for something important."

He looked baffled. "Well, that's, um, that's very clever, but I don't understand why… What's so important about this morning that you figured it useful to spit blood?"

"What's so important, at least to me, is something *I* don't understand. You have a secret that I've tried to explain to myself but can't."

"Me?" He said it like a boy nervously casting his mind back after someone's said: *'I know what you did.'*

Agnes leaned forward and tapped her little finger on the back of his big hand. "Remember, you promised to answer my question."

He shrugged acknowledgement.

"What baffles me, Dr. Schultz, is: here you are, a big, strong, handsome, intelligent, educated, personable gentleman…"

He blushed a little and looked down, but didn't seem displeased.

"… and yet you shamble around here like a whipped dog, barely raising your voice, and let the McKenneys treat you like a slaveboy."

His bashful blush blazed into a full-faced flush. He stood up and turned away as though looking for a way out, running one hand through his thick golden hair.

Agnes said: "We made a deal – I answered *your* question."

He murmured bitterly: "Yeah, well, that's what got me where I am – I made a deal." He glanced down at her, then looked away again and began to slowly pace the room. "It was a business deal, McKenney & Company, equal partnership. But a few months back I and Henry – my esteemed half-brother, Sheriff Henry McKenney – had a falling-out about… Well, when I say 'about politics' it sounds superficial, but it was fundamental. It has to do with the current state of Red River, all of Rupert's Land for that matter, and The Company, and what direction we should go in… Well, and not to sound too grandiose about it, but..." another shade of red seeped into his face, and he seemed about to stammer. "One of the reasons we came to Red River was to, in our own small way, help to build The British Empire. Or so I thought.

"Henry sold out his principles for a mess of pottage from The Company – his appointment as Sheriff by The Company's puppet Council of Assiniboia. The difference of opinion is so fundamental that two men holding such opposing views can't live under the same roof. But, you see, I have no other roof to live under except this one. All the assets I've managed to accumulate, all my income, is tied into McKenney & Company."

"But you're also a medical doctor. Surely you could set up a practice in the colony that would bring you an income that had nothing to do with McKenney & Company."

Dr. Schultz cleared his throat as though things were a bit more complicated than that, then said: "Well, um, one of the miscalculations I made when I immigrated here, was not thinking that The Company already has its own medical doctors in place here, and the locals are used to going to them, or getting quack remedies from midwives and old medicine women. But I could still make some income off my medical training by opening a pharmacy, and a general store along with it – Lord knows, after working my way through medical school as a store clerk I know more about that kind of business than Henry does."

"Then why don't you? It sounds like an excellent plan to me."

"Because that takes capital, and like I said, Miss Farquharson, whatever capital I've managed to accumulate belongs to McKenney & Company."

"But... didn't you say McKenney & Company is a partnership?"

Dr. Schultz nodded his leonine head. "Technically I'm the Junior Partner, but when Henry and I first drew up the papers back in Upper Canada, we agreed that he and I would share fifty-fifty in all profits and losses."

"Then if you dissolve the partnership, fifty percent of the assets and capital belong to you."

"You think I haven't thought of that? Henry'd never agree."

"He doesn't have any choice, it's the law. He's the bloody sheriff, isn't he? If he doesn't do what the law says, he'll have to arrest himself."

Dr. Schultz stopped his distracted pacing and turned to look down at her with his mouth hanging open and his blue eyes blinking. After a moment he said: "You're amazing."

CHAPTER 17

On the first day of the new school year, Hugh looked around for Andy Gunn and couldn't find him. Andy didn't come in late, which wouldn't've been unusual, he didn't come in at all. Hugh couldn't figure it; what with the drenchy August this year and no hint of frost yet, it would still be a couple or three weeks before school got bumped sideways for the harvest. Maybe there was something wrong at Andy's father's farm. When the schoolday ended, Hugh went up to Mr. MacBeth – reminding himself not to call him 'Uncle Hector' – and said: "Excuse me, sir, but I was wondering if you knew why Andy Gunn ain't – isn't – here. Has he come down sick or something?"

"Not that I know of, Hugh, but he won't be coming back to school. His family decided that he's learned more than enough about reading and writing and basic arithmetic to get along as a farmer with a little hunting and fishing on the side. So from now on he'll be occupied helping out on his father's farm till he marries and starts a farm of his own."

That sounded like an excellent idea to Hugh, and he said so at the supper table, adding: "Andy's fifteen and I'm almost. Only difference is he was born in August and me December."

Da said: "Donald is *six*teen and still in school. And after, um, one or two more years he… *may* go on to St. John's College when it opens again."

Hugh almost said: *'If it opens again,'* but decided he needed a few more years under his belt before he started correcting his father. The college offshoot of St. John's church had been a going concern through most of Hugh's lifetime, but shut down a few years ago for reasons Hugh didn't trouble himself about, just was thankful for – probably its economic kiss of death was when they decreed that the sons of families who'd left St. John's church for Kildonan kirk were 'no longer welcome' at St. John's College. The possibility of St. John's College reopening, and being more open, was a constant threat hanging over the heads of boys whose families couldn't afford to send them away to colleges in England or Upper Canada. There were several Young Ladies' Finishing Schools at Red River that girls could go on to after finishing their basic education, but most girls didn't seem to mind going to school.

Hugh said: "But Donald's smarter'n I am."

Mum said: "Never say that, Hugh. All of you children are intelligent, just in your own different ways."

"But that's what I mean, Mum. Donald might, I dunno, maybe be a Councillor of Assiniboia or a clerk with The Company or something. He'll get more good out of school nor I would. My kind of smarts, if I got any, is for being a farmer with a bit of hunting and fishing on the side." What he really meant was 'hunting and fishing with a bit of farming on the side,' but it sounded better the way Uncle Hector had said it. "I don't need a lot of book learning for that."

Da said: "Hugh, it may be that by the time you, um, reach your majority, life won't be as... *simple* as farming with a bit of hunting and fishing on the side. Things change."

"But people are always gonna need to eat, Da, that ain't gonna change. So there's always gotta be somebody doing the farming and hunting and fishing."

The upshot was that Hugh would keep on at school this year, and if he still wanted to drop school they'd talk about it again next fall. A year seemed several lifetimes away to Hugh, but he was sure it wasn't long enough to make him change his mind as the seasons changed around him. Once the snow and ice locked in it was the season for sociability, and that meant surprise parties. At Red River surprise parties were a surprise to the host. On the appointed evening a horde of sleighs and carrioles and snowshoe walkers would descend on the lucky victim's house, all loaded down with food and drink and extra buffalo robes to lay on the floor for those who planned to stay the night.

Hugh had been to a few surprise parties, but only as a child hanger-on, back when Granda's fingers were still supple enough to play the fiddle in public. Mum and Da didn't go in much for social rambunction, except Kildonan weddings and Hogmanay, and the regales after Christmas Midnight Mass when St. Boniface Cathedral was packed with people of all stripes and religions. But now there was going to be a huge surprise party for a huge man and his not-much-smaller wife, and Donald was now old enough to go without parents or grandparents to shepherd him, so Hugh figured he was, too. After some discussion, the household decision-makers decided that Hugh was, yes, but Aleck not yet.

The target house was five or six miles west of The Forks, so Hugh and Donald started before sundown, travelling in a cart-sled pulled by one of the family's shagganappi ponies. First they crossed the river into Kildonan to pick up two of the Bannerman boys and their sister and a few assorted Mathesons, ending up with a cart so jammed with stewpots and food baskets and people that Hugh found himself pressed up against Betsy Bannerman, but she didn't seem to notice.

To reach the crossroads west the surprise party party first had to go through the Village of Winnipeg, as some people were starting to call it. All it consisted of so far was McKenney & Co's 'Noah's Ark,' the new house and store William Drever had built almost flush to its eaves, Dutch George Emmerling's hotel, and a snow-covered mound of lumber for the big new store old Andrew McDermot meant to build next summer in place of the ramshackle sprawl of tacked-together log cabins that'd been good enough since before Hugh was born.

Hugh found it funny that they were proudly calling their offshoot little village Winnipeg, since it was Cree for muddy water, or a swamp. What he didn't find funny was what he heard as the cart-sled passed through: two male voices shouting so loud and angrily that the sound cut through the wooden walls of Noah's Ark. Hugh said: "Tabernac, somebody's gonna get killed."

John Bannerman said: "Not a bit of it. I go past here oncet or twicet a week, hauling firewood from my father's woodlot to the fort. Often as not I hear the two of 'em going at it like that – Sheriff McKenney and Dr. Schultz, and sometimes Mrs. McKenney gets in on it – yelling about partnerships and money and I don't know what all. Been going on all winter and they ain't killt each other yet."

Hugh was willing to take John Bannerman's word for it, but it still seemed to him that if two people kept on shouting at each other that viciously, eventually one of them was going to pick up an axe handle and put an end to it. But a moment later the sled was away from the buildings and the voices, and Hugh forgot about it as Donald clucked the pony into a trot. The night was sparkling cold, with stars in the snow dunes on either side of the packed-snow road. Hugh said to Donald: "You could set 'er to a gallop. With the runners skimming along so slick, the weight don't mean nothing to her."

"It does to us. One bad bump and we'll topple over." Good old Careful Donald, ever the eldest. Hugh thought it would've been good of good old Donald, though, to've told him he meant to hold to a trot before Hugh spent a finger-freezing afternoon levering up the cart-sled and painting the runners with river water to make a slick-skimming coating of ice.

Others coming up behind their sled weren't as careful as Donald, or had no need to be. A couple of low-to-the-ground carrioles behind fast trotters got stuck behind them until the road widened enough to pass and start racing again. A cutter loaded with Company people had a harder time getting around the sled box, but managed. Out on the unbroken snow a dog carriole went by, with a fur-cloaked old woman in it and a driver on snowshoes popping his whip over the team's heads.

As their destination hove into view, Hugh could already hear the fiddles and the laughter. Deer Lodge was a long, three storey wooden house surrounded by barns and sheds and fenced pastures, including the paddock where the proprietor kept half a dozen buffalo. People kept telling the man he was crazy to keep buffalo as pets, but he'd say the time was coming when the only buffalo left on the plains would be his little herd and their descendants. Nobody would've called James McKay crazy to his face if he weren't so affable. A couple of years back a cart carrying a couple of newlyweds fording the Assiniboine had got bogged to the axles in sucking gumbo; James McKay had come along and lifted the cart out of the mud, newlyweds and all.

A bonfire showed Hugh that the big yard was already filled with sleds, carrioles and cutters, and people bustling in and out of the house. A lower, longer fire burned under a whole steer sizzling on a spit. Turning the spit was a man not much taller than Hugh but three or four times wider, with an immense head, curly black hair and a big black wooly beard. It occurred to Hugh that James McKay looked like the front half of a buffalo with arms.

As Hugh and the others climbed off their sleigh shouting surprise-party boisterisms, Mr. McKay slapped his forehead and said: "Sacré damn – more? You sure fooled me! Get into the house and get warm." Hugh thought it a bit too much coincidence that the McKays had just happened to've butchered and bled a steer, and rendered a firepit blaze down to cooking coals, just in time for the surprise to get sprung on them. But he didn't want to spoil the fun any more than Mr. McKay did.

Inside the house, all the furniture in the parlour and the dining room had been pushed back against the walls, and the long dining room table was covered with steaming plates and platters and a huge bowl of hot punch. Hugh filled a plate with slices of ham and grouse, boiled potatoes and carrots and a few pickled beets, and squatted in a corner to watch the dancers. At the moment, the fiddlers were playing a quadrille or some other complicated foreign dance Hugh didn't understand, and there were only a dozen or so people weaving patterns on the floor. But soon the fiddles and Indian hand drum switched back to the standby Red River Jig and the floor filled up with people bouncing up and down with their feet flying and their arms stiff by their sides. Granda had told Hugh that the Irish jigged the same way, without moving their arms, and explained it was for the same reason – when you've got forty dancers crammed into a fiddler's kitchen, flapping arms could be a problem.

Hugh picked out Betsy Bannerman dancing with a halfbreed boy, which Hugh thought nothing of except to notice the fact – after all, their hosts were halfbreeds, too, as were a good many of the surprise guests. Hugh was more interested in noticing Betsy Bannerman's legs when her jouncing skirt bounced up toward her knees and sometimes beyond…

And then another dancer stepped onto the floor, and all the other girls disappeared.

Hugh hadn't seen Wauh Oonae Nancy Prince since he'd stood stupidly in the snow watching her pony carry her away after he'd kissed her. Through much of the time in between, she and her family would've been gone on the summer and fall buffalo hunts, and there weren't many occasions when people from Kildonan and people from St. Peters way down river got together. Although the lives of everyone at Red River overlapped at times, the different parishes had their own ways of living. It took a lot of time to run a farm or a buffalo hunt or a community fishing operation. And even just within Kildonan, everyone was so busy tending their own gardens that Hugh had cousins he didn't see for months on end except at church.

Nancy Prince was dancing on the far side of the room from Hugh, and the momentary gap in the crowd of dancers between them soon closed again. Hugh set his half-eaten plate aside and stood up on a bench pushed back against the wall, pretending to be just looking around to see where his brother had got to. He moved his head from side to side but kept his eyes on her. She was wearing a red calico blouse with purple and red silk ribbons sewn on to make a shimmering yoke. When her hair bounced back with her jigging, silver hoops gleamed at her ears. In his dun-coloured homespun shirt and brown corduroy Sunday trousers, Hugh felt like a wren looking at an oriole.

Wauh Oonae was dancing with a Metis boy in a beaded buckskin vest – as much as anybody could be said to be 'dancing with' doing the Red River Jig. The Metis boy was actually more along the lines of a young man; he looked to be a couple of years older than her and Hugh, and half a foot taller. Hugh told himself not to think foolish thoughts – she was obviously swimming in waters that were way out of his depth.

But then the fiddlers and the drummer paused for a drink and the dancers turned into a milling, thinning crowd, some heading for the food table and some just drifting around. Telling himself not to do it, Hugh stepped down off the bench and threaded his way through the wanderers and knots of joking gossipers. When he got through far enough to see her standing with a group of brightly-dressed, laughing men and women, he decided he should swerve off – it would be too much embarrassment if she said: *'What was your name again?'* in front of other people. But just then she happened to step away from the group and stand alone, so he kept on his course.

He was almost up to her when the fiddles started up again and he saw the young man in the beaded vest a few feet the other side of her, setting down his cup and starting toward her. Hugh was about to give up and turn away, but just then she happened to turn slightly, so her back was to the beaded vest and her front to him. He took the last couple of steps and said: "Hello, Nancy Prince."

"Hello, Hugh Sutherland."

That soft alto voice, somehow perfectly clear through all the noise around, did him in. He said: "Would you like to, um," then swallowed and blurted, "dance with me?"

"Oh, I don't mind, me whatever."

She held out her hand as though the proper thing was he should lead her to where they were going to dance. Instead of just moving to the nearest patch of unoccupied floor, he led her to the middle of the oversized wooden gyrating sardine tin, so he could hold her hand a little longer. He found a few square feet of open space and let go of her hand with reluctance – not just for letting go of her hand, but because he only now remembered he wasn't much of a dancer.

He started to bounce his feet up and down in what he hoped was generally the same time as the music, reminding himself to not try anything fancy. She, of course, was magnificent, her crown-beaded moccasins sometimes pounding out the same triplets as the fiddlers' fingers, sometimes flashing up and down as she cocked a knee to bring her ankle across her other knee in the quarter-second before that foot had to hit the floor again. Part of the etiquette of the Red River Jig was that you shouldn't be seen to be looking closely at what your partner was doing, or what anybody else was doing, but maintain a steady gaze into the middle distance as though in a half-trance. But Hugh soon discovered it was possible to see up close while appearing to be focused away, just by concentrating on your peripheral vision. He could see that Nancy Prince's unbound hair was flying up and down beside her face like a raven's wings; that the flapping of her hair-wings wasn't just because her feet were bouncing her up and down but because the front of her ribbon-woven blouse was bouncing like two demons; that there was a mole just beside her left earlobe…

Red River Jig etiquette also allowed for some lateral movement and turning, so that sometimes you and your partner would be dancing shoulder-to-shoulder, sometimes back-to-back, sometimes face-to-face. The lateral movement meant a room packed with jiggers was bound to have a few collisions. But with everybody's arms down at their sides, all that meant was a shoulder bumping a back and a tossed-off "Pardon me," or "Sorry," or, if you happened to be really good friends, "Clumsy oaf."

Wauh Oonae called over the noise and across the arm's length between her and Hugh: "You dance good," and laughed. Hugh turtled his head between his shoulders and almost stopped dancing – or his fumblefooted attempt at dancing – then realised she wasn't laughing at his fumblefeet, she was just letting out the bubbles of laughter built up by the music and the dancing and the company. Hugh laughed, too, and began to believe he was going to be able to keep on dancing with Nancy Prince all night long. But then she stopped dancing. She fanned her face with her hand and said: "It's hot in here. Think I'll go outside and cool down."

Hugh mumbled: "Oh, um, yeah," not sure whether he should head off farther into the crowd or just stay standing there till she was gone.

She turned to go, then looked back over her shoulder with a little wrinkle in her forehead that might've been perplexity. "You coming?"

"Oh! Yeah, I'll just... go get my coat." To someone from another climate it might've sounded ridiculous to get your coat to cool off, but there was a difference between cooling off and freezing off parts of yourself.

It took Hugh a frustrating few minutes to dig through the mounds of coats in one of the upstairs bedrooms before he finally found his own; the search was complicated by having to work around several sleeping babies and played-out toddlers nested in the mounds. When he finally hustled outside onto Deer Lodge's long front porch, Nancy Prince wasn't standing there waiting for him. He looked around. There was no one on the porch, and no one in the yard, just the horses and sled dogs standing or lying in their traces, all snugged close together for warmth. There wasn't even anyone beside the glowing firepit and the spitted steer left to sizzle on its own through its last cooking stage. Then he spotted her, not all that far away. He'd only missed her because her white capote blended with the snow, except the red and green HBC blanket stripes above the hem. She was standing in the yard looking up at the sky.

As Hugh stepped out from under the porch roof, he saw what she was looking at. The Northern Lights were fairly common at Red River in the winter, but the common variety was a pale, shivery, silvery green. Tonight was a real rip-snorter – blazing reds and blues and purples and rich greens, rippling and shimmering like firelit icicles hanging from God's eaves.

Hugh stood silently by Wauh Oonae for a moment, looking up, then murmured: "Boy, that's something." As soon as he'd said it he felt like an idiot. In the first place, she obviously wasn't a boy, and then to say something was something was saying nothing.

She said: “It sure is.” She said it almost in a whisper, and Hugh understood why. It seemed wrong to speak too loud, like raising your voice in church.

“Gran said that back in the Highlands, they called them the Merry Dancers.”

“We call ’em the Ghost Dance.”

“Huh. I wonder if ghosts can be merry.”

She shivered, and pointed her mittened hand at a nearby shed. “That’d be out of the wind.”

On the lee side of the shed, the air was still cold but didn’t bite. They stood with their backs leaned against the shed wall, looking up at the waving curtains of flame. Hugh said: “Seems as everybody’s dancing tonight, even the ghosts. Some in there,” pointing his thumb over his shoulder, “they’ll likely dance all night.”

“Some.” She bent down to pick up a mittful of snow and licked it, saying: “I should’ve drunk a couple quarts of something before coming out.”

“Me, too.”

“Why, ain’t you all cooled off, yet?”

“Not so much.” Hugh would’ve known better than to say anything of the kind if he’d been recess-roughhousing in the snowy schoolyard, or skating on the river with his brothers and sisters. But Nancy Prince still went ahead and did the ‘you asked for it’ he would’ve expected in those circumstances: she laughed and mashed her mittful of snow across his nose and eyes, the proverbial washing-your-face that was the coup de grâce for the defeated in a snowball fight.

Hugh sputtered and blinked, swerved around and pressed one hand against her shoulder to pin her against the wall, scooped up snow with his other hand and did the same to her. She was laughing and protesting, trying to bat his face-washing hand away, and he was laughing and crowing, both of them three years old. And then he was kissing her, and they weren’t three years old anymore. His arms of their own accord slid around her back and hugged her to him. He could feel her arms twine around his back and press, too, as though if he and she just pressed hard enough they could push and pull each other through the layers of wool padding between them. He was surprised that it didn’t feel strange to be kissing Nancy Prince and hugging her body to his; it seemed like the most natural thing in the world, and all the other moments of his life were strange.

Hugh didn’t want to stop kissing Wauh-Oonae, but he didn’t want to smother her, either. He eased back just enough that he could see her face, and brought one hand up to brush her wet hair back from her eyes with the dry back of his mitten. He whispered: “Too bad the Merry Dancers picked tonight to put on such a beautiful show. It’s wasted.”

“‘Wasted’?”

“Wasted on me – I got something much more beautiful to look at.”

She lowered her eyes, blinking. He dabbed the back of his mitten against the corners of her eyes where the snow-melt seemed to be seeping in and out. He planned to kiss her again right soon, but as long as her eyes were down he had an up-close opportunity to gorge his eyes on her. It occurred to him to ask Mr. MacBeth next schoolday whether that was where 'gorgeous' came from. Then again, explaining where the question came from might get complicated.

Hugh tugged off his right hand mitten so he could trace his naked fingertips along the line of her cheekbone and jaw. But his out-of-line little finger got itself twisted in her hair. He started to pull his hand away, embarrassed about his crooked finger, but she brought one hand up to take hold of his wrist and softly kissed the knuckle that hadn't mended right.

"What the hell are you two doing out here in the cold?" boomed out of the dark. Hugh jumped away from Nancy Prince and turned to see the squat, hulking form of James McKay advancing toward them. Amazing that someone that heavy could walk so softly.

Mr. McKay laughed, "You're just doing what I'd be doing if I was your age. But if the cold gets in your blood, rubbing noses is going to break 'em off. Here," he reached in his capote and came out with a leatherbound flask, uncapped it and handed it to Hugh. "Just take a couple little sips. *Little* sips. Yep, I don't know if the old Earl of Selkirk ever thunk it through, but bringing in a bunch of colonists from the Scotch Highlands, some of them was bound to bring some ancient knowledge with 'em."

Hugh sniffed at the flask and took a very tentative sip. It tickled his nose and burned his throat. He coughed and tried to exhale the heat and handed the flask to Nancy Prince, who tilted it to her mouth as though she knew what to expect. Then she handed the flask back to Mr. McKay, who took a large swallow before putting it back inside his coat, saying: "Well, I better be on about my business," and carried on toward the necessary at the far side of the yard, half-singing a song about: *'Whisky, whiskey, Nancy Whiskey…'*

Once the burning in Hugh's throat had settled down, he did feel a little warmer, and a little bolder. But when he turned to Nancy Prince, she took one mitten off to touch his cheek with her bare hand and said: "We better be getting back inside."

"Oh, um, yeah, I guess so."

As they headed back, she tugged her mitten back on and reached her right hand over to take hold of his left. They walked mittened hand in hand across the yard and up onto the porch, and Hugh caught himself wondering whether other boys would think she was pretty or not and change their estimation of him accordingly. He told himself he deserved a cuff on the scruff, at least, for that line of wondering, and that Wauh Oonae's estimation of him would rightly drop through the cellar if she knew it had crossed his mind.

As it was, he and Nancy didn't go back into the house holding hands anyway, because they had to let go to deal with the door. Once inside, Hugh pointed at the stairs and said: "I'll go put my coat back. Want me to take yours?"

"No. Thanks. It goes somewheres else."

"Well, I'll go put mine away…" But on his way up the stairs he met Donald coming down, with his own coat on.

Donald said: "Where the deuce have you been, I've been looking all over. Come on, everybody's ready to go."

"Go? We just got here."

"You call two hours 'just got here'? Come on, it's a long way home and we all got chores in the morning."

"Well… I just gotta tell somebody I'm leaving."

"Okay, you go tell 'somebody,'" Donald smirked, "but remember we'll all be waiting on you out in the cold."

Hugh found Wauh Oonae over by the banquet table, getting herself a cup of punch. He said: "Uh, the people I came with, they, um… I have to go now."

"Oh. I'm staying the night."

"Oh. Um… I have to go."

CHAPTER 18

On a fine mid-summer evening, Schultz stood gazing at his new home as the workmen packed up their tools and the last scrap-ends of lumber. He'd selected his site on the south-east corner of the Portage Trail and the main road north, looking across the crossroads at Noah's Ark on the north-west corner. Any traffic coming from the Fort Garry landing heading north or west would encounter Schultz's store before McKenney's – or Drever's or McDermot's or A.G.B. Bannatyne's. Since the Portage Trail was generally assumed to be the northern boundary of The Company's reserve land around Fort Garry, the salubrious location just south of the crossroads was technically trespassing. But not by much, and once construction had started it would've been too much of a fuss for The Company to tell him to tear it down, which was what Schultz had counted on.

The head carpenter came up to him and said: "Well, she's all snug-tight now, Doctor. Time to settle up."

"She's 'snug-tight' a little later than we agreed upon." He had planned to be open for business weeks ago, but it had been a brutal summer, over a hundred degrees in the shade all through July and parched like a bake-oven. So any outdoor labouring had been confined to the first few hours of the morning and the last few hours of evening.

"I couldn't do anything about that, Doctor, no more'n the farmers could do anything about the locusts this year. Hardly a head of grain left standing. Matter of fact, the evil summer prob'ly got you a better building – half the good men I was able to hire on would've been too busy tending their crops if they'd had any crops to tend."

"Well, give me the bill and we'll discuss it."

"The bill? We had a handshake deal."

"Of course, but I still need a bill for my business records."

"Well… I guess I could get the wife to write something up."

"Good. Do that and bring it around to me."

The head carpenter went back to the knot of waiting men, and Schultz could hear the beginning of unhappy murmurings, but that wasn't his problem. Schultz went back to admiring the front of his new building. It was certainly solidly built, possibly more solidly than if he'd been able to afford his first intentions. He'd had to settle for crude traditional Red River squared-log post-and-beam construction, instead of proper frame and clapboard like Noah's Ark. Hand-hewn local planks, or imported lumber from a St. Paul's sawmill, were just too damned expensive and complicated. It sourly reminded Schultz that one of his and Harry's plans had been to build a sawmill at Red River. All those winter nights kept warm by building future ventures across the kitchen table, and it had all come out to this.

Schultz turned to look across the crossroads at what 'this' was. The sign above the entranceway to Noah's Ark no longer read *McKenny & Co.*, but *McKenny & Sons*. Schultz couldn't even bear to think of Harry as Harry anymore, but as some foreign entity called Sheriff Henry McKenney.

Schultz turned his back on McKenny & Sons and went into his own store. He stood for a moment breathing in the smell of fresh-cut lumber, looking around with satisfaction at the kegs, crates and bales waiting to be unloaded onto the empty shelves and the apothecary counter in one corner, then got a crowbar and started prying open crates to see what was where. He'd had to pay for the whole shipment COD, but that had only cost him a shuffling of numbers in The Company's banking ledgers, the only bank for several hundred miles. The line of credit to McKenney & Co. from Frederick E. Kew Investment Brokerage of London had grown to £2,000, which meant a thousand pounds to each partner upon dissolution. Technically, the money would have to be paid back with interest eventually, but London was a long way from Red River. Some of that line of credit had already been spent on building and stocking Noah's Ark, but since that establishment fell to Henry's share, Schultz still was entitled to half of two thousand.

Despite *McKenney & Sons*, *McKenney & Co.* still existed on paper. Schultz hadn't yet formally and officially dissolved the partnership, and wasn't going to until he'd first got his hands on as much of his 50% as Henry was willing to give up without a fight.

Looking around at the crates and barrels he'd already opened – enamelled tin dinnerware, rock candy, felt hats, axe- and hammer-heads – Schultz knew that the responsible thing to do would be to start unpacking them onto the shelves. But he didn't feel in a responsible mood; he felt a little celebratory. Only there was no one to celebrate with.

He climbed the stairs to the second floor, where one room was to be his examining room and the others his living quarters. It was still Spartan quarters till he accumulated more furnishings, but he'd been living there comfortably since the building was roof-tight – a lot more comfortably than living under Henry McKenney's roof. His plan was to expand from the back of the building to a large, attached warehouse with rent rooms above, but that would have to wait until the store was a going concern.

Schultz poured a little brandy in a cup, topped it up with water from the washstand pitcher, and sat down at the narrow writing desk set by the window. The window faced west, so at this time of year it still had sunlight and would till nine o'clock and more. From the back of the drawer he took out a cheap, cardboard-bound, schoolchild's scribble book, and leafed through it till he came to an empty page. Tapping his front teeth with a pencil, he let his mind wander in irresponsible directions, and then began to print:

The moon was blue, the sky was green,
The river rats cavorting,
When, sailing in a soup tureen,
Froggy came a-courting.

The boy stood on the burning deck
Of cards with one ace missing.
He rung a bell-rope chicken neck
And –

"Hello," cut in on Schultz from behind. He jumped in his chair, one hand automatically splaying across what he'd been scribbling, and turned around blushing like a boy who'd been caught playing with himself – which, in a way, he was. The voice had come from Agnes Campbell Farquharson, who was wearing a pretty, hooded, light green travelling cloak over a print dress and was standing in his bedroom doorway. Nestled in her arms was an unlabelled, dark green wine bottle with half its cork sticking out.

Schultz had managed to see Agnes Farquharson occasionally since she and her family moved out of Noah's Ark. He'd danced with her at the New Year's Regale at the Stone Fort, and made a habit of walking all the way to the Middle Church every Sunday so he could exchange a few words with her in the churchyard. The Sunday fiction he held up was that he preferred to travel by shank's mare for its healthful benefits, when the fact was he knew he looked ridiculous astride one of the stubby little local ponies and he was damned if he was going to church in a Red River cart. A civilized carriage and cutter were due to be delivered to him on the next voyage of *The International*, but the dry summer and low river meant the next voyage wouldn't be till next year.

Schultz stood up quickly, saying: "Forgive me, Miss Farquharson, you surprised me."

"Forgive *me*, Dr. Schultz, I didn't mean to startle you. Mrs. Burton –" the Burtons were the family who'd rented the Farquharsons the temporary home they'd been living in for a year now –" makes a remarkably tasty rhubarb wine, and she kindly allowed me a bottle to bring you as a housewarming gift."

"That's very kind of you, thank you – but, the workmen only just finished, how did you know it'd be done today?"

"Oh, a little bird told me." She came close enough to hand him the bottle, then glanced at the scribble book on the desk. "Did I interrupt you writing a letter?"

"No, I, um…" He felt his face reddening. "It's just, um, some things I write from time to time, just for my own amusement. Nothing really."

"Do you mind if I have a look?"

"Well, I…" Part of him very much minded the idea of her seeing his ridiculous scribblings, and part of him hoped she would like what she saw. Before he could begin to make up his mind, she'd already sat down and started reading the open page.

After a moment, she let out a giggle and said: "Why, Dr. Schultz, who would've thought you are poetical?"

"Well, it's, um, just nonsense, really. Silliness."

"Of course it is – delightfully so. People need a little silliness in their lives. You should finish it and have it printed in *The Nor'Wester*. The editor could hardly refuse you." She had a point there. William Coldwell was now the editor as well as publisher, and was having a rough go of it. James Ross had embarked for Upper Canada to pursue a law degree, and had sold his share in *The Nor'Wester* to Schultz for a surprisingly small infusion of ready cash and a promissary note.

Schultz said: "Um, that's very kind of you, Miss Farquharson. Your enthusiasm is, um, very gratifying. But I don't think writing nonsense verse in a newspaper is the best advertisement for a Doctor of Medicine."

She smiled, pink lips showing just the tips of her little white teeth. "Publish it anonymously. You'll be giving readers a bit of levity in their drab lives, and only you and I will know who the poet is. It'll be another secret between us."

"Hm," Schultz nodded. "You might have something there." He became aware that she and he were alone in his bedroom with a bottle of wine for housewarming.

Then a voice called up from downstairs, "Found him yet?" Miss Farquharson's father.

Miss Farquharson crossed to the doorway, elucidating on the way, "Mr. Burton kindly lent Father and I his carriage to come give you a housewarming." Then she shouted down the bare hallway in a bellow surprisingly loud for such a small frame, "Yes! We'll be down in a minute!"

Schultz said: "Well, there's cups downstairs…" and caddied the bottle of rhubarb wine behind her. Downstairs, he fished three enamelled cups out of a straw-packed barrel – vowing silently that someday soon he would pour wine for Agnes Farquharson in leaded crystal – and they toasted his new home and enterprise and made small talk. Miss Farquharson showed a surprising and gratifying interest in how he planned to set up the store, what kinds of goods he'd imported, every detail short of the déclassé subject of actual pounds, shillings and pence. Mr. Farquharson finished his wine rather quickly and tapped his empty cup on the counter, as though he didn't want to stay long but also didn't want to leave anything in the bottle to spoil and go to waste.

With his cup refilled, Mr. Farquharson looked around the bare shell of a store and said: "Damn fine looking place. All it needs is a few coats of paint. I see it in forest greens – very big in London this year, forest green, and I just happen to have the right powders on hand."

Schultz considered saying that a free paint job of the entire building would almost equal the Farquharsons' unpaid bill for room and board at McKenney's Lodging House. Schultz had suggested to Henry, and Henry hadn't argued, that the whole of the Farquharsons' account be factored into the Junior Partner's half of McKenney & Co's assets and debits. Schultz hadn't mentioned that fact to any of the Farquharsons, but he suspected that the younger

Miss Farquharson had divined why Sheriff McKenney had suddenly stopped trying to serve writs on her father for debts owed McKenney & Co. It was another little secret, though an unspoken one, between Agnes Campbell Farquharson and Dr. John Christian Schultz.

Schultz decided to leave it unspoken and just said: "Well, um, I thought I'd leave the place unpainted for now… to let the wood season. I'll have to have the exterior protected against the weather, of course, but it'd be a waste of a professional's talents to trouble with a few coats of whitewash that any halfbreed handyman could slap on for a few shillings."

Mr. Farquharson shrugged, "Suit yourself," and eyed the bottle again, which now had only a dab of murky sediment in its bottom. "Well, I told old Burton we wouldn't be long – best we get him back his chariot."

As Agnes Farquharson re-fastened her travelling cloak, she said: "I think the store looks elegant with just the bare wood, and it will set off the stock so much better. I think you've made a good start, Dr. Schultz." Her blue eyes fastened directly on his, their gaze meeting on about a forty-five degree plane. "A very good start, indeed."

After the Farquharsons were gone, Schultz felt more energised than he had an hour ago. Instead of going upstairs to finish his poem, he started stocking the shelves and continued by lamplight. By one o'clock in the morning he had the shelves stocked and ready for business, even down to a supply of cheap cotton handkerchiefs behind the counter. The habit at Red River was that if one went to the store for a half-pound of tea or sugar, one also bought a cotton handkerchief to carry it home in.

Schultz carried one of the lamps up to his bedroom but still didn't feel like sleeping, so added on another couple of stanzas to finish his poem before turning in. He was wakened by the arrival of the mildly intelligent young man he'd been training as a stock boy and store clerk. The lad had learned the rudiments tolerably well, but had yet to deal with actual customers. They came in droves as soon as Schultz unlocked the front door, but mostly for curiosity – it wasn't every day a new store opened at Red River. But many of them had enough conscience to buy at least a little something to justify their curiosity. By the time Schultz closed the doors at the end of the day, he felt he just might be able to make a go of it. He'd never been in business on his own before, always as an employee, or Henry's junior partner. He wasn't sure whether the pride outweighed the fear.

After making himself a supper of cold ham and a boiled potato – the dry summer made potatoes a luxury at Red River this year – Schultz wandered over to the *Nor'Wester* office with his new poem in his pocket, jauntily rehearsing subtle ways to introduce it to the editor. But the spring in his step came unsprung when he came within sight of where he was going.

The newspaper office and print shop were both in the same square little, rent-free cabin on the Ross property – even though James Ross had departed, Coldwell's wife was still Granny Sally Ross's daughter. Hitched to the ring by the cabin door was a standard-issue scruffy Red River pony wearing a non-standard issue saddle: an American style cowboy saddle, instead of the English or homemade saddles most Red River riders favoured. One Red River resident who did favour an American western saddle was Frank

Larned Hunt. In between working his farm and the occasional revival of his law practice – even more occasional than Schultz's medical practice – Frank Larned Hunt sometimes contributed articles to *The Nor'Wester*, and sometimes poems. *Real* poems, not childish nonsense. Schultz wasn't about to present Coldwell with his lame Edward Lear imitation while Hunt was there. But Schultz could come up with perfectly legitimate reasons to look in on the enterprise he part-owned, and maybe Hunt wouldn't stay for long, so Schultz pulled open the door.

Coldwell looked up from behind a stack of newspapers on his desk – *real* newspapers, not the four-page *Nor'Wester*. "Oh, good evening, Schultz."

Schultz nodded, "Coldwell, Hunt."

"Evenin', Doctor."

It seemed to Schultz that Hunt leaned on the 'doctor' more than his American drawl accounted for, but he let it pass. Coldwell tapped on the stack of newspapers in front of him and pointed at the one in front of Hunt, saying: "They finally got the freight from the last cart train sorted out, and brought me two months of our back subscriptions –"

"The *foreign* newspapers," Hunt interjected, "New York *Times* , Toronto *Globe...*"

"Hunt's helping me skim through them, to sort out what's worth culling for *The Nor 'Wester*."

"How goes the American war?"

"Endgame. The Union Army's almost at Atlanta, might be there by now – the recentest issue's a month old."

"Not necessarily checkmate," said Hunt. "Don't count out Robert E. Lee till he's surrendered or dead."

"Only a matter of time. And *that*, Schultz, old man, gives thee and me more cause to celebrate than just the impending ending of a foreign war. Maybe even Hunt can be persuaded to join in for conviviality." Coldwell fished a bottle and a glass from a desk drawer and scoured around for other glasses, finding one on top of the typeface cabinet and another on the lip of the printing press, "It's finally sinking-in to the patchwork little colonies of British North America that when the Civil War ends they'll be sitting right next door to a country with the largest standing army in the world, and nothing for that army to do. Idle hands...

"It would only take a few malcontents in Nova Scotia or New Brunswick – and there's always malcontents – to invite the Americans in, give some legal pretext, and the United States Army could swallow any of the Atlantic colonies before breakfast. The Atlantic colonies have been jawing about forming their own Union for years to no effect. But *now*, with this extra bit of impetus, they're conferring again this summer, *and...*" Coldwell's eyes glittered. "Upper and Lower Canada have asked to have seats at the conference table, to talk seriously about forming a federation of all British North America."

Schultz was stunned by the suddenness and glory of it. If all the British colonies south and east of Rupert's Land were one entity, then the next logical step was Rupert's Land itself.

Coldwell poured a dollop of precious imported whiskey into each of the three glasses and the three men automatically raised them in a toasting gesture. Schultz and Coldwell spontaneously and simultaneously came out with: "Canada!"

Hunt only muttered: "If you say so," but happily drained his glass. When he set it down, he said: "I know what you gents are thinking, but don't count out the United States of America. Remember, I was born and raised down there. I was still living there when they took California and the whole south-west from Mexico. South-west, north-west, what's the difference?"

"The difference," Schultz said, "is that the Spanish Empire is not the British Empire."

Coldwell said: "Here, here."

Hunt shrugged as though he could say something more on the subject but wouldn't, and went back to leafing through his stack of newspapers. Schultz had been hoping that once Hunt had had a free drink he'd head home so Schultz could show Coldwell his 'anonymous' poem, but Hunt seemed to be settling in. Coldwell's news, though, had made the poem seem a trifle of no immediate import, and had also revitalised Schultz when he'd thought he was tired from the opening day of his store. So he busied himself with starting to set the type for the page Coldwell had already composited for the next issue.

Schultz liked picking through the little metal blocks of letters and blanks and lining them up on the page frame, choosing larger and smaller typefaces as per Coldwell's notes. And he liked the printers' jargon he'd been picking up from Coldwell, wherein 'k-legged' meant knock-kneed, or drunk, and 'a comely toonitch' was a pretty woman, since compositer's shorthand for a girl-child in the birth notices was two nitches, =, and a male was a wunitch, - . It was a kind of secret language that put Schultz in mind of the ancient origins of the Freemasons, as explained to him when he was recently initiated at Fort Pembina. In most other parts of the world he'd still be a very junior member of The Order, but here he was Worshipful Master of the brand new Northern Light Lodge, the first Lodge in Rupert's Land.

Schultz more than liked his quick advancement in The Ancient Order of Freemasons. Even back in college days in Canada, he'd noticed how a secret phrase or secret hand-sign – secret to him – could gain a man instant access to a banker's inner sanctum or a Public Works Committee's private deliberations. Of course, that wasn't the purpose of becoming a Mason; the purpose was to become a humble student of eternal moral truths and universal brotherhood. But brotherhood was a natural part of commerce, as naturally as a part of a publication like *The Nor'Wester* was to publicize that there was now a Lodge at Red River, where men of substance and good will could gather free from the prying eyes and ears of the uninitiated.

The page Schultz was typesetting was Page 4, the back page of the next issue, so there were some filler snippets and a few paid advertisements. One of the ads made Schultz stop and push the type tray aside.

!FOR SALE!
American-made Carriage and Cutter, and a Fine
Trotting Horse (gelding). Horse Twenty Pounds
Sterling, Carriage and Cutter Ten Pounds Each,
or Thirty-five Pounds the Lot!!

Schultz pointed the item out to Coldwell and said: "You may have to find something else to fill this space."

"But he's already paid for the ad!"

Pulling off his typesetting sleeve guards and reaching for his coat, Schultz said: "If you end up having to fill the space, he'll have got his money's worth. If I don't come back here tonight, consider it a done deal." On his way out the door, Schultz tossed back: "Good." 'Good' was printers' shorthand for 'good-night,' and was the customary salute when leaving 'chapel,' the printing shop. Schultz liked customary things. They were a kind of comfort in a world where brothers turned against you, and success or failure were a hair's breadth apart.

The address in the ad was 'Batchelors' Hall, Fort Garry.' The bottom rim of the sun was nearing the western horizon, but Schultz calculated that with the length of his legs and a brisk pace he could make it to Fort Garry while there was still light in the sky, so the advertiser couldn't protest against a business call at night. Halfway between the village of Winnipeg and Fort Garry, Schultz could see that the north gate – stone gatehouse centring wooden walls – was closed. Which meant he'd have to walk all the way around to the main gate facing the Assiniboine. But the inconvenience put Schultz in mind of a very encouraging fact. Back when Sir George Simpson, longtime HBC Governor In Chief, built the Stone Fort as The Company's North American headquarters, he'd let the old headquarters at The Forks decay into a minor trading post. But trade and traffic so naturally gravitated to The Forks that he'd eventually had to build another, smaller, stone fort there. Some years after that, he'd had to give in and add on the log-walled section, to house the Governor of Rupert's Land and all his staff, relocating the headquarters to where it had been relocated from. Not even the Little Emperor could change the fact that everything flowed through The Forks. The Forks was a lodestone, a pole star, a magnet that drew all compass points toward it. And John Christian Schultz's new establishment, with all his prospects, was located right by The Forks, at the crossroads.

The front gates of Fort Garry were still open when Schultz got there. Beyond the gates was a large open square hedged by wide, tall, hip-roofed buildings: warehouses, counting rooms, servants' quarters, Governor Mactavish's house, Dr. Cowan's house... The 'houses' were like the housemaster system in books Johnny Schultz had read about the English Public Schools built for boys who were born successful. Governor Mactavish and Dr. Cowan and the other senior officers didn't really need four or five storeys and several dozen rooms to house their families, but their houses included less palatial quarters and a mess hall for the employees they uncled.

All the houses were settling in for the night, so Schultz's boots echoed on the boardwalks built for times when the earth was knee-deep mud or buried in snow. He went up a set of wooden steps to the open doorway of the junior officers' quarters. Beyond the doorway was a long, broad hall dotted with tables sporting newspapers, books, cups, pipes and tobacco pouches, dry-fly tying gear… Lined along both walls were doors to the sleeping chambers. A few clerks and traders were still up, playing cards or reading magazines. Schultz spotted the one he was looking for – a young man in a velvet smoking jacket – and headed toward him, nodding back at those who said: "Evenin', Dr. Schultz," as he passed by.

"Mr. Shadforth."

The young man in the smoking jacket looked up. "Oh, Dr. Schultz. Nice to see you, old man. Haven't seen you since… Was it New Year's at the Stone Fort?"

Schultz nodded and got right to it, "I was helping typeset the next issue of *The Nor'Wester* and saw your advertisement. I might be interested."

"In which – the carriage, or the cutter, or the horse?"

"Perhaps all three."

"Oh. Well, that's jolly good, but it's a little late for doing business."

"There's still daylight."

"Oh. Well, I'll just fetch my boots, shall I? And we'll go 'round the stables so you can have a gander."

On the way to the stables, Schultz said: "Is The Company posting you elsewhere, then?"

"Not a bit of it. I've bought out my contract and posting myself home. Too bad I didn't make up my mind until too late for the brigade to the bay, so as soon as I've wound things up here I'll have to take a deuced cart train to St. Paul and travel all the way across country to Montreal. Or maybe even New York, if I get east too late in the shipping season. But even at that, I hope to be back in London by Christmas."

Schultz smiled to himself: Seller had just told Buyer that Seller was pressed to sell soon. Schultz had known plenty of Shadforth's type back in medical school, born to privilege – not necessarily fabulously wealthy, but they'd certainly never had to mend their own shirtsleeves and keep their suitcoats on at sweltering garden parties to hide the fact. It grated on Schultz that they had no idea how easy they had it, but part of him pitied their naivete. All of him, though, was determined that someday they'd be presenting their cards to his doorman. Schultz said companionably: "Two years in Rupert's Land were enough for you?"

"Not a bit of it. It's a grand life for a single chap. Excepting times when a boat brigade or cart train comes in or goes out, the clerking leaves plenty of free time, and here we are in God's own hunting park. But my father sent me a letter by the spring packet… Seems The Company's Directors in London sold out all their shares to some sort of consortium or other –"

"The International Financial Association," Schultz contributed. Another characteristic of the Shadforths of this world was that they didn't pay much attention to details which weren't immediately and obviously pertaining to their social circle.

"That's the ticket. Well, those chaps back there," Shadforth thumbed over his shoulder at Bachelor's Hall, "think it's just a change of brass nameplates in the London office, and it'll still be business as usual here on the ground. Not a bit of it, according to Pater. He says The International Financial Association is more interested in real estate than the fur trade, and the on-the-ground Partners won't be Partners anymore. The only fortunes left to be made are on the London Stock Exchange, so home I go. And it seems it ain't just Pater's view of the situation; Governor Dallas is doing the same thing I am."

"*Governor Dallas* is?"

Shadforth stopped short a few steps short of the door into the stables, and furrowed his brow. "Oh dear, maybe that's still supposed to be on the Q. T. Well, it'll be common knowledge deuced soon. Governor Dallas has decided to take an early retirement. Nothing wrong with his health, but he's cashing in his chips, or his shares, and leaving North America behind. So, Governor Mactavish will be Governor of Assiniboia *and* The Company's Governor of Rupert's Land, at least for a time. No doubt the locals will be happy about that, since Mactavish has been in Rupert's Land since donkey's years – not a foreigner like Dallas – even married to a daughter-of-the-country, as they say. All abstract to me now, old man, so on to the business at hand."

Shadforth ushered Schultz into the cavernous Company stables, where the remnants of daylight didn't penetrate much and the air was rich with hay and oats and horse manure. Shadforth led Schultz to one corner and said: "Well, here's the goods, I'll call the ostler to bring a light…"

The Metis ostler obediently brought a lantern and stood mutely holding it while Schultz looked things over. Schultz hardly considered himself an expert judge of horseflesh, or of carriages and cutters, but he managed to point out enough frayed spots on the carriage upholstery and harness that the price of thirty-five-pounds-the-lot came down to twenty-seven pounds, five shillings and sixpence. A bit of wear and tear wouldn't've been enough to bring the price down that low, if Schultz hadn't been armed with the knowledge that Shadforth was intent on winding up his affairs in time to be in London before Christmas.

Once the price was agreed, Schultz said: "Deuced handy that your destination's London. My investment broker's Frederick E. Kew of London. I'll write you out a draw on my letter of credit, and once you're in London you can pop by Kew's and he'll give you the cash."

"Well, um, that sounds a trifle inconvenient –"

"Not a bit of it. More convenient for you to not have to carry the cash; more convenient to me since I do have a retail business to maintain and you know how scarce cash money is around here – except The Company's paper shillings, and they'd do you no good in London. A note from me to Kew's as good as gold, and if the only fortunes left to be made are on the London Stock Exchange it won't do you any harm to have an acquaintance with Frederick E. Kew of London. A done deal."

"Well, um –"

"Excellent. Here's my hand on it. I'll write up a bill of sale and my note to Kew and bring them down tomorrow. And of course I'll have to leave the horse and conveyances here till I can get a carriage house builded behind my place – shouldn't be more than a week or two. Pleasure doing business with you."

On his jaunty walk home, Schultz considered sending a message by the next cart train to St. Paul, cancelling the order for the cutter and carriage due to arrive C.O.D. on the next steamboat. On second thought, given that the next steamboat likely wouldn't be till next year, if the carriage makers did make the shipment he could refuse payment, on the reasonable grounds that a year's delay voided the order. He could generously offer to take the delivered goods off their hands at half-price, leaving them the option of paying the exorbitant return freight and no sale. Then he could sell off either the new carriage and cutter or Shadforth's, with no time pressures to prevent him from holding out for the best price. But whatever happened, he now had a fine trotting horse, carriage and cutter to cut a good impression throughout the settlement, and to take Miss Agnes Farquharson for Sunday afternoon rides in all seasons.

Schultz didn't go in much for self-congratulation – it was bad luck to congratulate oneself for having run a good first lap when the race was barely begun. But looking back on the long day from opening the store to his sunset walk home from Fort Garry, he allowed himself to accept Miss Farquharson's assessment. He'd made a very good start indeed.

CHAPTER 19

Kate MacPherson knelt amidships of the dugout boat while her grandson Donald paddled from the stern and her grandson Hugh from the bow. Hugh's paddling was frequently interrupted by leaning forward to break a path through the skin of ice growing on the river. The mid-October snow had mostly melted off the ground, but it had just been an early calling card that King Winter was on his way, as the crackle and splash of Hugh's ice-breaking attested.

Kate felt a little sorry for Purple Hugh these days. His father had decided that if Hugh would rather work on the farm than go to school, then he was going to *work*, from dawn till dusk. Kate hoped John would keep it 'dawn to dusk' as the days got shorter, and let go of the rule when the days started getting longer again, since it seemed obvious by now that Hugh wasn't going to be worked out of his determination to be done with school. Father and son were each as stubborn as the other, in those rare circumstances when Hugh wasn't happy to just drift with the tide. Kate couldn't imagine where they got it from.

Someday soon, Kate planned to get John to admit it was lucky for all of them that Hugh hadn't gone back to school this year. She and Sandy had both slowed down somewhat since turning eighty, and Janet had her hands more than full with thirteen children and the thirteenth colicky and frail. And John's life hadn't been his own this autumn, thanks to the plague of locusts decimating everybody's crops. Somebody'd had to persuade the Council of Assiniboia and The Company to suspend the tariff on grain brought in from Minnesota, so there would be seed for next year. There hadn't been starvation at Red River since very early days, before the people who lived different ways realised that if they weren't all in the same boat they'd be in the same casket. When the crops failed, there was always the buffalo hunt and the fishery, and vice versa. But food distribution didn't happen by magic, and Point Douglas John Sutherland was in the perfect position to be the go-between for the Kildonan farmers, the Metis hunters and The Company, being a Kildonan man living on the 'French' side of the river. Kate had no doubt her son would rather spend his time wrestling a plough than sitting in Council meetings, but he had a fatal flaw which meant he'd always be called upon in times of trouble: people trusted him.

When the boat reached the west bank, the boys angled it sideways so she could reach her 'Jacob's Ladder' – a shagganappi rope with hand loops knotted into it, hanging from a tree close by the shore. It had miraculously appeared one Sunday morning several summers ago, after she'd started experiencing increasing difficulties getting up off her knees to step out of the boat. No one had admitted to putting it there, but she had small doubt it was Hugh, because he usually paddled her across alone so was the most likely to notice. And because, well, it was the kind of loony thing her Christmas Boy would do.

Once Kate was safely upright ashore, the boys pushed off, calling that they'd see her in the afternoon. She turned up the path to the road, holding her cloak closed against the north wind and holding her Bible to her breast. The Bible was the same one that had come across the ocean with her half a century ago, in the crowded, typhus-ridden hold of a ship not built to carry passengers, and she still marked her place with the brown silk ribbon her grandmother had embroidered in silk thread: *'Lord teach me to pray.'* Kate chuckled darkly to herself – He most certainly had done that. If the Highland Clearances hadn't been enough, she would've learned when the ship's doctor died of the typhus and left no one to take care of the sick but volunteer nurse Kate MacPherson, or when so many died in the blink of an eye at Seven Oaks and she'd had every reason to believe her husband had been one of them, or when the flood of '26 swept the whole settlement away and left the colonists shivering and starving on the high ground at Stony Mountain…

But her prayers had been answered, unlike so many others', and she had no idea why hers and not theirs. Even the frosted grass crunching under her shoes was a blessing, since she had to be alive to feel it and hear it. Even the grey and glowering autumn sky was a blessing to look at, with its slowly drifting clouds rippling soft shades of charcoal to dove, and the foggy pearl of the morning sun beyond the cloudbanks.

Kate's eyes came down out of the clouds to fasten on the fence of the Willow Creek Bannermans' place up ahead, with its friendly, thigh-high boulder by a corner post. Back in the Highlands, every crofter's home had a Wanderer's Stone beside the door, where travellers could perch and rest. Kate was just as glad that the Willow Creek Bannermans had modified the custom to their roadside fence; she preferred to keep to herself on Sabbath mornings. She had her regular stopping places along her walk to kirk: the Bannermans' boulder, the stump of an old oak tree a ways farther along, the upturned, crack-hulled dugout canoe that the Polsons never got around to sawing up for firewood… From what her legs and lungs were telling her when she was still more than a few strides shy of the Bannermans' boulder, maybe it was time she scouted out some intermediate rest stops.

Kate heard hoofbeats and wheels coming up behind her. She shifted to the side of the road and looked over her shoulder. It was Dr. Schultz with his trotting horse and carriage, wearing a blue derby hat over his neck-length bronze hair. She nodded over her shoulder for politeness' sake and kept on walking. But he reined in his horse when he caught up to her, so it seemed the polite thing to do was for her to stop, too.

He tipped his hat and said: "Good morning, Mrs. Sutherland. On your way to church?"

"Aye." *'I'm two miles from my home on a Sunday morning, where the devil else would I be going?'*

"Well, I'll be passing by Kildonan Kirk on my way to the Middle Church."

Kate just nodded. It seemed odd that he'd be going all the way to St. Paul's Church when he lived in St. John's parish, but she had no doubt he had his reasons and they were none of her concern. It annoyed her that he said 'Kildonan *Kirk*' instead of what came natural to him.

Dr. Schultz shifted over from the middle of the carriage seat, patted the empty seat beside him and said: "It's a long walk on a frosty morning. Since I'm going that way anyway..."

She was going to say: *'I'd rather walk,'* but that sounded like an insult. Dr. Schultz started to reach his hand out to help her, but she took hold of the ironwork rims and levered herself up onto the padded leather seat. He thoughtfully waited till she was settled before flicking the reins to start the horse trotting again.

As the carriage jounced along – though much less jouncy than a Red River cart – Dr. Schultz made conversation, saying he was looking forward to the snow when he could try out his new cutter, and asking after the health of 'Mr. Sutherland, Senior,' and how the grandchildren were getting on at school. He did seem genuinely interested in all the doings of her family, and Kate wasn't sure why she tended to reply as curtly as civility allowed. There wasn't anything obviously dislikeable about Dr. Schultz – he was certainly a handsome young man, in a smooth-jawed sort of way, and he was well-spoken without flaunting his education. But for some reason she felt uncomfortable sitting on a carriage seat beside him.

There was at least one definable reason for feeling uncomfortable – it was much colder riding in the open carriage than walking. She doubled the front of her cloak, pulled its hood tighter and acknowledged there was some sense in Dr. Schultz wearing a buffalo coat even though they were still a few days shy of November. She let her gaze drift sideways, to the homes and farmyards between the river and the road – winter bedded kitchen gardens and snug thatched houses and barns, where only yesterday she and her new husband had had to fight through untouched tangled brush to find a piece of land that satisfied him, nearby the rest of the colony but not part of it. It had taken him and her some bickering before she understood he'd had enough of being part of something in the British Army.

With her higher field of vision from the carriage seat, and not needing to keep an eye on the ground in front of her feet, Kate's eyes travelled up the threads of smoke from the hearth fires of Kildonan. The wind had died for now, and in the still air the grey-white smoke went up in straight lines from the chimneys toward the grey-white clouds. 'Cloud machines...'

Hugh couldn't have been more than four or five years old, because he'd had to stand on the blanket box to see out the little window in the upstairs hallway. It had been a day much like today, with a low roof of cloud blanketing the sky – except it must've been further on in the winter, because Hugh had had to rub and breathe on the frost-crocheted glass to clear a space he could see out of. Kate, coming out of one of the bedrooms with a sheetful of laundry, had asked him what he was looking at, and he'd said: "The cloud machines are working."

She'd bent down to see what queer fancy had got into the boy this time. Peering out across the river through the porthole he'd made in the frost, it did appear that the smoke from Kildonan's chimneys was going straight up to the clouds – she was quite sure it must be an illusion, the smoke surely dissipated long before it got that high. But since the clouds and the smoke were the same colour, and the clouds covered the sky to the horizon, it did look like they met. And once a body'd got Hugh's strange notion in mind, it did look like the chimneys were pumping up stems of cloud that spread and joined together when they got high enough, like a giant mushroom farm with the edges of the caps melding.

"Mrs. Sutherland…?" Kate was back in the carriage again, and it was Dr. Schultz's voice. She looked to her left, but he wasn't there where he had been. She looked to her right. The carriage had stopped and Dr. Schultz was standing there to give her a hand down. She couldn't very well refuse his hand this time without being baldly graceless, so she let him help her down and thanked him. As he swung back up onto the carriage seat, he said: "Since they changed the time for Sunday Services at St. Paul's, I'll be coming along this road your time most Sundays. And the cutter oughta be an even smoother ride than the carriage. Well, do give my regards to Mr. and Mrs. Sutherland the younger, and young Hugh, and the rest of the family. *Gittup*."

As Dr. Schultz's carriage clattered away, Kate wondered why she didn't at all fancy the idea of riding in one of Dr. Schultz's conveyances most Sundays to come. It was just kindness on his part, after all, to save an old woman a long walk. Perhaps she was just being stiff-necked against being thought of as an old woman. It crossed her mind, though, that there might be something aside from kindness in Dr. Schultz's mind. If a relative newcomer to Red River wanted to become accepted and trusted by the people of Kildonan, he could do worse than to be often seen riding in his carriage beside Kate MacPherson. *'You don't think much of yourself, Catherine MacPherson,'* said a voice inside her head, *'do you?'* She replied that she didn't have to think much of herself in particular to consider that possibility about Dr. Schultz. The plain fact was she was one of the few left of the original Selkirk Settlers, so the descendants of the others were bound to look at her with some respect, even if not particularly deserved.

Kate walked on into the kirkyard, mindful of the occasional patch of ice – snow was so much more trustworthy. One disadvantage to getting a ride from Dr. Schultz was that she was here earlier than usual, there was no one else about. But smoke was coming from the chimney pipe behind the bell spire, so Dr. Black had already built fires in the Carron stoves and gone back to the manse for his breakfast. So the inside of the kirk was bound to be much warmer than the outside, but it felt like giving-in to go sit inside alone when in only a few minutes there'd be the usual pre-service gathering of neighbours in the kirkyard. So she continued wandering among the rows of gravestones angling out from the kirk.

There weren't all that many gravestones yet – less than fifteen years had passed since the people of young John Black's first parish built him a stone church with their own hands, and for the thirty years previous they'd had to bury their dead in St. John's cemetery. Unlike St. John's, or the other churches at Red River, the graves weren't in a separated cemetery but close by the front and sides of the church, so eventually the path to the front door of the kirk would be flanked by rows of those who had gone before. The headstones weren't just names to Kate; they all had faces and voices she remembered.

She heard a tiny *mew* that might've been two frozen twigs rubbing together. It came again. She went and looked in that direction. Partway up a leafless, hoarfrosted, grey-barked tree was a lump of brindled grey with a dab of white frosting. It might've been a burl swelling out the skin of the tree, but it wasn't. It was a kitten – maybe the product of one of the innumerable barn cats in the settlement, or maybe someone's pampered house cat had snuck into the woods to birth her litter.

Kate reached up, but the crotch of the tree the kitten was hunkered in was a bit too high for even her undainty height and length of arm. Kate scrabbled her gloved fingertips against the bark to try and rouse its curiosity. The kitten looked at her and mewed, but didn't move. Maybe it couldn't move; maybe it was frozen to the tree and only needed a pair of warm hands cupped around it to thaw it free.

Out of all Kate's horrible memories of the Highland Clearances, the worst was of her cat, MacCrimmon. When the bailiffs set her parents' cottage on fire, so the family would have nothing to sneak back to, hidden MacCrimmon had bolted terrified out of the house just before the roof caved in. Patrick Sellar, the Countess of Sutherland's Factor, had scooped up MacCrimmon and lofted him back into the flames. One of the bailiffs had next-to stove in Kate's skull with his pistol barrel when she went for Sellar.

Looking up at the quivering kitten in the tree, Kate didn't debate whether it was better to die by fire or by ice, because she wasn't going to let it happen this time. She looked around the kirkyard. There was still no one in sight. Maybe in a few minutes families would start arriving with cartfuls of agile young boys, or maybe it would be somewhat more than a few minutes – she had no way of knowing how much time Dr. Schultz's carriage had shaved off her usual walk to church. And she had no way of knowing how long the kitten had been trapped up the tree, bare to the wind and frost, or when it had last put some fuel in its belly. There might not be much longer before the cold worked its way into its tiny heart.

Kate spotted the edge of a pile of logs behind the church, waiting to be sawn up into stove lengths. There might be a sawhorse there. She went and looked and found two, one nestled on top of the other. She carried the top one back and set it against the tree.

The kitten was mewing louder and more often now. Kate murmured: "Ssh, my dear, don't fret, I'm coming," and checked-over the top crosspiece on the sawhorse to make sure there were no slippery patches of ice or frost. Then she bent one creaky knee, teetering on her left leg while pulling her right shin with one hand to help get her foot high enough, and levered herself up standing on the sawhorse, holding onto the tree trunk for balance.

The kitten looked to be just within her arms' length now. She let go of the tree trunk and reached both her hands up.

But when she'd carefully checked over the sawhorse crosspiece for patches of frost or ice, she hadn't thought about the soles of her shoes that had been walking over frost-coated grass. Her right foot slipped off the sawhorse, she made a grab for the tree trunk too late, lost her balance and fell straight back onto the frozen ground. There was a bomb-burst of pain in her right hip, and then the pain and everything else was gone.

She came back to herself lying in the spring heather beside Kildonan Burn, with the side of her head still throbbing from the bailiff's pistol barrel, and MacCrimmon's screams of terror still echoing in her ears. But no, this ground was wintry hard, and that had been half a century ago. She tried to sit up, but the movement brought another burst of pain from her right hip, like two sawblades grinding their teeth against each other. The kind dark closed over her again.

When she awoke the next time there were feet all around her – feet in moccasins, in boots, in home-sewn shoes – and voices were murmuring to each other to move back and give her some air, or to crowd in tighter and keep her warm. The Reverend Dr. Black was crouched beside her, saying: "Mrs. Sutherland…? Catherine, can you hear me…?"

"Yes, I – *Uh!*" Just the slightest movement brought that grinding pain again. Kate clenched her teeth and tautened the corners of her eyes – bad enough to be a foolish and helpless old woman, damned if she was going to be a blubbery one.

Dr. Black said: "We fear you may have broken your hip. A couple of lads are galloping to Fort Garry and St. John's, trying to find Dr. Cowan."

"The kitten…?"

"Pardon me? I'm sorry, Catherine, I couldn't make out what you said."

She unclenched her teeth. "The kitten… in the tree…"

"Ian Bannerman got her down and has her snugged inside his coat."

"Ah. Good. But you must get her some milk."

"I'll see to that as soon as –"

"*Now!* No telling how long the poor thing was – *Uh!*" It would just top things off perfectly if the bloody little kitten went and died.

Mrs. Black's unseen voice came from somewhere above and behind her crouching husband, "I'll fetch a saucer of milk from the manse."

"And meanwhile," Dr. Black said to Kate, "we'd best get you up off the cold ground and back home." He called over his shoulder: "Angus…?"

Angus Matheson's voice called back: "Just ready now, Dr. Black."

The fence of feet and legs on one side of Kate moved back and Dr. Black stood away, to make room for a makeshift stretcher cobbled together with poplar poles and a blanket. As they laid the stretcher down beside her, Kate looked beyond it to the gravestones standing nearby and said: "Might just as well save carting me back and forth."

Dr. Black and helping hands clearly did their best to shift her onto the stretcher without jarring her hip, so she did her best to keep from crying out when the edges of the broken bone grated together. Once they'd loaded her onto a cart, someone handed her the Bible she'd set aside to climb onto the sawhorse. She laid it on her belly, crossed her hands over it and watched the sky go by, occasionally turning her head to peer through the cross-hatch of cart-rails to see how far they'd got so far. Whoever was leading the carthorse seemed to be taking it slow so as not to jar her too much on the lumpy road. She wasn't sure she wouldn't rather have a quick succession of sharp and hideous pains than a drawn-out series of merely hideous pains.

There was a game she'd made up when she was a little girl suffering toothaches, or when the straps of the peat basket felt like they were sawing her arms off at the shoulder. The game was called 'You think this is bad?' and consisted of harking back to times in the past that were worse than the present. So now she reminded herself of the long, late-winter march along the coast of Hudson's Bay, when the ship that brought the colonists from Scotland had put them off at Fort Churchill, two hundred miles north of where they were meant to go, and they somehow had to get to York Factory before the spring brigade of York Boats left for Red River. And before that there'd been the weeks on the Scottish seacoast, where she and all her neighbours had been herded to their new 'lands' of rock and sand, with nothing to eat but handfuls of millet soaked in the drawn-off blood of their starving cattle, and no hope in sight…

"She's in here!" called a voice from in front of the cart. Kate heard running footsteps approaching from farther ahead. Donald, Hugh, Morrison and Aleck appeared through the grid of the cart sides and fell-in walking beside it, panting.

Hugh said: "Are you all right, Gran?"

'Of course I'm not all right, idiot child.' Kate said aloud: "Passable, lad, passable."

Donald said: "Father's coming along, too. He stuck to walking so Granda wouldn't try to run."

Kate nodded and closed her eyes and went back to reminding herself of times when she would've gladly traded places with her current wretched state. There'd been that terrible first winter at Red River, when the harvest had been so scant that all the colonists had to trek down to Fort Pembina with Chief Peguis's people to try and survive till spring, crammed into dilapidated old hunting cabins near the buffaloes' wintering grounds… And the winter before that had been even worse: makeshift huts outside Fort Churchill, with Kate MacPherson doing her ignorant best to nurse the many still delirious with Ship's Fever, and there was one set-aside hut gradually filling up with frozen corpses stacked waiting for the ground to thaw enough to dig graves. On the other hand, among her patients had been lamed-but-game, ex-Private Sandy Sutherland –

"Catherine…?"

Kate opened her eyes and there was Sandy Sutherland's hand, gripping a cart rail, and beyond it was the rest of him – though a grizzled version of the him at Fort Churchill – limping along beside the cart. His face had even more worry in it than the time-stamped map of worry lines she'd seen beside her pillow that morning. He said: "Which side?"

"The right side."

"Ah. Then once you're up and about again, we'll be a matched pair." He said nothing more, but put one hand through a space in the cartwall grid and walked along beside the cart holding her hand.

One of the neighbours, Jean Baptiste Lepin, was waiting on the riverbank with his homemade skiff – wider and longer than the Point Douglas Sutherlands' dugout canoes. Kate clutched the sides of her stretcher, feeling useless and ridiculous, as they carefully loaded her onto the boat, unloaded her on the other shore and carried her up to the house. Janet had already brought down a feather mattress from upstairs and laid it in one corner of the kitchen; John and Sandy said they'd soon have a bedframe cobbled together so Kate would be up off the floor while her hip was knitting back together. Janet brought her a dram from the bottle of medicinal brandy, which softened the pain a bit but didn't mollify the aggravation of everybody being hushed and fussing over her.

Dr. Cowan came and very gently probed around Kate's hip with his fingertips, though not gently enough to keep her from embarrassing herself with gasps and winces. He pronounced that it was definitely a broken hip and the only thing for it was to stay abed and let it heal. Kate said: "It's my comeuppance."

Dr. Cowan said: "How so?"

"All my life I've been able to lord it over other women because I'm so much taller than most. A normal-heighted woman wouldn't have had so far to fall."

Dr. Cowan chuckled and shook his head. "At your age, Mrs. Sutherland, a midget falling off a footstool would break her hip."

A while after Dr. Cowan left, someone else came to the door. Kate heard Janet say: "Oh, Dr. Schultz – Dr. Cowan's already been."

Dr. Schultz spoke lowly, a sick-room voice, but it was still clear enough for Kate to hear from the far corner, "Ah. Well, I'm sure I could add nothing to Dr. Cowan's diagnosis, but a second opinion sometimes makes a patient feel more secure..."

"She's sleeping just now."

Kate silently blessed her intuitive daughter-in-law, and closed her eyes so Janet wouldn't be a liar. When she closed her eyes, her mind's-eye picture of Dr. Schultz in his black buffalo coat somehow twisted its shape into something like a vulture – hunch-shouldered and perched on a high place, watching and waiting.

Dr. Schultz said: "Well then I won't disturb her, rest is the best cure. But since I'm also a pharmacist, I brought along something... This little bottle is laudanum, tincture of opium. One drop in a glass of water to ease the pain, three drops for a long night's sleep. No charge."

"Oh no, Doctor, we couldn't –"

"I insist. You'll be easing my conscience a little. You see, I gave Mrs. Sutherland a ride to the kirk in my carriage, and I can't help but feel that if I'd left her to her regular routine she would not have had an accident."

"I'm sure that's not so, but thank you."

As soon as Dr. Schultz was gone, Kate called from her bed on the floor: "Janet, I think I'll try some of that, please." One drop in a glass of water did distance the pain, and she even managed to doze a little through the afternoon. Perhaps Dr. Schultz wasn't all that bad after all.

But when night came, Kate couldn't sleep, even after everyone had gone up to bed but John and Janet, who were tiptoeing around banking the fires and snuffing the candles. Whenever Kate felt sleep creeping near, she would try to grab it and clutch it to her, and the timid beast would scurry away again. Finally she realised the problem. Except for the occasional few nights when Sandy went off into the deep woods eastward to cut building lumber, or some like expedition, she hadn't slept alone in fifty years. Fortunately she realised it just as John and Janet started up the stairs – another minute and it would've been too late to call out softly: "Janet, dear, I think I'll try those three drops now, please." That did the trick.

It turned out Kate didn't always have to sleep alone, or at least not nap alone, because it seemed like her invalidness was a trade-off for another member of the family, which to Kate seemed like more than a fair trade. Mary Ann, who'd been colicky and worrisome all six months of her life, suddenly became a healthy baby. When it came time for Mary Ann's afternoon nap, Janet would tuck the gurgling and cooing little bundle in beside its grandmother. Kate didn't have to worry about rolling over in her sleep and crushing the wee thing, because any attempt to turn over – waking or sleeping – would set her hip on fire.

November turned into December, and still Kate's hip didn't seem to be healing much. She could sit up for awhile, if there was someone handy to prop pillows behind her, but that was about it. She could knit simple patterns lying down, or peel potatoes and carrots, but other than that the hands that had always been busy with something were the devil's playground. An increasing feature in her good-night prayers was asking for patience.

One morning Kate was jarred awake by a sound from above. She only guessed it to be morning – the windows were still dark and the only light in the room was from the embers in the hearth and stove, the ones in the stove casting red bars of light through the grate. The sound didn't come again, and Kate thought back to try and identify what she'd heard. It hadn't been a loud sound, but a wrong sound, something like a stifled shriek.

A candle came down the stairs, followed by Janet wearing a shawl over her nightdress. Janet usually dressed for the day before coming downstairs. Janet was holding a wadded handkerchief pressed over her mouth and nose, and the candlelight glittered on streaks running down from her eyes.

Janet slumped into the nearest chair at the table and took the muffling handkerchief away from her mouth. But still the sobbing sounds were muffled, held in so as not to alarm the children. Kate said softly: "Janet, dear, what's happened?"

"Oh! Oh, I'm sorry, I didn't mean to wake you, Gran..." As soon as they'd started having children, Janet and John had fallen into the habit of calling Kate and Sandy Gran and Granda, just as they called each other Mother and Father.

"You didnae wake me. What's happened?"

"Oh, it's... Mary Ann. I..." Janet twisted the sodden handkerchief in her hands, and her voice choked in on itself. "I... gave her her midnight feeding and... she was fine, she was happy, she went to sleep with a... with a smile on her face. And... when I looked in her cradle this morning... She's dead."

"Oh dear. Oh my poor dear." Kate covered her mouth with her hand and blinked against the tears welling up.

"I don't..." Janet whispered hoarsely and helplessly, "I don't know what I did wrong, what I didn't see... I don't *know*."

Kate felt her spine stiffen and the moisture in her eyes and the back of her nose quickly drying away. She patted the side of her bed and said: "Come here, dear. Janet...? Please."

Janet came and perched on the side of Kate's bed. Kate enveloped Janet's left hand in both of hers; Janet's right hand was occupied with the handkerchief. Kate said: "If the good Lord decides to take one of his little angels back sooner, He has His reasons, and they have nought to do with anything we do or don't do. Cradle death is beyond any doctor's understanding. Elizabeth McKay, I remember, woke up one morning to find her wee son dead, and she was a better mother than ever I was. Same with your Aunt Christina, though you'd've been too young to remember. And... you mustn't ever say a word of this to John, we never told him, but... he had an older sister. She died while I was carrying him. There she was one morning in her crib, cold and still. When you and John were wed, I made Sandy promise to never tell you of her, for fear you would not trust me with your children."

"Oh, no – who could I ever trust more than you? That wasn't your fault!"

Kate put her hand up to the back of Janet's neck under her unbound hair, and gently pulled her down so her head was on Kate's shoulder, and they both wept. Kate looked at the ceiling and said in her mind in Gaelic, the language the Good Lord was most likely to understand, *"Well, if lying's always a sin, it's less of a sin than bootless guilt."* She gave herself a reminder to be sure and tell Sandy as soon as they next had a chance for a murmur alone, in case Janet should murmur something to him about Mary Ann gone to meet her infant Aunt. And something else occurred to Kate that had nothing to do with God and Heaven, but she couldn't shake the old superstitions. Mary Ann had been John and Janet's thirteenth child.

Kate couldn't go to the funeral, and in the weeks following couldn't find a way to tell the children it was all right for them to go on living after their baby sister had died. Even on New Year's Day, when a group of painted Indians came as always to dance luck into the home and get their presents of currant oatcakes, the children were laughing and clapping one minute, and the next sombre and confused. When the Indians had gone on to the next house, Sandy said: "Well, Miss MacPherson, you've been slugabed long enough. Bring it in, lads."

Donald and Hugh bustled outside without bothering with their coats. Kate looked around. There were stifled giggles and anticipation, but no one would give her a hint. Hugh and Donald came back in carrying a wooden armchair, the chair she'd usually sat in at the table. She'd noticed some time ago that it was gone, but had assumed it had just been set out of the way while she was still taking her meals in bed. The boys set it down on the floor, Hugh butted the heel of his hand against its back, and instead of teetering on its front legs or tipping over, the chair glided forward, and kept on gliding. As the chair came past the table, Kate saw that it had miniature cartwheels fixed to its legs, the back ones bigger than the front. Everyone was laughing at her gaping astoundment and she didn't mind a bit.

Hugh called over the laughter: "Granda's been working at it in the barn for weeks."

Sandy said: "The spokes would be an embarrassment to an honest carpenter, but they hold."

John gently lifted his mother out of her bed and onto the chair. There was a ledge built onto the front legs for her to prop her feet on, and the back wheels were just high enough to get her hands on the rims. She gave the wheels a push and it moved – it didn't turn very well, but it moved. She propelled herself around the room laughing like an idiot, and everybody else was laughing with her. But they didn't know the entirety of what she was laughing at. Part of her laughter was at her old lies coming home to roost: when she did get healed enough to go back to kirk on Sundays, how was she going to explain that her husband's arthritis was too crippling for him to come to church but not so crippling he couldn't finick together a set of working wheels fixed to a chair?

January became February, and still the most movement her hip would tolerate was a few halting steps from her bed to the chair. On a Saturday when most of the family was outdoors, John, Hugh and Donald came back inside looking mischievous. Hugh said: "Get your cloak, Granny, we're going skating."

Ignoring her protests that they'd all gone mad, they bundled her up warm, and Donald – who was bigger than his father now – picked her up and carried her outside. She stopped flailing as he started down the path to the river, and instead clung to his neck for dear life. As the path levelled out on the river, and vertical and horizontal became themselves again, Kate loosened her death grip enough to look around. At one corner of the piled-up snow surrounding the wide swath of ice that the Sutherland and Inkster boys kept clear, stood the bane and balm of Kate's existence: Sandy Sutherland. He was standing beside a contraption shaped something like a chair, but only planks pegged to a frame. It stood on two roughly-bevelled, gleaming wooden runners – gleaming with ice to help them slide.

John and Donald settled her onto the contraption and tucked a quilt around her, while Hugh sat in the snow to strap his skate blades to his shoes. Then Hugh stood up and put his hands on the backrest, the others stood back, and she was gliding over the ice with the fresh wind blowing through her hair. Children were skating all around her, laughing and calling her name and falling happily on their wool-padded bottoms. Out on the snow, another bunch of children were playing fox-and-geese on a tramped-down maze of pathways. The cloud machines were working.

Her skate chair halted and her Christmas Boy crouched in front of her, saying: "What's wrong, Gran? Was I going too fast? Why are you crying?"

"Oh, it's… It's not fair, Hugh. I've had such a lucky life, so many blessings. And I fear it cannot be the same for you and all the others. I fear I've used up all the family's good luck on myself."

CHAPTER 20

Hugh was digging last year's cow manure into this year's garden – horse manure carried too many weed seeds – when he heard the voice. The voice would've taken him by surprise even if he'd been thinking in the present, but at the moment he'd been chuckling to himself remembering something his Granda had once said to him: *"When ye're cursing pulling weeds in the hot and muggy sun, try and remember how much shit other people had to shovel to make the garden."*

Most farmers at Red River said the soil was so rich and deep it didn't need manuring, and just dumped their barn-scrapings in the river. Not the Point Douglas Sutherlands. As Gran put it: *"If you do not feed your land, eventually it will stop feeding you."*

Over the past eight months as the only school-age child at home, Hugh had spent so much time talking to his grandparents – or listening to them – that sometimes the present seemed less real to him than the days of the Fur Trade War, when a farmer would be tending his fields with one ear cocked for the sound of galloping hoofbeats that could mean Mr. Grant's wild riders coming to burn the colony. So it caught him off guard when a clear, alto voice called from behind him: "Hallo, Hugh Sutherland."

It also caught him off balance, about to lever another wad of manure off the wheelbarrow. He swung his off-foot back, let go of the homemade manure fork so he could pinwheel his arms to realign himself, and just managed to keep from falling into the dollops of manure he'd already spread across the tilled earth.

It was Nancy Prince, sitting on her buckskin-spotted pony with her black hair glossy against the soft green haze of budding trees. She put one hand up to her mouth to cover a giggle and said: "Sorry, I didn't mean to scare you."

"No, I was just, um…"

"Working. You're always working, every time I pass by – chopping wood, hoeing in the garden, ploughing in your field across the river."

"Every time?"

She shrugged. "Oh, you know, sometimes I have to ride by on the other side of the river, or in a canoe going fishing with my brothers. But today I had to come right here. My grandfather wants to meet you."

"Your grandfather?" When Hugh said just 'my grandfather,' people assumed which of the two he meant. But he wasn't sure what to assume with Wauh Oonae.

"My father's father."

That would be Mr. King, the famous and infamous and fabulously old Chief Peguis. Hugh said somewhat nervously, "Why?"

"Because he wants to."

"Um… When?"

"Now."

"Well, um, I'd better, um… Just a minute." Hugh propped his manure fork and hoe against the wheelbarrow and went into the house. On his way there he noticed something strange, and one reason why Wauh Oonae's 'hallo' had caught him so much off guard. The dogs were lounging in a patch of sunlight by the house. They hadn't barked when Nancy Prince walked her horse into the yard.

Before stepping into the house, Hugh scraped most of the mud off his boots on the cast iron blade fixed beside the doorstep. But he knew he hadn't got it all, so once inside he stopped and stood just past the door. Da was gone away to a Council meeting for the day, so Mum was who to ask. She was sitting at the table making a ball out of the wool wound around Christina's outstretched hands. Gran was in her wheeled chair at the other end of the table, trying to do the same thing with James, whose hands and patience were both smaller than Christina's. Mum turned toward the doorway when Hugh came in, turning her chair rather than twisting her swollen midriff – poor little Mary Ann wasn't going to be Hugh's last sister or brother.

Hugh said: "Um, Mum, I aren't finished the garden chore yet, but someone just now come to tell me someone wants to see me."

"Who wants to see you?"

"Mr. King."

There was a pause. Mum and Gran looked at each other. Then Gran looked at Hugh and said: "*That* Mr. King? Chief Peguis…?"

Hugh nodded.

Mum said: "Why does Mr. King want to see you?"

"I dunno, me whatever. Just – someone just come and told me Mr. King wants me to go see him today."

Mum said: "Who came and told you?"

"His granddaughter."

Mum and Gran looked at each other again. Then Gran said: "Hugh, if – Yes, Jamie, you can put your hands down, but don't fidget them or we will have to start over… Hugh, if Chief Peguis wants to see you today, then you must. He can't have many days left, though the Lord knows people have been saying that of him for donkey's years. But you must take something with you, mayhap a pinch of your grandfather's tobacco –"

"No," Mum put in, "Hugh's still too young to be bringing someone tobacco. But the Indians all like berry-brittle. Take one from the pantry, Hugh."

Hugh tugged off his boots, reached down his Cree shoulder pouch from the wall of coats and hats and such hanging on pegs, and padded to the pantry. He rummaged through the shelves of baskets, birchbark rogans and crockery until he found the leathery cakes they'd made last fall by mashing wild berries in wooden pans and letting them dry. Over the winter, Mum would occasionally break pieces off one for the children to have with dinner, with a little sugar when there was sugar to be had. There were three red ones left and two purple. Hugh tucked one of the blueberry ones in his pouch, added in a half-wheel of bannock and went back to the door. Instead of tugging on his boots again, he slipped into his moccasins – he only wore stiff-soled things on his feet when he had to, and he didn't have to for riding. As he stepped out the door, Gran called after him: "Tell Mr. King Catherine MacPherson says porridge beats pemmican when your teeth go."

Nancy Prince had climbed down off her pony and was sitting with her back against the old oak tree, holding Cheengwun's halter rope, with two of the dogs pillowing their heads on her outstretched legs. Hugh said: "Sorry, I thought I'd just be a minute."

She cocked her head at him curiously, like the dogs did when they encountered something odd, then shook it. "No matter." She got up and walked with him to the pasture fence, which simplified matters because the farm ponies came over to investigate Cheengwun. Hugh bridled and saddled Brownie, and he and Wauh Oonae set off north at a bouncing trot; there was a lot of road between St. Boniface and St. Peters, or The Indian Settlement. So much road that Hugh wondered whether she'd set off from St. Peters in the middle of the night, to get to the Point Douglas Sutherlands' by mid-morning.

When they saw a clear stretch of road ahead of them, they'd kick their ponies into a gallop, then let them slow down to a walk to breathe themselves out. Then they could talk without straining their voices, but Hugh couldn't think of much to say. He very much wanted her to explain the mystery of why Chief Peguis would want to see some Kildonan farmboy, but when he'd asked her that before it hadn't got him anywhere. He very much wanted to ask her some other things, too, but settled for: "So, um, did you have a good winter?"

"Pretty good. Colder'n last winter, eh?"

"Yeah, but not as much snow."

"No, not as much snow."

That made him feel particularly foolish, and wondered if she was thinking the same thing – usually colder winters came with less snow than less cold ones, as any fool knew. He said: "Well, and, uh, last summer's buffalo hunts, they went pretty good, too?"

"Pretty good. An uncle of mine got killed."

"Oh, I'm sorry, I, uh…"

"It's all right – he wasn't an uncle I knew real good. And it happens – running buffalo ain't like killing steers."

"No, no, I guess not." He couldn't think of anything else to say. He hadn't seen her since the winter night he'd kissed her out behind James McKay's shed. Since then he'd kissed other girls: Betsy Bannerman last New Year's, and Janet Gunn in a dark corner at George Matheson's wedding party. Now, riding along beside Wauh Oonae, the other kisses made him feel a little ashamed of his flightiness, but also a little more experienced. It also made him wonder whether she'd kissed other boys since then.

After another stint of galloping, when the sun was starting to work its way down from the top of its spring arc, Hugh began thinking seriously about the half-wheel of bannock in his pouch. Nancy said: "There's a stream up ahead, we can stop a minute to water the horses and take a quick bite to eat."

"Huh. How'd you know I was just now thinking about something to eat?"

"Your stomach told me."

"Oh."

"Hey, another couple miles and my stomach'd be talking to yours. I mean, um – There, just ahead, you can see where the trail dips down into the trees..."

A wooded hollow wouldn't've been the best place to stop once the mosquitoes and flies came to life, but this early in the year it felt protected and hushed – no sounds penetrated but the sighing of the pines and the burble of the little stream. They slid down off their ponies and let them nibble at the stream and the fresh new greens around it. Hugh pulled the half-circle of bannock out of his Cree beaded shoulder pouch, wishing he'd brought more. Wauh Oonae produced a flat stick of dried meat and a small knife from her Ojibway quillworked shoulder pouch, clamped one end of the stick in her front teeth, sawed it off with her knife, then handed the stick and the knife to Hugh. As he started sawing, she said around her mouthful: "Watch your nose."

Hugh handed back the dried meat and knife, and bit down hard on the piece in his mouth. His teeth told him he'd made a mistake. Wauh Oonae giggled and said: "No, it's *real* dry, you got to wetten it," and sucked in her cheeks to show she was squeezing mouth-juice into it.

Hugh broke a piece off his bannock and handed it to her. They sat chewing dry bannock and dried buffalo, washing it down with handfuls of creek. Hugh took the cake of dried blueberry mash out of his pouch, weighed it in his hand, then shook his head sadly, "No, we can't – it's for your grandfather."

"Here." She neatly sliced off about an inch of it and handed it back. "I won't tell if you won't tell." The little extra bit of flavour did help the woody buffalo go down.

Hugh would've gladly stayed in that hollow with Nancy Prince all day, but as soon as the food was done she put her knife back in her pouch and said: "We better get going." They let the freshened ponies have a good gallop, then slowed as the trail turned twisty.

The road wound through a long stretch of woods, with St. Andrews rapids heard but unseen off to the left. Then there was a break in the woods and a very small farm on the river side. An oddly chunky young man and a larger, older man were hoeing in the garden patch. The odd part of the boy's build was that his back was long for his legs, and his shoulders three times as wide as his hips. But that was far from freakish at Red River. A lot of Metis family trees were rooted in old voyageurs, and the North West Company had preferred paddlers with strong backs but short legs to take up less room in its freight canoes. This boy carried it to extremes, though, like he'd been bred through a long line of short-legged men.

The boy turned to look at the horses passing by, leaning on his grounded hoe. Then he suddenly began to wave enthusiastically, churning his right arm back and forth above his head and bouncing up and down like a jumping-jack with his left hand on the hoe haft. He whipped off his hat to wave it, and the sun glinted on metallic blonde hair.

Wauh Oonae said: "That's Norbert."

"Huh? Parisien?"

"Yep."

Hugh just had time to stand up in his stirrups and wave back before the woods cut them off from view. He sat back down on his saddle and said: "I wouldn't've guessed – he's got so much bigger since I saw him last."

"So have we."

"I hope he understands we didn't have time to stop and say hello."

"I'm sure he does – as much as Norbert understands anything the same ways other people do. That's where I stayed last night, and he was all excited you'd be passing by today, but I think he forgot till he saw us, and even then it taken him a minute."

"Huh. Strange they live out here in the middle of nowhere."

"Not so strange – they're in the middle of his father's hunting grounds. Long time ago Norbert's father got his leg broke on the buffalo hunt, so he can't ride no better'n a white man. So he cuts wood – sells a lot of firewood to The Company."

The woods petered off and the road passed by the big stone and whitewashed timber houses of Little Britain, and the Stone Fort across the river. As the riverbank lowered, the trail angled toward it, and soon they were riding along a strip of well-worn ground between the river and log cabins with brown children playing in the yards. Every cabin had one or two birchbark canoes or a wooden boat pulled up on the shore in front of it. Wauh Oonae turned her pony in toward a log cabin considerably bigger than the others – actually several cabins joined together, with a buffalo hide tipi and a bark wigwam on either side. As Hugh and Nancy climbed down off their ponies, she said: "Back at your place, when you came back out of your house, you said you was sorry – sorry it took you longer to talk to your people than you figured. Don't say that to my grandfather."

"But, uh, he wasn't even there."

"I mean don't say 'I'm sorry' about anything. My grandfather's lived next to white people a long time, but he's still Saulteaux-Ojibway. An Ojibway can't ever say 'I'm sorry' for something that happened. It'd mean he thinks so much of himself he thinks he can make things happen, or not happen. Things just happen. You understand?"

Hugh wasn't sure he did, but said: "Okay."

Nancy Prince stepped to the cabin door and opened it without knocking. Hugh followed her inside. Although it was a warmish day, it was a good deal warmer inside. A strong fire was burning in the hearth, and an old woman was bending over a steaming pot of something fishy. There was a long table with at least a dozen chairs and no one in them. The only light was from the fire and a couple of parchment windows.

Wauh Oonae proceeded past the old woman without saying anything and Hugh followed her, toward what looked to be a pile of rags and old blankets heaped near the other side of the hearth. As his eyes adjusted to the light, he saw it was an old man lounged on the packed-earth floor, propped against a woven willow backrest and smoking a meerschaum pipe. Spread in front of him were several mats of woven rushes dyed in varicoloured patterns, the same kind of 'Indian mats' that were on the floor at home.

Nancy sat down on one of the mats in the pretty posture of Indian women: leaned on one hip with her legs tucked up against her other hip. Hugh sat down cross-legged on the mat next to hers. He tried not to stare at Chief Peguis, but it wasn't easy. Mr. King's face was like a crumpled pancake of old leather, with two holes where his nose used to be. His nose was said to've been bitten off by accident, when he tried to separate two young men fighting in a wigwam, and one of the grapplers thrashing around on the floor mistook it for the nose of the man trying to strangle him. That had happened before Hugh's grandparents came to the Selkirk Colony, and even back then Chief Peguis had said to the young man who'd bitten off his nose: *"Don't feel bad, I'm an old man, it won't be long people will laugh at me for having no nose."* By all reckoning, he was at least ninety years old now.

Hugh sat waiting. No one said anything. There was no sound but the soft crackle of the fire, and Mr. King's wheezing breathing and sucking on his pipe. Hugh couldn't think what he was supposed to do. After a while, he pulled the cake of blueberry leather out of his pouch and extended it toward Mr. King. An eagle claw of a hand came out of the folds of the layers of blankets, took the cake and brought it close to the muddy black and yellow eyes. Hugh remembered that the few Indians who lived to grow old usually started growing blind, from years of living in smoky tipis.

Chief Peguis sniffed at the cake through the holes in his face, then tucked it away in a pouch or pocket somewhere under the blankets and said: "Huh. I should give something to you… Maybe I think about it." His voice was like the rattle of autumn leaves, but there was still a trace of resonance within it, just enough to carry across the space between him and the mats horseshoed in front of him.

Hugh said: "My grandmother said to tell you Catherine MacPherson says porridge beats pemmican when your teeth go."

"Huh." It might've been a laugh. "She is the one we used to call Big Red. Powerful woman. Some of my foolish young men used to think not much of your grandfather – skinny little fella, and lame… I would told them, if there was any use tell such young men anything, 'A man who's husband to such a woman, you gotta think that's some man.' And he came back from Seven Oaks – not many white men did."

Hugh heard a kind of jingling behind him and turned to look. The old woman from the fire was coming toward them with a silver tea tray – the jingling was the empty cups and saucers. Seen up front, she wasn't such an old woman after all. She set the tray down on the floor between Mr. King and Nancy Prince and went away.

Wauh Oonae poured from a silver teapot into two china cups and a pewter mug with a big handle, then handed the mug to Chief Peguis and one of the cups and saucers to Hugh. There was no milk or sweetener, but from the fumes that had come out of the pewter mug when the hot tea went in, there'd already been some extra flavouring in Mr. King's cup. Hugh was happy to have plain tea, or anything wet – his mouth was dry from trying to think of what else he could say to Mr. King, and still having no idea why Nancy's grandfather wanted to meet him.

Chief Peguis smacked his lips and his gums after his first sip, then said: "Your father, Hugh Sutherland, he is on the Council of Assiniboia. What he say about what I been saying about our land?"

Hugh wondered if that might be the reason he'd been summoned, but it seemed a stretch. He and everyone else in the settlement that could read knew of Chief Peguis's declarations published in *The Nor'Wester* over the last few years: that the treaty he'd signed with the Earl of Selkirk fifty years ago had just been a good-faith agreement to sell land to Lord Selkirk when he came back to Red River. Since the Earl had never come back – went and died young in France – the Saulteaux's tribal lands had never been sold. Or so said Mr. King.

Hugh said: "Um, would if I could, sir, but I can't tell you what my Da thinks about all that 'cause I don't know. He don't talk about what goes on in Council meetings, unless it's a funny story, at least not around the supper table. But my Gran and Granda both say you're up to something."

"'*Up* to something'?"

Hugh thought maybe he'd gone too far, but then he saw out of the corner of his eye Wauh Oonae smiling, even though she was looking down at her teacup. A wash of old stories came back to him, usually told with a chuckle around the hay-common campfire waiting for midnight, or on the riverbank waiting for the fish to bite: that Chief Peguis's sacred 'ancestral lands' hadn't been Saulteaux land until he moved his tribe in from the east only a year or two before the first Selkirk colonists arrived; that when the Anglican missionaries had been about to relocate from St. Peters and take all their Church Missionary Society money with them, Mr. King had written to the Society headquarters, mentioning by the way that half his tribe still hadn't converted to Christianity and there were a lot of Catholic missionaries lurking around… There were too many stories for Hugh to remember all at once, but they all came to the same point. He said: "Um, well, sir, both my grandparents say you're a wily old bugger who'd pull any trick out of a hat if it'd gain an inch for your family or your tribe."

This time Chief Peguis definitely did laugh. When he'd wheezed his breath back he said flatly: "The problem with white people is the ones as would be easiest to do business with are never the ones you have to do business with." He tilted the pewter mug to drink the last of his tea, then held it out to his granddaughter. When she took it from him, he twitched his head in the direction whence the not-so-old woman had brought the tea tray. Nancy shook her head. Chief Peguis sighed and the blanket folds over his shoulders shrugged. Wauh Oonae re-filled the mug from the teapot and handed it back to him.

With both hands wrapped around the warm mug, Mr. King said: "In other days, Hugh Sutherland, I would wait a few more years before I tell my granddaughter fetch you to me. But now… It is a long way from here to White Horse Plains, but I think the ghost horse is coming for me soon anyways. Some nights, I hear his hooves, walking slow around my tent."

"You think Mr. Grant has been riding him long enough?"

Chief Peguis's head twitched, and the age-smoked eyes fixed on Hugh more sharply. "What you know of Mr. Grant?"

"I shook his hand once. When he was sick and dying, Gran and Granda took me and my brother out to Granttown at White Horse Plains to meet him. And, I've heard a lot of stories, from my grandparents."

"You listen to your grandparents talk of old days?"

"Sure." It seemed like an odd question – who wouldn't? "More now that I'm out of school and home all the time."

Chief Peguis's eyes drifted to his granddaughter, then shifted to the middle distance and he nodded. "Too many young people today got no time to listen – too busy. But if no one hears – all the things that did happen, all the good things, all the bad things, all the mistakes, they never did happen. The children that do listen, they are a treasure to us, and will be a treasure to the ones that did not trouble to listen till it was too late."

Nancy Prince had lowered her head and her eyes bashfully. There hadn't been enough sun yet this year to darken her skin too much for Hugh to tell that she was blushing. But a shy smile dimpled the blush, and Hugh figured if she was a kitten she'd be purring.

Mr. King's eyes shifted back to Hugh. "So, you and your brother shooked the hand of Mr. Grant…"

"Just me. My brother was too afraid."

"Huh. Your brother was wise to be afraid. Grant was the most dangerous man I ever met, in all my days. But you were wiser not to be afraid. He was never a danger to anyone who meant no harm to his family or his people. Wahpeston," Mr. Grant's Cree name, "was a complicated man. Are you a complicated man, Hugh Sutherland?"

Hugh was a little bit pleased and a great deal surprised to be called a man, but he didn't know what was the right answer to the question. So he just told the truth, as far as he could figure it. "No, I don't 'spect so, from all I can tell and what other people seem to see. I mean, *things* can get complicated, and I confuse easy, but if anything I figure I'm prob'ly more simple than I should be, me whatever."

"There are many worse things to be. What do you want, Hugh Sutherland?"

Hugh naturally looked at Wauh Oonae for some clue as to what that wide question might be about. Mr. King let out a throaty rumble that might've been a chuckle, and for some reason said: "Uh-huh, I can see *that*. But what I mean to ask you is – damn, what's that crazy thing white people say…? Oh, uh-huh. What you want to be when you grow up? Doctor, lawyer, Indian Chief…?"

"Well, uh, I dunno – guess I'm short on ambition. Guess eventually I'll get a farm of my own, a *small* farm – you get too big you got no time for hunting and fishing and just going for a ride to nowhere in particular sometimes. And I guess I'll get a…" It was Hugh's turn to blush, he could feel his face hottening up. "… a family, if I'm lucky."

"That is all you want to do, is live?"

"'Fraid so, that's all." Hugh was about to add 'sorry,' but caught himself. "Told you I was simple-minded."

"Huh." The noseless head bobbed slowly back and forth, like Chief Peguis was thinking something over. Then the bobbing stopped and he said: "You got a long ride home, Hugh. Wauh Oonae will stay and talk with me awhile."

Hugh stood up and looked down at Nancy Prince. She looked up at him and nodded he should go, but she was smiling and her eyes were glistening.

As Hugh started turning to go, Chief Peguis said: "Hugh Sutherland – you brought me a present, and I said maybe I should give something to you. I think I already did."

Hugh didn't quite know what was meant by that – maybe it would explain itself later – so he just nodded and went on his way. Everything outside had a soft, golden glow to it, as happened sometimes in the last hour of a clear day when the sunlight came straight across the prairie. One thing he knew for certain was true among the answers he'd given Chief Peguis – that he was easily confused – because he had no idea what had just happened, or why.

He didn't think about it in the stints when Brownie was galloping – too busy keeping his seat and watching for anything on the road ahead. But when they slowed to a trot or a walk, he mulled it over. He didn't believe mulling was his strong suit, but there was nobody could do it for him.

He tried on the possibility that the reason Mr. King had sent Nancy Prince to fetch him was that business about the Council of Assiniboia, and what Hugh might've heard of Da's opinions on Chief Peguis's land rights declarations. But it didn't fit. The more Hugh tried to make it fit, the more it seemed that he'd been right when it'd first occurred to him: it was too much of a stretch. And Mr. King hadn't seemed at all disappointed when Hugh said he didn't know tiddlywinks about Da's opinion of the Saulteaux land claims; he'd just casually gone on to another topic of conversation. Even though Chief Peguis was 'a wily old bugger' who could hide or dissemble any emotion, there was no practical reason for him to exercise his wiles on a sixteen year old farmboy.

With that possible explanation for the summons eliminated, Hugh tried to think of another and couldn't – except for the one that had been lurking at the back of his mind but was too impossibly beautiful to think out loud. But since he couldn't come up with any alternative… Nancy Prince Wauh Oonae was pretty obviously her grandfather's sunshine. If she'd talked to him about the boy she hoped to marry in a few years, and if Chief Peguis figured he wouldn't live to see it, or even next winter… *"In other days, Hugh Sutherland, I would wait a few more years before I tell my granddaughter to fetch you to me…"*

Hugh kept telling himself he was being swell-headed and ridiculous, but he couldn't stop. He started seeing pictures of a snug little house by the river, with him and Nancy hoeing in their garden, and black-haired, green- and dark-eyed children playing in the yard…

He eventually realised that the light wasn't golden anymore, it was almost gone, and that he'd been letting Brownie plod along at a walk for some time. And there was a gnawing in his stomach that even daydreams couldn't override. If he'd been on the Kildonan side of the river he could've stopped at any house and asked for a bit of bannock. Even on this side of the river, he could've knocked on any door if he was in trouble, but an hour past suppertime and still a ways to home hardly qualified as lost in a blizzard.

It was way too early in the year for any kind of berries. But there was still just enough sunlight left that he could stop and search the roadside for wild greens: goosefoot or pigweed or dandelions. There was a better use for the light, though, so instead of stopping he kicked Brownie into the last gallop they could have before it came full dark.

By the time they reached the stream where he and Nancy'd stopped for lunch, now moving at a cautious trot, a half moon was half up over the horizon. Hugh turned off the road to let Brownie and him have a short drink and a quick breather. The creek water slightly blunted the teeth chewing in Hugh's stomach, but as he trotted on through the treacherous moonlight – there one minute and cloud-masked the next – past the warm yellow lights of parchment-windowed houses and successive barkings of yard dogs, another gnawing came on him. Soon Wauh Oonae would be gone on the summer buffalo hunt, and then the autumn hunt, and before and after those he'd be working dawn-to-dusk helping Da get the fields planted and then the harvest…

By the time Hugh got home, the house was dark except for a pale light through the back windows of the ground floor. He unsaddled Brownie by starlight and went inside. The light was a lone candle on the little bedside table Granda had made for Gran. As Hugh came through the door, she laid down her Bible and said: "Your mother left out a cold supper." On the table was a cloth-covered plate of bread and cheese. Gran beckoned him with one hand, so he carried the plate and a chair over beside her bed. She said: "How is Chief Peguis?"

"Um…" he stalled to chew and swallow. "He thinks he'll die soon, but he seems pretty cheerful about it."

"Well, he's had a life and then some. And how is his granddaughter, Nancy Prince?"

Hugh almost choked, but coughed the wad of bread and cheese out of his throat, mashed it quickly with his back teeth and swallowed safely. "Um, how did you know that's her name?"

"Well, that is the same girl who let you ride on the back of her horse back and forth from the Corbett trial, is it not?"

"How did you…?" Then Hugh stopped himself from finishing a foolish question. Of course Gran knew, and so did everybody else at Red River looking for a topic of conversation to chew up a few minutes of a winter evening. "Yes, Gran. Nancy Prince. Wauh Oonae." The names tasted sweet in his mouth. He'd never spoken them aloud to anybody else before.

"Hugh…" Gran's voice was pained, but not like the pain from her hip, more like she had something painful to say. "You like this girl…?"

"Um, well, uh, yeah, I'd say 'like' don't touch on it, Gran."

"And she likes you?"

"Uh, well, I'd say… I think so, I hope so, I guess so." He thought back over the only 'possible explanation' he'd been able to come up with. It was embarrassing and thrilling to say aloud, "Yeah, I'd say she does."

"Hugh… it's nice that you have friends, especially pretty girl friends at your age. But you must know it can't ever go any further than that."

She might just as well have slapped him. Suddenly the possibility he'd started to believe became ridiculous again; there must be something he'd misinterpreted about the day. "Why not?"

"Come now, Hugh, you know why not."

"Um, no, I…" He put his half-full plate on her bedside table and pinched his eyes shut. "I'm sorry, Gran, I really don't… understand."

She put one large, gnarled hand out to rest on his left hand resting on his knee. "She is different, dear. Different from us."

He opened his eyes again. "Different? How do you know? You've never met her."

"I don't need to to know that. All the people in the Indian Settlement – St. Peters – they are different from us."

Hugh drew his hand out from under his grandmother's and pushed himself farther back in his chair. Gran looked different than she had all his life, and up until just a moment ago – now craggy and crabbed and cold. All that fine talk about skin colour and so on meaning nothing, but when it came down to it the talk meant nothing. He said, in a more distanced voice than he'd ever expected to use with his grandmother, "What do you mean 'different'?"

"You know as well as I do, Hugh, you don't need me to spell it out."

"I'm afraid I do, Gran. How are all the people at St. Peters different from us here?"

"It's as plain as the nose on your face, Hugh – they're Church of England." Gran closed her mouth on that pronouncement, but promptly opened it again. "Hugh, stop laughing, ssh! For Heaven's sake, Hugh, you'll wake the house! What's got into you?"

CHAPTER 21

Agnes Campbell Farquharson stepped out the front door of Dr. Schultz's White Store, looked down the empty road leading to Portage la Prairie and the September sunset – wild rose pink sky ribbed with burgundy clouds – then looked up and down the empty road leading from Fort Garry to the Stone Fort, then stepped back inside, bolted the door, turned the chained door sign so the Open side faced inward, and went upstairs to Dr. Schultz's bedchamber. She'd been living there all summer, since Dr. Schultz had employed her to mind the store while he was gone to Canada. Technically he'd employed her father, but as per usual if any Farquharson was going to take on actual responsibility for anything it would be Agnes or her sister, and Laura wasn't exactly suited to dealing with a raft of strangers across a shop counter on a daily basis. And Agnes didn't exactly mind spending the summer sleeping in Dr. Schultz's bed and perusing his personal possessions and private papers.

Agnes was aware that some people at Red River thought it humourous that Dr. 'British Empire' Schultz – who trumpeted constantly that the only worse fate than Rupert's Land continue being ruled by The Company would be joining the United States – had climbed into bed with the White Stores Company of Minnesota, U.S.A. But as far as Agnes was concerned, it was immature to not understand that politics was politics and business was business and never the twain shall meet – except in circumstances where they could grease each others' wheels. And American politics were a particularly strange and savage brand. Anyone who doubted that had only to look at the news that had come north in the spring, just as Dr. Schultz was about to embark westward: the Americans had finally stopped killing each other wholesale and ended their Civil War, so then they'd turned around and killed their President. Never enough blood.

Up in Dr. Schultz's bedroom, Agnes stripped off her day dress and corset and relaxed into the Chinese silk kimono she'd added to her father's bill at a New York City millinery shop the day before they took the train west. She went into the kitchen – an oversized room with an oversized table, waiting for the day when waves of immigrants would arrive needing temporary lodging in the unoccupied rooms above the store and warehouse – and ate a boiled egg for dinner, along with a half-slice of bread and a bowl of the purple berries called 'saskatoons,' which the Indian women came around bartering this time of year. It was a pleasure to be able to eat what she wanted when she wanted, instead of being tied to her father's and sister's mealtimes, not to mention doing much of their cooking for them.

After dinner, Agnes took out the day's pencilled receipts and inked them into the big ledger: *2 oz. Plug tobacco, 1 small jar Epsom salts, 1/2 lb. Pig lead, ditto gunpowder, 3 yrds calico...* Then it was time for recreation and research. She went back into Dr. Schultz's bedchamber and looked around. There wasn't anything in there she hadn't thoroughly gone through already: his business records, his wardrobe, letters from his family in Upper Canada and other correspondents... She thought it quite likely that she knew more about Dr. John Christian Schultz and his activities and relations than he knew himself. She carried her lamp into his examining room across the hall. She couldn't see anything in there, either, that she hadn't already inspected more than once and carefully put back exactly as she'd found it. But there was one thing she'd expected to find and hadn't.

She knew from Dr. Schultz's personal papers that he'd been enrolled in the medical school at Queen's College, Kingston, Upper Canada from 1858 to '60, and then at Victoria College, Coburg, Upper Canada during the term of 1860 - '61. But among those papers there was no certificate of graduation, no diploma, no medical degree. Of that she was certain, but she wasn't certain she might not have missed a piece of paper when examining his examining room. So now she went through the room once more, turning every page in his medical texts, taking every last article out of his doctor satchel and the lone drawer in his doctor desk, even getting up on a chair to see if there might be something propped atop the window frame she couldn't see... After she'd meticulously combed through the whole room, she took an overall survey from the doorway to see if there were any places she might've missed. None. It wasn't there. "Well, well," Agnes murmured to herself. "Well, well."

Partway through the next morning she heard gunfire, a lot of it. Since there were no customers at the moment, she went upstairs to get a wider field of vision, leaving the halfbreed part-time stockboy to mind the shop. Not that she completely trusted him, but she knew he knew she knew the entire inventory down to the last straight pin and twist of tobacco. If the stockboy hadn't happened to be on duty, she would've sat on her curiosity rather than going upstairs. She wasn't about to adopt the slipshod habits of the locals, wherein customers might wander around in an untended store, sometimes finding articles the storekeeper had said weren't in stock, while all the while the shopkeeper might be out back splitting firewood.

From Dr. Schultz's bedroom window, Agnes could see Fort Garry. In front of it, little toy men were firing guns in the air, and so were others on the other side of the river. There was a lot of colour on the east bank, and a lot of carts milling about, and the ferry and a York boat were crossing toward them. So the latest cart-train was back from St. Paul, quite possibly the last one of the year.

Agnes checked her hair in the mirror above the washstand. It was still neatly ribboned at the back of her neck, making a wavy, dark halo around her face. There were a few escaped strands, but she decided they correctly conveyed the impression that although she cared about her appearance, she wasn't obsessed with frivolities when there was work to be done. She went back downstairs and debated whether it would be more effective if she were rearranging stock shelves, or sweeping up. Then a better idea occurred, so she hurried back upstairs to fetch the big ledger book and rescue yesterday's pencilled, scrap paper receipts from the wastebasket.

A few months previous, soon after Agnes had taken charge of Schultz's White Store, she'd come across a long, shallow, empty wooden crate that had originally been used for transporting half-a-dozen rifles, and she'd set it face-down behind the counter, to put the counter-top at waist height instead of breast height. Now she stepped up onto it, smoothed out the sheaf of crumpled receipts beside it and took up a pencil to tic off the entries as though double-checking. She knew she wouldn't find any mistakes; one of the unfeminine attributes she tried to hide from dashing young army officers and such was that she was very good with figures, and not the kind they would be interested in.

She expected it wouldn't take long for Dr. Schultz's long legs to cover the ground between Fort Garry and his home, and she was proven right. When the shop door swung open, jingling the bell above it, she was certain it wasn't a customer – there'd be no customers today, with all the excitement of the cart-train coming in. But she looked up from the ledger with her shopkeeper's smile on, saying: "Good morning, how may we help – Oh! Dr. Schultz!"

He did look splendid, in a new suit of grey broadcloth only slightly dappled with travelling dust, and a broad-brimmed felt hat which he now swept off. He also looked a little surprised and confused. "Oh, Miss Farquharson, I, uh, wasn't expecting…"

"Father had another job of work offered him for the summer, and he couldn't be in two places at once, so I volunteered."

"Oh. Well… that was very good of you, but, I'm sorry – if'n I'd had any idea it would take up *your* time I would've made other arrangements."

Agnes made a mental note that 'if'n' would have to be corrected when an unobtrusive opportunity arose, but just said: "Not at all; I've been glad to do it. Spending the summer away from the family's been a bit of a holiday. And it's been useful to the family that I work off at least some of the debt we've incurred. I like to be useful."

"Well, I, um… thank you."

Agnes smiled. There were few things she found more pleasant than a big strong man being abashed in her presence, and she'd never met a bigger, stronger man than Dr. John Christian Schultz. She tucked her pencil into her hair and said: "I was just double-checking yesterday's receipts against what I entered in the ledger last night. My first month or so here I spent my evenings going over the past accounts and found a few errors – only the kind of minor misadditions an overbusy man might make at the end of a long day's work – but they all balance now."

The screeching of several Red River carts intruded from the south. Dr. Schultz said: "Oh, that'll be my freight consignment – I told the Train Captain if he didn't have it here the same day as me I'd start docking the freight charges. I could hitch up the carriage and drive you home and then deal with –"

"Oh, you'd best not leave the drovers waiting, they'd get surly – surly or drunk, or both. And if I attend to the waybill, you'll have your hands free to speed the unloading." Preempting further discussion, she stepped down from her crate and proceeded back through the banks of shelves behind the counter to the cavernous warehouse beyond. He followed her.

Agnes found it more than pleasant to have the two of them working together: she checking off items on the waybill as they came in, he hoisting crates that two drovers couldn't lift. He'd stripped off his suitcoat, and she could see the muscles in his back straining the seams of his waistcoat. When the last bolt of cloth and barrel of molasses had been tucked away, and the drovers hurrying back to their homecoming, Dr. Schultz said: "That was thirsty work, Miss Farquharson," and looked around the stockroom. "I think there was a keg of sherry on the waybill…"

"South-west corner, on top of the crate of Ladies' Footwear." While Dr. Schultz malleted a tap into the bunghole, Agnes delicately pried open a crate marked Tea Service and fished two china cups out of the straw. She perched on a crate across the aisle from Dr. Schultz, sipping her sherry and looking around at the kegs and crates of money-to-be in the dust-flecked, golden light through the loading gate. She said: "It appears you've had a very successful journey."

"Passable, as far as business goes. More than passable in other ways."

"Oh? In which ways?" Even if he'd been intending to go on anyway, there was no harm in encouraging him.

"I was lucky enough to have some conversations with some important men – some *very* important men, who will soon be even more important."

"I wouldn't say 'lucky.' They obviously thought it in their best interests to have conversations with you." He blushed a little. That was one of the advantages of blonde men: they were so much easier to read. He waxed quite animated, going on about Eastern politicos and newspapermen, and Agnes began to see why it mattered whether the end of the U.S. Civil War spurred the Atlantic colonies to form a federation with Upper and Lower Canada. A much larger Canada would be much more able to absorb Rupert's Land, which would mean much more immigration and much more money to be made by people who'd staked land first. And more than money. Back in the Caribbean, she'd been aware of more than a few individuals with no more pedigree than a yellow dog, who now were Sir This and Lady That – Builders of Empire.

When Dr. Schultz's carriage reached her family's 'temporary' abode, and he stepped out to give her a hand down, Agnes let her hand linger in his a little longer than was strictly necessary, and let her fingertips trail across his palm as they parted. He asked if he might give her a ride to church this Sunday, and she allowed as how she would be amenable to that. She went to the door smiling, knowing that when he laid his head down tonight his bed linen would smell of her eau de toilette.

As soon as she'd pulled the cabin door partway open, she saw and heard that she should jump inside quickly and pull it shut, before Dr. Schultz caught a glimpse through the open doorway. Her sister, in a greyish, once-calico, sack of a dress, was ladling boiled potatoes and onions into two tin bowls. Her father was lolling back with his feet on the table and the back feet of his tilted chair digging into the dirt floor, with a pilfered HBC mess cup in his hand and no shirt on over his union suit.

Her sister looked across the table at Agnes and said: "Well?" Agnes blinked at her. Laura dropped the ladle into the pot, held out her open hand and said again: "Well?" It was only then Agnes remembered that being employed to take care of Dr. Schultz's store all summer meant that he was supposed to pay her.

CHAPTER 22

Hugh heard Donald say: "Just cut through the skin, no deeper – a straight line about a hand's-breadth, then a circle around the limb and peel the skin off that far," and looked up. Twelve year old Angus was painstakingly trying to follow his oldest brother's instructions. The boys-before-the-girls were sitting by the riverside peeling poplar poles for fence rails. Poplar fencing stayed straight, didn't crack and didn't rot for years, *if* the bark was off. The brothers were more or less paired off between the more and less experienced. Responsible Donald had of course made himself responsible for first-timer Angus; Aleck was leap-frogged down to Hector; and Hugh had Morrison, who didn't need any instruction.

"*Or*, Angus," Hugh offered up, "you can cut one straight line the length of the pole and work your circles out from there." That was the approach he and Morrison were taking, and once the straight line was cut they'd start cutting and peeling circles from either end. Whoever reached the middle first got to keep one grey-green circlet to mark the score, while the rest were tossed onto the growing pile that would dry for firestarters. So far they had three apiece. Although Hugh had the advantage of two years' more experience and hand strength, he was also more likely to get distracted by the cloud calls of a wedge of geese heading south, or even just the feel of the snakeskin poplar bark and the smooth slick wood underneath.

Donald said: "People who butt in on people trying to educate other people deserve a cuff on the scruff."

"People who spend too much time in school got nothing worth eddy-cating anybody about."

Aleck laughed with a *'so there'* edge that was sharper than Hugh had intended to bring out with his foolery. You had to be careful with Donald's disposition to take things to heart. So Hugh said: "But if anybody's wanting a cuff…" He popped his latest hand's-breadth circlet of bark onto his wrist, then popped it off again and tossed it to Donald, who batted it out of the air. "Anyway, Angus, pay me no mind – lotsa different ways to do anything."

The poplar pole peeling was a bit of a sit-down Da had allowed the boys, something useful they could do that didn't involve their whole bodies swinging scythes or toting sheaves or swinging wood-and-chain flails to thresh the grain off the straw. The harvest was done except for the winnowing, and there was just the right kind of wind today to make that easy. So the rest of the family was up in the farmyard, gathered around a huge old sheet of sailcloth spread on the ground, scooping wheat up into the air and letting the breeze carry away the chaff.

Hugh said: "Well, after the last ten days 'off,' you scholar-boys should be glad to be dragging your wore-out bones back to school. Well, school or college." St. John's College had indeed got back in business, with a loosening of the 'Anglicans Only' rule, just in time for Donald to be finished with Kildonan School. But Donald didn't seem to mind.

Aleck said: "What should be and what is be don't always meet."

Hugh found it annoying when Aleck talked like some shagganappi stubble-jumper. Aleck knew better than that. In fact, Hugh was finding a lot of things about Aleck annoying these days. Although Aleck's hair and hairline were straight, he'd taken to brushing it straight back, which Hugh only did because it was the only thing you could do with semi-curly hair and a premature widow's peak. And Aleck had gone back to wearing moccasins instead of 'bull shoes' – the thick steerhide home-cobbled boots most boys graduated into once their feet stopped changing sizes every two months – echoing Hugh's opinion that smoked buckskin moccasins were much better for rain and snow than bull shoes.

Donald paused his knife and said to Aleck: "What's that supposed to mean?"

Aleck said: "It means I aren't going back. I'm done with school."

"Uh... what's Mum and Da say about that?"

"I aren't told 'em yet. I'll tell 'em tonight after supper." Then Aleck abruptly got up and stomped away, as much as anyone could stomp in moccasins.

Donald looked at Hugh and Hugh at Donald. Donald said: "Wuff-wuff, Hugh."

Hugh nodded and said: "Wuff wuff." The exchange was a kind of pack-signal the boys had fallen into so long ago Hugh couldn't remember where it came from. Depending on the tone, it meant: 'This situation feels strange/weird/scary/fun/promising, eh? ' – 'I'm with you.' Although the tone varied, the correct vowel-pronunciation never did, halfway between 'roof' and 'rough.'

After supper, after the children from Angus on down had gone up to bed, Aleck made his announcement, and before anybody else could put a word in added: "I'm the same age now as Hugh was when you let him stop school."

There was a pause, and then Mum said: "But, Aleck, you went back to school after this summer with no complaints."

"I thought I'd give it a try. I've been thinking about this a long time, but thought I'd give school one more try. But now as we've had the harvest break I've decided I'm not going back."

Da said: "Oh, *you've* decided, have you?"

Mum cut in quickly with: "But your Uncle Hector told me you'd only need one more year in his school and you'd be ready to go on to St. John's College."

"And what's Donald learning at college? How much use am I gonna have for Latin and Greek and Algebra in my life?"

Donald said: "That isn't the entire curriculum. And anyway, Latin can be useful for a career in the law, and algebra for accounting."

"Well maybe I don't *wanna* be a Company clerk or a lawyer or something. Maybe I just wanna be a farmer with a little hunting and fishing on the side."

Da's eyes sidled at Hugh, and what was in them wasn't pleasant. Mum said: "Maybe, though, Aleck, you'll find after a little more time at school that you actually want to do more than farming. You've always been very good at your lessons, very quick to learn things and remember them. You're very young yet to be making a decision about the rest of your life."

"I'm the same age Hugh was when you let him decide."

"Well, it's different for Hugh –"

"*Why?*" Aleck's face and his voice were ablaze. He flailed his arms and practically shouted: "Why is it always different for Hugh? Why does Hugh always get to do things nobody else gets to do?" Then he lowered his arms and his head and murmured: "Sorry, didn't mean to raise my voice…"

There was a pause, and then Granda said: "The lad should hae been a lawyer."

Da said: "He might still be. Your grandfather is right, Aleck, that we can't… *dispute* that what is fair for Hugh is fair for you. But, you may find, um, after a while, that what is… *right* for Hugh isn't necessarily right for you. There's no shame in changing your mind, better that then, um, sticking to something just for the sake of sticking to it. If it turns out you… *eventually* decide to go back to school, no one will think any less of you – quite the opposite."

Aleck said: "Okay, then. Thanks Da. Thanks," and he nodded at the adults in general. "Well, it's been a long day – a long *ten* days. Good-night."

A moment after Aleck was gone, Da said: "Donald, you and Hector and Morrison must be tired, too."

"Not so much, I thought another cup of – Oh, yes!" Donald put on a big yawn and a stretch. "Come on, boys, it'll be an early morning."

After Donald, Morrison and Hector went up the stairs, Hugh felt four pairs of adult eyes boring into him. "I didn't have nothing to do with it! First I ever heard of it was this afternoon, and that's the God's honest truth."

Da seemed to weigh that for a moment, then said: "I believe you, Hugh, that you didn't, um, encourage your brother to not go back to school, but are you sure you didn't *dis*courage him from going back? Rubbing his nose in the fact that you don't have to… *study* anymore?"

"No!" Hugh thought back to make sure. All that he and his brothers had said about it over the last year had been bits of back-and-forth jokes that'd been just as likely about him having to do more farmwork as them still having to do schoolwork. "No, sir, I did not. Fact is, if I'd knowed he was thinking this way I would've tried to talk him out of it. I think you're right, Da, that what's good for me ain't necessarily good for Aleck. But *try* talking to Aleck…"

Gran said: "Why don't you, Hugh? Try. If he'll listen to anybody, he'll listen to you."

Hugh looked at the ceiling and exhaled as though someone had just asked him to roll a boulder up the riverbank. Actually, he'd rather've taken on that. The notion that he was anyone to give advice to anybody gave him the wooly shakes. But Gran had asked him to try…

After Hugh had felt his way up the dark narrow boxed-in stairway and turned the little dogleg at the top, he saw a glow of light ahead. That would be the candle that the first boys to go to bed carried up and set on the blanketbox under the bedroom window, for the last boy to come to bed to blow out. Hugh moved toward the candle, carefully picking his way since the boys' bedroom had grown a mite crowded over the years. Now there were three homemade two-layer bunk beds in it – an arrangement Granda said the British army used for saving barracks floor space – and a trundlebed pulled out from under one of them for Willy, Jamie and Roddy to sleep on horizontally. Now that Granda was the sole inhabitant of their grandparents' room, it might've seemed sensible to move one of the double bunks in there, but that would've been admitting that Gran's hip was never going to heal enough for her to ever climb a flight of stairs again.

Aleck's bed was the bunk under Hugh's. Hugh could see by the candlelight that Aleck's eyes were closed, but he was lying stiffly on his back and his breathing wasn't sleep-deep. Hugh perched on the edge of Aleck's bunk and whispered: "Aleck…?"

Aleck's eyes came open, but only partly – the same kind of defiant slits as the straight, tight set of his mouth. His mouth stayed closed. Hugh whispered: "Uh… you know I got no right to be telling anybody they should do this or shouldn't do that. Specially 'bout something like going to school. But… you're much better at books and figures and things nor ever I was. Warn't much of a loss to anybody that I didn't get more schooling. Barely enough room up here," tapping the side of his head, "for what I *did* get. But you… maybe Da's right, maybe if you stuck at it a little while longer you'd find you don't really want to quit going to school."

"Why shouldn't I quit? *You* did. *You* always get to do whatever you wanna do. Running around screwing Indian girls –"

Hugh's right hand shot out to grab his little brother's throat, and his left hand cocked into a fist. The next instant, Hugh made both his hands go slack and snatched them back against his chest in horror. Aleck's eyes were opened wide now and then some, and his head pulled back as far as his neck could stretch. Hugh whispered: "I'm sorry, Aleck, I… But it's not like that. Don't… don't talk about things you don't know about."

"*I'm* sorry, Hugh. I won't."

"Well… get some sleep. You're gonna need all you can get if Da rides you like he did me last year."

"That bad?"

"Worse."

"Huh. Wuff-wuff, Hugh."

Hugh nodded. "Wuff wuff."

In the days that followed, Hugh would've said Aleck worked like a dog, except that the Point Douglas Sutherland dogs had it pretty easy. Hugh wasn't sure what his own attitude was, whether he wanted to sneak Aleck a hand while Da wasn't looking, or whether he wanted Aleck to give in and go back to school. He could see Aleck was wearing down, physically.

One morning after breakfast, Da said: "I want you to run an… *errand* for me, Hugh. Or, um, paddle me an errand. Always better to be, um, stocked-up, rather than buying supplies by dribs and drabs. So, if you would please take one of the dugouts to Fort Garry, where they can just… *deduct* this from the, um, credit in our account."

Hugh glanced at the pencilled list, and could see why Da didn't want him carrying the stuff across on MacDoog's ferry:

1 small keg gunpowder
2 canisters percussion caps
4 pigs lead

Hugh glanced across the table at Aleck waiting to be assigned his torture for the day, then said: "Sure, Da, but maybe better if it's not just me. Two paddlers'd make the canoe less tippy."

Da looked suspicious, but then nodded. "Yes, Hugh, good point. Aleck, if you, um, wouldn't mind giving your brother a hand with – ?"

"Sure, Da."

Hugh took the stern paddle, since it was customarily the older brother's privilege to do the steering, and since Aleck's laboured way of attacking the water meant Aleck would've been well advised to let even Morrison or Hector take the stern. Going against the current up the Red and around The Forks into the Assiniboine wasn't easy, but Hugh was quite sure Aleck found it a holiday compared to what Da might've dreamed up for him for today. Like maybe shifting the stack of logs seasoning for next winter's firewood so that all the bottom logs were on the top, 'to let them air out better.' Hugh's back and shoulders remembered that assignment.

The slope of the bank from the Assiniboine to the gates of Fort Garry was a wide swath of permanently tramped-down earth. Hugh stopped at the top to look back across the river. Through a gap in the trees on the other shore, he could see south-west onto the open prairie. Wauh Oonae was out there somewhere, hundreds of miles beyond that flat horizon, with the gun-bristling caravan of the Red River Buffalo Hunt.

"Hugh?"

"Hm? Oh, yeah, sorry, Aleck, let's go in."

'In,' beyond the vaulted cave of the gatehouse, was the usual bustle of people and languages. On the oval lawn at the centre of the central square, a few late-blooming flowerbeds showed colour around the wheels of cannons. The Company officers did love their flower gardens, especially since it was the Company servants who had to tend them. The Company's retail store was in the south east corner, first building on your right when you came through the gates.

Hugh turned to start in that direction, but a long knife blade and a black horsetail fly-whisk flared in front of his face. Beyond the knife and whisk was a painted snarling Indian. Hugh stepped back. On second look he saw that the Indian wasn't snarling but grinning, and the whisk was a scalp tied to the pommel of the knife. Hugh didn't know much from scalps, but it did seem to him that this one was finer-haired and longer than you'd expect. And since the man gleefully flashing it around was Saulteaux, the scalp was probably Sioux. The Saulteaux man was crowing: "I am the warrior and this is the knife who took this scalp! Ha! Yes, me!"

Hugh nodded politely, and the Saulteaux warrior moved on to show off his trophy to other admirers. They muttered things like: 'How nice for you,' and went on about their business, or skirted around him while he was accosting someone else. But Hugh noticed that there was one person who wasn't moving anywhere, just standing staring at the waving scalp, a Metis named Francis Desmarais.

There were a lot of Desmaraix around Red River, so many Hugh couldn't remember one from another. Francis Desmarais, though, stuck out because it was rumoured he had some sort of secret tie-in with the Sioux, while most other Red River Metis ran with the Cree and Ojibway.

Before Hugh could start himself and Aleck moving toward the store again, Francis Desmarais moved. He snatched the scalping knife out of the Saulteaux's hand, and then there were a couple of flashing blade movements, sort of a cross between stabbing and slicing, like an expert fish-fileter. The Saulteaux clamped his arms across his midriff and looked down. Blood was oozing out between his forearms, and mixed with the red broth were sickly-slick white sausage lengths tinged with pink and purple. Hugh had gutted pigs before, and cleaned the guts to make sausage casings. But the pigs had been dead and bled before gutting, and this was a human being.

The Saulteaux turned and walked stiffly through the open door of the general store. Hugh heard him say to the stupefied clerk behind the counter, "Gimme some cotton," and saw him making sewing motions with one hand to make the dim white man understand he meant cotton thread. Then the Saulteaux collapsed on the floor.

Some noises off to Hugh's right turned his head in that direction. Some Company men were warily closing in on Francis Desmarais, who was brandishing the bloody knife with its attached scalp and declaring: "I gave him as much warning as he gave her!"

Hugh felt a movement on his left; Aleck starting to step forward toward the store. Either Aleck was thinking of helping the downed Saulteaux, or of carrying on with the errand Da had sent them on. As stupid as the second possibility sounded, Hugh could understand it – the world had suddenly turned so strange and unreal that one way to get through it was to mechanically carry on with whatever real thing you were doing before it flipped. Whichever impulse Aleck was following, the Sutherland boys couldn't be of any help and the store would be open other days. Hugh threw his arm up in front of Aleck's chest to stop him, and turned back toward the fort gates.

Neither one of them said a word as they rode the current through The Forks and down the Red. As they rounded Point Douglas, Aleck looked back and said dazedly, "Wuff wuff, Hugh."

Hugh nodded, "Wuff wuff."

The gutted Saulteaux's friends did find a needle and thread and sew him up, but they couldn't get all his innards back in and he died the next day. Francis Desmarais had to be tried for murder; whatever killings and scalpings that happened out on the prairie stayed there, but this had happened in the heart of Assiniboia, inside the walls of Fort Garry.

Hugh and Aleck didn't have to testify, there were so many other witnesses. But Hugh heard immediately, as did everyone else at Red River, when Judge Black brought down the only verdict and sentence the circumstances allowed: Guilty and Death. And then the trouble started.

Judge Black had pointed out that Governor Mactavish had the legal right to commute the sentence. So the murdered Saulteaux's brothers and cousins camped outside the courthouse and declared that if Francis Desmarais stepped out the door to go anywhere except the gallows, they'd carry out the sentence themselves. Francis Desmarais's brothers and cousins declared that any Saulteaux who laid a hand on him would pay for it, and that they weren't too happy with the court of Assiniboia passing a death sentence on someone who'd only murdered a murderer.

Hugh could almost see the cloud of tension Da carried around with him, except when Da was away to yet another emergency council meeting. Apparently Bishop Taché could no more order the Desmarais clan to back off than Chief Henry Prince could order the Saulteaux camped around the courthouse to stand down. Family and blood trumped tribes and religions. When Donald asked Da why the Chief and the Bishop didn't step in and disarm the situation, Da said: "I don't know much, Donald, about, um, being a… *leader*, but I do know this: if you want to… *maintain* your authority, you don't go issuing orders you know won't be obeyed."

Came a day when Da's tension changed. He was still tight and nervous, but in a hopeful kind of way – though what he might be hopeful about he wasn't saying. A few days later a messenger came from across the river. Da murmured with him in the doorway for a minute, then came back in grinning all over and announced: "It's done."

Mum said: "What's done?"

"Francis Desmarais is gone. Governor Mactavish commuted the death sentence to banishment from Red River, for life. Actually, that was, um, decided a few days ago, but kept secret till other… *arrangements* could be made. Late last night the, um, prisoner was… *smuggled* out of the courthouse and rushed west to The Company's post at Portage la Prairie. They'll keep on moving him west from, um, post to post, and let him loose at New Caledonia in the Rocky Mountains."

Hugh wondered for only a moment whether that would satisfy the Saulteaux. When he thought about his own self getting uprooted from his home country and banished forever from his family and friends and the places he knew, it didn't seem like a light sentence. It made him think of his grandparents exiled from the Highlands, but at least they'd come in company with some of their own people.

Even in the general relief that The Company and the council had managed to keep a blood feud from getting started, Hugh could still see that Saulteaux staring down in blank surprise at his intestines oozing out between his fingers. That picture, and the few seconds that came before it, kept coming back to Hugh at unpredictable moments. Although he couldn't say in exactly what way, he had a feeling that the John Hugh Sutherland who'd walked in through the gates of Fort Garry that sunny day was different from the one who walked back out. Just a couple of flashes of a knife blade out of a blue sky.

CHAPTER 23

Schultz finished sweeping the last of last night's accumulation of yellow and brown leaves off the front steps of the White Store. In the embryonic village of Winnipeg there wasn't one tree big enough to relieve a puppy, but it seemed the prevailing night-winds conspired with all the trees along the riverbank to give the citizens the illusion they were living in an arboreum. Or maybe it wasn't prevailing easterlies at all, just errant gusts that overnight swept onto his steps the same leaves he'd swept off the previous morning.

Schultz sloped his broom and looked at the infinity of prairie spread in front of his front door: autumn grey-brown speckled with glinting patches of frost. The sky was speckled, too, a delft of fluffy little white clouds herding to the horizon. The clouds all sat on the same level, like dumplings on a glass tabletop. It was a pretty enough picture, in a barren sort of way, but Schultz had more useful things to do than look at pictures.

Back inside, he perched on the stool behind the counter and opened up the ledger he'd closed last night. He wasn't expecting many customers today, nor any day in the immediate future, but in a few weeks there was going to be a rush like Niagara and he meant to have his credit accounts all lined up for easy access. The weather was cold enough now, or almost, for meat to freeze and stay frozen. And that meant that somewhere out on the plains the Red River Buffalo Hunt was getting ready for its last few runs of the year.

From Schultz's thirdhand understanding of the mechanics of the buffalo hunt, for the last while the caravan would have been trailing the herd at a distance, waiting for the Captain of the Hunt to declare the time was right to fill their carts with 'green meat.' When Schultz had expressed skepticism to old Andrew McDermot that the wild Metis would hold themselves in check within sight of their prey just because some elected Captain told them to wait, McDermot had shrugged and said: "Mr. Grant," as though that were all that needed saying.

"He's long dead, isn't he?"

"Yeah, but his laws ain't. Oh, I doubt even Grant could've got the woollier ones to abide by his hunt rules if the rules didn't make good sense. That's a whole, wide ocean out there," McDermot had waved his arm in the general direction of the prairie that Red River perched on the coast of, "if you don't heed the words of your captain and your navigator, you're sunk."

Like McDermot and all the other storekeepers at Red River – even The Company's retail store – Schultz extended credit to the buffalo hunters between hunts. He meant to have them all alphabetised and toted up before the hunt came home with cartfuls of frozen meat and winter-thick buffalo robes to turn into debt paydowns, imported goods and cash. Even hunters who took their carts to Fort Garry could wind up bringing cash into Schultz's White Store, since Governor Mactavish had abolished ex-Governor Dallas's edict that The Company would only pay in credits for its own stores.

Schultz opened the ledger to the half filled-out sheet of foolscap he'd left in there as a bookmark, licked his indelible pencil and picked up where he'd left off the night before: *Lepine, J., £2, 3s, 2d… McBeth, R, £4, 5s, 4p…*

The bell above the shop door jingled and in came a shy young blonde wearing the ubiquitous, dark blue homespun cloak of the Kildonan women. It turned out all she wanted was three ounces of Chinese tea, "And a small bottle of my grandmother's tonic, if you please – Bergen's Sass-perella." That explained why she'd walked all the way to Schultz's White Store from Kildonan, instead of shortening her errand at McDermot's new store, or A.G.B. Bannatyne's. The one advantage Schultz had over his competitors was the medical dispensary, and as long as customers had to come in to his store for their pharmaceuticals they might as well buy their tea and sundries while they were at it.

Schultz didn't know the other, herbal ingredients in Bergen's Secret Recipe, but he did know there was a pinch of sulphur, a tincture of cocaine and a touch of alcohol. That should keep the old girl perky. The marriageable-age granddaughter didn't correct him when he called her 'Miss' as he handed her purchases across the counter.

After the pleasant young miss left the store, Schultz thought about her. Her voice still carried traces of the pretty, Gaelic lilt her grandparents or great-grandparents had brought across the ocean. The summer colouring of her fresh, outdoor complexion hadn't faded yet, and there was something fetching about honey tan with sun-polished blonde hair. There would certainly be advantages to taking a Kildonan woman to wife. Not only would she be very capable and knowledgeable in all the practical facets of living at Red River, any man who married into an old Kildonan family would immediately cease to be a foreigner.

Schultz told himself to stop moonbeaming. If there was one thing he should've learned from the people in his hometown, it was that a man should get himself a good start in life before thinking of marrying. He'd seen too many bright hopes and shining prospects buried under a day-to-day treadmill of earning pennies to feed the children and pay the rent on a leaky hovel.

Besides, his life was more than full at the moment. What with the Masons and *The Nor'Wester* and various other ventures and adventures, he hardly lacked for companionship. Some evenings when there was nothing scheduled he hoped there wouldn't come a knock at the door, so he could have at least a little time to himself.

But there was a different kind of companionship, the kind that didn't require any wariness. No matter how convivial the social gathering, or how earnest the mystical promises of universal brotherhood, Schultz was always aware that competitiveness and private agendas were still in play. If he hadn't known that before, Henry had taught him. If your own older brother and sworn business partner could turn his back on you when the wind shifted, anyone could.

Schultz had caught glimpses of that other kind of companionship in moments alone with Miss Agnes Campbell Farquharson, when she happened to come into the store when no one else was there, or taking her back and forth to church in his carriage – which fortunately didn't have enough seating for her father and sister to fit on comfortably. Not that he wasn't always on good behaviour with Miss Farquharson, polite and unpresumptuous. But somehow he could say things out loud to her that he never would've to anyone else – some things he hadn't even *thought* out loud. Ever since the day they'd traded secrets – she with her coughing blood and he with his shamefully helpless position in McKenney & Co. – there 'd been a kind of trust between them, a feeling they were fellow travellers through a hostile world.

But then, there was that Toronto alderman's daughter Schultz had danced with at a garden party last summer. Even if she got snatched up before he got set up sufficiently to be a worthy catch, there were others of her ilk coming along. Schultz was perfectly aware that Society – the circles of wealth and power and public honours – was much like the Ancient Order of Freemasons. Even though there were tiers and hierarchies within it, the essential fact was that either you were a member or you weren't. Marrying into one of the families that were would accomplish the same thing as marrying a Matheson or MacBeth at Red River, and Upper Canada was a much bigger world than Red River.

Schultz knew he had a long hill to climb before he could propose himself to any alderman's daughter, and the climb was in tiny steps. Steps like making sure he had his credit list in order before the chaos of the Red River Hunt's homecoming. He looked to where he'd left off, and added: *Morin, B...* "Bear down," Schultz said to himself. "Bear down and bear up and you're bound to get where you're bound."

The shop bell jingled again. Schultz looked up, with his proprietor's smile on. The customer didn't look very promising: a scrawny old man with a scraggly beard and a much-patched coat. As the fellow proceeded stiffly toward the counter, Schultz saw that he wasn't that old after all, just moved with the painful gait of arthritic or brittle-dry joints. "Dr. Schultz...?"

"Yes."

"I read your notice in *The Nor'Wester*, and my wife said I should come see you, me. I brung a note from Father Ritchot."

Father Ritchot would mean the man was from St. Norbert parish, south of The Forks. The note read: 'I attest that Joseph Sinclair is truly in poverty.' Schultz had run an advertisement in *The Nor'Wester*, offering to provide free medical care to those who couldn't afford to pay for it, provided they brought written proof from their clergyman.

It wasn't the same as Dr. Bird's ridiculous bugaboo about publicly-funded health care for all the public, it was charity. *'Though I speak with the tongues of men and of angels, and have not charity, I am become as sounding brass, or a tinkling cymbal.'* Besides, it was good public relations. Schultz couldn't remember exactly how he'd come up with the idea, but it was an excellent one.

Schultz looked from the note to Joseph Sinclair, whose eyes were drooping and who had both hands planted on the counter as though he needed all the strength of all four limbs to stay upright. There was no smell of alcohol about him; there was a slight odour of something resembling putrefaction. There were a few small red splotches on his face, but the skin wasn't broken.

Schultz always kept a couple of chairs behind the counter, in case of conversations longer than 'That'll be two shillings.' He lifted one over the counter and reached over to set its feet on the floor. "Have a seat, Joseph."

"Thank you, Doctor."

"What seems to be the problem?"

"Well, I got bad soreness in my elbows and knees and all, hurts to move. And I get wore down so easy. Couldn't go on the buffalo hunts this year, can't hardly even work in the garden – hoe a little and I got to sit down. And sometimes I get a bit feverish."

That could fit a lot of different diagnoses. Maybe the best approach would be a little general conversation, draw him out, make it seem like a consultation and then send him on his way with a free small bottle of patent medicine – there was one brand that wasn't selling anyway. "Been married long, Joseph?"

"Some while." There was a shy smile. "Twelve years come December."

"Any children?"

"Yes." There was a wide grin. "Ten, and another on the way. Gotta keep Genevieve fed good to grow it good."

The grin was the first time Joseph Sinclair had opened his mouth wide. Schultz realised that everything Joseph had said so far had been said with his mouth fairly tight, lips covering his teeth. The wide grin had shown Schultz that there were gaps in the teeth, and the ones remaining were askew, as though loose in the gums. The gums looked swollen and sickly, and oozing a bit of blood. Schultz said: "How well do *you* eat, Joseph?"

"Oh, good, I eat good, me." He seemed evasive. "Well, gotta be soft food since my teeth, you know… But I eat good."

"And no one else in your family, your wife and children, have the same symptoms? The same problem?"

"No, no, just me." That wasn't evasive, that was definite.

"Um, I have to fetch something upstairs, won't be a minute. Just call up the stairs if someone comes in, would you?"

"Sure, Doctor."

Up in his examining room, Schultz looked in the index of one of his medical books and found the right page. The symptoms under the heading fit perfectly: *General debility and lethergy, soreness or bleeding of the gums, subcutaneous bleeding, and pain in the limbs.* Schultz could understand why Father Ritchot, or the Grey Nuns in their St. Norbert mission, hadn't guessed what Joseph Sinclair was suffering from. Who would've guessed, in the midst of all this plenty – green gardens, golden fields and 'God's own hunting park' – that a man could've come down with scurvy? Schultz could guess how. Joseph Sinclair had probably been living on stale bread and water for months now, or as long as the family had been in straitened circumstances. Likely at family mealtimes he would push the food on his plate around enough to make it look like he'd eaten some, then dole out the rest to his children and his wife. If his wife packed him a lunch to take out to the fields, he would secretly give it to the children.

Schultz thought of the two stoneware jugs that had come with the last freight consignment he'd get till next summer. Lemon juice was a very expensive article this far from anywhere. Expensive and lucrative, because a number of local ladies liked to be able to say: 'Milk or lemon?' just like the hostess at a tea party in a London salon. The impulse to give some of it away made Schultz feel guilty of foolishness and irresponsibility. Not only would he be giving away what had cost him dearly wholesale, he would be giving away the profit he'd make by selling it retail. But then, if word got around that Dr. Schultz had cured Joseph Sinclair's mysterious ailment, it certainly wouldn't do any harm to his practice and his pharmacy. There now, that wasn't so childish after all.

Schultz funnelled a mid-sized bottleful from one of the stone jugs. When he handed the bottle across the counter, he said: "I want you to take this home to your wife and tell her that Doctor's Orders are you must drink two ounces in a cup of water every day until it's all gone. Now, this'll put you on the mend, but it's not an entire cure. You must –" Something caught in Schultz's throat and caught him by surprise. There was something about the fact that there'd be a father who'd do what Joseph Sinclair had been doing for his children, that choked Schultz up. He cleared his throat and went on. "You must eat better, Joseph – fresh greens, root vegetables, meat, fish, barley soup, the same food you feed your family. Better there be a little less to go around than you try to live on next to nothing. Because you won't live that way for long. You're no good to your family dead, Joseph."

Joseph looked down and slowly nodded his head.

After Joseph Sinclair had gone with his bottle of lemon juice, Schultz opened the account book to pick up where he'd left off. Then he paused and nodded to himself. If he'd had any doubts about one of his thoughts on the subject of marriage, they were gone now, because he'd just seen living proof. Joseph Sinclair seemed a reasonably bright and competent fellow, and obviously had enough education to be basically literate. And here he was starving himself to scurvy so his wife and children would have a little more to eat. Because he'd gone and got himself married before he was in any position to do so. No, husband and father was a good state for a man to aspire to, but not before his other aspirations had borne fruit.

CHAPTER 24

In the dawnlight, Hugh headed east from Red River, with his moccasins crunching the ice crystals in the hayfield marshes and the crust of the year's first snow worth mentioning. The days were getting short and he had a long way to go, and would need at least a couple hours of daylight when he got there. He'd debated riding one of the horses, but he would've had to leave it tethered or hobbled in the woods for hours on end while he was half a mile away, and there were wolves in the woods. Not so many wolves that the odds were heavy they'd stumble across his horse, but Hugh didn't like any odds when it came to the thought of a tethered and helpless pony torn to pieces by a pack of wolves.

So instead of riding, Hugh was striding or jogging along wearing a homemade shoulder harness – usually used for dragging firewood logs to the sawhorse – towing a half-loaded toboggan on a shagganappi line long enough to let his legs swing freely. There was just barely enough snow on the ground for the toboggan to slide, but among the gear strapped onto it was a pair of snowshoes, because you never knew what the sky might bring tomorrow and he'd feel a right fool to find himself miles from home in knee-deep snow and no snowshoes.

He had no doubt any passing Indian would call him a fool already, for not hitching the toboggan to a dog. But Hugh didn't fancy the idea of a lone, tethered dog with a pack of wolves any more than a lone, tethered horse. And no farm dog living could be trusted to keep still and quiet within sight and sound of deer.

The sounds of farm animals and human voices faded behind Hugh, leaving just the crisp tick-tock of his footsteps, the swish of the toboggan and the sighing of the wind. Back among the trees and buildings along the riverbank, the wind was known to stick its nose in at times, but out on the prairie it was always there. Not a storm-wind today, at least not so far. The sky was just about cloudless, and the paler blue along its rim matched nicely with the pale gold of bleached-out wild hay poking through the snow and twinkling with frost. The blue and yellow seemed leached out of each other, separated, waiting for the time they'd join together in summer green.

Hugh left his eyes and ears and legs to their own devices and let his mind wander into what-ifs, as people said it was prone to do of its own accord. He wondered if the day might've been even pleasanter with some of his brothers along; that way they all could've come on horseback and left one of them in camp to guard the ponies. But all of his younger brothers who were old enough to go a-hunting were stuck in school. Except for Aleck, who was stuck in the same grind Da had put on Hugh last year. And poor Donald was stuck in college, even after manfully serving his full sentence in Kildonan school.

But now as Hugh had some open space away from people to think about it, college probably wasn't as much of a hardship for Donald as it would've been for him; and a few days and nights in snowy woods looking for a buck deer probably wasn't as much of a pleasant prospect for Donald as it was for him. As Gran said: "Donald's favourite moon is aye the Harvest Moon, and Hugh's is the Hunter's Moon" – the big, orange moon that came after the harvest was done and before the winter started whittling away the wild creatures' stock-up of fat meat.

It did seem odd to Hugh that the closer he and his older brother grew to adulthood, the farther they grew apart. Donald was born to be a farmer, and prone to be a well-educated one. Hugh didn't mind a bit of farming, as long as you didn't get too carried away with it. The point of farming was to grow your own food so you didn't need much money, not to bust your back and your brains growing bigger yields to make more money.

Hugh laughed aloud alone out on the prairie, at the hilarious notion that adulthood and 'Purple Hugh' were ever likely to come within hailing distance of each other. But, like it or not, he'd be seventeen this Christmas and he'd butchered the excuse of saying he was still just a schoolboy. In one very important way, though, he wished he could leapfrog over the next few years to where responsible adulthood would be upon him. He could hear himself saying to Nancy Prince: *"Wauh Oonae, I'm of age now, and so are you, and I've scouted out a nice piece of unclaimed riverfront land just up the Assiniboine where we could build a house and..."*

Then again, it might not be necessary to scout out unclaimed land along the Assiniboine. While it was true that Kildonan and all the other parishes along the Red had got populated so thickly over the generations there was no unclaimed land left wider than the back end of a horse, Point Douglas was as wide as several standard riverfront allotments. Because Da was an only child, Point Douglas had never been divided. Kildonan people didn't follow their French neighbours' habit of divvying up their land among the children until the original farm was just a band of ribbons running back from the river. Kildonan people followed the Highland habit that the youngest son would stay at his parents' home when he married, care for his aging parents and inherit the undivided farm – the older children had to fend for themselves, and likely many of them preferred it that way. But since Point Douglas was so much wider than the other original allotments, it likely *would've* been divided if Da had had a brother, but since he hadn't...

Even if Roddy proved to be Hugh's youngest brother – which was an open question, since Mum had brought Mary Ann Bella into the world only last week – it'd still be at least another fifteen or sixteen years before Roddy got old enough to marry and take over the farm, and Da likely wouldn't mind having a grown son nearby to help out the meanwhile. A little house on Point Douglas would be far enough apart from Mum and Da's place that Wauh-Oonae wouldn't feel bossed around...

So in that case, Hugh could start with: *"Nancy, I'm of age now, and so are you, and my family's agreed that you and me could put up a house of our own on Point Douglas..."* No, that sounded too dry, too matter-of-fact. Maybe: *"Nancy, my love, I'm of age now, and so are ..."*

No, that sounded too offhanded, too sure he had the right to call her 'my love.' Maybe he should just start with: *"Nancy, I've loved you since the day I first saw you –"*

Maybe she would cut him off there with: *"Oh, Hugh, I've been waiting seven years for you to say that..."* It tingled him, hearing her voice in his mind's ear. Then again, she might just as likely cut him off with: *"Are you out of your goddamn mind, Hugh Sutherland? There's a Metis man – a man, not a boy – I've known on the buffalo hunt for years and years, we just been waiting till I get old enough to marry."*

Hugh turtled his head between his shoulders, pulled himself back to the real world and felt his cheeks growing hotter than frostbite. He focused himself on the raggedy smudge line between snow and sky that was the border of the wooded country, and broke into a loping jog to eat up some distance, trying to keep his gait smooth to keep the toboggan from bouncing. By the time he slowed to a walk again, the smudge line was starting to show colours: dark green spruces, silvery-grey trunks of poplars and birches, and blood red veins of basketbushes. He bit off a couple of chunks of jerked beef from the stick in his pocket and chewed them up as he walked, stooping to scoop up a scant handful of snow to wash them down. No matter how thirsty you got, you had to remember that eating snow would give you cramps, but one mouthful to wet your mouth wouldn't hurt.

Once into the woods, Hugh threaded his way to a spot he'd scouted when he'd been out riding in the spring, before the warming weather brought out the blackflies and mosquitoes and only a damn fool would go riding in the woods. It was a stand of poplars by a stream, and two of the good-sized trunks were only seven or eight feet apart.

The first thing to do was build a fire. Beside one of the tallest poplars was the mound of stones he'd piled up in the spring – hunting for stones in snow-covered frozen ground would've been ridiculous. He built a fire ring, scooped out the snow inside it and went looking for deadwood. He didn't have to look long – one of the big old poplars in the stand had died and fallen, taking a few neighbouring spruce trees with it. That was how poplars operated: if a male and female poplar managed to grow up in a neighbourhood of spruces or pines, they'd start to propagate, with poplar saplings springing up among the evergreens. Then one of the full-grown poplars would die and fall, taking out some of the evergreens with it and opening up sun- and earth-room for the younger poplars to thrive. Within as little as ten years, you had a poplar grove where a spruce thicket once had been. Hugh knew it could happen that quickly, because he'd seen it from start to finish, from the day Granda had tapped him on the shoulder and said: "Ye see those two young poplar trees among the pines there? Aye, ye'll live tae see the day when that's all poplars and no evergreens. Maybe even I will."

Hugh chuckled to himself, remembering Granda going into a rant about an article in one of the old Illustrated Magazines from the Red River Library. A highly-educated

London philosopher had written that vegetarianism was better for the soul, because the animal kingdom was constant warfare, predation and killing, while the plants were a peaceable kingdom of earth, sunshine and rain. Granda had ranted: *"Anyone who thinks plants dinnae fight and kill each other has never walked through a wild forest or tried tae grow a garden! Yon plant life is just as much warfare as the wild beasts, they just take more time at it."*

While ruminating and chuckling, Hugh was taking branches off fallen spruce and poplar, reminding himself to swing his axe up at the base of a limb instead of down into the crux. It seemed more logical to chop down into the V, but would take twice as long with the spring of the branch working against you. The next step was to cut a few handsbreadth lengths off one of the poplar branches and shave them into fuzz-sticks: chunky stems with wooden petals. Then he was ready to build a fire, or try. He did know how to make a spark with flint and steel, or even two dry sticks of balsam fir, but given the frosty air and dwindling daylight he blessed the inventor of sulphur matches and soon the fire had graduated from spruce needles tinder to twigs to fuzz sticks to branches he had to break over his knee. Once a few hunks of tree trunk were on and burning, Hugh filled his cooking pot with snow, propped it on a fireside stone and got up to start building his house.

The saplings between the twin grown poplars had to be taken out, and some of them were tall enough to be long enough to reach across the gap between the two trunks. Hugh uncoiled a shagganappi rope from his tobogganed gear and went to work lashing poles to trees and poles to poles. At least he didn't have to peel the poles for the present purpose.

As Hugh's eyes watched his arms and fingers work, his mind wandered off again. It had its doubts whether going deerhunting alone was the sanest idea he'd ever had. He'd rambled alone many's the time, in the woods or out on the prairie or along the riverbank – fishing or hunting or just stretching a pony's legs – but that had always been within home-for-supper distance, or at least home-for-bedtime. And he'd camped in the woods many times, on woodcutting or hunting expeditions. But that had always been with various mixes of his brothers and Da or Granda, or with the Lagimodières, the sons and grandsons of old Jean Baptiste, the man the Crees called Great Hunter, late husband of Gran's old friend Madame Marie Anne Lagimodière.

Even though Hugh'd only been a tadpole when the old courier de bois took his last journey, he clearly remembered a gusty winter night in front of the fireplace, Granda and M. Lagimodière puffing pipes and drinking funny-smelling tea, and could still hear the smoky-drawling voice: "I tell you, Sandy, this place we live on, The Forks, it's Big Medicine, and big trouble. Oh, I know we ain't seen no trouble but tempest-teapots since the Fur Trade War, but there was wars fought over this place long before then. I been all over the west country, from Thunder Bay to the Rockies, from the Athabaska to the Mississippi – hell, you been over some of it with me…"

"A little," Granda had put in, as always keeping his own accomplishments from sounding like accomplishments.

"And this place where the rivers join is where all things meet and come together, or come apart. Where the forest meet the prairie, where the river roads north and south meet the rivers east and west, where the deer-hunting Ojibway meet the buffalo-hunting Sioux… But no Indians ever did make a homecamp here, at least not in my time.

"Oh, the Crees still gather here every autumn time for a dog feast and making medicine, but they don't live here. Because they know…" M. Lagimodière's voice grew dark and spooky. "They don't name this place the Miskoussippi, Blood Red River, for nothing. I'm a good Christian, me, but sometime I think them Indians ain't so far wrong that what happen at a place stay in it, that the ground you walk on remember. But don't tell my wife I said so."

Hugh's fingers brought him back to the present, by reminding him that they were numb and mitts were no good for tying knots. He went back to the fire, where the potful of snow had melted down to a thumb-width of water. He scooped more snow in and warmed his hands over the flames. When he splayed out his fingers, he saw again that the little finger on his right hand still stuck out crookedly from where Dr. Schultz had splinted it years ago. He rarely noticed it anymore, except sometimes when it got in the way. At least his nose had healed straight, or as straight as it had ever been, although Granda warned him that when he grew old the fracture lines would come back to haunt him.

When his fingers came back to life, Hugh went back to knotting shagganappi rope around poplar pole joins. Once the framework was done – a slanted checkerboard drawn by a drunkard – Hugh went to cutting armfuls of spruce and pine branches and weaving them through the poles and rope to make an evergreen-thatched lean-to. Then more boughs for his mattress: spruce boughs with the curved side up so they'd be springier, then a layer of fir boughs to even them out. On top of that he laid an old buffalo robe, wool side up, and another one wool side down, with a woolen HBC blanket sandwiched between them.

While doing all that, he'd been periodically going back to the fire to feed it and the pot and warm his hands. The pot of snow was now a pot of English tea stretched with kinnikinnik – country tea – and a corner of berry leather for sweetening. Hugh poured some into his tin cup, tossed a spruce bough onto the fire to flare up light, and stepped back to have a look at what he'd done. It looked pretty good: a snug bed with a grounded awning woven tight and thick enough to keep out the wind and snow, broadside facing a fire that was close enough to warm it but not so close as to set it on fire – he hoped. He was quite pleased with himself, but also aware that anyone who spent more time hunting than farming could've done it twice as good in half the time, even Norbert Parisien. On second thought, he took out that 'even,' reminding himself of what Wauh Oonae had once told him: *"My Grandfather says Norbert is one of God's Blessed Fools – seems so simpleminded and then you turn around and he's found good fishing where no one thought there was any."*

Hugh knew that all this fussy shelter-building would seem foolish if he got lucky right off tomorrow morning, but not so foolish if he had to stay a few days and the weather turned nasty. To that end, he knew he really should build a reflector – of stacked green logs or something – at the back side of the fire circle, or else half the fire's heat would drift away from him. But he was tired and cold and hungry and it'd be easier in daylight. So he fried up some chunks of berry-flavoured pemmican and flour, settled some thick logs on the fire and piled a few sticks of firewood within arm's reach of his bed.

The first thing he'd done on reaching his camping spot had been to unlash his blanket-wrapped gun from the toboggan and lean it against a handy tree, just in case. It was an old smooth-bore double-barrelled percussion-cap gun – more or less a shotgun, except it would fire a musketball if you wanted it to. Which was why most people thereabouts preferred that kind of gun to a fancy rifle. You could load one barrel with a ball and the other with birdshot, and if you stumbled across a deer or a duck you were ready. Hugh tucked the gun in under the top buffalo robe and blanket, then crawled in behind it. There was no danger of it going off accidentally; it took an effort to wrench the hammers back even when you wanted to fire it.

With his coat balled up for a comfy pillow, his cocoon soon warm from his body heat and the fire, and the soothing smells of pine and spruce needles and woodsmoke caressing the back of his nose, Hugh expected to be asleep in a minute. And he almost was, but then he heard something somewhere beyond the fire – a scratching, clicking sound. He told himself it was just winter-brittle branches rattling in the breeze. But then came another sound: a kind of low groan, or grunt. He cursed himself for not taking two minutes to hang his foodsack from a tall bough away from the lean-to; but the fire should keep the smaller creatures away, and the bears were all asleep by now – or should be.

The groan came again, or maybe it was a growl, from somewhere back behind and to the right of the fire. Hugh told himself he was being a baby, it was just some heavy tree limb surrendering itself to the cold and settling in for the winter. But that didn't stop baby from imagining hunger-crazed Sioux snuck north to steal what they could along the edges of Red River, or remembering ghost stories that were laughable in daylight and gruesome fun around a campfire when you knew come bedtime there'd be other sleepers between you and the circle of darkness.

He started to reach out for the arm's length pile of nightwood, to toss a couple of smaller sticks on the fire and widen the light, then stopped and pulled his arm back in: "You start that and you'll be up all night squinting at shadows."

Now he heard a skittering sound, or maybe just imagined it in the hiss and crackle of the fire. His ears were stretched wide open and tingling. It occurred to him too late that he hadn't thought about one good reason to bring a dog along, regardless the extra complications. If a dog wasn't barking, you knew there was nothing out there. Then again, a dog might've made him even more twitchy, barking at a whiff of skunk from three miles away, or a chipmunk rolling over in its sleep, or at nothing at all. Couldn't blame them for that; dogs were only human.

Hugh chuckled to himself, and then asked himself just how impressed Wauh Oonae was going to be when they were married and went out hunting and fishing together and she discovered her husband was a farmboy frightened of the woods at night. Then again, when he and Nancy Prince were husband and wife she'd be snuggled in his lean-to beside him and he wouldn't be afraid of anything. He saw ahead to times when they'd be camped out in the woods or on the prairie and he'd be teaching their children how to build a lean-to, or how to tell the difference between a wolf's trail and a big dog's... Hugh hadn't learned much of that kind of thing from his father; to Da the woods were a place to get firewood and lumber, and the prairie a place to get hay. So, given that Hugh had had to pick up woodscraft where he could, and Wauh-Oonae he been born to it, he had to admit there were likely more things she could teach their children than he could. Likely many things she could teach *him*...

The next thing Hugh knew, his toes were cold and his eyes were open to daylight. He chucked a few of the smaller sticks from his arm's-length pile into the fire circle, hoping there were still enough embers to catch, and pulled his pillow-coat in to warm before putting it on. Once the fire was going good, he baked a wheel of bannock in his frypan, ate half of it with cheese and put the rest in his coat pockets, then picked up his gun and made his way through the woods to the stream – but not before knotting his second rope around the top of his food bag, tossing the other end over a tree limb twice his height and hoisting temptation out of reach.

There was a skin of ice on the creek, but not so thick yet that delicate deer hooves couldn't break it to get a drink. The streambanks were a tangle of willow and spruce, so instead of trying to fight through it Hugh worked his way along parallel to the thicket, weaving slowly through the bush and scanning the ground ahead of him. After awhile he thought he saw something and stopped, then took one step further and crouched down. About a pace-and-a-half in front of him was the print of a deer's hoof in the snow. There was another to his right and to his left, and what looked like a little pile of pellets farther along. Without crossing the trail, Hugh moved closer to the stream. He saw a swatch of barely-regrown ice, with no snow on it, at the near edge.

Hugh went back to camp and busied himself with keeping the fire going, rolling a knee-high boulder up behind it as a reflector, eating a lunch of pemmican and bannock, and taking a nap. An hour or so before dusk he went back to the deerpath by the stream, this time pulling the toboggan behind him. There was a handy scrub oak as far from the deertrail as the range of his gun and marksmanship would allow. He sat down with his back against the tree, tossed a pinch of snow up to make sure he was downwind of the path, and lit a pipe of store tobacco and kinnikinnik, which worked just as well for stretching tobacco as tea. He hadn't yet worked up the temerity to try smoking at home, except out behind the barn or on the riverbank when no one else was likely to stumble across him. So he was only slowly learning to keep a pipe slowly burning.

The pale winter sunlight was almost gone when Hugh saw a movement off to his left: an antlered buck walking down for his evening drink. Hugh very carefully put down his pipe and lifted his gun off his lap, reining his movements to stay gradual and even, despite the kicked-up gallop of his heart. As he cradled the gunstock into his shoulder he reminded himself that the right-side barrel was the one loaded with a musketball, and he didn't want to complicate the venison with buckshot unless he had to. He cautiously pulled back the right-side hammer, but when it clicked, Mr. Deer disappeared.

As the buck vanished over a bush as tall as Hugh with one spring, Hugh caught a flash of white. Whitetail deer tended to have twice the home range as mule deer, about a square mile, and were geniuses at making themselves invisible, especially at this time of year when everything was dun-coloured and white. But square mile or no, whitetails were also creatures of habit and not much memory. Mr. Deer would be back.

On his way back to camp, it occurred to Hugh to wonder why he didn't feel annoyed or disappointed. Then he realised that The Wilderness Madness had snuck up on him. 'The Wilderness Madness' was a name Hugh and his brothers had coined for what can happen to a seemingly-sane person spending time in the bush or on the plains. You didn't notice it happening, and the first sign it had happened would be something like sitting back for a moment after lunch to watch the cloud-shadow ships scudding across the prairie waves, and then discovering you were watching the sunset and hadn't fallen asleep and hadn't been pondering anything in particular – just perfectly content to sit there and let the breezes play around you.

Now as The Wilderness Madness had set in, Hugh's time became a fluid kind of thing, and his thoughts – when he bothered to think at all – flowed in no particular direction: "I might should set some rabbit snares to stretch out my provisions... Nancy gets dimples beside her eyes when she smiles... sounds like there's something out there beyond the firelight, if it's got any sense it'll come in closer and get warm... wonder why it's warmer on clouded-over winter days than when you can see the sun?... we'll name the first boy Sandy and the first daughter Kate, unless Wauh Oonae's got strong wishes for other names, though I misdoubt she'll push for 'Peguis'... glad I thoughten to bring Da's second-best axe file along, thinking ahead for a change... funny how I'd no-chance eat plain flour and lard at home, but tastes good balled onto a stick and roasted over a campfire... maybe summer after next, when Morrison and Hector are big enough Da can spare me for awhile, I'll go on the buffalo hunt, good way to get some set-aside money to get me and Nancy started out, and they say you don't have to be a good shot for running buffalo just a good rider and Wauh Oonae says I ride pretty good for a white man, though they say running buffalo's like riding through a thundercloud with horns... funny how you don't notice how your nose gets clogged up with the smells of farms and people till you get out in the wild air for awhile, not that there's anything wrong with home smells, but – *Deer!*"

Hugh was sitting with his back against the scrub oak and his pre-cocked gun across his knees. The sun had gone down, but the full moon – The Hunter's Moon – had risen above the trees. Last night – or the last couple of nights; Hugh couldn't remember – the sky had been so thick with cloud the moon was only a vague glow, but tonight the moonglare on the snow etched the world in a clear, blue-white light. Hugh didn't need cat's eyes to make out, ahead and to his left, Mr. Deer ambling daintily down to his drinking place.

Just ahead of the deer's line of march was a clump of brush between Hugh's tree and the deerpath. When the buck disappeared behind it, Hugh rose quietly to his feet, tugging off his right mitten with his teeth, and raised the gun to his shoulder. Mr. Deer reappeared on the right side of the tangle of brush, then stopped and turned his head to look at Hugh.

Hugh knew the deer couldn't see him against the black of the scrub oak, or at least not clearly enough to tell he wasn't part of the landscape, otherwise it would've sprung away. But he also knew that if he moved his gun barrel even the couple of inches he needed for a heart shot, the deer would be gone before he pulled the trigger. So he stood stock still staring into the soft, dark eyes in their winter-grey cowl, with the white bib beneath and the proud antlers above. Impossible that anything could look so delicate and so strong at the same time. It seemed a crime to kill it. But then, this buck had had more of a life than any of the meat steers raised on the farm. And Mr. Deer wouldn't hesitate to pillage Hugh's family's garden of the vegetables they needed to put by for the winter. Still, it seemed a pity…

The deer moved its head and took a step forward. Hugh moved the gun and pulled the trigger. When the smoke cleared, the deer was gone. Hugh pushed his way through the brush. The deer was lying on its side with one leg twitching and a black hole drilled just behind its shoulder. Dead before it hit the ground. Hugh wiped the mist out of his eyes, cut the lovely throat to bleed it out, and went back to where he'd left the toboggan.

When Hugh came back to the deer, the snow in front of it was steaming with blood. He reloaded the empty gun barrel and put a fresh percussion cap on its nipple, in case the blood smell drew wolves, then went to work by moonlight with his thin-bladed skinning knife and thick-backed sheath knife. He cut off the antlers to be sectioned and drilled for buttons and coat-toggles, then cut the legs off just above the knee, cut off the head and made a long slice from throat to tail to peel the skin off and scoop out the innards. By the time he'd cut the body into quarters and loaded them and the hide on the toboggan, the moon was starting her way down. He washed the blood off his hands with snow – there'd been no need for mitts with all the heat coming out of the deer's body – and headed back to camp, leaving the head and guts and shanks for the other meat-eaters.

When Hugh got back to camp, he was surprised that he didn't feel in the least bit tired, or at least definitely not sleepy. He built up the fire and looked at the moon – still another couple hours of moonlight. What the hell. He broke down his camp, loaded up his toboggan and started home.

The moon was down and the sun not yet up when Hugh saw the windowlights of early risers winking on ahead of him. He was much closer to the river and home than he thought he'd got; maybe the Wilderness Madness was messing with his sense of time and distance. A few more minutes' trudging and he discovered there was something he should've thought of when he decided to head straight home instead of spending another night in camp: yard dogs who smelled deer blood and whose owners weren't yet up and about enough to keep them in the yard. Packs of them came running from Hugh's left and right, baying and snarling and trying to tear off everything lashed to the toboggan. Hugh threw off his harness and kicked at them, yelling threats or commands or just yelling. He thought of unwrapping his gun, but he didn't want to shoot someone else's dog, and even if he did, what was he going to do if he fired off both barrels and the rest of them didn't run away? He was almost weeping with frustration – so close to home, but if he kept on pulling the toboggan the dogs would get at it, and if he stayed there trying to drive them off they'd get around him eventually, and they were getting so crazy with blood-smell and pack mentality they might start tearing at *him*...

And then another pack of roaring dogs came running from straight ahead, the home dogs. Behind the dogs came Da and Donald, and Aleck, Morrison, Hector and even Margaret, all brandishing shovels or brooms or rakes or axe handles. Behind them came Granda stumping along on his cane and bellowing Gaelic curses at the sassenach invaders. Mum was no doubt tied to keeping the breakfast porridge from burning, but Hugh had no doubt Gran would 've been in the thick of the rescue party if she could still walk.

Once they were safely in their own yard, and the rest of the family unloading Hugh's camp gear and venison for him, Granda said: "Aye, Hugh's the lad. I just wish old Jean Baptiste was still alive, so I could rub his nose in whose grandson grew up to be the hunter."

CHAPTER 25

"St. Agnes Eve – Ah, bitter chill it was!..."

Agnes Campbell Farquharson peered out the frost-damasked window, murmuring the lines she had by heart without memorising:

"The owl, for all his feathers, was a-cold;
"The hare limped trembling through the frozen grass,
"And silent was the flock in woolly fold..."

The window was in one of the buildings clustered around and behind St. Boniface Cathedral: college, students' dormitory, Bishop's palace, priests' quarters, nuns' quarters... The interior of the whole, vast cathedral had needed painting, and since Agnes's father was a housepainter by trade he'd got the job, along with free board and room for himself and 'dependents' for the months and months it would take him to do it. Knowing her father, Agnes had no doubt he could stretch it out for many months, unless a better opportunity came along. Of course, the arrangement meant they'd all had to convert to Catholicism and pretend they'd been intending to do so anyway, but pretending wasn't foreign to the Farquharson family.

The nuns who'd given Agnes her formal training in how to be a Catholic had naturally told her of *Saint* Agnes, who'd been martyred more than a thousand years ago because she refused to marry the man chosen for her, and declared she was the bride of Christ. On the anniversary of her martyrdom, January 21, the nuns would bless two lambs in the chapel, then shear them and weave their wool. But one of the older nuns had told Agnes informally about St. Agnes' Eve. At midnight on St. Agnes' Eve, a maiden who'd performed the proper ritual would see a vision of her fated bridegroom.

There was something else Agnes had learned that also wasn't part of her official lessons from the Sisters of Charity, the Grey Nuns. She hadn't learned it from anything said to her, just by observation. For all their meek and mild manner, the Grey Nuns would make the average Sicilian Black Hand Society look pallid. They'd been at Red River for a quarter of a century now, and an entire generation had been educated by the Grey Nuns, nursed through sicknesses by the Grey Nuns, been fed through times of famine by the Grey Nuns... When the Grey Nuns spoke, the Bishop listened, and so did The Company.

And the toughest, drunkenest, rantingest buffalo hunter on a tear would turn into an apologetic toddler if a Grey Nun looked disapprovingly at him.

At the moment, though, Agnes wasn't thinking of the Grey Nuns, but of what one of them had told her. And the darkening grey sky this January 20th meant that it was now St. Agnes' Eve.

Maybe it was all superstitious mumbo-jumbo, but she'd seen enough evidence among the natives in Guiana that mumbo-jumbo could have tangible effects, that someone could be bound to someone else forever by invisible threads and ceremony. It wasn't all that far-fetched – after all, that was what a wedding was, a ceremony, and people generally acknowledged that it had its effects. Besides, once the New Year's Regale at Fort Garry was done with there wasn't much to do at Red River except wait out the winter, and a bit of superstitious ceremonialism was at least something to do.

So when the bell rang for the evening meal, Agnes walked to the dining hall looking only straight ahead as the good Sister had whispered to her and as Mr. Keats had said in his very, very long poem: *"Nor look behind, nor sideways…"* If someone called to her from behind, she would have to stop and turn full around to see who it was. The Farquharsons' table stood a little ways apart from those of the boarding students, and the one for the bachelor workmen who lived in the buildings they cared for. Agnes stopped behind the chair she usually sat in and announced to her father and sister: "I don't much feel like dinner tonight."

Her father said: "Feeling poorly are you, Aggie?" She'd hated that nickname ever since she was old enough to wear long skirts, but she knew the more she showed annoyance the more it tickled him to use it.

Without turning her head to look at him, she said: "Not so much, Father, just not much like eating. I think I'll lie down awhile."

"Best have a little lie-down," he said as she was already turning to make her way out of the dining hall. She went down the corridor staring straight ahead, up the stairway at its end and along the fourth floor corridor to the rooms that were the Farquharsons' for the duration. The door to Agnes's room had been left open to let a little heat in from the hallway. She closed it behind her, sat down on the bed to warm the nightgown laid out between the covers, and took up a beaded deerhide pouch filled with fresh sprigs of balsam fir. Separating the sprigs into single twigs, she tied them end-to-end with white silk thread – virginal white and evergreen – until she had a strip of balsam fir slightly longer than the width of her bed. She found it surprisingly difficult to do without looking sideways – having to stand up, turn around and kneel beside the bed instead of turning her head whenever she couldn't put her hand on where she'd last set down the coil of thread – but she managed.

Agnes put the unused sprigs back in the pouch, set it on her night stand at the farthest corner from the burning candle, stood up and undressed. Once she was naked and shivering – St. Agnes' Eve was also said to be the coldest night of the year – she fastened the balsam belt around her waist with a cursory twist-knot, quickly pulled on her nightgown and scurried into bed. Lying on her back with her eyes pointed straight ahead at the candle-flickered ceiling, she whispered: *"As, supperless to bed they must retire, and couch supine their beauties, lily white.."* A great deal of the rest of the poem was bosh, but she remembered the germane parts. She especially liked: *"their beauties, lily white."*

The balsam fir belt prickled the small of her back and tickled her belly, but wasn't nearly as uncomfortable as she'd feared. She felt a bit more silly than lily, but also a bit deliciously pagan, despite the fact that it was Sister Marie France who'd told her the secrets. What was supposed to happen next was that the maiden was supposed to go into a kind of holy trance and keep her eyes focused on the ceiling, or rather *through* the ceiling to what was above and beyond. In the case of St. Agnes herself, and ostensibly Sister Marie France as well, the vision most devoutly to be wished was of Our Lord And Saviour. But Agnes had something less lofty in mind, and suspected Sister Marie France would've, too, if the opportunity had arisen.

Agnes moved her right hand up to the locket watch she'd bought on her father's pay-you-next-week credit the day before they took the train from New York City. The chain was just long enough that she could raise it up to read it without shifting her eyes or bending her neck. Only a quarter of eight, still a long night to wait. But Agnes did find it encouraging that she was actually feeling a bit ethereal; maybe there was something to the spell. Or maybe not so much ethereal as a bit dizzy from going *supperless to bed.* In Red River winters one's body furnace burnt a surprising amount of fuel surprisingly quickly, which was useful for maintaining one's girlish waistline but not so useful for trying to go past dinnertime without dinner. But to Agnes's way of thinking, whether 'ethereal' or 'dizzy' didn't really matter, either way it was a kind of trance. After all, saints and shamans fasted to bring on visions. And, to her way of thinking, the spell could work on both the visionary and the envisioned. So any means of helping it along was fair game. With that in mind, she closed her eyes to see if she could conjure up a few clear memory-pictures to prime the pump…

"Agnes…?" It was a female voice, and Agnes smelled soup. As her eyes popped open, she just barely caught herself from turning her head toward the voice and the odour of buffalo meat steeped in onions and sage and carrots and potatoes.

Instead of replying, Agnes hoisted up her locket watch to eye level. A quarter of nine. Agnes slipped the watch and her hand back under the covers and, still keeping her eyes on the ceiling, said: "Yes, Laura?"

"I brought you a bowl of soup, the Sisters were making some up ahead of time for Sunday."

Agnes had to swallow the saliva squirting out from the hinges of her jaw before saying: "Thank you, but I still don't feel like eating."

Her sister came and hovered over her, bringing the soup smell even closer. There was definitely parsley in the mix. Laura set the soup bowl on the night stand, perched on the edge of the bed, put her hand on Agnes's forehead and said with genuine concern for a change: "Does your tummy hurt?"

"Not so much. I just don't feel like eating."

"Well, you don't have a fever. Does your neck hurt? You can't seem to turn your head –"

"Oh, it's just a bit stiff. Maybe I kinked it."

"Well, you should try a sip or two of nice, warm soup, Aggie." The graceless nickname wasn't quite as grating when Laura said it, maybe because it sounded less patronising in a female voice, or maybe just because she never used it in public. "You'll feel better."

"I can't, really, but thank you."

Laura sniffed and said: "Funny, it smells kind of foresty in here. Pine or something."

Agnes had heard that there were sisters who shared secrets with each other, but that certainly wasn't the case with her and her inevitably-spinster, stiffly awkward older sister; more of a prim maiden aunt than a sister. So Agnes just said: "Oh, when I was taking the air this morning I came across a balsam fir and thought it would be nice to have that perfume in my room. You can see there's a few sprigs in the pouch there…"

"What a clever idea. I might maybe try that in my room, and maybe Papa's room, too. Well, I'll leave the soup here –"

"No, please Laura, the smell makes me – " ravenous "– a bit nauseous just now."

"'Nauseous'…?" Another tincture crept into the concern in Agnes's sister's voice. "Is there something you haven't been telling me, Aggie?"

"No, I just… don't feel like eating."

"Well… I'll look in on you again before I go to bed."

"Thank you, Laura."

Agnes's sister left the room, taking temptation with her, although its odour still lingered for a while. Agnes was glad to've slept away one of the hours, but apprehensive she might fall asleep again, a danger she hadn't factored into her plan. If she did fall back asleep, and if her sister chose to let her sleep when she looked in on her again, St. Agnes' Eve and all the trouble she'd gone to would be gone for nought. She shifted from side to side to prickle the balsam needles against the small of her back and tingle her more awake, then widened her eyes and focused on the ceiling: amber candlelight playing across the plains and elevations of rough-daubed plaster. The way to stay awake was to concentrate on why she was staying awake: her future.

Mrs. John Christian Schultz would not only have a handsome, clever, virile, charming husband, she would also be proprietress of a general store, pharmacy and lodging house, but that was only the beginning. If – no, *when* – Dr. Schultz's prognostications came true, and the Hudson's Bay Company's territories opened up to all the land-starved sons and daughters of Empire waiting to pour in from the east, Mrs. John Christian Schultz would be proprietress of the profits from vast acres purchased as wilderness and sold as farmland. She could see herself in a silk gown – or, rather, in a corset and smallclothes trying to choose from a walk-in closet filled with silk gowns, and a maid to help her choose.

But that was only the beginning. The powers that be in Upper Canada would need men whom they knew, and who knew the lay of the land, to administer the new territories for them. And who fit that description better than John Christian Schultz?

He had spent part of his time in Upper Canada last summer talking with 'some very important men.' It wasn't fantastical to imagine he'd be a Member of Parliament someday, maybe someday even *Sir* John Christian Schultz. She could see herself at the head of a receiving line, wearing an apricot taffeta gown, with men two feet taller than her bending over her hand and murmuring respectfully: "Lady Schultz…" No, not apricot, navy blue would bring out her eyes more –

"Aggie…?"

It was her sister again. Agnes lifted her watch again. Seven minutes after ten. Miraculously, she'd dreamed away almost two hours without falling asleep. It was still a little early for what she had planned, but if her sister was looking in on her on her way to bed, it was now or never.

Her sister said: "Why are you looking at your watch?" with a tone that implied people who were truly ill didn't care what time it was.

"To see if I'd fallen asleep again since you were last here. I've been checking every quarter hour or so. It seemed to me that if I had fallen back asleep, then the pain was passing, or at least wasn't bad enough to keep me awake. But I haven't slept."

"Your tummy hurts?"

"Yes, and, as you surmised, so does my neck. I still can't turn my head. I'm sorry to be troublesome, Laura, but I'm afraid you'd best send for a doctor. There's always one of the cathedral caretakers up on duty all night, ever since the old church burnt down, and I'm sure he wouldn't mind taking a little jaunt in the fresh air. Fort Garry's gates will be shut for the night by now, and Dr. Cowan's probably asleep anyway. But Dr. Schultz will likely still be up…"

After a short pause, Agnes's sister said somewhat drily: "You want me to fetch Dr. Schultz for a pain in the neck?"

"And in my stomach – my stomach feels like it's chewing itself to pieces," which wasn't that much of an exaggeration. She could tell that her sister was wavering – after all, it wasn't the spitting-blood trick. Agnes gave out a little moan and murmured wanly: "Please, Laura."

"All right. I'll see if anybody's still up and about, and if not I'll go myself. Can I get you anything?"

"No, just… Dr. Schultz. Thank you, Laura."

Once her sister was gone, Agnes looked at her watch again and calculated: roughly a half-hour for someone to hike along and across the river to Dr. Schultz's White Store, maybe ten minutes for Dr. Schultz to gather his medical bag and get himself garbed for outside, and a half-hour back… That would put his arrival at about half-past eleven; much too early. That would mean she'd have to stall him for half an hour. But maybe he'd choose to hitch up the cutter instead of walking, which would shorten his travelling time but actually take longer overall when harnessing time was factored in. Then again, it might take her sister some while to find a willing messenger still up and about, or to give up and decide to go herself, and Dr. Schultz might not arrive till *after* midnight. Both

Sister Marie France and John Keats had been very specific about midnight, although naturally Mr. Keats had put it more poetically: *"the honey'd middle of the night."*

Agnes didn't much like worrying about what might or might not happen, she much preferred to make things happen. But at the moment she couldn't think of what more she could do to make what she wanted to happen happen, it was just a question of time. She rolled her posterior from side to side again to prickle the small of her back with needles to keep herself awake, and put her mind on the distant future when the village of Winnipeg would be a city, a city with a railway terminal, and thousands of people on the boardwalks would tip their hats when Lady Schultz passed by in her carriage...

Agnes had worked her way up to meeting Queen Victoria when she heard heavy footsteps coming along the corridor, with the slow-but-fast cadence of long legs striding quickly. She looked at her watch. Eighteen minutes before midnight. There was a knock on her door, and his voice penetrated the barrier, "Miss Farquharson...? It's Dr. Schultz..."

"A moment, please... I'm... indisposed..."

She could see him through the door in her mind's eye, with the Viking red-gold curls at the back of his neck mingling with the red-black curls collaring his buffalo coat, and a dusting of snowflakes on both. She'd hardly seen him at all this winter, except for the New Year's Regale; the carriage or sleigh rides to and from church every Sunday had come to an end when the Farquharsons relocated to St. Boniface Cathedral. But since she could envision him so clearly now, maybe all that the secret ceremony required was for her to hold that picture until midnight, even if he only took ten minutes to examine her and was gone before the hour struck. But no, the spell had to work in both directions –

"Miss Farquharson...?" The knock came again.

"Just another moment, please." Her stomach growled and groaned in a very unpoetical way, making her doubly glad she'd stalled Dr. Schultz a moment longer. She rubbed her belly to quiet it, working the tips of her lower fingers in under the girdle of balsam fir.

"Miss Farquharson...?"

"Yes. Come in." She couldn't stall him forever. It was an effort to not turn her head to look when she heard the door open and close and his bootsteps approaching her bed. His face entered her field of vision, bending over her concernedly. There was a slight golden haze along his jawline; he hadn't paused to shave before coming to her aid. If – *when* – she had him in hand, she would have to elucidate to him that if there were an evening official or social function, he should shave after dinner as well as before breakfast.

He said: "Your sister tells me you're having some difficulty turning your neck...?"

"Yes, Doctor." She was also having some difficulty calling him 'Doctor' with a straight face, given what she'd found in his personal papers last summer – or rather hadn't found.

"And a loss of appetite, some pain in your... midriff...?"

"That, too."

"Hm..." As her sister had done, and as he'd done on his first examination of her two-and-a-half years previously, he put his hand on her forehead, held it there for a moment and said: "Hm… Doesn't seem to be any fever…" Then he ducked out of her field of vision and she could hear him opening his satchel and slotting together his wooden stethoscope. She had no idea of what listening to her heart and lungs might have to do with pains in her stomach and neck, and likely neither did he, but she took the opportunity to quickly raise her watch to her eyes again. Eight minutes until midnight.

Dr. Schultz coughed discreetly and said: "Um, Miss Farquharson, if you would please…"

Agnes didn't turn her head or sidle her eyes, but she could see on the periphery of her vision that he was kneeling by the side of her bed holding up his listening tube. She unfurled the covers on that side down to her waist, and he pressed the wide end of the tube against her ribcage through her nightgown, and cupped the other end to his ear. Her stomach chose that moment to let out a long, gurgling growl that must've near-deafened him. It was her turn to cough discreetly, trying to cover the growl and the sudden blush she could feel. He didn't comment, just held the stethoscope to his ear a moment longer, then murmured: "Hm," and leaned back to take the instrument apart and put it away. While he was occupied, she raised her watch again. Four minutes.

Dr. Schultz stood up and then stooped again to perch on the edge of her bed, saying: "I'd best have a feel of your neck." His huge, work-callused hands settled tentatively and tenderly on either side of her head, the thick fingers probing gently. "Hm… Well, I'll have a little try at turning your head, shall I…?"

"No! Just, not just yet… Maybe if you massage it a moment longer – I can feel it starting to soften up…"

"Very well…"

She lifted her watch between his forearms and up to her eyes. Eleven fifty-nine, and the second hand at the bottom of its sweep. She started counting off in her mind: *One thousand, two thousand…*

Dr. Schultz's red-gold eyebrows knit together, and he said confusedly: "Why do you look at your…?"

Agnes didn't answer. When she got to *twenty-eight thousand* she closed her eyes, then opened them again. And there was his face hovering above her at midnight on St. Agnes' Eve. She felt a smile blossoming across her face, and said in her mind: *"You're mine."* She rolled her head luxuriously from side to side, hearing the tiny crackles of her neckbones, and there truly was a bit of pain in there from holding her head in one position for so long. She said: "Thank you, Dr. Schultz. You have the healing touch."

"Um, yes, well… seems there was just a kink in the cervical vertebrae…" He seemed to suddenly become aware that he was sitting on her bed and had been massaging her neck. He stood up, stepped back and said: "And then, about your… digestive tract…"

"Oh, I'm sure that will be fine now, too. Now that I can turn my head again, I don't feel so queasy."

"Good, yes, there are… anatomical connections and interactions that modern medicine still don't understand." He turned his head, and his eyes rivetted on something. She followed his eyes to the crucifix on the wall, then back to him. He looked as tortured as the little wooden Jesus on the wall. He tore his eyes away from it, but didn't look at her. He said: "Miss Farquharson, I… Dammit, I – pardon my French – but, I don't want to pry into what's none of my business, but I do think we're well enough acquainted that I have some right to ask about something so… perplexing." It sounded like 'perplexing' was the mildest term he could come up with, and he'd had to reach for it.

"What is it you find so perplexing, Dr. Schultz?"

"You and your family, this… *conversion.* All this Romishness. I mean, I could understand some ignorant farmgirl brought up with the priest's thumb on her neck, or some halfbreed buffalo hunter impressed with incense and Latin chants, but *you…?*"

Agnes was about to laugh and tell him the conversion was only so her father could get the contract for painting the cathedral, and would likely only last for the duration, but caught herself. It hadn't occurred to her what a powerful card she held in her hand, or even that that trick was on the table. She said meekly: "We don't all have your advantages, Dr. Schultz. Those of us who see little hope of glory in this life must look to the next. I'm not a young maiden anymore; if I'm going to be an old maid I might as well do it in a convent and be a bride of Christ." She thought of adding 'like St. Agnes,' but decided that might be tipping her hand.

Dr. Schultz said: "My… 'advantages'?"

"Just look at you. You're a big, strong, handsome man with a good education, keen intelligence and high ambition. You'll go far."

"Do you really think so?"

"I know so."

"Will you go with me, Agnes?"

"Where?"

"Wherever I go." He crouched by her bed and enveloped her hand in both of his. "Will you marry me, Agnes? Oh, I should speak to your father first."

"Yes, John."

"Yes, of course, you're right, I should've thought that I should speak with your father before –"

"I *said* 'Yes, John.'"

"Oh! That's wonderful! Thank you!" He squeezed her hand so hard she thought he was going to break it, then leaned forward to kiss her. But at that moment her stomach chose to let out a growl like a grizzly bear. He leaned back quickly, saying: "I'm sorry, I forgot you're not well – and if anyone should know, because that's why I'm here, and glad I am of it, not glad you're not well, but…" He stood up. "I'll look in on you again tomorrow, shall I?"

She nodded.

He gestured tentatively at the decidedly unProtestant wall crucifix and said: "So, you'll have no more need of… all that…?"

"Not once we're married."

His forehead puckered.

"My family will still be living here for the foreseeable future, so *I* will still be living here. I can't very well go live with *you* before we're married."

He nodded at the sense of that, and more – in understanding that of course she would have to pretend to go along with the priests as long as she was eating their bread and sleeping under their roof. His nod reminded her of the real reason they were meant to be married: they understood each other in so many ways. He'd just needed a little push.

He said: "Well, you need to get some rest, I hope you're feeling better tomorrow. So... until tomorrow."

"Until tomorrow."

After the door closed behind him, Agnes waited until his footsteps faded down the corridor, then jumped up, threw on her dressing gown and went to see if her sister had left out that bowl of soup.

Agnes awoke in an unfamiliar bed that was somehow familiar. She groggily realised that it was Dr. Schultz's bed, and she was taking care of his home and store while he was in Canada for the summer. Then she realised it was the next summer, and the morning after her wedding night. Oh, yes... She smiled all over and wrapped her arms around herself, since there was no one else in the bed to do it for her.

Her husband was standing at the washstand with his broad, long back to her, shaving. It occurred to her that it might be a good idea for him to grow a beard. Not a hedge-growth bib, but a closely-trimmed beard that would accentuate the proud prow of his jaw and give him a bit more maturity. Besides, when his face was looked at straight on, his eyes were a size too small for the size of his head, and a beard and mustache would mitigate that. When she found an apt moment to broach the subject, she could point out truthfully that she would be the one making the sacrifice, since it was her face that would suffer the stubble of the prickly growing-out stage.

He husband glimpsed her sitting up in his shaving mirror and turned toward her, wiping his razor. She became aware that the bedclothes were all rumpled and tangled and so was her hair. He said brightly: "Oh what a mangled bed we leave, when first we practice to conceive," and then turned red as a radish.

"Yes, I'm afraid I'm probably looking a bit bed-raggelled."

"You mean 'bedraggled.'"

"I meant what I said."

"Oh. Oh! Good one. Maybe Anonymous should use it in one of his *Nor'Wester* poems – anonymously, of course." He towelled the last errant flecks of lather off his face and put away his razor, saying: "Actually, I was hoping you wouldn't waken till I'd done shaving. No doubt I'll get used to it, but at the moment it's... hard to concentrate. Well... my dear, shall I go put on a pot of tea while you're... freshening up?"

"Thank you, John. No!"

"Oh, um, you'd rather something cold – ?"

"Tea would be lovely, thank you. I meant no I can't call you John. John is so common, and there is nothing common about you. John Christian Schultz… I think I should call you 'Christian,' as in Pilgrim's Progress." Back in a girlish religious stage she'd read John Bunyan's dreary book more than once, parts of it so many times she could still see the words on the page. "You're no Pilgrim, thank God, but you're certainly going to progress."

"How could I not, with you beside me, Aggie?"

CHAPTER 26

Sandy Sutherland sat in the sun sipping cold tea for a hot day. A waft of breeze from the riverside trees convinced him he'd rather be sitting in the shade. With both hands on the head of his walking stick for leverage, he creaked to his feet and limped toward the path down to the river. The sun's heat did seem to've done his knee some good, though not much. Funny how a moment's accident could change a man's life forever, though he had to admit it was the luckiest thing that ever happened to him, though it took years for that to prove true.

The pain in his knee put him back at Corunna on the coast of Spain, where he was one dot on the thin red line on a night that was a Devil's Dream of flares, rockets, cannon flashes and screams, including the scream of Private Alexander Sutherland when a French bayonet drove into his knee –

"Hello, Granda."

It was Hugh, sitting on the riverbank with an H-shaped wooden spool of fish line in his hands. Sandy looked down at his grandson and laughed, because it was quite possible that if Hugh hadn't broke in on his memory, Private Sutherland would've kept on limp-marching straight into the Red River.

Sandy eased down sitting on the cool grass, with his back against a shaded tree trunk and his right leg stretched out straight in front of him. He squinted to focus his rheumy eyesight along Hugh's fishing line to a bottle-cork float in the deeper water. "Any luck then, lad?"

"Just a couple little suckerfish I'll give to the dogs, if the barn cats don't run 'em off. Prob'ly better luck as the day cools, knockin' wood."

"Well, it's nae so easy fishing here as it was before it got so populated. Ye could fill a boat of an evening. Mind you, we were never much for angling, just net-fishing – get as much provisions as ye can as quick as ye can. I hear the fish are still just as thick up on the lake, in a good year."

Sandy took out his pipe and tobacco pouch and so did his grandson. Sandy had been relieved that Hugh had ceased being secretive about his smoking ever since he'd started to grow a mustache. It meant 'Granda' no longer felt constrained to make noise when walking around to behind the barn, or down the river path. It wasn't much of a mustache, just black peach fuzz, but it seemed Hugh had fallen for the old wives' tale that growing out the peach fuzz and then shaving it off made the real whiskers come sooner. Then again, maybe old wives did know more about whiskers than old husbands; they'd generally had to kiss more of them.

Sandy peered through his pipe smoke at Point Douglas across the river. He remembered smoke *on* Point Douglas: thick, black smoke and flying soot, and he and his new-wed wife scrambling with buckets and blankets and spades to confine the fire to the half-acre of prairie grass that was going to be their first field.

But the wispy, pale, pipe smoke was less like that smoke than like mist. There wasn't often a mist on the Red River, not like a Highland river. Back in County Sutherland there was almost always a morning mist or evening mist on the River Ulidh and Kildonan Burn, when they weren't frozen. But it hadn't been mist the night ex-Private Alexander Sutherland came limping back into the glen he'd only left because the only choice open to him was to go for a soldier. The mist that night had been smoke from all the crofters' homes put to the torch by the agents of their own Clan Chief. The same kind of black mist had spread over the Red River the day the North West Company and Cuthbert Grant's Metis burned the colony and sent the colonists rowing north along the same rivers and lakes they'd rowed south from Hudson's Bay two years earlier. Or was he remembering the second time that happened, in which case it would've been three years…?

Sandy waved away his pipe smoke and the memory, and blinked his eyes away from those smoke-choked rivers to the peaceful one in front of him. The Red wasn't like a Highland river at all. She was wide, slow and muddy instead of swift, clear and rocky. She didn't have the dangerous look of a Highland river, but was more dangerous than all. Sandy could see himself at the stern of a dugout canoe, paddling out the door of their little house on Point Douglas, with Kate in the bow ducking her coppery red mane to pass under the lintel the flash flood waters were reaching for, and black-haired wee Johnny amidships between them – or maybe it had been black-haired wee Hugh…?

"I don't think so, Granda."

"Hm?"

"I don't think it was me in the boat, it must've been Da."

"Oh." Sandy hadn't been aware he'd been remembering aloud. "Aye, I'd say ye're right, it wasnae the flood of '52 but the flood of '26. A much smaller house then and washed clean away, smashed to flinders by the ice floes. Well, I hear ye hae a fond lass, Hugh."

Sandy's not-so-wee grandson, Kate's Christmas Boy, squirmed and said: "I think so, maybe, me whatever."

"Ye *think* so? What the de'il's thinking got to do with it?"

"Well… I'm still a couple years too young to talk to her serious, and she's the kind of girl – well, for all I know about that kind of thing – I'm thinking she's the kind of girl that you either get serious or get lost."

"Huh. That's the good kind. It's a lucky man that lives the old toast."

"'The old toast'...?"

"Aye. 'May your first love be your last.'"

"Um, was it, uh..." Hugh gave a tug on his fishing line, to bob the bobber and the baited hook up and down, and kept his eyes on the river. It seemed blatantly obvious to Sandy Hugh was just trying to give the impression he was concentrating on fishing, as though the subject of females was just idle conversation. Being young was hardly worth the price of being so painfully transparent. "Was it like that for you and Gran? Your first loves was your last?"

"Well..." It was an unfair question, bringing back images of a lamed and futureless ex-soldier and a woman too gawky-tall and self-willed for most men. "It wasnae the same for your Gran and I as for most wedded couples, Hugh. Though we knew each other as children, a little, but in the years most people would hae been courting I was far away, marching wherever His British Majesty took a fancy. So your Gran and me were both firm-set in our single ways by the time we became a couple.

"Being in a marriage and being in love are no' the same thing – I dinnae mean to say they are mutual exclusive, but... I needn't tell ye your Gran's a strong-willed woman, and I can be stubborn at times. We had our set-to's. Slashed my arm with a knife once."

"You did?"

"No, she did."

"*Gran?*"

"Well, I deserved it... more or less... All I mean to say, Hugh, all I *can* say, is I suspect that a young couple that's grown up acquainted with each other will have a smoother time of it than your Gran and me in our first years. Not that there isn't always some skirmishing, but..."

"Why'd Gran slash your arm with a knife?"

"Oh, your father had jet black hair like yours, before he started greying early from too much thinking and worrying." Sandy shook his head at the memory of his own gormless stupidity. Married late or not, he'd still been young and foolish. Sandy-haired Sandy Sutherland and red-haired Kate MacPherson had been married eight years before they'd had their first child – which turned out to be their only child – and the child had jet-black hair. And so did Grant: Cuthbert Grant, Mr. Grant, 'The Chief of All The Halfbreeds.'

Sandy had always been a bit suspicious of the courtly relations between his wife and Grant. And for the first ten years of marriage he'd carried festering suspicions that Catherine MacPherson had manipulated him into marrying her because she knew he was the only colonist who came with a freehold deed, not just a leasehold. Because he knew he was no prize in himself.

One autumn day when Kate happened to be cutting up a turnip, it had all come out. When Sandy's rant got to the point of pointing out that John had black hair – unlike either of his official parents but like Grant – Kate had lashed her right arm out at him in rage, perhaps unaware that the paring knife was still in her hand. Oddly, the blood and their mutual shock had washed away all that had been festering in him. Not that there weren't still things to be sorted out over the years, but he never again doubted that her heart and soul were bound to his as much as his to hers.

Sandy said aloud: "Your great-grandfather, Hugh – your Gran's father – had black hair, too."

Hugh said: "Oh," in the polite way of well brought up young people when old people come out with odd leaf-bits off the family tree. But by then Sandy had already been taken by another memory, one that was always lurking whenever conversation or recollection touched on Mr. Grant, one that he'd never spoken of in any detail.

It was a sunny day fifty-one summers ago. Sandy was standing with a bayonet-fixed musket at one end of a ragged skirmish line of two dozen colony men, most of whom had never faced an armed enemy in their lives. On the other side of the wildflowered, honeybee-humming meadow of Frog Plain was a line of fifty Metis horsemen, and more of them coming up from the woods along Seven Oaks Creek. Big young Grant rode out of the woods and took up his place at the centre of the line of horsemen. Even at that distance, Sandy could read the expression in Grant's gleaming black eyes when they settled on Governor Semple at the centre of the line of colony men, because it was exactly the same thought Sandy was having: *"Is it possible that any two-legged creature could be this boneheaded stupid?"*

There was an attempt to parley that turned into a shouting shoving match between Grant's envoy and the governor. Then someone fired a shot and the meadow exploded in gunshots, powder flashes, smoke and screams. When the smoke cleared enough to see between its drifting shrouds, half the colony men were down already and the men from the other side of the clearing were running forward with hatchets and knives. Your only hope to live was throw down your empty musket and run for the river, charging blindly through the smoke with your right leg swinging like a stick of wood and bullets buzzing past you like bumblebees…

Sandy's brittle old bones shivered in the sun and he pushed the memory away. But, oddly, now as he'd happened to remember Seven Oaks just after remembering Kate slashing his arm, it seemed they were the same thing. Not that there hadn't still been things to be sorted out over the years after Seven Oaks, tail-ends of skirmishing and negotiating, but the Fur Trade war had ended there. The hearts and souls of everyone with either had been seared by the horror of that day, and no one had to imagine any longer what might happen if they didn't find a way to make peace. It seemed a general principle that people couldn't really see that other people had blood in them, too, until some of it got spilt. It seemed a pity, but…

"What was that song, Granda?"

"What song?"

"You were humming a song I never heard before. I heard you sing a lot of songs, but never that one, or I don't remember, me whatever."

"Oh… I dinna ken. My singing voice has grown so cracked and wandery – not that it was all that true to begin with – it might hae been a tune ye heard a hundred times before but cannae recognise in my mangling."

A truer voice sang in Sandy's inner ear:

"For a' that, and a' that,
"Our toils obscure and a' that…
"A man's a man for a' that… "

He said aloud: "Ye know, lad, it's only natural for Kildonan folk and Indians to feel a kinship. Deep-thinking philosophers hae said that Highlanders are The Noble Savages of Europe." Hugh looked like maybe the old man with the gamy leg was pulling his. "It's aye true – I read it in a book, and writ by a foreigner at that. Nae doubt even the English would agee – except the 'noble' part."

The crude-carved spool of fish line in Hugh's hand suddenly tried to jump into the river. Sandy tried to make a grab for the line, but his elbow seized up. No matter – Hugh snagged a tighter, two-handed hold on the wooden H before it had quite jumped away. No matter except that Sandy felt like a useless old bundle of sticks. Hugh jumped to his feet and Sandy stayed sitting, watching his grandson play the fish by backing up the bank with the line taut and walking forward again rewinding the line. When the cork float reached the shoreline, Hugh threw his arms up over his head, jumping backwards, and out popped a fat trout with its bronze scale armour glistening in the sun.

Sandy crowed: "A trout Hugh! No one's taken a trout out of this over-fished old river since… since – I dinna ken – since auld lang syne! If ye get it up to your mother quick, there's just time to have it cleaned and cooked for supper."

Hugh dropped the still-flopping fish into the Saulteaux basketwork approximation of a creel, latched the lid and reached down to give his grandfather a hand up. Sandy waved him off, "No, no – I can still get tae my feet without a hand. Go show your mother your plunder while it's still fresh."

Sandy cricked his neck around to watch his near-man-sized grandson bound up the path, trying to remember what it felt like to move without pain. Or without 8,000 connotations and remembrances that distracted a man till he forgot what move he'd meant to make.

Sandy did see one advantage, though, to his gammy leg. At times when his knee was flaming up again, he hardly noticed the aggravation in his finger joints, wrists, elbows, ankles… He hoisted his walking stick up to hook its crook on a handy tree limb, and hand-over-handed himself upright. Once on his feet again he had to pause and catch his breath before following his grandson up the path.

The trout would've been big enough to feed a whole family in the Highlands, where so many children died in infancy, but with seventeen mouths around the table it was just enough to make a tasty side-dish to the mutton and new potatoes and fresh-picked peas. When the dishes were cleared away and the tea and tobacco came out, John announced to

Janet at the other end of the table, in a voice that included anyone else who cared to hear, "At the Council meeting this afternoon, Mother, Governor Mactavish had, um, discovered a few more... *factual* matters about Alaska and Canada. Hm, funny to think that not too many years ago we, um, wouldn't hear of what happened in the outside world this spring until next spring, but now with the American railways and telegraphs...

"At any rate," John leaned forward with his elbows propped on the table and trellised his hands. Sandy leaned forward, too with his eyes on his son. John didn't often get in a mode of having important secrets to impart. "It seems the Act creating the, um, Dominion of Canada was passed in London on March 29th, and the sale of Russian Alaska to the United States was signed on March 30th. Strange... *coincidence*, don't you think?"

Sandy, and the rest of the family still at table, looked around to see if any head was nodding 'Ah-hah! ' But nobody seemed to have any idea what their father, son and husband seemed to think was obvious. Finally Janet said: "'Coincidence,' Father...?"

"Yes, a bit much for coincidence. It's, um, almost like they're in a race – in fact they *are* in a race, and we're the prize."

Hugh said: "I wouldn't call us much of a prize. Not Donald and Morrison, at least."

Morrison said: "Somebody give Mr. Purple a cuff on the scruff."

John said: "I mean *all* of us," waving his arm wide. "All of Rupert's Land. As of March 29th there is now a... *Dominion* of Canada, and as of March 30th Alaska is, um, part of the United States. Now... don't you think that any, um, true-blue American thinks it's a... *pity* that poor, little Alaska is stuck way up there so far from the rest of the United States, with all the empty space of Rupert's Land in between? And that any, um, red-blooded Canadian thinks it's a pity that their new Dominion is... *confined*, to a little strip of land along the St. Lawrence River and the seacoast, when there is all the empty space of Rupert's Land to the north and west? Hm?"

Donald said, in his grave, college-man way, "Do you think there's going to be a war, Da?"

Janet said: "You see, Father, you're upsetting the children," which looked to miff Donald a bit.

John said: "I'm sorry, Mother, I hadn't meant to. Um, no, Donald, I'm sure there won't be a war. Quite sure. After all, the new, um, Dominion and the United States are both... *democracies*. They have to answer to their people."

"Buying and selling Alaska and its people," said Kate, "seems not so democratic to me."

"I don't guess the Eskimoes," Hugh put in, "much care whether they sell their furs to Cossacks or Yankees."

"I don't guess anybody asked 'em," said Aleck.

"Whatever happens," John pronounced, "it's going to happen fast. Or as fast as such... *large* events can happen. Or so it seems to me, from, um, what little I know of that kind of thing. Maybe they'll negotiate to, um, divide the territory between them, or maybe... I don't know."

Kate said: "Or it may be that The Company will hold fast to its rights to the land, and change will be allowed to happen at a natural pace, as it has the last forty years here."

John looked doubtful, but didn't argue with his mother. But the seeming fact that two foreign countries were jockeying to get into Rupert's Land led inevitably into the old question of what should be done with Point Douglas. The question seemed abstract and distant to Sandy, as did everything else at the moment. He'd fallen into an eerie fancy that came over him at times: *'Maybe I died at Corunna, or in that fever-heat, frozen hut outside Fort Churchill, or at Seven Oaks, and maybe all since has been just a death-dream...'*

Nonetheless, dream or not he had to treat it as real. So he again told his son that a piece of land to call your own was worth more than any schemer's schemes, but he wasn't in a mood to speak harshly to anyone and was so tired that, once the subject had run its course, it seemed he fell asleep in his chair. He didn't know for how long, but one minute Kate was in her wheeled chair across the table from him and the next moment he was rubbing his eyes and she was gone. She was in her bed in the corner with her Bible and candle. John and Janet and the boys-before-the-girls were still at the table or in chairs by the hearth, but none of them made comment on the fact that the old fella seemed to've nodded off.

Sandy planted his hands on the table to push himself upright and go say good-night to his wife. But when he got to the edge of her bed, the toe of his indoor, sheep's fleece mocassin bumped against something metal. She said: "Oh, that is just my goffering iron – the wee girls were playing with it this afternoon, though I would not let them try it in the fire. Just nudge it under the bed."

He did, remembering the day in 1820-something when she came back from The Company's store brimming with delight that this year's shipment had included goffering irons. Goffering irons were the cast iron contraptions that all Highland women used to make starched curls on the white linen caps they wore to kirk. All of the colony women had lost theirs in the years of house-burnings and evictions and take-only-what-you-can-carry. But it wasn't the prospect of getting a goffering iron again that had made Kate so giddy she'd come home laughing and crying. It was what the prospect of a new goffering iron brought her to realise: after going without anything but the meagerest necessities for so many years, she could now actually use some of their potatoes to make starch.

All of that came back to Sandy in a blink, as he toe-nudged the ancient goffering iron back under her bed. Kate had lain her opened Bible face-down across her breasts and clasped her hands over it. They were large hands, bigger than his, or at least the fingers were longer. Even parchment-skinned, dabbed with liver spots and knob-knuckled with arthritis, he could still see the strength in them, and the gentleness they could touch with despite the pad of work-callus that covered the palms and finger-fronts. He gestured at her Bible and said: "I'd hae thought you'd hae it memorised by now."

"Mostly. The 'begats' wear me out."

He reached to take hold of one of her hands; she raised the near one to save him bending down. He squeezed her hand and said: "I hope you sleep well, Kate *Ruadh*," – Red Kate.

"You, too."

When Sandy'd carried his candle up the stairs and was stepping into his room, the candlelight and his eyes caught on something he'd learned to ignore. Donald Gunn had had two copies of a certain issue of The London Illustrated News in the Red River Library, so had allowed Hugh to snip out an illustration and Hugh had pinned it to Sandy's bedroom door. It was an imaginative depiction of the glorious stand of the 42nd Highlanders against Napoleon's army at Corunna. Sandy muttered: "Damn fools," – not Donald Gunn or Hugh, Hugh'd just been trying to please his grandfather. The mutter meant the myriad of two-legged creatures who thought glory meant marching behind a regimental band in a victory parade. Damn fools – the glory was in seeing the field outside your front door waving with golden barley where once there'd been nothing but prairie twitch-grass and bramble, in seeing your sweat-soaked, beautiful wife holding the red and wrinkled baby to her breast, in binding the last patch of roof-thatch onto your own house you'd built with your own hands... He thought of going back downstairs and telling Hugh that, but it would sound too much like an old fool's sermon and, anyway, the stairs were steep and Sandy was too tired. So tired.

As he closed the bedroom door and set the candle on the blanket box, it occurred to Sandy that there was something he could tell Hugh that wouldn't sound like a sermon, because it was just plain fact. It was a terrifying fact, though, or would be to most young people, so old people kept it to themselves. But Kate's Christmas Boy was one young person who might not find it terrifying, maybe even encouraging. Maybe tomorrow Sandy would find an opportunity when no one else was in earshot, and tell Hugh the Great Secret: *"We're all just children walking around in Big Folks' clothes."* Maybe tomorrow.

Sandy took off his trousers but was too tired to change into his nightshirt, his day shirt would do. When he settled into the bed that had been his and Kate's, the feather mattress billowed up around his whittled-down body – nothing left of him but gristle and bone. Not surprising, when he considered how far he'd travelled. He'd come a long way from County Sutherland and Corunna and Seven Oaks and the starvation camp on Hudson's Bay, and a few other dire circumstances along the way. So many times he'd have called anyone daft who predicted his life would come to include a fine son and daughter-in-law and a horde of grandchildren. And a fine piece of land with his name on the deed. And a snug house big enough for all the family. And a larder that was never empty. And Catherine MacPherson. Sandy smiled in his sleep.

CHAPTER 27

Schultz was working in his newspaper print shop when a tentative knock came at the outside door. *The Nor'Wester* was truly and entirely *his* newspaper now; he'd bought out his partner in a fire sale – literally – when the log cabin print shop cum office burned to the ground, taking the printing press with it. Dapper William Coldwell had interpreted the heap of smouldering slag as a sign to hie himself back to Upper Canada – or rather, the Province of Ontario in the Dominion of Canada now. Schultz expected to be seeing him again soon, since that was where Dr. & Mrs. J. C. Schultz were going on their slightly-belated honeymoon.

The Nor'Wester's new printing press was an old one that had long ago been through the fire: a fire that didn't quite destroy the old offices of the St. Paul *Pioneer* but ate away enough wood that the cast iron printing press fell through the floor of the second storey, smashed through the floor below and wound up in the cellar. Its broken print bed had been more or less repaired by a blacksmith, but was so warped that the proprietors of *The Pioneer* gladly parked it in a back room as soon as a replacement could be procured from back east, and were more than happy to get rid of it when the proprietor of the burned-out *Nor'Wester* came scrounging around for any printing equipment he could get his hands on. Newspaper offices did seem to have an attraction for fires, maybe something to do with cigars and stacks of newsprint.

So when the knock came at Schultz's print shop door, he was happy to leave off trying to shim the blacksmith-butchered print bed level yet again. He opened the door to a shimmering summer day and a young man with curly black hair brushed back from a widow's peak, blue-green eyes and a juvenile attempt at a mustache. Schultz took a moment to quickly leaf through his mental files; Agnes had been encouraging him to exercise his inborn talent for remembering names and faces, as it would be very useful in political circles and public life. Schultz said chipperly: "Why, it can't be young Hugh Sutherland all grown up!"

"Not all, Doctor, me whatever." The voice was anything but chipper, and the green eyes were downcast. He held out a folded piece of paper. "Da sent me to give you this to print in the next *Nor'Wester*, said to send around the bill when you know how much."

Schultz unfolded the piece of paper. *Point Douglas Alexander Sutherland died peacefully in his sleep, aged 83 years…* "Ah," Schultz said in a sombre tone, "I'm sorry for your loss."

"Well, he had a good run, didn't he?" but there was a choke in the voice. "I better be getting home."

Schultz called: "Extend my condolences to your family," at the retreating back, then closed the door and contemplatively fluttered the piece of paper against the knuckles of his left hand. *"Well, well,"* he said to himself. *"Well, well…"*

It wasn't a long walk from the print room of *The Nor'Wester* to Schultz's White Store – just out the back door of the print room straight into the stock room, across the stock room and into the back of the store. Schultz saw that his wife was busy with a customer out among the display shelves – after six weeks he still wasn't used to thinking or saying 'my wife' – so he stopped behind the counter and waited. He didn't at all mind waiting and watching his wife. It tickled him that the customer could only see a trim little woman in a lilac-print day dress, while Schultz could now clearly see what was under the dress. She wasn't as small as she looked with clothes on, large enough to accommodate him, and his experiences with professional women back east – and semi-professional, darker ones out west – had taught him that the large scale he was built on extended to all parts of his anatomy.

His wife noticed him standing behind the counter, and her pretty brow furled – women's intuition. She called the stockboy over to finish dealing with the customer and came toward the counter. Schultz held up the piece of paper and said: "Old Alexander Sutherland – *Point Douglas* Alexander Sutherland – died in his sleep last night."

"Oh, my," her right hand made a tiny, abortive gesture that Schultz suspected was the impulse to cross herself. After an entire winter of trying to make the appearance of Romish behaviour instinctive, it was bound to take a while to slough it off completely. Schultz knew he'd gotten off relatively easy in the indoctrination department. The priests' way of thinking was that the bride would be the one who raised and taught the children, so all the groom had to do was go through the motions. Another factor that had simplified the wedding process was that Henry and Lucy McKenney had gone to England for the summer, partly to further Henry's business schemes and largely because a trip to the centre of civilization was the carrot Henry had been holding in front of Lucy through seven years in the wilderness. So the sticky question of whether the groom's brother should be invited to the wedding hadn't come up.

After aborting her Catholic hand gesture, Schultz's wife settled for saying: "God rest his soul," which was appropriate for any religion. She added: "And maybe hers soon, too – the bereft's, the widow's. I've heard it said in general of old married couples who've lived together most of their lives, it's often the case that when one of them dies the other doesn't live much longer."

"Yes," Schultz nodded gravely, "I've heard that, too."

"Do you think we should go to Mr. Sutherland's funeral, Christian? To show our respect?"

"Huh. That's a good thought… my dear." He'd almost said 'Aggie,' the family nickname that he didn't know she loathed until a few nights ago. They both had a few things to unlearn. "But I'm not sure. Kildonan funerals have an odd sort of, um… fashion… manner of doing things…"

"Protocol."

"They send out invitations –"

"Invitations to a funeral?"

"I suppose it's as much an announcement as an invitation – though I'd lay odds all of Kildonan and half St. Boniface knew by breakfast time Point Douglas Alexander Sutherland was dead. I suppose no one would object to someone joining the funeral procession without an invitation, but it's a long walk to Kildonan kirk." He thought it unnecessary to point out aloud that her short legs weren't exactly made for long marches, although perfectly serviceable for other purposes.

"Walk?"

"Yes, part of the protocol for Red River funerals – well, I don't know about the Catholic side, but… They think it disrespectful for a coffin to be placed on any sort of conveyance, it has to be carried on pallbearers' shoulders from the death house to the cemetery. In this case they'll have to put it on a boat to get it across the river, but it'll still be a long walk from there."

"They won't be walking fast."

"That's true. That is true. But the funeral usually doesn't happen until three days after the deceased… deceases." Their honeymoon plan was to start the long journey east day-after-tomorrow.

"We can alter our agenda. That's one advantage to not having a steamboat schedule to be tied to."

"It is at that." There hadn't been a steamboat on the Red River since halfway through the American Civil War. Well, there was a steamboat *on* the Red – *The International* decaying at her moorings. The war and the Sioux and a few other complications had piled up until the binational consortium that owned her finally ran aground on a disagreement: the American business partners wanted more northbound passenger fares; The Company did not want a bunch of immigrants stomping around its stomping grounds. So the only steady traffic between Red River and St. Paul was once again the hellishly slow cart trains. So Schultz had purchased a sidesaddle from an old gentleman in Little Britain whose wife wouldn't be needing it anymore, a horse from The Company's herd that was almost as tall as his own carriage- cum saddle-horse, and a docile pony to carry tenting gear. The journey down the Crow Wing Trail to St. Paul might prove to be the most romantic part of the honeymoon.

Schultz said: "Well… putting in an appearance at the funeral does sound like a good idea, even if it means putting ourselves off a couple of days. If you're amenable."

"Of course I am. I'm always amenable to my own ideas."

Schultz smirked at her, then tweaked the end of her pretty little nose and went back to the print room. That evening brought the usual confabulation of like-minded fellows in the Common Room above the White Store, including Dr. Walter Bown and Mr. Thomas Spence. Bown had a broad face and broad, neck-muffler beard and was a dentist who'd emigrated west from Upper Canada some years before Schultz, but into the American west. His unfortunately publicly expressed sympathy with the Sioux at the time of the Minnesota Massacre – *'can't hardly blame 'em '* – had impelled him to re-emigrate north, before the Americans found a rail to ride him out on. Dr. Bown wasn't exactly a geyser of initiative, but rumour had it he didn't need to be because he received a handsome annuity from family in England, a rumour Schultz found very interesting.

Thomas Spence seemed intent on providing a contrast to Walter Bown. Spence had a long face made longer by a narrow beard and was an energetic newcomer who'd been and done many things – or so he said – lawyer, surveyor, political organiser… The one thing Bown and Spence and the others who gravitated to Schultz's had in common was a certainty that Rupert's Land should be part of Canada, and they'd been riding on a wave of enthusiasm ever since the news came of Confederation. The enthusiasm of their plans and prognostications was ratcheted up by the certainty that barely a hundred yards away, in a back room of Dutch George Emmerling's hotel, a group of American immigrants and adventurers were talking up schemes to get Rupert's Land into the embrace of Uncle Sam.

Schultz announced to the assemblage at his table: "I've been thinking about the Prince of Wales –"

"Do tell."

"Well, it's public knowledge that he's coming to Canada next year – the Royal Visit will more or less put the seal on the fact of the new Dominion. Ha! Just occurred to me – the Royal Seal, indeed. At any rate, what if…" Schultz had to pause to absorb the enormousness of what he was about to say. "What if he came here?"

There was an awed silence. Then someone said: "Who? The Prince of Wales?"

"Yes!"

"Here?"

"Yes!" Schultz nodded vociferously and pounded the tip of his forefinger up and down against the tabletop. "Here! At Red River!"

"Why… why would he do that?"

"Because we asked him to, we invited him. We," Schultz circled his hand in the air inclusively, "the loyal British subjects and Canadian citizens of Red River. And because a visit here from the Prince of Wales would underscore to all the world that – The Company be damned – these territories are and always will be part of the British Empire."

"I dunno," someone muttered, "he must get invitations from little groups of loyal subjects all over the world…"

"And it's one thing," someone else put in, "for His Royal Highness to take a ship from London to Canada and up the St. Lawrence River, but it's a hellish long ways overland to here."

"You know…" long-faced Thomas Spence drawled from his end of the table, in a way that turned all eyes and ears toward him. "I spent the first twenty years of my life in Great

Britain, and I can tell you for a certainty that all Britons have a great awe and affection for The Noble Redman, or what they imagine him to be. An invitation to the Prince of Wales from the Chiefs of all the tribes around Red River…"

Eyebrows were raised and heads nodded in interest, but then round-faced Dr. Bown said: "Old Chief Peguis likely would have gone for it, that sort of high malarky was his stock-in-trade, but since he has gone to The Happy Hunting Grounds…"

Agnes, the only female at the table, said: "How would they know?" All eyes turned toward her, but unlike most women she didn't shrink from being the centre of attention of a group of men discussing politics. "What I mean is, how would they know in England? How do they know if the Chiefs around here are named Yellow Buffalo or Green Otter or Fat Bear With The Sun In His Eyes?"

There was a momentary pause for that to sink in, then Schultz started applauding and laughing, and so did all the other men. Tactical practicalities tumbled out from all directions: the White Store's stock included several varieties of coloured ink, even gilt, that could produce a document of barbaric splendour; one or other of the halfbreed boarding students at St. John's College could be hired to translate the invitation into Cree or Ojibway, and the original English version could be enclosed to His Royal Highness as the 'translation' of the 'original'; Spence's background in writing up legal and surveying documents made him just the chap to mock-up the 'original' of the invitation on birchbark…

It took them all that evening and the next to hammer out the actual wording, but they eventually reached consensus that it was impossible to improve on:

To the Firstborn of our Great Mother, across the Great Waters.
Great Chief, whom we call Royal Chief,
We and our people hear that our relations, the Half-breeds and the Pale-faces, at Red River, have asked you to come and see them the next summer. We and our people also wish you to come and visit us. Every lodge will give you royal welcome. We have the bear and the buffalo, and our hunting grounds are free to you; our horses will carry you and our dogs hunt for you, and we and our people will guard and attend you; our old men will shew you their medals, which they received for being faithful to the Father of our Great Mother. Great Royal Chief! if you will come, send word to our Guiding Chief at Fort Garry, so that we may have time to meet and receive you as becoming our Great Royal Chief.

It was going to take Spence a while to get the work done, so the next day and evening were relatively quiet around the White Store. The following morning Schultz's wife woke him a little earlier than usual, by tickling his nose with butterfly kisses with her eyelashes. Still only half-awake but laughing, Schultz put a hand on her waist to pull her back into the nice warm bed. But she pushed away from him, saying: "We have a funeral to attend, remember?"

Schultz grumped out of bed, washed and shaved himself and dressed in his rarely-worn black suit, thankful that at least stiff cellulite shirt collars weren't de rigeur at

Red River funerals, a soft collar would do. His wife asked him to button up the back of the black dress she'd never worn except when fitting it. Only six weeks living above the White Store and already she'd made three dresses which incidentally served to advertise the store's selection of bolts of cloth. Well, his mother had always told him to marry a woman with clever hands.

He said: "I'd rather *un*button it," but nonetheless found it rather pleasant working his fingers up her lithe-muscled back. After fastening the top button, he lifted her hair and bent down to kiss the nape of her neck.

They had a quick breakfast of local bread and cheese and imported marmalade and tea while the stockboy hitched up the carriage; walking in the funeral procession didn't mean they had to walk to the starting point. As the carriage neared Point Douglas, Schultz saw that there were a number of saddlehorses and ox carts hitched to the trees fringing the riverbank. He muttered: "Damn fool – I mean darn fool – I should've known."

"Should've known what, dear?"

"I thought they'd land the boat further downstream, by St. John's churchyard – that's where old Mrs. Sutherland started walking from the day I met her on the road to church and she broke her hip. I should've known they'd paddle the coffin boat against the current so they could start Point Douglas Alexander Sutherland's funeral march from Point Douglas." But Schultz soon realised his mistake was a piece of luck, because of another thing he should've known: farm folk start their days early. By the time he'd got the carriage maneuvered in among the carts and saddlehorses, and the horse hitched to a tree – with its harness loosened and a sprinkling of oats among the grasses at its feet – the funeral procession had already formed up and was filing past him. If they'd started from farther down the road, he would've been too late.

First came the Reverend Dr. Black in his black robe and white tab-collar, with one of the church elders walking alongside. Then came the shrouded coffin, balanced on the shoulders of John Sutherland, Hugh Sutherland, and what Schultz guessed were the other two oldest Sutherland boys. All four pallbearers had an empty-handed man walking alongside. Behind them came a Red River cart, which would've been a scandalous breach of protocol except for what it carried: white-haired, ramrod-backed Kate MacPherson in a wooden armchair, with what must be the youngest of her grandchildren in her arms. Beside the cart walked a black-shawled woman who looked almost as old, with one hand on a cart rail within reach of Widow Sutherland's.

Agnes whispered: "That's Madame Lagimodière – I used to see her at Mass, and the Sisters often talked about her. The only white woman who's lived here longer than Mrs. Sutherland."

After the cart came the younger Mrs. Sutherland with another one of her sons, then the rest of her children and then friends and relations, all two-by-two. There were a surprising number of crucifix-wearing Metis dotted here and there, prompting Schultz to wonder if there might've been even more if so many weren't gone on the summer hunt.

As the tail-end of the procession finally passed, Schultz offered Agnes his arm and they fell into line. Given the height difference between his elbow and hers they couldn't exactly walk arm-in-arm, more like forearm-in-upper-arm, but it was workable. Agnes was proven right that her short legs would have no difficulty keeping up; he had more difficulty keeping his long legs to the proverbial funereal pace. But at least it was still July. In August the roadbed would be a dust bed that all these footsteps would turn into a cloud for those at the back of the line to eat.

It seemed they hadn't walked very far when Dr. Black at the head of the column called: "Relief!" and everyone halted.

Agnes sotto voce asked what was going on. Schultz, who could see over most of the heads in front of them, said in an in-church murmur: "It looks like… Yes, the men who were walking beside John Sutherland and his sons stepped in to put their shoulders under the coffin, and the Sutherlands are stepping out." As the rustic cortege started moving again, the four Sutherlands stood waiting to fall in behind the cart with the rest of the family, while four other men from farther back in the line came forward to walk beside the new pallbearers. It happened several more times along the route, but unlike the Sutherlands all the other pallbearers who'd been relieved in turn fell back to the end of the line, so the Schultzes soon had several pairs of men walking behind them.

When the road bended to accommodate a bend in the river, Schultz could see the coffin lengthwise for a moment, and noticed something he thought he'd noticed when the coffin was first carried past him on Point Douglas but hadn't been sure then because of the dappling shadows from the trees. In all the Red River funerals he'd seen before – angling his carriage off the road to let them pass by, or happening to glance out his office window as a procession made its way from Fort Garry towards St. John's church – the coffin had always been shrouded with black cloth. This one was, too, but on top of the black cloth was a length of tattered faded cloth that was mostly black, but had patches of blue and green so dark they were almost black.

When he mentioned that odd fact to Agnes, the man in front of them swivelled his head back to say: "It's the plaid of a common soldier of the 42nd Highlanders – The Royal Black Watch." As the man faced front again, he muttered: "Aye, he's almost the last of them."

Schultz said: "The last of the 42nd Highlanders?"

The man glanced back with an expression somewhere between pity and annoyance, but said patiently, "No, the last of the Auld Ones, the original Selkirk Settlers. Kate MacPherson and one or two others, and then they'll all be gone."

When they got to Kildonan church, as the coffin was being carried inside and the rest of the procession stood waiting, several of the widow's grandsons lifted her and her armchair off the cart, and then her son wheeled her through the door. It soon became apparent that there wouldn't be room in the church for everyone, so Schultz and Agnes stayed standing in the churchyard along with several other clumps of mourners, where they could hear Dr. Black speaking and the choir singing through the open door. Some of the others in the churchyard sang along, but since the hymns were in Gaelic, all Schultz could do was stand there with his eyes fixed ahead in what he hoped was an appropriately solemn expression. He had no doubt Agnes was doing the same, but probably carrying it off better.

When the coffin was carried out to the cemetery and everyone gathered around the open grave, Schultz was surprised to see a white tombstone lying in the grass waiting to be set in place. Usually a fresh grave would only have a small wooden cross or temporary marker until a stonemason had had time to carve a gravestone.

Dr. Black said a few more words and another Gaelic hymn was sung, then a piper in fringed buckskin trousers and a tartan vest played *The Flowers of the Forest* as the coffin was lowered down. What counted was that at one point in the proceedings, Schultz caught John Sutherland's eye and nodded sombrely at him, and Sutherland nodded back – so John Sutherland had registered the fact that Schultz had taken the trouble to come to his father's funeral.

With that accomplished, and the crowd beginning to drift away – no doubt many of them planning to make their way to the Sutherland farm with platters of cold meats and baskets of home baking – Schultz figured he and Agnes were free to head back to the carriage and home. But then he noticed that a kind of informal receiving line had formed up in front of the church, with old Mrs. Sutherland in her wheeled armchair and her son standing behind it. He murmured to Agnes: "This will only take a minute," and steered her in that direction.

It took more than a minute, but not much. Most people were being brief and, by and large, those who had the most to say would say it at the Sutherland homestead later in the day. The last in line before Schultz and Agnes was a tallish middle-aged man in a quillworked deerskin jacket, with greying hair brushed back from a widow's peak to show off the kind of profile Spence had meant by Britons' romantic imagination of The Noble Redman: chiselled cheekbones, schooner-prow chin and Roman nose. Schultz thought there was something familiar about him beyond the standard magazine-story image.

The Indian and John Sutherland exchanged nods, then the Indian bent toward old Mrs. Sutherland and held out what looked to be a dried braid of hair cut off the head of an ash-blonde little girl. He said: "This is sweetgrass, Mrs. Sutherland –"

"I know what it is, thank you. I will burn it over my husband's grave. You're a Prince, aren't you?" Now Schultz placed him: Henry Prince, the Chief of the Saulteaux at St. Peters since his father Mr. King passed on. It occurred to Schultz that it might tickle the Prince of Wales if the name of one of the chiefs on the invitation was Prince. Then again, the Royal Family were probably a bit too ticklish about that sort of thing.

Henry Prince said to old Mrs. Sutherland: "My father always said your husband was the second toughest of all the Selkirk Settlers – next to you."

"I think you inherited your father's tongue, Mr. Prince. I cannot say whether you got your father's nose – Lord knows who got it."

"Oh, we know, but he was long dead long before my father."

"Your father was very helpful to us in those early days."

"And you to him."

"And it is very kind of you to come all the way from St. Peters for my husband's funeral."

"It was very kind of you and your husband to come all the way to St. Peters for my father's funeral, especially with travel so difficult for you. We of St. Peters and Kildonan may not see each other very often, but we watch over each other and we know each other. In fact, I have suspicions that a grandson of yours and a niece of mine know each other better than they are letting on. And now your husband and my father are watching over us all."

Schultz was very pleased with the lucky impulse that had prompted him to not leave a few minutes ago. Because of it, when it came time to approach the leaders of St. Peter's Parish about some acres of surplus scrubland, he could begin by saying: *"You remember me, Chief Prince, we were both at old Alexander Sutherland's funeral…"*

Schultz was jolted out of his musings on the future by the realisation that in the present the multi-hued quillwork on Chief Henry Prince's jacket was no longer in front of him, and it was his turn. He said: "Mr. Sutherland, Mrs. Sutherland, we're sorry for your loss."

John Sutherland said: "Good of you to come, Dr. Schultz."

"This is my wife, Agnes."

Old Mrs. Sutherland nodded in Agnes's general direction, but the age-paled blue eyes stayed fixed on Schultz. The eyes sparked and the old lady rasped with a strange intentness: "I know you."

"Of course you do, Mrs. Sutherland. I'm Dr. Schultz." He thought of reaching out to reassuringly pat one of the gnarled hands clawed on the chair arms, but then thought better of it. "I gave you a ride in my carriage to the kirk the day you had your unfortunate accident. And I'm proud I'll be able to say to future generations that I also met your husband face-to-face, once or twice – one of the last of the Auld Ones."

"I wish you could have met Mr. Grant face-to-face."

Schultz was quite touched, and felt welcomed into the bosom of the community more than ever before. When Red River people spoke of a 'Mr. Grant' with no further definition, there was only one man they meant, and although Cuthbert Grant had been dead more than a decade, it was still a name to conjure with. And here was one of the original settlers telling Schultz she wished he could've met him. Schultz smiled, "I wish I could've, too."

"Do you? Well, if wishes were horses… But I do truly wish you could have met up with Mr. Grant."

"Well, there are many other people waiting to offer their condolences. Our deepest sympathies, Mrs. Sutherland, Mr. Sutherland. Come along, Agnes."

When he and Agnes had started down the walkway between the files of tombstones, Agnes hissed under her breath: "Old witch."

"Eh?" Schultz was about to ask her what she'd meant by that, when something caught his eyes. He veered off the path, saying: "Just a minute."

"*Another* minute?"

The grave had been filled in, and Hugh Sutherland and one of his brothers were setting the gravestone upright in its slot and pressing sods down around it. Schultz approached them, saying: "Hello, Hugh."

"Oh, hello, Dr. Schultz." The lad's voice was low and slow, and his eyes looked dull.

"It's none of my business, and I don't mean to intrude, but… I don't think I've ever been to a funeral where the gravestone was already prepared."

"Oh, Granda had it made a couple years ago, secret-like, case'n he went first. Gran didn't know about it till he… weren't here anymore. You see, he figured she might figure he was being too sentimental in public-like. But once it was done, she couldn't change it except to get a new one made, and this one was already bought and paid for, so… All the stonecutter had to do now was chisel in the numbers."

Schultz looked at the inscription:

In memory of Alexander Sutherland
Who departed this life
July 13th 1867
Also
of his beloved wife
Catherine MacPherson
who died
aged

On the long walk back to the carriage Agnes didn't seem talkative, so Schultz didn't attempt to make much conversation. Glancing down at her, he could see her lips were grimly pressed together and her jaw clenched. He understood: women's dress shoes just weren't as comfortable as the everyday boots men could get away with at a funeral, at least a funeral at Red River. As soon as they got home, Agnes went straight upstairs, no doubt to take her shoes off and soak her feet in cold water. The stockboy told Schultz that Mr. Thomas Spence had dropped something off for him. Schultz carefully unwrapped the butchers' paper package on the counter.

It was a sheet of buckskin-coloured birchbark rind, with the Invitation in Cree – or maybe Ojibway – written up in multicoloured inks. The heading was in the red-white-and-blue of the Union Jack, all the capitals were gold, and a curlicued gilt border framed the whole. Perfectly splendid, in the way of barbaric splendour. Enclosed with it was the English 'translation' on vellum paper in scholarly black ink.

All in all, Schultz felt he could say it had been a very productive day, although he couldn't say it aloud, of course, on such a solemn occasion.

The next day, Schultz and his wife finished the last stages of their packing, to get an early start in the morning. Schultz said: "Here's a jolly thought, my dear. This summer we're going to Canada, but next summer, or maybe the next at the latest, Canada will be coming to us."

CHAPTER 28

Hugh's grandfather had been in the ground two weeks when the summer buffalo hunt came home from the plains and the night was filled with fiddles and laughter – and the occasional gunshot – from the homes north and south of the Point Douglas Sutherlands' and from the traders' common around Fort Garry. Donald, Aleck and Morrison went to help out with the dancing, but Hugh stayed home to try and get a full night's sleep for tomorrow. He didn't, but it wasn't because of the clamour outside.

After doing his morning chores and eating his morning porridge with the rest of the family, Hugh carried a kettle and his shaving equipment out to the summer washstand beside the doorstep, as he had every second or third morning since the weather got warm. While his hands in the basin worked lye soap, hot water and a pinch of lard into lather, he studied his semi-mustached face in the polished steel mirror above the washstand. Around Red River, whiskers helped tell one man from another. How would you know it was the Reverend Dr. Black without the wreath of beard that came down from his jawline and left the rest of his face bare? Or Point Douglas John Sutherland without the wooly beard that put his blue eyes in an oval picture frame? Or Mr. A.G.B. Bannatyne without the thicket beard that spread outward as much as downward? Or, maybe someday, John Hugh Sutherland without his mustache: a medium mustache that was neither pencil-thin and showy in a fussy way, nor thick and showy in a bushy way?

But not yet. When he'd worked up something resembling lather in his hands, Hugh didn't just spread it onto his cheeks, neck and chin, but also into his peach-fuzz mustache. He liked shaving and washing in the fresh air, with birdsongs and cattle murmurs accompanying the razor scrapes, but he had to shut out awareness of all those pleasant side-elements when he brought the razor to his upper lip. He'd never shaved off anything thicker than sparse stubble before, and he was hardly a dab hand with a straight razor yet. When he washed off the leftover flecks of soapy foam and looked in the mirror again, he got an unpleasant surprise and muttered at his reflection: "Shoulda thoughtena that, shoulden you?"

The silky, silly, boy's mustache was gone – to hurry up the change to real whiskers, he hoped – but in its place was a strip of white skin across the middle of his summer-tanned face. If he'd had the sense to shave it off a week ago, the skin would've blended in by today. Too late now.

Hugh sluiced out the basin, tossed the soapy water into the yard and carried his razor and towel back up to his grandfather's room, which was now his and Donald, Aleck and Morrison's room. Aleck's general grey mood was harder to ignore with just the four of them bunked together, but Hugh did have to give him points for stubbornness for outlasting Da's attempts to work him so hard he'd wish he was back in school. But Hugh could distinctly remember feeling light and free when Da gave up and eased up on him, whereas Aleck seemed as down and dogged as ever. Well, Aleck wasn't who Hugh was thinking about today.

Back downstairs, Hugh ducked into the pantry to cut a hunk off a wheel of cheese, wrapped it and a half wheel of bannock in a cloth and put them in his fishing creel with his fish-line, hook case, knife, pipe and tobacco. Mum was standing at one end of the kitchen table kneading bread dough to go into the summer oven outside; Gran was sitting at the other end in her wheeled chair, slowly peeling potatoes. Hugh said: "I done all my morning chores, so I figured I'd walk down river a bit and try another fishing spot."

Mum paused in her kneading and looked at him with an oddly raised eyebrow. She said: "Oh, going fishing, are you?"

Gran said loudly: "What's he say?"

Mum raised her voice, "He says he's going fishing."

"Oh, going fishing, is he?"

Hugh said: "I packed some bread and cheese, so if I'm not home till milking time don't worry about me."

Mum said: "No, I won't worry about you."

On Hugh's way out the door, Gran called after him: "Good luck with your fishing, John Hugh."

Hugh detoured to pull a couple of carrots out of the garden and then headed for the road, shaking the earth off the carrots before tucking them in his creel. A mile or so north, the river road crossed the rough-beam bridge over the creek where Norbert Parisien had trapped two fat catfish five summers ago. This summer was a lot less dry, so Hugh had a tight squeeze working his way downstream between the water's edge and the overhanging tangle of willow and alder. Finally he gave up and just stepped into the stream, edging forward carefully with the pleasant tingle of cold water tugging at the backs of his knees and trying to pull him off balance. The stream widened and deepened considerably just before it met the river, but the riverside trees shaded out the undergrowth so there was open space on the creekbank to climb out onto before the bottom dropped away.

Hugh sat down on a bed of moss, draped his sodden moccasins over a rock to dry and looked around him. Although the widened-out pool was near the riverbank, the curtain of trees and brush was thick enough to hide it from the river, and it certainly couldn't be seen from the road. The stream flowed fast enough that it wasn't a mosquito hatchery. The air was cool and mossy and tinged with the rustling of leaves and the burbling of the creek and red-winged blackbirds. Almost a perfect place to be on a summer day, lacking only one thing.

Since there was nothing he could do to hurry that along, Hugh opened his fishing creel, took out his pipe and tobacco and sat smoking and waiting. After awhile he told himself he was being foolish, it wasn't going to happen. He decided that if nothing happened by the time he'd smoked his pipe out, he would take up his fishing creel and go see if there were other fish in the river. But when his pipe sucked cold, he told himself he should stay waiting until his moccasins had dried. Himself chose to ignore the fact that he'd just be stepping his dried moccasins back into the creek anyway. He knocked the ash out of his pipe and re-packed it. He'd barely got it going again when he heard an intermittent clopping and splashing sound approaching.

Hugh debated whether to stand up, but decided it would be better to be just sitting there puffing on his pipe. Out of the green and dappled sunlight through the willows arcing over the stream came a black-haired girl on a spotted buckskin pony picking its way carefully along the streambed. She had bright brass earrings, and a green bead necklace over her calico blouse. Where the stream and the bank widened out, she clucked Cheengwun out of the water, and Hugh stood up as she swung one leg over the horse's back to slide down to the ground. She said: "Wakiye, Hugh Sutherland."

"Wakiye, Nancy Prince." He took a step toward her. "I thought maybe you weren't coming."

"It's a long ride."

"Oh, yeah, it is." Of course it was, and he'd been sitting there stupidly stewing in his own self-centred juices while she'd probably been riding since dawn. His right hand made a tentative move forward. Her left hand came forward and the hands took hold of each other, sending a surge of strange sensation up Hugh's arm. She stepped in a little closer, just close enough that her breasts touched his chest, and he lowered his head and carefully kissed her mouth. Then she turned sideways and sat down where he'd been sitting. She still had hold of his hand, so he sat down beside her.

Wauh Oonae said: "I'm sorry about your grandfather."

"Huh. You know, when I said that to you, I thought it was a stupid thing to say, but I couldn't think of anything else. But it's not a stupid thing to say, not from this end."

"It wasn't to me."

"I guess it sorta helps that someone else cares about it. It does. But, it's funny… I don't – didn't – feel so much sad, not like you'd expect, more sorta… numb."

"I know."

They talked about her last two months away on the buffalo hunt, and his last two months at home, and the funny thing Aunt Somebody-or-other said, and whether the willow leaves floating by looked more like tiny York Boats or tiny canoes, and sometimes they didn't talk at all. Sometimes Hugh had his arm around her shoulders and her head was snuggled into the hollow of his neck; sometimes they moved a few inches apart so they could look at each other.

After awhile, Hugh said: "It's funny – you're easy to talk to."

"So are you. Why's that funny?"

"Well, 'cause the first time I tried, I mean even just to say hello – back when Norbert trapped the catfish – you seemed so, uh… unreachable. Sorta silent and distantish. All closed in."

"I was scared."

"'Scared'?" The idea of Nancy Prince being afraid of anything seemed ridiculous. "Scared of what?"

"Scared of saying something stupid."

"*You*?"

"Well, of saying something… wrongly. I knew you'd been going to school for years, and knew about speaking English proper."

"*Me*?" He laughed; she blushed. "Well, I guess you sure learned different since then."

"I learned you don't care. About that kinda thing."

"Well, it ain't like I got any choice, me whatever. Born with a wooden spoon in my mouth." Uncertain why he felt uncertain, Hugh's eyes lit on the pipe he'd set aside when he'd stood up to greet her. He put it in his mouth and struck a match. Wauh Oonae delved into the shoulder pouch she'd set aside when she'd sat down, and came out with a pipe of her own. She wasn't the first woman he'd seen smoking a pipe, although Kildonan girls didn't go in for that sort of thing. She seemed more experienced at keeping it going without thinking about it than he was.

They sat side-by-side with their shoulders and knees touching, puffing smoke into the air rather than each others' faces. After awhile, Hugh said: "I been thinking that maybe… Well, not this year but maybe next year… Maybe I' ll come on the buffalo hunt."

"No!" She pulled away from him.

"Why not? You said I ride pretty good for a white man. I can likely borrow a buffalo runner from the Lagimodières' string. With a good buffalo runner, all you got to do is stay on and the horse does all the work. That's what they say. And I figure you don't have to be a crack shot, galloping along so close beside a buffalo you can almost touch it."

"It's too dangerous."

"How? There aren't been any trouble with the Sioux since the White Horse Plains Hunt whupped 'em good way back in Mr. Grant's day. Ain't that true?"

"It ain't the Sioux. Galloping in with a thousand thousands of stampeding buffalo – legs get broke, horses get gored, men get trampled… Every year, it seems, we bury at least one man out on the plains. And more'n a few of them were longtime hunters who'd run buffalo a hundred times before. Or maybe you'd get lucky. Maybe your horse wouldn't trip in a gopher hole. Maybe you'd just be one of the ones whose guns exploded from shooting too many times too fast. Maybe you'd just lose a few fingers, or a hand."

"Well, I gotta do *something* to try and get a little money together –"

"Why?"

"So I can move on out."

"'Move on out'?" Her voice had gone cold. "Where?"

"I can't stay living in my parents' place forever. I'm gonna need *some* kind of money to start up a place of… my own, and around here the buffalo hunt's about the fastest way to do that."

"Maybe not." The sudden coldness had gone out of her voice as quickly as it came in, but she still didn't sound agreeable. "Maybe that's not so anymore. Even in just the few years I been doing the adding up for my father and brothers, I seen there's fewer bags of pemmican and less hides every time. A *lot* less this time. Some hunters are saying the Eastern herd's just about hunted out and it's time to move west to the Qu'Appelle and South Saskatchewan."

Hugh felt a twinge of panic. "Is that what your father's saying?"

"Oh no, he's pure Saulteaux, he'd never leave his father's country."

That wiped away the panic, but cleared the way for another fear: that maybe Wauh Oonae wasn't saying the real reason she didn't want him going on the buffalo hunt, and the reasons she *was* saying were just excuses. For five or six months of every year she was away on the plains, and he had no way of knowing all she was doing out there, or who she was doing it with. But then she said something that turned the fear in his chest into warm mush: "You said you weren't thinking of coming on the hunt till next year anyway. So we'll talk about it again next spring."

Nancy raised her arms over her head and arched her back with a bit of a grimace, and Hugh had to admit his own back was getting stiff from sitting up with no backrest. She lay back on the moss with one arm under her head and her ankles crossed. Hugh stretched out on his right side with his right elbow cocked to prop his head on his hand so he could look at her. He tentatively reached out his left hand and rested it on her belly. She didn't seem to mind. Through the thin calico her belly felt warm and soft and taut at the same time. He could feel her pulse resonating against the palm of his hand, or maybe it was his own pulse echoing off her.

Wauh Oonae turned her head to look at him and her eyebrows furled quizzically, as they had a few times when he'd looked at her looking at him today. She said: "What happened to your mouth?"

"Huh?"

She raised her free hand to skate a fingertip along the skin between his nose and upper lip. He'd forgotten about the mustache. "Oh, I, uh – they say if you grow out baby whiskers and then shave 'em off, real whiskers'll come sooner. So I grown out a sort of mustache, and then shaved it off this morning."

"Why'd you shave it off?"

"Looked silly. Like I said – just boy's peach fuzz." He'd never seen a peach, and doubted anyone he knew had, but that was what people said. "Didn't stop to think it'd look even sillier the first few days after I shaved it off."

She smiled. "You look fine to me, John Hugh Sutherland."

Hugh felt an agitated rumbling against the palm of his left hand. He sat up, saying: "I brung some cheese and bannock."

"I brought some buffalo sticks."

They sat munching bannock and cheese and smoke-dried buffalo, washing it down with handfuls of fresh-flowing water. Hugh took out his two carrots, sluiced off the last few stubborn, clinging crumbs of earth in the stream, and handed one to her. He started eating his carrot the same way he'd always ate fresh carrots, but after his first few nibbles Nancy Prince said: "What are you doing?"

"Oh, um..." He felt foolish again. "You see, uh, there's two parts of a carrot. There's the orange part that's the most of it, and inside that there's a yellow part that's a lot sweeter. So if you can take off mosta the orange part in little bites, you can peel the rest off the yellow part and get the sweetness all at once. The marrow, like."

She looked doubtful, but imitated what he was doing and seemed delighted when the yellow carrot-within-a-carrot came free. Even the spiky yellow tendrils that poked out into the orange part peeled free intact. She munched it up and grinned around the sweetness in her mouth, leaning forward to tug on his ear and laugh, "Yellow, orange and Purple Hugh."

Then they stretched out on their backs side-by-side, looking up at the blue blaze of sky in its ragged frame of treetops. After awhile, Hugh said: "No clouds to watch today."

"Oh, prob'ly some somewheres, in a sky as big as ours – just not in this little patch. Phew, I thought it'd be cooler down here in the shade by the water."

"Prob'ly is – I mean cooler'n elsewhere. Must be like a bake-oven out there in the open today."

"Yeah, and only just a warming-oven down here." Nancy sat up and took off her necklace and earrings. Then she stood up, kicked off her moccasins, unfastened her beadwork-hemmed skirt and let it fall around her feet. The hem of her calico blouse hung down a hand's-breadth below the join of her thighs, or where Hugh imagined they joined.

Wauh Oonae stepped out of her skirt and into the pool, wading forward carefully until the water was licking her thighs, then flopping forward in a semi-dive. She ducked her head and came up laughing, swinging her head back so her hair was a long black pinwheel spinning out sparkling droplets. She swam around in a half-circle till she was facing Hugh with her hair plastered to the sides of her head, the front ribbons following the contours of her cheekbones. She called out: "Come on in, it's delicious."

Hugh didn't have to be asked twice, and he knew his shirttails hung down past embarrassment when they weren't bunched up by his trousers. But when he stood up to unbutton his trousers, he realised that in certain conditions of maleness, a man wearing only a long shirt was in more humiliating circumstances than a woman wearing the same. He could hear his Granda saying: *'That's why God invented sporrans, lad.'*

Hugh turned sideways so mostly his back was pointed at Nancy Prince, affecting to be having some difficulty with his trouser buttons, and once he had his trousers off he sidled into the water on an angle that still kept his back to her, pretending it was easier to keep his balance if he planted his feet sideways. As soon as the water was even remotely deep enough, he crouched down into it and pushed off swimming. The cold water soon wilted his problem away, now that it didn't matter.

It took only one kick and arm-stroke to get to the middle of the pool where Wauh Oonae's head was magically floating, with the hair that wasn't plastered to it radiating out from it on top of the water or billowing in dark coils beneath the surface. When he got near to her he discovered why she wasn't having to tread water: she was standing on the bottom of the deepest part of the pool. When he did the same, his shoulders cleared the surface. He also discovered she'd been right about the water: after the initial shock it was cool rather than cold, and there wasn't much current with the momentum of the stream spread out wider and deeper.

He stepped a little closer to her, moving slowly against the resistance of the water, and raised one hand to cup the side of her head. She stepped in very close and he lowered his head and kissed her. It quickly turned into a different kind of kiss from the shy and careful one that morning. His arms came around her back and pressed her next-to-naked body tight to his. Her arms clasped his back and pressed him to her with surprising strength. His hands roamed up and down her back and hips and shoulders and the back of her head, and hers his, discovering each other. He broke away from her mouth to catch his breath, and bent a little lower to kiss the side of her neck. She was making soft little moaning sounds, and he supposed he was, too.

He shifted very slightly sideways so they were still more-or-less pressed together but he could get his right hand between them to close over her left breast. The same sort of strange surge travelled up his arm as when their hands touched that morning, only this time it was more like heat than warmth. She sighed deep in her throat and rocked her hips against him. He moved his hand down from her breast to the side of her hip, then her thigh, then up the inside of her thigh. His eyes had closed themselves as though they'd decided he didn't need them at the moment, but every now and then he cracked them open to get a look at her. Her eyes were closed, too – long black lashes and smooth, copper eyelids – but she looked impossibly more beautiful than ever, with a flushed glow in her skin, her neck arched back, and her mouth going from half-open to open in rhythm to some inner drumbeat. At one of those instants between kisses when he was looking at her, he saw her eyelashes starting to flutter apart, and quickly shut his eyes.

Hugh wasn't certain exactly how to proceed, but he thought he had a general idea, although he wasn't doing much thinking at the moment. He got his legs between hers, moved his hands to cup her hips and lifted her a little – not all that difficult with her body buoyed up by the pond – then bent his knees, pulled her against him and began to slowly lower her while straightening his knees. At the last instant she shrieked "No!" and tore away from him, churning backwards and spitting like a cat, "You think all us halfbreed girls just a fast fuck?" Then her face contorted in on itself and she reached both hands out toward his face. "Oh, Hugh, I'm sorry – you're not like that, I know. Just… I known too many girls with a baby and no man."

"You'll have one if you'll have me – but I ain't quite a man yet."

"Parts of you are." She moved toward him, blushing and not quite meeting his eyes. "Just because we can't… doesn't mean…" She pressed her body against his at a kind of half-angle, as he had with hers a few minutes or hours ago. "My hands are clumsy..." 'Clumsy' isn't the word he would've used. "Not like yours..."

He took the hint. She gasped again and rolled her head back and forth across his shoulder, sometimes nibbling at his neck and ear with half-bite kisses. But after a moment or two he realised that he was more interested in feeling her than her feeling him – at least a little more interested. And there was another factor. With what her hand was doing, he could feel himself building up to an explosion, and he could think of nothing more embarrassingly crude than splattering onto her. He shifted so that her back was to him and his left hand could explore her breasts, her belly, her neck, while his right hand was between her legs. But it turned out that the back of her body rubbing against the front of his was having the same effect as her hand. Then it occurred to him that they were up to their necks in water, and whatever came out of him would be washed away in an instant. He let himself go.

An instant later, the spell was broken and he was just an ignorant farmboy standing behind a girl beyond his reach. He'd thought he'd learned long ago what it was to feel shy, but realised now he hadn't had an inkling. She turned toward him, put both hands on the sides of his head and kissed him very slowly. Then she moved her head back just far enough that they could see each other, and said: "I love you, Hugh Sutherland."

"I, uh... well, you must know."

"Know what?"

"I love you, Nancy Prince Wauh Oonae."

She smiled and blinked her eyes and there looked to be something like tears in the corners of them, or maybe it was just the water dripping out of her hair. Then she said: "Your lips are turning blue."

"Yours, too. Yeah, I hadn't noticed, but... I guess we been standing in cold water a while."

"Come on." She took his hand and led him out of the pool. They found a patch of sunlight big enough for both of them to sit in. Hugh waited till the sun had cooked the edge off the chill on his skin and shirt before putting his arm across her shoulders and snuggling closer again.

Wauh Oonae suddenly laughed and pointed at the pool. "By rights it should be giving off steam."

Hugh pointed to his still-damp sleeve and the vapour that the sun was baking out of it, saying: "*We* are," and she laughed harder.

They talked some more, about all kinds of things and nothing. Hugh had meant it when he'd said she was easy to talk to, but realised now he hadn't really known what ease and warmth was. When the shafts and patches of sunlight in the hollow faded to shade, Wauh Oonae said: "I better be getting back, it's a long ride to St. Peters."

"Yeah, and I said I'd be home before suppertime."

As he was tugging on his trousers and she her skirt, she said: "It won't be but ten days or so before the autumn hunt sets out, and it'll be a busy ten days – getting all the pemmican and hides sold, and stocking up what we need for two or three months on the plains. So I might not see you again till October-November."

"I'll miss you till then."

"Someday we won't have to."

Autumn turned out to be unusually late and drawn-out, which Hugh and everybody else at Red River knew meant the Hunt would stay out longer shadowing the herd till it was safe to take green meat. But to Hugh and everyone else at Red River, the late fall also meant a longer battening-down season, that time between harvest and freeze-up when farmers run around like squirrels, working down a mental list from 'What Absolutely Has To Be Done Before Winter' to 'Be Nice If We Got That Done Before Winter.' So Hugh was kept more than busy with bucksawing stovewood, re-railing the paddock fence, ferrying boatloads of manure across to Point Douglas, running the thornbush chimneybrush up and down the kitchen and parlour flues…

One early morning in late November, Hugh got moving before everybody else for a change and came downstairs to find his eleven year old sister Catherine sitting on Gran's bed crying. It wasn't unusual to find Catherine on Gran's bed – on a lot of cold mornings Katy would wake up in the dark and sneak downstairs to snuggle in with Gran. But it was unusual for Gran to be sitting up and stroking Katy's hair and crooning things like '*There, there…* 'while Katy was keening: "I don't *want* them to take you away."

Hugh moved toward Gran's bed, saying: "What's wrong, Katy-love?"

Gran's head jerked toward Hugh with startled eyes. Then she dropped her eyes and shook her head, murmuring: "Old fool… You sounded just like… Well, it does seem to be my morning for hearing voices."

Hugh perched on the bed beside his sister and put his hand on the shoulder Gran's hand wasn't on. "What's the matter, Katy?"

"I…" Katy snuffled and choked and Hugh gave her the clean handkerchief he'd just put in his pocket. "I came downstairs to snug in with Gran… and she woke up and said… she said…"

"I only told you the truth, my dear." With Hugh now there, Gran lay back down, and Hugh could see from the pain in her face how much it had cost her to sit up to comfort her granddaughter. "I had just been with the angels. They were coming to take me away if you had not wakened me. I heard them singing as they were coming for me."

Katy wailed: "But I don't *want* the angels to take my Granny away."

Gran said: "Better them than the others, my dear."

A few mornings later, Hugh's Gran didn't wake up. The winter had made up for its late arrival with a vengeance, so she didn't have to be put on a boat to start her last journey. But the quick freeze-up also meant a fire had to be built beside Hugh's Granda's still-fresh mound of earth, to thaw the ground enough to dig.

Hugh couldn't tell whether there were more people in the funeral procession than for Granda's, but there certainly weren't less. The atmosphere, though, was a little different. At the gathering of neighbours after Granda's funeral, the stories Hugh had overheard through his numbness were of a reliable but quirky man who kept himself to himself. After Gran's funeral, Hugh overheard more than a few people of Da's generation delivering variations on: "I remember my father saying, 'Aye, ye can tak all yerr Governors an' Captains an' Lairds, an' stuff them in a sack – the Sergeant Major wha kept us marrching was Red Kate MacPherson.'"

On Christmas Eve the Point Douglas Sutherlands went to Midnight Mass at St. Boniface Cathedral as always, just as always many of their Catholic neighbours would stop by the Sutherlands' for Hogmanay – although this Hogmanay Hugh planned to be away at the Stone Fort for the New Year's Regale, where Nancy Prince was likely to be. As the Sutherlands were stepping back out onto the trampled snow around the steps of the cathedral – Hugh carrying suddenly-sleepy Roddy, whose eyes had been kept wide by gilt altarpieces and Bishop's robes and sparkling incense-wafters – a soft but sonorous voice called from behind: "Bon Noel, Monsieur Sutherland, Madame Sutherland…"

Hugh and the rest of the family turned to see a dark-mustached young man buttoning a well-tailored buffalo coat over a satin-cravatted, charcoal wool suit. Da said: "Bon Noel, Monsieur Riel. Welcome home."

The young man smiled. "I think I am not yet of so dignified an age to be 'monsieur' to you. Joyeux Noel Donald, Hugh, Alexander, Morrison, Hector, Angus, Margaret, Catherine, William, and to you four born while I was in foreign lands – I'll learn your names at Hogmanay."

Hugh murmured back: "Joyeux Noel, Louis," along with the others of the family old enough to recognise who was Merry Christmassing them. Louis Riel Jr. had grown up a nearby neighbour to the Point Douglas Sutherlands since the year their house wound up on the east side of the river. His father, Louis 'Irish' Riel, had married a daughter of Jean Baptiste and Marie Anne Lagimodière and built a house close by his in-laws. But eight or nine years back, the Bishop had arranged for young Louis to get educated in far-off Lower Canada, so any Sutherland from Hector on down wasn't likely to recognise him. They'd place the name, of course – Louis Riel Jr. was the kind of person that gets talked about.

Louis said with grave courtesy: "I wanted to extend to you my deepest condolences, Monsieur Sutherland. I know what it is to lose a father, but a mother, I cannot imagine the devastation." That made Hugh remember his grandmother's voice speaking of 'circularity.' Three or four years back, 'Irish' Riel had died at about the same age Da was now, and a few months after that word came to Red River from the east that his son had quit the seminary school. The 'circularity' was that Louis Senior had been a failed seminarian, too. In fact, he'd failed at almost everything, except being an apparently decent husband and father. He was sometimes unkindly called 'The Miller of The Seine,' because he'd inveigled The Company and the Church into buying him the machinery for a textile mill and a flour mill and maybe some other kinds of mills as well, and had somehow managed to never mill anything anyone would buy.

The one thing 'Irish' Riel had been good at, outside of raising a family, was agitation. Hugh had heard many stories, and had seen for himself, that whenever the Metis or anybody else had a hate on for The Company, there was M. Riel at the front of the crowd. But in his last years Louis Sr. had suddenly started saying good things about The Company, instead of yelling they were tyrants who needed overthrowing. Hugh remembered Da at the supper table remarking on the strange changeover, and Granda saying: *"'Tis no strange at all; he just finally started seeing the alternatives."*

Da said to the only Louis Riel he could say anything to anymore: "Thank you, your sympathies are appreciated," and took off his mitten to shake the proffered hand. "I expect we'll be seeing more of you. You'll be staying around for good now?"

"For good, I hope."

As the family crossed the snow-packed compound to the patiently-waiting sled ponies, Mom said to Da: "Did you know he was back?" in that tone that carried in it: *"And if so why didn't you bother to mention it to me? Remember me, the mother of your children, the woman who bakes your bread and darns your socks? Yoo-hoo."*

Da said: "No."

"You didn't seem surprised to see him."

"I wasn't. Seminaries and law schools and big cities be damned, he's a Red River boy, I knew he'd be back eventually. Besides, his mother's here."

That got Hugh thinking on circularity again, and that Granda's chuckle on the day Hugh brought home the venison was specifically about Louis Riel Jr. Although Louis was a better-than-good horseman – he'd taught Hugh a few things when Hugh'd got big enough to get onto a pony's back by himself – he'd never gone out on the buffalo hunt, and was a different species from the wild Metis boys wee Hugh had admired. Hugh remembered tagging along with a group of older boys from the Lagimodière clan – the ones about Louis's age – setting rabbit snares in the riverside woods, and seeing Louis and his mother walking by on the deep-worn path to the cathedral compound, for Mass or Confession or lessons or whatever else happened to be doing at church that day. Reliable word had it that the first words baby Louis learned to speak weren't 'Mama' and 'Papa,' but 'Jesus' and 'Mary' and 'Joseph.' There was a lot admirable about Louis Riel Jr., and Hugh was sure Granda would've been the first to admit it, but that was who Granda'd meant by: "I wish old Jean Baptiste was still alive, so I could rub his nose in whose grandson grew up to be the hunter."

CHAPTER 29

Agnes inched her bedsocked feet out onto the floor, then quickly stood up, flung on her dressing gown and made a dash for the washstand. She broke the skin of ice in the water pitcher with the ebony handle of her hairbrush, filled the basin and splashed her face – a faster and more effective wake-up than a morning cup of coffee, though she would've preferred to have the choice. She looked at her face in the mirror and saw that the only hint of red was the ice water flush, so her husband's beard had finally grown out past the wiry, chafing stage. A few more weeks and it would be time to start trimming and shaping it.

Behind her, she could hear Christian stirring the embers and putting some wood in the little iron stove that heated their bedroom and sitting room. By now the halfbreed shop assistant would have come in and stoked the store stoves, so it should be warm downstairs by the time they got dressed and breakfasted.

The kitchen was warm already, with the cook stove well fed and coffee put on by a delightful article the Schultzes had brought back with them from Canada. Elizabeth Louise McKenney was sixteen years old and Christian's half-niece, daughter of Henry McKenney's full brother. Eliza had been familiar with Red River since before Agnes ever saw the place; her father had tried to make a go of it as a working partner in McKenney & Co, but after one winter they'd moved back east. Eliza was a bit taller than Agnes, her hair a bit darker and thicker, her eyes liquid brown instead of bright blue, and her personality much more accommodating and pliable than Agnes knew her own to be. Despite those differences, Agnes had quickly decided that Eliza would be the younger sister she'd never had. Certainly more of a sister than gawky dismal Laura.

The store was indeed already warmed by the time they came downstairs, but there was no sign of any customers yet. Which was just as well, because there was something Agnes wanted to talk to her husband about, and not when anybody else was about. Eliza was nearby, counting ceramic beads out of a large box into a smaller one that would fit under the counter, but Agnes didn't mind Eliza overhearing; it might be good for her to hear and see how one went about helping a man make up his mind to follow a certain course of action.

Agnes hopped up and perched herself on the counter – something she never would've done if there'd been customers about – and chirped: "Christian, don't you think it's time to have a talk with the Point Douglas Sutherlands, about Point Douglas...?"

"Don't you think it's a bit too soon yet, my dear?"

"It's been well over a month since they put that dear old lady in the ground – and with Christmas and New Year's to help get over their bereavement. I'd call that a decent interval."

"I might, too, but... You haven't lived among these people quite so long as I have, Agnes. They don't like to be pushed."

'Neither do you,' Agnes thought, *'but I'm pushing you.'* "You've said so many times yourself, dear – since Confederation and Alaska – that the Dominion is going to have to move on The Company soon, before the Americans move in. Well, if immigrants from Canada start pouring in before you've made arrangements about Point Douglas, even a back-country bumpkin like John Sutherland will see for himself the opportunity you saw at a glance. And once he sees it for himself, why would he want to deal with partners or middlemen? For that matter, how do you know that Henry McKenney or some other unscrupulous people aren't already trying to worm their way into Point Douglas and steal your chance?"

"I wouldn't call John Sutherland a bumpkin."

Agnes could think of several other things she'd like to call John Sutherland. She hardly knew the man, but she did know he'd been appointed when her husband was disappointed. Recently a member of the Council of Assiniboia had died unexpectedly – more unexpectedly than most – and by far the most qualified candidate to take his place was obviously Dr. John Christian Schultz. Christian had done everything appropriate to put himself forward, beginning with a letter printed in *The Nor'Wester* from an unspecified 'Five Prominent Citizens' begging the proprietor of *The Nor'Wester* to take the vacant council seat. But The Company's Governor Mactavish had whispered in the ear of Assiniboia's Governor Mactavish, who appointed Company-friendly John Sutherland on the pretext that his long experience as an alternate councillor had prepared him for the position. "Whether you would call John Sutherland a bumpkin or not, dear, doesn't alter the point I'm trying to make. The point is –"

At that point the shop bell jingled and Agnes jumped down off the counter. But it wasn't a customer, it was her half-brother-in-law, Sheriff Henry McKenney, looking even larger than usual in a buffalo coat and wide hat. The proprietor of McKenney & Sons General Store didn't make a habit of shopping at Schultz's White Store. Any slim doubts whether it might not be a social call were dispelled by the fact that there were two other large men with Henry McKenney.

One of the men was one-armed, middle-aged Constable Mulligan, whom The Company had recently appointed the only full-time constable at Red River, specifically assigned to the village of Winnipeg. Mulligan had been one of the Chelsea Pensioners posted to Red River twenty years ago, and stayed on after the posting ended. The only possible logic Agnes could guess behind making Mulligan Constable was someone's theory that even the most obstreperous drunkard wouldn't turn violent on a grey-haired man who'd lost an arm in the service of Queen And Country. Agnes didn't recognise the other large man flanking Sheriff McKenney, but suspected he was a Special Constable sworn-in for the day.

Christian said crisply to his half-brother: "What do you want here?"

"It's not what I want, it's what John Inkster wants. Two hundred and ninety-six pounds, eight shillings and fourpence. He's been waiting patiently for eight months, finally ran out of patience."

Agnes recognized the numbers, both monetary and monthly. The money figure was her husband's partnership-half of what McKenney & Co still owed Frederick E. Kew of London. The summer after Agnes arrived at Red River, Frederick E. Kew himself had shown up there, quickly procured a judgement against the ex-partners in the Court of Assiniboia, then delegated John Inkster as his collection agent and hied himself back to civilization. Stalwart stolid John Inkster had let himself be fobbed-off with excuses for two years, then launched another trial which judged that the junior ex-partner of McKenney & Co. must pay up his share immediately. That 'immediately' had been proclaimed eight months ago, a month before Agnes walked down the aisle of St. Boniface Cathedral.

Sheriff McKenney held up a folded piece of heavy vellum. "I have a copy of the Court Judgement from the trial last May –"

"*Trial?*" Christian spat. "I wasn't even here to defend myself!"

"Well, *I* was in St. Paul when the Kew trial happened here, what's the difference?"

"The difference is *I'm* not in The Company's pocket, or pockets. The Company's court made damn sure *you* got justice, but *me* – I been calling for a new trial, a fair trial, they ain't listening!"

Agnes had noticed before that her husband's proper English went out the window when he became agitated, but now did not seem a time to draw that to his attention.

McKenney sighed through his big black, frost-dusted beard. "You can't put this off forever. Face up to it, Johnny –"

"Don't you 'Johnny' me, Sheriff McKenney. Here's The Company's Sheriff come with a judgement from The Company's court to make me pay half the debt for McKenney and Company. What about Henry McKenney's half of the debt?"

"You know damn well I paid my half straight to Kew when I was in England last year."

"I know damn well I only got your word for that."

"I got a piece of paper in my desk, signed by Frederick E. Kew for payment received."

Agnes put in loudly: "But how *much* did you pay?"

Her husband caught on immediately. "Yeah, Henry, how do we know you didn't tell The Company you paid Kew *all* that was owing, not just your share, so when The Company's court gets my half they'll just hand it over to you?"

McKenney's head wobbled and eyes blinked several times, in a manner that might come from stupefaction at a sudden phantasmagoria, or from shock at being found out. Agnes suspected she knew which. He said: "Look, John – *Doctor* Schultz – it's perfectly understandable you might not have two hundred and ninety-some pounds sterling in your back pocket. If you pay out a little on account, and draw up a schedule of payments, I'm sure Inkster will be satisfied."

"Not one penny!" Agnes's copper-crowned husband roared, jabbing one forefinger high in the air. He really was magnificent when his blood was up. "Not one unjust farthing! I demand a fair trial!"

Sheriff McKenney said: "All right, John, if that's the way you want it. The order says 'or seizure of goods in lieu of payment.'" He pointed to the set of platform scales on the counter – a very expensive piece of machinery, even without adding-in the exorbitant freight costs to get it to Red River in one piece. "Mulligan, that looks like a good place to start. I'll get the door."

Eliza was standing behind the counter and the scales, but seemed utterly flummoxed as to what she should do. Agnes moved to position herself between the constables and the scales, but the next instant the scales didn't matter. Henry pulled open the shop door, Christian sprang forward and slammed it shut again, and McKenney threw his arms around Christian to lift him aside – a feat that very few men at Red River could've accomplished, but Sheriff McKenney might have if Christian hadn't grappled with him and tripped him up. The two of them fell on a stack of flour sacks, punching and gouging at each other and raising a white cloud. The constables forgot about the scales and went to help their sheriff. As the three of them piled onto Agnes's husband, she grabbed a broom and flailed on their backs. Constable Mulligan's one arm flailed back and knocked the broom out of her hands. Even with five arms and six legs against Christian's two and two, they were cursing and sweating to hold him down. McKenney raised his hatless head, frantically glancing around, and Agnes saw his eyes fasten onto a shelf hook holding a coil of twine. She darted forward to snatch it away, but his hand got there first.

When the three bullies raised her husband back to his feet with his hands bound behind his back, Agnes spat at Henry McKenney, "He's your *brother*, how can you treat him this way?"

McKenney, still catching his breath, grunted: "Goes both ways, Agnes," then planted his broad right hand on Christian's broad left shoulder. "Dr. John Christian Schultz, I'm gonna have to arrest you for assaulting officers of the court in pursuant of their duties. Mulligan, you stay here and make sure nothing gets sold or taken away till this gets sorted out."

They draped Christian's buffalo coat over his shoulders and escorted him outside, with his face redder than his hair but his head still held high. As Constable Mulligan closed the door behind them and turned back into the store, Agnes said to him: "You'll leave, too."

"No, ma'am."

"This is private property, belonging to my husband and I. If I tell you to leave and you do not, you are guilty of trespassing."

"No, ma'am. I've been ordered by the sheriff to stay here and guard these premises. I'm only doing my duty."

Agnes swept her eyes around the store, looking for some inspiration on how to take hold of the situation. Eliza was still standing blankly wide-eyed behind the counter, no help at all. Well, Eliza could hardly be blamed for getting a bit stunned at seeing her supposedly grown-up Uncle John and Uncle Harry wrestling on the floor. But someone was going to have to do something...

Agnes worried her lower lip with her front teeth, then called loudly: "Pascal!" The head of the halfbreed shop assistant rose warily over the bank of shelves in a far corner. "I want you to fetch some boards and nails and board over the front door so no one else can barge in here. Where's Hamish?" Hamish was Pascal's cousin, hired on as a temporary extra pair of hands. Labour came cheap at Red River in the first few months of any given year, when the remnants of income from the autumn buffalo hunt had all been pissed away over Christmas and New Year 's, and the summer hunt still too far off to borrow against.

Pascal said: "He's out in the side-shed – I mean 'ox-illery warehouse' – re-stacking of some things."

That gave Agnes an idea. She said: "Well, Constable Mulligan, if your duty is to make certain none of our goods and chattels get removed, you'll want to see them all. Do come along, please." She drew on her maroon-striped, heavy woolen cloak and led Constable Mulligan out the side door.

Set a ways apart from the main building was a newer, squared-log cabin where they stored gunpowder and kerosene and whatever overflow from the stockroom wouldn't get harmed by the cold. As Agnes and Constable Mulligan crunched their way across the snow toward it, he said: "I don't mean you no ill-will, Mrs. Schultz, I'm just trying to do my duty."

The door of the auxiliary warehouse was standing open to let light in. Agnes glanced to make sure Hamish hadn't taken the padlock inside; it was hanging loose and open in its bracket on the doorframe. Hamish was working with his coat and mitts on, making room in a corner to stack empty crates that could someday be used for either kindling or shipping if not left out in the weather. Agnes said to him: "There's something I want you to help Pascal with in the store."

"I won't mind working a bit in the warm today, me whatever."

Once Hamish was gone, Agnes pointed to the corner farthest from the door and said to Constable Mulligan, endeavouring to keep her voice level, "If the court is determined to confiscate enough of my husband's goods to equal two hundred and ninety-some pounds, there is something in that corner you should itemise." She stayed at the doorway until Mulligan was almost to the far corner, then yanked the door closed, quickly lifted out the padlock so she could close the hasp over the bracket, snicked the padlock back into place and clicked it shut. She shouted through the door: "Guard away, Constable Mulligan, don't let any of those items out of your sight, do your duty! I'd advise you not to strike a match in there!"

Back at the main building, Pascal and Hamish had got a good start in at boarding over the front door and first floor windows. She told them to leave the side door alone and sat down on the stool behind the counter to make a list. She estimated a dozen men would be enough, but listed twenty names on the assumption that some would be too cowardly and some would be too occupied for such short notice. By the time she'd done her list, and Eliza'd helped her copy several different versions of a message on several sheets of paper, Pascal and Hamish had finished with the windows. She sent Pascal riding west and Hamish walking north, then went up to the kitchen where she and Eliza went to work with the halfbreed maid-cum-cook putting together a very large supper for a lot of hungry men.

When she got a moment to sit down between food preparation, Agnes chose one of the armchairs by the south windows of the common room and gazed out across the snow at the courthouse where her husband was shackled in a prison cell. She wouldn't have been able to see the old courthouse behind Fort Garry, but Governor Mactavish had last year decreed the erection of a new, stone courthouse halfway between the fort and the crossroads, ostensibly because the old, wooden one had grown too rundown and the population grown too large for it to serve adequately. But Agnes had no doubt another reason was to show that The Company's reserve land around Fort Garry was going to stay reserved, a stone-hard warning to anyone planning to push the boundary any farther than the White Store. The new courthouse certainly looked more inviolable than the old one. Agnes had plans to violate it tonight.

The fat, halfbreed cook – fat cooks were always a good recommendation – came out of the kitchen with a question that put Agnes back in the realm of feeding the troops. By lamplighting-time in the afternoon twilight, some of them had already arrived. Brown-bearded Dr. Bown was standing looking out one of the common room windows and remarked: "There is a horseman coming from the courthouse. It looks like… Yes, it is: Sheriff McKenney."

Agnes and the others crowded to the windows. Sheriff McKenney slowed his trotting horse when he got close enough to see the door and windows boarded up, then reined it to a halt when he got closer. He stood in his stirrups to yell: "Mulligan…?" The yell probably echoed across the prairie, but was only a muffled mutter through the walls and windows of Agnes's home.

There was much laughter in the common room when McKenney's head turned sharply toward what was probably a plaintive voice responding from the side shed warehouse. He swung his horse in that direction, trotted to the shed and climbed down, then stood at the padlocked door with his fists on his hips in a perplexed posture. One of the men at the windows said: "Should've thought to bring a crowbar," which brought more laughter.

James Stewart from St. James said: "*We* will," which brought even more laughter.

The dumb show through the windowpanes grew active again, with the sheriff going back to his horse to draw his rifle from the saddle scabbard, then back to the shed and aiming at the padlock. The sound of the gunshot made Agnes jump: dumb shows weren't expected to include loud noises. McKenney kicked the door open and Constable Mulligan came out, moving very stiffly and trying to bat some circulation into his torso with his one arm. The sheriff helped him up onto the horse, slapped its rump to send it trotting back down the road to the courthouse and followed along on foot, still carrying his rifle.

With the show over, Agnes served out another round of beer; she was saving the whiskey till midnight. By midnight there were fifteen in the common room, including her. She poured a tot of whiskey for each man. Dr. Bown raised his with: "Storm the Bastille!" and all downed their whiskeys with one gulp, then trooped downstairs buttoning their coats. The cutter was hitched up and waiting, as were a cart-sled and several saddlehorses. Agnes rode in the cutter, leading the way to the courthouse and its jail cells.

There was one grey-bearded half-awake halfbreed jailer on duty; Agnes wondered if he were the same one in the grand stories of her husband and James Stewart freeing the Reverend Griffith Owen Corbett. Were he or not, he was just as easy for three men to intimidate into a corner while the rest carried on to the cells. Agnes called out: "Dr. Schultz?" Calling each other 'Dr. Schultz' and 'Mrs. Schultz' in public was a habit they'd started when they were still giddy about actually being man and wife, and had developed into a way of being intimate with each other while sounding like they were maintaining a dignified distance.

From behind one of the heavy, padlocked doors came: "Here, Mrs. Schultz! I'm in here!"

Dr. Bown had the crowbar. After a moment of fidgeting either end against the sides of the padlock hasp, he muttered: "There is no space, no cavity, I can't..."

Someone said: "Should've thought to bring your tooth-drill," and there was laughter.

James Stewart stepped forward to take the crowbar. After a moment of metal clicking against metal, he said: "Well, it's, um, considerably more solid than the lock on the Reverend Corbett's cell – they've put the blacksmith through his paces since then. And it's set back into the wood, so there's no space to start the bar in, as Dr. Bown said."

Someone else said: "Should've thought to bring a hammer." No one laughed.

Agnes had no doubt her husband had the strength to wrench the crowbar in without a hammer, and snap the lock off with one tug, but he was on the wrong side of the door. She looked around. At one end of the corridor in front of the cells was a stack of lumber, and at the front of the stack was a piece of heavy beam about as long as she was tall. Agnes called the men's attention to it. In a moment Dr. Bown, Mr. Stewart and two others had it lined up like a battering ram in front of the cell door and as far back as the width of the corridor would allow. Agnes called: "Dr. Schultz, stand back from the door!"

Dr. Bown chortled, "At your word, milady."

"One, two, three – Charge!"

The concussion sent splinters flying from the door and bent it inward a little, but it still stood. The second charge smashed it off its hinges and sent it crashing down. The dust and splinters settled and there stood Agnes's husband, looking none the worse for wear except for a scrape on one cheek he'd got from rolling around on the floor with the sheriff and two constables. He stepped out across the door, bent down to wrap his arms around her and picked her up, laughing, "Robin Hood never had such a Maid Marian. Home to the greenwood – or the White Store."

It turned into a glorious night of whiskey and laughter – and a few other things when Agnes and her husband retired to their chamber, leaving those of the rescue party with too long a ways home to bed down on the floor of the common room or in one of the beds in the empty rooms waiting to be someday filled by paying lodgers. Agnes felt a bit woozy the next morning, but not so much that she couldn't help Christian compose the copy for a special edition of *The Nor'Wester*, reminding him of details such as his wrists having been bound so tightly they bled, and that it was clear Sheriff McKenney meant to pocket the money ostensibly owed to Frederick E. Kew, with the collusion of The Company's kangaroo court. Agnes had been at Red River long enough to guess that many of the local citizens would take the special edition with a grain of salt, but copies of every edition of *The Nor'Wester* went to newspapers in Canada, who were often happy to fill page space by simply reprinting an interesting story from the western wilds.

Walter Bown, James Stewart and a couple of the men from Headingley stayed on at the White Store in case Sheriff McKenney returned in force to make a re-arrest – though what they would do if he did was an open question. Agnes found she had to work to keep her own spirits up through the day, much less anybody else's. Eliza looked like she was having second and third thoughts about the wisdom of leaving Amherstburg, Ontario. Last night and yesterday had been a bit of a sleigh ride on anger and excitement; now they could only wait to see what The Company, the Governor, the Council, the Sheriff et al were going to do in response.

Late in the day came the answer to that question. An emergency meeting of the Council of Assiniboia issued a notice that three days hence a force of one hundred special constables would be appointed, composed of men willing to act without question on the orders of the Governor and Council. At this time of year it wouldn't be hard to drum up volunteers; Red River was filled with half-savage buffalo hunters willing to do anything for a free drink and a few shillings. This didn't seem like fun anymore.

When Agnes and her husband were alone, she said: "Christian, do you think perhaps if you offered to stand trial again on the suit John Inkster is pursuing for F. E. Kew, they might let slide the resisting-arrest and assault and jail-break and all that?"

"I've already asked for a new trial time after time. And even if they did, it'd still be just my word against *Sheriff* McKenney's, and we're back where we started."

A while later, she said: "Christian, when Mr. Kew was at Red River, did he come by the White Store?"

"Uh-huh. Once at least, maybe twice, I disremember."

"Did you have anybody working for you in the store then?"

"Must've – I can't run the place by myself."

"Do you remember who it was?"

"Why? Does it matter?"

"It might."

"Um… let me think… summer of '65… all the buffalo hunters and their families out on the plains, so it wouldn't've been cheap labour… Sabine."

"Ah," Agnes nodded. That would be Herbert Sabine, who'd been brought to Red River to do some surveying for The Company and stayed on after his contract was done. "Sabine did some surveying for you, too, didn't he?"

"Some."

"Land that might prove valuable…?"

"Could very well be, if – *when* – Rupert's Land becomes part of Canada."

"Land that Sabine might have an interest in…?" Christian squinted one eye at her as though he were beginning to get a notion of what she was getting at. "What if Herbert Sabine were to testify in court that he was working here the day Frederick E. Kew came to pay a call on you, and he saw you pay Mr. Kew all the money you owed him – no papers signed, just a handshake deal, gentleman's agreement? And what it if, when you apply for a retrial now, you could say you have new evidence which proves Inkster's suit is unfounded – evidence you couldn't produce at the first trial because you weren't here to defend yourself…?"

"Well… I don't think I'd want to tell them exactly what that evidence might be, yet – wait to spring it on them at the trial."

"Good plan." John Inkster – a great-grandfather, but still known as 'Orkney Johnny' – had a reputation for dogged honesty, not for being fast on his feet. "But in the meanwhile, if you and the court can come to some sort of agreement about a future trial, The Company and the Council might call off their dogs."

"Hm…" Christian scratched his beard thoughtfully, which to Agnes's eye was a much more mature and sage-looking gesture than a man rubbing his naked jaw. "I suppose I'd best ride over to Herbert Sabine's place and have a conversation with him – a *subtle* conversation. But as to that other conversation you were talking about when all this started, I think now's not a time for me to be having a conversation with Councillor John Sutherland."

The notice that had gone out from the Council asked for all men willing to have their names on the list of one hundred special constables to assemble at Fort Garry. On the appointed day, three hundred men showed up. The Governor thanked them and explained that the current disturbances had been resolved, since the Kew vs Schultz case was going to be retried at the next quarterly session, but the names of the three hundred were taken down for future reference and each was paid a day's wage of ten shillings for showing up. Agnes remarked to her husband: "That's a hundred and fifty pounds out of The Company's and the Council's back pockets. Two days like that and they could have paid off your debt and saved everybody all this trouble."

On the day of the trial, Agnes sat in the front of the visitors' gallery, as close as she could get to Christian sitting alone at the Defence table. Looking across at the homespun backwoods farmers and Indian traders in the jury box, Agnes saw the page in *Pilgrim's Progress* listing the jury judging John Bunyan's Christian: *'Mr. Blind-man, Mr. Malice, Mr. Enmity, Mr. Liar…'*

After the venerable Mr. Inkster presented the by-now old legal papers from Mr. Kew, Dr. Schultz called one witness: Mr. Herbert L. Sabine. Once the witness had been sworn in, the defendant said: "I believe you have something to say to the court on this matter."

"Well, yes. You see – Your Honour, jury members and all – two-and-a-half years ago, summer of '65, I was employed as a clerk in Dr. Schultz's White Store. One sunny afternoon I was sweeping up the store and Dr. Schultz was working on some ledgers at the counter, when in come a gentleman in a white linen suit and a straw hat. Well, visitors to Red River all the way from England get talked about, so I knew it was Mr. Frederick E. Kew. Mr. Kew went up to the counter and he and Dr. Schultz talked pleasantly awhile, then Dr. Schultz took out the strongbox, counted out two hundred and seventy-five pounds and handed it to Mr. Kew. They agreed that that money was paid on the debt, but would be kept quiet and not marked on the note."

A murmur went through the courtroom. John Inkster's white-whiskered mouth opened and closed like a landed fish. Judge Black said: "Mr. Sabine, why ever would they want the debt payment kept quiet and not marked on the note?"

"Well I don't know, Your Honour. That's not my business."

Judge Black ran a hand over his bald crown, scratched his grey beard and said: "Mr. Sabine, you don't know *that*, but you *do* know the amount was two hundred and seventy-five pounds. How much do you know, as distinguished from what you might *think*, of this singular transaction?"

Agnes's husband leaped to his feet, bellowing: "I object to The Court harassing and badgering this witness and... and... putting him in a false position in front of the jury!"

Judge Black turned red, but Agnes could see he knew he was snared in his own rules. It wasn't up to the impartial judge on the bench to cross-examine a witness; that was up to the agent for the plaintiff, and at the moment John Inkster was obviously too flabbergasted to get a word out. All Judge Black could do was charge the jury to exercise their best judgement on the basis of the evidence, and let them retire to do so. After deliberating for an hour, their verdict was that since it had been stated under oath that Dr. Schultz had already paid out two hundred and seventy-five pounds, and the total debt was two hundred and ninety-six, Dr. Schultz owed Mr. Kew a total of twenty-one pounds. That night was a very enthusiastic one in the private chambers of the proprietors of Schultz's White Store.

Agnes found out later that Governor Mactavish was so disgusted by the trial that he'd immediately sent off a dispatch to London, empowering Frederick E. Kew to draw two hundred and ninety-six pounds from the governor's personal account. Agnes saw immediately that Mactavish's 'honourable' motive was just a cover-up for his true and venal motive: trying to uphold the illusion in London that The Company was upholding British Justice in Rupert's Land.

Christian and his friends didn't have the kind of money a man like Mactavish could afford to toss around, but they did have *The Nor'Wester*. Agnes enthusiastically helped them compose ringing phrases for articles about the perfidious, lying ways of The Company and its puppet Governor and Council: *'the artful dodges made use of by a tyrannous Government.'* She especially liked *'there is no crime more infamous than the violation of truth,'* and pointing out to readers that without truthfulness *'every man must disunite himself from others, inhabit his own cave, and seek prey only for himself.'* But best of all was: *'A falsehood is no less an untruth, whether coming from the lips of a Secretary of State, from a Senator at Washington, from a State Senator, from a Chamber of Commerce, from a partisan Newspaper, or from a hod carrier!!'* That ought to get their attention in Ottawa and Toronto, and, yes, even London.

CHAPTER 30

Hugh loved a funny story. Especially one that was more or less true. Best of all were ones that were so ridiculously funny they couldn't possibly be true at all, but were entirely. One snowy evening Da came home late from a Council meeting and gravely announced to the family: "It seems, um, the settlement of Portage la Prairie… no longer… exists. Wiped off the map."

Mum said: "Pardon me?"

"Portage la Prairie is gone. Vanished off, um, the face of the earth. In its place is… The Republic of Manitoba."

Hugh could at least makes sense out of 'Manitoba': a Cree word meaning something like *'the voice of God whispers in the waters,'* although he knew the Cree notion of God wasn't the same as the Reverend Dr. Black's. The word apparently came from the burbling, drumming noise made by a couple of pebbly islands at the narrows of Lake Manitoba and gave the lake its name. But Hugh couldn't fathom what 'Manitoba' had to do with Portage la Prairie, except that the lake was a day's ride due north of there, or this 'republic' business.

What it all had to do with, Da explained, was Mr. Thomas Spence, who'd immigrated from Canada two summers ago and then last summer relocated from Red River to Portage la Prairie. "Mr. Spence soon discovered that Portage la Prairie is just west of the, um, eastern border of Assiniboia. So, *technically*, Portage la Prairie isn't under the legal… *jurisdiction* of the, um, Governor and Council of Assiniboia. That gave Mr. Spence an idea, and some… *cronies* there went along with it. They have declared that… Portage la Prairie and several hundred square miles west of it is now The Republic of Manitoba, with Thomas Spence its President!" Da barely managed to sputter out the last words before laughter took him and shook him up and down in his chair.

Some of the others at the table laughed with him, some of the others just scratched their heads. Hugh might've thought Da was making it all up, except that making things up wasn't exactly in Da's line. Hugh said: "Well… back when me and Donald was about Willy's age, us and Aleck and Morrison built a poplar-pole fort back in the woods, and declared it was Castle Sutherland and Donald was the prince and the rest of us was knights."

Aleck actually smiled, not something he did a lot of anymore. But Donald looked like he didn't care to be reminded of such childish things. Da, though, pounced on it gleefully, "Exactly! But you didn't levy taxes, did you?"

"Taxes? No, I didn't think of that, me whatever."

"But Mr. Spence – I mean President Spence – did. Well, what's the first thing a government needs? Why, a courthouse and jail, of course. But building... *buildings* costs money. So it came to pass that there went out a decree from President Spence that all the Republic of Manitoba shall be taxed." Da burst into laughter again, which caused some of the others around the table to glance at each other sideways. Da was generally good-tempered, but not the belly-laughing kind.

When Da had quietened down again and was wiping his eyes, Mum said a little worriedly, "So what are the Governor and Council going to do about it?"

"Nothing. Neither is The Company – except for the, um, Factor at the Portage post telling the... *Republic's* tax collector to come back when he had a written order from the Governor of Rupert's Land. Other than that, well, we'll all just... sit back and shake our heads at the shenanigans."

Not many days later, Da came home from doing business at Fort Garry with the news that the Republic of Manitoba was no more. It seemed that one of the citizens of the Republic was a shoemaker named MacPherson – "Odd," Da slipped in, "how many troublemakers are named MacPherson," – and he not only refused to pay the tax, he noised around that the taxes were only going to buy whiskey for President Spence and his buddies. So President Spence sent a couple of deputies to arrest Shoemaker MacPherson for Treason. After a bit of a scuffle the deputies dragged the shoemaker back to the tavern that was the temporary court of the Republic of Manitoba, and the president put the traitor on trial. But then a couple of MacPherson's friends burst in waving pistols, the candles got knocked over, there was a gunshot in the dark and the president bawled: *"For God's sake, men, don't fire, I have a wife and family!"* The trial ended with the president and his court getting chucked out into the snow.

"And thus endeth," Da concluded sombrely, although he seemed to have some trouble keeping a straight face, "the Republic of Manitoba. I, um, expect we'll soon see President Spence back at Red River, working as a store clerk or errand boy."

Now Da let his laughter go, rocking back and forth in his chair, and Hugh laughed with him, although Hugh's laughter was a bit reined back by trying to get his mind around the weirdness of it all. Hugh did let his laughter have its head, though, when Da leaned over to punch him on the shoulder in a 'Can you beat that?' gesture – a gesture more one-man-to-another than man-to-boy.

When their laughter settled down somewhat, Mum said: "But I don't see what's entirely funny, Father, about people firing guns at each other. Someone might've been killed."

Da chortled, "Don't you worry, Mother, from the condition I hear they were in, the only danger they would've been in was if they, um, weren't aiming at each other." But Da's chortles died down and his voice grew softer, not really sombre as much as thoughtful. "It is odd, though… brought something to mind… There've been a number of odd things these last few years, and this, um, business at the Portage being odder than odd made me think – pointed up… It, um, occurred to me that people who come here from the east, they've lived all their lives under all sorts of… *restraints*, a constable on every corner, laws against spitting on the street or having a cup of beer on Sunday –"

Mum cut in: "*You* would never drink beer on the Sabbath."

"No, but not because there's a… *secular* law against it, and if my neighbour chooses to do so, that's his business. I was just, um, thinking of an explanation, imagining…"

Hugh was quite sure that imagining didn't come easy to his father.

"… trying to imagine what it would be like to grow up in a place with a, um, regular legislature, whose whole… *raison d'être* is to legislate, telling you what you can do and what you can't do. And then people from there come here, where there are no restraints – so long as you don't put a… *crimp* in The Company's trade, or cut a hole in the ice without putting up a warning pole – and some of them… go stark, staring mad."

Hugh couldn't think of anything to say to that, and it seemed Mum didn't either.

"Well," Da brightened, "but as long as all it means to us is… free entertainment…"

Hugh was all in favour of free entertainment, or anything free. Some of his appointed chores around the farm were more in the line of freedom than of something he was obliged to do. The next day was a Wednesday, and the free-est of those so-called chores. Da wasn't much for winter riding, so from November till May the only exercise Montrose would've got was the occasional jaunt across the river to Fort Garry or the new courthouse or the post office in A.G.B. Bannatye's store. So every winter Wednesday when there wasn't an all-out blizzard, Hugh would saddle Montrose in the morning and set off north up the river road for a good few hours' run. What Hugh hadn't mentioned to his parents was that whenever possible Nancy Prince would be riding south along the river road on Wednesday morning. In the tree-cracking cold, it wasn't possible for them to do much but a little kissing and a lot of dreaming out loud about what kind of house they would build, how many cows and chickens they'd need to start with, whether they could get by with just a fireplace until they could afford to buy an iron stove… But that was more than enough for Hugh, for now.

This Wednesday, though, there were no gunshot-cracks of icebound trees, and a twittering flock of madcap black-capped chickadees had actually ventured out of the woods to see if there were any frozen berries on the roadside bushes. Hugh figured whatever the thermometer temperature was would probably have felt chilly to him last fall, but after four months of real cold it felt like sitting-in-the-sun weather to him. Maybe it would to Wauh Oonae, too, if today didn't turn out to be a day she couldn't get away.

The answer to that 'if' came up sooner than Hugh'd expected. He hadn't ridden half a mile before he saw a smaller horse and rider coming toward him. She must've set out before dawn. Nancy had grown out of her white HBC blanket capote and now wore a dark blue one with a black stripe around the hem and cuffs, but Cheengwun was still buckskin with a white-spotted rump. Wauh Oonae pushed the hood back off her glorious, blue-black hair as the horses came nose-to-nose and halted. Hugh was about to climb down off Montrose so he and Nancy could have their good-to-see-you kiss and body press, but she didn't jump down off her pony, instead turned Cheengwun's head and starting him walking back north. Hugh flicked Montrose's reins to fall in beside.

Nancy flicked her eyes sideways at him, then said tightly, "We have to go to St. Peters."

"Oh. What's happened?"

She kept staring straight ahead, but a flush crept into her winter-paled cheek. "My parents say it's time they met you. Well, my mother says, but my father says 'okay' like always."

"Okay."

She didn't laugh. She nudged Cheengwun into a trot and then a gallop, which Hugh thought thoughtful of her, since he would have a lot of miles to cover back and forth to St. Peters and a short day to do it in. He let Montrose play hoof-thunder music for awhile, then slowed him to a walk again, partly to let him breathe himself out and partly to let Wauh Oonae catch up. The stubby, Indian ponies had more stamina and toughness than an Irish Hunter crossbred like Montrose, but legs half a foot longer made a difference over a mile or so.

When Nancy had caught up and fell in beside him, Hugh said: "Maybe it's time you met *my* parents, too."

"No! That is – not yet. Better we wait till we got everything all ready, or close-to, so it's not just a... dream. I wouldn't think it time for you to meet *my* parents yet, but... I shoulda kept my big mouth shut." She shut her mouth and set her horse running again.

When next they slowed down, Hugh said: "I don't see as it'll be much of a problem. I ain't exactly Prince Charming..." He thought of making a joke out of Prince Charming and the Prince family, but decided she didn't seem in much of a mood for jokes. "...but I got two arms and legs and only two eyes. Your folks and me'll talk a bit about the weather and the fishing and maybe have a cup of tea and that'll be that."

"May be."

Wauh Oonae's closed-in mood made Hugh a good deal less confident than he was trying to sound. He was beginning to wonder if there was something she wasn't telling him. Then a dab of colour in the white field to his right caught his eyes. He'd already noticed that the banks of snow on either side of the trampled-down road were lower than they'd been last week, and now, off in the middle of that field where there were no trees to block the sun's warmth, in the lee of a snow dune, there was a dappling of blue deeper than the ghost of blue that haunted sunlit snow. He stopped his horse and pointed, "Look, Wauh Oonae..."

In the interval between his saying and her stopping, Cheengwun had moved a few steps ahead. Which was just as well, since she was on his left and Hugh was pointing to his right, and her shorter horse would've made it difficult to see past him and Montrose.

He said: "You see? That blue there…? Crocuses!" Although they were only dots of colour from that distance, he could see them clearly in his mind's eye, and feel their fur-coated petals. He figured there had to be a hummock there, or some sort of rise of ground, so the seeming-even plain of snow in the lee of the drift was actually thinner at that spot.

One corner of Nancy's mouth tipped up slightly, in what might be something like a smile. She said: "Not blue exactly. They got a touch of a purple hue."

"Well… it's a hopeful sign, anyways."

"Let's hope so. Come on," she urged her pony back up to a trot.

They were galloping again when they passed by Norbert Parisien's family's place. Norbert was in the yard helping his father load cordwood onto a sled. Hugh waved his arm over his head as they whipped past, then wished he hadn't, because Norbert dropped his end of the log to wave back and Hugh could hear Norbert's father's cursing even over the hoofbeats. But from what Nancy had said in one of their long and wandering conversations, that didn't mean Norbert's father was mean to him, just got exasperated at times.

They passed through Little Britain, and past the Stone Fort and St. Peter's church across the river. Hugh half-expected Wauh Oonae to turn in at the cluster of joined-together cabins where he'd met Chief Peguis, but she rode on by. He wondered who was living there now – probably the widow, or widows, and the younger children of Mr. King's old age.

A little farther on, Nancy did turn her pony off the road. There was a low-roofed, squared-log cabin with a clay chimney. The weather-greyed logs showed a few patchy remnants of a coat of whitewash long ago, and some of the clay chinking between the logs was cracked and peeling. A few scruffy dogs rose out of their nose-to-tail curls in the snow, then lay back down again. Near them a buffalo skull lay sideways: glossy black horns and matte white bone where it wasn't yellowed by territory-marking. Dark-haired children barely dressed for the weather stopped chasing each other around the yard and stood and watched Nancy and Hugh ride in.

Wauh Oonae walked her pony around to the south side of the cabin, where a stand of brush gave a windbreak for the horses while still letting the sun shine on their backs. There was a deerhide nailed to that wall to stretch and dry, and a few rusty traps hanging beside it. When Hugh and Nancy were down off their horses, she said as though she wasn't sure whether she'd be more foolish to say it or not say it, "They can't stop us, not when the time comes, but… better for all if they don't try." She headed around the corner toward the cabin door.

Hugh rounded the corner and stopped. On the far side of the yard, sitting with her back against a tree, was a leather-faced suety middle-aged woman smoking a pipe. She had an old buffalo robe propped below and behind her and seemed to be keeping half an eye on the children, particularly one reddish-haired boy running with the darker ones.

Wauh Oonae had stopped and turned to see why Hugh had stopped. He said: "Shouldn't we go say hello to your mother?"

"That's not my mother. That's my sister."

"Oh." Hugh was glad that only Wauh Oonae had heard his idiot assumption. After all, in his own family there was almost twenty years between the oldest child and youngest.

As if she'd heard what he was thinking, Nancy said: "She's four years older'n me. She's back from out west on a 'visit.' Prob'ly soon she'll head back west with whoever happens to be goin' that way, goin' with anybody who happens to be goin' anywhere. She thought she was a wife, but she was just a muffin."

Hugh knew the shagganappi meaning of that word from listening in on old fur traders. A muffin was an Athabaskan woman a trader took up with while he was stuck in an outpost on the Athabaska, or an Okanagan woman when he got reposted to the Okanagan Valley, 'just a little something to tide me over.' When 'so-and-so's muffin' was said by the old Company men who'd chosen to retire to Red River rather than abandon their country wives for civilization, the phrase had a cutting edge to it, and the sharpness wasn't intended for the woman in question.

Wauh Oonae said: "Come on," with an undercurrent of *'let's get this over with.'* When she pulled the cabin door open and gestured Hugh forward, he closed his eyes as he stepped inside. It was a simple trick he'd made up for himself, but he'd found it worked pretty well. The principle was that if you're going from bright light into dimmer light, if you shut your eyelids for a few seconds, then instead of going from bright light to dim light your eyes would be going from total darkness to dim light.

The only light beyond the doorway came from a couple of parchment windows and the fireplace where a broad-beamed woman was cutting onions into a pot. The one-room cabin had almost no furniture, just a small homemade table and two chairs in a corner. Hugh imagined the family took their meals sitting cross-legged on the buffalo robes and Indian mats strewn around the dirt floor, but that would only be for the slim half the year when they weren't taking their meals sitting cross-legged on the prairie inside a protective circle of buffalo hunters' carts.

The air was thick with a long-steeped smell of old sweat, fish, tobacco, half-cured leather, woodsmoke, fried lard and a touch of wet dog. Hugh figured that the air inside everybody's home got pretty thick over the winter, you just didn't notice your own. But the winter-battened smell inside Wauh Oonae's home was several layers above noticeable; a one room cabin where the whole family did their indoor living and no doubt slept on the floor.

There wasn't much on the walls. A couple of guns lay on wooden pegs set up beyond children's reach. There were a few empty pegs that Hugh figured were for the guns of some of Nancy's brothers, who were likely up at the lake fishing or out on traplines. Outside of the woman at the fireplace, the only person in the house just now was a black-haired man sitting at the table carving an Indian flute and trying the sound of the first two holes to gauge where to put the next one.

Hugh understood now why Wauh Oonae had been reluctant to have him meet her family. These were the real Red River people: plonk them down anywhere in the deep woods or way out in the prairie with only an axe or a knife, come back a week later and they'd have a snug shelter, a fire with a rabbit roasting over it, a steaming brew of Indian tea, and a sure sense of how to find their way home when they got around to it. And he was just a farmboy who 'rode pretty good for a white man.'

Nancy said: "Papa, Nimaama, this is John Hugh Sutherland." Wauh Oonae's mother came forward from the fireplace, wiping her hand on her skirt, and shook Hugh's hand. Her greying hair looked to've been brown, not black, but Metis's stew of races made for all sorts of colour combinations. Hugh'd heard it said that if you wanted to know what your girl was going to look like when she got older, look at her mother. But Hugh couldn't see anyone as active as Nancy Prince ever getting that plump, although there were traces of her cheekbones under her mother's layers of fat.

Wauh Oonae's father nodded at Hugh and gestured at the empty chair across the table from his. Hugh went and sat down. Mr. Prince twittered on the flute, shrugged, set it down on the table and pushed it and the knife and shavings aside. Whichever of Mr. King's wives had been this Mr. Prince's father, it couldn't've been the same as Chief Henry Prince's. This one was blocky and broad, not tall and sharp-featured.

Nancy's father gazed in Hugh's general direction and said: "Cold ride?"

"Not so much. We saw some crocuses." Hugh regretted it as soon as the words left his mouth, sounding like a five year old trumpeting he'd seen a squirrel.

"Good sign," Mr. Prince nodded. "Good sign."

Wauh Oonae appeared at the table with two tin bowls of rubaboo, the stew made from pemmican and whatever else the cook found to hand. In this case it was onions and some sliced carrots, which suggested that for all the Princes' buffalo hunting and woodsy ways they still kept a vegetable garden and root cellar. Hugh started to get up to give Nancy his chair, but she shook her head, saying: "I'll go help my mother," and set the bowls and spoons down in front of her father and Hugh.

Mr. Prince took a couple of unhurried spoonfuls without saying anything, so Hugh did the same, glad to get something in his stomach after the long time since breakfast, but finding his stomach a little knotted. Eventually Nancy's father said: "I hear you left school before you was done. Why's that?"

Hugh gave his reasons and wasn't sure whether Mr. Prince approved of them or not. Then they talked about the weather, and how good the rubaboo tasted, and the good and bad points of 'English' horses versus shagganappi ponies. Despite the sounds of fire-poking and domestic conversation from behind him, Hugh got the distinct impression that four other ears were hearing every word spoken by him and Mr. Prince. He managed to sneak a glance over his shoulder once and saw that Nancy was cooking in the pretty fashion of Indian women: sitting on one hip with her legs tucked up against the other one, with pouches of wild herbs and spices spread out within her reach, stirring and sniffing a smaller pot that had replaced the stewpot on the firehook.

Hugh noticed Mr. Prince glance in that direction, too, but not downward toward his daughter, more upwards, along a line where Mrs. Prince's eyes would be standing. Then Mr. Prince looked at the tabletop, drummed his fingers on its rim, blew out a worn-down breath and said: "My father told me some years back you're a good lad, and I'd say he's right, though not a lad anymore –"

"'Fraid I still am somewhat, sir."

"But... Well, I know you're fond on Nancy, and she sure is on you." The corners of Hugh's mouth jacked up and outward so hard his back teeth hurt. He dropped his head to hide his idiot grin. "*But...* 'fond' don't change the way that... there's... differences..."

"'Differences,' sir?"

Mr. Prince looked pained and looked at the ceiling. "Well, it was one thing in the old days when the fur trade was booming, and scads of lonely young men brought in from the Orkney Isles and such... And even today, some might say as a for instance, there's your Reverend Dr. Black married a daughter of Okanagan woman Granny Sally Ross – but Henrietta was brought up the daughter of Alexander Ross, so the differences weren't all that different... But, well, Kildonan people usually stick to themselves, their own kind, and folks from St. Peters ain't that same kind. They're, we're... *different*..." Mr. Prince looked straight at Hugh with a kind of beseeching expression. "You understand what I mean, eh?"

"Yes, I do, sir."

Mr. Prince looked relieved.

"I've thought about it a lot, and I figured out what to do about it."

Mr. Prince looked confused.

"If needs be, I can convert."

"'Convert'?"

"Well, my folks wouldn't like it, but Anglican ain't all that different from Presbyterian. Heck, they went to the Anglican church their ownselves all those years till Dr. Black came here."

Mr. Prince goggled at him, then roared into bellows of laughter, pounding his fists on the table. When Mr. Prince finally managed to catch his breath, wiping tears off his cheeks, he said: "You'll do, John Hugh Sutherland, you'll do just fine. And here's my hand on it."

CHAPTER 31

As the snow around Schultz's White Store rotted away and the crocuses were choked out by patches of new mint green grass, Schultz decided enough time had passed since the winter's legal friction that he could initiate a conversation with Councillor John Sutherland. Schultz would've preferred to wait a little longer, but – as Agnes kept pointing out with undeniable accuracy – events in the larger world weren't going to wait on J. C. Schultz's convenience before they started moving and shaking Red River. So since Pascal went across the river to St. Boniface every Sunday anyway, and soon would be gone for months with the buffalo hunt, Schultz crossed the Rubicon and got Pascal to deliver a note to the Point Douglas Sutherlands: inviting Mr. John Sutherland Esq. to stop by the White Store at his convenience to discuss a matter that might prove mutually beneficial.

The next day, Hugh Sutherland came into the store and only glanced around long enough to spot Schultz behind the counter. As young Sutherland approached, Schultz noticed that the lad had filled out somewhat since he last saw him, and so had his mustache. Not that it was walrus thick or Chinaman long, but it did look like real whiskers instead of sooty cobweb. Schultz rubbed his own beard reflexively and was glad he'd waited to grow facial hair until he didn't have to suffer through the ridiculous wispy stage.

Hugh Sutherland said: "'Mornin', Doctor. Da asked me to stop by since I was coming acrosst for the Post Office anyways..." Schultz wondered if that might not be a pointed reference, pointing out that the Post Office had been awarded to A.G.B. Bannatyne's store, not his. "Tricky coming crosst the river these days, with ice chunks still floating down, but I guess that's why people 'round here got in the habit of using dugouts stead'n of birchbark canoes. Da says he'd come by here day after tomorrow afternoon, if that's convenient for you."

"Certainly. Do tell your father I look forward to seeing him."

"Yep." Hugh Sutherland turned to go, then stopped and cocked his head, looking out the big front window. He said: "Spring's coming on fast. Soon be time for buffalo hunters to make up their minds if they'll be going along on this summer's hunt or not."

Schultz didn't have a figment of what that observation was meant to mean to him, if anything. Maybe it was meant to point up the fact that soon the store's hired help would be gone and there wasn't a damn thing Schultz could do about it. Or maybe there was some other undermining reason to the remark. Schultz just said: "I suppose so," and nodded as Hugh Sutherland waved over his shoulder on his way out the door.

Wednesday after luncheon, Schultz put on his three-piece business suit, then changed his mind and doffed the jacket for woolen wrist-to-elbow sleeve protectors and sat down at the common room table behind an open ledger, ink bottle, pen and blotter. The ledger in question, the one for the pharmacy stock and sales, was perfectly up to date, but John Sutherland wouldn't know that. On second thought, Schultz got back up to fetch several other ledgers from his desk and stack them beside the open one, to show that his business interests were many and varied. Then he sat waiting, rehearsing in his mind the various tacks the coming conversation could take.

He heard a rustling behind him and turned to see his wife emerging from the corridor to their chambers and the empty lodgers' rooms. She'd changed out of her brown shop dress into a pink and green striped day dress, with a frilled but businesslike bib apron over it. She stopped beside him, put one hand on a table corner and the other on his shoulder, and said quietly, as though keeping one ear cocked toward the stairway, "Christian, my dear, I don't mean to be intrusive, but… You have a natural tendency to think in terms of what is just and right and fair, and I love you for it, but sometimes it leads you to take less advantage of an opportunity than you are entitled to. So there is one thing I would like you to keep in mind, if it isn't there already. John Sutherland didn't build Point Douglas, or earn it, he just inherited it. You and I inherited nothing. Besides, how much do you think the Indians got for Point Douglas?"

Schultz heard boots coming up the stairs, and John Sutherland's: "Hello…?" echoing in the staircase.

Agnes skipped away towards the kitchen as Schultz stood up, pen in hand, and called back: "Yes, in here." John Sutherland emerged from the staircase wearing an HBC blanket coat and homespun wool trousers tucked into the tops of his knee-high boots – standard male fashion for a place where either snow or mud or both needed slogging through more often than not. "Good to see you, Mr. Sutherland."

"Dr. Schultz." They shook hands across the table. "I came in through the store, but your clerk, or, um, the young lady behind the counter, told me to just head on up."

"My niece, Miss Mckenney."

A flicker of surprise crossed John Sutherland's bland face, at the incongruity of someone named McKenney working in Schultz's White Store. Schultz would've explained if asked, but John Sutherland just said: "I, um, hope I'm not interrupting your work…"

"Not at all – the adding and subtracting never ends, so it's a relief to get a reason to put it away for awhile. Do sit down; just drape your coat over a chair." Schultz closed the ledger and inkpot, then went to wipe the pen and realised it was still dry. He assured himself John Sutherland wouldn't notice and went through the motions. "It's good of you to come, what with the river still bobbing with ice and all. I would've offered to come to you, but I thought we'd find it easier to discuss business where there aren't children running in and out and so on."

"You thought right. Never short of… distractions 'round home."

Agnes came in from the kitchen carrying a tea tray including a plate heaped with the Peak Freens Assorted Biscuits they usually rationed. While the teapot finished steeping, Agnes sat and chatted with John Sutherland about his children, surprising Schultz with the depth of her interest in the Point Douglas Sutherlands' domestic life. After she'd poured – 'one lump or two' was a nice touch for a place where sugar usually only came in sacks if at all – she surprised Schultz much further by standing up with her cup and saucer and saying: "Well, I'll leave you men to talk business. If you need more tea and biscuits, I'll be just next door puttering in the kitchen."

As Schultz watched his wife's pink and green back disappear through the doorway, he realised what a brilliant move she'd just made: she had just removed John Sutherland's wife from the equation. He turned back to John Sutherland and said: "I guess you've guessed what I wanted to discuss with you. Point Douglas."

Sutherland murmured: "Mm-hm," around the bit of biscuit he was chewing, then washed it down with a sip of tea and said: "What do you have in mind?"

"Well, first off it's not just what *I've* got in mind, but what a lot of other people have in mind. You've seen what's happened to the village of Winnipeg in just a few years. Not long ago there was nothing at the crossroads but Noah's Ark – Henry McKenney's place. Now there's my store, McDermot's, Bannatyne's, Drever's, Dutch George Emmerling's hotel, Monchamp's tavern, the harness shop, Ashdown's tin shop… And it's going to increase geometrically. I know for a fact there are two American brothers planning to put up another hotel here next summer. I'll be building a separate drugstore soon, since my little pharmacy counter can't accommodate the stock and the trade. And you know better than I do that the Reverend Black is going to build a second church here this summer. When the Presbyterian Kirk commits itself to a prediction that a locale is going to grow, you know it's not idle speculation."

Sutherland nodded silently, clearly mulling over what Schultz had said but taking a damn long time to mull. It occurred to Schultz that women might consider John Sutherland a handsome man, with his high, rounded forehead, broad but not sharp cheekbones, clear blue eyes, and a grey beard not unlike the Persian lamb some fashionable women back east were starting to wear on their collars. But there was something unmanly about him. Although there were crow's feet around the eyes, and worry-furrows creasing the forehead, there was still something boyish about the face. A man in his late forties should have more of a hardened look to him. But a boyish guilelessness wasn't the worst attribute Schultz might find in a potential business partner. Especially one who came with all the material assets the business would be built on.

When John Sutherland finally did speak, it was to say: "I grant you all that, Dr. Schultz, about the… *village* of Winnipeg…"

For an instant, Schultz thought Sutherland was being disparaging about the '*village*,' then reminded himself of John Sutherland's habitually odd and sometimes halting way of speaking. When he paused in the middle of a sentence and then emphasized the next word, there wasn't necessarily a reason behind the emphasis.

"... but, Point Douglas is a ways away from the village – not a long ways, but a ways."

"That is precisely its advantage, Mr. Sutherland." Schultz's enthusiasm couldn't be contained in a chair. He pushed off from the table, stood up and paced around the common room. "The village will naturally cluster around the crossroads and then expand along the Portage Trail and the main road north," stretching his left arm out sideways and his right in front of him by way of illustration. "Now, at the moment it's perfectly amenable that McDermot built a house nearby his store, and Bannatyne the same – I mean to do the same myself, don't mean to live above the store forever. But where we are now is going to become the centre of a large commercial district, and who wants to live in the centre of a commercial district? I mean, who that can afford not to?

"To the *north* of the Portage road and *west* of the main road north, there's nothing but bald, windswept prairie. *South* of the Portage road is The Company's reserve lands around Fort Garry. But just to the *east* of the north road is Point Douglas. Wealthy businessmen – and there are going to be a lot of wealthy businessmen here – will pay handsomely for building lots in a tree-lined residential area with lots of river frontage, where they can raise their families in peace and quiet and still be in easy reach of their businesses."

Schultz forebore to extrapolate into his longer-term vision for Point Douglas. Point Douglas had been gnawing at him since he'd first got to Red River, and he'd believed it was because of the future he'd just outlined to John Sutherland. But even while believing that, he'd still had the niggling feeling there was something else about Point Douglas, something he wasn't quite seeing. It was only when he and Agnes went to Canada last summer that he'd finally seen Point Douglas. In the drawing rooms and business clubs of Toronto, Schultz and Agnes had heard a lot of speculation that if the new Dominion did acquire the Hudson's Bay Company's territories, there would sooner or later have to be a rail line extended from Ontario to the new west. After all, Canada couldn't very well keep on using the American rail lines and still call itself a sovereign country.

Schultz had realised that such a railroad would have to cross the wide Red River somewhere, literally no way around it. And 'somewhere' was bound to be somewhere near The Forks, where there was already an outpost of civilization and where traffic had naturally flowed since long before civilization. The Red River narrowed considerably where it horseshoed around Point Douglas. Whoever owned a sizeable portion of Point Douglas was going to come into an immense amount of money when the railroad came through. But there seemed no necessary point in pointing that out to Point Douglas John Sutherland.

John Sutherland nibbled another tea biscuit, brushed a few crumbs out of his beard, took another sip of tea and said: "I did grant you that the village of Winnipeg is, um, bound to grow – but, maybe not near so much as you're saying. The only way a private business can... *survive* here – aside from taverns, and how many of them can our population support? – is to undercut The Company, or bring in specialty goods The Company doesn't import. That kind of narrows the possibilities. I mean the possibilities of... *lots* of wealthy businessmen hereabouts."

"But The Company's days are numbered. It can't last."

"It can't? It's lasted almost two hundred years so far."

"I mean it can't last in its present form, lording it over half of North America like some..." Schultz struggled for a strong enough term. "... Sultan – Oriental despot. It's becoming obvious to people in Toronto and Ottawa, and London, that The Company's so-called government can't keep order any longer." Schultz caught a sudden glint in Sutherland's eyes, and realised that some people might think the main reason The Company was having trouble keeping order was one John Christian Schultz. So he quickly shifted from the messy past and present to the future: "It's only a matter of time before the Dominion of Canada brings peace, order and good government to Rupert's Land. Then the population and the business possibilities will start booming, and a lot of well-off businessmen are going to be looking for a handy place they can get away from the boom in their off-hours. The only place that fills the bill is Point Douglas."

"Maybe." John Sutherland shrugged his shoulders and Schultz noticed that although Sutherland's shoulders weren't nearly as broad as his own – few men's were – they were considerably thicker: forty years of swinging a scythe, pitching hay and splitting firewood. "But if, as you say, some foreign government is bound to take us over..." Schultz considered objecting to 'foreign,' but let it slide. "... it could just as easily be the United States of America as the Dominion of Canada."

"Never. The Empire would never stand for it."

"No? The Americans have their ways. We're not so, um, ignorant or careless of the outside world as you might think. Even back in the days when... *packets* of newspapers and magazines and letters came in only once a year, they still came in, and got circulated – and six months of winter gives you a lot of time to read and discuss..."

Schultz didn't know where Sutherland was heading, if anywhere, but years of buying and selling had taught him that sometimes it's useful to let the other fellow ramble on. So he stopped pacing, crossed his arms patiently and cocked his head in a listening attitude. Something about the shape of John Sutherland's face looked like he should be wearing spectacles, but wasn't. It was annoying.

"American settlers gradually... *emigrated* into Mexican lands until there was enough of them to scream loudly enough about, um, living under tyranny, that the American army came in and... *liberated* them. And back when I was about my oldest sons' age, there was a... *crackpot* American soldier of fortune came here, but a crackpot with a, um, large store of money and arms from somewhere. His plan was to get Mr. Grant to take his soldiers of the buffalo hunt down to Santa Fe and help, um, liberate the Indians there from the Spaniards. But Mr. Grant saw right off what the... *unspoken* part of the plan was. Once the Spaniards had been, um, driven out of Santa Fe, the Americans would have an excuse to come in. And once Red River people had become... *enmeshed* in matters south of the border, the Americans would have an excuse to come north of the border. Uncle Sam has had his eye on us for some time.

"And now here, Dutch George Emmerling still, um, considers himself an American, and... *talks up* the United States to everyone who drinks at his hotel. And didn't you say there were two brothers from the States planning to put up a new hotel here next summer – ?"

"It won't happen!" Schultz realised he was shouting, with his fists in the air. He sat back down and picked up his teacup; it rattled in the saucer before he could steady his hand. "I'm sorry, Mr. Sutherland, I shouldn't be talking to you about politics, except insofar as it affects the business at hand. I meant, of course, not that the new hotel won't happen, but the North-West getting swallowed by the United States. But for our present purposes, it doesn't matter which duly-constituted, foreign government takes over governing Rupert's Land..." That was a hard pill to choke down, but not as hard as scotching golden prospects over a matter of principle. "... the village of Winnipeg is still going to turn into a hub of commerce and industry overnight, and Point Douglas is going to be a very desirable residential address."

John Sutherland scratched his beard and said: "Maybe... What do you propose?"

"A partnership. You have the land, I have the business apparatus and connections – I could already name you several men of substance in Ontario who'd be interested in relocating here if The Company's stranglehold got loosened. First step, Point Douglas will have to be surveyed into building lots – I'd pay for that. And I'd buy two lots from you right off, to put my money where my mouth is. After that it's fifty-fifty. How's your tea?"

"Hm?" Sutherland looked into his cup. "Oh, almost dry."

Schultz considered offering something stronger, but it was hard to guess which Presbyterians took the kirk's precepts entirely to heart. Schultz himself had got into the habit of never taking a drink in public, except among his closest confidantes, in keeping with the strict temperance principles of the Orange Lodge that ruled Ontario the way the Catholic church ruled Quebec. So, taking the better part of valour, Schultz just lifted the teapot and stood to lean across the table to refill John Sutherland's cup, then sat back down and waited for what Sutherland had to say.

John Sutherland didn't say anything, just sat sipping his tea, running a fingertip back and forth across the left side of his mustache and gazing pensively at the window behind and beyond Schultz's shoulder. So eventually Schultz said: "It might not seem I'd be bringing fifty per cent worth into the bargain, but real estate's worth what the market will bear. When things start booming here I'll be right in the middle of it, seeing whose business is doing better than the other fellow's and when's the right time to offer up a building lot for sale. You see, if all that the general public knows about my involvement with Point Douglas real estate is I'm acting as your agent, I can tell 'em: 'I'm sorry, Tom, I've tried to pry another lot loose from Mr. Sutherland, but he's not sure he wants to sell any more.' And then, when the time is right, I tell the highest bidder: ' You're in luck – Mr. Sutherland's decided to let one more lot go.'"

Schultz winked, but Sutherland didn't wink back, making Schultz worried he might've gone too far for a man with a rustical concept of honesty. John Sutherland was much older in years, but younger in some ways. "I know it sounds like sharp business practices, Mr. Sutherland, but believe me, anyone who'll be able to afford a building lot on Point Douglas will be a pretty sharp businessman himself.

"Regardless how the details play out, I can guarantee you I can get three or four times as much per lot as you could by selling them yourself. At the least." And some of those lots could be bought through blinds by John Christian Schultz, to be built up as temporary rental properties or left fallow, waiting for the coming of the railroad. After all, the lots would only cost Schultz the fifty per cent that was Sutherland's share, and that would be fifty per cent of what Schultz told him was the best price he could get.

John Sutherland finally spoke again, but not in a way that clarified anything. He said: "I have sons."

"You certainly do, and fine lads they are."

"The eldest, Donald, is a scholar – may be a… *schoolteacher* someday, maybe even a college teacher. But Hugh has, um, no interest in scholarly matters or business or the like. I was thinking I might let Hugh put up a… *house* on Point Douglas and eventually, um, deed over half the land to him."

"Hugh's the wild one, isn't he? Oh, I don't mean that in a tut-tutty kind of way. I mean he'd rather ride bareback across the prairie than in a carriage on a graded road." Sutherland nod-shrugged that that was more or less accurate. "Then Point Douglas is not a place where Hugh would want to live – or it won't be, soon." Schultz realised the palms of his hands were sweating, so he surreptitiously wiped them on his trousers. This was bloody hard work. "That quiet little section of the main road that runs across the base of Point Douglas – in a few years it's going to be crammed with boarding houses, livery stables, millworkers' homes… To a businessman from a city in the east, living a little ways back from that road on a treed lot overlooking the river will seem peaceful and pastoral. But to someone like Hugh, it'd be like living next door to a blacksmith shop. And a tavern on the other side.

"With your half of the sale of just one of those lots, Hugh could set himself up on a fine piece of land twice the size of Point Douglas, just a few miles south along the Red or west along the Assiniboine. The same goes for all your children – that is, the ones who wouldn't rather use the money to go to university in Ontario or New York, or even England!"

Schultz let some slack into his reel and leaned back to see which way the fish was going to jump. Sutherland sipped his tea again, looked at the window again, rubbed a fingertip back and forth across his mustache again, then said: "You talk a good fight, Dr. Schultz – maybe too good. I'm not the, um, quickest-witted man alive, and I'm not used to… *speculations*. I'll have to ponder on this awhile."

"Of course, of course – I'm confident the more you look at the proposition the better it'll look. Take your time, but keep in mind that once things start booming here they'll boom fast."

"I will. Please thank Mrs. Schultz for me for the tea and biscuits – very fine."

As soon as John Sutherland had disappeared down the staircase, Schultz got up to get the brandy bottle from the sideboard and poured a slug into his teacup. Agnes came out of the kitchen and said: "Well…?"

"Counting chickens is bad luck, but… if he comes back with 'sixty-forty,' or even 'seventy-thirty,' we got him."

CHAPTER 32

Once the fields on Point Douglas had been sown with oats, barley and wheat, and the other seedtime necessities more or less dealt with, Hugh figured that if he put things off any longer it'd be too late to talk to his parents before he talked to Wauh Oonae. He'd imagined his way through the conversation so many times he wasn't going to get any better prepared. So, mid-morning on a mousy-skied day, he left Aleck to finish hoeing up the kitchen garden and went into the house. Da and Mum were sitting at the table with cups of tea. As Hugh came through the door, he heard Mum say, sounding uncannily like Gran, "If you sup with the devil you'd best use a long spoon."

Hugh paused and stood waiting, expecting that if they hadn't heard him open the door they would've heard him close it. But they didn't seem to've noticed, and their backs were angled to him. Da said to Mum: "Well, Mr. Grant made a deal with the devil, to keep, um, this country… *free* as long as possible."

"Yes, and look what it got him."

"Oh, that wasn't all… *due* to that. My mother used to say Mr. Grant was born with a broken heart."

Mum turned her head sideways and her eyes happened to light on the doorway. "Oh, Hugh, I didn't hear you come in…" Da turned toward him, too.

Hugh said, a little embarrassed it might seem he'd been sneaking a listen, "I only just did. Um, there's something I oughta talk to you and Da about, but if I'm interrupting…"

Da and Mum looked at each other and then back at Hugh. Mum said: "Not at all – it's a long conversation that'll probably go on by fits and starts all summer. Sit down, I'll get you a cup."

Hugh sat down at the table and fidgeted with his pipe while Mum was fixing him a cup of tea, then told himself to get on with it. He said: "You know, I can't go on living here forever, I mean here at home – should come as a relief to you. Oh, I'm not planning on doing anything drastic right soon, still a long ways off…" He was planning on maybe next summer, when he'd be almost twenty-one years old, but next summer seemed a long ways off. "But before I can think of it as anything more'n daydreams, I gotta get a little money together to get myself set up."

Da and Mum looked at each other again. Mum scratched the side of her nose with a forefinger. Then they looked back at him. Mum said: "To get *yourself* set up…?"

"Well, um," Hugh could feel himself blushing, "like I said, I can't really think about it for real till I get a bit of a stake together." Hugh felt a bit ridiculous talking about 'getting a stake together' like a grown man setting off on an adventure, but the scary part was that that was just about exactly what he was.

Da said: "You know we'll help you out when the time comes – you've spent enough years helping us out."

"I appreciate that, Da, thank you, and I'll surely take you up on it… when the time comes. But you got a dozen others you're gonna have to help set up when their time comes – you can't do everything for all of us. And I seen too many fellas a bit older'n me get part of their start by buying a plough or other things on credit – from The Company or McDermot's or wherever – and then they're stuck trying to pay it off and they can't deal with anybody else till it's paid off, and they end up buying a few more things on their credit tab, building up new debt faster'n they can pay off the old, till eventually they might just's well be wearing a leash and collar. I want to start clean."

Da nodded and said: "That's very wise, Hugh."

Hugh ducked his head and looked down at the table – of all the things he'd ever expected his father to call him… He swallowed and said to the tabletop: "Around here there's only two ways I know of to get a quick lump of money, or Company credit as good as money. One's The Company's brigade to Hudson's Bay and back –"

"*No!*" came out of Mum with such a suddenness it brought Hugh's head up again. It wasn't a verdict 'no,' more of a horrified one.

Da said sombrely, "It's not for… *whimsy*, Hugh, that the Cree name for York Boats is 'The Back Breaker.'"

"I know that, Da. I seen big, strapping young fellas row out with the brigade in the spring and come back in the fall all hunched-over like old men. Anyways, I don't think my temperment's suited to being stuck on a York Boat all summer long – I get antsy enough just an afternoon fishing out on the lake, where I can't step out the boat and stretch my legs whenever I feel like it. And anyways, this year's brigade's already gone and I figured you'd want me to help with the planting. But now, Donald'll soon be off school all summer, and Morrison and Hector, and Aleck's here all the time…"

"Yes," Da said unhappily, "Aleck's here all the time." Hugh knew Da wasn't unhappy to have Aleck at home, but to not have him in school.

"So," Hugh got down to it, "the only other way is the buffalo hunt." He heard a small gasp from his mother but bulled on. "I can likely borrow a buffalo runner from the Lagimodières, and Granda's old smooth-bore carbine's about the same as most of the buffalo hunters use. If I club in with the Lagimodières, and they make the pemmican and carry it on one of their carts, they can take a percent of my buffaloes as payment and I'll still come out with a good chunk of money laid away – I don't intend on drinking or gambling it away like so many do." Although arrangements involving the Lagimodières were true possibilities, Hugh was hoping that all those practical details except the buffalo runner and gun would actually involve the Princes, but that wouldn't be entirely up to him.

Mum said: "Father…?" Da had both hands on the table and was looking into his tea cup. Hugh had heard of people reading fortunes in tea leaves. "You can't let him go."

"Why not, Mum? You'll have plenty of help here with –"

"Because it's too dangerous!" Mum had tears in her eyes, and she wasn't the weepy sort. But Hugh couldn't tell whether it meant she was frightened or angry or sad – maybe all three. "You know that every year some of the buffalo hunters come home maimed or crippled, or don't come home at all – just a little wooden cross somewhere out on the plains."

"But most of them come back just fine. And so will I. I'm a pretty good rider, Mum – aren't been throwed off a horse since I was little. There's a lot of buffalo hunters been going out every summer and autumn for twenty, thirty years and never got any worse than a few scrapes and bruises."

"They don't have any choice! That's the life they were born to, and they have to take their chances. But you…"

Da finally spoke, though still looking down at his teacup. "There's no need to argue it out today, because there's a… *reason* I very much need you to be here this summer, Hugh. You and all the boys, and girls."

That was a tack Hugh wasn't expecting. "Why's that?"

"The locusts."

"The locusts?" Last summer a cloud of grasshoppers had descended on Red River and eaten half the crops. It hadn't been as bad as the time before, three or four years back, and neither time had been a Biblical disaster, because even a medium-good harvest meant stacks of grain in wise farmers' lofts to carry over from one year to the next. Hugh had heard it said after last year's plague of locusts that twice within five years meant it likely wouldn't happen again for another ten. Even if that cheery prognostication proved too optimistic: "But, Da, they never come two years in a row. Just like the rabbits and the partridges and that – one year there's so many you're tripping over them, then the next year none and it takes a few years for them to build up to too many again."

Da raised his eyes from his teacup. "But last summer, if you… *recall*, the grasshoppers didn't fly away again, or not many of them. They came late in the summer, late in their lives, and most of them, um, died in our fields."

"Yeah, well I won't soon forget raking 'em up."

"That means they laid their eggs in our fields – or, um, might have, there's no way to know for certain until they… *hatch*. We had a late, mild autumn and it's been a dryish spring, that's perfect, um, conditions for…" Da was looking and sounding grimmer than Hugh could remember him being, or maybe Da'd been that grim sometimes before and just didn't show it to the children. "It happened here once before, before you were born. And your grandparents told me it happened once before that, before I was born. If it happens this summer we're going to need all the hands we can get."

Hugh felt all his plans and dreams slipping away into a chasm. He told himself they were just being postponed. "All right, Da. There'll be another hunt in the fall."

Mum said: "We'll talk about it then."

When Hugh told Wauh Oonae he couldn't go on this summer's hunt, she didn't seem all that disappointed. When he said he'd likely be able to go on the autumn hunt, she said: "We'll talk about that then." So he kissed her good-bye and went back to lumping his way through farm chores. With four boys over sixteen at home, and the crops already in the ground, there wasn't all that much work that needed his hands put to it. But going fishing along the river or riding across the prairie wasn't as satisfying as it used to be. He felt like he'd finished one stage of his life and was ready to move on to the next, but the world wouldn't let him.

Every morning before breakfast, Hugh went down to the river to look across at Point Douglas. The green needlepoint dots of new sprouts on the black ground soon became a green haze as the sprouts grew into sprigs, and then a green sheet as the shoots grew leafy and tall enough to blot out the ground. On days when Hugh and Da or the other boys went across to see if there were enough weeds to warrant bringing the whole family over for an afternoon of rooting out invaders, or to solidify the fence across the base of Point Douglas that protected the crops from roaming livestock, there was no sign of grasshoppers.

One morning when Hugh looked across the river, the fields seemed a slightly different shade of green. He thought it must just be natural maturing on the way from green to gold, or maybe the morning light was coming in at a slightly different angle than yesterday. Then he saw that Point Douglas was moving – not side-to-side or up and down, but quivering, like the shoulder of a frightened horse.

Hugh ran up the riverbank, shouting: "Da!" and he and Da and Donald jumped into the nearest canoe and paddled furiously across. When they climbed the other bank, Hugh saw that every plant had nodules of miniature grasshoppers on it, gnawing away, and more were boiling out of the ground in all directions.

Da shouted at Donald, "Go back and bring everyone!" then wrapped his fist around a locust-covered grain stock and squeezed, and started stomping on the ground. Hugh followed suit, using both hands and both feet, wishing for once he had boots on like Da instead of summer moccasins. The first time he squeezed a fistful of grasshoppers – crunchy shells and spewing innards – he was glad he hadn't had breakfast yet.

The family had two canoes, so it didn't take long for Donald and Aleck to ferry everyone across. Almost everyone; Mum shouted at Da: "I left Katy to look after Mary Ann Bella," and then saved her breath for the work at hand.

Hugh's hands were coated with slime and bits of clinging carapace. He didn't want to wipe them on his pants, just shook them off as best he could and kept on going. When he glanced back, the stalks he'd just crushed clean had new grasshoppers on them, and more were vomiting up out of the ground through the mat of the ones he'd stomped.

One of the younger children shrieked: "They're biting me!" another one was crying and another one was retching.

Finally Mum shouted: "John!" and everyone stopped and looked at her; it was more than strange for them to call each other anything but 'Father' and 'Mother' in front of the children. "It's no use. We're just making ourselves sick and crazy to no purpose."

Da lowered his head, then nodded and waved his hand toward the boats drawn up on the riverbank. Before taking up a paddle, Hugh washed his hands off in the river and wiped them on his trousers. As he and Aleck paddled a boatload of brothers and sisters back home, Hugh wondered sourly why Da had needed him to stay home this summer when there was nothing they could do about the grasshoppers anyway. He soon found out. After a few days of grasshoppers everywhere – crawling in under the house door or down the chimneys, making an undulating carpet across the barnyard – the locusts had eaten everything there was to eat that they could get at. Then they began to die.

It didn't take long for Hugh to realise he'd been wrong in saying he wouldn't soon forget raking up dead grasshoppers last summer, because last summer was weak tea compared to this. And last summer they'd just dumped the locusts in the river; this summer would've turned the Red River into a green swamp. Da came back from an emergency council meeting and said: "Dr. Cowan says the... *effluvia* from hills of rotting insects, is an invitation to disease for the entire community, um, especially in this summer's heat. It seems the only solution is to burn them, but the, um, smoke would be just as unhealthy. The Company will... *furnish* men and carts to ferry the locusts out onto the prairie and burn them there."

So Hugh and his brothers hauled load after load of dead grasshoppers to join the mounds piling up against the walls of Fort Garry. Once the grasshoppers were gone, Da grew less grim, even chipper, saying: "Well, we'll just have to eat more pemmican this winter – shouldn't be long before the summer hunt gets back." Before that came to pass, Da came back chuckling from Fort Garry one afternoon with a newspaper under his arm, a fatter newspaper than *The Nor'Wester*. "Listen to this! I never would've believed it, but...

"Dr. Cowan, you see, gets newspapers from Canada. He, um, showed me this, and I asked if I could borrow it. You remember that... *ridiculous* nonsense that Thomas Spence and Dr. Schultz got up to, sending an invitation to the Prince of Wales from the, um, Indian Chiefs of Red River...? Well, listen to this...

"'*A Dispatch has been conveyed from the Secretary of The Governor General to Mr. Thomas Spence of the Red River Settlement, enclosing a Dispatch from the Colonial Secretary in London. The Duke of Buckingham and Chandos desired Mr. Spence to inform the Chiefs of the Red River Tribes that their invitation had been presented to the Prince of Wales, who desired that his sentiments of satisfaction, on receiving their address, should be communicated to the Chiefs. It was added that His Royal Highness was unable to visit their country, but would have been much gratified had it been in his power to comply with their invitation.*"

Hugh laughed so hard he had to hold his ribs. Aleck said: "I don't see what's funny about pulling off a lie to the Prince of Wales."

Donald said: "From what Archdeacon McLean's been teaching us in History, a few Princes of Wales pulled off a few whoppers of their own." Aleck just put on a bland face and shrugged, as he tended to do whenever someone pointed to the education he'd walked away from.

Mum said, as though someone had just stepped on her grave, "Father... What if they believe it all?"

"Who? Believe what?"

"The people in Canada, and London – if they'll believe that ridiculous nonsense they'll believe anything. What if they believe everything that's printed in *The Nor'Wester*? Like the story that the people of Red River – *us* – rose up and freed Dr. Schultz from jail when The Company and the sheriff tried to cheat him... And you remember that mass public meeting where all the people of Red River unanimously elected... whatever his name was... to be our spokesman to the Colonial Secretary?"

"Sandford Fleming."

"Well, *we* know there weren't more than five people at that so-called public meeting, and this Mr. Fleming has never stepped foot at Red River, but the people in Canada and London don't know that. What if they took *The Nor'Wester*'s version as gospel? What if they take it *all* as gospel?"

Da folded up his newspaper and said: "I wouldn't worry, Mother – *The Nor'Wester*, um, sinks its own ship every time. In one sentence they'll say The Company is too... *tyrannous* and powerful, and in the next sentence say The Company is too weak and... *ineffectual* . Anyone can see that."

"Anyone who takes the trouble to look twice."

Hugh couldn't figure what was making Mum so agitated. But apparently Da could, because he said: "It's still not a worry, Mother. Even if everyone in the east is completely, um, deluded about what goes on here, Canada is still a... *parliamentary* democracy, and so is Britain. So if some... *arrangement* gets made that the Dominion takes over from The Company, there will have to be elected representatives from here to the Canadian Parliament. Whoever gets elected from here – in a real election – will set them straight soon enough. Now, what's for supper? Bacon and eggs again, I hope."

Since the buffalo hunt wouldn't likely be back for another two weeks at least, Hugh took his gun into the woods to hunt for rabbits and partridges. There were none. He sat beneath a likely tree all day and nothing moved but chickadees and sparrows, and even if he'd been a good enough shot to hit one of them there'd've been nothing left but feathers. Same thing the next day. He set some snares, something he usually wouldn't do until the rabbits had their winter fur and fat, but caught nothing.

It seemed what he'd so cleverly said to convince Da there wouldn't be a plague of grasshoppers this year – that all varieties of creatures had their cycles, and when there was a plaguey lot of one kind one year they'd bottom out the next – had come back to haunt him. It was a year when both the rabbits and the partridges had bottomed out.

Hugh tried to count back to the last time either had – old hunters said it was usually seven years – but the years blended together and it wouldn't change the fact anyway.

Just when everyone was getting truly gloomy, the buffalo hunt came home early and spirits lifted – until they saw the cart train straggling in with all the hunters still wearing their dusty travelling clothes, not a ribbon or brass earring to be seen. That night there were no fiddles or feux de joie echoing up and down the river. Next morning when Hugh went to the hidden pool by the creek mouth, Nancy Prince was there already. Her cheeks and the skin around her eyes were hollowed out, making her eyes look even bigger and darker. She said: "I'm sorry, Hugh, I'm not very lively. Should be better in a week or two."

"What happened?"

"We couldn't find the herd – or it wasn't there. Old hunters said it had happened before, when the herd goes way far west or stays south all summer. But some others said the Americans are killing so many there ain't no herd no more. We never take along enough food for the whole time, 'cause there's always so much buffalo to eat, so…

"We had to leave one of our carts out on the prairie 'cause we killed the ox to eat. The last few days before we got to Pembina we was eating prairie dog stew, and not much of that. We thought once we got back here there'd be plenty of food we could buy or borrow from the farmers, but…"

"Yeah, I know."

"I can't stay here long – we're packing up to go straight to the lake and get some fish in."

That last meant that Hugh saw a bright side to it all when Mum said over supper: "After we've cleared away, my dears, we'll have to sort out who gets to go down to the lake with our fishnets, and who gets to stay here and mind the farm." At Red River, 'the lake' meant Lake Winnipeg; if you meant the other big lake farther away you said 'Lake Manitoba.' Lake Winnipeg was a mighty long lake, but people coming from Red River to fish wouldn't want to go miles and miles north on it to set up their camp. So people of the Point Douglas Sutherland camp and the Prince camp would be bound to run into each other…

"We had to do that one summer, or autumn," Mum went on, "when Donald and Hugh were still babies and the house was still on Point Douglas. You remember, Father, when the hailstorm took out all the crops and the buffalo hunt was still out on the plains…? I'd never have believed I could eat that much fish – fried fish, boiled fish, fish rolls battered in flour… I guess it was only a few weeks, till we had enough dried fish to fill out the larder for the winter and the buffalo hunt came home, but it seemed like forever. If we were Catholic I'd've banked enough Fridays to last the rest of my life."

That helped narrow down Hugh's competition to be part of the fishing party. But before they got set to set off, other people who'd already gone down to the lake came rowing back upstream in boats no heavier than they'd started with. There were virtually no fish to be had this year.

Da sat shaking his head slowly, murmuring: "It's never happened before. Never. When the crops failed, there was the buffalo hunt. When both failed, there was the fishery. When the fishery failed, there was the buffalo hunt and the crops, and the small game. But never all failed the same year. Never."

After that, the family didn't see much of Da. He was either at the courthouse or Fort Garry, meeting with the council or The Company, or going around and about Kildonan making notes about who was in the direst straits. Word got out to the wide world about the Red River famine, and pledges of money started coming in from Relief Committees in Canada, Britain and the States. Hugh and the other boys-before-the-girls helped Da move cartloads of imported grain and root vegetables from Fort Garry to the kirk, which was the logical distribution centre for all of Kildonan, just as St. Boniface Cathedral was for St. Boniface. Hugh overheard Da and Dr. Black murmuring that the hard part was going to be convincing Kildonan people that they weren't being beggarly by taking food they hadn't grown or paid for.

Da seemed to loosen up a little once the actual relief money, not just pledges, started showing up. At supper in early September – which would've been a much later supper in any other September, since only sunset stopped the harvest work – Da said jauntily to Hugh, "Well, it looks like you're going to be able to, um, accumulate your start-up capital without getting gored or trampled."

Hugh could see Mum smiling at herself at her end of the table. He said: "How's that, Da?"

"Well, you know the government of Canada has been... *starting* to cut a road west from, um, Lake Superior to the edge of the plains...?"

Hugh shrugged. He vaguely remembered hearing something of the sort a year or so ago, but Lake Superior was something like a thousand miles from his life, and miles were much longer in wooded, boggy, bouldery country than the prairie. He expected he'd be a grandfather by the time he saw that road come out the west side of the woods, if ever.

"Well," Da said, "as a combination of that, um, Dominion public works project, and to bring wage money into Red River in our present... *troubles*, they've decided to start a second expedition from this end working east. They'll be bringing a work crew from Ontario, but will be, um, hiring on a few local labourers as well. Dr. Schultz is... *acquainted* with the superintendent, and says it could be arranged that one of those local labourers be one of my sons. So, the... *question* is, which of my sons is it to be? Donald will be back in college by then, and you have, um, something in particular you want some money for. So..."

"Well, that's just..." Hugh felt a little guilty about getting the good out of so many other people's ill wind, but, "That's just... grand. Thanks, Da."

"Oh, you'll have to work for it, and winter work in the woods isn't much fun. But over the, um, course of the winter, you should be able to lay away as much money as you could on the buffalo hunt, even in a... *good* year, and at least you'll come home with all your fingers – if you don't freeze them off."

Aleck said: "I could go, too. I can swing an axe as good as Hugh now, and there ain't much to pick between us for size anymore."

Da said: "You know better than 'ain't,' Aleck. As I said, a place for *one* of my sons on the road crew can be arranged. Hugh has plans for something he wants to do once he gets a little money together. Do you have plans?"

Aleck lowered his head and attacked his boiled potatoes like his fork was an axe.

When Hugh and Aleck were sitting out back smoking their pipes and watching the sunset, Hugh said: "Da won't be needing help with the harvest this fall..."

Aleck snorted: "That's for damn sure."

"So why don't you go back to school? Just one more year and you could go on to college."

"I wish to hell everybody'd stop nagging at me about that."

"I'm not nagging..." although Hugh wasn't entirely sure he wasn't; Aleck had the uncanny ability to turn people's intentions back in on themselves, even Da sometimes. "But... you ain't like me, Aleck, and that's somethin' to be glad about. Me, I can be perfectly happy just weeding the garden and milking the cows..." Well, it would be 'perfectly' once Wauh Oonae was in the picture. "But you, you're always *thinking*, and you got nothing to think about here except barley and turnips and... shovelling out the barn. You can do big things, Aleck, think big thoughts, not like me. You ain't happy moping around the farm, so why don't you –"

Aleck stood up and walked away.

It was late autumn when the expedition from Canada arrived, in a cart train sent to meet them at St. Paul. The carts were crammed with barrels of salt pork and sacks of flour. Da told Hugh he was to report to the paymaster at the end of the week at Dutch George Emmerling's hotel, but by the end of the week the Canadians had relocated to the lodging rooms above Dr. Schultz's White Store.

The road was to start heading east from Oak Point, or Prairie de Chêne as the people who lived there called it, at the west edge of the wooded country. Oak Point was at least half a day's ride south-east of The Forks, on a good day on a good horse, so the first order of business was to cut a big enough clearing for three long, barracks tents to house the work crew where the work was. Hugh wasn't sure canvas would prove to be the best idea come January, but the forest would take the edge off the wind, maybe there'd be enough snow to bank up natural insulation against the side walls, and each tent had two square squat cast iron woodstoves that wouldn't lack for fuel since taking down trees was what the crew was there for. And Hugh wasn't there for making decisions or expressing opinions.

Hugh had spent days cutting brush before, but he found there was a numbing difference between working for your family and working for wages. The wages for most of the local crewmen were paid out in the government salt pork and flour warehoused in Dr. Schultz's store, and Dr. Schultz had thoughtfully opened an off-shoot of his store in a cabin at Oak Point, to sell all kinds of extras on credit against the records kept by the paymaster. But Hugh's wages, minus his rations, were paid in cash banked with his father.

Hugh felt a little guilty about the special treatment, but mollified it with the fact that most of the locals on the crew would've used cash wages to buy salt pork and flour for their families. Da had enough cash and credit stored away that he wouldn't need Hugh's wages to help feed the family through this leanest of winters. And the special arrangement meant that when Hugh rolled wearily into his blankets at night, he could hug the fact that the last time he'd seen Nancy Prince he'd been able to say with certainty: "Come spring I'll talk to Da about Point Douglas, and if he's got other plans for it we'll start looking around for a piece of land of our own." For his first few nights in camp, Hugh was taunted and haunted by the songs of whippoorwills – wauh oonaes – but he missed them when they headed south.

Not all of the Red River residents on the crew were just choppers of trees and sledgers of boulders. Thomas Spence was hired on to help the superintendent with the superintending, and Herbert Sabine with the surveying. As for the Canadians, it took Hugh awhile to get used to their sharp, twangy voices and the fact that they only spoke English, so even when there was a more fitting word in Gaelic or French or Cree, he had to make do. But he was shy of talking too much, anyway, and the Canadians were generally a likeable lot once he got used to them. Or, rather, they were grown men who were what they were, and 'likeable' wasn't up to a nineteen year old farmboy.

There was big Tom Scott, six or seven years older than Hugh, almost as tall as Dr. Schultz but rangier. He had freckle-coloured hair and a temper, and the surest way to get his Irish up was to call him Irish. But he was the kind of foreman who did as much heaving and hauling as any man on his crew.

Mr. Snow, the superintendent and head surveyor, didn't give orders loudly, just clearly. Oddly, some of his surveying, and some of Mr. Sabine's, wasn't along the line of the road but around and beside it, sometimes with Dr. Schultz along for company. Hugh didn't spend a lot of time mulling about it – the only thing he knew about surveying was that he didn't know anything about surveying – but one of the older Red River men on the crew muttered: "Oh aye, they intend to be lords of all they survey."

But by far the most curiosity-inducing of the Canadians was the paymaster, Mr. Charles Mair. Newspapers from London and New York had dubbed him 'The Canadian Poet,' which some Red River rascal had said was like 'The Australian Bagpiper.' Mr. Mair was about the same age as Dr. Schultz – close enough that he'd actually gone to the same medical school as Dr. Schultz, but had left early to go into another line of work so stayed plain Mr. He didn't look particularly poetical – sort of short and dumplingy, with thin brown hair and a long mustache joined to underjaw sidewhiskers that made his round head look even rounder – but Hugh wasn't dead sure what a poet should look like.

On one of Hugh's Sundays home, Da happened to have the lone copy of Charles Mair's book – *Dreamland and Other Poems* – that was circulating through the community. Apparently they were a rare commodity even in Canada, because of a fire at a printing shop in Ontario. Printers did seem to have a problem with fires.

It wasn't the first book Hugh had held in his hands written by someone he'd shaken hands with; old Alexander Ross had written three. And Hugh was acquainted with a number of people around Red River who made up songs and tunes and comical rhymes, but real live published-type poetry was a different kettle. Frank Larned Hunt had written a few published in *The Nor'Wester* and eastern magazines, but not a whole book.

Hugh hunkered down by the parlour fireplace with Charles Mair's book and took a crack at the first poem, *'Dreamland'.* It was dotted with poetical words like 'lissome,' 'myriad ' and 'undulary,' and the only way he could tell for sure it was about sleeping and dreaming was the title. But he stuck with it and finally, near the end of the long, long poem was a dream he could recognise, because he'd had it himself more than once.

... with keen desire,
I took her eyes' wild light into my soul.
I claspt her spirit form, and drunk her breath,
And then our lips, more near than life and death,
Clung to each other in silence, and control
Vanished as snowflakes vanish in the fire.

Hugh had never dreamed of Nancy Prince being so drunk he could taste it in her breath, but it sounded like it might be fun. And he liked the thought that even poets liked to lose control at times, but most of the rest was beyond the ken of a simple farmboy and temporary bushwhacker. Hugh put the book back on Da's reading table and decided he'd just take it on the word of people with more brains that Charles Mair wrote fine poetry.

As Hugh set the book down, though, it did strike him as odd that the only other real poem he'd ever looked at close wasn't difficult at all to understand. And it must have pretty good poetry credentials, because Uncle Hector had said it had made Red River famous throughout the English-reading world. It was called *The Red River Voyageur* and painted a picture of a lone boatman way out in the middle of wild nowhere. But then he hears a far-off sound that makes him smile and feel less lonesome, the bells of St. Boniface Cathedral carrying miles and miles across the prairie. Odd, too, now that Hugh thought of it, that the Greenleaf Whittier fellow who'd written it was American. Odd that an American poet had written about Red River and the Canadian Poet hadn't, given that the Canadians were always preaching that Red River was an orphan Mama Canada yearned to adopt. Well, maybe Charles Mair would write about Red River after he'd been there for awhile.

As it turned out, Mr. Mair had already started writing about Red River, but not poetry, and it didn't turn out well for Mr. Mair. He'd been writing letters to his brother in Ontario, telling him all about the nature of life at Red River. His brother decided that the letters were so clever and educational they should be published in *The Toronto Globe*, and so they were. Seems it hadn't occurred to Charles Mair's brother, or to

Charles Mair, that there were subscribers to the *Globe* at Red River. The papers didn't get there till a few weeks after their date, but they did get there.

Opinion was divided at Red River as to whether the opinions in Charles Mair's letters were downright condescending or outright insulting. It didn't help that the occasional *'(*****)'* suggested something even worse had been edited out. Mr. Mair might've got off with a few dirty looks if he'd had the sense to leave the women well enough alone. But one of the letters went and said: *"Many wealthy people are married to half-breed women who, having no coat of arms but a 'totem' to look back to, make up for the deficiency by biting at the backs of their 'white sisters.' The white sisters fall back upon their whiteness, whilst the husbands meet each other with desperate courtesies and hospitalities, with a view to filthy lucre in the back ground."*

Three letters were published in the *Globe* over three Saturdays in November. By late January those issues had all made their way to Red River, and made the rounds. In early February there was a freak warm snap in a winter that'd been gratingly cold even by Red River standards, so Superintendent Snow decided to give the crew a few days off to enjoy it. On Hugh's first day home, Da asked him if he'd mind riding Montrose across the river to the post office in A.G.B. Bannatyne's store.

When Montrose reached the north edge of the village of Winnipeg, Hugh slowed him to a walk to take in all the odd and pleasant sights as they ambled along. There was the new Red Dog Saloon, proprietored by Bob and Hugh O'Lone, two brothers from some place in New York City called Hell's Kitchen. There was white-haired Andrew McDermot on the porch of the new store he'd relocated to when customers started gravitating to the crossroads. Hugh remembered Gran saying that the secret of Andrew McDermot's success – besides his Irish affability – was that the only commodity he didn't trade in was secondhand coffins. Mr. McDermot was currently playing his favourite game, pretending to be dozing in the sunlight on his porch chair with his beard resting on his hands propped on his walking stick – but any child who walked by would have its ankle snagged by the walking stick, and then a fistful of candy from a laughing old Irishman. And there, crutching down off his horse in front of Dutch George Emmerling's hotel, was Enos Stutzman: the big-torsoed, top-hatted lawyer and customs agent from Pembina, who'd been born without legs but with enough energy to make up for them. Hugh remembered someone saying: "Enos Stutzman has three gods: money, whiskey and public schools."

All in all, Winnipeg was getting to be a downright interesting place to visit. Hugh hitched Montrose to the long rail in front of A.G.B. Bannatyne's store and went inside. Mrs. Bannatyne was behind the counter. Local legend had it that the reason young Andrew Graham Ballenden Bannatyne had quit working for The Company only a few years after they'd brought him over from the Orkneys, was that junior clerks weren't allowed to marry and he'd been smitten by one of the Cree-Irish daughters of Andrew McDermot. Some said what had actually smitten A.G.B. was his could-be father-in-law's money, but Hugh didn't think that was all there was to it.

Before going to the counter to ask if there was any mail for the Point Douglas Sutherlands, Hugh drifted over to the display shelf of china dinnerware. The blue and white Old Willow dishes turned out to be not any less expensive than at McDermot's, but he knew Nancy liked them…

The murmur of other customers suddenly stopped. Hugh heard the shop door close and turned to look. Charles Mair had come into the store and was heading toward the post office counter and Mrs. Bannatyne standing very still behind it. Annie Bannatyne didn't have a long reach, being not tall to begin with and currently very pregnant with her fifth or maybe sixth child, Hugh disremembered. As Charles Mair approached the counter, she said to the stockboy in a flat and business-like voice: "Dick, hand me down that horsewhip there."

Mr. Mair stopped in mid-stride and looked from side to side for someone to tell him it was a practical joke. He said: "Now, madame, ha ha, but really…"

Hugh said: "I'd run, Mr. Mair – she ain't funnin'."

Mr. Mair still didn't get it, until he got the first whip-crack across the side of his head. Then he ran, and Mrs. Bannatyne ran after him. Hugh and everybody else in the store went out onto the front step to watch her chasing him down the snowy road. Mr. Mair gained a lead on her quickly, given her shorter legs and delicate condition. But without a ceiling and walls to cramp her swing, she could still get a few good licks in from even ten or fifteen feet behind him – and his behind was what she concentrated on until he got out of range.

As Annie Bannatyne turned back to her store, walking slowly to catch her breath, Andrew McDermot called out loudly enough to be heard over the laughter and applause, "Annie, how many times do I have to tell ye not to flail a horsewhip at a horse's ass?"

Da and Mum laughed till they wept when Hugh told them the story. Then Mum stopped laughing and said: "John…"

"Uh-oh," passed through Hugh's mind, *"it's 'John' again…"*

The same thought must've passed through Da's, because he turned to Mum with a serious expression erasing his grin. She said: "I wish that were all there was to it, but there was something else in Charles Mair's letters… You remember him telling all *The Toronto Globe's* readers that the stories about a famine at Red River were hugely exaggerated, that the only people even a little short of food were the halfbreed buffalo hunters, and that was just because they were too lazy to farm…?"

Da shrugged, "Well, just more ignorance. He's had his horsewhipping for it now."

"What if it wasn't ignorance? What if he knew perfectly well it was a lie, but told it anyway."

"I don't think so, Mother. Why would, um, Charles Mair, or anybody, want to… *propagate* such a –"

"Maybe because if Charles Mair or anybody wants to make a lot of money selling land here to immigrants from Ontario, it's best to not let people in Ontario get the idea there've been hard times here."

"That's… that's…" Da shook his head and couldn't seem to come up with a sufficiently impossibly evil comparison to say what that would be.

"I seem to remember," Mum obviously more than 'seemed to,' "you grumbling last month that it was all well and good for the Ontario government to vote five thousand dollars relief money for Red River, but the money had yet to show up. Has it yet?"

"Well, no, but –"

"You think it ever will, after The Canadian Poet told them it wasn't necessary?"

A few weeks later, an edition of *The Toronto Globe* carried a notice that the Red River letters from Charles Mair had been merely sketchy speculations never intended for the public stage. Hugh never did hear whether the relief money from Ontario ever arrived or not, but then neither did he ever hear Da say: *"You see, Mother, you were wrong about that."*

CHAPTER 33

Agnes sat atop a swaying barrel on a screeching Red River cart, angling her sun parasol against the blaze of the prairie sky. The heat made it difficult to stay clearheaded with the short shallow breaths her corset constricted her to, but like the drovers she'd put aside her loose and dusty travelling clothes for the arrival home. Christian, striding along beside the cart to stretch his legs, was wearing the new dove-grey suit hand-fitted by a tailor in Toronto, and the imported Panama hat that wasn't at all like the raggedy straw hats farmers wore.

As the crown of St. Boniface Cathedral's belltower hove into view, it occurred to Agnes that she was a different person from the one who'd watched that spire disappear in the spring. That other person now seemed so young and unsure of herself. After six weeks in Toronto and Ottawa in the company of Cabinet Ministers, railway magnates, wealthy land speculators – all of whose wives were eager to hear of life in the untamed west, and highly admiring of a woman brave enough to plant the first sprigs of civilization there – Mrs. John Christian Schultz had no doubt she had a place in the world. On her first, rushed trip to Canada, two summers ago, most of the time had been spent introducing Christian's new bride to his family and childhood haunts a distance away from the centres of power. And anyway, the powerful men of Christian's acquaintance had been at that time preoccupied with finalising the details of Confederation. A lot of things had changed in two years. Changed and moved forward.

The cart train reached the east bank of the Red, and the unearthly shrieking of its wheels mercifully ground to a halt. Agnes was quite sure she'd never have to hear that sound again, at least not up close and for days on end, because plans were afoot to finally have a steamboat back plying the Red next summer.

Christian reached up and lifted her out of the cart. It was one of her favourite feelings, when his huge hands cupped her armpits and wafted her over the cart rails down to the ground, and it was about the only thing she would miss about never travelling by cart train again. She reached back through the trellis of cart rails for the smallish carpetbag she'd kept close beside her for the whole journey back. Christian said: "You don't need to carry that. They'll bring our luggage over by tomorrow at the latest, and all you might need before then is already at home."

"No." She suppressed an impish grin. "I'll need this."

"Well... then I'll carry it for you."

She considered, decided there was no chance he could try to sneak a look inside without her spotting him and stopping him, and handed it over. Once across the river they walked arm in arm up the road from Fort Garry. A few people passed by on horseback or in carriages or on foot. Some of them nodded in greeting or said welcome-back, but some didn't, even though Agnes knew damn well they knew the Schultzes by sight and name. Well, in not very long those people would be tipping their hats whether they wanted to or not.

Once past the courthouse, Agnes could see the White Store up ahead, with the little yellow brick pharmacy beside it and the half-finished walls of the big brick house next door. An enterprising local had got the idea that Red River clay would be good for making bricks, and Christian had been his first customer. Not only was it more substantial construction than wood, the brick buildings were a poke in the eye to Henry McKenney. McKenney & Sons had, at great expense, imported the machinery to set up a sawmill on Lake Winnipeg, to ship lumber up to The Forks for the coming building boom. It was a plan Christian and his half-brother had hatched together, back in the days of McKenney & Co.

Agnes squinted ahead to see whether Tom Scott and Charlie Mair had let her down or come through with the surprise she'd requested. Sure enough, standing in the angle between the store and the pharmacy was a pole like a clipper ship's mast without yardarms, towering over the roofs.

Christian halted in his tracks and muttered: "What the devil...?"

Agnes said brightly: "Well, let's go see."

As they got closer to the sky-needling pole, Agnes could see there was a double line of thin rope running up it – she'd made a point of advising the men they'd find it easier to affix the top pulley and thread the line before they raised it – and that it was planted firmly in the ground, with a mound of stones around its base. She stopped a few steps in front of it so Christian, with his arm threaded through hers, had to either stop, too, or drag her. He stopped. She unthreaded her arm and said: "Open the valise, Christian."

He sidled a suspicious glance at her, then set the carpetbag on the ground and crouched to pull its jaws apart. Inside and on top of the few other things she'd packed in for filler was what had been on the bottom till last night brought the announcement they'd reach Red River today: a red fabric diagonal sewn onto a white diagonal joining a red and white L on a navy blue background. Any British subject, and half the rest of the world, would have recognized the partial pattern immediately as a folded Union Jack.

Christian muttered: "Well, I'm... blowed."

Struggling to keep from giggling before the surprise was complete, Agnes said: "Unfurl it, Christian." When he got it halfway unfolded she took the other end so they could open it completely without letting it touch the ground. Emblazoned across the central red bar in big white letters was: **CANADA**.

Christian stood shaking his head in wonder at the flag stretched out between them, murmuring: "How did you… how could you manage to…?"

Bubbling over with mischief and joy, Agnes tried to sound matter-of-fact, "Well, when we were in Ontario you were gone so often to business meetings and gentlemen's clubs, it was easy to make arrangements for the flag without you noticing, and do a little seamstressing on the sly. As for the flagpole – the road crew at Oak Point are in the business of cutting down trees anyway, and it's Canada who's paying them, so it didn't seem a lot to ask if while we were gone they happened to come across a very tall pine tree…" She trailed off as he stepped forward with a moist glint in his eyes, furling the flag around his forearm. He stooped to kiss her very warmly.

When her mouth was free again, she whispered: "Put it up, Christian."

"Hm?"

"The flag – our flag. Let's fly it."

It took a bit of improvising with grommets and rope ends – a more efficient mechanism for attachment and detachment would have to be come up with, but this would do for today. When the flag reached the top of the pole, the ever-present prairie wind stretched it out and then played with it, the scarlet, deep blue and sparkling white curling and shimmering like dancing Aurora Borealis. Agnes looked toward Fort Garry. Although The Company's Red Ensign was only a red dot above the distant fort, she was quite sure the new flag and flagpole were noticeably higher.

She looked to her husband. He was gazing up at the flag with an awed smile on his face and his hand over his heart in a civilian salute. She began to sing softly:

In days of yore, from Britain's shore
Wolfe the dauntless hero came…

Christian joined in, his strong baritone enabling her to sing louder – she knew her singing voice was better for accompanying than leading, although she could sing strongly enough to lead when she had another voice underscoring hers.

And planted firm Britannia's flag
On Canada's fair domain.
Here may it wave, our boast, our pride,
And joined in love together…

A third voice joined in from somewhere behind them. Agnes looked to see Charles Mair coming out of the side door of the White Store, marching toward them and singing with them:

The thistle, shamrock, rose entwined,
The Maple Leaf Forever.

The three of them stood side by side looking up at the flag with their hands over their hearts, lifting their voices across the prairie:

The Maple Leaf
Our Emblem Dear,
The Maple Leaf Forever,
God save our Queen and heaven bless,
The Maple Leaf Forever.

There was much backslapping and welcome-homes, and then up through the store to the living quarters and a few toasts to journeys' ends. Agnes noticed on the way through the store that the stockboy was standing behind the counter, not Eliza. Odd. Eliza turned out to be up in the common room and had set out four glasses and two decanters: whiskey for the men and sherry for the ladies. Eliza looked a bit flushed, and maybe just a tiny bit dishevelled. Interesting. It hadn't been all that odd that Mair had been at the White Store to welcome the proprietors home; cart trains travelled slowly and he wouldn't have needed much advance warning to get there from Oak Point before them. But Agnes now wondered how long he'd been there before them, and how often over the course of the summer.

As the four raised their glasses, Charlie Mair said with gusto: "Canada First!" The other three chorused it and drank. Agnes wondered whether Eliza knew the full meaning of the innocuous-sounding toast. The Canada Firsters were a very select and secret society formed in Ottawa on the heels of Confederation. Its handful of members consisted of The Canadian Poet and several military men and administrators of public works. And, as of last winter, Dr. John Christian Schultz. Their almost-blasphemous motto and raison d'être was: *'The Queen and The Empire, aye, but Canada First!'*

Agnes was grateful to Charles for initiating Christian into the Canada Firsters so soon after another secret society dear to her husband's heart had cruelly collapsed on him. The Northern Light Lodge of The Ancient Order of Freemasons was no more, or at least in abeyance. There had been no formal dissolution or crisis, but too many of the lodge members – A.G.B. Bannatyne, Judge Black, William Inkster… – had just stopped coming. There'd been no explanation, and Christian had been too proud to seek them out and ask them, though Agnes knew it had hurt him terribly. Agnes knew the explanation, but hadn't voiced it to her husband. No matter how much the Schultzes tried to contribute to life at Red River, they were never going to be accepted as part of the community. Fair enough; soon enough those tables were going to turn.

Christian recharged the delicate, leaded-crystal toasting glasses and raised his with a sombre: "Absent friend." Agnes, Charlie and Eliza solemnly repeated it, but Agnes wondered again whether Eliza knew exactly what she was toasting, or knew it wasn't a slip of the tongue that Christian had abbreviated the traditional 'absent friends.' The absent friend was the beautiful, brilliant and beloved Thomas D'Arcy McGee, the poet and Member of Parliament who'd inspired the Canada Firsters. Agnes knew D'Arcy McGee was beautiful from the newspaper photographs of a man with thick wavy dark hair, dark brooding eyes and sensuous lips. She knew he was brilliant from newspaper articles on his oratory. And she knew he was much beloved from the newspaper reports of his state funeral and the thousands of mourners. Agnes had been very much looking forward to meeting D'Arcy McGee when she and Christian travelled east this summer, but in the spring a midnight assassin's bullet had cut short his life. The murderer was a fanatical member of the Fenian Brotherhood, as if they weren't all fanatics: Irish Republicans who believed any harm done to the British Empire would help their cause, and had hatched a plan to get the English out of Ireland by holding Canada ransom. D'Arcy McGee had roused the Fenians' hatred by speaking out against them, and speaking for making the Dominion an even stronger arm of the Empire by absorbing Rupert's Land. The murder of D'Arcy McGee had brought home to Agnes that the endeavour her husband was engaged in wasn't just a parlour game.

Although Charles Mair was engaged in the same endeavour, parlour games were always part of the equation when he was around, and now Agnes was wondering what kind of parlour games he and Eliza had been up to. Despite Mair's physical resemblance to a squirrel or prairie dog, he could be as secretive as a fox. It was impossible to tell whether he had any suspicions about 'Dr' Schultz's medical degree, and Agnes wasn't about to ask him. Even though Mair hadn't graduated Queens Medical School either, he had studied there, and was the kind to squirrel away alumni records. Christian's story now was that although he'd taken most of his training at Queens, he'd finished up his degree at Victoria College and Oberlin, Ohio. Agnes had never told her husband she knew damn well he didn't have a medical degree from anywhere, but it wasn't a bad idea for a wife to know a few things about her husband that her husband didn't know she knew.

As Agnes took charge of pouring the third toast, her husband said: "Turns out you picked the right uncle, Eliza, to move west with. In not very long your Uncle Henry is going to be out of a job. I'm going to be appointed Sheriff of Red River."

Charles Mair raised his glass with a hearty: "Congratulations!" but it seemed to Agnes there was an undercurrent to the word.

Agnes said: "That's only the beginning – an interim position. In a few years, once we've had enough immigration from Ontario – so that a majority of the population here is familiar with the ways of democracy – there will be elections to the Canadian Parliament from here. So..." She shrugged the obvious conclusion.

The Poet mused: "'Sheriff Schultz' – has a ring to it. When's that happen, I mean when does Rupert's Land become part of Canada?"

Christian said: "It's a done deal. The Government of Canada pays The Company three hundred thousand pounds to relinquish its title, and The Company gets to retain a land reserve around each of its posts. But, pragmatically, it'll take a few months for the Prime Minister to appoint a Lieutenant Governor for the territory, and to appoint the Lieutenant Governor's staff – Attorney General, Treasury Head and so forth – and then for the Lieutenant Governor and his staff to get here."

Eliza said: "Hm. A ready-made government; just waltz in and take over."

That seemed to Agnes to be an odd way to put it. Maybe Eliza had been spending more of the summer with some backwater locals than with Charles Mair, or minding the store.

Charles Mair scratched his mustache with four fingertips and said through his knuckles: "Um, it does seem a trifle odd, don't you think… that if such a monumental arrangement has been signed, and overseen by the Imperial Government… that there's been no official announcement? I mean to say – I've had letters from friends in Canada referring to rumours, and seen articles in newspapers from Toronto referring to rumours… But there's been no formal announcement from the Imperial Government, or The Company, or the Government of Canada. Doesn't that seem a trifle odd?"

Christian said: "It's a done deal, Mair. You can take my word for it."

"Well, if you say so, Schultz old man. But, speaking of done deals…" Charlie sidled his eyes at Eliza, who blushed and lowered her head and then gave it a little nod. "Your alluring niece and I have a little secret, which she's just freed me to divulge. Miss Elizabeth Louise McKenney and Mr. Charles Mair are engaged to be married."

That took Agnes aback; Eliza was barely eighteen and Charles Mair thirty-one, two years older than Eliza's 'Uncle John.' But the Canadian Poet had good prospects beyond his poetry, and had probably sown as many wild oats as he was going to sow. Eliza could do worse, especially around Red River. So after only an instant to adjust, Agnes joined in the kissing and hugging and the toast of "Congratulations!" which explained the odd undercurrent when Charlie'd said the same to Christian.

Eliza's affianced explained further, "Well, we'll have to wait till arrangements with the road expedition can be rearranged. Can't very well be Mister and Missus with Mister stuck out in a bush camp as often as not. But as you said, Schultz – or maybe I should start calling you Uncle John? – a lot of changes are in the offing, a lot of opportunities."

"But I won't have to change my underwear," Eliza giggled. "Handy." Agnes blinked at her. "Oh, ever since I learned first-stitch embroidery, I put a monogram on all my, you know, underthings. Eliza McKenney, Eliza Mair – it's still E. M."

Agnes would've giggled with her if there'd been just the two of them, but it was hardly an appropriate subject for mixed company. Obviously Eliza got a bit more than tipsy on a few thimblefuls of sherry. Which also explained that odd thing she'd said earlier, about 'just waltz in and take over.' That put Agnes a bit more at ease; she didn't like things she couldn't explain.

"Oh, by the by," Charlie Mair glossed sideways, "thought you'd like to know how McKenney & Sons sawmill has been prospering while you were gone." There was an undercurrent again, but this time it seemed less like holding something back than holding something in. "Brilliant idea: sawmill on the lakeshore close to virgin forest; plenty of fish in the lake to feed the workmen; lakeboat-cum-riverboat to do the fishing and to ferry the lumber upstream to The Forks. First-rate idea."

"It should be," Agnes said, "it was Dr. Schultz's."

"Mrs. Schultz tends to give me credit for everything. Take note, Eliza." But Agnes could tell that her husband wasn't jolly about Eliza's fiancé shovelling McKenney & Sons onto the table.

"Yes, brilliant concept," Charles Mair went on, "and the senior McKenney commissioned a schooner to be built, and so it was, and a fine schooner it is. But... the senior McKenney overlooked, or forgot, a couple of factors. One is that a sailing vessel might be dandy for a large lake, where you can tack with the wind, but not so dandy for a river. Two is that a schooner has a much deeper draft than a flatboat steamboat – too deep to get past St. Andrew's rapids, except in spring floodwaters and then the current's too strong for a wind-ship to fight upstream. So, all the sawmill profits are being eaten up by the cost of carting lumber from the Stone Fort to The Forks. So sad. Brilliant concept, just forgot a couple of little details."

Agnes's Viking husband burst into such wild Viking laughter that he had to prop his broad hand on Charlie Mair's narrow shoulder before he could recover himself enough to pour one more toast. When the glasses were raised, he bellowed happily, "To absentminded enemies!"

CHAPTER 34

Hugh stopped swinging the bush scythe that was threatening to pull his shoulders out of their sockets, stood it on its head and propped his hands on its butt end to breathe himself out. Time he paused anyway, to put his whetstone to the blade for the tenth or twelfth time since breakfast. But as soon as he stopped moving, he discovered that he'd worked his way out of range of the smudge fire that was supposed to be keeping the mosquitoes off the crew. He took his half-smoked pipe out of his pocket and once he'd got it going the bugs stayed away from his head. Anyone who couldn't fathom why the Indians thought tobacco sacred and powerful had never been out in the bush or tall-grass prairie in the summer.

Hugh looked back toward the rest of the crew to see if he'd gone and forgot himself again and got too far ahead. Not quite. But best he take his time smoking his pipe out and then sharpening his scythe. Way back on his second or third day on the job, Tall Tom Scott had taken him aside and explained in a kindly way that hired labour wasn't in the business of getting the job done as fast as possible, but of putting in a decent day's work for a decent day's wages.

Before Hugh'd finished smoking his pipe, a loud voice called: "That's it for today, lads!" Hugh looked down the line to where Tom Scott was looking at his pocket watch. Tall Tom raised his voice again even louder to carry over the axe whacks and bent-back grunts. "That's it for today and this week!" Saturdays always ended early, so the men could get back to Red River in time to rejoice through Saturday night and repent through Sunday.

Back at camp, some of the Metis workmen were getting gussied up already; the Canadians and the clutch of American army deserters on the crew would wait till they got back to their hotels and boarding houses in Winnipeg. Hugh had nobody to get gussied up for – Nancy Prince was gone on what he hoped would be the last summer buffalo hunt she'd have to go on. So he could wait to shave the week of bristly stubble off his cheeks, and trim his mustache, until he could do it at his ease at home after supper. But he did join in with the group of men stripping off and jumping into the pond behind the camp. Hugh was a firm believer in the old hunters' maxim that frequent bathing robbed you of the protective layer that nature intended between your skin and biting insects in the summer or biting cold in winter, but he was aware that his mother was of a different opinion.

The homeward bound cart Hugh ended up in also carried Tall Tom Scott, along with a few Canadians and one of the Americans whose stomach for army life had run out before their terms of enlistment. Fort Pembina was just a short ride south of the Medicine Line, as the Indians called the 49th Parallel that magically separated American law from British law. That short ride could not only give a soldier his freedom, but also a good horse, revolver and carbine – all courtesy of the U. S. Army. Hugh couldn't imagine making a move that would separate him from his home and family forever. But then, he couldn't imagine joining an army in the first place, unless it was to defend his home and family from some threat he could see on the horizon.

Hugh stood at a corner of the jouncing cart, looking outward at the sea of grass dotted with oak bluffs. Among the windblown, green waves were swatches of blue harebells, golden asters, orange coneflowers, purple thistles, blazing pink fireweed… He wouldn't've known for sure the breeds of flowers just from the colours, except that he knew this was their part of the summer. He imagined that if it wasn't for the screeching of the cart hubs he could hear the trilling of a meadowlark, a sound he missed working in the woods.

But Tall Tom Scott's voice was louder than a meadowlark's, or the cart hubs', when he took in mind to raise it: "It ain't right, lads! Fifteen dollars a month. We should be getting more."

One of the other Canadians said: "Fifteen dollars is what they're paying the crew at the east end of the road. I got a letter from Thunder Bay – my brother's working on the crew cutting west from Lake Superior, and he says they're getting fifteen a month. Standard wage."

"Standard wage *there*," Tall Tom raised his voice another notch, "not here. Any local man doing this kind of work around here'd expect twenty dollars a month. Ain't that right, Hugh?"

Hugh still wasn't accustomed to being asked for a grown man's opinion by a grown man, even though his mustache wasn't peach fuzz anymore. He said: "Well… I don't know much from dollars, me whatever. Pounds and shillings is all I know, and I don't guess I know a lot about them. But I do know I'm getting four pounds a month, and from what I heared here and there, somebody doing this kind of work for The Company'd expect four-and-a-half to five pound. But that's part because –"

"*You see?*" Tall Tom cut him off and went back to group-talk. "Four-and-a-half to five pounds is more like twenty dollars than fifteen!"

One of the Canadians said: "I heard Superintendent Snow's actually getting paid-out *eighteen* dollars a month per man by the government, and he's pocketing the difference."

The American deserter said: "I wouldn't mind the wage so much, 'cepting we got to draw our provisions from Schultz's store, at prices set by the good Doctor Schultz and pure-as-the-driven Superintendent Snow."

Tom Scott said: "Yeah, we're busting our backs on a snow-job," and almost everyone laughed. Hugh didn't, just turned to look out at the passing countryside again. Maybe Tall Tom and the others were right. Maybe they were all being cheated, and wet-behind-the-ears John Hugh Sutherland was a fool not to care. But even if it truly was short wages, he had almost enough saved up to set up him and Wauh Oonae in a place of their own. Once Nancy Prince was Nancy Sutherland, the rest of the world could pretty much go hang.

The carts reached The Forks and the men all jumped out with that strange, Saturday combination that Hugh had come to recognise as worn-out from work but het-up for play. Most of them headed for the ferry across the Red, but Hugh and a few others shouldered their rucksacks and walked north along the road to homes on the St. Boniface side. As Hugh came into the yard, Da and Donald, Aleck, Morrison, Hector and Angus were coming up the riverbank from working the fields on Point Douglas. After some sparring and joking, and washing-up in the basin by the doorstep, Mum called 'her men' in for supper. Hugh sat in the same place he'd sat in since he was old enough to sit properly at the table, only now in the armed chair that had been his Granda's. The clatter of forks and knives and platters punctuated the chatter about the day and the past week, small events coloured by lifetimes of putting icicles down each others' backs, laughing at each others' stories and licking each others' wounds. There was a tableful of food that tasted like food, instead of the basic fuel served up from the road crew cookhouse. And when Hugh was leaning back smoking his after-supper pipe, Christina Ellen without saying a word climbed onto the arm of his chair and laid her head against his chest, and Hugh – without saying a word – draped his free arm loosely around her. Well, maybe not *all* the world could pretty much go hang.

When the younger children went up to bed, the summer sun still cast enough light to shave by. Hugh carried a kettle of water to the outside washstand and went to work with his storebought lather brush, genuine shaving soap and new razor. He hardly ever nicked himself at all anymore, though he was still a bit queasy about scraping the razor across his Adam's apple. He was just about done when he heard a horse walking into the yard and turned to look.

It was Louis Schmidt, a Metis a few years older than Hugh. The German name didn't single him out. Way back around the time of Seven Oaks, Lord Selkirk had got a troop of footloose Swiss Mercenaries to come west by offering them free land as well as wages. Most of them had migrated south after the first couple of winters, and after realising they'd have to *work* their free land, but the few who'd stayed on had married local girls, and now the Schmidts and the Kleins were as standard-issue Metis as the Lépines and the Grants. Louis Schmidt was one of the other two boys sent east along with Louis Riel for higher education. But unlike Louis Riel, Louis Schmidt had come straight back to Red River as soon as his essential schooling was done.

Hugh said: "Bon soir, Louis."

"Good evening, Hugh. Is your father still up and about? I know it's late to come calling, but I've come from a meeting..."

"Sun's still up, and so's he. I'd show you in, but…" Hugh gestured his razor at his half-lathered chin.

"No need." Louis Schmidt climbed down off his horse and looped the reins through the iron ring set into a corner of the house so that a visitor's horse could have the choice of being on the lee side of the south or west wall, depending on the weather. Hugh went back to shaving as Louis Schmidt disappeared into the squared-off, wooden nose between the house door and the outside door. When Hugh went back inside with his beaded buckskin shaving kit under his arm, Da and Louis Schmidt were sitting in the parlour with mugs of tea. Donald was in there as well, just listening, so Hugh figured he'd be allowed. Louis Schmidt was saying: "So you see, Monsieur Sutherland –"

"John. My father was Monsieur Sutherland."

"Well, so you see… Jean, if *I* go to Governor Mactavish, or if Father Ritchot goes or someone like that, it will seem like a delegation, something formal and political. But *you* – you're a Kildonan man living on the St. Boniface side, you represent nobody but yourself. And given all your years on the council, and all your work on the famine relief, you can just knock on the governor's door anytime and he'll ask you in for a cup of tea. And you can ask him, saying it's just to resolve your own confusion, for your own peace of mind, whether there is any truth to the rumours that Rupert's Land has already been sold – that *we* have been sold – to Canada."

Da said: "I wouldn't have to do any… *pretending* about that. It truly is, um, bedamned confusing, to have the Canadians here telling everyone we're now part of their country, and yet no… *official* announcement. Unsettling, to say the least. You'd think between the, um, Imperial Government, and the Canadian government, and The Company, *somebody* would issue some kind of decree. If there was anything to decree." Then Da went back to sipping his tea very slowly. Hugh couldn't count the number of times Da had driven him crazy by slowly sipping his tea before getting to the meat of a matter. Finally Da said: "You may… *overestimate* how easy it is for me to get in to see the governor – there are a lot of calls on his time and he's, um, not in the best of health. But, tomorrow after Sunday Services, I'll stop by Fort Garry."

Louis Schmidt exhaled: "Thank you," and his shoulders lowered as though they'd been hunched under an uncomfortable weight. "You understand – with rumours feeding on rumours, and Dr. Schultz bragging that soon he'll be running things here…"

Da nodded, "I understand."

"You, Jean, have some business dealings with Dr. Schultz. Do you think it is true, what some people say he is hinting at? Some people say Dr. Schultz is representing himself as a confidential agent of the Canadian government. Do you think he truly is that – the Canadian government's agent at Red River?"

"Well, Dr. Schultz and I are, um, hardly in each others' pockets. But, I would think, if someone was a… *confidential* agent, he'd want to keep it confidential."

Louis Schmidt laughed and nodded and then grew thoughtful again. He took a pipe out of his pocket and held up it and one eyebrow. Da nodded. While priming his pipe,

Louis Schmidt said: "The few years I was out east, some things changed here. Were I to go back east and try to explain that to people there, they wouldn't believe me, because they wouldn't believe or understand what I'd say had changed. My years growing up at Red River, there was a word I never heard, in French or English. When I came back, it had become part of everyone's vocabulary. The word is 'politics.'"

Da chuckled and shrugged, but didn't say anything. It seemed to Hugh – and he guessed it seemed the same to Da – that Louis Schmidt was working up to saying something further, or maybe weighing whether to say it. Louis Schmidt puffed his pipe a moment, then took it out of his mouth, looked straight at Da and said in a lower, thicker tone: "And there is something people *here* don't understand about the east, about Canada. There is a sickness there, a festering scar they can't stop scratching, a scar that runs along the border between Ontario and Quebec. I was there just long enough to see this sickness, and feel a bit of its effects, but not to catch it – but it is very contagious. There, you are either French or English, you have no choice. You are for your side and against the other side, there is no in between."

Da said: "Well, the east and west sides of the Red have always had their spats and disagreements –"

"No," Louis Schmidt shook his head fervently. "Those were family squabbles, I'm speaking of tribes – tribal warfare. It is a never-ending war, French against English, Catholic against Protestant, Red against Blue. And men who wish to make themselves important encourage it – you cannot be captain of a team unless you have a team, and an opposing team.

"Oh, I make it sound silly," Louis Schmidt shrugged his pipe-hand, sending up a puff of smoke, "like a schoolyard game. And it *is* that silly, but… If that disease comes here, you will see neighbours who have worked beside each other all their lives suddenly looking at each other across the borders of their fields with suspicion. Suspicion of the other tribe makes people stick to their own, and once tribal warfare starts… A Cree warrior is just as proud of scalping a Sioux woman or child as a Sioux warrior. After all," Louis Schmidt shrugged, "if you kill an enemy girl-child you kill all the enemy warriors she might have borne if she grew to be a woman."

Hugh could see Francis Desmarais in front of the public store in Fort Garry, waving the bloody scalping knife and shouting: *"I gave her as much warning as he gave her!'* Da said: "But they're… *savages*."

Louis Schmidt just raised an eyebrow, and Da looked a bit embarrassed. Louis said: "Not so long ago the Americans – who are not so different from us, except they've had 'civilization' much longer than us here – spent four years killing each other, brother against brother."

Da said: "That couldn't happen here."

"True, there's not enough of us to last four years."

Hugh knew he didn't get exactly what-all Louis Schmidt was getting at. But he did remember Granda saying, and Gran helping him say it – back when the Reverend Griffith

Owen Corbett was on trial – that there was a 'sickness' no one who'd grown up at Red River would understand. And Hugh had a feeling Louis hadn't just been talking to express himself, when he'd gone on after Da had agreed to do what he'd come to ask him to do. There was some particular reason Louis Schmidt wanted to get something across to Point Douglas John Sutherland, or maybe all the Point Douglas Sutherlands.

When Louis Schmidt had finished his pipe and his tea and gone on his way, Da said: "Hugh, let's you and I go for an evening walk." In past years that would've meant a lecture, or worse, but Hugh was quite sure he'd grown too big for that sort of thing, and hadn't done anything particularly wrong lately anyway. Quite sure.

They didn't walk far. Mosquitoes' distant ancestors seemed to've figured out that people liked to sit outside watching Red River sunsets, when the whole infinity of sky blazed red, purple and gold, and had handed down that knowledge through the generations. But the tramped-down ground of the farmyard wasn't as rife with stingers as the tall grass and riverside woods, so Da just walked to the horse corral, leaned on the fence and took out his pipe. Hugh did the same.

After awhile, Da said: "So when are we going to meet this girl of yours?"

"Soon, I s'pect – I hope. She's kind of superstitious – or shy, I guess, or scared, I guess – about making things... formal before everything's for sure. The practicalities, I mean. How much've I got saved up now? Last count was twenty-five pounds eight shillings, wasn't it...?"

"Twenty-seven nine now. I expect it will be an even thirty by the end of this month."

Hugh laughed out loud and shook his head at the wonder of it all. "Thirty pounds should be more'n enough to get me and Nancy set up. The Pritchards've always got a stock of squared timbers dried to sell; we'll need to put in a vegetable garden, but that and the house won't take up much of Point Douglas, hardly a bite out of the fields, and we'll..." Hugh trailed off; his father didn't seem to be brimming over with enthusiasm.

"Um, Hugh... about Point Douglas..." Da proceeded to clean out and refill his smoked-out pipe, which seemed to require his eyes fully concentrated on his fingers. "Your mother and I have decided... it will mean we'll be able to be more, um, help to you, in a... *monetary* fashion, a few years down the road... We'd long planned that Point Douglas would be divided between you and Donald. It's not Highland tradition, but this isn't the Highlands, and times are changing – by the time Roddy and Jamie would get old enough to, um, take over from, and take care of, their... *aged* parents, Red River would be a different world..."

Hugh couldn't figure what Da was driving at, but Da seemed to be driving the long way around and didn't really want to get there. Hugh cocked his head and waited.

"But now... *times* are changing even faster than we'd, um..." Da stopped fussing with his pipe and took the bit in his teeth. "Whichever way the wind ends up blowing, Point Douglas won't be farmland much longer. Dr. Schultz and I have entered into an agreement to divide Point Douglas into building lots and sell them once the inevitable wave of immigration pushes up the price of land – prices that would seem unimaginable today. But today, you and your Nancy can still, um, find a piece of farmland for next to nothing, and be… *assured* that you – like the rest of the children – will have access to, um, a large amount of money once Point Douglas is sold."

Hugh had to blink a few times. "What's Donald say?"

"Oh, it's all a bit more… *theoretical* to Donald. It seems likely that he and Christy Matheson will, um, decide to start a household of their own someday, eventually, but Donald was always slower to act than you. Which is why I thought I'd best talk to you now, instead of putting it off any longer, to see if you and your Nancy might be able to find… *alternatives* to Point Douglas."

"Well sure, Da, we can easy find a place along the Assiniboine, or further up the Red. Anyways, that'll mean we won't be in your hair so much."

"Or we in yours. You'd've been too young to remember, but things were pretty… *testy* between your mother and grandmother the first few years, until they, um, got their borders all surveyed. An old sea captain who'd done some trading in the Orient told me that the, um, Chinese… *writing* symbol for peace is a woman in a house, and the symbol for war is two women in a house."

Hugh laughed, and Da winked and half grinned and then quickly looked away. "Well…" Da sounded a bit relieved, as though he hadn't been looking forward to this conversation. "When the… *time* comes, you might have a, um, house-building crew with some experience ready to hand. I've traded a building lot on Point Douglas for a prime lot in Winnipeg, right by the crossroads, that Dr. Schultz has rights to. Once the harvest's done, I and the older boys will start building a storefront with living quarters above. Or maybe by then you'll already be, um, off the road crew and on the construction crew. What are your plans?"

"Oh, depends on the buffalo hunt. If this summer's hunt's as bad as last year's, Nancy won't go out on the autumn hunt and we'll get right to it. If this year was good again, she'll go out on the fall hunt one last time, lay a little bit more money aside. She ain't no fool so far as money and such – since years back, all the buffalo her father and brothers kill, and all the pemmican and buffalo robes her mother and sisters and her make from 'em, she's the one totes it all up and keeps account."

"Hm. You do know, or I imagine you've… *guessed?*… that your mother's found out virtually all there is to know about Wauh Oonae Nancy Prince. Everybody at Red River knows someone who's known by someone else, and the winters make for… *conversation.* By all accounts she's, um, a very fine young woman. I look forward to meeting her."

"I look forward to that, too," and Hugh decidedly meant it – because that would happen when the date was set, the preacher booked and Nancy therefore no longer terrified of getting pregnant.

When the Point Douglas Sutherlands got home from kirk the next day, Da asked Hugh to saddle Montrose for him, and then set off for the ferry crossing to Fort Garry without taking a bite out of the cold lunch Mum had put together the night before. It wasn't till mid afternoon, when Hugh was sitting by the roadside with his rucksack of clean socks and other sundries he'd need for the week, that Da and Montrose came back along the road. Hugh said: "I'll help you brush him down – Henri and Henry'll see my sack and shout." In the barn, with Hugh working on Montrose's port side and Da the starboard, Hugh said: "What'd Governor Mactavish say?"

"He says it's nonsense. Oh, he says it's certain that The Company and, um, Canada have been having… *discussions* in London, but the rumour that an agreement was signed and sealed months ago is ridiculous. After all, since they made him governor of Rupert's Land as well as Assiniboia, William Mactavish *is* The Company in North America. It's impossible that the, um, proprietors in London would sign such a… *monumental* document without informing him, even if only after the ink was dry."

A modified pig call: "Hue-eee!" came from the direction of the road.

Da said: "I'll finish up. Have a good week, son."

"You, too, Da," and Hugh ran to the road where Henry and Henri were standing by their own rucksacks making jokes about spending too much time in the privy.

Two weeks later the buffalo hunt came home and the world turned lovely again. When Hugh told Wauh Oonae that Point Douglas was no longer a possibility, she didn't seem all that disappointed. Maybe she'd been having the same thoughts as Da about mothers- and daughters-in-law and close quarters. She said: "Jean Claude MacGregor said when this fall's hunt is done he's packing up his family and moving west to the Saskatchewan River country, where there's already a lot of Metis who found Red River getting too civilized for them – 'les sauvages,' the priests call them. Even though this year's hunt's been much better'n last year, Monsieur MacGregor figures it won't stay much better much longer, but the western herd's still going strong. So he'll be selling off his place on the Assiniboine, nearby Big James McKay's Silver Heights, where we watched the Northern Lights and you telled me I was beautiful."

"Well, that was just a plain fact, I just don't know how I got up the guts to say it out loud – maybe the little nip Mr. McKay gave us from his flask."

"Oh, so it was the whiskey made you think I was beautiful."

He grinned and buttoned her nose, "Don't push it, Nancy – I already told you it was just a plain fact."

"So would you like to have a look at it?"

"At what?"

She buttoned his nose and said: "At Jean Claude MacGregor's farm, you moonias."

Hugh had already arranged with Paymaster Mair to take a few days off when the buffalo hunt came home, and deduct them from his wage. Wauh Oonae arranged to borrow a couple of ponies from a cousin who lived on the west side of the Red. After breakfast, Hugh paddled one of the family's dugouts across to meet her and they set off west along the Portage Trail.

Jean Claude MacGregor turned out to be about halfway between Hugh's age and Da's. His wife was hanging laundry in the yard, and a clutch of children were chasing dogs chasing chickens. Jean Claude MacGregor's 'farm' was a hunter's farm: just a house and barn, vegetable patch and some fenced-in pasture. The squared-log house looked basically solid, even though it was corner-notched instead of post-and-beam. It definitely needed a coat of whitewash, and some of the roof thatch looked iffy, but other than that Hugh knew he didn't have a clue about appraising houses. The standard practice of buying a property at Red River – except for freehold-deeded properties in places like in Kildonan or Little Britain, or the land Lord Selkirk granted outright to old Jean Baptiste Lagimodière – was just to pay for the improvements: buildings and tilled gardens and such; the land itself was just there.

Jean Claude MacGregor wanted ten pounds for the place, not including the milk cow, but Da had already promised Hugh a heifer anyway. Hugh said he'd have to think it over, and that he and Nancy would have to talk it over. Jean Claude MacGregor said: "Of course, of course. If you can't make up your minds before the fall hunt goes out, I'll tell anyone as asks, you got first dibs. And if anyone offers me eleven or twelve pounds I'll give you a chance to better it before I make the deal."

On the ride home, Hugh felt totally gobsmacked – as his Gran would've put it – at the wondrous impossibility that he was riding beside the woman who would be his wife and talking about the place that could be their home. They agreed that they would each ask their parents their opinions of the price. Hugh said: "One thing for sure, if we do buy the place I'll buy some sawmilled lumber and put in a floor – I'll not have you raising children on a dirt floor."

Wauh Oonae's summer-browned cheeks got a trace of pink in them.

A little farther down the road, Hugh said: "You know, some while back Da shifted over to this new strain of wheat, like most Kildonan people are growing now. It's got shorter necks and bigger heads, more grains. But, you know, the old kind of wheat – tall, tall stocks – it don't need near as much weeding, 'cause it stands over the weeds and gets the sun, and the stocks are long enough for roof-thatch. Sounds like a better idea to me."

"Whatever you think. I don't know anything about raising wheat."

"I don't know anything about raising children."

"Nobody does."

A little more farther down the road, she said: "If the price does get agreed on, don't you be handing him any money till you got a signatured piece of paper."

"Monsieur MacGregor seems like a fella we can trust."

"Trust nobody; trust nothing. The river ice you ride a sleigh across today will give way under your moccasins tomorrow. The minute you feel safe is the minute things'll turn on you." She shrugged. "Everybody lies."

"I don't."

Wauh Oonae didn't say anything, but didn't make a point of not saying anything. She didn't look at him, but didn't pointedly not look at him. Hugh considered the many Wednesdays he'd pretended to be just taking Montrose out for 'exercise' when he was truly going to spend time with Nancy Prince. Or more than a few times in his younger years when he hadn't gone out of his way to be entirely truthful to his parents or his schoolteacher. But those were just little fudgings for convenience. Maybe people who told bigger lies thought the same of theirs.

Da said, and Mum nodded, that if Hugh offered Monsieur MacGregor eight pounds he'd take nine. Hugh wanted them both to have a look at the place and see what they thought, and Da said they could likely borrow Dr. Schultz's carriage for the day. But by the time that day could get co-ordinated, the autumn buffalo hunt set out and Hugh had to make what he promised himself would be his last long-time farewell to Wauh Oonae. Although Hugh was more than disappointed that things would have to wait to get finalised, he consoled himself with Jean Claude MacGregor's word that he wouldn't sell the place without talking to Hugh first. Even if he didn't have it in writing.

When Hugh and Mum and Da got out to the MacGregor place there was no one there. No doubt some neighbour was coming over morning and evening to milk the cow and feed the chickens while the MacGregors were gone on the hunt. Mum said there was definitely a leak in one corner of the house, and Da said there should be a milk shed outside of the barn, but they both said it would be a snug home with a little work. Mum got a little teary at the prospect of Hugh moving so far away, more than two hours if you factored in crossing the Red. But Hugh pointed out that he'd been farther away six days a week since last autumn, and made her laugh by saying soon he wouldn't be carrying a sack of laundry when he came through the door.

Through Hugh's next week at work, Tall Tom and others kept making jokes about moon-eyed Sutherland tripping over things and forgetting where he'd left his axe. Hugh didn't mind. He didn't mind much of anything. He was seeing the corner of roof-thatch that needed replacing, seeing his hands weaving thatch-grass together, seeing Nancy picking strawberries in their garden, seeing Wauh Oonae naked in the firelight from their own hearth… It was all going to come true right soon.

But then… The next Saturday, when Hugh came home Da was waiting for him in the parlour. Mum poured Hugh a cup of tea and pointed him in that direction. Once Hugh had got sat down, Da said: "There is, um… there is an… *expedition* come from Canada. A surveying expedition, led by a Colonel Dennis, come to survey… *all* the land around Red River. Colonel Dennis, um, formally asked Governor Mactavish's permission to proceed, which obviously means we are still under the… *jurisdiction* of The Company, and the rumours we've already been sold to Canada are just, um, worth what rumours usually are worth. Nonetheless, this Colonel Dennis – like Superintendent Snow before him – housed himself with Dr. Schultz, as though taking his cues from him. That made some people around here a bit… *edgy*. So, instead of starting at The Forks, Colonel Dennis has, um, taken his expedition down to the forty-ninth parallel to lay a… *base-line* and is working his way north from there."

Hugh wanted to say: '*So?*' but that seemed a bit flip in the face of Da's inexplicably grave manner, so he said: "Well, then he's not getting in anybody's way."

Da's blue eyes fixed on Hugh as though Hugh'd just asked how to tie his shoelaces. "Hugh, you can't buy Jean Claude MacGregor's farm."

"Huh? What...? *What?* Why not?"

"I mean not yet, not until, um, things get sorted out."

"What things?"

"Listen, son..." Da spoke more slowly, leaning on the words as though he would've made them all one-syllables if he could. "There is a Canadian survey team doing a land survey of the Red River area for the Canadian government."

"So?"

"So... We have a deed to Point Douglas, signed to your grandfather by the Earl of Selkirk, whose... *indisputable* right to hold or sell that land is, um, a matter of record with the Imperial Government. And we have a deed and bill of sale for this, um, piece of land our house stands on, signed by Jean Baptiste Lagimodière, whose widow... *holds* a deed signed by the Earl of Selkirk. Do you think Jean Claude MacGregor has a deed to his place?"

It seemed an odd question. "He's been living there for years, everybody knows that."

"The Canadian government doesn't know that, not on paper."

"Oh!" Hugh almost laughed with relief that that was all Da was worried about. "We'll have it on paper for sure, Da. Nancy'd skin me alive if I handed over our money to Monsieur MacGregor without getting a signed bill of sale from him."

"But does Jean Claude MacGregor have a deed giving him the legal right to sell you that property? Or is his only... *right* that The Company, and the neighbours, had no objections to him putting up a house on that piece of land?"

Hugh figured he probably knew the answer to that question, and so did Da. But he couldn't figure anything that needed saying about it.

"Look, John Hugh... If we are going to be... *annexed* by Canada, you might've paid your nine pounds to Jean Claude MacGregor and, um, got your bill of sale from him... But next thing you know there's a family of Canadian immigrants with a Canadian government deed to that property, and if you don't... *clear-off,* the Canadian police or Canadian army will clear you off."

"Do you really think that could happen?"

Da rubbed his forehead, covering his eyes with his hand, and rasped out: "I don't know... I don't know... Nobody seems to know what the fuck's going on."

CHAPTER 35

Dr. Schultz sat trying to be patient with John Sutherland. Sutherland was dithering about starting construction of his Winnipeg storefront and lodgings, and the first nail driven would nail down the deal giving Schultz title to a double lot on Point Douglas. Which would pretty much lock in the plan to have Schultz act as real estate broker for Point Douglas.

They were sitting in Schultz's summer office, on the ground floor behind the store; the upper storey was no place to do business in the heat of the day. The summer office had been the print shop of *The Nor'Wester* until Dr. Schultz sold *The Nor'Wester* to Dr. Bown, who'd moved the press and equipage to a new building a few doors down the main road. It was a smooth arrangement: Walter Bown's remittance from his relatives in England had taken the paper off Schultz's hands, and Bown still came to him for advice and 'suggestions' of what to print in it.

The arrangement with John Sutherland wasn't going quite so smoothly. Schultz said: "But you couldn't ask for a better location, Mr. Sutherland – practically at the crossroads of the Portage trail west and main road north."

"It's not the, um, location that hesitates me, Dr. Schultz, it's the… *surety* of the land title."

"As I've told you before, and it still remains true: the gentlemen I know in Canada have assured me that any land titles I hold will automatically be entered when the Canadian Land Office starts its registry here. And those gentlemen," Schultz tipped in a companionable wink, "are in a position to make certain of that."

"But," Sutherland scratched his beard, "that'd be a… *certainty* only if we become part of Canada –"

"There's no 'if' about it. It's a done deal."

"If it's a done deal, why hasn't there been any official announcement?"

Schultz wanted to bellow: *'How the bloody hell should I know?'* but contained himself. Instead he said, in a tone that almost choked him to keep even, "I imagine they're waiting until the Lieutenant Governor and his staff have all been appointed, and their appointments verified, so they can announce all the details at once. But the transfer agreement between The Company and the Dominion has already been signed and sealed – you can take my word for it."

Sutherland didn't say he wouldn't, but he didn't say he would, either. Schultz got up and took a pewter pitcher from a side cupboard, then stepped past the curtain of mosquito netting that allowed him to leave the outside door open to the morning air. As he dipped the pitcher in the rain barrel by the doorway, he glanced at the height of the sun and decided it was time to close the door. The cool earth under the floor could mitigate a little, but not if he left the door to the blast furnace open. But he lingered by the rain barrel an instant longer to savour the sounds drowning out the wind and songbirds: hammers and saws and lumber thumps and workmen's shouts, from all directions, as new businesses, warehouses and homes rushed to double the size of the village of Winnipeg again before winter set in.

Back inside, Schultz set the pitcher on the table between his chair and John Sutherland's, then reached down two glasses and a bottle of whiskey. When he uncorked the bottle and held it up inquiringly, Sutherland nodded, "Thank you," and held up his right hand with the tips of thumb and forefinger about a quarter inch apart.

Once seated again, and his mouth moistened, Schultz said: "Look at it this way, Mr. Sutherland, even if you're not inclined to take my word for it – which I don't find insulting, we're doing business after all – you have other assurances. Your building will be directly across the road from the kirk…" Last summer the Reverend Dr. Black and his congregation had put up a mission church in Winnipeg, next-door to the Red Dog Saloon. "… and you'll be directly next-door to the headquarters of Colonel Dennis's survey expedition. Any carpetbagging shyster trying to swindle away legitimate land claims would have to deal with them as well."

Sutherland pursed his mouth around his latest mouthful of barely-whiskeyed rainwater and raised an eyebrow. Schultz said: "And if that's not enough assurance, the Sisters of Charity have put up a school on this side of the Red, within the bounds of the village of Winnipeg."

Sutherland wrinkled his forehead and looked *'That's hardly news'* at Schultz. "So you see," Schultz extrapolated, "any dispute about the validness of property titles in Winnipeg, would have to include property held by the Sisters of Charity."

Sutherland laughed and nodded, saying: "You do have a point there, Dr. Schultz – no one in his right mind tries conclusions with the Grey Nuns. And any, um, fool that did would find himself soundly spanked right quick."

"So, shall we sign the papers? I've had them drawn up and waiting for weeks."

"Well…" Sutherland's wide, round head sunk forward between his much wider, rounder shoulders, annoyingly like a bull trying to make a decision. "I couldn't start… *construction* soon, anyway. Not until after the harvest. Not just because me and my, um, older boys will be over-busy with farmwork, but so will the MacBeths; brothers-in-law and nephews. We've put up barns together before, I don't… *imagine* this'd be much different. And I'll have to, um, price out all the lumber and such, see if I have enough cash and Company credit on hand to cover it all."

"That's not the way to go about it," Schultz blurted before realising he was patronising an older man. "No, I mean, I'm sure that *was* the way to go about it, and a good way, too. But *now*... First off, for lumber there's McDermot's sawmill just a few hundred yards from here." One of old Andrew McDermot's sons had delightfully put up a steam-driven sawmill on the west bank of the Red. Delightfully because not only was Henry McKenney stuck with a watermill on Lake Winnipeg and a schooner not suited to ferrying lumber upriver, there was now another lumber mill right where all the building was going on, and a mill that could run when the rivers weren't running. "I have no doubt that young McDermot would sell on pure credit to Councillor John Sutherland. *And* there's an added advantage to your new building being cheek by jowl with Colonel Dennis's.

"Colonel Dennis's building isn't only his headquarters office, it's also meant to house the survey crew, but it'll be damn close quarters, and the entire crew will have to be housed in Winnipeg once they've worked their way north from the border. I suspect Colonel Dennis would be very interested in a building going up next door. He can requisition funds from the Dominion Government to subsidize the construction; you let out rooms to some members of the survey team, with their rents paid by the Dominion Government; and when the survey expedition goes back to Ontario or moves on further west, you have the building to yourself, just as you would if you'd built it yourself – except that this way the Canadian Government has built it for you."

John Sutherland's blue eyes had grown as wide as the prairie sky. He said: "Well, I... It's a lot for me to take in... It's, um, a different kind of world from what I'm used to."

"It *is* a different world here now, Mr. Sutherland, or will be soon."

"Well, I don't mind... *confessing*, Dr. Schultz, that you've given me a lot to, um, ponder on – and anyone that knows me will tell you I ponder rather... *ponderously*."

"I doubt that, sir. But I'll gladly undertake to talk to Colonel Dennis on your behalf, next time he's in town – as for the lumber pricing, you're no doubt better acquainted with the McDermots than I." Schultz got up from the table and went to his desk. "But those are details. As long as you're here, we might as well sign the agreement now and attend to the details as they arise. Let me see now, where did I put it...?" Schultz knew precisely which drawer the relevant papers were in, but made a show of hunting for them, so as not to give Sutherland the impression that getting his signature was the first thing on Schultz's mind. "After all, I can't very well approach Colonel Dennis about a possible arrangement without I've got written proof that there's something to arrange."

"Oh, there's still plenty of time – as I said, I couldn't, um, start construction until after the harvest anyway."

"But if we can make an arrangement with Colonel Dennis, there's a good chance he'd set some of his men to constructing the building according to your specifications, and then you wouldn't have to wait, nor use up the time and labour of yourself and your sons and brothers-in-law and nephews."

"Well..." Sutherland stood up and set his empty glass on the table. "I still have to think it over, and talk it over. Sorry to be so, um, slow, but it's a new way of thinking about things and I was never all that fast at thinking in the ways I'm used to. But, it's not right to leave you... *hanging* too long, so I'll be back to see you in a week or two."

As soon as John Sutherland was gone, Agnes came in through the doorway to the store and said: "Well?"

"He has to think about it a little longer."

"Damn farmers. Well, come upstairs and I'll fix you some lunch, you'll want to be fed and fit for the meeting."

"Oh, yes, of course, thank you." In concentrating on reeling in John Sutherland, Schultz had temporarily forgotten about the meeting that afternoon. The Company had allowed access to the courthouse for a public meeting to air opinions on what direction the village of Winnipeg, and the Red River Settlement in general, was headed in.

As Schultz and his wife circuited behind the store counter to get to the stairway, a male voice called from the front of the store: "Dr. Schultz…?"

Schultz stopped and looked in that direction. Coming toward him was James Stewart, the St. James Parish schoolteacher who'd led the liberation of the Reverend Griffith Owen Corbett from imprisonment, and whom Schultz had helped liberate, and who'd helped liberate Schultz in turn. "Mr. Stewart, good morning – or afternoon, I suppose it is now, just."

Stewart came to a halt on the other side of the counter. He seemed a bit agitated and had obviously just ridden a dusty road. He'd suddenly become middle-aged since the last time Schultz had seen him. "Good afternoon, Dr. Schultz, Mrs. Schultz. I wonder if I might have a word with you?"

Agnes said: "We were just going up for luncheon, would you care to join us?"

"That's very kind of you, thank you, please." It came out so eagerly Schultz wondered if it was pure accident that Stewart happened to show up just at mealtime. Upstairs in the common room, over a cold chicken luncheon, it came out that Stewart was in a bit of a bind – more than a bit, for a man of forty with a wife and children. It seemed that ever since the Corbett and Stewart jailbreaks, the St. James school board had been secretly looking for someone else to teach their children. Now, even though the flow of immigration from Canada was still just a trickle, the trickle had been enough to bring in a suitable candidate. So James Stewart was suddenly out of a job. And he and his family would soon have to be out of the house that came with the job. Stewart had come to ask Schultz if he'd heard of any openings in or around Winnipeg.

Agnes, who'd been delicately nibbling while they'd been wolfing, said: "Dr. Schultz…?"

"Yes, Mrs. Schultz?"

"Weren't you saying just yesterday that you wished you could find a reliable man to clerk the pharmacy, so you wouldn't have to be constantly scooting back and forth to keep an eye on things? And do you remember the head carpenter's house…?"

It took Schultz a minute to place that 'the head carpenter's house' meant the cabin that the head carpenter of the warehouse addition to the White Store had thrown together near the riverbank so he could live on-site for the duration. Schultz said: "Well there's a possibility, Mr. Stewart. If you care to take on the clerking position you could also take on the empty house, on a rent-to-own basis. The house will no doubt need some refurbishing, but it's basically sound."

Stewart beamed. "Thank you, Dr. Schultz."

"Oh, thank Mrs. Schultz, it was her idea." And a grand idea it was. After deducting Stewart's 'house' rent from his wages, Schultz would have a competent and mature clerk at a bargain.

Stewart volunteered to accompany Schultz to the public meeting. Agnes stayed home – political meetings were not places ladies wanted to be present. Stewart made the walk to the courthouse in shirtsleeves, carrying the shiny-elbowed wool suitcoat he'd have to put on inside to look authoritative. Schultz barely felt the heat in his summer-weight linen. As they progressed to the courthouse, Schultz couldn't help but feel some satisfaction at his own progress. Only a few years ago, Stewart had been a leader in the movement to free the Reverend Griffith Owen Corbett, and Schultz just a fellow-traveller. Now Stewart was *his* fellow-traveller.

The courtroom was already packed with murmuring and gladhanding men, some of whom had obviously taken their lunch at the Red Dog Saloon, or Dutch George's, or Monchamp's. Schultz made his way to the raised platform where a few chairs had been set out for the convenors of the meeting. Charlie Mair was already there, looking a bit the worse for wear from his long morning's gallop from Oak Point. There was a large empty oaken captain's chair beside Mair's chair. Thoughtful of Mair to take an ordinary chair and leave the large one for the larger man. Schultz sat down in it and surveyed the assemblage.

There weren't many old-stock Kildonan men in the room. Farmers tended to have other things to do on August afternoons than attend meetings, which was one of the reasons Schultz had wanted to hold the meeting in the afternoon. A smattering of Metis were in one corner, men too old or disinclined to be gone on the autumn buffalo hunt. There were a few Company men here and there. There were even a few men who'd come all the way from Portage la Prairie; ex-President Thomas Spence sat on the far side of the room from them.

Charles Mair looked at his watch, stood up and called the meeting to order, several times. Judge Black had declined to attend and chair the meeting, on the grounds that since The Company paid his salary, his opinions on The Company's land's future might not seem impartial. Schultz missed his presence. Sheriff McKenney and one-armed Constable Mulligan perched at the back of the room gave some semblance of lawful authority, but Judge Black could silence a room with one flare of his dark-browed eyes.

When the general hubbub finally toned down enough for Mair to make himself heard clearly, the Canadian Poet made an uncharacteristically short speech about the beauteousness and natural advantages of the land they were inhabiting, leading into the rhetorical question of whither they meant to go with what nature had given them. He was only interrupted once, when he said: "There is obviously a need for mass immigration to build a vibrant economic life here –"

"What's wrong with the life we got now?"

Schultz couldn't pick out exactly who had called that out, but the voice had a Gaelic-flavoured lilt to it, so not all Kildonan farmers were farming this afternoon. Mair flustered and blustered something about progress being inevitable, then managed to find a segue back to his prepared speech, which ended with Psalm 72: "He shall have dominion also from sea to sea…"

That was Schultz's cue to stand up and wax eloquent about the sheltering and civilising qualities of the new Dominion and the Empire. But before he could take his cue, a sharp and sonorous voice from the crowd commandeered the floor: "I got something to say about that."

It was the legless, jaw-whiskered, American lawyer, Enos Stutsman – still wearing his flat-crowned, narrow-brimmed, semi-top hat indoors to add some inches to his stubby profile. Stutsman crutched himself up out of his chair and stumped up and down the courtroom aisle, regaling the audience with: "Systems of federal government may seem abstract and distant, but they infect the lives of honest men and even lawyers." That got a laugh. "And I don't say *infect* accidentally. Now, the framers of the United States Constitution operated on the principle that anyone who wants to have power over you is not someone you should trust. So American democracy is built on checks and balances – an elected Senate balancing States' Rights against the federal House of Representatives, a President whose appointments to the Supreme Court must be approved by Congress, and so on.

"Whereas in the Canadian Parliament there is an *appointed* Senate – appointed by the Prime Minister and rubber-stamped by the Governor General appointed by the Monarch. A Prime Minister with a majority in Parliament is an unfettered despot, free to pass any law or edict that strikes his fancy, so long as the members of his own party don't vote against it – which would bring down the government and cost said members their jobs and their pensions. Canadian so-called democracy is in fact a dictatorship that merely changes dictators every five or ten years; in American democracy, even the President is answerable to other elected individuals who don't have to toe his line. Anyone who cares to dispute those facts is welcome to try."

As Enos Stutsman lowered himself back into his chair, there was applause and cheers, and not just from those who'd come to Red River from The Land of The Free. Some jeers fought against the cheers, and a few voices managed to cut through the general clamour:

"U. S. A. – the land of bilk and money!"

"Aye, they don't need elections, they have assassinations!"

"Like your D'Arcy McGee?"

"That was a Fenian, not a Canadian!"

Charles Mair was on his feet again, shouting: "Gentlemen, gentlemen, order please!" When some semblance of order was restored, Mair proclaimed: "There is no need to dispute Mr. Stutsman's so-called 'facts,' because the matter is entirely abstract. The fact is that Red River and all of Rupert's Land is already a part of Canada –"

Mair was drowned out by shouts of *"Who says?"* and *"Show me the paper it's written on – and I don't mean the bloody Nor'Wester!"* Someone at the back of the room – Schultz couldn't see who with so much of the crowd up on its feet, but the voice sounded suspiciously like Henry McKenney – began to sing to the tune of 'The Maple Leaf Forever': *"The make-believe, the make-believe, The make-believe forever…"* Other voices joined in; there was laughter and catcalls; Mair flapped his arms and his mouth, but it was impossible to hear him through the din. Some pushing and shoving broke out. Enos Stutsman swung a crutch at someone.

Schultz stood up, stepped back behind his chair, raised his right leg to plant his boot on the chair seat, wrapped a fist around each chair arm and pushed down with his leg while his arms pulled upward and outward. The solid oak chair split to flinders with a rending crash that echoed in the room like a cannonshot, sending splinters flying and leaving Schultz holding a spindle-studded cudgel in each hand. The courtroom was suddenly silent. Charles Mair said, without having to raise his voice to be heard, "Um, I believe Dr. Schultz has the floor."

Someone in the crowd drawled: "I'd say he has the chair." There was laughter at that, but not a threatening kind of laughter, quite the opposite.

Schultz began with: "Now that I have your attention…" But now that he had it, there wasn't much he could do with it. There were no more outbursts, but plenty of sidetracks. One old gentleman suggested that if The Company truly wanted to get shut of its responsibility for Rupert's Land, there was a third option besides joining Canada or the United States. Rupert's Land, or at least Assiniboia, could just become a Crown Colony, like so many others around the globe. Not a few men in the courtroom thought that an interesting idea, and there was no convincing them that it was only an idea that meant nothing because the case had already been closed.

When Schultz got home and his wife asked him how the meeting had gone, he said: "Around in circles. I made a mistake – well, Mair and Bown and I – arranging a public meeting before there's been official notification of the transfer of Rupert's Land to Canada. But who would've thought a month ago there wouldn't've been some sort of proclamation by now? I can't understand why not."

Agnes said: "Maybe something's gone wrong, some complication that –"

"No!" Schultz bellowed, "Nothing's gone wrong! It's a done deal!" He caught hold of himself and lowered his voice. "I'm sorry, my dear, I don't mean to take my frustrations out on you."

Agnes said sweetly: "I know you don't, and I know you won't. You're not the kind of man who would abuse his wife in any way. You're far too intelligent for that. Intelligent enough to realise that every man, no matter how energetic, must eventually close his eyes and go to sleep." Agnes's eyes shifted from Schultz to Eliza on the other side of the table, as though what she'd just said was something her 'little sister' should take note of.

"Eliza!" burst up from downstairs, and then "Eliza!" again, accompanying a pair of boots clattering up the stairs. It was Mair, who'd detoured to pick up his mail and

Superintendent Snow's at Bannatyne's. He had a sheaf of letters clutched against his narrow chest, and his free hand was brandishing an opened one. "It's from Mr. McDougall, the Honourable William McDougall, Dominion Minister of Public Works!" The Canadian Poet was tripping all over his words. "They've offered him to be Lieutenant Governor here, and he wants me to work for him, his headquarters'll be at Fort Garry, and that means... We can get married!"

Agnes and Eliza broke into the same sort of overexcitement as Mair, but Schultz was removed for a moment, considering what else Mair's news meant. Charles Mair was a kind of protege of the Honourable William McDougall – it was McDougall who'd lured Mair out of medical school, to do research in the Parliamentary Library on the legalities of Canada acquiring Rupert's Land. And now Schultz's niece would be the wife of a member of the new Lieutenant Governor's inner circle.

Apparently the Lieutenant Governorship wasn't official yet, still some details to work out. But McDougall was confident of it enough to instruct Mair to meet him at the railhead at St. Paul around late September. It was decided that Mair and Eliza would make that their honeymoon journey, the same as Schultz and Agnes two years earlier. Except that Charlie and Eliza wouldn't be travelling on horseback but in a little, two-seater carriage called a democrat – bought in the U. S. of A., appropriately, to ferry Superintendent Snow and Paymaster Mair to Red River last fall.

But that plan meant the wedding had to happen soon. Fortunately Agnes and Eliza had already started working on the wedding dress. Agnes seemed to take delight in big-sistering Eliza on the subject of salubrious camping spots along the Crow Wing Trail, and probably a few other subjects Schultz wasn't privy to.

Eliza McKenney became Eliza Mair in St. John's church on the morning of September 7, 1869. She and her new husband were set to set off south immediately after the wedding breakfast. But before climbing into the carriage, the groom took Schultz aside and murmured, holding up a folded piece of paper, "Wondered if you'd do me a favour, and give this to Superintendent Snow? Don't feel like I should be doing business on my wedding day."

Schultz unfolded the piece of paper and took a glance. It was a bill to the Department of Public Works for goods purchased from the Hudson's Bay Company: *'For brandy, tent, bacon & cash paid for horse – £28, 7s, 6d – to HBC.'* Schultz folded it up again and said: "Certainly, nephew."

"Much thanks, Uncle John."

After the newlyweds had departed – amid much crying and laughing, in the way of women at weddings – and the guests started going their separate ways, Schultz stepped over to Superintendent Snow and said: "Mr. Snow, Mr. Mair asked me to give you this."

Superintendent Snow unfolded the note, took a look, and his eyes bulged. "*What?* He's billing the Department of Public Works for his bloody honeymoon?"

"Well, he *is* going to meet the ex-Minister of Public works, soon to be Lieutenant Governor of the North West Territories. And last I heard, from Paymaster Mair, one of your sons was still on the payroll of your road-building expedition."

Superintendent Snow didn't say anything further, just folded the piece of paper back up and put it in his waistcoat pocket. But as September wore on and the leaves turned, there was still no official announcement that the Honourable William McDougall was indeed now Lieutenant Governor of the Dominion's North West Territories. Not even an official announcement that Rupert's Land had indeed been transferred to Canada.

CHAPTER 36

"Watch your back, Hugh!"

Hugh paused the axe poised over his right shoulder and looked over his left shoulder. Tall Tom Scott, who'd yelled, and one of the Desmarais brothers on the crew, had just about chopped through a sixty foot birch tree about forty feet behind Hugh. From the angle they'd alternated their cuts on either side of the trunk – Tall Tom chopping high and Malcolm Desmarais low – it should fall well to Hugh's left, but surprises happened. Hugh lowered his axe and cocked the springs in his knees to jump left or right. Tom Scott planted his knobby-knuckled hands around the birch trunk, planted his big boots wide and pushed. The tree fell in the direction it was supposed to, taking down a few saplings and ripping off a few branches as it crashed to the ground. Out of the crash came another sound, a clanging from the west.

Hugh planted his axe in a stump and joined the rest of the crew ambling back toward where they'd started that morning, footsteps hissing through the autumn leaves. Although the trees were bare, and everything a bleak grey-brown, it was the best time of year to be working in the woods: no snow yet, but enough frosty nights to've cut short the lives of all the flies, tics and mosquitoes, and good riddance to 'em.

The clanging came from a rusty piece of pipe hanging from the rail of a Red River cart, and an equally rusty rod that one of the camp cooks was whanging it with. Hugh joined the line for tin bowls of salt-pork-and-vague-vegetable stew. He'd never properly appreciated homecooked food till he'd had to live on the kind made in huge vats. But as soon as the autumn buffalo hunt came home he'd be done with eating road crew food for good. Provided the confusion about land title registry got resolved, and it surely must be sorted out by then. Surely the autumn buffalo hunt would be bringing home his future, and by New Year's the homecooking he'd be eating would be Wauh Oonae's, in their own home. But thinking about the future too much would awaken yearnings that made it harder to slog through the present day-by-day.

Tom Scott and a clutch of other Canadians and a couple of the American deserters were squatted on the roadbed doing more talking than eating. Hugh found a roadside tree to plant his back against, not close enough to be part of the group but close enough to hear what they were saying – although some things were said loud enough he could've heard them in Fort Garry. Tall Tom was saying: "Two months! Two bloody months! He must've heard back by now, if he did what he promised."

One of the ex-Americans growled: "Two *weeks*'d be more'n long enough – given the rail line through the States."

"We've been patient more than long enough, lads," Tom Scott proclaimed. "You know there's only one way we can get Snow to pay attention."

One of the Desmaraix who had little English murmured in Bungee to Hugh: "What's they say?"

Hugh told him: "Sounds like here we go again."

The Desmarais rolled his eyes toward the sky. Hugh shrugged his shoulders and his arms. Two months earlier, at lunchtime on a sunny day, the Canadians and Americans on the crew had finally grown fed-up with constantly chewing over the same complaints about low wages, wages paid in overpriced goods from Dr. Schultz's store, and rumours they were actually getting higher wages on paper but someone was pocketing the difference. They'd decided there was only one way to get Superintendent Snow to pay attention. The concept of a 'strike' had been difficult for the local men to fathom. Not that they were blindly obedient by nature – Hugh had heard stories of mutinous behaviour on the York Boat brigades, and heard more than a few retired Company officers grumbling that at Red River they couldn't find a servant who acted like a servant. But the notion of stopping working and making everybody else stop, too, didn't make much sense when you were trying to get boats to Hudson Bay and back before freeze-up, or trying to get pemmican made before the meat rotted, or trying to get the harvest in before Ma Nature pulled any of a thousand cruel tricks. Enough men had wanted to strike, though, that the others had decided to go along with them and see what happened. What had happened was that after a day-and-a-half strike Superintendent Snow had promised to write a letter to the Minister of Public Works in Ottawa, detailing all the factors the men thought unfair, if they'd go back to work.

But now two months had passed and Mr. Snow had yet to tell them what he'd heard back from Ottawa, if anything. Tall Tom Scott said around his latest mouthful of salt pork and whatever: "We only got Snow's word for it…" he paused to swallow, his prominent Adam's apple going up and down, "that he even wrote the damn letter in the first place. And you know what Snow's word's worth."

There were grumblings of agreement and shouts of *"Bloody right,"* and *"Lying bastard."* Hugh didn't join in, but neither did he feel Mr. Snow's honour was necessarily worth defending. Last winter Superintendent Snow had been charged, convicted and fined ten pounds sterling for selling liquor to the Indians around Oak Point. Coincidentally, those were the same Indians who lived on the land that Mr. Snow and Dr. Schultz had been so interested in getting surveyed.

But the whole business of the road crew and everything to do with it had become a bit abstract to Hugh, and he knew it. He already had as much money put away as he needed to buy Jean Claude MacGregor's farm and get him and Wauh Oonae set up in it. He was just marking time and taking in a little extra till the buffalo hunt came home. The rest of the men on the road crew had a lot more stake in it than he did, and he could see which way the wind was blowing with them. So he took his empty tin bowl and tea mug back to the cook cart and retrieved his axe to carry it back to camp. He would've preferred to just carry on home, but the last strike had taught him that every man in the crew was to stick around, to show they were all in it together.

Nothing happened that afternoon or evening, but next morning Mr. Snow's assistant came to camp and read out the letter Superintendent Snow had received from the Minister of Public Works some while ago. The letter from Ottawa said that fifteen dollars a month was all that was allowed to be paid to general labourers, and that the Dominion Government had no doubt any arrangements for wages to be paid in goods from Dr. Schultz's store were fair and equitable. Then the assistant read out a letter Mr. Snow had written yesterday evening after he'd got the news the men were on strike again. It was a letter to the crew in general, and said that any man who was dissatisfied could come to 'The Depot' tomorrow and be paid all wages owed to him.

After Mr. Snow's assistant had read out the letter and got back on his horse, Tall Tom said: "I'm done with this slave labour anyway. There'll be plenty of other work for Canadians around here right soon, and a damn sight better-paying."

Next morning as soon as breakfast was done they hitched up the carts and almost all the crew piled on. Hugh packed along his canvas sack of extra clothes and moveables, not sure what to expect. He stood in a corner of the cart as usual, looking out at the world passing by. The woods had grown darker now with no lighter greens mingling with the spruce trees. There were a few gold and bronze leaves left on the birches and bur oaks, but not many – it looked to be an early winter. A wedge of geese flew over, heading south and so high in the sky you could only tell they were geese by their arrowhead flying formation, until a shift in the wind carried down their bugling travelling song. They reminded Hugh that by rights he should be taking his shotgun to the delta marsh where the Red met Lake Winnipeg and thousands of geese and ducks stopped by in the fall. Next year.

'The Depot' was a log house, office and storage shed built for the headquarters of the road-building project, in a pretty spot beside what some people called German Creek and some the Seine River. The new paymaster, Mr. Mair's replacement, came out the front door of the office and told the men to form a line and come in turn. Hugh could see through the front doorway, and by the light of the open back door, that there was a table with Superintendent Snow and his assistant sitting behind some piles of paper and a strongbox.

Hugh had been in the office before, and had wondered why it had been built as a sort of afterthought sticking out the side of the house, with its own front and back doors. Now he saw why. This must've been the regular routine at pay days; Hugh had never been to one, because his pay had gone straight to his father from Mr. Mair via Dr. Schultz. The men lined up at the front door, went to the table in turn and then out the back door – no bottlenecks or confusion.

Tall Tom Scott and his friends were naturally at the front of the line. They came around from the back door one by one, counting their money and calling to the rest of the line: "See you in Winnipeg, lads – the Red Dog or Dutch George's!" But before many other men had passed through the door, Hugh heard a wolfpack of shouting behind him and turned to look. Tom Scott and a half-dozen other Canadians and Americans were piling back out of the cart they'd commandeered to take them to Winnipeg and charging back towards the office, roaring curses. Tall Tom bellowed at the men still in line: "Three days short! All of us got paid three days short, and it'll be the same for you!"

The line of men tied itself into knots in front of the doorway, some yelling angrily, some standing in confused clumps. Tom Scott elbowed his way to the front just as Superintendent Snow appeared in the doorway, dressed for business in a frock coat and starched collar. Tom brandished a handful of banknotes and shouted: "Three days short! I can bloody count! It's three days short!"

"Of course it's three days bloody short! You were on strike the last day and a half, and a day and a half in August! Why should I pay you for not working? By rights I should've deducted the cost of your board for those days!"

They were yelling into each others' faces, made possible only because Mr. Snow was standing on the doorstep and Tom Scott on the ground. Tall Tom yelled: "You better pay us for those three days, or else!"

Superintendent Snow crossed his arms and said flatly, "Or else what?"

"Or else we'll… we'll…" Hugh could see Tom Scott glancing around and his eyes light on the river. "We'll fucking drown you!" Tom's big, gnarled hands took hold of Superintendent Snow's lapels. Mr. Snow tried to bat Tom's hands away, but several other pairs of workmen's hands took hold of his arms and legs. After almost a year of helping each other fell trees and move boulders, the men worked together well: in an instant Superintendent Snow was up and being carried flailing and hollering toward the riverbank.

Hugh drifted dazedly along the edge of the laughing mob, wondering if they really meant to throw the Superintendent in. The Seine River was nowhere near the size of the Red, but it was deep enough to drown in, had a good current, and swimming wasn't easy in boots and a frock coat. And although the water was still a month or two short of being iced over it was already icy. Mr. Snow's assistant came scurrying out of the office bleating: "Pay them, Mr. Snow, pay them!"

Just as they reached the riverbank, Superintendent Snow altered his shouted curses and threats into: "All right! All right, I'll pay it!" They set him back down on his feet. He straightened his collar and added: "But every man who takes pay for those three days will sign his name acknowledging the fact."

As everyone else headed back toward the office, Hugh went in the other direction. He lifted his bulge-bottomed canvas sack out of the cart where he'd left it and started walking. Angling across the prairie instead of following the roads, it would only be a few miles home. No need to line up for his wages, Da would get what was owed in the usual way, for the last time. John Hugh Sutherland had seen enough of Public Works, or any other kind of works that led to the kind of insanity he'd just seen.

After his legs got stretched out enough that he could taste the wild sage in the bottoms of his lungs, Hugh began to smile, and then to whistle a tune Granda used to play on the fiddle. After several times adding up the practicalities ahead of him – the amount of money he had banked with Da, the cost of the MacGregor place and the things he and Nancy would need to get started, and how much would be left over for a hedge against surprises – Hugh was pretty sure he could make himself a vow that could be kept: he would never work for wages again, and have no boss but Ma Nature. Well, and maybe Wauh Oonae on occasion.

By the time his feet were crunching through the stubbled Hay Common, and he could see the roofs of the Point Douglas Sutherlands' house and barn, the only thought in Hugh's mind was of bread and cheese – that and putting down the sack he'd been shifting from shoulder to shoulder. When he came into the yard, Mary Ann Bella – the only progeny left not old enough for school – was trying to throw a stick far enough for one of the dogs to bother fetching it. She squealed and ran toward Hugh. He crouched down so she could throw her little arms around his neck, and so he wouldn't have to try and pick her up with arms cramped dead. Aleck came out of the barn and said: "What are you doing here?"

"I'm done with the road crew."

"Why?"

"I'll tell you inside, I'm famished." Hugh picked up the cursed, awkward sack – handy for throwing into the back of a cart, but not for hiking – and headed for the house. Inside, Donald was following Mum around with a bucket of river clay while she explored the walls for any chinks that might've opened up over the summer. There hadn't been any for years, but nonetheless every autumn… Hugh had been her clay porter the last few autumns, but now Donald had gone as far as there was to go at St. John's College, unless he wanted to be a pastor or a missionary and an Anglican one at that. Morrison had been obliged to make sure there was still a Point Douglas Sutherland at St. John's College, and likely Hector would follow him there next year. Hugh had tried once to suggest to Aleck that he might not mind minding his younger brothers there – it would only take him one year of catching up at Kildonan school – but had quickly dropped the subject.

Mum seemed confused but not unhappy to see Hugh home in the middle of the week. When he told the story of Superintendent Snow being gathered to the river – in between mouthfuls of buttered bread and cheese – Mum clucked and shook her head, Aleck laughed and Donald seemed strangely distant. When Hugh ended with saying he was done working on the road crew, Mum said: "I think that's wise. Well, Donald, have you told Hugh your news?"

Donald said: "Um, well I… uh…" Hugh wasn't accustomed to seeing his one and only older brother turn shy on him. An older brother either said something to you or didn't, not 'um' and 'uh' around its edges. "Well… Christy Matheson has decided – I mean, she and I have decided… we'll get married."

It was Hugh's turn to be tongue-tied. He'd never before had to come up with the right thing to say to people he'd grown up with announcing their impending marriage. He said: "Well, I… uh… It's about time," and Donald snatched up the bucket of wet clay to dump over his head. Donald didn't actually dump it, of course – Mum would've skinned him alive and then made him scour the floor and Hugh's clothes – but what with Mum's shrieking and some laughter and some shoulder-punching, the moment was appropriate. When things had settled down again, Hugh said: "So have you found a place yet?"

Donald said: "Mm-hm, but it's not built yet, will be soon – you might have a hand in building it, since you won't be busy building roads. Da's got the timber already stacked and waiting, for a building on the Portage Road in Winnipeg. Sutherland & Sons will have some kind of business on the ground floor, Da and I've talked over several possibilities but we're waiting to see which way the wind blows. And we're waiting to start construction until Colonel Dennis's survey crew are relocated to Winnipeg. Colonel Dennis will set some of his crew to help with the building, and once it's done a few of them will bunk in there and Christy will get paid to cook for them. Then once the survey crew moves on – either further west or back to Canada – we'll own the building, I mean all us Sutherlands, and Christy and I will live on the upper floor and I'll work in whatever business Da decides is our best bet to put in on the ground floor." Donald winked. "In on the ground floor. Likely we can start construction in just a few days – Colonel Dennis's survey expedition have worked their way north from the border to almost the Assiniboine."

Hugh was a little ashamed at his own selfishness, but there was no denying what interested him most in Donald's news was if the Canadian surveyors were almost at the Assiniboine, they might have the land around Jean Claude MacGregor's place surveyed and registered before the buffalo hunt came home. It did seem odd to Hugh that Donald was excited about living in a business building in a town – a town growing so fast that in a year or two he wouldn't be able to see anything out his window but other buildings – but Donald had always been a little odd.

Da came home from a Council meeting at the courthouse before school was out, and instead of seeming surprised to see Hugh there just said right off: "Glad to see you have some sense. I know what, um, happened at the… *Depot* this morning, because Superintendent Snow left his assistant to finish the, um, pay-outs and galloped straight to the ferry across to the courthouse and got Judge Black to swear out a warrant against Thomas Scott and three others for… *aggravated* assault. So, when Thomas Scott and the others were ferried across on their way to, um, the Winnipeg taverns, Sheriff McKenney was waiting for them with Constable Mulligan and a half-dozen Special Constables sworn in for the… *occasion*. The four of them will spend the night in jail, and if they can find somebody to, um, go their bail tomorrow – likely one of the saloon-keepers, it would be a good… *investment* – they'll stand trial at the next Quarterly Session of the Court of Assiniboia. That is, if there *is* a next Quarterly Session of the Court of Assiniboia."

Mum said: "What do you mean?"

Da shook his head. "I don't know what the devil's going on with this supposed... *Transfer* any more than you do. Maybe by November our courts and our laws will've been, um, taken over by the... *Dominion* of Canada, maybe not."

Then there was a commotion coming up from the river and Hector, Morrison, Angus, Margaret, Catherine, Willy, Christina, James and Roddy were home from school, and the shadow of outside events was swept under by a raucous tea-and-biscuits before pre-supper chores. It was a rare slack-time in the farm year: the harvest done but the air not yet reliably freezing enough for slaughtering. So Hugh and Donald and Aleck decided, with permission, that they'd spend a day or two up at the delta harvesting ducks and geese. Next morning they loaded one of the carts with their camp gear, guns and the smaller dugout.

By the time the cart had creaked its way north to the head of the lake, there was just enough light left to make camp. Hugh was surprised by how much his brothers didn't know: which direction to angle the canvas lean-to, whether it's warmer to sleep on top of two buffalo robes or sandwiched between them... There had been a time when Donald and Aleck knew as much about the woods and the prairies as he did, but since then Donald's education had been cut short by school and college, and Aleck's by moping around the farm. But the only thing Hugh hated worse than other people telling him what to do was telling other people what to do, so he endeavoured to get his brothers to avoid making mistakes by 'helping' them.

Hugh borrowed a duck from a Metis family camped nearby, promising to replace it tomorrow, and spitted it on his muzzle-loader's ramrod over the fire. There were hundreds of hunters camped around the edge of the marsh, but even if every shot they fired brought down two ducks or geese, there would still be thousands left. Starting at dawn, in one day Hugh and his brothers brought down several times more birds than the family could use – they could've used more if the waterfowl didn't troublesomely time their migrations to be just before Ma Nature's cold storage kicked in. Hugh took a bunch of their birds over to a family of Saulteaux from St. Peters camped nearby, who were turning geese and ducks into smoked meat. Nancy Prince's father was a rarity in taking his family on the buffalo hunts; most people of St. Peter's parish spent their summers fishing the lake, and their autumns harvesting birds and wild rice from the marsh. These ones agreed to Hugh's proposition that if they went to the trouble of smoke-curing the birds he'd brought them, they could keep half and bring the rest to the Point Douglas Sutherlands'. He didn't make a count or ask for a receipt, it would more-or-less average out.

Next morning Hugh and his brothers broke camp and set off home again. Aleck had of course caught a cold after only two nights sleeping outdoors – he was really made for indoor work and brain work, but try and tell him that... It occurred to Hugh that the past year of working away on the road crew and only seeing the family occasionally had given him a sharper perspective of each of them; or maybe just that added year of age and experience had clarified his vision; or maybe he'd grown swollen-headed and developed too high an opinion of his own opinion. Whichever, there was no maybe that he felt both aggravated and sad at Aleck's attempts to be who he wasn't, like a short-legged kid built for paddling canoes who insists on running footraces. But there was something endearing in Aleck's stubborn refusal to give in. Hugh fervently wished, though, that he could find a way to get Aleck to give in, before Aleck got too locked-in to living a life pretending to be who he wasn't. And Hugh felt a certain amount of guilt and responsibility – somewhere back along the years he'd done something that had given Aleck the loopy notion that he wanted to be Hugh. Whatever it was, Hugh wished he hadn't done it.

While Hugh had been pondering his way through all of that, the cart had made its way into the stretch of woods-shrouded road between St. Peters and St. Boniface, and was passing by the one home on that stretch of road. Norbert Parisien and his father were bucksawing a log into splittable stove-lengths. Hugh asked Donald to stop the pony for a moment, jumped down, reached back through the cartrails to grab a couple of dead mallards by the neck and carried them into the yard. Norbert and his father stepped back from their work, leaving the saw standing halfway through the log. Norbert squinted and then shouted: "*Purple Hugh!*"

Hugh had no idea where Norbert might've heard that silly family nickname, but there was no telling how or what Norbert might pick up and what he might remember or forget. Hugh said: "Me and my brothers was up at the delta and got more ducks than the family can eat before they goes bad." Norbert's father looked a bit perturbed, like just because he had a gammy leg didn't mean he needed charity. "Both ducks together ain't near so big as the catfish Norbert give me once."

Norbert nodded and grinned, "Made a catfish trap – catfish corral." Then Norbert's father nodded merci and reached out for the ducks.

"Well, we better get the rest of them birds home in time for supper. See ya."

Norbert's father said: "See you, too, Hugh Sutherland."

When the cart came parallel to Kildonan Kirk across the river, Donald stopped the pony again and the three of them carried the dugout canoe and two fat geese down to the river. Hugh set off in the dugout while his brothers carried on homeward in the cart. At the manse he held the brace of geese out to Mrs. Black, saying: "If two's too many for you, ma'am, we'd be happy if you give one to your mother," the widow Granny Sally Ross. By the time he'd paddled home against the current, Mum had already got three of the ducks plucked and cleaned and sizzling on the spit in the fireplace, another in the cast iron oven box that fitted on top of the Carron stove, and the rest hanging in the ice shed – which was only slightly cooler than outside, now that the summer had melted away most of the ice that had been cut and dragged from the river last winter.

Mum seemed strangely pinched and quiet: not outright scolding anybody, but not exactly revelling in the prospect of roast duck, either. Hugh wondered whether there had been something that needed doing over the last few days while her three oldest boys were off playing Nimrod. Da had the latest copy of the Toronto *Globe* – well, the latest to get to Red River – and said to Hugh: "You've been working all last year for our new governor."

"How's that, Da?"

"Well, *Lieutenant* Governor. The *Globe*'s published the, um, names of the Lieutenant Governor and his staff… *appointed* to come out here from Canada and, um, take charge. The Lieutenant Governor will be the Honourable William McDougall, who was the… *Dominion* Minister of Public Works that Superintendent Snow was, um, reporting to. Odd, though, that we should read about it in a… *foreign* newspaper, when there still hasn't been any, um, official announcement to the people who live here, but I expect there will be soon –"

At that point, there was a clang when Mum set the big kettle back on the woodstove with more force than seemed strictly necessary. She didn't say *'oops'* or *'sorry'* or anything at all. Da looked mystified and then raised the newspaper in front of his face and kept quiet.

Supper was a grand demolishment of ducks, along with savoury spoonfuls of the wild rice that Da got a sackful of every fall in trade for a sackful of barley. Between chews and swallows there were many funny stories about the last three days in school and college and hunting camp, but Mum said virtually nothing. The younger children seemed oblivious, but Hugh caught Margaret sidling her eyes toward Mum's end of the table, so even a fourteen year old could tell there was something seething. After supper and a few details like cleaning up the dishes and fetching wood and water for tomorrow morning, and after bedtime for the school children and Mary Anne Bella, when there was no one left at the table but Hugh, Mum, Da, Donald and Aleck sipping their end-of-the-night tea, Mum said out of nowhere, "The *Honourable* William McDougall."

Da said: "Pardon me?"

"Just because I don't have anything hanging between my legs, John, doesn't mean I don't have anything between my ears."

'Oh, oh,' passed through Hugh's mind, *'she called him John, not Father.'* He snuck a glance at Donald and Aleck, whose eyes were asking the same question he was asking himself: *'Maybe I should think of something I should be doing somewhere else?'*

Da said: "Um…"

Mum said: "When you bring home the newspapers that get sent from Canada, I read some parts of them you don't: the Society Pages. It's foolish, I know, but it's something like a little girl playing dress-up, and we all have to be childish at times. So that list of the staff the Lieutenant Governor is bringing to rule over us – I've seen some of the names before. Captain D.R. Cameron, who is to be in charge of the police and military – Captain Cameron recently married the daughter of the Honourable Charles Tupper, a big chief in the Canadian government. J.A.N. Provencher, who's to be Secretary of the Lieutenant Governor's Council, is a nephew of Bishop Provencher. I'm sure if you read out that list to someone who knows all about who's who in the Dominion, you'd find that every one of them is the son-in-law or nephew or kissing cousin of someone with a big name in Canada."

"Well, that's not so different from The Company, Mother. I can't count how many, um, sons and nephews of... *Chief* Factors and Chief Traders were brought into The Company."

"Yes, but they had to *do* something. If they couldn't make a profit running a little wilderness outpost, they were set to stacking bales or sent back where they came from. These men coming from Canada don't have to do anything, except tell *us* what to do. And there isn't a damn thing we can do about it."

"I'm sure they're all men of ability."

"Oh, I'm sure. I'm going to bed."

After Mum had stomped up the stairs, Da sat looking at the table and seemed in no hurry to follow her. Da muttered: "Well... well..." and nothing more. Hugh had the feeling Da was in some agreement with some of what Mum had said, but especially *'there isn't a damn thing we can do about it.'*

In the morning, Hugh, Da, Donald and Aleck crossed the river with the boatloads of other Sutherlands heading off to school. When most of the scholars started walking north in the direction of St. John's College and Kildonan school, Morrison and Hector stayed behind, allowed a few days off to help with construction. Hugh and his father and brothers loaded themselves down with the tools they 'd ferried across, and walked south into the village of Winnipeg.

Several of Colonel Dennis's men were waiting there and had already set out stakes on the building site. There were stacks of squared logs of various lengths from McDermot's sawmill, all remarkably even-faced compared to the adze-squared beams Hugh was used to. Da and the foreman looked over the plans and then all went to work. The Canadians from the survey expedition were delegated to digging the marked postholes, because they didn't have even as much experience as Hector at Red River building.

The trick to putting up a house or barn at Red River was teamed lifting and lowering. Before that stage, you planted upright, squared-log posts securely in the ground, after two grooves had been cut along their lengths: on opposite sides for mid-wall posts, kitty-corner for corner posts. The squared-log beams were sized about four inches too long to fit between the posts, but the ends got carved into tongues to fit inside the posts. Then came the matter of lifting six- or eight-foot long, six- or eight-inch square beams up to the top of the posts, and lowering them down with the tongues in the grooves. It was only three- or four-foot beams in sections where posts had been planted closer together to accommodate doors and windows. You ended up with six- or eight-inch thick, solid wood walls, all locked together and supporting each other, without the need of iron nails or even many tree nails.

The Point Douglas Sutherlands had worked together so much they hardly even needed grunts to communicate that the hands on the other end of the beam wanted you to shift your grip, and they could mock and josh each other without interrupting the business at hand. Hugh noticed that although Da was as strong as ever, he tended to step back a little more than he used to, didn't push himself quite as hard as when he was still closer to forty than fifty. Hugh also noticed that the survey crew labourers worked hard enough, but with no sense of urgency. It reinforced his growing notion that the system of working for a boss for wages wasn't the best of arrangements.

The Point Douglas Sutherlands and the survey expedition labourers weren't the only ones who worked on the new building. A Matheson or an Inkster might pass by delivering something to the new little kirk across the road, or just stop by for a look, and chip in to tongue a few beam-ends or help lift a few into place, then stick around for a cup of tea before heading on their ways. One of those chipper-inners, Angus Bannerman, who was about halfway between Hugh's age and Da's, said at the tea break: "You know why there aren't been no official announcement yet of Canada taking us over? There's something the Canada government don't want to talk about and don't want us to think about. Leastwise not till they got their people here and in control. Taxes."

Hugh said: "Taxes?"

"Yep. Last year my total taxes paid was five shillings. That's my entire share for maintaining of roads and bridges, salaries for Judge Black and Sheriff McKenney and all, everything. Five shillings."

Da said around his pipestem: "You can thank The Company for that. Last year, like, um, most years, half the public outlay came from customs duties... *remitted* by The Company to the Council of Assiniboia. Well, The Company and the private traders..." he shrugged that hairs didn't need splitting.

"Even so," Angus Bannerman jabbed a finger in Da's general direction, "even if my taxes woulda bin double without the customs duties kicking in half, that'd be ten shillings. Even so, I got a letter last month from a cousin in Canada, and he told me he paid three pounds tax last year. Three *pound*. That's not just twice what I paid, that's more like ten times more! And my property's three times the size of his! Look, John," Angus was growing more animated-agitated, "you don't exactly get a princely wage for being a Councillor of Assiniboia..."

Da looked a little embarrassed at talk of other people's money going into his pocket. "It's, um, public knowledge – ten shillings a day for Council meetings on... *active* business. Most years that's forty shillings."

"Exactly!" Angus Bannerman jabbed his right forefinger at the air so forcefully that the tin mug in his left hand sloshed tea on his trousers. "'Cause you already make an honest living outta your farm! This here Governor McDougall and his on-too-raj, the only income they got is what they can squeeze outta us. And once we're part of Canada, the Canadian government's got the right to squeeze money outta us to spend in Ottawa, or Toronto, or Quebec. Right? And we ain't got no say in it. They can squeeze us till we howl, we got no voice!"

Everyone's heads turned questioningly toward the Canadian survey crew labourer who happened to be leaning his back against the stack of lumber nearest to the ones they were leaning their backs against. His shrug said clearly: *'I dig holes and chop logs.'*

So then Hugh's and everyone else's eyes naturally turned towards Da. Da said: "Think of it... *reasonably*, Angus. Do you, um, milk every cow in your herd bone-dry all of the time? No – when a cow calfs, you let the calf take her milk until it's, um, weaned, and every now and then you give her a... *drying-off* for a month or two, so she can build herself up again. You don't want to squeeze your herd dry all at once, you want to keep them healthy and producing, so that... um, so that..." He trailed off. His fingers rolled through the air slowly, then stopped and he looked down at the ground. Hugh remembered someone saying: *'They can't sell us like cattle that go with the land.'*

Angus Bannerman said: "Yeah, so you can keep on milking them."

Da didn't seem to have anything to say to that. But Hugh wasn't going to let any nigglings about vague future generalities get in the way of his tingling delight at the way his own real future looked to be progressing. The survey crews had worked their way so far north from the Medicine Line that they were starting in on the settled lands just south of The Forks, which was why Colonel Dennis could spare Da a few labourers who would've been setting up and moving base camps. There were two Majors under Colonel Dennis and he'd set each of the Majors with a crew to work either side of the Red. At the rate they were going, by the time the buffalo hunt came home the Major working the west side of the Red would definitely be across the Assiniboine, and Jean Claude MacGregor's farm would definitely be surveyed and registered.

There were rumours that the survey was being done in neat squares to accommodate the Canadian mapmakers, instead of the rectangles running back from the river as was the way of farms in Assiniboia. But Hugh was quite sure that any squaring-off wouldn't apply to land someone was already living on. Square farms didn't make sense. With a long, rectanglish field – what the old folks called 'runrig' – you had furrows twice as long so had to turn the plough around and start a new furrow half as many times as the same-size field in a square.

At lunch on the fifth day of building, with the walls almost done and the roof beam waiting to be raised, the chipper-inners were two Macleods, father and son. Mum always packed a little extra soup or bread and cheese into 'her men's' lunch, in case some volunteer happened to appear mid-morning. Between munches, the younger Macleod said to the surrounding munchers in general, "Coupla days ago I rode down to Little Britain, to take a coupla books back to the Red River Library for my mother and get a coupla more. Dotty Don Gunn said –"

"Ahem," Macleod Sr. cleared his throat with a loud grunt.

"That is, old Mr. Donald Gunn, he said there was something about the name of this William McDougall fella, the Lieutenant Governor, that stuck in his mind from way back. So he went to digging through the stacks of old Canadian newspapers in the library... Seems there's a place called Manitoulin Island, on Lake Huron."

Donald put in, for the edification of his less-educated brothers, "One of the Great Lakes. Manitoulin is the largest freshwater island in the known world."

"Well," the younger Macleod went on, "seems as about ten years ago there was a kind of little rebellion on Manitoulin Island, some people got killed, or almost killed. Seems the Canadian government decided to survey the whole island, so it'd be regulated ahead for new settlers, and register property deeds for the folks as already lived there. Well, the fella in charge made sure the surveying got done all right, and made sure the property deeds got registered – in *his* name, and the names of his friends and relations. That fella's name was William McDougall."

The Point Douglas Sutherlands looked at each other, but especially at Hugh. Hugh chewed his mouthful of roast beef sandwich and took a sip of tea to moisten it – the bread and beef had suddenly gone dry.

Next morning's tea break, a cart came up from the direction of The Forks, bearing one of the Majors and his survey team. Colonel Dennis stepped out onto the front step of the headquarters building while they were still climbing down from the cart. Hugh picked up his mug of tea and drifted over to lean against the corner of the Sutherland Building to see what he could hear.

Colonel Dennis said: "Finished already, Major?"

"No, sir – well, maybe in a manner of speaking. It's up to you."

"How so?"

"You said if there was any trouble with the natives – with the locals – we were to stand down and come straight back to headquarters."

Colonel Dennis knuckled his military mustache thoughtfully, then said: "What sort of trouble?"

"Well, sir, we were starting to work our way in through the common land behind the farms – what the locals call the hay privilege. We'd just got the chain stretched out and the markers set to take another reading, when up from one of the farms came walking about a dozen halfbreed young bucks, and walking purposeful. They were none of them armed, but they spread out in a kind of skirmish line and… stood upon the chain."

Colonel Dennis blinked. "They what?"

"They lined up side-by-each and planted both moccasins squarely on the chain."

Colonel Dennis blinked some more and furrowed his forehead, then seemed to light upon a line of approach. "Could you identify the ringleaders?"

"I don't know as there were any ringleaders, sir, they seemed to be all in it together. There was one that did the talking, but that might've been just because he spoke good English and seemed to know something about the law." Hugh wondered if that might be Louis Schmidt. "Well set-up young fellow, with a neat mustache and sort of reddy-brown hair."

Wrong Louis, Hugh corrected himself, *Louis Riel.*

"And there was another one," the Major went on, "a little older than the others and a good deal bigger. Must be six-three, six-four, shoulders two axe handles wide, black hair and beard…"

Ambroise Lépine, passed through Hugh's mind. He remembered Da saying in some adult conversation Hugh had been listening in on years ago: *"It would take a great deal to make Ambroise Lépine lose his temper, but I wouldn't want to be the ten men that did it."*

"But," the Major added, "the big fellow didn't say anything. And the one who did the talking didn't say much."

"What *did* he say?"

"'You go no further.'"

CHAPTER 37

Dr. Schultz sat at his kitchen table in his nightshirt and robe, looking out at the autumn night. With no light burning in the kitchen he could see shapes through the window by moonlight, and he hadn't needed more than moonlight in his kitchen to find the whiskey bottle, water pitcher and tin of imported English cigarettes. The cigarettes were ostensibly store stock, but the fact was most of the locals bought much cheaper leaf tobacco they could cut for themselves and mix with kinnikinnik to smoke in a pipe. One of the advantages of being a storekeeper was that anything he or Agnes wanted came wholesale, and on credit till the suppliers lost their patience and had to be given a bit of a pay-down as a sop.

One of the moonlit shapes Schultz could see through the window was a corner of the roof of his new brick house. The exterior was all complete and weather-tight, and over the winter the carpenters would put in the floors, staircases and interior walls, if all went as planned. If all went as planned…

Schultz was troubled by the fragility of plans. He was twenty-nine years old, and when he was fifteen he'd promised himself he'd make his fortune by the time he was thirty. His promise was tantalisingly close to coming true, but somehow the fact that it was almost within his grasp made every unexpected sidestep more unnerving than the many he'd had to make in the past.

A flicker of golden light from behind him tinged the silver moonlight. He turned to see Agnes coming from the bedroom in her nightgown and Chinese silk kimono, carrying a candle. The candlelight put an amber glow into her cream-skinned, heart-shaped face, with her unbound, thick dark hair melding into the darkness behind it. Schultz said softly: "Sorry, my dear, I couldn't sleep, didn't mean to wake you…"

She shifted the candlestick into her left hand, put her right hand on his shoulder – amazing how such a small hand could feel so palpably there – and said: "What's troubling you?"

"Oh, I, well, um, nothing in particular, just couldn't sleep…"

She reached down a glass, poured in a touch of whiskey and a filling of water and sat down across the table from him, in front of the window he'd been staring at. "Now, Christian, you didn't marry me so you could spend the rest of your life keeping a stiff upper lip and pretending all's well when it isn't."

"I didn't?"

"I'm not the kind of woman that needs to be coddled and protected, or needs to feel her husband's a kind of granite statue that never feels doubts or disappointments. Now, what's troubling you?"

"Oh, it's probably foolish to worry about it..."

"Well I don't know, I can't say, since you haven't told me what 'it' is."

"Oh, just a couple of things that, when added together..." Schultz ran his lower lip back and forth against the blades of his top incisors. "Those damned halfbreeds stopping the survey..."

"They won't stop it for long. In another two weeks or so the Lieutenant Governor and his staff will arrive, and things will be put in order. I think it was very wise of Colonel Dennis to suspend operations till then, don't you?"

"Well, yes, I suppose –"

"You suppose? What else would you have him do?"

"Well, yes, under the circumstances... That'll resolve itself soon enough, and if it was only that business about the survey –"

"*Were.*"

" – I wouldn't worry. But, Howe left today. Howe's gone, and didn't see me." The Honourable Joseph Howe had come all the way from Ottawa to see for himself what things were like at Red River, and in what soon would officially be the Dominion of Canada's North West Territories. Howe had let it be known that he hadn't come on government business, just a private inspection tour, but oddly hadn't inspected much of anything, as far as Schultz could tell.

What Schultz did know was that Joseph Howe was by far the loosest cannon in the Federal Cabinet. Howe had fought like hell to keep his home province of Nova Scotia out of Confederation, then when the Imperial Government over-ruled him he'd used his popular support to pry out more provincial autonomy than the Dominion had initially offered. Once that was a done deal he'd accepted a cabinet post in the federal government he'd fought against, so he could make damn sure its promises to the provinces were kept. Howe was sixty-some years old and word had it that last year's midwinter election in his home county had aged him even more. So why the hell he would travel all the way to Red River when he didn't have to, was beyond Schultz's understanding. Schultz was certain there was some understandable reason, he just couldn't fathom what it was, though he had some unsettling suspicions.

Schultz had extended a generous invitation for Howe to stay at the Schultzes' commodious home while he was at Red River. Howe had cordially declined, claiming the journey had been a bit much for an old man and he needed some time to recuperate in a private room in Dutch George Emmerling's hotel. Once ensconced, Howe had hardly ventured out of the hotel, except to hire Dutch George's stable-keeper to take him on a carriage ride to the Stone Fort and back, and on shorter jaunts to Fort Garry and a few other places. A very few Red River citizens had been invited to private conversations in his hotel room. Schultz hadn't been one of them, but he'd bribed Dutch George's desk clerk to inform him who was, and who the coachman had taken Howe to see.

Schultz growled across the candlelit kitchen table: "He could see the bloody Grey Nuns, but he couldn't see me."

"No need to feel insulted, Christian. If anything, that shows that Mr. Howe is perspicacious. Never underestimate the Grey Nuns – I saw that for myself in my time in St. Boniface. They're aptly named, truly the éminence grise of Red River."

"I'm not insulted – well, maybe a little bit, but… As you said, 'never underestimate,' and it seems the junior of the pair of Grey Nuns Howe had an interview with was Sister Marguerite-Marie Riel, sister to that Louis Riel who put his foot down on the survey chain. Bit of a coincidence, don't you think?"

Agnes looked gratifyingly disturbed at that, but it turned out to not be for the same reason Schultz was. "Christian, you're seeing phantoms. When I said Mr. Howe was perspicacious to seek out the Grey Nuns, I just meant that they know more than anyone about the warp and woof of the Catholic community here – how many people suffer from poverty, the general state of health and education, that sort of thing."

"I suppose, I suppose… But I just…" Schultz hesitated, unsure how far a man should go in confessing weakness to his wife. "I just have this uneasy feeling that… things are unravelling."

She reached across the table to put a hand on his drink hand, the one not holding a lit cigarette. "Have a little faith in yourself, Christian. You weren't made for the Slough of Dispond. When and if you see a definite difficulty, you will find a way to sort it out. Just as you did with the election problem in the spring."

"That wasn't just me, there were others that helped solve that."

"Don't underestimate your*self*, dear. No doubt there were others, but it was your letter that did the trick."

Schultz didn't argue; he was glad to be reminded he had reason to believe he could deal with unexpected problems. Back in the spring, when the sale of Rupert's Land to Canada finally looked to be an imminent reality, it had suddenly occurred to Schultz and Mair and the other Canada Firsters that if the Dominion government inaugurated elections at Red River as soon as the transfer was sealed, there wouldn't be nearly enough true Canadians yet resident to form a majority vote. Elected offices could wind up going to crude Catholic Metis, or autocratic retired fur traders, or the unlettered descendants of rough Highlanders. Once Red River was part of Canada, immigrants from Ontario would come pouring in, bringing their votes with them, but it might take a year or three for the trickle to swell to a flood.

So Schultz had penned a letter to a highly influential gentleman he'd become well acquainted with on his frequent sojourns back and forth to Canada:

"The greatest danger from the Hudson Bay influence will be in giving the franchise to our people at once. Theoretically fair and even necessary it is fraught with very great dangers till our people feel the change and we get an immigration of Canadians on Canadian principles. Our people will be satisfied with simply the local town and country self-government and to have No Elective Choice Whatever Over the Necessary Officers for these Positions."

Schultz couldn't remember whether it had been his brilliant idea, or Mair's, or Agnes's, to use 'our people' – defining him as a rooted member of the Red River community, not an interloper – but it had definitely been brilliant and helped do the trick. There would be no elections at Red River anytime soon.

Unfortunately, dredging up the memory of that brilliant success also brought to the surface the real reason Joseph Howe's visit to Red River was so unsettling. Joseph Howe had first become famous for leading the movement against 'The Oligarchy' – a few interconnected families that had ruled Nova Scotia for generations – and bringing in what was called 'Responsible Government.' His political history clearly indicated a prejudice against government by appointment, and a superstitious faith in the magic of elections. And Joseph Howe's current position in the federal cabinet was Secretary of State for Provincial Affairs, the regulator of relations between the nation and its provinces...

Schultz suddenly barked out: "Bosh!" and laughed.

Agnes bolted back in her chair, recovered herself and said: "What's bosh?"

"Me! Me and my hand-wringing and fretting – turning into a skittish old woman. Joseph Howe is Secretary of State for *Provincial* Affairs. The North-west Territories will be a *Territory*, not a Province, at least not in the foreseeable. Our Lieutenant Governor will only be answerable to the Prime Minister and the Governor General, and Joseph Howe's opinions are only his own opinions. Well, I hope the Honourable Mr. Howe enjoyed his little sightseeing tour, because that's about all it amounts to. In a week or two, William McDougall and his staff will arrive to take charge, and there's bugger-all Joseph Howe or anybody else can do about it."

Agnes smiled, then got up from her chair and came around the table to behind his chair. She reached her hands down over his shoulders to press his chest, and kissed the top of his head, her silk-clad breasts soft and substantial against the back of his neck. She murmured: "Now you're yourself again – not a man to stay in the Slough of Dispond for long. Can you come back to bed now?"

"Um, yes – yes, I believe I shall."

A few nights later, not long after sundown, a Metis gentleman paid a visit but didn't knock, just slipped in the side door and called up the stairs. Schultz called down: "Yes, come up." It wasn't an expected visit, but not unexpected, either. This particular Metis gentleman owed a substantial amount of money to the White Store and Dr. J. C. Schultz's Pharmacy next door. Schultz had worked out an arrangement whereby the debt could be gradually reduced without money changing hands, and further credit extended. Schultz gestured the gentleman to a chair in the common room and poured him a mug of beer from the barrel in the corner – it was always a mistake to give them whiskey, almost as bad as the Irish.

The Metis gentleman took a deep quaff, wiped the foam off his mustache and said: "There was another big meeting last night, in St. Norbert," which was the southernmost settled parish on the Red. "Mostly Metis, but not all the Metis, and not only Metis. Captains got picked and –"

"'Captains'?" Schultz snorted. "Captains of what?"

"Captains of Ten, like on the buffalo hunt. Well, the autumn hunt ain't back yet, but the voyageurs of the Portage La Loch brigade are, and the York Factory and Saskatchewan boat brigades, and they most of them been on the hunt a few times so they knows how it goes, the way Mr. Grant laid it down way back when. How it goes is: maybe three or four or five men will decided together they want somebody-or-other be their captain, and maybe he got a couple cousins who wouldn't mind him being their captain, and pretty soon you got ten men who will do what their captain tells them, and he does what the Captain of The Hunt tells him. Well, here it's not the Captain of The Hunt, but –"

"And just what," Schultz cut short the dissertation, "do these captains propose to do?"

The Metis gentleman reached into his greasy buckskin jacket and came out with a crumpled bit of paper, saying: "I got someone to write me a copy, telled him I wanted to show it my wife."

Schultz smoothed out the scrap of pencilled paper enough to read:

Dated at St. Norbert, Red River, this 21st Day of October, 1869.
The National Committee of the Metis of Red River orders William McDougall not to enter the Territory of the North-West without special permission of the above-mentioned committee.
By order of the President, John Bruce
Louis Riel, Secretary

Schultz laughed. "What 'National Committee'? What nation?"

The Metis gentleman looked miffed. "The New Nation. All the mix-blood people of the Northwest. We are not Cree nor Assiniboine nor white, but ourselves."

"Since when does that make a nation?"

"Since back in the days of Mr. Grant and Seven Oaks."

Schultz wondered whether the allusion to the Seven Oaks Massacre was meant as a jab. Not worth wondering. "Well, this Bruce and Riel and their playmates can put on paper mitres and prance around, that still doesn't make them the Pope. But I appreciate the information. I'll deduct three dollars from your debt."

"Merci, monsieur. And I should paddle myself back across the river before they wonder where I gone." The Metis gentleman sloshed down the last of his mug of beer and stood up. "But first, my wife she need more of that… stuff…"

"I can't go carrying a lamp over to the pharmacy and rummaging around – you said you don't want to attract attention. Come back tomorrow during business hours. I'll tell Mr. Stewart to accommodate you."

Over the next few days, rumours drifted in and out of the store, and Schultz tried to sift through the rumours with Agnes and Bown and Colonel Dennis and whatever other loyal Canadians happened to knock on the door after business hours for private conversations. One rumour that eyewitnesses could attest true was that the 'National Committee's' minions had erected a barrier at the south end of St. Norbert, barring the main road north from Pembina and the American border, the road The Honourable William McDougall and his staff were bound to take after making their way west from the railhead in the States.

That unfortunately brought The Honourable Joseph Howe back to Schultz's mind. It seemed too much coincidence that the timing of Howe's departure from Red River meant that he'd be travelling east toward the railhead at the same time the new Lieutenant Governor was travelling west from there. They were bound to meet somewhere along the road…

Schultz took himself by the scruff of the neck and reminded himself he'd already decided Howe had no power to interfere. Rather than letting himself be spooked by phantoms, he should focus his attention on the here and now. Some of the local Canadians were in favour of going to St. Norbert en masse and removing the barricade, but Schultz said it would be better to wait – soon the Lieutenant Governor would arrive and overawe the ridiculous National Committee with a show of lawful authority. And then Sheriff John Christian Schultz would deputise Special Constables to help him ferret out and arrest the ringleaders in whatever rat-holes they'd scurried away to.

There was an early snowfall that stayed. Schultz had become accustomed that there was usually a snowfall at Red River before Hallowe'en, but usually it didn't stay. The unusually early lock-in of winter made for some amusement in the common room above the White Store, since the halfbreeds guarding the road barrier wouldn't've expected it either, and would likely soon be slinking home with frozen toes.

Two nights after Hallowe'en, that Metis gentleman came calling again, and this time seemed more nervous than before. He said: "I must not to stay long, and best I not come again – not soon. The fat she's in the fire now."

"What fat? What fire?"

"They did stop Governor McDougall and his people at the border, just like that Order said. A couple of McDougall's people – young Provencher and a Captain Cameron – did ride on north by themself. When they come to the barricade at St. Norbert, this Captain Cameron did yell at the guard there…" The Metis gentleman crooked his forefingers under his nose like an upturned, military mustache and imitated an extremely British accent, "'Take down that blawsted fence!' Well, the man he did yell it at was Ambroise Lépine." The Metis gentleman shrugged as though that was all there was to say.

Schultz said: "So? What's that supposed to mean?"

The Metis gentleman blinked as though surprised Schultz couldn't understand English. "So, the fence she is still there, and Captain Cameron he is not – he gone back down the road to wherever Governor McDougall holed-up on south side of the Medicine Line."

CHAPTER 38

The morning after the autumn buffalo hunt got back to Red River, Hugh bolted a few bites of breakfast and then scuffled into his coat to go saddle one of the ponies. Just before he got to the door, Mum called: "Hugh!"

"Yes, Mum?"

"You will be careful…?"

"Don't worry on me, Mum – everybody knows I'm harmless." She still looked worried. "Yes, I'll be careful."

In the two days since the National Committee had halted the Lieutenant Governor at the border, things had become extremely strange at Red River. Neighbours were looking at each other sideways; groups of armed men trotted or galloped up and down the roads at night. Construction of the Point Douglas Sutherlands' new building at the corner of the Portage road and the main road had come to an abrupt halt. It was roof-tight now, and Da had figured they could safely leave off finishing off its insides for now, whereas for now *they* might not be all that safe in the village of Winnipeg, where the taverns of Canadians, Americans and Metis brushed up against each other. The Sutherlands younger than Aleck and older than Mary Ann Bella still went to school and college, but their whole route to and from was through Kildonan.

Da had come back from an emergency meeting of the Council of Assiniboia yesterday saying the Council had decided to make no decisions yet but wait to see what happened next. Everybody at Red River seemed to be waiting: waiting to see what Governor Mactavish and The Company's men in Fort Garry were going to do; waiting to see what Dr. Schultz and Colonel Dennis and the 'Canada Party' were going to do; waiting to see what Lieutenant Governor McDougall and his staff hunkered just across the border were going to do. One thing was certain: among the many cartloads of equipage the Honourable William McDougall and his people had brought with them were cases of several hundred brand new rifles and plenty of cartridges. Da had snorted disgustedly, "Anybody from here could've told the bloody idiot that the Metis freighters hauling his, um, luggage, would tell their brothers passing by, and long before he got here the… *news* would've got here, that the Lieutenant Governor coming to bring us… *peace* and good order, was bringing along enough guns to start a war."

Hugh saddled his pony slowly and mechanically. He'd expected that when the buffalo hunt came home this time, this *last* time for Wauh Oonae, he'd be bubbling over with joy, and fly galloping down the road at first light. Now he didn't know what to say or how to say it. He tried to work it out as he trotted north along the river road, but by the time he got to the little bridge and the wooded hollow where the stream flowed into the Red, he still hadn't come up with anything that didn't sound sickeningly disappointing.

He figured he'd have time to mull it over some more waiting for Nancy, since she had a lot farther to come. But she was already there, sitting with her back against a cutbank beside the half-frozen puddle that was a pool in melt-off or rainy times. She'd built a fire and laid a buffalo robe down and propped another one between her back and the bank. She stood up as he slid down off his pony and tethered it beside Cheengwun. Hugh and Nancy Prince took each other in their arms and kissed, then just stood holding onto each other, swaying from side to side and trying to say how much they were missed. But Hugh felt a certain awkwardness that wasn't just the awkwardness of not having seen each other for ten weeks.

They sat down side-by-side on the one buffalo robe and draped the other one across their shoulders. Wauh Oonae said by way of explaining the fire already built and the gathered deadwood piled up beside it, "I left while it was still dark – couldn't sleep anyways."

Hugh asked her how the buffalo hunt went and told her why he'd quit the road crew. She laughed about the crazy Canadians, but the laugh had an undercurrent of unease. That seemed an opening to start working his way sideways to what he was going to have to get to sooner or later. He said: "You heard about the Canadian Lieutenant Governor being stopped at the border…?"

"Mm-hm. Day before yesterday a few Metis gallopers met the buffalo hunt. Everybody's happy that the new Governor's kept out, but some are worried John Bruce and his National Committee maybe went too far. Canada's got an army, don't they?"

"Well, yeah…" Hugh wasn't too sure of the specifics. "A militia, anyway…" He half-remembered a funny story a few years ago, about the lunatic Fenian raiders from the U.S.A. actually winning a battle when the Canadian militia panicked and ran. Rumour had it that one of the panicky Canadian officers had been Colonel Dennis. "And I guess there's still some British troops stationed there. But Canada's a long ways away, and Da says he doubts the Americans would let a foreign army use their railroad and travel through their territory."

"There's other ways." Wauh Oonae sounded anxious and uncertain. "My grandfather told me that back in the old fur trade days the Canadians used to move hundreds of voyageurs and tons of trade goods, all the way from the heart of their country to Red River, in just half a summer."

"Yeah, but how many of those old voyageurs that knew how to do that are still alive? And anyway, I don't know if you can carry cannons in canoes." He tried to picture it, but couldn't. He felt a bit silly even thinking about armies and cannons and troop movements, much less saying anything about it, but everyone at Red River was talking that way these days. "So if Canada does get mad enough to send an army, they'd either have to sail around to Hudson's Bay and come down the rivers in York boats, or cut and haul their way through, I dunno, maybe hundreds of miles of spruce woods and rock and muskeg. And they can't be even making a try at either way with winter coming on. So that means… I mean, that and everything else means…"

Hugh paused to see if he could think of a way to avoid saying it, or of a better way to say it. He couldn't. He said: "That means that what we planned to do as soon as you got back – buy Jean Claude MacGregor's place, and us getting married and all – we can't do it." He felt her shoulders stiffen under his arm. "My father says –"

She whirled away from him and reared up onto her knees, her face a betrayed snarl. "Your father says what? That you can diddle all the Indian girls you want but you can't marry one?"

"What? No! He never said… anything like that, nor did my mother, and if they did I wouldn't listen. They know I love you, and they'll love you, too, once they get to meet you. What Da said – and other people are saying the same thing – is with the survey stopped and Canada not let in yet, but The Company maybe got no legality anymore, no one knows where land titles are going to be registered or how. So, we could buy Jean Claude MacGregor's farm tomorrow, and then find out next week our deed's no good, some Canadian or someone else got the legal title to it, we've spent the money we saved up for it and we got nothing.

"It ain't just us in that boat. Donald was set to marry Christy Matheson December Twenty-first, and now we don't know whether the building they were gonna live in'll be finished by then. Everything's stalled up, waiting. Maybe it'll all get sorted out in a few days, nobody knows. I dunno, Nancy, maybe if I was…" Hugh felt himself embarrassingly choking up, "Maybe if I was a bit stronger or brighter I could see a way around it, but –"

"Ssh," Wauh Oonae leaned forward and wrapped her arms around him. "Don't ever say that. You're the strongest, brightest man I ever met – my Purple Hugh. If we have to wait a little longer, well, we'll wait."

The fire had burned down dangerously low while they'd been rivetted on problems and misunderstandings. Hugh stirred the embers awake and cross-hatched a few thin sticks with a larger one on top, incidentally giving himself a moment to recover from his childish choking-up. Then he and Nancy settled sitting side-by-side again, with their backs against the buffalo robe padded cutbank. Nancy said: "Anyways, there's a good chance Monsieur MacGregor might not want to head west right away like he'd said. That National Committee is planning something big, and it's going to happen soon."

"What's going to happen?"

"I don't know. But those Metis gallopers that met the buffalo hunt was talking real excited and thoughtful to the Metis hunters about something they wasn't saying to us from St. Peters. Oh, they was friendly enough to us, but it was like they didn't trust us. And they're right not to."

"Why not?"

"Because my uncle the Chief, Pabator Kokorsis, he's like his father. The old stories about my grandfather say all he cared about was his tribe, the people he was responsible for. Back in the Fur Trade War he stayed just enough friendly to both the Hudson's Bay Company and the North West Company, that both sides thought maybe us Saulteaux was on their side. Until he saw for sure which side was going to win. My uncle's the same way."

"Well, I guess that's the way he should be."

"That's the way he *is*. Let's move closer to the fire so we can warm our hands."

Not long after Hugh got home, he learned what the 'something big' was the National Committee had been planning. Da had been called away to another emergency meeting at the courthouse. Hugh was just finishing a late lunch when he heard Da's voice approaching the house, calling Donald and Aleck to come inside with him. Hugh looked up to see Mum turn toward the door with a strangely anxious expression, as though she'd heard something in Da's voice Hugh couldn't. He saw her glance at the staircase to make sure Mary Ann Bella hadn't woken from her afternoon nap, and then mechanically proceed to lift the kettle onto the stove and crumple tea leaves into the tea pot.

Once Da and Donald and Aleck had got their coats and boots off and were seated around the table with Hugh and Mum and Da, Da said: "Well, um…" then breathed in and out and in again. "The Metis have taken Fort Garry."

Hugh looked at Donald and Aleck, who were looking at him and each other. Mum said: "What?"

"The Metis – well, I shouldn't say 'the Metis,' just, um, those that are following… *'President'* Bruce and his National Committee, but those are enough to… They came across the Assiniboine, or along the banks of the Red through the trees, just in, um, groups of three or four, so as not to look… *suspicious*. I don't know if they brought a little scaling ladder or two, but, hell, Ambroise Lépine could… *throw* a man high enough to get his hands on the parapet, and once one man's up there and, um, lowers a rope, and then another man with another rope… And you know Fort Garry – with all the tall buildings around the main square, no one sees the back wall, and there's no, um, sentries patrolling along the firing ledge there, unless there's some… *suspected* danger, and no one suspected…

"Well, some people are saying The Company suspected and did nothing to, um, prevent, but what was The Company to do? Call out Special Constables and make ready for, um, a siege and a civil… *war*…? Anyway, the men most likely to, um, heed the call and side with The Company, are the ones most… *against* Canada taking us over, and so are the very ones most likely to join in taking over Fort Garry to keep Canada out."

Da rubbed his temples with the heels of his hands and regained his thread. "*So*, when there were a hundred and more of them inside the walls – all, um, well-armed, of course – they told the guard at the front gates to… *step aside*, opened the gates to President Bruce and Secretary Riel and others waiting in the woods, and told Dr. Cowan – he's standing in as Chief Officer while Governor Mactavish is bedridden… They told Dr. Cowan that Fort Garry is now…" Da fanned out his fingers in finality, "… the headquarters of the National Committee."

There was a silence. Hugh could understand why no one else seemed to know what to say or think, because he surely didn't. The whole face of the world had changed. All his life 'Fort Garry' had been a passive kind of name, just a place to house The Company's men and goods, and all its cannons and stone walls were just to prevent the Sioux or Assiniboines or American whiskey traders from even thinking about raiding The Company's storehouses. Fort Garry had seemed no more a military installation than the compound of St. Boniface Cathedral. Now suddenly 'Fort Garry' meant a stronghold with armed sentries patrolling the walls, and gunners standing by the cannons. Cannons pointing outward at Winnipeg, Kildonan, St. Boniface…

"Apparently," Da parted the silence, "when Dr. Cowan asked Louis Riel what, um, this was all about, Monsieur Riel told him they'd come to guard the fort from an… *impending* danger, but wouldn't say what the danger was. So now, The Company's men and their families aren't exactly, um, prisoners, but no one can leave or enter the fort without… *permission* from the National Committee."

Mum said tightly: "What… what do you think they're up to, Father, this National Committee?"

"I believe they mean no harm –"

"No harm? Fort Garry is the *home* of The Company and its people. Would you call it no harm if men with guns moved into our home without a by-your-leave and tell us they'd decide who could come and go?"

"Well, so far as I understand they haven't, um, actually 'moved into' any of The Company's warehouses or living quarters. They're taking that… *principle* so far that the off-duty guards are bedding down inside the fort walls but outside the buildings, sleeping in the snow. They haven't, um, dispossessed anybody, just taken possession of the fort." Da brightened. "And now as you've got me thinking on those lines, Mother, taking possession of the fort may have been, um, a very wise thing for the… *National Committee* to do. For all our sakes.

"You see, the last couple of days I've been, um, worried about a… *possibility* I didn't want to worry you with. There was a chance that, um, Dr. Schultz and Colonel Dennis and a few others here, might've got enough… *hotheads* together, from Portage la Prairie and elsewhere, go down and get the Lieutenant Governor and his people and his… *arsenal*, and try to, um, force the barricade at St. Norbert. But now, you see – Fort Garry was to be the Lieutenant Governor's headquarters, and his… *residence*. So now, even if they could force past the barricade – which is unlikely, I doubt there's fifty men in the whole territory would, um, take up arms to bring the Canadian governor here. But they might've *tried*…"

Hugh got an image of dozens of men shooting and hacking at each other on the road south of St. Norbert, a stretch of road he'd ridden up and down a hundred times. He guessed that a few years back it might've been a hazy image, just variations on the time-smudged drawings of battles in old illustrated magazines. Now he saw clear, bright-coloured, queasy variations on that Saulteaux warrior trying to keep his guts and blood from pouring out through the hole Francis Desmarais had slashed in him.

"But now," Da went on, nodding with a kind of satisfaction, "even if, um, some people have been… *thinking* of forcing the Lieutenant Governor's, um, passage to Red River, now they are faced with the fact that there is nowhere here to bring him to. And, where else but Fort Garry could the National Committee, um, house all its armed men in one place, instead of… *scattered* throughout the settlement, where all kinds of flare-ups might happen? No, the more I think of it, Mother, the more it seems like… *taking* Fort Garry was the best way to keep things from getting out of hand. I mean, um, more out of hand than they are already."

"Nonetheless," Mum said, "when the children get home from school I'll tell them that from now on, for now, they go nowhere but straight to school and straight back home again – and definitely no venturing anywhere south of Point Douglas." She turned to Hugh, Donald and Aleck. "And the same goes for you three. Stay away from Winnipeg and Fort Garry."

"Of course, Mum."

"Certainly, Mum."

"Absolutely, Mum."

CHAPTER 39

Agnes sat by a sidetable she'd pulled next to a corner window in the common room, nibbling biscuits and sipping sherry by the light of a lamp turned down so low it barely cast a glow – any lower and the wick would've snuffed out. But turning the lamp any higher would've turned the window into an impenetrable black mirror. As it was she could see any movement outside through the ghost of her reflection, especially given a clear, moonlit night with the roads white with snow.

There was another ghost reflection beside Agnes's: that of Eliza Mair nee McKenney. Agnes glanced sideways to reassure herself Eliza was really there. That afternoon, Eliza and Charles had reappeared out of nowhere, or out of limbo, which seemed apt for a Catholic incarceration. They'd spent the last few days as 'guests' of the Grey Nuns' mission in St. Norbert, while the geniuses who manned the barrier for the National Committee tried to decide whether the Mairs qualified as residents of Red River or members of Lieutenant Governor McDougall's entourage.

Agnes and Eliza were sitting waiting for their husbands to come home. The corner window gave them a view north along Main Road – as people were starting to abbreviate 'the main road north to the Stone Fort' – or west along the short 'street' leading from the crossroads to the river, both of the routes their men might be taking from the public meeting at the Engine House. There were almost fifty buildings in the village of Winnipeg now, most of them wood and some of them quite close together; the dangers of a fire came clear a couple of years earlier, when old Andrew McDermot's new house burned down and no bucket brigade could save it. So through public subscriptions, and donations from The Company and the Council of Assiniboia, the village had bought a secondhand still-serviceable manpower-pump fire wagon and freighted it from St. Paul. Governor Mactavish had been so generous that the enterprise was christened 'Mactavish Fire Engine Company No. 1.' The building put up to house it and future engines was large enough and still empty enough to accommodate a public meeting.

Tonight's meeting was in response to a printed proclamation issued in English by the National Committee in Fort Garry. Walter Bown had refused to print it on the *Nor'Wester* press, so the Metis bullyboys had forced Dr. Bown at gunpoint to stand back and had brought in someone else who knew how to run the machinery. James Ross, ex-editor of

The Nor'Wester and ex-Sheriff and -Postmaster of Red River, had returned to his ancestral home after seven years in Toronto.

It seemed to Agnes an odd coincidence that a number of troublesome men had chosen to return to Red River just when trouble was about to start. It wasn't just that James Ross had suddenly taken it in mind to pack up his wife and children and new law degree and come home. Louis Riel, from what she'd heard, had only recently reappeared after ten years in the east. And William Coldwell, who'd sold *The Nor'Wester* to Christian when the original print shop burned down, and gone home to Ontario, had come back to Red River with the last cart-train of the year bearing a new printing press and plans to start a rival newspaper called *The Pioneer*. Fussy and fastidious William Coldwell still hadn't got *The Pioneer*'s printing press set up to his satisfaction, but James Ross had seen to it that the National Committee's proclamation got printed nonetheless:

> *The President and Representatives of the French-speaking population of Rupert's Land in Council (the invaders of our rights being now expelled) already aware of your sympathy, do extend the hand of friendship to you, our friendly fellow inhabitants; and in so doing do invite you to send twelve Representatives... in order to form one body with the above Council, consisting of twelve members, to consider the present political state of this Country, and to adopt such measures as may be deemed best for the future welfare of the same.*

The proclamation named ten parishes who were to elect one representative each, and two from 'the town of Winnipeg.' Agnes's husband and other loyal Canadians had tried to explain to their fellow citizens that sending representatives would be giving the National Committee an appearance of legitimacy. But the general opinion was in favour of at least having some conversation with 'President' John Bruce & Co. So, since the 'town of Winnipeg' would be electing two representatives regardless, it was patently obvious that one of those two should be Dr. John Christian Schultz. Tonight's meeting at the Engine House was to make that official and to select the other.

Either the meeting had gone on longer than expected, or something had happened after. Agnes and Eliza had spent the first couple of hours in their window seats enthusiastically catching each other up on the last couple of months, happy to have no men around to inhibit the conversation. But for the last while they'd been mostly silent. Neither one of them had said aloud that she was starting to get worried, but these were worrisome times.

Agnes spotted something moving on Main Road, a clutch of human beings walking south. She moved to blow out the lamp so she could see outside more clearly, then hesitated and just shaded the glow with her hand. Four men walking side-by-side, just silhouettes against the snow. There was no reason Christian and Charlie might not be walking back from the meeting in company with two other men, but...

Eliza leaned forward and said: "Is it them?"

"Oh, no, none of them's tall enough to be your Uncle John. And look at the way they're walking – moccasins, not boots." The silhouettes showed the barrels of guns crooked in arms or slung over shoulders. "It's the Night Patrol."

"The which?"

"The Night Patrol, sent out from Fort Garry every sundown since the National Committee took possession. They claim the reason they walk Winnipeg all night long is to make sure no riff-raff takes advantage of the current state of confusion to break into stores or steal horses. How thoughtful of them. A.G.B. Bannatyne has given them the use of his kitchen, even when everyone in the house is abed, so the Night Patrol can warm themselves between rounds. Rather an odd gesture on Mr. Bannatyne's part."

"Is it?"

"I'd say."

That gesture of A.G.B. Bannatyne's exemplified what Agnes's husband and Colonel Dennis and all the other loyal Canadians found most frustrating about the current situation. The locals of British stock were so intermingled with the Metis and Indians that it was almost impossible to draw clear lines. So Christian had seen at least one bright spot in the National Committee's proclamation: the fact they had defined themselves in black and white as 'the Representatives of the French-speaking population.' That would go a long way toward showing people in Ontario and the rest of the world that the insurrection at Red River was entirely on the part of the French halfbreeds, and probably encouraged by the Roman Catholic Church and Quebec.

The National Committee had been the subject of much animated conversation in the common room above the White Store, as Colonel Dennis and Christian and others had tried to pool scraps of information to get a picture of the three men at the head of it. Agnes had enjoyed those conversations, because her time in St. Boniface meant she'd seen and heard a lot of useful snippets to contribute. The resulting pictures were only sketches, but since the three men in question seemed rather sketchy themselves, that would do. 'President' John Bruce, despite his stout Scots name, was French Metis, about forty years old, an uneducated carpenter who'd sometimes acted as go-between for his confréres because he spoke serviceable English and several Indian dialects. 'Secretary' Louis Riel was in his mid-twenties, a preening Mama's-boy who'd come back from the east with his tail between his legs after failing as an apprentice priest and an apprentice lawyer. 'Adjutant-General' Ambroise Lépine was about thirty and it seemed his major qualifications as a military leader were that he was bigger and stronger than any of his 'soldiers'; no doubt his head was even thicker than his biceps. All in all, not exactly an impressive trio.

Agnes saw a lone man walking down Main Road, and when he passed by the Night Patrol going back in the opposite direction he showed a head taller than any of them. She blew out the lamp and pressed her nose to the cold window glass. No, it was *two* men – a much shorter one trying to keep up with the other's longer legs and sometimes falling behind. The tall one was definitely her Christian, striding quickly with his hands in his coat pockets and his barndoor shoulders hunched.

Agnes and Eliza moved the lamp and biscuits into the kitchen, put more wood in the stove, set the kettle to boil and took down the teapot and brandy decanter. By that time Agnes could hear footsteps thudding up the stairs, oddly heavily and ponderously – for all his size and weight, Christian's footsteps didn't usually thud. He loomed into the kitchen still wearing his coat and hat and snowy boots. Without saying a word, he flopped onto one of the kitchen chairs, creaking its joints, took off his fur hat and dropped it on the floor, took the top off the brandy decanter and poured brandy in his teacup without waiting for his tea. Charlie Mair appeared in the doorway looking a bit flushed and flustered, but purse-mouthed.

By way of starting some communication, Agnes said to her husband: "So, who's the other Representative?"

"Other?" He took a large swallow of brandy and exhaled the heat through his nostrils. "Other… They elected Henry McKenney."

Agnes could see how her husband would be annoyed at the prospect of sharing a bench with his half-brother and onetime business partner; they could barely share the same room together. But since it seemed a pill he was going to have to swallow, she said: "I suppose it was inevitable they'd be impressed with him being Sheriff all these years. Still, I would've thought they'd keep in mind his principles have shifted toward American annexation."

"Principles? Henry has no principles. The only reason he wants us to get swallowed into Yankee jurisdiction is he owes so much money to Canadian investors." Christian poured some more brandy into his teacup, then said with elaborate precision: "The elected Representatives to the National Committee from the town of Winnipeg are 'Sheriff' McKenney and Hugh O'Lone."

Agnes's head twitched on her neck. "Pardon me? I don't understand."

"Surely you remember Mr. Hugh F. O'Lone Esquire, late of Hell's Kitchen, New York City, co-proprietor of the Red Dog Saloon just across the road from us…? They elected him instead of me."

"That's preposterous!"

"Is it? Maybe it is, but I've seen this kind of thing all my life – men smiling in my face and shaking my hand, but when it comes right down to it I'm not a member of the club. Dammit I *built* this town!" Christian slammed his open hand down on the table, making the teacups jump. "Oh, you can say Henry was here before me, but if I hadn't talked Kew into investing, McKenney & Company would've gone under and Noah's Ark never would've got built. And if I hadn't taken all those trips to Canada, talking-up Red River, giving speeches, encouraging politicians and businessmen to look this way…" His fine, big, handsome face twisted up with rage and something else.

Agnes felt her own face burning at the unfairness of it all. She said: "I still can't believe they'd elect two Americans – well, one American and one who wants to be."

"I can. I should've known the meeting would be loaded – in more ways than one. Hugh and Bob O'Lone have probably been serving out free drinks all week. And old

Andrew McDermot and his sons are staying out of the whole business entirely, so there's a block of votes gone. Dammit, if I'd seen it coming I could've brought in some good Canadian lads from Headingley and Portage, put them up here so they'd be residents of Winnipeg…"

The kettle was singing. Agnes got up to fill the teapot, then went around the table to put her hand on her husband's shoulder. She said: "There'll be other meetings. You'll be ready for them then."

Two mornings later, shortly before the appointed hour of noon, Agnes stood at the south windows of the common room with her husband, Charles and Eliza Mair, Walter Bown and Superintendent Snow, looking across the windswept white wasteland at the courthouse where the Representatives and the National Committee were due to convene. Colonel Dennis likely would've been at the windows with them, but he'd gone down to Pembina to confer with the Lieutenant Governor, taking a back trail that didn't entail the barricade at St. Norbert. Rumour had it that Lieutenant Governor McDougall had hired Pembina locals to quickly build a large log cabin and he and his entire staff, and the wives who'd accompanied them west, were all living in it, crammed cheek-by-jowl. If true, it was a shocking state of affairs for people honoured by Royal appointments, and Agnes was sure the men responsible would pay for it.

Ranked on either side of the steps to the courthouse door were a hundred or so armed Metis, looking like a mockery of tin soldiers in their multicoloured blanket coats and beaded buckskins. As the delegates began to arrive, on sleighs or saddlehorses or on foot, the ragged ranks of Metis 'soldiers' fired their guns at the sky in something resembling a volley, the gunshots crackling in the crispy air. Charles Mair said: "Hard to tell sometimes the difference between a salute and a threat," but before the words were all out of his mouth there came another, deeper crash, a staccato rumbling. Agnes looked to Fort Garry – a toy fort at that distance – and saw puffs of smoke rising all along the north wall.

Superintendent Snow said: "They're showing us they know how to load the cannons."

Christian said: "Loading in a blank charge and touching it off ain't gunnery. When I was working the lake boats back in Ontario I watched the naval gunners training and, believe me, it's not a simple science."

By then the Representatives had all arrived and gone inside, the show was over and Agnes and the others went back to going about the business of their day. Which wasn't much, there wasn't a lot of retail commerce going on at Red River these days. But just in case an actual customer appeared, Agnes took charge of the counter while Christian and the stockboy attended to a large stock-shifting operation. Since the Superintendent of the road-building expedition currently had no crew to supervise, Mr. Snow lent a hand, and so did Charlie and Eliza.

The stock-shifting wouldn't have been necessary under normal circumstances. In a far corner of the warehouse was a padlocked enclosure for the barrels of imported spirits, including raw alcohol to be poured into bottles of dried herbs labelled 'Dr. Doyle's Tonic.'

Now some of the barrels were moved out onto the warehouse floor and replaced by the kegs of gunpowder kept in the 'auxiliary warehouse' – the set-apart shed where Agnes had once imprisoned Constable Mulligan. All of the guns and ammunition in the warehouse and on display in the store were moved into the enclosure as well.

The current stockboy was technically an English Protestant halfbreed, not French Catholic, but one never knew with those people. So when all the arms had been safely locked away, Christian put the key in his waistcoat pocket, handed Agnes the spare and told the stockboy: "If a customer wants to buy a gun or lead or anything of the kind, you tell him you're not sure we have any left in stock, then come and find me or Mrs. Schultz and we'll determine whether said customer is someone we want to sell firearms to. You understand?"

"Yessir, Dr. Schultz."

Freed from the counter, Agnes spent part of her afternoon helping her husband compose a letter to a gentleman in Portage la Prairie, another to a man in Headingley and a third to someone in St. James. It seemed Christian had taken to heart her encouragement that there would be other public meetings, and was determined that the next one would be loaded from the right side. But he kept glancing out the window at the courthouse, cracking his knuckles or drumming his fingers on the windowsill, helpless to affect the meeting that was going on there.

The evening brought a visitor at the side door, a graduate of St. John's College who held a part-time position clerking for Judge Black. Agnes poured tea while Christian reached down the whiskey bottle for added warmth. Their visitor blew on his fingers and said: "They wouldn't've let me in the courthouse, except I have to make ready for the Quarterly Session day after tomorrow. So they let me go into the back office and I left the door ajar."

Christian said: "Were you able to overhear much of the meeting?"

"All of it, what there was to hear. Oh, there was a great deal said but not much said, if you gather my drift. Most of it was James Ross trading insults with Louis Riel. The French want the English to stand with them to negotiate with Canada – negotiate terms for us becoming part of the Dominion. The English don't want to agree to do that until they know what terms the French have in mind; the French don't want to tell them the terms until the English agree."

Agnes could see her husband brightening at the stalemate, and at the fact that the two sides were already being referred to as the French versus the English, Riel versus Ross. That would help dispel confusing details such as one of the 'French' delegates being named O'Donoghue. She said: "So nothing happened at this famous Meeting."

"Oh, something happened, for sure…" The young man paused to drain the last of his teacup. Agnes poured him more tea and Christian pushed the whiskey bottle closer to his teacup. "Just before the meeting adjourned till tomorrow. What happened was, Governor Mactavish had written a letter meant to be read out to the assemblage – well, I guess he dictated it, I hear the consumption's got so bad he can't even sit up at a desk anymore. His secretary brought it to Sheriff McKenney, but half the meeting didn't want it to get read out and half did. The compromise was it would be read at the end of the meeting, and even at that, Sheriff McKenney had to remind President Bruce as he was starting to adjourn. After the meeting the sheriff took the letter over to Mr. Coldwell's office to be typeset and printed tomorrow."

Christian said: "And to Dr. Bown's office…?"

"Nope, I heard no mention of *The Nor'Wester*. I guess that letter'll be the inaugural edition of *The Pioneer*."

Christian jolted out of his chair and paced. "Look at my back, Agnes, do you think there's room left for any more knives?" Although he was technically no longer owner of *The Nor'Wester*, it was still his newspaper, and here it was being passed over in favour of his interloping, onetime partner.

Agnes said to the part-time court clerk: "What did the letter say?"

"Oh, it's long, I can't remember it all and I'd probably garble what I can remember. But… Governor Mactavish's secretary brought a couple of drafts of it and sat down to sort them out in the office behind the courtroom, the office I was working in. He left one of them there." He reached inside his coat and came out with several sheets of paper folded together.

Christian snatched the letter from his hand. Agnes said: "Christian…?" and her husband politely sat down beside her so they could read it together. Agnes skimmed it through quickly to get the gist, sliding the second and third pages out from under the first while Christian was taking it in word by word. *'Whereas I William Mactavish Governor of Assiniboia have been informed that a meeting is to be held today… I NOTIFY ALL WHOM IT CONCERNS… during the last few weeks large bodies of armed men have committed the following unlawful acts…'* Then there were four numbered paragraphs, delineating that said men had obstructed the liberty of travellers to and from Red River, had seized and detained imports of merchandise, had interfered with the public mails and had unlawfully taken possession of Fort Garry.

The final paragraph was so delicious that when Christian got to that page Agnes re-read it slowly to savour it. *'You are dealing with a crisis out of which may come incalculable good or immeasurable evil and with all the weight of my official authority and all the influence of my individual position let me finally charge you to adopt only such means as are lawful and constitutional and rational and safe.'* But on second reading it didn't seem as unequivocal as it had at first. It sounded like a father who didn't necessarily disapprove of the course his children were taking, just urged them to go cautiously. Governor Mactavish's wife was the mixed-blood, Catholic daughter of old Andrew McDermot, and sister to the Annie Bannatyne who'd horsewhipped Charles Mair, so Mactavish's personal sympathies might actually lean towards the group his factual children belonged to. But most of the rest of the letter seemed to state clearly that The Company's Governor of Assiniboia and Rupert's Land was ordering the National Committee to cease and desist.

When Christian had finished carefully absorbing the letter, he looked at Agnes and she at him, and she could see he was having the same thought she was. It wasn't a thought they should voice, though, while the young man who'd brought the letter was still present. Christian turned to him and said: "When Canada assumes its lawful position of authority here, I'll let it be known to some people I know, that you did this."

"You, uh, won't let anybody know before then…?"

"You have my word."

As soon as the visitor was gone, Christian stood up and reached for his coat, saying: "It won't necessarily keep Bown up *all* the night typesetting and printing, with me to help him – and he's got an apprentice bunking in beside the print shop…"

"Christian…?"

"Yes, dear?"

"You know it's not unusual for a newspaper to use an amalgamated name: *Herald-Tribune*, or *Times And Chronicle*, or the like…?"

"Um-hm."

"Since this Special Extra of *The Nor'Wester* will likely be printed and out in circulation before Coldwell finishes fussbudgetly setting up the first edition of *The Pioneer*, is there any law against *The Nor'Wester* re-christening itself '*The Nor'Wester And Pioneer*?"

He laughed. "You little dickens. No, as a matter of fact, there doesn't seem to be any law against much of anything around here these days."

The Special Extra Edition of *The Nor'Wester And Pioneer*, published to make public Governor Mactavish's 'Proclamation to the Inhabitants of Red River' – and incidentally including a statement from several unnamed 'Prominent Citizens of Winnipeg' urging the Governor to act on his own words – scooped the maiden edition of *The Pioneer* by a good eight hours. Agnes happily pictured William Backstabbing Coldwell chewing pieces out of his neat mustache in the office of *The Pioneer*.

The second day of the conference of Representatives and the National Committee stretched out very long, since the next day they would have to give up the courthouse to Judge Black for the quarterly session of the Court of Assiniboia. It seemed somewhat unreal to Agnes that with the air filled with insurrection, with the country officially under Canadian authority but the Canadian authorities kept out of the country, there should still be a toy court sitting to determine whether Matheson should be fined because his dog chased Inkster's sheep. But so it was. Christian sat up late, pretending to read but constantly glancing out the window toward the courthouse. So Agnes sat up with him, doing her needlework while he read to her from an odd new book titled *Alice's Adventures in Wonderland* . It seemed appropriate for the general atmosphere these days, and contained some delightfully nonsensical poetry not unlike the kind John Christian Schultz used to pencil when he was young and lonely and had time on his hands. As the Apostle said '… but when I became a man, I put away childish things…'

It was after midnight when Christian abruptly stood up, leaned closer to the window facing the courthouse, and said: "There they go, finally." He went to the coat tree at the top of the stairs and donned his long-skirted buffalo coat, saying: "Some of them are bound to be heading for Dutch George's or the Red Dog Saloon, I'll just go see what I can hear." But instead of starting down the stairs, he went into their bedroom. When he came back out a moment later and proceeded toward the stairs, he said: "I don't expect I'll be gone long, but there's no need to wait up for me."

Agnes was fairly certain why he'd detoured into the bedroom, but once he was gone she went to satisfy her curiosity. When she slid open the drawer of the bedside table on his side of the bed, the British-made Adams Pocket Revolver that lived there wasn't there.

Given that, and the current air of uncertainty, and the offhanded violence of the Mad Hatter's Tea Party, Agnes thought she was in no danger of dozing off while her husband was gone. But she woke up in her chair to the sound of him stomping snow off his boots at the foot of the stairs. By the time he'd got up the stairs she was awake enough to stand up blearily. He came and kissed her forehead before taking off his coat, saying: "I said there was no need to wait up." He smelled of stale beer and tobacco.

"I was worried."

"That's sweet of you, but I'm sorry you were." He went and hung his buffalo coat back onto the coat tree that had had to be screwed down to keep its weight from overtoppling it. He seemed somewhat jaunty; certainly much more so than the last time he'd clumped up those stairs late at night. When he came back coatless to the chair nearest to hers, the tavern smell was much less evident.

Agnes said: "What did you hear?"

"Well, it's excellent, my dear, excellent. Given we couldn't stop this Convention from taking place, or have a voice in it, we couldn't've asked for a better outcome. They've decided… nothing."

Christian grinned so wide she had to laugh.

"Apparently Chief Henry Prince, the Representative from St. Peters, didn't say a word all through yesterday's meeting and most of today's. Late in today's – tonight's – session, he finally stood up and said two things. The first was in reference to the smallarms and cannonfire salutes yesterday morning. He said that among his people it was customary to not bring guns to a peace conference. And he said that as far as he could tell, the convention was a lot of dilly-dallying to no purpose. They're to convene again on Monday, and my guess is if by the end of Monday they haven't made some sort of progress toward agreeing on a course of action, then the convention will end and the lines will be clearly drawn."

"Which lines?"

"The line between us and the French – or at least those French who've sided with the National Committee. I think this calls for a toast." While he'd been talking, too animatedly to sit for long, Christian had sprung up to reach down the precious bottle of Old Glenlivet from its cubbyhole at the top of the sideboard, set out two lead crystal glasses and dipped the small Delft water pitcher in one of the buckets the halfbreed cook filled every evening from the river before going home so the sediment would settle by next morning. Christian poured a wee dram of whiskey into each delicate-stemmed glass, added a dollop of water, handed one glass to Agnes, clinked his against hers and raised his with: "To Canada."

Agnes downed her dram dutifully – she actually didn't like the taste, but it was expensive so it must be good. Once she'd got her breath back, she said: "And then?"

"Huh? 'And then' what?"

"That's what I mean. Once the lines are clearly drawn between us and the others, then what?" Agnes heard a Cheshire cat saying, *'That depends a good deal on where you want to get to'* – Agnes In Wonderland – and decided she was still half asleep. She shook her head to clear it, but her question still stood.

"Then," her husband replied, "we gather together all the stout hearts and strong arms who see the only sensible course of action is to bring in the lawful government waiting just across the border, and once we make a show of force the National Committee will fade away like the bullying cowards they are."

'A show of force' made Agnes see the stacks of guns and ammunition locked in the warehouse just below. The implications were frightening, but also a bit thrilling.

The next day, the 18th of November, brought several of those 'stout hearts' from Portage la Prairie and Headingley – young men who'd immigrated from Canada in the last year or two to work on Superintendent Snow's road, or to stake out a farm before the transfer, or both. They took up residence in the lodging rooms above the White Store, so they would qualify as residents of Winnipeg for the next public meeting. The next day brought more of them. With so many mouths to feed, Agnes never would've stood for her husband's decree that the halfbreed cook had to be temporarily discharged – since one never knew who was passing along eavesdropping to whom these days – except that Eliza was there, and Mrs. Stewart came over to help, from the 'house' that was part of her husband's stipend as pharmacy clerk. And some of those stouthearted males were actually capable of peeling potatoes, under supervision.

That 19th of November was also the last day of the Quarterly Session of the Court of Assiniboia, likely its last sitting ever. The last case Judge Black tried was the charge of assault laid by Superintendent Snow against Thomas Scott and others. Agnes and everyone else in town heard the outcome even before Mr. Snow trudged back from the courthouse to his temporary lodgings above the White Store. Thomas Scott and one of the other road-crew strikers were each fined four pounds. The reason the news of the verdict travelled so quickly was that immediately after the sentence was pronounced, Thomas Scott remarked loudly and clearly: "It's a pity we didn't chuck him in the river and get our money's worth." Superintendent Snow didn't appear to see the humour in it.

CHAPTER 40

Schultz angled across the wide, snow-packed crossroads of the Portage Road and Main Road, heading for the Emmerling Hotel. Charles Mair was with him, and two of the lads from Portage la Prairie – people generally travelled in groups these days. The reconvened convention at the courthouse had just broken up for the day, and there was a good chance one or two of the Representatives from the parishes north of Winnipeg would stop at Dutch George's on their way home. The two representatives from Winnipeg would undoubtedly be at the Red Dog Saloon, and Schultz didn't fancy asking his half-brother for anything, even information. Another reason to opt for Dutch George's was that Enos Stutsman, the legless American lawyer, had hove in to Red River that morning and was staying at Dutch George Emmerling's establishment. Stutsman was as much of an American Annexionist as Henry or the O'Lone brothers, but he would do business with anybody.

The public room at Dutch George's wasn't doing a roaring business, but was far from empty. Schultz spotted Thomas Scott and a few of the other ex-road crew lads at a corner table and nodded in their direction; Scott nodded back. At another corner table was Enos Stutsman, with his back to the wall, his plug hat on and his crutches leaned against his chair. But standing at the bar with the snow not yet melted off his moccasins was an elegant-postured man with a black widow's peak and Van Dyke, long nose and aristocratic cheekbones: James Ross, ex-several offices at Red River, and now the convention representative for Kildonan. So Stutsman became a secondary consideration. Schultz strolled over to the bar and said: "Good evening, Mr. Ross."

Ross nodded and replied rather distantly, "Dr. Schultz." They'd been on the same side in the Reverend Corbett affair, but since then Ross's years in Toronto studying law and writing for *The Globe* had made Ross an unknown quantity. Some rumours had it that the reason Ross had got himself elected Representative was he was secretly working for Lieutenant Governor McDougall and hoped to sabotage the convention from within; other rumours had it that Ross was secretly in league with the National Committee, and only put up arguments to make it look like the meetings bore some resemblance to democracy. Schultz's own opinion was that James Ross would argue with Noah about whether the weather had turned dampish.

Schultz said: "Might I buy you a drink?" and Ross became more cordial. When the bartender poured two shot glasses of whiskey, Schultz said: "Leave the bottle," and Ross grew even more cordial. Schultz sipped at the harsh local poison; Ross downed his in one gulp and reached for the bottle. Schultz said: "So, any progress made today?"

"Depends on what you mean by progress."

"Well… was there much reaction to Mr. Stewart's petition?"

"Huh. You mean *your* petition."

"The heading signature was Mr. James Stewart's."

"No doubt, but I edited enough of your copy at *The Nor'Wester* to know your style." Ross had finished his second shot glass and was pouring himself a third. The drink had no noticeable effect on him, except to make his voice a bit more resonant. "There was no reaction to said petition, because it was ruled out of order and not allowed to be tabled at the meeting. Don't feel singled out – A.G.B. Bannatyne sent a public statement, declaring why he'd refused to sign said petition, and it wasn't allowed to be read out, either. The landscape's bristling with petitions; Colonel Dennis's bookkeeper's shopping one around, too."

Despite that, Schultz had no doubt Representative McKenney had specifically maneuvered the Stewart petition out of the meeting, since part of its substance was that Sheriff McKenney and Mr. H.F. O'Lone weren't properly representing the interests of the citizens of Winnipeg. He said: "So what *did* happen at the meeting?"

"A lot of shilly-shallying. Towards the end of the day, the representative from St. Clements stood up and said if we can't come to some agreement by the end of tomorrow's meeting, we might as well bring the Honourable McDougall up from Pembina so we can talk to Canada directly. Secretary Riel jumped up and shouted that under no circumstances would William McDougall be allowed to cross the border, neither in his official capacity nor as a private citizen."

Schultz wondered how much credence he could put in James Ross's perception of events. It was said Ross had been seldom sober since reappearing at Red River, which made Schultz wonder whether Ross had been always intending to come home once he'd got his law degree, or had discovered there was no place for a half-Indian lawyer in Toronto. But Schultz had noticed before with habitual drunkards that in time their features grew blurred, almost as if showing the outside world what the drunkard's blurred vision saw in a mirror. Ross's features were still sharp, so maybe his perceptions were, too. Schultz said: "And what did President Bruce say?"

"John Bruce doesn't say much of anything, just chairs the meetings and lets Louis Riel do most of the talking. Maybe Bruce says more in the backroom meetings. There's sure gonna be a lot of those tonight, all up and down Red River," Ross shook his head slowly, "maybe all night long. Even some of the representatives from the so-called French parishes are losing patience. If the National Committee doesn't come up with something substantial by tomorrow, this Convention is just going to fizzle away."

Schultz let Ross fill his glass once more, then picked up his bottle and his own glass and started towards Enos Stutsman's table. Despite his petition getting snookered, the news from the meeting was encouraging. He liked the sound of *'fizzle away.'*

There were two other gentlemen at Enos Stutsman's table. Stutsman looked up, waved his cigar sideways and they both moved elsewhere. As Schultz came up to the table, Stutsman drawled: "Well, *Doctor*..." putting an odd note of irony into the title. "Wondered when you were going to get around to me."

"Well, *Colonel*..." Stutsman was Honorary Colonel of some trumpery American militia or volunteer outfit.

The cigar pointed at the empty chair across the table and Schultz sat down, placing his bottle in the middle of the table. Stutsman appeared to be amused about something, and tossed a folded newspaper across the table. It turned out to be the latest edition of *The St. Paul Pioneer*, and the story it was folded to was an interview with a Canadian businessman who'd recently been making some arrangements at Red River and had left homeward just after the Lieutenant Governor was due to arrive. Said Canadian businessman declared that a hundred Red River halfbreeds had indeed ridden south to prevent the Honourable William McDougall from entering the territory, but half of them had deserted en route and the remaining fifty felt so foolish they'd turned themselves into an honour guard to escort him to Fort Garry, where the Lieutenant Governor and his staff took up governing Rupert's Land as they'd been appointed to do.

Schultz had to skim through the article again to make sure he'd read what he thought he'd read, then he looked up at Enos Stutsman in some confusion. Stutsman chuckled, "Shocking, isn't it, Doctor? Simply shocking, that untruths could be printed in a newspaper...?"

"But... I know the man they're quoting; he's neither a drunkard nor a fool; what would he possibly have to gain by baldfaced lying to the St. Paul press?"

Now Stutsman laughed aloud. "*Now* I understand you, Doctor – you have no trouble grasping the notion of lies printed in a newspaper, you just can't see a motive in this case. Well, my guess is that your Canadian friend was trying to keep ambitious Americans from getting the idea that the country north of the Medicine Line is up for grabs. But it's going to backfire on him – 'cause when folks south of the line find out this was a pack of lies, it's going to make the situation up here seem even more desperate. And it's not hard for folks down there to find out the Honourable McDougall's still cooling his heels in Pembina. Matter of fact, I had an interview with him and his staff there not two days ago."

Schultz refilled his shot-glass to try and appear nonchalant, and proffered the bottle to Stutsman. Stutsman was drinking beer, but shrugged and poured a dollop of whiskey into his tankard, saying: "Only way to drink this horse-piss."

Schultz took a small sip and said: "What occasioned you to call on the Lieutenant Governor?"

"Oh, there's some Chippewas north of the line I done some business with back when. They'd been planning to send a delegation to His Honourableness, but then after the Metis stopped him at the border they thought it might look like a conspiracy, like the Chippewa and the halfbreeds were in league with each other."

"And are they?" wondering: *'And are you?'*

"How would I know? Anyway, so the Chippewa just got me to write up what they wanted to say in a letter and hand it to him – basically that they were nervous because some white men had been surveying their lands, that their lands had never been sold to The Company nor anybody else, and they were looking forward to talking treaty with Himself when circumstances allowed."

Schultz was momentarily distracted by noticing that despite the name, Enos Stutsman actually looked like a cartoon Irishman, with his plug hat, bristly leprechaun sidewhiskers and potato-y face. It just needed a clay pipe in place of his cigar. Schultz had to glance away to get his mind off the image and back onto what was coming out of its mouth. Cartoon Irishmen be damned, it was best to be very alert when conversing with Enos Stutsman.

"So, I got to meet the whole Royally Appointed Government of The Dominion of Canada's North West Territories. Half of 'em ain't fit to govern an outhouse, and most of the other half I wouldn't turn my back on if there was half a biscuit on my plate. I got the feeling a lot of 'em'd just as soon head back to Canada instead of hunkering in a log cabin chewing pemmican, but McDougall won't let 'em go yet."

"He's right. The impediments to them taking their rightful positions at Fort Garry won't last long."

"You think not?"

"By the end of tomorrow's meeting the English Representatives, and even some of the French, will see this is fruitless, and that will leave just the so-called National Committee, and they can't stand alone for long."

"That's what you figure?" Schultz nodded authoritatively. "Well, I guess you'd know better'n me – you live here." Stutsman drained the remains of his beer in three long swallows and set the empty tankard down. "Well, it's been nice talking to you, Doctor, but somebody drank my beer."

Schultz started reaching for the tankard, saying: "I'll fetch it for you," but the sudden blaze in the cartoon Irishman's eyes stopped him cold. No one helped Enos Stutsman. Stutsman levered himself nimbly out of his chair with one crutch, picked up the empty tankard with his free hand and proceeded toward the bar with crutch and peg legs. Schultz looked around. Charlie Mair was in conversation with someone at the near end of the bar; the two stout lads from Portage la Prairie were at Thomas Scott's table. Schultz strode over to that table and plunked down the remains of the bottle of whiskey, saying: "There you go, lads, but go warily."

"That's mighty white of you, Doctor."

Mair had broken off his conversation and was waiting for Schultz at the door. There was still much to do tonight. Firstly, although it wasn't the first thing Schultz wanted to get to, with Mair's and Agnes's assistance he quickly polished up an anonymous column for the next edition of *The Nor'Wester*. He had a last-minute stroke of inspiration to work a 'news' item into the column by a 'Concerned Citizen of Winnipeg,' namely the news that Governor Mactavish was reported to be recovering from his recent long and severe illness. That ought to give a few people second thoughts about whether The Company and the Council of Assiniboia were going to lie dormant much longer. One of the major unfortunate circumstances that had made Red River ripe for nonsense like the National Committee, was that the two most authoritative figures in the territory – Governor Mactavish and Bishop Taché – weren't able to exercise their authority this winter; Mactavish because of his illness, and the Bishop because he'd been called to Rome for an Ecumenical Council. Schultz had to wonder, though, just how ill Mactavish actually was, or how necessary it had been for Bishop Taché to embark for Rome just before Red River went off the rails. Both The Company and the Roman Catholic Church could shrug, *"Well, when the cat's away, or incapacitated..."*

Once the copy had gone off with one of the new 'lodgers' to the *Nor'Wester* print shop above the stationary store across from Dutch George's, Schultz sat down in the common room to do what he'd wanted to do first: divulge and discuss his new information with Agnes, Mair, Superintendent Snow, James Stewart, and the dozen or so other loyal Canadians who'd taken up temporary residence above the White Store. There was a gratifying chorus of applause and huzzas when he told them that tomorrow's Meeting would be make-or-break for the National Committee and its Convention. That led to an animated discussion of what to do after the convention 'fizzled away.' Superintendent Snow didn't take much part in the conversation. Schultz wondered if Snow'd lost his nerve after his own men tried to drown him.

Agnes eventually pointed out that there was nothing for it but to wait and see what happened tomorrow, and that the fastest way to make that happen was a good night's slumber. After the activities of the day Schultz had every reason to be tired, but once abed he found he was too exhilarated and anticipatory to sleep. Agnes appeared to feel the same way, but found a way they could both work off their nervous energy – though they had to go about it quietly, with so many other people in the surrounding rooms.

The next morning brought James Ross calling in on his way to the convention. It seemed a pity that a young man of such promise – only a few years older than Schultz – should have such shaky hands in the morning, and it wasn't shivers from the cold. Schultz remembered hearing that James Ross's older brother, William, had been expected to inherit their father's offices and responsibilities, while the second son had grown up expecting to pursue whatever idle interests appealed to him. But William Ross had died unexpectedly, only a few years after the old man.

Agnes poured James Ross a cup of tea and Schultz added in a tot of brandy; Ross didn't say no. What Ross did say was: "I thought you'd want to know – well, you would know eventually, but I have cousins who come and tell me things before eventually but wouldn't come here... The National Committee has taken Fort Garry."

Schultz looked at Agnes and she at him. He could see she was as taken aback as he was, that Ross's dipsomanic disorientation had reached such a stage. She turned to Ross and said gently: "Yes, Mr. Ross, that was three weeks ago."

"No, I mean they've *taken* it. To keep men in arms for any length of time, you have to house them and feed them. Amazing they've lasted this long – sleeping in the snow and eating only what their families could bring them, while only a few steps away were The Company's snug, warm barracks buildings, and warehouses filled with exotic edibles and barrels of wine... Now the National Committee has taken full possession, moved their soldiers into The Company's buildings, taken the cash and records of the Council of Assiniboia, all the papers in the Land Registry... The National Committee promised Governor Mactavish The Company would eventually be indemnified for all the goods and provisions, but meanwhile he and all his people are prisoners."

Schultz felt a curious combination of iration and delight – irate that the rebels could commit such highhanded crimes; delighted that they'd put themselves so far beyond the pale. Ross drained the dregs of his teacup and set it back down on the saucer; it didn't clatter like it had after his first sip.

Ross topped up his tea and said: "Some of the Representatives are currently having private conversations about whether they should go to the meeting today, or whether they'd wind up taken prisoners as well, but I have a feeling they'll all show up in the end. I have it on good authority that the National Committee is going to put forth a proposal today that the people of Assiniboia form a Provisional Government."

Schultz spouted: "That's Treason!"

Ross sipped and shrugged. "Is it? Treason to whom? As I understand it, the date for completion of the transfer from The Company to the Dominion is December First. That's still a week away. Can one commit High Treason against a business corporation?"

Schultz declared: "The Hudson's Bay Company territories are under British Crown law, and always have been."

Ross said quirkily, "That's an interesting sentiment, coming from you. Well, the meeting's to start at ten o'clock and I'd best get there a few minutes early. Thanks for the tea."

After Ross had taken his leave, Agnes said: "What kind of game is he playing?"

"Game?"

"Why would James Ross come to tell us all that?"

"Well... there's no love lost between him and The Company. And his years in Canada may have given him an appreciation of the Dominion."

"Odd that he just happened to pick this year to come back."

"Not odd at all. A lot of people moved here from Canada this year, getting in on the ground floor on the eve of the transfer." Schultz glanced at the mahogany-cased clock on the rough-adzed mantlepiece. "Time we took up our seats in the loges."

There were now two chairs in permanent residence on either side of a sidetable in front of the window with the best view of the courthouse. On the sidetable were two pairs of opera glasses they'd bought for theatrical presentations in Toronto. Schultz was aware that Agnes seated had her lower field of vision truncated by the windowsill, but she could stand up if he saw anything of import. And if anything of import happened directly below them, they'd be alerted by the temporary lodger Schultz had temporarily hired on to mind the store. Which these days probably meant spending the day playing cards across the counter with his cronies.

There were several Metis guards on either side of the courthouse door. Representatives were arriving from the north and west, singly or in twos and threes – the ones from the farther parishes had bunked over with friends or at Dutch George's. Before going into the courthouse, they detoured to the south side of the building to hobble their saddlehorses or tether their sleigh horses. Chief Henry Prince arrived with his lone, ceremonial bodyguard – or at least supposedly ceremonial. But no one came along Main Road from the south, the direction of St. Boniface, St. Norbert and St. Vital.

Agnes said: "Perhaps they're all in there already?"

"Have you ever heard of the French being early for anything? No, I expect they're all conferring at Fort Garry before coming on."

The clock struck ten and still no sign of activity from the south, except a cart-sleigh that passed by the courthouse and kept on going. After a few more minutes, Agnes stood up, saying: "I'd best be conferring with Mrs. Stewart and Eliza about luncheon, and put a couple of our lodgers to work slicing cold ham and bread. Call me if anything happens."

Nothing did. After awhile, Schultz stood up and paced around the room, keeping his eyes on the window, then tapped himself a mug of beer, sat back down and lit a cigarette. Shortly after the clock struck eleven, a dark tongue snaked out of the mouth of Fort Garry. Schultz stood up and called: "Mrs. Schultz!" By the time Agnes got to the window, the tongue had defined itself as about three dozen men marching north toward the courthouse. Mair and Stewart came to watch as well. When the column from Fort Garry reached the courthouse, most of the three dozen went inside while a few stayed out to relieve the guards, who strolled briskly off toward the stoves and fireplaces of the fort. After a few minutes of nothing more happening, Agnes headed back toward the kitchen and Stewart wandered away to wherever he'd wandered from. Schultz sat down and lit another cigarette, staring at the mute walls of the courthouse until his eyes began to blur and he had to glance at the sky before training his eyes on the courthouse again.

Mair said: "What do you think's going on in there?"

"How the devil should I know? Oh, sorry, Mair – it's just… frustrating, knowing events are moving but not knowing in which direction and not being able to affect them. I'm not used to sitting on the sidelines."

"Think nothing of it, old chap, all our nerves are getting a bit frayed."

As the clock chimed noon, Agnes brought Schultz a sandwich – local ham, butter and bread and imported Worcestershire sauce. He sat munching by the window while the rest gathered around the long table and jabbered about everything from how soon the new Winnipeg residents' votes could be put to use, to the relative mildness of the winter so far. As Schultz set his empty plate aside, a movement through the window caught his eye, a dotted line inching north from The Forks. He stood up and squinted, then took up his opera glasses. The dotted line was a cart-train – or cart-sled-train it must be this time of year – about a dozen long. It passed by Fort Garry, then the courthouse, and kept on ambling north. As the cart-sleds passed by Schultz's window he could see that each one carried several large upright barrels, the barrelheads dusted with snow. He moved to a window on the north side of the common room and saw that the cart-train was turning to its right along the short road to the river. There was nothing along that road but William Drever Jr.'s junior-sized store, and the off-shoot school the Grey Nuns had built across the river from St. Boniface. Nothing except the loading doors to the White Store's warehouse.

The cart-train stopped. Schultz headed for the staircase. Agnes called from the table: "What is it?"

"I'm not sure – I think we have visitors." As Schultz reached the top of the stairs, he peripherally noticed everyone at the table getting up to follow him, some of them picking up the guns they'd leaned in the corners of the common room. Schultz's own pocket pistol had been transferred from pocket to pocket for a fortnight now, whenever he went out or came back inside.

The temporary shopclerk was starting up the stairs as Schultz was coming down. "Oh, Doctor – there's a delivery."

"Delivery…?" Still wary, Schultz stepped into the warehouse, unbarred the double doors of the loading dock and pushed one open.

There were several carters standing around outside, maybe some Schultz had dealt with before – hard to tell when they all wore thick black beards and blanket coats. One of them took a sheaf of papers out of his capote, saying: "Bonjour, Doctor. A shipment for Superintendent Snow, consigned to you, from the Canadian government. Salt pork."

One of the temporary lodgers who'd come west with the road crew said: "That'll be our rations for the winter, and provisions-wages for the local labourers. Or would be if we was still in business."

Schultz said confusedly to the head drover, "How did you get past the barrier, at St. Norbert?"

"They're letting most past now, so long as it ain't someone carrying guns or suspicious intentions."

Agnes said what Schultz was thinking, "Well, at least Governor Mactavish's Proclamation accomplished *some*thing." He wondered if she intuited the other factor he was thinking, something James Ross had said that morning, *'To keep men in arms for any length of time, you have to house them and feed them.'*

What with the drovers and the temporary lodgers and a couple of handy stout planks, it didn't take all that long to get the barrels of pork rolled off the carts and ensconced in the warehouse; the major part of the operation was re-stacking enough other goods to make room. When all was squared away and the big doors barred again, Schultz went back to his window. He hadn't been there long when a stream of miniature men came out of the dollhouse courthouse. He got his coat, went out onto the front step and leaned against the doorframe of the White Store, as though he'd just stepped out for a bit of fresh air and a smoke.

Schultz nodded or waved companionably at the Representatives passing by, even at Sheriff McKenney and Hugh O'Lone walking and talking together. O'Lone nodded back perfunctorily; Henry condescendingly grandly, with his thick dark beard split by a grin like the Cheshire Cat's. When finally James Ross came trotting by – Schultz didn't know his horse, but recognized Ross's puffy, leather-peaked fur cap – Schultz called out: "Mr. Ross! Stop by for a cup of tea?"

Ross looked from side to side, turned his pony and reined in beside the store's front step but didn't dismount. He said to Schultz in a voice timbred to not carry much farther, "What happened is the National Committee did propose we form a Provisional Government. Most of the representatives said we weren't empowered to do that, have to consult with the people of our parishes and then convene again at the courthouse a week tomorrow." Schultz nodded at the wisdom of saying so to stall and extricate themselves from such an insane idea. "That's all I can tell you. We've got to stop meeting like this; people are beginning to talk."

Schultz laughed at Ross's irreverent wit, but Ross shook his head and said in an even lower voice, "I'm serious. I've heard of rumours that my confabs with you must mean I'm secretly hand-in-glove with you and the Honourable McDougall."

"I never said such a thing to anybody!"

"I never said you did." Ross clucked his pony to start moving again, then reined it back in for long enough to say: "Oh, and Roger Goulet has been summoned to Fort Garry to speak with Secretary Riel, and to bring his files and records along with him. Thought you might be interested to know."

'Interested' was hardly the word. There were two possible reasons the National Committee might've summoned Roger Goulet, and two sets of files and records he might've been instructed to bring. Neither possibility was a comfortable one for John Christian Schultz.

Roger Goulet was The Company's surveyor, and he'd often said that The Company's survey chain had been in use so long it had likely stretched as much as six inches. A standard 'Gunter's chain' was sixty-six links equalling one hundred feet. Six inches over one hundred feet wasn't much, until people started to operate on terms of dozens of side-by-side lots, each two or three chains wide, and those were the terms Schultz had long been planning to operate on. And according to Ross, the National Committee had already taken possession of all the papers in The Company's Land Registry…

The second possibility was even more unpleasant. Roger Goulet was also the Collector of Customs for the Council of Assiniboia. Goulet had always given a certain amount of slack to the non-Company traders, on the sensible understanding that one didn't have the cash to pay duty on goods imported wholesale until one had sold them retail. Schultz had always taken as much slack as he could get, but over the last year he'd stretched it even further, on the sensible assumption that if he stalled until the transfer there would be no more Council of Assiniboia to dun him for back customs duties. But now, with the National Committee taking possession of all the Council's records, and needing all the resources they could get their hands on…

When Schultz went back up into the living quarters he beckoned Agnes into their bedroom, which was about the only place left they could have private conversations about private business. He'd found that sometimes just talking to Agnes about a difficulty he'd encountered, the mere act of defining it verbally, could lead to a solution. When he told her they might be facing a sudden demand for payment of back customs duties, she said: "We've dealt with bailiffs before," then laughed, "you remember poor Constable Mulligan locked in the warehouse?"

"This is different."

"Yes, it is – this time we have more than a dozen brave men lodging here, who'll stand up with you against Sheriff McKenney and his bailiffs."

"No, something else is different, it just feels different, I don't know… Ah!"

"What?"

"You see, my dear, we mustn't let the lines get blurred. It's very important that we keep it clear-cut to people here and in the outside world, that this insurrection is entirely on the part of the French. It'd get confusing if, in the middle of all this, an English sheriff and bailiffs came to enforce a court order against a fellow English-speaker. It's not unlikely the National Committee can convince Judge Black to issue a court order – he's fussy about unpaid debts."

The preemptive solution Schultz and Agnes came up with was to send a message to the National Committee, offering to provide the invoices for the shipment of government pork and immediately pay whatever duties were entailed. The messenger brought back a reply which seemed possibly positive: the Secretary of the National Committee considered the duties on the government pork to be a matter Dr. Schultz need not trouble himself over at present. But the messenger brought back something else not as welcome: four well-armed Metis 'soldiers' to stand guard over the government pork. Schultz remembered again what James Ross had said about provisions and men-in-arms. Agnes's verdict on the pork guards was: "Fine, let them stand around outside the loading doors till doomsday – there'll be nothing between them and the home of the north wind but a few spruce trees and shacks."

Over supper there was much discussion about the possibility of a Provisional Government getting declared when the convention reconvened next week. It seemed possible that those representatives from the English side with American leanings might get duped into voting for a Provisional Government, thinking that would make for a semi-official body for Washington to proposition. Schultz knew there was no point even trying to talk sense into Henry, but Hugh O'Lone was a possibility. He sent a message across to the Red Dog Saloon, inviting Mr. Hugh O'Lone to the White Store for a conversation with Dr. Schultz. The messenger came back saying: "Well, Doctor, uh, Mr. O'Lone said he saw no point talking to you 'cause, so he says, you and *The Nor'Wester* are most of the brine what put us in the pickle we're in now."

"Do go back and tell him that Dr. Bown's writings and doings have nothing to do with me."

The messenger came back with a two-syllable reply, verbatim: "Ha! Ha!"

CHAPTER 41

Janet Sutherland sat spinning wool, working the whirring wooden wheel that had belonged to her mother-in-law, and to the grandmother-in-law Janet had never seen, and had been made for her great-grandmother-in-law by her great-grandfather-in-law. Her great-grandmother-in-law had dragged it from a burning Highland cottage when the Campbells and the English soldiers came scouring the glens after Culloden; her grandmother-in-law had rescued it from another burning cottage in the Highland Clearances; her mother-in-law had carried it in pieces across the ocean and down to Red River, then up to the top of Lake Winnipeg and back again after the first burning of the colony and after Seven Oaks.

Janet hummed an old Gaelic spinning song while her family's winter evening hummed around her. Margaret was working the loom, with Christina perched beside her intently watching the shuttle go back and forth and moving her own hands in imitation. Willy was kneeling on the floor in front of a wooden tub of new-spun wool, happy in one of his favourite tasks: pouring sturgeon oil onto the wool from a birchbark rogan the St. Peters fishermen's wives sold it in, and squelching it through with his fingers. The oil made the wool easier to work, but had to be worked out again once the blankets were woven. But young cousins and second-cousins didn't seem to mind getting together to barefoot-stomp piles of blankets in a huge tub of soapy water and show each other their legs.

Catherine was at one end of the long table watching Roddy draw his alphabet letters with a piece of charcoal on a hank of brown paper from McDermot's store, showing him where he went wrong and coaxing him to try again. Roddy looked like he'd had just about enough for tonight of being governessed by his older sister. Farther along the table, Morrison had his head propped on one hand, staring down at an opened book from St. John's College, which didn't appear to be an open book to him. Hugh had angled a chair sideways to catch the light from Morrison's candle and was braiding strips of buffalo hide into a shagganappi bridle. Long before Janet was born, Kildonan people had learned to spiral-cut a buffalo hide into shagganappi. The buffalo hunters' wives were always glad to sell you shagganappi they'd already cut, but that was more costly.

Across the table from Hugh, Aleck was puffing his pipe and staring into space. His neatly-trimmed mustache was as maturely-whiskered as Hugh's now and the same shape, though red-brown instead of black. But subtract the mustache and the pipe and Janet could see Aleck exactly as she'd seen him so many times in the past: staring off into space with the wheels going around behind his eyes, and then coming out with the most surprising combinations of 'if this, then that.' Only now he didn't come out and say what he'd been thinking anymore, almost as though he was ashamed of it, since around the time Hugh left school. Aleck still laughed and roughhoused as any young man would, but he seemed determined to hide what made him different from the other boys. As if every one of the boys didn't have something that made him a little different from the others. It pained Janet to see her third son seeming uncomfortable in his skin, but John had cautioned her not to pester Aleck about it: "He'll come around eventually to what he wants to be and do – or he won't."

Morrison's college book reminded her of what her mother-in-law had told her Aleck sometimes did in the dead of night: sneak downstairs and light a candle to peak through whatever textbook Donald had left on the table. Aleck's Gran would always pretend to be asleep.

Farther along the table, Hector and Angus were playing checkers with the board and pieces their grandfather had carved after convincing their grandmother it wasn't the same thing as playing cards, or at least half-convincing her. At the far end of the table, Donald was studiously leafing through a rare new article – a seed catalogue – and comparing it to the Scientific Farming sections in old Alexander Ross's book about Red River.

Through the parlour doorway, Janet could see her husband at his cramped little writing desk going over some papers, no doubt including the dozen messages that had been hand-delivered to the Councillor of Assiniboia throughout the day. Curled up asleep on the parlour hearthrug – though not too close to the fire – was Mary Ann Bella snuggled with the housecat that had grown out of the kitten Janet's mother-in-law had crippled herself rescuing. The evidence of 'Gran' and 'Granda's' lives was still part of the family. The chair Janet was sitting in was her mother-in-law's old chair with the wheels removed. John had waited a year or so after the funeral, to give the children time to adjust, and then brought the chair back out of the barn, telling Janet that his mother would've been aghast at letting a perfectly good chair go to waste.

Unfortunately, remembering that reminded Janet that when Dr. Schultz had first started making advances about Point Douglas, and John's parents had been dead against it, she'd pointed out to John that in a few years they'd be dead period and whatever happened to Point Douglas wouldn't distress them. That had made it complicated for her when, by the time it came true, she'd developed her own uneasiness about Dr. Schultz and his schemes.

Donald set down his seed catalogue and said: "So, did you hear anything around college today about what might be happening with Fort Garry and Winnipeg and the National Committee and all?" He'd tried to make it sound like an impersonal question about the general state of affairs, but Janet knew Donald had a very personal interest.

He was still hoping that the situation could be resolved, and their building in Winnipeg finished, in time for him and Christie Matheson to be married before the end of the year. Janet feared it was going to be Donald's first full-blown, adult-sized disappointment. But better it should come when he was still young and limber. As for how deeply Hugh was disappointed about his Nancy Prince and the home they'd almost had in their grasp, it was hard to tell. Hugh hadn't volunteered to talk about it, and it was hard for Janet to introduce the subject of someone she'd never been introduced to. Hugh had always found it easier than Donald to shrug off drastic changes in the weather – too wet to plough, you can always go fishing – but it seemed to Janet Hugh hadn't been laughing as lightly lately.

Donald's 'idle' question had been put out to the room in general, but the only ones who could answer it were Hector and Morrison. Angus had another half-year at Kildonan school before it would have to be decided whether he'd go on to college or not. And maybe by then Dr. Black's venture to establish a Presbyterian college would've taken root, and Angus wouldn't follow his brothers into St. John's either way.

Morrison looked up gratefully, not sorry to be interrupted, but was still blinking his way out of his book. Hector said without raising his eyes off the checkerboard, "There's a lot of opinions and talk around the college – Second Years trying to let on to us First Years they've got some better idea of what's going to happen, but they don't. Like Ian Gunn said to me, it all depends on what the Frogs do."

Janet took her foot off the treadle and clapped her hand on the spinning wheel to stop it, at the same time saying: "Hector Sutherland! You will not use that word in this house!"

"What, 'Frog'?"

"I told you!"

"Aw, Mum, it's just a word – I don't mean any harm by it. I've seen grown men call each other Frog and Limey face-to-face, and neither one takes offence."

"When you're a grown man you can decide for yourself whether you know someone well enough that they can call you Haggis-eater without you taking offence, then you can call them Frog – face-to-face. But I warn you, if you guess wrong about the wrong person, you'll get your ears boxed or worse. Meanwhile, you'll not be using that word under this roof."

"Yes, Mum."

Janet worked the foot treadle again. As the whirring of the spinning wheel started up again, so did the clicking of the loom – Janet hadn't realised it had stopped – and the squilching sound of oil and wool. Those sounds melded with the crackle of the hearthfire and Janet's favourite winter sound of all: the muffled undercurrent of the north wind outside when all her family were snug and safe inside.

Then Aleck said loudly, "Do you remember when Hugh made us all eat frogs' legs?"

Janet looked to see if Aleck was being deliberately cheeky – he'd been doing that occasionally lately – but some of the girls and younger boys were going *'ew,'* the older boys were laughing, and Hugh was saying: "I didn't *make* you."

Aleck said to Willy, "You'd be too young to remember, but Angus was there."

Angus said: "No I weren't – I was smart enough to run home."

Margaret said: "*I* wasn't."

The children's voices were tumbling over each other. Hugh cut through the laughter with: "You swore honour-bound not to tell."

Donald said: "That was ten years ago – Statute of Limitations."

Aleck turned toward Janet. "You see, Mum, Hugh had got us playing French Explorers…" That sounded believable; even though Donald was the oldest, it was usually Purple Hugh who'd come up with the imaginary games the others followed. Not because he was bossy, or thought his ideas better than others', but because when he got enthusiastic about hunting hippopotamouses it was hard not to get caught up with him. Hugh always did everything with abandon. Well, everything he wanted to do.

Janet's seven oldest – excepting Angus who'd claimed not to've been there, and Hugh who was the accused instigator – paraded out the story:

"Hugh'd read or heard somewhere that French people –"

"French people in France."

" – ate frogs' legs. It was a wet spring –"

"Musta been summer, or it woulda just been tadpoles."

"No, it was –"

"Anyway, the low ground back in the hayfield was half-swamp, and filled with frogs –"

"Big, fat leopard frogs."

"Well, big to us."

"We caught a buncha them and killed them with a stick."

Catherine and Christina went *'ew,'* and: "You *killed* them?"

"Well, it was a big stick, just one whack apiece."

"Then we cut off their legs –"

"No, *you* did – you and Hugh."

"And Hector snucked back home and 'borrowed' the little kettle."

"No, I didn't, it was Morrison."

"When I got back to the swamp with the kettle, Donald and Hugh had got a fire going –"

"We got the water boiling and dropped the frogs' legs in –"

"Hugh made some tongs with a green twig."

"When the skin started to peel off, we lifted 'em out and nibbled."

Janet felt her gorge rising, but forced it back down. She said: "Well, at least they'd be boiled clean."

"They didn't taste half bad – kinda like soft chicken."

"But not much more'n a nibble on each leg."

Hector said: "I think in France they must have bigger… amphibians."

There was a pause, as though that was the end of the story, but then Hugh contributed straight-facedly, "And then the next day…"

"Oh, yeah! Next day Granda made himself a cup of tea with the small kettle, took a sip and said –"

Donald, Morrison and Margaret chorused: "'There's aye something fishy about this tay'," Margaret so sputtering with laughter she could hardly get it out. Then all the children burst with laughter, even the ones too young to have been there.

Janet shook her head, and kept her mouth pursed to keep from laughing with them. When she could make herself heard, and keep her voice even, she said: "Naughty children. Naughty, naughty, naughty children. I hate to think what other mischief you may've got up to behind my back."

Donald said: "Well, there was the time we –"

"No," Hugh cut him off, shaking his head. "There's no Statue of Imitations on that one."

John came out of the parlour carrying the sleeping bundle of what would undoubtedly be their last child. After Mary Ann Bella was born, there'd been a couple of years when Janet deeply regretted dismissing her own mother's Hot Flashes as exaggerated, middle-aged foolishness.

John said: "I'd say it's past bedtime for Catherine on down." A year ago it would've been 'Margaret on down,' and a year from now it would be 'Willy on down.' But Margaret did go upstairs, to carry Mary Ann Bella to bed, then came back down as the last of her younger brothers and sisters were going up, squeezing past each other in the narrow closed-in staircase.

Janet moved the spinning wheel back against the wall and went into the pantry for some bread and cheese and blood sausage. There was always a late night nibble for those whose mornings would start with an hour or more of chores before breakfast. Hector looked at what she'd put on the table and said: "What, no amphibian legs?" and Janet cocked her hand as if to swat him.

When that spate of laughter had died down, and John was still pretending to be mystified about it – Janet knew darn well he would've heard the whole story from the parlour – Morrison said while munching, "You think we still got to keep the channel clear for getting across the river?"

Aleck said: "When I got tonight's water the ice 'round the hole still warn't a hand thick."

Janet knew Aleck knew it should've been 'wasn't,' but he seemed determined to speak as though he'd never seen the inside of a school, even though properly intelligible English actually came more naturally to him.

John nodded, "I'd say another week at least, just to be safe."

Donald said: "All those messages today, Da... Are people telling you they want to go in for a Provisional Government, or that they figure it's too drastic?"

"A lot of, um, uncertainty is what they're... *voicing*. I won't have any voice in the, um, Convention of Representatives next week, and meanwhile people aren't sure if I'm still a Councillor of Assiniboia – that is, whether the Council still has any... *standing*. I'm not sure myself. One thing I do know is that every, um, parish, will be holding its own Public Meetings this weekend, to decide what stand they want their representative to take."

John looked away from everyone, and at something no one else could see. "A Provisional Government... I don't know... As you said, that would be a drastic step." It seemed to Janet, from the way her husband had started a couple of threads and then dropped them, that there were one or two things he didn't feel at liberty to tell.

Aleck said: "I read somewhere, or heard somewhere, that under International Law any people that finds itself with no effective government has an inalienable right to form its own." Then he seemed to catch himself, feeling the eyes around the table seeing him let slip a side of himself he'd been striving to hide, even from himself. "Well, but all that business about laws and stuff don't mean a pinch of coonshit next to people doin' whatever they dang feel like doin'. Cut me another hunka bread, please, Mum."

Janet did so, keeping her own thoughts to herself about Provisional Governments and so on. What mattered to her was that the plan to bring in appointed foreigners to rule over her children's world had been knocked on the head, at least for now, and for that she was thankful to the National Committee. Whatever form the next steps took, it looked likely now that Red River would be able to peacefully negotiate a fair deal for her children. As long as nobody went and did something childish.

CHAPTER 42

Schultz had to admit there was one good thing about the seditious talk of a Provisional Government – it meant there would have to be another public meeting of the residents of Winnipeg. And that would finally give a chance to make use of the temporary lodgers, who were getting restless hanging around to no apparent purpose. The meeting was in the Engine House again, and as before the crowd lent the wooden cavern a tavern smell of male-sweaty wool and leather, tobacco and alcohol, except with an untavernish dankness from the breath-misting excuse for indoor temperature. There were several men in chairs on the makeshift stage of upturned packing crates. The man standing beside Schultz nudged him and murmured: "Look at Hargrave."

Schultz looked to J.J. Hargrave, Governor Mactavish's gentlemanly young secretary – born and bred in Rupert's Land and educated in Scotland – sitting with a studious expression and posture, as though waiting for a Royal Geographic Society lecture to begin. The man who'd nudged Schultz chuckled, "I betcha a dollar he's not carryin' pertection. And another dollar he don't know he's the only man here that ain't."

Schultz laughed, "No takers," and nestled his hand around the revolver in his coat pocket, glancing around at some of the other men leaning on much thicker walking sticks than needed to support their weight. He did wonder, though, how it was that Hargrave had been allowed to leave Fort Garry, when all the other officers of The Company were held prisoner within its walls.

The appointed Chairman, A.G.B. Bannatyne, called the meeting to order and called on Sheriff McKenney to deliver the report of Winnipeg's elected Representatives. Henry reported that the two choices on the table were to either form a Provisional Government, or to carry on for now with the old government of The Company and the Council of Assiniboia. No mention was made of the third choice: to bring in Lieutenant Governor McDougall and proceed with the legal transfer agreed to by The Company, the Dominion and the Crown. Schultz shouted to that effect, and so did several other voices salted through the crowd. Henry ignored them and sat back down as though he'd said all he had to say.

J. J. Hargrave stood up and addressed the crowd in his mild way, "Governor Mactavish's proclamation of ten days ago expressed The Company's position on the current state of affairs, and I have nothing to add. But, rumours and false assumptions are the greatest enemies of our peace, so I've been asked to introduce a speaker who can dispel them. Gentlemen – the Secretary of the National Committee, Mister Louis Riel."

As a shadowed figure stepped from a back room toward the stage, there was hissing and booing from Dr. Bown and others. Schultz joined in. Other voices shouted: "Shut-up and let the man speak!" and Bannatyne called repeatedly for order. Riel took the stage and just stood waiting for the crowd to quiet down.

The Secretary of the National Committee was wearing a natty double-breasted black buffalo coat that stopped at mid-thigh, and matching hat. He doffed the hat, disclosing thick dark chestnut waves, and unbuttoned the coat, disclosing a grey wool suit with a purple satin waistcoat. Word had it that his mother had sold her milk cow to buy him that suit. He began to speak in a measured, sonorous voice that filled the Engine House. His English was perfectly intelligible if a trifle tortuously convoluted, but Schultz guessed the same was true of his French.

What Riel said, though he took a long time saying it, was that the current so-called 'government' of The Company and the Council of Assiniboia had never been constituted to contend with this volatile a situation and was incapable of doing so; that a Provisional Government was necessary to maintain order and negotiate with Canada; and that the National Committee would not coerce or interfere with the rights of anyone in Assiniboia.

There was applause at several points during Riel's speech – Schultz noticed even Mair applauding at one point – and more applause when he thanked the assemblage for their kind attention and bade them adieu. Riel and Hargrave left the stage together for the back room – and Schultz strongly suspected straight out the back door to a squad of armed and waiting Metis horsemen. There was something unholy about Riel and Hargrave appearing together. Maybe the National Committee and The Company were up to something.

After Riel's departure, there were several gassy speeches from the floor that added nothing. Tempers were fraying, men were mumbling insults at each other and shouting outright things like: "Shut up and sit down!" and "Bullfeathers!" Schultz could feel his heart pumping faster and his breathing growing deeper, and all the men and objects in his vision took on a sharper clarity and deeper colour. Much longer and the place was going to blow.

Finally Chairman Bannatyne shouted: "Gentlemen!" enough times to make himself heard. "We all know all the arguments by now. The question is: do you want to vote now on whether to empower our Representatives to join a Provisional Government, or do we adjourn to ponder on it for another day or two?"

That was the opening Schultz had been waiting for. He bellowed: "Mr. Chairman! Before we vote on anything, shouldn't we determine what constitutes a resident of the Town of Winnipeg? There are plenty of men who live here but aren't property owners."

"That is true, Doctor. Do you wish to make a motion?"

"I move that any man who's resided in our town for a week has the right to vote."

Mair managed to shout his Second just before the Engine House erupted in a bedlam of bellowing voices, out of which Schultz could pick out the occasional word like 'preposterous' or 'legitimate.' Men were pushing and shoving, and fists were being cocked. Schultz shouted at Bannatyne, "*'Chairman'?* You couldn't Chair a ladies' sewing circle!"

A single roar of "Order!" from the direction of the stage actually accomplished its purpose. It wasn't that the voice was louder than all the other voices combined, but after seven years as Sheriff people had learned to identify that voice as the voice of the law. Schultz had to admit it had been wise of Henry to just use his voice to get attention, instead of firing his pistol in the air.

Sheriff McKenney declared: "A meeting is nothing but a mob when there's no respect for the chair, and our chairman has been insulted. I believe this meeting has adjourned itself to re-convene another day. Correct, Mr. Chairman?"

"This meeting is adjourned." Schultz doubted that the move had as much to do with Bannatyne's injured sensibilities as the palpable fact that in another minute or two one of those shaking fists was going to connect with someone else's nose, and then all hell would break loose. When the meeting spilled out onto the road, wind-driven ice crystals quickly cooled tempers down to thoughts of homefires and hot toddies.

The next morning brought an invitation to another Public Meeting that afternoon, *'to decide the question before the meeting of last evening as to who are to be considered as entitled to vote.'* This meeting wasn't at the Engine House, but in the large open room on the second floor of Dutch George's hotel. After a few preliminaries, Sheriff McKenney moved that all householders and property owners, and six months' residents, be allowed to vote at public meetings. Schultz jumped up with: "Mr. Chairman! I move an amendment to the motion – that any man who's been resident of our town for three weeks be entitled the right to vote." It wasn't as good as one week, the motion he'd initiated at the Engine House, but that had been a negotiating position, and if there were a clear-cut end in sight the temporary lodgers could be induced to camp out at the White Store a little longer.

Then W.B. O'Donoghue rose to propose an alternate amendment, and everyone paid particular attention. It wasn't because O'Donoghue was a particularly commanding presence: a few years younger and a few inches shorter than Schultz, with pale Irish hair and eyes, sharp cheekbones and wispy goatee. There was a gauntness to O'Donoghue, and an unnatural brightness in his eyes, but those were more likely to solicit concern for his health than command respect. The reason everyone in the meeting paid particular attention was that O' Donoghue was there representing the Sisters of Charity at their Winnipeg school, where he was a teacher of mathematics. The bloody Grey Nuns again.

O'Donoghue's amendment was that *seven months'* residence be the qualifying factor. That amendment and Henry's motion were quickly put to a vote and carried. Schultz protested that they hadn't voted on his amendment, and his had been tabled first. But the verdict was that since the motion had already been carried, any further amendments would be out of order. Schultz was furious at the perversion of democracy – *and he'd offered to compromise, dammit!* – but it was obvious he'd get no justice there.

The next couple of days were a guessing game, with various of the lodgers coming back from jaunts through town with observations like: "I saw O'Donoghue going into Bannatyne's house – not Bannatyne's *store*, his *house*..."

"James Ross's horse was tethered in front of McKenney's all afternoon..."

"Someone spotted the O'Lone brothers comin' out the Grey Nuns' school..."

But the third morning brought a rumour that seemed to emanate from everywhere and nowhere in particular: Colonel Dennis had made his way back from Pembina to the Stone Fort, and he'd brought with him a Queen's Proclamation, which had been despatched by Her Imperial Majesty to Lieutenant Governor McDougall with instructions that it be issued to the inhabitants of Rupert's Land. A proclamation from the Queen directly to her subjects was like Moses bringing down the tablets from the mountain; there was no higher authority and no quibbling. But it was only a rumour until the late afternoon twilight, when someone called Schultz's attention to the windows facing south along the Main Road. A couple of dozen Metis horsemen were trotting north, and the very tall one in the lead was undoubtedly Ambroise Lépine, the War Chief of the National Committee.

As they trotted past, Schultz shifted to the windows facing north and practically pushed one eye through the glass trying to see between the new buildings flanking the road. Stewart said: "What are they doing?"

"They're stopping in front of Dutch George's. No, across the road from Dutch George's."

One of the lodgers said: "Think a few of us should go down there and see what they're up to?"

Schultz thought about that a moment. "No, better we don't stick our noses in – or stick our noses out. We'll find out soon enough."

Soon enough, Walter Bown came up the stairs from the side door to the second floor of the White Store, slumped onto a chair in the common room and said: "Well, that's torn it."

Schultz said: "Torn what?"

Bown thanked Agnes for the cup of tea she poured him, furled his fingers through the thick, curly beard that made winter scarves unnecessary, and said: "Well, I have been camped out all day in the *Nor'Wester* office, waiting. I expected that if the rumours about Colonel Dennis and the Queen's Proclamation were true, somebody would be bringing a hand-copy from the Stone Fort to *The Nor'Wester* – maybe the damned *Pioneer* as well – to be typeset and printed off as fast as possible. But who showed up was from Fort Garry, Ambroise Lépine and a batch of –"

"I know – we saw them pass by."

"Well, they have shut down *The Nor'Wester* and *The Pioneer*, placed armed guards on the printing presses – in fact, the *Nor'Wester* print shop is now a guardhouse, so the night patrol and the guards on the government pork can have a handy place to warm their toes and play cards."

Mair said: "But that's private property! They have no bloody right!"

Schultz said: "Well… but it does strongly suggest President John Bruce and company believe the rumours about the Queen's Proclamation are more than rumours. If they just wanted to shut down the newspapers on general principles, they would've done it before now. No, the National Committee is suddenly very much afraid of something." Schultz found himself smiling, but the smile faded against the fact that the National Committee had effectively prevented what they'd feared, namely the Queen's Proclamation printed and circulated throughout the settlement.

Agnes reminded Schultz, and informed the rest of the company, that they had a printing press stored somewhere among the odds and ends in corners of the White Store's warehouse. Back when the old *Nor'Wester* press burned with the old office, Schultz had bought a small hand press from the Church Missionary Society, to keep the paper in some sort of circulation until a replacement press could be found and freighted from St. Paul. Mair said excitedly, "We could send a rider to fetch a hand-copy from the Stone Fort, and under cover of night –"

Schultz cut off Mair's flight of poetic enthusiasm by informing him, and reminding Agnes, that although they did have a press they had virtually no type. Any of the hand press type that could be jigged to fit the *Nor'Wester* press had gone with it when Bown moved the operation from behind the White Store to above the stationary store.

Bown shrugged, "It may be of no import anyway. Just because the National Committee believes in the Queen's Proclamation does not mean it is necessarily true. The whole settlement has turned into a nail box these last weeks." Some of the others in the room looked at each other confusedly, but Schultz knew that a 'nail box' was traditional printers' jargon for a place of back-biting, gossip and rumour-mongering.

There was a clatter on the stairs, and one of the temporary lodgers returned early from his assigned duty. He was a young Canadian who'd come west this summer to start a farm in Headingley, and Schultz had given him some money to spend the afternoon drinking in the Red Dog Saloon – though only enough for beer, and not enough of that to fuddle his hearing. He paused at the top of the stairs to catch his breath, then said: "A messenger came to fetch Hugh O'Lone. Seems someone delivered a copy of the Queen's Proclamation from the Stone Fort to Fort Garry, and all the delegates are summoned to hear what it says."

Agnes said: "Well, that would take it out of the realm of rumour."

Schultz said eagerly, "Did the messenger say what the proclamation says?"

The eavesdropper shrugged. "Not that I heard. Just told O'Lone to come to the courthouse."

Schultz went to the south-west corner of the room and clasped his hands in his armpits. Here he was once again standing at the window gazing at the outline of the courthouse fading into the gathering gloom, trying to hatch out something he could *do*. The way this was playing out, all that the general public would know of the Queen's Proclamation would be what the Representatives chose to remember of what portions the National Committee chose to read out to them.

Schultz barely partook of his dinner. As the plates were being cleared away, he heard an approaching cacophony outside: a male voice singing loudly and drunkenly in English. The Metis pork guards outside the loading doors laughingly called out rude suggestions to the singer. Then there was a thumping and stumbling on the staircase, and slurred bellowing echoing in the stairwell. Schultz stood up and faced the top of the stairs, as did some of the other men at the table; a couple of them went to fetch their guns from a corner.

The young man who emerged from the staircase was an apprentice-journeyman printer named Winship, whom Bown had hired from Canada. Winship was in a shocking state for so early in the evening, his hair dishevelled, his coat misbuttoned, and Schultz could smell the whiskey across the room. But as soon as Winship accomplished the top of the stairs, his stumbling stoop disappeared, he straightened his back, put a finger to his lips, came straight to the table across from where Schultz was standing and said: "I need to ask a favour – the loan of a few, small, paper boxes you may have in stock, though I may not be able to return them in the same condition. I need them to help me print off the Queen's Proclamation."

That brought exclamations of astonishment and surprise, which Schultz and Agnes shushed by indicating the direction of the Metis guards outside who might be able to hear any loud voices inside, depending on how hard the wind was blowing. Someone helped Winship off with his coat, someone else pushed forward a chair for him, Agnes poured him a cup of tea and Schultz slid the brandy decanter toward it, since it was now evident that most of the whiskey smell came from his coat and not his mouth.

In answer to Bown's immediate question, Winship said: "No, the *Nor'Wester* print shop is still shut down and guarded. But… You were right, Dr. Bown. That is, that if the rumours were true someone would bring a hand copy of the proclamation to *The Nor'Wester*. The messenger saw the Metis guards, guessed what that meant, and detoured to the public room of Dutch George's, where I happened to be. We hatched out a plan…

"It's only natural that I should return occasionally to the office and print shop, since my cubbyhole of a bedroom is right beside. I offered to move some cabinets of type and so on into a corner, since they weren't going to be used anytime soon, to give the guards more room for their card table and a wider space around the stove. During the process I snuck a few handfuls of selected type into my pockets, including enough Bold for PROCLAMATION, and filled a double-galley with more type. But the galley was too big to conceal in my coat, so I left it hidden in my bedroom, delivered the loot in my pockets to my partner-in-crime, then borrowed an oversized overcoat from an accommodating gentleman at Dutch George's and went back to the print shop."

Eliza Mair squealed: "You went *back*?" in admiration and apprehension. Schultz found himself feeling somewhat jealous of Winship, weedy mustache and all. Not, of course, that Schultz begrudged someone else being the centre of admiration, and Winship had certainly earned it. But weedy Winship had found a way to *do* something, while Schultz had been laid-up above the White Store hatching plans that led nowhere.

Winship said: "Oh, there really wasn't much danger. Unless I made it glaring obvious, the guards had no reason to suspect me of pilfering type when I have no press to use it with."

Agnes piped-in: "We have a press! A small hand press, but it's workable."

Schultz said regretfully, "I think the pork guards would get a bit suspicious if we started rummaging through the warehouse in the middle of the night, and it would take a bit of rummaging. But come daylight –"

"No need," Winship shook his head, "We have the proclamation three-quarters set up already, in a back room down the road from Dutch George's. We hit upon the idea of using paper boxes for type cases, and we'll print using the planer method." Schultz had a vague understanding that although in modern printers' lingo a 'planer' was a wooden block used to level type, 'the planer method' was an archaic, labourious printing process of pressing and pushing a wooden block across the back of a page whose face was on the inked type. "It'll likely take us all night long to print off a few hundred copies, but it can be done – except, we've run out of paper boxes…"

"We won't have to rummage for those," Schultz volunteered. "And then Dr. Bown and I can come with you and help with the printing."

"I appreciate the offer, Doctors, but these days in Winnipeg every move you make is marked – especially you, Dr. Schultz. We don't want to be drawing attention until the job is done."

"This is ridiculous!" Agnes stood out of her chair and slammed her little fist on the table. "That we should be skulking about the streets of the town we built! There's more than a dozen stout, brave men here, and all of them armed. We could march en masse to that back room, help Mr. Winship with the printing while the rest stood guard, and what are the Frenchmen going to do about it?"

"Um…" Winship spread his ink-imbued fingertips along the edge of the tabletop and said carefully, "I admire your spirit, Mrs. Schultz, but, um… There is a reason the National Committee fears the proclamation getting out, the same reason we'd best keep on skulking until that happens, the same reason Colonel Dennis chose today to send the proclamation from the Stone Fort. Today is December First, the date the transfer to Canada was to be finalised –"

Agnes snorted: "As if the French will pay any attention to that."

"Oh, they will, Mrs. Schultz, and so will everybody else at Red River. Everything is going to change around here once the Queen's Proclamation is out and about."

Schultz tentatively reached out an open hand, and said what he'd been looking for an opening to say since Winship first said he had the proclamation, "Might I… read it?"

"Oh, I didn't bring it with me, Doctor, just in case. But I can tell you the gist. There are a lot of whereases and so on, referring to the legal history. But essentially, Her Imperial Majesty proclaims that as of December First, 1869, Rupert's Land is now and henceforth the North West Territories of the Dominion of Canada, and its governance is in the hands of Her Majesty's good and trusted servant, Lieutenant Governor William McDougall."

There was an outbreak of cheers that was quickly hushed to a lower volume but no less enthusiasm. There was much backslapping and Schultz was nearly thrown off his chair by Agnes hurling herself onto his lap and flinging her arms around his neck.

Winship said: "There's more," and everyone leaned in to listen. "My friend from the Stone Fort informed me that Colonel Dennis informed him of the Honourable William McDougall's intentions for today, intentions that were no doubt carried out. A proclamation isn't official until it's been proclaimed, logically enough. So, sometime today, our Lieutenant Governor came north from Pembina, just far enough north to be across the border and within Rupert's Land – that is, the North West Territories – then climbed out of his sleigh, and read out the proclamation."

Schultz felt himself getting a little choked-up, and had to clear his throat. There was something noble in the image of the faithful servant of Empire standing alone, reading out Her Majesty's words to the wind-swept prairie and frost-rimed poplars who would have no more comprehension of the significance than many of the human denizens of the Dominion's new territories.

When the printed copies of the Queen's Proclamation came out, they were all over Red River before the National Committee knew it had happened. The loyal Canadian shopkeepers and businessmen affixed copies to the front doors of their establishments. Schultz begged enough from Winship to practically paper over the front door of the White Store, while still leaving two copies to pass around the common room.

Superintendent Snow looked up from the copy he was perusing and murmured: "That's odd."

Schultz said: "What's odd? If you mean the printing – using upside-down commas when they ran out of apostrophes, and upside-down f's when they ran out of j's – well, it's a miracle they got it printed at all, and none of that affects the substance of it."

"No, I mean... the *timing* is odd, the time-frame. Some of the 'whereases ' in here are obviously meant to shore up the legitimacy of McDougall's authority, as though that's been challenged."

"Well, it *has* been, in case you haven't noticed what's been going on here lately."

"But... it's been less than a month since McDougall got stopped at the border, and then there was another couple of weeks before it came clear the National Committee wasn't just going to melt away. That leaves less than two weeks. That's awful quick for the news to've got to London, and for Her Majesty and her Ministers to've composed this proclamation and got it to McDougall in Pembina."

Schultz sighed, "There *is* a Transatlantic Cable now, Mr. Snow, and the telegraph station in St. Paul isn't all that far from Pembina." Beyond the physical fact that Snow's hair was starting to live up to his name, he was showing other signs of calcifying earlier than his forty-some years warranted. Some men just couldn't accommodate the fact that the world of their youth had changed.

Snow snapped his fingers against the proclamation, which seemed a bit lèse-majesté. "This'd be one helluva long telegram."

"I think Her Majesty could afford it."

"But… look," Snow pointed to the bottom of the proclamation. "It says 'Signed: J. A. N. Provencher, Secretary,' no other name."

"Yes, and right underneath it says 'God save the Queen,' and at the top is the Royal Arms – quick thinking of Winship to pilfer that plate – and 'Victoria by the Grace of God,' etcetera. Of course only the secretary affixed his name at the bottom, to certify he made a fair copy from the telegram. Honestly, Snow, I don't know what you're driving at." Despite Snow's staunch British Canadian heritage, he had been born in Quebec and educated in New York, and Schultz was beginning to wonder if Snow hadn't picked up some strange infections along the way.

Snow mumbled: "I don't know… I just… it just seems a little odd…"

Schultz ignored him and went back to dusting off the hand press, which had been rummaged out of the store room in case of need. Need came that evening, in the person of Winship with another messenger from the Stone Fort. The hand press and Winship's pilfered type were wanted at the Stone Fort to print off another proclamation – this one in the form of a communication from Lieutenant Governor McDougall to Colonel Dennis, meant to be circulated as an addendum to the Queen's Proclamation. It seemed the Lieutenant Governor was appointing Colonel Dennis Deputy Governor, and empowering him to raise an armed militia.

Schultz said: "We're done with skulking," and sent a couple of the temporary lodgers to inform the various Canadian business proprietors and those ex-roadcrewmen still residing at Dutch George's. By the time Schultz and Mair had got the cutter hitched up and the hand press stowed aboard, there were thirty or forty armed men gathered in the lee of the White Store, on horseback or in sleighs or cart-sleds. Schultz kissed his wife good-bye, saying: "I should be back tomorrow or the next day. If I thought for one instant you'd be in any danger here, I wouldn't go." The National Committee and its minions wouldn't dare to harm a female, and Superintendent Snow had opted to stay behind to provide a male presence.

Once the column was out of the shelter of the town, they ran smack into the full force of a blizzard driving snow into their faces, and the Fahrenheit thermometer outside the White Store had read twenty below without the wind. It was a glorious night. Someone with a strong tenor voice began to sing into the teeth of the gale, and Schultz and others joined in:

"We are soldiers of the Queen, me boys,
"The Queen, me boys, the Queen, me boys,
"We are soldiers of the Queen, me boys,
"We are soldiers of the Queen!"

CHAPTER 43

Hugh was helping Mum move the last of the breakfast dishes to the washtub, and most of his brothers and sisters were getting into their coats and high-top moccasins at the door, when Da announced from the table, "There'll be no school today, nor college, either." Hugh'd had the feeling all through breakfast that there was something odd coming.

Some of the children at the door cheered, some looked puzzled. Her Royal Whyness said, of course, "But why…?"

Da said: "Does it matter?" bringing some delighted laughter. "I'll tell you later – but meanwhile, I waited to tell you till you were dressed for outside because you'll still need the fresh air and exercise you would've got walking to school. So go outside and run around and play for an hour – the river's safe for sliding down the bank on that old buffalo hide now. But I'll need you two college boys to help me with something inside. The rest of you run along now, and take Mary Ann Bella with you."

They quickly bundled up their toddling sister and scooted happily out the door. As soon as there was no one left in the house but the older boys and Mum and Da, Da said: "Right, I want every gun and powder flask and bit of ammunition in the house on the table. Quickly now."

His tone said 'no questions,' so Hugh and the other boys hurried up to their rooms to fetch their own guns, and lifted down the ones on wall pegs in the downstairs. By the time everything was piled on the table it made a motley collection, including Granda's old army musket and an equally ancient, double-barreled, big-bore, flintlock pistol that Hugh had never seen before. Mum pointed at it and said: "Is that the famous 'horrible ugly-looking' horse pistol you pointed at the men trying to take you hostage when they were rioting to break James Stewart out of jail?"

Da gaped at Mum. "I never… *mentioned* that was me."

"Come, John, this is Red River, everybody hears everything."

Hugh hadn't heard it, but then he hadn't been in on adult conversations in those days. He'd certainly heard the story, and remembered it: a horseback chase onto the prairie behind Fort Garry, the pursued man suddenly stopping his horse and turning to face his pursuers, levelling a 'horrible ugly-looking' horse pistol at them and telling them the first man to put a hand on his bridle would surely die. But it had never crossed Hugh's mind for a second that that coolly dangerous man might've been stolid and solid old Point Douglas John Sutherland.

Da mumbled something about having got the pistol years ago from a buffalo hunter as surety on a couple of bags of flour for hunt provisions. The buffalo hunter hadn't made it back from the hunt, so Da had just tucked the pistol away and mostly forgot about it. Mum shook her head with a complicated smile and patted Da's reddening cheek. Da cleared his throat and got back to business, "Now, we need every gun clean and limber and loaded – ball or buckshot, not birdshot. I'll tell you why while we're doing it."

Hugh picked up his own double-barrelled smooth-bore, which was already cleaned and oiled as always, but he checked the action anyway before tamping in powder, patch and ball, surrounded by the sounds of metallic clicking and cleaning rods snicking in and out. Da said: "Late last night I was brought some news, it may turn out to be only a rumour, so many flocks of rumours flying around these days, but… Do any of you boys recognise the name George Racette?"

Hugh did, but he left it to the oldest to speak for all of them. Donald said: "The renegade?" and Da nodded. Hugh had heard more than a few stories about Racette's dealings with the Indians, and if half of them were true George Racette was a nasty bit of business.

Da said: "What I've been told is that Racette has gathered together eleven hundred Sioux warriors and is on his way here. It's exactly what Governor Mactavish feared when we were going through that nonsense with the Reverend Corbett and James Stewart. The Crees, and even the Assiniboines, have been dealing with The Company for so many generations they wouldn't throw that away for what they could loot in one raid, but if the Sioux ever got the idea we were fighting among ourselves and vulnerable… I imagine if the Sioux do come we'll drive them off quickly enough, just as long as we're ready."

Hugh realised there was something surprising about the way Da had been speaking, since the moment he'd announced there'd be no school today. Except for that mumbly moment when Mum caught him out about the horse pistol, Da hadn't been stumbling and fumbling with what he was trying to say, just saying it. That seemed to somehow connect with the surprising fact that Da had been the man who'd turned the tables, and the horse pistol, on the pack of horsemen chasing him. And now it seemed to Hugh that Mum hadn't brought up that story just because the pistol appeared on the table, or because she couldn't resist interrupting the urgent business at hand, but because she was trying to communicate something to her husband and her sons. Marriage and motherhood seemed a complicated business. But now didn't seem like a time to sit down and ponder on that, or anything else.

Mum said: "Governor Mactavish and Ambroise Lépine have sent out scouts across the prairie, so if the Sioux *are* coming we'll have plenty of warning."

Hugh weighed a couple of things, including that the old horse pistol had been brought out of hiding, then said: "I gotta get something from the barn." He threw on his capote on the way out the door but didn't bother to toggle it, just held it closed until he got into the warmth of the barn. Up in the loft, the barn cats' eyes gleamed from the shadows, patrolling for meals lured by the sacks of barley and wheat and oats. Hugh stopped under a particular rafter, leaped up to grab it, and hung there by his left hand while his right hand fumbled in the thatch and came out with a flour sack that clinked and had a noticeable weight to it.

When Hugh stepped back into the house, shifting the flour sack from hand to hand as he shrugged off his coat, all eyes at the table were on him. Mum, Morrison and Hector didn't look; they were at the stove and Mum was carefully pouring molten lead from a thick-walled, spouted little pot into bullet moulds the boys were holding. But once the current bullet mould was safely hissing in a pan of water, they looked, too.

Hugh clunked his flour sack down on the table, reached in and pulled out a U. S. Army dragoon's revolver, a tin of percussion caps, a powder flask, a bag of .44 calibre, rough-edged lead bullets, a bullet mould and a spare cylinder. He said to the questions in the eyes, "Uh… Sorry, Da, I was kinda… sneaky about this. Back in the summer, one of the deserters on the road crew desperate-wanted ready cash for whiskey and poker, and Mr. Mair wouldn't give him any more advances, and the fella said he didn't plan on ever using this again, so… I got Mr. Mair to advance me and dock it from my pay the next couple months bit by piece, under 'provisions and sundries.' I guess I… guess I felt a little foolish spending money on something like this, when I was s'posed to be saving up to buy MacGregor's farm and get set up."

Da said: "It was your money, Hugh."

Hugh shrugged, then hefted the revolver and pulled back the hinged rod lined under the barrel, freeing the cylinder from the frame. "You see, you load both the cylinders and keep one in your pocket, so if you fire off all five shots and need more right away, you just switch cylinders. Me and Donald tried it out back in the woods last summer." Out of the corner of his eye, Hugh caught a look of betrayal flicker across Aleck's face – that Hugh had trusted Donald with the secret and not him. Hugh wanted to tell him it was nothing personal, there were just naturally things you told older brothers and not younger ones, and vice-versa. But Hugh knew it was pointless to try, he just seemed to keep stepping on Aleck's toes, and trying to tell Aleck he was only imagining sore toes just made it worse.

Once Hugh had loaded both cylinders and locked one into place, he said: "Uh… Da, today's the day I'm s'posed to exercise Montrose…"

Mum and Da looked at each other. It had never been said aloud, but Hugh was pretty sure they both knew 'exercising Montrose' meant meeting up with Nancy Prince.

Hugh said: "If the Sioux do come, they'll come from the south or the west, and I'll be riding north on the east side of the river. If I hear any kind of alarm I'll gallop back here and go with you, or follow you, to wherever we're going to line up to meet them. You said yourself we'd have plenty of warning." Hugh felt a bit out of his depth talking about 'lining up to meet them,' but it did seem logical that the plan would be to intercept the Sioux before they got in among the houses.

Mum said: "All right." Her eyes flicked to the revolver on the table and then back up at him. "But you take that with you."

The revolver was too long to fit into the pocket of his blanket coat, so Hugh put it back in the flour sack and tied the sack to his ceinture flechée. It bounced a bit against the back of his leg and the side of Montrose's saddle blanket, but not enough to aggravate either of them. When the bridge across the frozen stream down to the hollow came in sight, he could see Wauh Oonae up ahead and on foot. She was walking Cheengwun up and down the road to keep them both warm; the wind had calmed down after last night's blizzard, but the air was still cold enough to crack trees. Hugh slowed Montrose's gait so that when they got up to her he could stop and climb down for a hello kiss and squeeze. But before he could, she vaulted into the saddle, called: "Come on, there's something I want you to see," and kicked Cheengwun into a gallop back north.

When they slowed their horses to a walk again, to let them catch their breath, Hugh said: "What is it?"

She shook her head, "You have to see it – up near the Stone Fort." She seemed tense, but then everybody did these days.

"You heard about the Sioux…?"

"Uh-huh."

"You think it's true?"

"I don't know – the Sioux don't tell the Saulteaux their secrets any more than they tell white men. My father says the Sioux would have to be pretty desperate-stupid to try a raid on Red River, but they just might be that desperate. People here'd drop their differences for awhile pretty quick if they saw the Sioux on the horizon."

"Huh. Maybe the Sioux'll end up doing us a favour."

"Huh?"

"Well, like you said, if people here saw the Sioux on the horizon, they'd stop spitting and spatting about Provisional Governments and Lieutenant Governors and what-all. And I'm thinking if people have stood up beside each other to fight off some real danger, they're less likely to squabble amongst each other about stuff that don't matter. Oh, I know some of that political stuff matters, but maybe the Sioux'd help show us the difference between what matters and what don't."

Nancy Prince burst out laughing. Hugh ducked his head and glanced sideways at her, feeling like an idiot for waxing philosophical when he didn't even know how to spell it. But although her eyes were fixed on him with amazement, it wasn't necessarily amazement at what an ass he could be, and she was shaking her head with a complicated smile. She said: "Goddamn, Hugh Sutherland, sometimes I swear – well, I guess I just did… Sometimes I swear if a doctor told you he was gonna have to cut off your foot, you'd say 'Well, that'll save me half the cost of moccasins for the rest of my life.'"

He didn't quite know how to take that. Apparently she saw he didn't, because she reached one mittened hand across the gap between their horses to touch his arm, and said: "That ain't such a bad way to be. Fact is, it's lucky for me – 'cause your same eyes that always see good possibilities are the same eyes that look at me."

It took Hugh a moment to hear what Wauh Oonae had said; he'd been busy watching her mouth form the words. He said: "Huh. Well, um… Say, you ever meet this Racette fella?"

She shivered, and not from the cold. "No."

"I know the Sioux call him Shawven, but –"

Nancy giggled and said the name again in what Hugh guessed must be the proper way. It sounded almost the same as the way he'd said it, but compounded the sounds in a different way than Cree or Ojibway, a way Hugh couldn't quite catch. So instead of trying to imitate it, he just went on, "… but I don't know what it means. Do you?"

"Uh-huh."

"Well…?"

"I don't think I should say them kind of words around you till after we're married."

After another stint of trotting and galloping, Nancy said: "What's in your bag?"

Instead of telling her, Hugh tugged his right mitten off with his teeth, untied the flour sack from his ceinture flechée and reached his hand in. The revolver had got turned upside-down with the jostling, but there was no danger of it going off unless it was double-cocked and that took some doing even when you intended to do it. So Hugh just wrapped his bare hand around the body of the gun and pulled it out. A stab of scalding heat shot through his hand, and he didn't so much drop the revolver as throw it down. He reined in Montrose, looked at the palm of his hand for blisters that weren't there, and realised it hadn't been heat but cold, a cold so sharp it burned. Which was just about what anybody with any sense would expect from a piece of metal that'd been sucking-in thirty or forty degrees of freezing for an hour or two.

Hugh shoved his right hand into his coat and under his armpit, and climbed down awkwardly to retrieve the pistol. Wauh Oonae was laughing so hard she could hardly get out: "That's some powerful defence – any Sioux nearby would've run like hell from the whoop you let out."

Hugh warmed the revolver in his mittened hands before tucking it inside his coat, and it still sucked some of the warmth out through his wool shirt and sweater. When he was back on board and the horses walking forward again, he told Nancy how he'd come to possess a U. S. Army Colt's revolver. She said: "It's a good thing to have."

"Yeah, I can use it to cool the ice house."

They clucked the horses into a faster gait for another mile or so. Hugh didn't mind when the drumming hooves and jouncing made for minimal conversation, it made it less likely he'd say something stupid and it was pleasant enough just to be riding alongside of Nancy Prince. Next time they slowed, she said: "There's a new song, have you heard it? It's called 'The Ballad of the Trials of An Unfortunate King.'" There was a sly twinkle in her voice.

"No, I don't think so."

"It's pretty long, I prob'ly can't remember it all…" She began to sing in a shy, quavering alto that got stronger as she got safely through the melody a few times, and as Hugh got the gist and began to laugh. She sang partly in French and partly in English, and partly in la-las when she forgot a line. The song was about a king who came with his royal retinue to assume his throne in the north-west country. Unfortunately, the people he'd come to rule over wouldn't let him into his country, so he had to camp out south of its border. More unfortunate still, the king hadn't thought to bring any money with him, expecting to loot all he wanted from his new subjects, so he had to beg firewood and pemmican from the foreigners he was stranded among. Hugh especially liked the part about the poor, unfortunate king not being able to sit on his throne – word had it that the Honourable McDougall had shipped west a very fancy and impressive Governor's Chair – and had to settle for a throne with a hole in the seat.

When the song was done, or at least when Nancy said: "That's all I can remember," Hugh hooted with laughter and clapped his mittens together. He sputtered: "Wherever did that come from?"

"Nobody knows, just came from everywhere all at once. But since it came first in French, and for other reasons, most people think it musta been Pierre Falcon."

Hugh certainly knew the name, but it was a name out of history and fables. Pierre Falcon had been brother-in-law to Mr. Grant, and had made up the songs that helped make up the New Nation, including 'The Ballade of Seven Oaks.' Hugh said: "I didn't know he was still alive."

"Oh yeah – must be eighty years old now, but still lively. When the news got to White Horse Plains about the Metis barricading St. Norbert, old Monsieur Falcon's grandsons had to hold him down from grabbing his gun and jumping on his horse – 'Just let me kill another Englishman before I die!'"

The next walking stretch when Hugh and Wauh Oonae could talk again, they were almost to the stretch of thick woods that closed around the river road, but not quite. With the riverbank poplars and alders reduced to bare twigs, Hugh could see the road on the other side of the river. A lone horseman was on it, trotting south: a very large man on a very large horse. Not that the man was particularly tall, but tremendously wide. Hugh said: "Funny, that looks like Mr. McKay – James McKay."

"Ain't two like that."

"But… I heard James McKay had took his family down to St. Joe across the border, to wait out the strange times going on up here."

"And *I* heard James McKay can't cross the border, 'cause the Americans still want to arrest him for being friendly with the Sioux in the Minnesota Massacre. Tomorrow I'll prob'ly hear James McKay's gone to London to marry the Queen. Onliest things you can believe these days is what you see with your own eyes, and I see James McKay trotting his horse south on the west side of the Red River."

"Huh. Well, you'd know him better. I hardly never seen him up close, me whatever. Well, except for that time he gave you and me a drink of whiskey, at the surprise party, when we was looking at the Northern Lights… Well, that was a long time ago…"

"Oh, I still remember. Always will. That was the first time you told me you loved me."

"I couldn'ta been *that* drunk." Hugh had an immediate intuition that that hadn't come out right. "I mean is, I can't believe I was brave enough to say that then."

"I didn't say you said it, I said you told me."

"Oh." He let the soft thudding of the horses' ambling hooves on road-packed snow fill the silence for a moment. "I do, you know – love you."

"And I love you."

"Do you?"

"Didn't I just say so?"

"Well, you *said* it, but you didn't *told* me."

She lashed the trailing end of Cheengwun's halter at the side of Hugh's head, which he took to be a signal to kick Montrose back up to a gallop.

They were trotting when they passed by the cabin in the woods where Norbert Parisien lived. There was no one in the yard, but on the right side of the road there was a kind of gully in the snow that snaked into the woods, and a freshly-trampled path along its middle. Hugh figured the gully was where Norbert and his father and draft horse had tamped down the winter's accumulation so far, hauling logs out of the deeper woods, and the new tracks were over what had drifted in with the blizzard.

That set Hugh's imagination wandering along another side path. When they slowed for another breather and dismounted to unbow their legs, walking stiffly along the road leading their horses, he said: "It's amazing handy about firewood, ain't it?"

"Uh… what is?"

"Well, you gotta let it age for awhile, dry out, eh?"

"Uh… yeah."

"And you wanna cut it in the winter when there's no sap in it, so it won't gum up your chimney. And you wouldn't wanna be in the woods in the summer anyways, 'cause the bugs'd eat you alive, and besides, in the summer you got so much to do around the farm. So you'd want to cut your wood in winter anyways – but hey, coincidence, that's also the best time to get the best-burning wood, and let it sit and age even better through the summer.

"I mean is, there's all these different, unconnected… things about firewood and bugs and farm seasons and what-all, you'd think there's bound to be some confliction somewhere along the line. But there ain't, it all fits together perfect. Amazing handy."

Hugh didn't know whether he'd expected her to join in his amazement, or laugh at his goofy ideas. What he definitely didn't expect was for her to murmur almost inaudibly, "You got a lotta faith in things. Come on, we still got a ways to ride."

The road had almost reached the end of the woods when there was a crash of gunfire up ahead: more than a few guns, firing more or less at the same time, the sound so sharpened by the cold Hugh couldn't guess how far away it was. He reined in Montrose, whipped off his right hand mitten and shoved his hand in his coat for the revolver, pulse pounding in his ears. Wauh Oonae said: "No, don't worry. Come on, you'll see," and nudged Cheengwun back into motion.

As they came out of the woods, Hugh could see the pink-grey sprawl of the Stone Fort ahead across the river, and what appeared to be a coven of black spiders milling around outside the south wall. When he got closer, he saw that they were men on foot. Closer still, and he could hear someone barking orders. They formed a line and fired their guns more or less in unison – puffs of grey smoke drifting up to join the blanket of cloud.

When Hugh and Nancy got to where they were directly across the river from the marching men, she halted her horse, so so did he. The men – Hugh figured near a hundred of them – weren't dressed like soldiers, but seemed to be trying to act like ones. They formed a kind of double line facing out onto the prairie, the front line kneeling, and then fired another fusillade at the horizon. Hugh said: "What the hell are they doing?"

"Practising."

"Practising? For what? For the Sioux…?"

"Maybe partly, now, but they would be anyway. There's men there from St. Andrew's Parish, St. Johns, Little Britain, Winnipeg, even some from St. Peters. And the ones you see ain't half of them."

"But… if they're not practising in case of the Sioux, then what are – ?"

She cut him off a bit impatiently, but there was something besides impatience in her voice. "They're practising to march down to Fort Garry and take it back from the National Committee."

Hugh thought about it for about two seconds, then said: "Nah. That'd be crazy, marching up against stone walls and cannons –"

"They can take along their own cannons from the Stone Fort, they been practising with them, too."

Montrose shook his head, jingling his bridle chain. Hugh absently rubbed one mittened hand up and down the glossy black neck to reassure the one with horse sense they wouldn't stand still in the cold for long, while his eyes stayed trained on the lines of men marching up and down the new-tramped parade ground outside the Stone Fort. Maybe Colonel Dennis and his volunteers knew what they were doing – after all, what did John Hugh Sutherland know about military matters? But it did seem to him unnecessary that anyone at Red River be thinking about military matters at all, unless and until the rumours about Racette and the Sioux turned out truthful. And he remembered that when his grandfather talked about his soldiering days – on the rare occasions when Granda could be talked into talking about them at all – it was with a strange mixture of pride and disgust.

Nancy Prince said: "Let's get outta here."

"Hm? Oh, yeah, cold for standing around in the open –"

"No, I mean let's get out of *here*, away from here, away from Red River." She spoke quickly, like it was something she'd worked out in her head and had to get across to him in its entirety: "I got cousins in the Saskatchewan country, and along the Qu'Appelle – there's just as good land there as here. Or we could just stay with them until the craziness here is over. The winter ain't really locked in bad yet, if we left tomorrow we could be there by mid-December, even if we get storm-stayed a day or two along the way."

It was a lot to take in all of a sudden. Hugh couldn't think of anything to say, except: "But… we're not married yet."

"I don't care."

That would've set him back on his heels if he'd been standing. Nothing else she might've said would've convinced him so immediately that *'Let's get outta here'* was a long way past a whim. He turned Montrose around and nudged him in close, nose-to-tail with Wauh Oonae's pony – over the years Montrose and Cheengwun had learned to tolerate each other. Hugh peeled off his right hand mitten and softly skated his knuckles down Nancy's cheek, lifting off the tear dangling on her cheekbone. He said as gently as he could and still be heard, "I know things are crazy around here just now, but they're bound to sort themselves out. If I thought there was any chance of anything bad happening to you here, I'd be packing up my camp gear right now."

"I'm not afraid of anything bad happening to me – though what I *am* afraid of is worse than anything that might happen to me." She reached up one mittened hand to his bare one, brought his hand to her mouth and kissed the back of it. "If the men here march up to Fort Garry, that's a long ways from St. Peters, but you'd be right in the middle of it."

"I got no plans to enlist in anybody's army, Nancy, believe me – except against the Sioux, if they come."

"But if people start shooting guns at each other right around your home, you and your father and brothers will have to do something."

"Well, all the more reason I shouldn't go running off on my family right now. But nothing's gonna happen except this kind of marching around in circles, and people yelling at each other in meetings."

"You got more faith in people's brains than I do. You told me about when the roadcrew men picked up Superintendent Snow to throw him in the river… What if Mr. Snow had had a gun on him and shot one of the men trying to grab him? All hell woulda broke loose and you woulda been in the middle of it."

"Well…" Now that she'd brought that up, he could remember standing on the edge of that crowd in astoundment that grown men could carry on like that. "But Mr. Snow didn't have a gun on him, or maybe he even did and was too smart to use it, knowing all hell woulda broke loose. I know there's bound to be some idiots over there," pointing at the toy soldiers across the river, "but there's bound to be some people with sense there, too – same as in Fort Garry. Things'll get sorted out."

"Maybe. I got a bad feeling about this."

"Well… but what you're saying, I mean about us taking off, it's a lot to think through all of a sudden. Another week won't lock the winter in much worse'n it is now. And who knows, another week and things here might be sorted out." He glanced up at the pale white patch of the sun in the grey sky. Already the sun was working its way down from as high as it got this time of year.

Nancy read and replied to that glance. He was getting almost accustomed to the fact that she and he could reply to things the other hadn't said. She said: "You got a lot further to get home than me. Next week, then."

"Yeah, next week."

CHAPTER 44

Agnes and Eliza were among the stock shelves behind the White Store's counter, unpacking a few small freight boxes from back in the warehouse. Unfortunately, one of the boxes contained Cuban cigars to be shifted into a humidor and the glass jar on the counter. Unfortunate because as soon as the lid was lifted and the pungency wafted out, Eliza belched and gurgled and gasped, "Oh no! I never know what's –"

"Go!" Agnes barked. As Eliza clattered up the stairs toward her bedroom and the bucket that lived there, Agnes called after her, "And lie down awhile after. I'm fine here."

Agnes was partly jealous of and partly sorry for Eliza. On the one hand, Agnes had now been married two-and-a-half years without getting pregnant, while Eliza had been married barely two-and-a-half months. On the other hand, carrying and bearing children truly was a burden when the parents' lives hadn't yet reached a state of some security. The Mairs no doubt had thought their future was secure, as had the Schultzes, until the barrier went up in St. Norbert. *'Well,'* Agnes scolded herself, *'that won't be up much longer, will it? Just carry on with the task at hand.'*

She was halfway through unpacking a box of spindled silk thread when the shop bell jingled, so she went to take up her customer-welcoming stance behind the counter. It wasn't a customer, it was a half-dozen Metis carrying guns. In their lead, unarmed, was the Secretary of the National Committee, Louis Riel. Agnes had only seen him from a distance before, but there was no mistaking the well-brushed, wavy chestnut hair, thickish mustache, and the way the rougher-looking men around him all followed his lead, taking off their hats as he did when she came into view. Up close, she could see the mustache was so neatly trimmed the contours of his upper lip still showed, that he had a heart-shaped face with a dimpled chin, and that he looked more French than Indian. She reminded herself that that last shouldn't have come as a surprise, since she'd heard that the self-appointed spokesman for the halfbreeds was actually only one-eighth Indian at most. He said: "Bonjour, Madame Schultz."

"My husband isn't here."

"Ah, but we were wondering if another man might be."

"Pardon me?"

"Are you acquainted with a gentleman named George Klyne?"

Agnes was inclined to reply: *'What the hell business is that of yours?'* but Riel was being courtly and cordial so far, so she decided to play along and see where he was going. "I've heard the name, that's all."

"Ah. Despite the name, George Klyne is Metis, but unfortunately he is also a traitor."

"To whom?"

"To his people, and all the people of Red River."

"How so?"

Riel waggled a finger at her and smiled. "Ah, Madame Schultz, I am not one who believes anyone who wears skirts is dull-witted." She refrained from saying: *'That would include priests?'* "You can add up more than shop accounts. I know that your husband is at the Stone Fort, and so is Colonel Dennis. Someone who knows this country much better than any Canadian brought Colonel Dennis back here from Pembina by backtrails that are not being watched, and is carrying messages back and forth to McDougall. We wish to ask George Klyne whether he might have some intuition as to who that someone might be."

"Then why come here?"

"Your husband is closely tied to Colonel Dennis and the 'Honourable' McDougall, and someone is paying George Klyne to run errands – Monsieur Klyne is certainly not doing it out of principle. It would not be illogical to suspect Klyne frequents these premises."

"Perhaps not illogical, but incorrect. There is no George Klyne here. You might have better luck looking for him at the Red Dog Saloon," where the O'Lone brothers kept sawed-off shotguns behind the bar in case of unwelcome intruders.

"Perhaps you are mistaken, about who is or is not here. This is a large building with many rooms, no doubt there are at least several rooms you haven't looked into today." Riel half-turned his head and raised a forefinger over that shoulder. "Adjutant-General, if you would proceed, s'il vous plait..."

Agnes looked past Riel to the man she would've noticed first if Riel hadn't been fronting the group: considerably taller than Riel, maybe even taller than her husband, with a swarthy face so chisel-featured he looked like an Indian with a beard. The hand he raised to wave his confréres forward was immense and cris-crossed with old scars. Agnes had never seen Ambroise Lépine up close before, either, but didn't need to have him introduced. It wasn't just his size; she had never seen a man so casually certain that any man or group of men who offered him trouble was making a mistake. Consequently, his face bore a peaceful expression that expected no trouble and offered none. Agnes was quite sure that if she were male and had any brains at all – the two didn't always go together – mild-mannered Ambroise Lépine would've scare the pants off her.

As Lépine and his men started toward the shop counter, obviously intending to pass behind it to the warehouse and staircase and ransack the building, Agnes flung her arms wide and shouted: "No! This is private property! You have no right! Show me a search warrant!"

Riel said: "It is true, Madame Schultz, that we have no search warrant. But where are we to get one? There is no court of law at Red River anymore, no government – a situation I am trying to remedy, but George Klyne is interfering with my efforts."

"George Klyne is not here!"

"Hm. Perhaps. Or perhaps the lady doth protest too much."

There was a thump of booted feet cascading down the stairs from the common room. Lépine looked to Riel; Riel flicked an answering glance out of the corner of his eye and minisculely shook his head. Agnes read the unspoken conversation: Lépine had wondered if that might be George Klyne trying to bolt out the side door; Riel had answered that if it was, the pork barrel guards outside the loading doors would nab him.

Superintendent Snow came out from among the banks of shelves between the shop counter and the stairway, looking slightly dishevelled and with his right hand behind his back. He stopped at the counter and said: "Oh. Monsieur Riel."

"Bonjour, Monsieur Snow."

Ambroise Lépine said gently, but with a much more guttural accent than Louis Riel's English, "What do you got in your right hand, Mister Snow?"

Mr. Snow very slowly and deliberately brought out his right hand holding a revolver, which he was very careful not to point in anyone's direction. He set it on the counter and said: "When I heard Mrs. Schultz's voice raised, I feared someone might be trying to take advantage of her in these troubled times. Obviously that's not the case."

"Just so," Riel nodded. "We are looking through the village of Winnipeg for a man named George Klyne."

"I am vaguely acquainted with the gentleman, but he's not here."

"So said Madame Schultz, and I do not doubt her honesty nor yours. But, as I said to her, this is a large building with many rooms, someone could be in one of those rooms without your knowledge. I pledge we will not disturb you, just a quick scout through."

Riel moved around the counter, Lépine followed him, and the rest of the hunting party followed Lépine. Agnes could see there was no point trying to stop them, so she fell in beside Riel to keep an eye on them. Behind the aisles of shelves behind the counter was a kind of squared-off hallway, with the door to the outside on the left, the staircase to the living quarters on the right, and the door into the warehouse straight ahead. Riel pointed, "That is the door to the warehouse?"

"Yes."

"We'll start there." As Riel led the way through the doorway, Agnes saw Lépine flick a forefinger at one of his followers, who took up a stance at the foot of the stairs in case someone tried to sneak down them and out through the store while the rest were in the warehouse. It surprised her a bit that these rough and unruly buffalo hunters were so well-disciplined that it only took a tiny gesture for one to understand the leader and obey. But then, this small party accompanying Lépine was no doubt the elite among his 'soldiers,' and probably so inbred they practically shared the same brain. And it was too early in the day for them to be much inebriated.

Inside the warehouse there was enough light through the windows to make out the general shapes of things, but the sunlight didn't carry much warmth and the small stove in the corner barely kept the cavern above freezing. Agnes wrapped her shawl tighter around herself as the Metis went around prodding into corners and peering behind crates. Riel stopped beside a rank of large barrels, wrapped his knuckles against one of them and said to her: "This would be the famous government pork…?"

"Yes."

"Well, your husband always said he would be first in line for pork-barrelling."

Agnes didn't reply. She knew from imported newspapers that 'pork barrel' was the Canadian colloquialism for government graft, and insiders fattening on public money. If that was a sample of Louis Riel's celebrated elegant wit, she could live without it.

A hint of a smile lifted one corner of his mustache. "Do you know, madame, the answer to the ancient riddle: 'If money is the root of all evil, why doesn't it grow on trees?'"

She unpursed her mouth just enough to let out: "No."

"It does, but it takes grafting." He didn't seem to have expected her to respond, just continued walking along the row of barrels, rapping his knuckles on the top of each. The search party worked its way to the back of the warehouse and the planked-off corner where the store's stock of guns and gunpowder was locked away. Riel fingered the padlock and said: "This is where you keep firearms?"

"We are a general store, and around here that means we do a fair bit of trade in firearms and ammunition." She caught Riel and Lépine glancing at each other, and wondered if they had truly only come looking for George Klyne, or also to map out how many weapons were in and around the White Store. Fortunately, most of the guns belonging to Christian and the lodgers had gone with them to the Stone Fort. Or perhaps unfortunately – Riel and Lépine wouldn't have got past the store counter if a dozen armed men had thundered down the stairs with Superintendent Snow.

Riel let go the padlock and shrugged, "Well, I doubt George Klyne has locked himself in there." Lépine chuckled and Riel led the way out of the warehouse and up the staircase.

Agnes grew increasingly offended as the rough-handed Metis rummaged through the common room, and even more so when they moved into the kitchen. She began to help them out by opening the stove and calling to the searing coals: "Are you in there, George Klyne?" or picking up a chicken thawing on the counter and calling into its vent hole: "Come out, George Klyne!" Riel chuckled, which she wasn't certain was annoying, or a sign he appreciated that although she couldn't stop the invasion of her privacy, at least she could ridicule it.

One thing she was certain of, from his general demeanour and fastidiously groomed appearance, was that Louis Riel had no small opinion of himself. She remembered from her St. Boniface days that one of the more acerbic nuns had said that Louis Riel's mother and sisters 'worshipped the ground he walked above,' or maybe it was 'worshipped the water he walked on,' Agnes disremembered. At that time, Riel had been a thousand miles from Red River and had been for years, but he was still a topic of conversation in the convent, and very little of it even remotely acerbic. One of the nuns' favourite stories about Louis Riel's inborn saintliness was that his grandmother had been on the threshold of entering Holy Orders when Jean Baptiste Lagimodière proposed marriage. Well, Agnes knew how that game went, and saintliness didn't figure into it.

When the search party came out of the kitchen and Ambroise Lépine reached for the first doorknob down the hall, Agnes erupted: "No! That is my private chamber – myself and my husband's."

Riel said: "I understand, madame, but you must understand that that very fact might've made it seem a good place for someone to sneak into and hide when he heard us downstairs. But, only I will go in there." He seemed to reconsider that. "Well, myself and one other."

Lépine told off one of his men to stay with Riel, then led the others to explore the rooms down the hallway. As Riel reached for the doorknob, Agnes stepped in front of him and opened it herself, then stepped inside and aside to let them enter. Inside was a small sitting room with a chaise lounge, easy chair, stove and writing desk, and a beaded curtain in the doorway to the bedroom. Riel stopped in the middle of the sitting room and turned to face her. He said: "You have made a warm and pleasant home here, Madame Schultz, and it shows the love you feel for it. All people here love their home, even if it is only a bark wigwam on a lakeshore. People here have lived for generations with a freedom people in the east cannot comprehend – I know, I have been in the east and seen its machinery…"

Agnes found herself having a very strange experience. Everything seemed to have disappeared except Louis Riel's dark eyes, which were glistening and dancing. His eyes and his voice: "The people of Red River and Rupert's Land have paid for that freedom with their blood, and their benign sufferance of each others' differences. No doubt they must lose some of that freedom, as the world encroaches, but that does not mean they must become slaves. I intend no impediment to anyone's honest hopes and aspirations, but I hope your husband can understand – before too late – that the people who live here did not buy their rights and freedoms lightly, and will not sell them lightly."

Then the eyes flicked away to glance around the sitting room again, and whatever strange spell had been cast was broken. The 'soldier' that Lépine had delegated to stay with Riel crouched to look under the sofa, then stood up and shook his head. Riel headed for the bedroom doorway. Agnes followed him through the curtain beads rattling and clicking together, and Riel's henchman followed her.

While the henchman crouched to look under the bed, Riel opened the wardrobe where Agnes's dresses hung. She felt her face heating with embarrassment and anger. Riel slowly stuck his hand in between two silk dresses, far enough to tap his fingertips against the bare back of the wardrobe, then pulled his hand back out and carefully closed the door.

Riel turned to his confrére getting up off the floor, they both shook their heads and went back through the beaded curtain. Agnes followed them back out into the hallway and closed the door behind them. All down the hallway, individual Metis were coming out of individual doors and shaking their heads at their captain. Lépine led them back to Riel and said: "No one here, excepting one young woman who is ill – the morning sick. Not so bad as my wife, but no fun."

Riel said: "You did not disturb her…?"

"No, no – just looked in and then closed the door again."

"Good, good, you are naturally gallant." Then Riel shrugged, "Ah well, de-Klyned here, on to Bannatyne's. I do apologise again, Madame Schultz, for so rudely intruding upon your privacy. But I hope you understand that we are working to achieve peace and justice for all people of Red River, and most are working with us. But a few, for reasons of their own, are working to prevent that, and we must perforce be a little rude at times to intercept their intentions."

Agnes accompanied Riel and his minions down the stairs, to make sure they left through the side door and not through the store with its shelves of pocketable goods. Looking at the back of Riel's head two steps below her, a strange imp in her head whispered: *'His hair is chestnut and yours hazel, maybe you're both nuts.'* The disjointedness of the day had definitely made her a bit giddy. Halfway down the stairs, Riel commented to her casually over his shoulder, "Looks to be a harsh winter, and still a long way from St. Agnes Eve."

She almost tripped. Riel immediately reached back to steady her, but she caught her balance before his hand could touch. She said: "Pardon me?"

"'St. Agnes Eve – Ah bitter chill it was!' Said to be always the coldest day of the year. You must have heard that saying when you were living in the convent, since it is your Name Day."

"That was a long time ago."

"Really? I wouldn't have thought so long… Well, it was a loss to the Church when you unconverted your conversion, Madame Schultz. But, as you must have noticed, at Red River we go to whatever church we choose, and no one thinks any the less of those who make a different choice. Again, my apologies for the intrusion, and thank you for your co-operation. Do tell Dr. Schultz I'm sorry we missed him."

Christian came home a few hours later, along with all the men who'd accompanied him to the Stone Fort. He was furious to learn of the Metis 'visit,' and apologetic that he'd left her alone to face it. She said: "Oh, I don't believe I was in any danger of any insult or injury – at least not as long as Monsieur Riel was here."

"*'Monsieur'* Riel? Courtly gentleman, is he?"

"Well, in a Gallic and garlic sort of way. But that doesn't change the invasion of our home."

"Bloody right it doesn't," and he immediately sat down and penned a statement of protest to President John Bruce, and two copies for the two Representatives for Winnipeg. The statement reported plainly that Louis Riel and a dozen cronies had forced their way into Dr.

Schultz's home while he was away and ransacked it, *'even tampered with the privacy of my wife's chamber.'*

Once the messengers had gone to deliver that message, Christian leaned back with a hot toddy in the company of the common room to tell Agnes and Superintendent Snow the news from the Stone Fort. "Lieutenant Governor McDougall's proclamation is being printed as we speak, but postdated a few days until that creaky old hand-press can run off enough copies to paper the settlement with them. I jotted down a few phrases while I was helping Winship set the type."

He reached into his waistcoat pocket, tugged out a much-folded piece of paper and unfolded it. "Ahem. To begin with, the Lieutenant Governor of the Dominion of Canada's North West Territories proclaims that Colonel Dennis is commissioned his *'Lieutenant and Conservator of the Peace.'* Then, *'whereas large bodies of armed men have unlawfully assembled on the high road between Fort Garry and Pembina,'* Colonel Dennis is empowered to *'raise, organise, arm, equip and provision a sufficient force… and with said force to attack, arrest, disarm or disperse the said armed men as unlawfully assembled and disturbing the public peace…'*"

A thrill passed through Agnes's body. Those men who'd stomped their greasy moccasins through her home today were going to be running in them tomorrow, or some tomorrow soon.

"And then, Colonel Dennis adds a short proclamation of his own." Christian's voice began to rise as he read it out, and partway through he rose out of his chair. "*By virtue of the above commission from the Lieutenant Governor I now hereby call on and order all loyal men of The North West Territories to assist me by every means in their power to carry out the same and thereby restore public peace and order and uphold the supremacy of the Queen in this part of Her Majesty's dominions.*"

Agnes applauded and cheered and so did everyone else in the common room, even the ones who'd likely already read the proclamation at the Stone Fort. It would be one thing to read those words on paper, and quite another to hear them boomed out by that golden-haired giant with his fist in the air, and bedamned to what the government-pork guards outside might overhear.

When the applause and emotion subsided enough, Agnes proclaimed: "Time to raise the flag!" The Sundays and holidays raising of the Canada flag in front of the White Store had been set aside since the Metis captured Fort Garry.

Superintendent Snow said: "Um, don't you think that might be a little premature – red flag to a bull and all?"

Agnes looked to her husband, who was rubbing his beard thoughtfully. He said: "Mr. Snow might be right, my dear. You see, we all of us who went down to the Stone Fort are now enrolled in Colonel Dennis's militia. But our orders were to return home for now and await further orders. I don't expect we'll have to wait long, once this proclamation is out. But I don't think we should do anything in the meantime that the French might see as a poke in the eye."

"Well, there are other ways to raise a flag."

Supper was an excited babble of possibilities and expectations, momentarily interrupted by the arrival of Dr. Bown. He declined the offer of a plate, but accepted a cup of tea and sat sipping silently until the table was cleared and cigars being passed around. Then Dr. Bown said: "Well, I didn't want to spoil your meal, so… I've come from the *Nor'Wester* office, where I was summoned – and 'summoned' is the proper word – by representatives of the National Committee, or Convention of Delegates, or whatever it's called this week.

"They wanted me to print something off for them on the *Nor'Wester* press. At the same time, another hand copy of the same was brought over to Coldwell at *The Pioneer*, two presses being faster than one. Coldwell had no choice – couple of Metis with buffalo guns asking him 'pretty please' – but I had the excuse that half my type has been spirited away. What they wanted me to print is called 'The List of Rights.'"

Christian said: "List of *what*?"

Agnes said: "Whose rights?"

Bown shrugged, "Everybody's, I guess – a list of the conditions under which the people of Rupert's Land will agree to become part of the Dominion of Canada."

Christian snorted: "*Conditions*? It's already happened! Didn't they read the Queen's Proclamation?"

"I guess it didn't take. Apparently all the delegates from all the parishes – including our two from Winnipeg – are pretty much agreed on what they want, just disputing whether the list should be presented to McDougall in Pembina or sent straight to Ottawa."

Agnes said: "What do they want – free beer on Sundays?"

"Well," Walter Bown furled his fingers through his pelt of a beard, "they wouldn't let me keep the hand-copy, since I wasn't going to print it, but I had to go through it carefully to show I didn't have enough type on hand to print it… Let's see how much I can remember… representation in the federal government, namely Members of Parliament elected at Red River and in short order… Uhm… all local officials to be locally elected –"

"That's ridiculous!" Christian laughed, "The appointments have already been made – and the few that haven't will be appointed by the Lieutenant Governor once he gets here!" Agnes didn't like to shush her husband in public, but she would have if he hadn't left off his interjection so Dr. Bown could go on with the list.

"Let's see, what else do they want… that the people of Rupert's Land have the right to elect a local legislature, which shall conduct its business in both English and French –" That brought snorts and groans from all around the table. "Um… that the Dominion guarantees to negotiate treaties with all the various Indian tribes… Oh, and that the Dominion guarantees that within five years Red River to be connected by rail to the nearest rail line east, the railway land grants to be determined by the local legislature. All land titles, in fact, are to be regulated by the local legislature, and all existing occupation of land to be respected."

Agnes could see her husband's head slumping. Altogether, that tinplate List of Rights could wipe away everything he'd built and worked for in the last ten years.

Dr. Bown said: "Well, that's about all I can remember. There were some other clauses about local judiciary and so on, but the details escape me."

Christian raised his head again, and his eyes were bright and glistening. Agnes told herself she should've known her Viking wouldn't succumb that easily. He said: "It's not hard to see why 'Sheriff' McKenney and Hugh O'Lone and the other American annexionists would vote for this shopping list. When Ottawa replies *'This is preposterous,'* they'll have an excuse to plump for Washington.

"Well, boys…" he looked around the table. "All in all, it sounds to me like time to man the barricades."

All around the table there were nods, fist-thumpings and *Aye*s. Christian turned to Agnes in her perplexity and said: "You see, my dear, on the long ride back from the Stone Fort today, there was plenty of time for discussion of what might happen when Colonel Dennis's call to arms becomes public. For one thing, the French will realise that the government pork would go a long way toward provisioning Colonel Dennis's loyal militia, and likely they'll send a force from Fort Garry to confiscate it…"

Although he was speaking directly to her, he spoke in a strong enough voice to fill the room. Periodically, the rest of the men murmured words of agreement with what he was saying.

"And when Colonel Dennis does march out of the Stone Fort – well, a lot of Canadians in and around Winnipeg are scattered and defenceless, easy for the French to take hostage before he gets here. And there's no doubt it would be a great advantage to Colonel Dennis to have a secure bastion already in place close to Fort Garry, in advance of his line of march.

"Add to all that what happened to you here today, and now this 'List of Rights' giving the world the false impression that everyone at Red River defies the Queen's Proclamation, and I think you'll see – I hope you'll see – we have only one reasonable course of action: to barricade ourselves into this building, along with any other loyal citizens who care to join us, and defy the defyers. We have plenty of provisions and arms, I don't believe we lack for courage, and we know we're standing up for the rule of law."

Agnes smiled and put her hand on the big, capable shoulder. She said: "I'd call that raising the flag."

He lifted her hand off his shoulder and kissed the back of it, mustache hairs tickling her knuckles, then stood up and moved toward his coat, saying: "It's still early in the evening, I'll pay a call on some of the Canadian store owners along Main Road. They won't know yet about Colonel Dennis's call to arms, or what happened in our home this morning – which could happen in their own homes tomorrow. Maybe some of you other lads would care to drop in for a tipple at Dutch George's and the Red Dog – but mind your words to anyone you don't think we can count on, and be careful not to be overheard."

Christian came back a couple of hours later and told Agnes that some of the men he'd spoken with had pledged to come to the White Store tomorrow, and some had said they'd have to think it over. There wasn't much sleeping done in and around the White Store that night, the inhabitants were busy turning it into Fort Schultz: boarding over the windows to just firing slits and loopholes, moving furniture and bric-a-brac out of the way… The freight doors to the warehouse already had a stout bar across them, but the side door had to be reinforced. The stock of Carron stoves in the warehouse provided cast iron armour plating. And all the guns and ammunition in the padlocked corner of the warehouse were brought out and distributed, or stacked on the common room table in wait for the volunteers that would arrive tomorrow.

At one point, Charlie Mair laughingly called from the window he was boarding up: "Schultz, come have a look at this." Agnes trailed along behind her husband and pushed in front of him when they got to the window; he could see over her head perfectly well. Standing in the middle of Main Road in the moonlight was the night patrol, staring at the front of the White Store and the windows above. They weren't actually literally scratching their heads, but they might as well have been. Mair chortled, "They know the little Canadian beavers are busy at something, but they don't know what."

Christian said: "They'll know tomorrow." After a moment the night patrol shrugged at each other and went on about their rounds.

In the morning, men carrying blanket rolls and guns began to arrive and were passed through the guards downstairs up to the common room, where Agnes sat at the big table with a pencil and a list and a rough diagram of the layout of the second floor, trying to sort out sleeping space. Once the list grew past thirty, she realised that some of them would have to bunk in on the floor of the store, or even the warehouse. Not all of the men who came up the stairs were footloose adventurers by any means. James Ashdown owned a hardware store, Arthur Wright a harness shop, Joseph Lynch and John O'Donnel were both MDs, William Kitson was a schoolteacher…

Agnes was just getting used to an atmosphere filled with male jokes and discussion and the metallic sounds of firearms preparation, when the common room went quiet. She looked up and followed everyone else's eyes to the top of the stairs, where three ex-members of Superintendent Snow's roadbuilding expedition were standing. In the lead was tall rawboned Thomas Scott. Agnes's eyes and everyone else's went to Mr. Snow, who'd been sitting with his back to the staircase and now was standing and turning to see what everyone else was looking at. When he saw who it was he stood still and raised his chin a little.

Thomas Scott took two long strides toward Superintendent Snow, thrust out his open right hand and said: "Canada." Mr. Snow nodded, held out his own right hand and manfully shook Tom Scott's. Agnes could feel tears in her eyes, and had to bite her trembling lower lip.

Agnes's list had reached forty when the common room went silent again, but a different kind of silence, a different kind of uncertainty. Someone cocked a gun, sounding in the stillness like a hammer hitting an anvil. Emerging from the staircase was Sheriff McKenney's minion, one-armed Constable Mulligan, whom Agnes had locked in the store-shed two winters ago. The question was, what was Constable Mulligan doing here today – serving some trumped-up warrant? Agnes stood up as Constable Mulligan approached the table. He stopped in front of it and said: "Bygones is bygones, Mrs. Schultz. I've come to enlist."

She had to stand on tiptoe to kiss him on the cheek.

CHAPTER 45

Point Douglas John Sutherland was crouched in the barn very carefully daubing warm pine tar on the ulcerated hock of Old Queen Bessie, the matriarch of his cattle herd, when the dogs in the yard set up an unholy ruckus. John glanced at his fourth son, who was standing behind him watching how it was done. Morrison nodded and picked up his father's double-barrelled gun and his own leaned against a stall, while John levered his stiff knees straight. John remembered his father talking about the early days of the Fur Trade War, when any sensible colonist had walked out to his fields carrying a hoe in one hand and a musket in the other. Bloody nuisance, and most likely the intelligence about Racette and the Sioux had no intelligence to it. But until that was known for certain…

When John and Morrison came out of the barn, two Kirk Elders were helping each other down from the back of a cart-sled, and the dogs were quietening down. On the other side of the yard Donald, Hugh and Aleck were putting their own guns back in the buffalo robe wrap lain near where they were cutting and splitting firewood – the continuous crack of the axes was why John hadn't heard the sled pony's hooves. Morrison said: "I can finish up for you in here, Da, I was watching how you were doing it."

"Thank you, Morrison." John crooked his gun in his left arm, tugged his right mitten back on and moved toward the sled, reminding himself to take a look at Bessie later on to see if Morrison should be congratulated or carefully corrected. Horses and children had to be corrected gently enough that it didn't bruise their spirit. Dogs and children had to be corrected obliquely enough that they didn't feel humiliated in front of the rest of the pack.

John shook mittens with the elders and invited them inside. It was obvious they had some urgent reason to come jouncing across the river and down the froze-rutted road in a stand-up sleigh, but just as obvious that it'd be ridiculous to stand in the cold discussing whatever it was. Inside the house, most of the schoolchildren were sitting around the table with the books and slates their mother had condemned them to even though there would be no school until the Sioux threat was resolved. Janet was over by the fireplace with Margaret and Angus, standing up stiff-frozen bedsheets just brought in from the line. John called from the doorway as he kicked off his barn boots, "We have company, Mother."

Janet came dusting her hands on her apron, made her greetings and welcomes and said she'd serve tea in the parlour. All perfectly cheerful, except she slipped John a worried look that asked what the elders had come for. He twitched one eyebrow to tell her he didn't know, yet.

Once the two venerable gentlemen were ensconced and John had stoked up the parlour fire, the senior elder said: "We've come tae ask ye forr a favourr, John – a favourr tae the whole community."

The junior elder – barely seventy-two, if John remembered right – said: "Ye may hae heard that Dr. Schultz and forrty-some other Canadians hae barricaded themselves inside his store and taken up arms."

"No. No, I hadn't."

"Well, now ye have."

At that point Janet carried in a tray with the teapot, cups and homemade biscuits and berry leather. She looked around at the three men and didn't stay to wait for the tea to steep and do the pouring. The senior elder said: "Ye've no doubt hearrd, John, that Colonel Dennis is at the Stone Forrt training volunteers tae march in order and fire in volleys and such?"

"I have." John shrugged. "I guess if they've got, um, nothing better to do… And it doesn't do any harm to give out the idea there's some sort of… *organisation* around here, besides the National Committee at Fort Garry."

"Perhaps it would do no harm," the senior elder said gravely, "if Colonel Dennis intended to stay at the Stone Forrt. But what he intends is to march on Forrt Garry with guns and drums and drive out the National Committee. Dr. Schultz and his four dozen hae made a forrt out of the White Store to prepare the way."

John blinked at the senior elder, not sure whether the thin grey lips between the naked chin and sidewhisker-wings had actually formed the words he'd heard. John shifted his gaze to the junior elder, who nodded his head that those were the facts. A strange tingling feeling started up along the backs of John's hands and arms, and he felt a little queasy. His eyes lit on the teapot, and he judged it had steeped long enough to be strong enough for the elders. He poured three cups and handed two to the elders, along with the biscuit plate. When he leaned back in his chair, the air of unreality hadn't gone. If anything it had got worse, watching the two sober old men sipping tea – the senior elder daintily dipping-in a square of berry leather to soften it for his gums – while John's inner eye clearly saw gangs of armed men fighting each other through the farmyards of Kildonan, stray bullets flying through kitchen windows, barns burning, men from the east side of the river galloping across to help their brothers fighting on the west side, and if a child from one side were to be killed by a bullet from the other 'side'…

John remembered his father saying of the brutal skirmishing and sniping around the colony in the early years, that the one fortunate thing was no child was ever killed, because then peace and forgiveness would've been near impossible. He also remembered asking his father whether it had been a colonist or one of Mr. Grant's men who'd fired the first shot at Seven Oaks, since it was a matter of some debate among John's generation. John's father had replied: *"Does it matter? It could hae been a passing duck hunter and the result would hae been the same."*

"Regardless when Colonel Dennis," the senior elder mumbled around his mouthful of biscuit, "purrsues his intentions..." He took a large slurp of tea to help him swallow, then went on, "Dr. Schultz's Castle Belligerent is already a challenge and a threat to the men in Fort Garry."

"And that, John," the junior elder contributed, "is why we hae come tae ask ye a favour."

John said bewilderedly, "What can I do?"

The senior elder said: "We must make it known, to Colonel Dennis and the National Committee, that we of Kildonan will not assist or enlist in Colonel Dennis's militia. That might gie Colonel Dennis second thoughts on how strong a force he can raise, and make President John Bruce and company less nerrvous. Since ye hae lived on this side the river twenty years, many of the Metis in Forrt Garry are your neighbours, ye can speak wi' them easily."

"But first," the junior elder said, "we must hae a Public Meeting to determine that that *is* the opinion of all in Kildonan. The Reverend Dr. Black will take no part in politics or such-like temporal matters –"

"As is only fitting," the senior elder put in, "for a Meenister o' The Kirk."

" – but he has agreed to let the kirk be used for a Public Meeting tomorrow evening. If you agree to stand up, after services tomorrow Dr. Black will call on you and you can announce the Public Meeting."

"But... I'm not the elected Delegate. Shouldn't it be up to James Ross to call a public meeting?"

The two elders looked at each other, purse-lipped. The senior elder looked down and brushed a biscuit crumb off his lap. The junior elder said: "Young Jamie has his qualities, but he's not the man his father was. One of the qualities Jamie Ross is short on is moderation."

"Yesterday," the senior elder said as though it pained him to say it, "James Ross told a public meeting at St. Andrew's Parish that two hundred and twenty 'Scotchmen' were ready to march to Dr. Schultz's store to help defend the government pork from confiscation. We sent a message to St. Andrew's today that as far as we 'Scotchmen' were concerned, the government pork could go to the de'il."

"Ye're the right man to call a public meeting, John, being a Councillor of Assiniboia."

"But... I'm not a Councillor anymore, because there is no Council anymore. The Queen's Proclamation wiped out The Company's... *jurisdiction* as of December First, and that includes the Council of Assiniboia."

"But ye hae *been* our Councillor up until then, and people are accustomed t'ye carrying that responsibility. Ye can call a public meeting and take the chair o' it and nary a man in Kildonan will gainsay it."

There was a pause, and then the senior elder said: "So, *will* ye?" as if John had a choice.

As usual, John didn't get a chance to talk privately with his wife until they were tucked up in bed. Or in this case until she was; he was perched on the edge of the bed still wearing his trousers and day shirt. When he'd explained what the elders had told him, and asked him, Janet said: "Pork and pemmican."

"Pardon me?"

"You know how they sometimes call the Fur Trade Wars 'The Pemmican War' – because so much of it had to do with the two companies fighting over who got the pemmican…? It seemed silly till I got old enough to understand that men can't be paddling boatloads of furs and trade goods all day long and hunting for food at the same time. Fifty years ago it was pemmican, now it's government pork."

"I suppose so, but, um, provisions are much less of a… *scarcity* now. Not that the government pork doesn't… *matter* in itself, but it's also more or less an excuse for, um, a lot of other things."

"But all those things could lead to the same end as the pemmican did, couldn't they? Only much worse now. Because there are so many more people here now." She left off, as though waiting for him to say something to that. When he didn't, she said: "It's close, isn't it, John?"

He considered pretending to her that all was well, as some said a man always should to his wife. He looked down at her, with her silvering hair brushed-out and radiating across the pillow from a face grown rounded with blur-edged features in what was called 'the pregnancy mask,' which seemed to become permanent after the first four or five. John knew, from long winters reading his way through the Red River Library, that if he told someone from any other part of the world that his wife had borne fourteen children and only one had died, they would've said he was lying or lucky. But that was just the way things were at Red River, or what Red River had been all his lifetime. He said: "Damned close. Teetering on the edge."

She sealed and tightened her lips for a moment; the only lips he'd ever kissed as man and woman. Then she said: "It won't happen, not so long as there are enough men like you around to hold it steady. Now come to bed before the warming brick loses its heat and I have to suffer your cold feet."

In the kirkyard the next morning, the weekly standing-around to trade news started earlier than usual and went on until the last possible minute. It probably would've even if the weather hadn't suddenly turned mild, barely five below by the Fahrenheit thermometer. Some of the men in the kirkyard were saying Dr. Schultz had been proven right to barricade himself and his cronies and their guns inside the White Store, because the National Committee was now confiscating all the guns in the other shops in Winnipeg, and now any man who appeared on the road with a gun would be stopped and asked where he was going. Others said that Dr. Schultz's actions were the reason other guns were being confiscated.

It was Janet Sutherland who finally came back out onto the front step and yelled at the men still standing in the kirkyard, "For God's sake, does Dr. Black have to come out and ring the schoolbell?"

As the men headed into the kirk, one said to John: "She may only be your mother's daughter-in-*law*, but some'ut seems to've rubbed off."

At the end of the service, Dr. Black asked if anyone would like to address the congregation. John stood up and announced the Public Meeting for that evening, then went home with the family and hurried back for the end of the afternoon service to make the same announcement. After supper, he and his sons from Hector-up climbed onto one of the cart-sleighs, and the pony expressed its displeasure that the Point Douglas Sutherlands didn't seem to know if they were coming or going today.

The kirkyard was filled with sleighs and saddlehorses, and the kirk with men ranging from white-bearded to dewy-mustached. Rather than climbing into the high pulpit, John took up a stance on the step in front of it and called the meeting to order. To his great relief he discovered he didn't have to do much speaking, just maintain that everybody else only spoke one at a time.

A vaguely-familiar young man in one of the front pews stuck up his arm and John nodded at him. The young man stood up and said: "I don't see why not get enlisted in Colonel Dennis's militia. I hear he's paying an enlistment fee plus daily wages, and that's more'n anybody else is paying around here these days. And, after all, the Queen's Proclamation means we're Canadians now, don't it? So joining the Canadian Militia'd be our duty…"

John looked over at his five oldest sons in one of the square box pews at the side of the pulpit, and tried to not picture them marching dutifully into gunfire. Donald, of course, wouldn't take any course of action his father advised against. But John could see Hugh enlisting for the sake of an adventure, and Aleck would follow wherever Hugh went. But then, Hugh wouldn't stick five minutes with someone telling him 'left-right-left' and the proper angle to slope his musket.

The young man who had the floor was in mid-sentence when a considerably older voice cut in from the back of the hall, "Is that you, Tom Matheson? It sounds like your voice, but I can't recognise by the back of your head and you're talking like there's nothing in it. What, you'd take a musket and bayonet to shoot and stab the boys you hunted gophers with, and who pulled you out the river when you fell through the ice? Or have them shoot and stab you?

"And for what? For the glorious Dominion of Canada? Canada didn't ask our opinions when they decided to buy us, or decided who would govern us. And now they want us to help them put in place what they and they alone have decided upon? Stuff that for a dead chicken."

Essentially and eventually that turned out to be the consensus of the meeting. The question remaining was who would convey that message – in politer terms – to Fort Garry and the Stone Fort. It was decided that since Point Douglas John Sutherland was well-acquainted with many families on the St. Boniface side of the river, and somewhat acquainted with Colonel Dennis from putting up a building next to the survey expedition's headquarters, he was the logical person to bear the message to both forts tomorrow. John glanced at a pew on the other side of the pulpit from his sons, and saw the two elders who'd visited him yesterday nodding at each other contentedly. He'd been had.

But next morning while John was letting his breakfast settle and pondering politic ways to say 'stuff that for a dead chicken,' waiting till the last minute to have Montrose saddled and brought out into the cold, a young Bannerman came across the river with a folded broadsheet in his pocket. "Da said you'd want to see this, Mr. Sutherland. There's hundreds of 'em in Kildonan and St. Johns and all, but Da figured they might notta got to your side of the river."

John thought at first it must be the List of Rights that had been posted and distributed yesterday, and the young Bannerman had wasted a hike. But when he unfolded the broadsheet, one glance at the top told him it wasn't. *'By His Excellency the Honourable William McDougall... Lieutenant Governor of the North West Territories...'* It was in the form of a long, formal letter to Colonel Dennis, appointing him *'conservator of the peace'* and authorising him to raise a militia to *'take, disperse or overcome by force'* the group of armed men currently interfering with lawful authority.

That wasn't all that different from what the two elders had said Colonel Dennis was up to, except that this proclamation took it out of the realm of rumour. But there was a shorter, added proclamation from Colonel Dennis which changed the situation entirely. *'I hereby call on and order all loyal men of the North West Territories...'* That wasn't a call for volunteers, it was a direct command from the deputised representative of the authorized representative of Her British Majesty. The wording wasn't open to interpretation: any man who didn't obey the order to enlist was therefore not a loyal subject of the Crown, and thereby placed himself outside the law.

John sat at the table for a long while, with his elbows propped on either side of the broadsheet and his hands on his temples, watching the phrases jump off the page. Finally he looked around and saw Margaret passing by. "Margaret, do go out and ask Hugh to saddle me one of the ponies, please."

Why one of the ponies and not Montrose was because where John had decided to go, his mount would likely have to stand in the open for some while, and even though the weather had milded up somewhat it was still better suited to a shaggy shagganappi pony than big sleek Montrose. Why Hugh and not one of the other boys was because the ponies tended to come to Hugh more easily, instead of playing chase-me-'round-the-paddock. John thought of tucking the proclamation away somewhere, instead of leaving it out in the open where the boys could see it – the boys who would be 'men' in terms of Colonel Dennis's order. But they were bound to hear about it from passersby, and better they should read it than get it secondhand garbled.

John angled the pony up onto Point Douglas, where the riverbank was more sloped than sheer, and turned south along Main Road. At the north edge of the town of Winnipeg, several armed Metis were standing around a fire of scraps of lumber from a half built house nearby – or maybe it wasn't only scraps; who was going to tell them to keep their hands off his lumber? As John approached, two of them stepped out onto the road with their guns at the ready. "Halt! Oh, Monsieur Sutherland, I did not recognise you not on your big black horse. Something happen to him?"

"No, but where I'm going my horse will have to stand outside awhile…"

"Ah, yes them big English horses got their good points, but not made for this climate. We're supposed to stop anyone goin' in or out of Winnipeg, and ask 'em where they're goin'. So, where you goin', if you don't mind me askin'?"

"A.G.B. Bannatyne's." John figured that including the Christian name – or the initials that passed for Bannatyne's Christian name – would make clear he meant Bannatyne's home, not his store.

"Good, that's good; maybe you and Monsieur Bannatyne together can talk some sense into some people – things been pretty jumpy down at Fort Garry today." John suspected that 'pretty jumpy' was an understatement for the howl that went up when today's proclamation reached the National Committee.

A.G.B. Bannatyne's house was a good quarter mile north-west of Dr. Schultz's place, but through the gap between Monchamp's tavern and 'Mercer's Watchmaker & Fancy Store' John could see a goodly number of Metis and ponies milling around on the open ground just north of the White Store. He suspected there were as many more on the west side, south and east. It didn't help matters that his field of vision crossed a snaggletoothed jaw of black, charred timbers sticking out of the snow. The ruins were nothing more sinister than the remains of old Andrew McDermot's new house, which had accidentally burned down half-built a few years ago and left till someone else got around to building something else there. But John could hear his mother whispering Gaelic warnings about omens.

Another shagganappi pony was already tethered to one of the iron rings set into the front wall of the Bannatyne house. John hitched his pony close to it for company and mutual windbreak. The door was answered by dumpling-cheeked Annie Bannatyne, not carrying a horsewhip today. She said: "He's in the kitchen," and led the way.

Thicket-bearded A.G.B. Bannatyne was taking his morning tea with goateed, widow's-peaked James Ross. There was a whiff of alcohol from James Ross's end of the table, but it was said there was rarely a day that Mr. Grant hadn't smelled of alcohol, and he'd managed to get one or two things done. Bannatyne looked up from his teacup and nodded, "John."

"A.G.B. James."

"John."

Mrs. Bannatyne set out another cup and sat down to go back to her knitting, which in the present circumstances unfortunately put John in mind of Charles Dickens's Madame Defarge. Mr. Bannatyne said: "I take it you've seen the latest proclamation."

John nodded, "And it's waylaid me from what I was delegated to do. We had a public meeting last night –"

Ross put in: "So I heard."

"– and today I was to carry a message to Fort Garry and the Stone Fort."

Bannatyne said: "That message being…?"

"That no Kildonan man will enlist in Colonel Dennis's militia."

Bannatyne said: "Excellent, that'll take some steam out of their sails." James Ross said nothing – after all, it was him who'd told St. Andrew's Parish that 220 'Scotchmen' were ready-aye-ready to defend the government pork. "And it'll help unknot some sporrans in Fort Garry."

"You think it would?"

"I know it would."

That certainty from that perspective was a large part of what had brought John to the Bannatynes' before taking a guess at what to do next. A.G.B.'s personal credentials were such that every corner of the community felt he was more or less one of their own: he'd worked for The Company, he was foreign-born but not Canadian, and his wife was native-born and part Indian. Virtually everyone in the settlement passed through Bannatyne's store at one time or another, and freely expressed their opinions across the counter. So it was a pretty safe bet that if A.G.B. thought Kildonan taking a pass on Colonel Dennis's recruiting drive would help calm down the community, it would.

John said: "Well, I'm glad to hear that, but I don't know how Colonel Dennis might take the message, after today's proclamation. Who knows, he might even take it in mind to arrest me for treason." He said it lightly, but wasn't sure how lightly he meant it.

Ross said: "Seems to be an arresting kind of day today. Lépine's patrols finally found George Klyne this morning, escorted him to Fort Garry for incarceration. Handy place to improvise a jail, Fort Garry – the warehouse windows already have bars in them to prevent pilferage. Do you know Patrice Bréland?"

John didn't see how George Klyne and jails led to Patrice Bréland as night follows day. Maybe perpetual pickling had indeed addled 'young Jamie's' brains as much as some would say. But he gave James the benefit of the doubt and just said: "Barely – I know his father better, from sitting on the Council." Patrice Bréland was a grandson of Mr. Grant's, and Patrice's father Pascal had inherited Mr. Grant's position as Magistrate of White Horse Plains. Magistrate Pascal wasn't in evidence these days; the minute the barricade went up on the road from Pembina he'd decided this would be a good year to winter on the Qu'Appelle. Which some said proved he was weaker than his late father-in-law and some said proved he was wiser. "Patrice is one of the Delegates from St. Francis Xavier, isn't he?"

"Was. This morning he went back home and wiped his hands of the National Committee and all."

John looked from Ross to Bannatyne. What had changed between yesterday and today to make Patrice Bréland jump ship on the movement he'd been part of since the beginning? Maybe it was the proclamation about and from Colonel Dennis, maybe it was something else. Either A.G.B. and James didn't know either, or they weren't saying. The ground had gone fluid this winter.

A sharp crash like a gunshot jolted John up off the seat of his chair, almost toppling it backwards, and his heart leaped into a gallop without passing through a trot. Bannatyne and Ross had much the same reaction, A.G.B.'s hand jerking in mid-sip and spilling tea down his beard. A hip-high Bannatyne child appeared in the kitchen doorway, lugging the family Bible and saying: "I'm sorry, Mama – I was tryin' to reach my pitcher book and this just felled down."

Annie Bannatyne said: "That's all right, dear, no harm done. Just put it up on the dining room table for now." Then she looked around at the three men in her kitchen, said: "A little jumpy, are we?" and went back to her knitting.

John, A.G.B. and James Ross laughed at each other, then James stood up and said: "I'll tell you how jumpy *I* am – I've arranged to remove my wife and son to stay with my sister and Dr. Black for a few days, and I'd best get to it."

John said: "And your mother?"

Ross snorted, "Fat chance getting Granny Sally Ross to leave her home because of a possible commotion. About as much chance as getting Annie Bannatyne to."

Mrs. Bannatyne put in: "Damn right," above the clicking of her needles.

Ross paused on the way to his coat and the door and said: "So you'll take that message to Fort Garry, A.G.B.?"

"Directly."

John said: "What message?"

Ross said: "Oh, last night seems to've been a meeting kind of evening. A.G.B. and I met with Hargrave and a few others, which was why I couldn't be at your meeting." John suspected that wasn't the only reason, but let it pass. "We came up with a proposition for the National Committee – Bannatyne'll tell you; I have a wife and child to parcel up and transport."

When Ross was gone, John said to Bannatyne, "Proposition…?"

"Oh, it's fairly simple, in two parts. First part is that the 'English' delegates – for lack of a better term – will undertake to keep Colonel Dennis pacified, ditto Dr. Schultz. Second part, that a joint delegation go down to Pembina to discuss the List of Rights with McDougall. Everybody with any sort of sense is doing all they can to keep this thing from blowing up. Last night Ross wrote a letter to his old boss at the Toronto *Globe*, telling him it would be a mistake for Canada to send a military force here –"

"I didn't know Canada was thinking of doing that – and *how* the hell are they thinking of doing it in the middle of winter? Oh, sorry for interrupting."

A.G.B. waved off the apology. "I don't know what they're thinking of, but better to tell 'em it's a bad idea before they think of it. I do know the Toronto *Globe* pulls some pretty heavy strings down there. The other thing James said in his letter was that the Dominion should grant the French here as many concessions as it can stomach, and thereby save the settlement."

John could understand why the French-speakers of Rupert's Land would want a few basic rights guaranteed in writing before opening the door. Louis Riel Sr. had been one of the leaders of a long agitation against one of Judge Black's predecessors, who'd bragged about his facility with languages such as Latin, Hebrew and Ancient Greek but refused to hear testimony in French. John could remember one occasion, when he was about Hugh's age, when the only reason said Judge wasn't shot dead on his bench by an exasperated Metis was that Mr. Grant was there to step between them. Rumour had it that in later years Mr. Grant sometimes expressed regret for stepping in.

What John couldn't understand, or wasn't sure of, was whether James Ross's dispatch to the Toronto *Globe* was what it seemed on the surface – a message from a concerned citizen only interested in preserving the peace – or whether Ross was secretly working with the National Committee. Ross's speech to St. Andrew's about '220 Scotchmen' being ready to fight didn't exactly fit with preserving the peace. And then there was the odd fact that Governor Mactavish's secretary J.J. Hargrave had been among those Ross and Bannatyne had met with last night. All the other officers of The Company were prisoners within the walls of Fort Garry, while Hargrave was allowed to roam free…

John wasn't accustomed to thinking in terms of hidden motives and under-the-surface, and he didn't want to become accustomed: it hurt his head and aggravated his stomach. But one thing was mercifully clear, as he said to Bannatyne, "Well, if all the parish delegates are going to tell Fort Garry and the Stone Fort that they don't want Colonel Dennis beating war drums, there's no need for me to." So he got back on his pony and rode home.

Donald and Morrison were in the house when he got there; Hugh, Aleck, Hector and Angus came in quickly from the barn and yard. Donald sat at the table with the proclamation in front of him and the rest of the boys-before-the-girls standing behind him. Donald said: "It's hard to misinterpret, Da. *'I hereby call on and order all loyal men of the North West Territories…'* That's from the Queen's duly authorized representative. Legally, either we go to the Stone Fort and enlist, or we've set ourselves outside the law."

John spent a moment mentally cursing the day they sent Donald to college, then explained that the elected delegates were working to mollify the situation, so there was no need to act until it was seen what came of that. That seemed to satisfy the boys for now, so John went and sat alone in the parlour. After a moment Janet came in from the main room and pulled a chair up close to his. He said in a voice that wouldn't carry beyond the doorway: "I don't know…"

"Don't know what?"

"Well, *that* list is endless, but… I don't know whether the, um, reason I'm not delivering the… *message* the public meeting charged me to deliver, is because it makes sense to, um, wait to see what comes of the delegates'… *proposition*, or because I'm afraid."

"Afraid of what?"

"Afraid that Colonel Dennis might, um, clap me in irons – or so might the National Committee, for that matter – now that that bloody… *proclamation* has stirred things up even worse. All us little mice going 'Who will bell the cat?'."

"You're not a mouse, John – no more than was your father, or mine for that matter. They neither of them went looking for trouble, but they did what needed doing. I'm just glad you didn't take after your *mother*, or I'd be worried you'd go stomping down to the Stone Fort and box Colonel Dennis's ears. And now what *I* need to be doing is get some soup on the table for all my boys and girls."

After a couple of bowls of buffalo and barley soup and a few slabs of fresh buttered bread, John felt a little insulated from all the agitation on the other side of the river. As the dishes were being cleared away, he said to the table at large, "Well, that was absolutely delicious, but I think it's time we, um, added a little… *fish* into our diet."

Donald said: "You think it's time, Da?"

"The ice is, um, thick enough for skating and sleighing – I'd say it's thick enough for fishing."

Everyone flurried into their outside clothes except Janet, Margaret, Catherine and Willy – they would maybe join the expedition after the dishes were done. John snagged one of the utility poplar poles leaning outside the door and headed straight down to the river, knowing the older boys would organise what was needed from the barn.

A little ways downstream from the stretch of ice kept cleared of snow for skating were two pole-marked holes about thirty paces apart, east to west. John had made sure that the ice-planted poles were 'at least six feet high,' as specified in Article XV of the Laws of Assiniboia, the holemaker *'being otherwise liable to make good all injury which such pole might have been expected to prevent.'*

There was an inflated sheep's bladder floating in each of the two holes, and since last cleared an inch-thick skin of ice had formed between the bladders and the foot-thick ice all 'round. By the time John broke up the skin with his pole, his oldest boys were coming toward him carrying a rolled-up fishnet. Unseen under the ice was a long shagganappi rope with each of its ends tied to one of the bladder floats. Once one end of the rope was tied to a top corner of the fish net, it was simply a question of feeding the net into the east hole while the rope was drawn out from the west hole, and tomorrow draw out several dozen gill-netted fish. Some of the fish would be eaten fresh – the suckerfish by the dogs – some would be stored frozen in the meat shed, or given away to neighbours, and the net would be hung in the barn loft to dry and wait for next time.

Simple in theory, but setting the net did take a while. What with keeping the younger children back from the edge of the holes, coordinating the drawing-up and coiling of the rope at one end with feeding-in the net at the other, occasionally correcting Margaret's authoritative explanation of the process to her most gullible brothers and sisters, and going back and forth to the house in relays to thaw fingers and toes, the job wasn't quite done when December's early twilight descended. A male voice hailed out of the gloaming: "Hallo, Mr. Sutherland."

John looked up to see one of the Inkster boys approaching – well, not a boy anymore, a young man. John stood away from uncoiling the net and Donald took his place. "Hello, Colin."

Colin Inkster stopped in front of John and said: "Da saw you were out here on the river and thought you should know what we just heard of. The National Committee, or whatever you call the Metis holding Fort Garry, they just arrested two men, or took them prisoner or whatever you want to call it. Thomas Scott and another Canadian named McArthur or something."

"What? Why…?"

"Some say Scott and the other fella went down to Fort Garry under a white flag to talk peace and got prompt locked-up instead, white flag and all. But some say Scott and the other fella figured they could just stroll across to the Red Dog Saloon from the White Store carrying guns, and instead found themselves taken prisoner for being part of Dr. Schultz's barricaded little army. Either way, they're locked up in Fort Garry now."

John went numb, and his mind wandered to James Ross mentioning that the barred warehouse windows in Fort Garry made it handy for a jail. Those warehouses could hold a lot of prisoners. But that thought was just an idle sidelight to the wretched reality Colin Inkster had presented him with. It was one thing to arrest a Metis like George Klyne, or to keep The Company's officers confined to Fort Garry, but Thomas Scott and the other were citizens of the Dominion of Canada. When the news reached the Stone Fort Colonel Dennis would go apoplectic. There were no more maybes.

John said: "Donald, can you see to it the net gets set right…?"

"Yes, Da."

"Hugh, saddle Montrose for me, please."

"Yes, Da."

"Aleck, please go across to your Uncle Hector's –" he saw a cloud cross Aleck's face at being sent to his former schoolteacher's, but this wasn't a time to hesitate over a young man's convoluted feelings "– and ask him if I can use the schoolhouse for a public meeting tomorrow morning at, say… nine o'clock, and if so to circulate notice." The reason for the schoolhouse and not the kirk was to signify the meeting wasn't just open to members of Kildonan Parish, and since the schoolhouse wasn't being used for school these days anyway…

"Yes, Da."

John didn't take his boots off on his way into the house, figuring Janet would forgive him under the circumstances. He went straight into the parlour, to the locked drawer in his writing desk, took out the infamous 'horrible ugly-looking horse pistol' and tucked it in his coat, keeping his back to the parlour doorway so no one would see what he was doing. Janet's voice came from the doorway, "John…?"

"Yes, my dear – I'm afraid it's time to bell the cat, or try to."

"Yes, Hugh ducked in and told me. I put some bannock and cheese in a pouch for you."

"Thank you." He paused on his way out the doorway to kiss her, something they rarely did in front of the children.

She said: "Go carefully."

"I will. It's a long ride to the Stone Fort, so don't worry if it gets late and I'm not home yet."

John had expected Hugh to be waiting outside holding Montrose's reins, and so he was; he hadn't expected Hugh to be sitting on a saddled pony. There was an unnatural bulge in the middle of Hugh's capote, just above the ceinture flechée. John didn't have to ask what it was; Hugh had obviously found time to do a little quick and secret rummaging of his own when he ducked into the house, or maybe the barn. John said: "What do you think you're doing?"

"I thought you and Montrose might want some company."

"No – that is, it's got nothing to do with wanting or not wanting company. You're not coming with me."

"But, Da –"

"No! And that's final." John took Montrose's reins, climbed into the saddle, let the horse walk carefully down the slanted path to the river and then nudged him into a trot towards Fort Garry. By staying on the river he could avoid dealing with the road guards and night patrol in Winnipeg. On both sides of the river were warm-looking squares of amber light from the windows of buildings and homes, and a good deal more light on the right side once he'd passed the Sisters of Charity school: the watchfires of the Metis encircling Dr. Schultz's store, their dancing flames throwing grotesque elongated man-shadows across the snow.

A little farther along John became convinced someone was following him. Montrose's trotting hoofbeats were muffle-edged by the snow packed down by carrioles and sleighs and other horses, but the other hooves John was hearing definitely weren't just echoes off the riverbanks. He halted Montrose and turned around, slipping his right hand inside his coat.

It was Hugh. John stabbed a pointing finger at him and barked: "I told you to stay home!"

"No, you didn't, Da. You just told me not to come with you. Well, I'm not riding *with* you, am I? I'm just… riding along the river, me whatever."

It was rank and shameless disobedience, made even worse by the fact that John found it hard not to laugh. But what was he going to do – turn his full-grown son over his knee? Instead, he turned his horse around again and trotted on toward Fort Garry. After a moment he heard the different trotting rhythm of the smaller horse following along. John sighed, raised one mittened hand over his shoulder and beckoned forward. The pony's gait quickened until John's prodigal son was trotting along beside him.

The gates of Fort Garry weren't yet closed for the night, but a Metis guard was marching back and forth in front of the gatehouse to keep his feet warm. As John and Hugh approached, he stopped marching, shifted his gun into one hand and held up the other. "Halt! No one gets in tonight!" A wide beam of orange light momentarily shone through the stone-vaulted gatehouse tunnel, as a second Metis stepped out of the guardhouse to back up his confrére.

John reined in Montrose and said: "I have a message that the people of Kildonan have entrusted me to deliver to President John Bruce." It seemed to John that the two guards glanced at each other oddly when he said 'John Bruce.' "It's important."

"No. No one gets in tonight."

There was another momentary gleam of orange light, but this one much thinner, since the frame of Ambroise Lépine filled most of the guardhouse doorframe. His soft-edged, deep-chested voice echoed in the gatehouse tunnel, "Bonjour, Point Douglas."

"Bonjour, Ambroise. I have a message I must deliver to President Bruce." Again, it seemed to John that something odd flickered across Ambroise Lépine's face at the mention of Bruce's name, and the two guards glanced at their captain with hooded eyes.

Lépine said: "No one passes in tonight – direct orders. But, if your message isn't very long, you can tell it to me and I swear to deliver it immediate and straightway to the President and Secretary before I have time to get it muddled and mixed-up." He crooked a beckoning finger toward the left side of the gatehouse. "We take a little walk, okay?"

John handed Montrose's reins to Hugh, climbed down and walked with Ambroise Lépine along the tramped-down snow fronting the front wall of Fort Garry. Once they were out of easy earshot of the guards, Ambroise said: "So?"

"The message is that no man of Kildonan will enlist in Colonel Dennis's militia to take up arms against our neighbours."

"That's certain?"

"Certain. We had a public meeting last night, and that was the resolution I was charged to bring to Fort Garry and the Stone Fort."

"Good. That's very good. When people don't know what other people might do, they start imagining. And when people get too scared of each other they do stupid things. How did Colonel Dennis take your news?"

"I haven't told him yet; I'm going there next."

"Ah. Well… Good luck there. I only hope Colonel Dennis has some wisdom. If not… We of Red River are not enemies, Point Douglas Jean. But any man who gives harm or insult to anyone of Red River *is* my enemy. And here's my hand on that."

John tugged off his right mitten to shake the huge hand held out to him. Ambroise Lépine's handshake grip was limper than most men's; he was afraid of crushing fingers.

The ride to the Stone Fort started at a gallop to eat up the miles, so there wasn't much talk until it came time to let the horses walk and breathe. When they did, after a bit of conversation about how bright the stars were and how cold that likely meant tomorrow would be, Hugh laughed and said: "That's funny."

"What's funny?"

"Well, sometimes, uh, on some of the days I take Montrose for his exercise, once in awhile I'll meet up with Nancy Prince…"

"Oh, really?"

"And she'll be riding on her short little Indian pony and me on big tall Montrose, and me'n her'll be talking, and I never quite realised till now – she must get some crick in her neck."

"I imagine she's used to it by now – even though it's just once in awhile." John decided not to elevate his eyebrows any further; it was a rare circumstance when Hugh said anything at all about his Nancy. "But I imagine she was disappointed when all this… trouble overthrew your plans."

"She ain't the only one. You woulda met her by now – hell, I mean heck, she woulda been your daughter-in-law by now, and her and me living on our own place. But all this confusion around here is bound to end soon, eh?"

"Well, it might not seem *soon* to someone –" John was going to say 'your age,' but decided that might put a crimp in the surprising ease between them, " – in your circumstances. But, it can't go on much longer." John did believe that to be true, but the question was whether things were going to explode before they got resolved, and the resolution be a matter of picking up the pieces. For the moment, though, he was more interested in having an actual conversation with this young man who'd been hunting rhinocerosauruses with a wooden gun only yesterday.

Hugh said: "Well, like I told Wauh Oonae – and I try to tell myself – a few weeks, or even months, don't seem like all that much when we got the whole rest of our lives."

"So you have no doubts, that… she's the one?" Using the word 'love' seemed a bit heavy-handed in a conversation between a near-fifty year old father and twenty year old son. In fact, John wondered if even his hedging hadn't been too intimate.

"Well, uh, I… Nancy's like… um… it's sorta like… uh… I mean… When I'm with her I don't wanna be anywhere else."

"Ah."

"Was it like that – I mean *is* it like that, with you and Mum?"

"Um… often. There are… other times, occasionally, in any marriage. Your mother can be a bit unreasonable at times." Hugh laughed in a way that showed he got the joke, as any sensible man would, and also showed John that he and his second son now had the kind of offhanded understanding he'd eventually had with his own father. It had taken a lot longer with John and his father, but John was aware that was the fault of his own tendency to mistake dry for serious. John laughed along with Hugh, then said: "I think the horses have cooled off enough now."

There were other between-gallops conversations on the way to the Stone Fort, ranging from the state of the currently-pregnant cow to the time Margaret fell in the pickle barrel. Not particularly profound or intimate conversations, but the kind John couldn't have with any of his children when all the rest of them were bubbling around, or when leaning on a scythe to catch his breath before the next row. He found himself feeling a strange contentment. It occurred to him that his life had reached a point where, if it were cut short now, his older children and his widow would take care of the younger ones perfectly well, and all his children already had a good start on growing up to be as happy as human beings could reasonably expect themselves to be. Well, all except Aleck, of course, but there seemed nothing anyone could do about that, except Aleck.

John's contentment dissipated when they reached the Stone Fort. A voice from above the barred gates called down: "Who goes there?"

"John and Hugh Sutherland – Point Douglas Sutherlands."

"Open the gate!"

When John and his son plodded their weary horses into the fort, a man John vaguely recognized from one of the parishes north of Kildonan came forward eagerly, saying: "The Point Douglas Sutherlands! Have you come to enlist?"

"Not exactly. I've been sent to bring a message to Colonel Dennis."

"He's in the Governor's House."

"Thank you. Hugh, will you take care of the horses?"

"Yes, Da."

John climbed down and walked – a little stiffly after hours in the saddle – toward the pink stone and whitewashed timber edifice that the Little Emperor, Sir George Simpson, had erected for the refined young wife he'd imported from Scotland. John could remember how deeply all of Rupert's Land had been offended by the callous way Simpson had shunted off his Metis wife, but no one dared say a word about it within earshot of The Little Emperor. Except, of course, Mr. Grant, and it had proved to be a long step on the road toward Mr. Grant and The Company parting company. No governor had lived in the place for a quarter of a century now, but it was still 'The Governor's House.'

A uniformed guard – John recognized him as one of the Canadians who'd come west with Colonel Dennis's survey expedition – informed John that Colonel Dennis was in a strategy meeting, ushered him into a deliciously warm front parlour and went and knocked on an inner door. After a few moments, one of the two Majors from the survey expedition came out that door, nodded companionably to John on his way through the parlour, and the guard said: "You can go in now."

Colonel Dennis was fully rigged-out in his splendid green-and-gold uniform, except that the top button of his tunic was unbuttoned and his scabbarded sword leaned against his desk, or whomever's desk it had been before Colonel Dennis moved in. Which brought something to mind John hadn't thought of before, or heard anybody mention. The Stone Fort was still The Company's property. Whatever might be the other details of the deal that sold Rupert's Land to Canada, The Company undoubtedly kept ownership of its own forts and trading posts. Colonel Dennis had most definitely not asked Governor Mactavish's permission before taking possession of the Stone Fort, any more than the National Committee had asked permission before taking over Fort Garry. But just now did not seem the time to bring that up to Colonel Dennis.

Colonel Dennis said: "Pleasure to see you, Mr. Sutherland. Do sit down."

John doubted Colonel Dennis's pleasure was going to last long, but sat down in the indicated chair. Well, as John's mother had always said: *'Bad news is best served quick,'* but as his father had always added, *'Ye neednae serve it with vinegar.'* "Last night, Colonel, there was a public meeting at Kildonan kirk. The decision of the meeting, and the message I was instructed to bring to you, was that no man of Kildonan will enlist in your militia."

Colonel Dennis blinked, and his colour began to rise. "But that was before any of you had seen the proclamation I issued this morning – that the *Lieutenant Governor* and I issued."

"True. But the decision still stands."

"That proclamation wasn't *inviting* you to take up arms to restore order, it was *commanding* you to – in the name of your Queen and Country!"

"Well, um, there seems to be some question, Colonel, as to whose country it is."

"*What*?"

"And, um, there is a general feeling that…" Now the delicate matter of how to say 'stuff that for a dead chicken' politely. "… that what you are planning to do, and what Dr. Schultz is doing, will not restore order but destroy what little order is left."

Colonel Dennis stood up from behind his desk, buttoned his gold-leafed collar and went and stood looking out the night-blind window, with his hands clasped behind his back and flapping against each other. John wiped his own sweating hands on his winter weight wool trousers.

Colonel Dennis said: "So what you're telling me is that every man-jack of you in Kildonan is an arrant coward."

"No. We're all of us prepared to fight eleven hundred Sioux, if they come. If you think that qualifies us as cowards, you haven't met many Sioux."

"You realise I'd be perfectly within my lawful authority to have you clapped in irons here and now."

"I do." John was inclined to not say any more. Either Colonel Dennis had an ounce of brains within that close-clipped skull, or he didn't. As Ambroise Lépine had said, *'I only hope Colonel Dennis has some wisdom.'* But then John considered the fact that he didn't only have himself to consider. Hugh was trapped inside the Stone Fort, too. So he spelled it out, "And *you* realise, Colonel, that clapping me in irons would be driving every man in Kildonan straight into the arms of the National Committee."

"Are you threatening me?"

"No." John was quite sure that, if anything, he'd understated the fact. He liked to think he didn't think too highly of himself, but he'd worked hard all his life to be a relatively decent human being who had fair dealings with everyone he dealt with. And being a Councillor of Assiniboia meant he hadn't just dealt with people in Kildonan. If Canada were to court-martial someone as harmless as Point Douglas John Sutherland, a lot of currently-neutral people in Rupert's Land were going to have second thoughts about the transfer. Including Point Douglas John Sutherland.

"Well, you've delivered your message. Go scuttle back to your wife and hearth and home."

John rose from his chair, feeling the heat rise in his face. "Colonel Dennis, you're not in Toronto now, or Ottawa, or London. You might do well to remember that the only scuttling-away that's been going on around here has been on the part of your eminent Lieutenant Governor."

The long ride home in the frozen dark quickly cooled John off enough to be astounded at his own temerity for saying those parting words to Colonel Dennis. The only explanation he could come up with was that the ghost of his mother had taken possession of his tongue. But then again, his supposedly cooler-headed father probably would've said the same things he'd said, except with a few choice Gaelicisms thrown in for spite.

At the meeting in the schoolhouse the next morning, John reported that he'd delivered the message, but that he didn't know how it might affect Colonel Dennis's plans. Even so, he could feel the meetings' relief that he'd belled the cat for them and come back with his ears and tail intact. But there was still an uneasy feeling in the air. A Matheson stood up to say there were even more gun-carrying Metis in and around Winnipeg this morning than yesterday. A Pritchard reported a rumour that President Bruce had come down ill, so ill he couldn't take his seat at the council table, which made Louis Riel temporarily the head of the National Committee. John thought that might explain the sidelong glances between the guards and Ambroise Lépine at Fort Garry last night, but that was too ephemeral a detail to put out to the meeting. Far too many ephemeralities and rumours floating around already.

After the meeting, John dropped in at the manse, where James Ross had detoured to look in on his wife and son. John and Ross were trading opinions of rumours with Ross's Scottish wife and half-Okanagan sister when a wondrous thing happened: Colonel Dennis arrived at the manse from the Stone Fort, and not at the head of his militia. The only man who arrived with him was the nephew he'd promoted into his Rupert's Land survey expedition back in Canada.

Colonel Dennis accepted a cup of tea and said: "I know there was a pubic meeting in the schoolhouse this morning." Which made John wonder whether Dr. Black's ecclesiastical abstention from politics might not extend over sending messages. Or maybe it had been James Ross. "It seems to me, that as a duly-appointed public official, I should be guided by the will of the public. The question is: what *is* the will of the people? Mr. Sutherland, did this morning's public meeting alter the message you conveyed to me last night?"

"No, sir."

"Well, then we know the will of the people of Kildonan. But Kildonan isn't all the people of Red River…"

Judge Black was sent for, and a few other men who could be relied upon to know which way the wind was blowing in their segment of the community. As the little gathering in the manse parlour waited for them to arrive, John allowed himself to believe, for the first time in days, that the banks of the Miskoussippi weren't going to run red with blood again this time. He heard a horse galloping up to the manse, but it was sooner than expected and Judge Black had never seemed to him to be a galloping sort of man. It wasn't Judge Black, it was one of the Metis stockboys who worked for A.G.B. Bannatyne. "Mr. Sutherland, Mr. Bannatyne sent me to fetch you urgent. I went to your house, but they said you was still down here."

"What is it?"

"Don't know, me whatever. But since he said you in partic'lar, I'm guessing it's got something to do with all those men from your side the river that's holding Fort Garry."

A.G.B. Bannatyne wasn't the kind to say 'urgent' lightly. And whatever Judge Black was going to say to Colonel Dennis was going to be said whether Point Douglas John Sutherland was there or not. John brought Montrose out of the shelter of the manse carriage house and galloped south.

There were a number of men already gathered in the Bannatynes' kitchen, including Dutch George Emmerling and young Colin Inkster. A.G.B. said: "Glad my man found you, John. I got pretty good credentials for communicating to folks from the St. Boniface side, but not a patch on you."

"What's happened?"

"Temporary-President Riel's writing up an order to Fort Schultz to surrender or else."

"Or else what?"

"Or else the Metis around the White Store will start shooting."

"But… the Metis are all out in the open, and Dr. Schultz and his men all barricaded behind strong walls…"

Colin Inkster said: "Oh, the Metis will have *some* cover – the shell of Dr. Schultz's brick house, the Reverend Young's house, the ruins of McDermot's house…"

"Anyway," A.G.B. waved away the detail, "four or five hundred buffalo hunters blazing away at once…? Schultz and his friends might knock down a few in the meantime, but eventually they'll blow his barricades to sawdust – and anyone behind them."

"But… I've just left Colonel Dennis, and I'm sure he's going to give up his plan to march on Fort Garry. So there's no reason for Dr. Schultz to hold out."

"Way I hear it," Dutch George put in, "Colonel Dennis already twice sent orders to Schultz to take down his barricades and stop waving the flag, and Schultz wouldn't listen."

The plain fact that George Emmerling was one of the worried men gathered at Bannatyne's helped sink John's short-lived optimism. It was no secret that Dutch George wanted the North West Territories to become a territory of the United States, not Canada. A wholesale gun battle at Red River would give the American army a perfect excuse to come north and restore order. Yet here was Dutch George Emmerling among the men trying to prevent that from happening. The only explanation John could think of was that Dutch George saw the same terrible possibility he did: if some people were killed in and around the White Store today, then tomorrow a friend or cousin of one of the dead would go gunning for a friend or cousin of one of the killers, and the day after tomorrow...

John said to A.G.B. Bannatyne, "So what do you want me to do?"

"Well, we've all of us here decided, that together we'll stand surety for Schultz's property and possessions – and the same of anyone else in there – if they surrender. Problem is, to get the Metis to let us pass in to deliver that guarantee. That's where you come in."

"Well... I'll try..."

"Mr. Sutherland," said Colin Inkster, "out of all the us-and-them-ing going on around here these days, there's one thing I know for certain: they trust you."

Bannatyne said: "And that's a damn rare commodity these days. If I could bottle some for sale I could retire. Well, gentlemen, it's not a long walk to the White Store, if we all go together we'll look like a proper delegation."

John wasn't sure he liked the sound of 'we all go together.'

"But..." Bannatyne added, "No guns. And that includes you, Emmerling."

"Nobody'll see it under my coat."

"They will – you walk different."

Dutch George said: "Oh, hell; oh, well..." and unbuckled the gunbelt that Americans seemed to think part of standard business attire. He put the holstered gun on Annie Bannatyne's kitchen table, where it was joined by Colin Inkster's shotgun, someone else's hunting rifle, and several handguns. John felt left out that he'd left his 'horrible ugly-looking horse pistol' at home today.

As they all trooped out the door, buttoning coats, A.G.B. said: "You'll walk up front with me, John, if you would – less chance they'll mistake us for the vanguard of Dennis's militia and start shooting," which John didn't find particularly encouraging.

The day had turned relatively mild; the snow under John's boots crunched instead of squeaked. A little ways before the Portage Road and the Red Dog Saloon there was a log fire burning on the open ground just left of Main Road, a couple of hundred yards north of the White Store, and a dozen Metis warming their hands around it. A grizzle-bearded scarfaced gun-toter whose sons used to chase minnows with Hugh and Donald stepped onto the road and said: "Bonjour, Jean. Where you fellas figure you're going?"

"We're hoping to convince Dr. Schultz and his friends to give up this nonsense, if you'll let us through to talk to them."

"Well, I'd sure to hell like you to try, but it ain't up to me –"

"Here they come!" came from a look-out south of the fire. John's eyes followed the look-out's pointing arm. He could see there were other clumps of Metis on either side of Main Road south of the White Store, but they didn't appear to be coming or going anywhere. But, passing the courthouse from the direction of Fort Garry was a large group of men on foot and horseback.

John's grizzle-bearded neighbour, Normand Lagimodière, said: "That'll be Riel and them. That's who it'll be up to, but he won't come further along the road into gun-range of the store. So, you fellas come along with me." As they walked south, other well-armed

Metis stepped out from the lee side of Drever's store and the new store The Company had put up in competition, but they stepped back when the escort waved them off. Just a casual winter's morning constitutional along Main Road, but John did notice that the guide stayed on his right side, so that John and Bannatyne were always between Normand and the White Store.

Louis Riel was in the front of the column coming from Fort Garry and, as Normand had predicted, they'd stopped just north of the courthouse. John could see Riel's eyes flicking across the group of men approaching him and registering that Normand Lagimodière was the only one armed. John said: "Bonjour, Monsieur Riel –"

"Now, now," Riel waggled a gloved finger at him and smiled, "I told you two Christmases ago, Monsieur Sutherland – Monsieur Riel was my father, I will always be petit Louis, to you."

"Well, Louis…" and John explained what he and Bannatyne and the others were come to do.

"Blessed are the peacemakers," Riel smiled even more broadly. "It is providence, Monsieur Sutherland, that brings you here precisely now. Another few minutes and I would've had an envoy deliver this," he reached inside his coat and came out with a neatly-folded sheet of vellum, "but I believe it will be even more effective coming from you, and with the added news you bear."

John unfolded the paper and held it up so that Bannatyne could read it with him, and Colin Inkster and Dutch George craning over their shoulders.

Dr. Schultz and men are hereby ordered to give up their arms and surrender themselves. Their lives will be spared should they comply. In case of refusal all the English Halfbreeds and other natives, women and children are at liberty to depart unmolested. [Signed] Louis Riel, Fort Garry 7th Dec. 1869. The surrender will be accepted at or 15 minutes after the order.

As John folded up the paper again, 'petit Louis' said: "If they can't be persuaded to sign their names as accepting that, please do come back out as quickly as possible. I should think there's no need for Monsieur Emmerling and the others to go in with you, just you and Monsieur Bannatyne should suffice." Dutch George and the others didn't argue. Riel reached into his coat again and came out with a gold pocket watch. "Fifteen minutes."

John said: "You mean, fifteen minutes after we pass through the door and can present them with the order."

"Of course. Excellent point."

On the long walk to the White Store, A.G.B. murmured: "Funny Lépine wasn't there."

"Hm?"

"Ambroise Lépine. I didn't see him, did you?"

"No."

"Hard man to miss if he's in eyeshot. Odd they'd be getting ready for a shooting war and Lépine not around." A few steps farther on, when they were almost to the store's front steps, Bannatyne murmured less distinctly, as though to himself, "Well, there's bound to be a few idiots in there, but at least a few semi-level heads, like O'Donoghue."

"O'Donoghue? I wouldn't've thought he'd be in there."

"Good God, no. I didn't say *O'Donoghue*, I said *O'Donnell* – damned fuzzy Irish names. Dr. O'Donnell, new-come from Canada just in time for all this mess. But he brought his wife and children with him, so he's less likely to play at Alamo than some footloose young fools."

The door of the White Store swung open as John was reaching for it. He and Bannatyne were tugged inside, and a bank of store shelves heaved back into place across the doorframe. Standing behind the counter was Dr. Schultz, with a half-smoked cigar in his mouth, a shiny new-fangled Winchester repeating rifle crooked in his arm, and the butts of two revolvers poking up out of the waistband of his trousers. There were bags under the blue eyes, and the curly red-gold hair had gone lank and straight from too long indoors with no bathing. But the eyes still had a jaunty glint to them, a bit too jaunty for John's comfort, and he said cheerfully, "Good morning Mr. Bannatyne, Mr. Sutherland. As neither of you appears to be armed, I'm assuming you've not come to join us."

A.G.B. said: "We don't have much time – not our choice. There've been things going on outside you don't know about, things that make it sensible for you to give up the siege and surrender. I and Emmerling and others will guarantee the safety and security of your property – if the National Committee expropriates anything of yours, we'll make it up to you."

Dr. Schultz's eyes sidled at the two young men who'd moved the door barricade back into place, and he said around his cigar, "Sounds like something we should discuss upstairs." John and Bannatyne followed him through the ranks of shelves behind the counter, many of them now empty. In the alcove at the foot of the stairs, an unshaven young man with a rifle was peering through a loophole cut into the boarded-over side door. Dr. Schultz said to him, "Same as ever?"

"Yep, just standing around their fire, except more of 'em than before. I'll sing out if anything changes."

"Good man."

Upstairs, the air was thick from too many people shut in for too long. A baby was crying down the hall. Men were playing cards at one end of the common room table, with guns leaned against their chairs. Several children were scampering about, maybe Dr. O'Donnell's, maybe one of the Canadian storekeepers' – there'd been so many newcomers in the last year John couldn't keep track. Mrs. Schultz greeted John and Bannatyne as though they'd just dropped in for tea, and then, in fact, said she would just step into the kitchen and put the kettle on.

John unfolded the surrender order and handed it to Dr. Schultz. Dr. Schultz's eyes skimmed across the lines and then he read it aloud, loudly. Throughout, there were laughing shouts from the other men in the room:

"Hereby *ordered?*"

"Spare our lives – that's big of him!"

"Who the hell does this Riel think he is?"

"One volley from us and the frogs'll hop away."

"Fifteen minutes by whose watch, if they can read one?"

"All we gotta do is hold 'em off till Colonel Dennis and the boys from the Stone Fort get here!"

There was a general movement of men and guns toward the boarded windows. John said very loudly, "Colonel Dennis isn't coming!" That quieted things enough that he could make himself heard without yelling. "I just spoke to him this morning. He can't get enough local volunteers to make a strong enough force to attack Fort Garry." Colonel Dennis hadn't actually come to that conclusion by the time John got called away, but John figured it a pretty safe bet he had by now. If he hadn't, well, then the Recording Angel could add Point Douglas John Sutherland to the long list of falsifiers around Red River these days.

There were mumblings and grumblings and spat-out words like 'cowards,' 'craven,' and 'bastards.' Charles Mair said brightly, "If Colonel Dennis isn't coming, we can go to him, and the Stone Fort. If we make a dash for it, catch the French by surprise, they likely won't come after us once we're in Kildonan." Which didn't make John feel very comfortable at all.

Superintendent Snow said, the first thing he'd said since Dr. Schultz started reading the surrender order, "They got horses. They'd run you down before you got a hundred yards." It did seem a bit odd that Mr. Snow said 'you' instead of 'us,' but John wasn't about to cavil.

A male voice John didn't recognise called from the corner of the common room nearest Fort Garry, "I think you'd better come have a look at this, Doctor."

Dr. Schultz said: "What's that, Doctor?" as he headed in that direction, so John guessed the other must be Dr. O'Donnell.

John thought of retrieving the surrender order, but it seemed perfectly safe in the middle of the table. So he trailed after Dr. Schultz and found an unoccupied loophole to peer out of, then said to Bannatyne, "There's your answer."

"Answer to what?"

"Why we didn't see Ambroise Lépine." Several carts had come up from the direction of Fort Garry, and a crew of men were bustling around them under the direction of the unmistakably towering figure of Ambroise Lépine. They were unhitching the carthorses so they could slope the backs of the cartbeds down to the ground, which was fairly standard procedure for unloading heavy items. But the items they rolled off the carts weren't standard: several good-sized cannons aimed point-blank broadside at the White Store.

Dr. O'Donnell moved away from his window, calling: "Mrs. Schultz, would you happen to have a pen and ink handy?"

"Certainly, Dr. O'Donnell. What do you need them for?"

"To sign my name on that order of surrender. And I'd suggest somebody grab the nearest white bed-sheet and wave it out a window."

Mrs. Schultz dropped the tea tray and clutched her belly, wailing: "Oh, oh, oh! And I'm so near to my confinement," over the crash of crockery. John wouldn't've guessed her to be pregnant, but some women didn't show as much as others and she was wearing an uncorseted loose day dress. And he was hardly familiar enough with the configuration of her figure to notice changes. Odd, though, that it was young Mrs. Mair, not Mrs. Schultz, whose complexion showed that slow-bake glow John had learned to recognise as another bun in the oven. Mrs. Mair was just standing quietly with her arms crossed under her breasts, gazing into the middle distance.

Dr. Schultz rushed to scoop up his fainting wife and carry her into their private chambers. He came out a moment later, but John could still hear Mrs. Schultz crying and moaning. Dr. O'Donnell said concernedly, "Does she need attending?"

"No, no," Dr. Schultz shook his head, "just the shock combined with morning nausea. Mr. Bannatyne, Mr. Sutherland, would you please inform 'Monsieur' Riel that we will disband and remove our barricades, on the condition that all be allowed to retain their arms and return peacefully to their homes."

So it was another long, tense walk out of the White Store and back in again, only to inform Dr. Schultz that the only terms and conditions of surrender were those already spelled out – *'Their lives will be spared...'* – and that the gentlemen around the cannons were getting impatient. Dr. Schultz was inclined to dicker further, but Dr. O'Donnell said: "Give me that blasted pen," and signed his name to the surrender. Every other man present shuffled forward to follow Dr. O'Donnell's example, excepting John Sutherland and A.G.B. Bannatyne – and, oddly, Superintendent Snow, who seemed to think the entire business had nothing whatever to do with him.

Soon Fort Schultz was filled with armed Metis jovially disarming the garrison and patting them down for hidden weapons. All the male occupants were to be marched to Fort Garry for incarceration – except Superintendent Snow, whom Louis Riel pronounced merely happened to've been lodging there. John noticed Dr. Schultz and others shooting sidelong glances at Mr. Snow when that pronouncement was made.

Mrs. Schultz shrieked from her bedchamber that she couldn't bear to be separated from her husband. Mrs. Mair, Mrs. Stewart and Mrs. O'Donnell expressed the same sentiment, except they didn't shriek it. Riel informed them that Dr. Cowan and other Company officers with houses in Fort Garry had generously offered to lodge any married prisoners in their own homes. Since Mrs. Schultz was apparently in no condition to march anywhere, a carriole was found and brought to the White Store's front door.

When Mrs. Schultz came out into the common room, leaning on her husband's forearm, 'petit Louis ' said: "Oh no, Madame Schultz, it is far too cold a day for anyone to go from here to Fort Garry in just a light dress, especially in your delicate condition. If you will permit..." and he slipped off his coat and draped it over her shoulders. She didn't thank him, but she didn't shuck it off, either. As the Schultzes proceeded toward the stairway, John saw Louis Riel cock his head with his eyes focused on Mrs. Schultz's back in his coat, then glance oddly at the doorway to the Schultzes' private chambers. It was only a moment, but seemed an odd one.

John stood on the front steps of the White Store with A.G.B. Bannatyne, watching the prisoners within a cordon of armed Metis marching south along Main Road – Dr. Schultz pulling the carriole with his wife swaddled inside it in Louis Riel's coat. A.G.B. Bannatyne exhaled a breath that sounded like he'd been holding it for a week, and said: "Well, John, I know you're not much of a drinking man, but I've got a bottle of Old Islay at home that's been waiting for a deserving occasion, and I'd say we've earned it."

The whiskey went down well with the echoing explosions of cannon- and gunfire from Fort Garry, celebrating the fact that the only gunpowder touched off at Red River today was blank charges. But the next evening John was summoned to the White Store again. A.G.B. was there already, along with Louis Riel, Ambroise Lépine, several other Metis, and Superintendent Snow still in residence. Riel said: "Ah, Monsieur Sutherland, I want you and Monsieur Bannatyne to please witness the inventory I am making, so no one can say anything was taken that shouldn't be…"

The inventory party went through the store, the warehouse and the common room, finding guns and ammunition hidden behind counters, under flour sacks, inside kitchen cupboards… Finally Riel stopped at the doorway to the Schultzes' private quarters, and said to Superintendent Snow, "Has anyone been in here since the surrender?"

"Just me, just to feed the stove."

"Well, let us see what Madame Schultz was delivered of in her confinement."

In the Schultzes' bedroom, Riel cocked his head and gazed at the bed with the same curious gaze he'd directed at Mrs. Schultz's back the day before. He said: "Monsieur Sutherland, may I ask you a question? Do you remember I loaned Madame Schultz my coat yesterday?"

"I do."

"Oh, I should have said 'two questions.' The second is: if you were in a sickbed and had to be transported somewhere in a carriole on a winter's day, would not your first thought be, without even thinking, to take along one of the blankets and quilts covering your bed, to bundle in around you when you were bundled into the carriole?"

"Well, um, yes, I suppose it would be."

"Just so. Adjutant General, please to strip the lady's bed." Ambroise Lépine and one of his soldiers peeled the blankets and sheets off the Schultzes' bed, Ambroise carefully folding each one and piling them on top of a dresser.

'Petit Louis' said: "Well, well… Does it not seem a pity, Monsieur Sutherland, Monsieur Bannatyne, Monsieur Snow, that poor Madame Schultz must sleep upon such a lumpy-looking mattress? Adjutant-General…" he made an upward motion with one hand and Ambroise Lépine flipped the feather mattress away, exposing the planked underpinning. "Well, well… I would say she is no princess, and that is no pea. You witness me adding to the list: '2 fourteen-shot rifles, 1 breach-loader, 5 six-shooter revolvers, 1 double-barrelled pistol, 100 cartridges…'"

CHAPTER 46

With school and college back in business, Hugh had more room and time to himself on weekdays. He did miss a little having Willy, James and Roddy traipsing around with him when he checked his rabbit snares, but only a little: with them tramping and talking he hadn't been able to hear the woods. And he hadn't felt comfortable answering their questions about the best kind of slip knot to tie, and the best way to bend a sapling so it would snap up sharp enough to break a rabbit's neck and high enough that wolves and foxes couldn't reach it. Hugh didn't feel comfortable teaching anybody about anything, since he knew that whatever he knew was only patched-together bits and pieces, and that the way he did things wasn't necessarily the best way to do them, it was just the way he did them.

On nights when he hadn't got himself bone tired enough to forget that by rights he should be lying beside Nancy Sutherland-nee-Prince in their own bed in their own home, he'd try to remind himself he wasn't the only sufferer: Donald in the bunk above him was seeing the date he'd set with Christy Matheson fast approaching, but it was going to pass on by like any other December 21 in any other year. But that just reminded Hugh that barely yesterday, when Wauh Oonae had still been away on what was meant to be her last buffalo hunt, he'd been looking forward to getting a giggle out of her by saying there was at least one good reason to make it a double wedding: December 21st was the longest night of the year. Damned bloody stupid politics and governments getting in the way of people's lives.

But at least there was now a general feeling around Red River that things were going to get sorted out, now that the campaign to start a civil war had been knocked on the head. Colonel Dennis had given up and snuck back to his Lieutenant Governor at Pembina, leaving few tears behind. There was a little sympathy for the garrison of Fort Schultz now imprisoned in Fort Garry, but not much. The prisoners weren't going to freeze or starve to death, and as long as they were locked up they couldn't shoot at anybody. There was a petition circulating to get Dr. O'Donnell set free, since December was the season for little children to come down with colds and influenza and croup. No such petition had been issued for Dr. Schultz.

December was also the season for birthdays in the Point Douglas Sutherland household: Donald on the 12th, Morrison the 17th, Hugh 25th, Aleck 30th. Kildonan people didn't make as much fuss over birthdays as the more Englified folk in Little Britain – maybe a new penknife or hair ribbon, and the birthday boy or girl got to decide what kind of berry tarts Mum would make for after supper, if it was a kind she could get her hands on.

A few days after Morrison's birthday, Hugh went across to Bannatyne's store to get the mail. Not that the Point Douglas Sutherlands were expecting any letters, but Da had taken out subscriptions to the Toronto *Globe* and St. Paul *Pioneer* to try and track what the outside world was thinking and saying about the situation at Red River, if anything. It did strike Hugh a little odd that the mail should still be coming and going, in a place where things were so agitated and confused that people couldn't get married. But then, if the National Committee or Lieutenant Governor McDougall or anybody else had crimped-up Red River's only connection to the rest of the world, all the squabbling factions and parishes would've united in one big lynching party.

As Hugh was getting the bundled newspapers from Mrs. Bannatyne, Mr. Bannatyne came over to the postal counter and said: "Well, Hugh, you've saved me the trouble of writing up a note, and one of my stockboys the trouble of carrying it across the river. I've got a piece of news for your father, news that won't be in those newspapers yet. The Honourable William McDougall and his entourage have departed Pembina and headed back to Canada."

"Huh. Guess it was getting pretty cold for them in a cabin on the prairie and winter setting in."

Mrs. Bannatyne said: "Or pretty hot for them."

"Huh?"

Mr. Bannatyne said: "You see, the other part of the news for your father, is that the Queen's Proclamation, regarding the transfer of Rupert's Land to the Dominion of Canada, is expected to be issued in the new year."

"Huh? But it was already. I saw it three weeks ago – there was copies all over Red River."

Mr. Bannatyne said: "I saw it, too. Our esteemed Lieutenant Governor has a salty reception waiting for him in Ottawa."

Mrs. Bannatyne said: "That'll be nothing to when the Queen hears about it. Mama spank."

"Huh? Sorry, I, uh, I don't understand…"

"Your father will."

But when Hugh told his father, Da said: "I don't understand."

Mum said: "I do. Although it's hard to believe…" She trailed off and contemplated a far corner of the room, with her mouth pursed-in like she'd just bit a handful of chokecherries.

After a moment, Da said: "Well? What is?"

"What are the possibilities? Only one, so far as I can see. It's a plain fact that Governor McDougall issued the Queen's Proclamation three weeks ago. And now it seems a plain fact that the Queen's Proclamation won't be issued until sometime in the new year. So…"

Da looked stunned and shook his head, murmuring: "No, it's not poss… He wouldn't…"

"Can you think of any other explanation?"

Hugh said: "Who wouldn't? What?"

Mum turned away from dumbfounded Da and said: "You remember back eight or nine years ago, Hugh, when you decided your penmanship was getting so smooth you could make it look like somebody else's? So one day when you wanted to go fishing, you brought a note to school saying you were needed to help around home, and pretended the note was from me?"

It wasn't a memory Hugh was fond of – even at that age he should've kept in mind the schoolteacher was his mother's close cousin – but he nodded.

"Well, that's pretty much what the Honourable McDougall did with the Queen's Proclamation."

"So that proclamation," Da seemed to've found his voice again, and it was the kind of voice that didn't bode well. Hugh was getting adjusted to the fact that when things got complicated and difficult, Da stopped hesitating and groping for words, "has no legal standing – no more than any other fraud and forgery. And that means…" Da's eyes went abstracted, like he was adding up figures in his head. The sum total he came out with was: "What a bloody mess." Da rubbed his eyes and the sides of his head. "Since that proclamation of December First is null and void… Legally, the transfer of Rupert's Land to Canada hasn't actually happened yet. But meanwhile, The Company's been officially told it's not in charge here anymore. So who is?"

Hugh didn't have an answer for him, and it seemed Mum didn't, either.

"Oh well," Da brightened, "at least one thing's certain. Whatever else might be said about John Bruce and Louis Riel and the provisional government, if the Lieutenant Governor they kept out thinks forging the Queen's name is the way to govern, they did us all a favour." There was now officially a Provisional Government at Fort Garry – well, official in that it had its own flag, with a fleur-de-lis and a shamrock on it and a few other things Hugh couldn't make out from outside the fort walls. But whether that Provisional Government was in charge of anything besides Fort Garry and the barrier on the Pembina Road was open to debate.

But December wasn't just the month for children's flues and Point Douglas Sutherland birthdays, it was also the season for kick-ups, as the old fur traders called dancing parties. No amount of politics could interfere with the necessity for a blow-out rather than a blow-up through the long locked-in winter. There was one party in particular Hugh was interested in. The night before Christmas Eve was going to be a surprise party for old Donald Gunn, keeper of the Red River Library in Little Britain.

Since Little Britain – properly St. Andrew's Parish – was the last parish down-river before the Stone Fort, Hugh figured there was a good chance someone from St. Peters might show up there.

When he and Donald and Aleck got to the Gunn place, there was already music bursting out of the big stone house, and the thump of jigging feet. Hugh added his coat to the hillock in the front hall and went looking through the crowd. He hadn't gone far when a voice called: "Hugh!" But it was a male voice, and unrestrainedly loud, louder even than necessary to carry over the bedlam. Hugh turned and looked in that direction.

At one end of the long table of food and drink stood a waist-high barrel of oysters. Hugh had seen oyster barrels before, at New Year's regales at Fort Garry, and even eaten an oyster or two. Standing on one side of the barrel was a frock-coated man, likely a Company officer from the Stone Fort, with his leather-gloved left hand holding a closed oyster shell, and his bare right hand plying an odd-shaped flat-bladed knife. On the other side of the barrel stood brass-haired, broad-shouldered, stubby-featured Norbert Parisien. Norbert grinned, shoved his bare left hand into the barrel and came out with a dripping, barnacle-studded oyster. Hugh figured that after all Norbert's years of swinging an axe it'd take more than a few little barnacles and rough shell-edges to cut through his palm. Norbert flourished an ordinary hunting knife and said: "Want one, Hugh? He taught me how to do it."

The Company man snorted. "'Taught' him, hell. The lad's a dab hand with a knife."

Norbert's knife blade slid into the shell, made a twisting motion, and the top half of the shell flipped off and splashed into the barrel. Norbert proudly held out the oyster on the half shell, Hugh thanked him and concentrated on getting the edge of the shell up over his lower lip and tipped properly so the oyster and all its juice slid into his mouth. He was just starting to swallow when Norbert looked past him and shouted: "Nancy!"

Fortunately, the oyster slithered straight down to Hugh's stomach before he could choke. He turned around to see Wauh Oonae coming through the crowd, looking beautiful in a purply calico dress, with polished brass hoops gleaming through her blue-black hair. She could've been wearing a flour sack as far as Hugh was considered – it'd been months since he'd seen her in anything but a baggy blanketcoat and duffle leggings. He stepped toward her shyly, and he knew her well enough now to see that she, too, was a bit shy about being together with so many other people around. He reached out tentatively to touch her hand, and bent to kiss her on the cheek. She smiled and squeezed his hand and kept hold of it.

Norbert said: "Want one, cousin?" and held out another shucked oyster. She deftly lifted the shell to her mouth and tipped it back, as though she'd done it a hundred times before. It occurred to Hugh that she probably had, since she'd likely been to a lot more regales at the Stone Fort than he had at Fort Garry.

Nancy handed the shell back to Norbert and said to Hugh, slyly, "We better not eat too many of those – yet."

Before Hugh could think of anything to say to that, a tenor voice on the far side of the room started bellowing a song that cut through the fiddles and bore no resemblance to what they were playing. Hugh laughed, "There goes Jimmy-from-Cork again. Last week there was a kick-up at the Engine House, and Jimmy-from-Cork got so enthusiastic they had to herd him to Fort Garry and lock him up for the night. Guess it'll be the Stone Fort tonight. It's kinda encouraging."

"Encouraging?"

"Well, you know, there's all this talk and worry about Provisional Governments, and Lieutenant Governors, and 'What's gonna happen?' But Jimmy-from-Cork is still getting silly and locked-up for the night, the meadowlarks'll still come back in the spring, the Red River's still running north to Lake Winnipeg – even though you can't see it under the ice…" He started feeling a bit ridiculous for waxing philosophic. "You know what I mean…?"

"Yes." She smiled again; it made him feel worthwhile to make her smile. "We're going to be all right. All this other business is just a little interruption."

"Well, um…" He was going to add *'Let's hope so,'* but that would've spoiled things. What with the fiddles and dozens of thumping feet and the general commotion, Hugh had to talk louder than he'd like to, and he guessed the same applied to her. But since even at that they had to lean in close to hear each other – which Hugh didn't mind at all – he figured no one else was overhearing. "I'm glad you, uh… I thought maybe you'd be here tonight, but I wasn't sure."

"I thought maybe you would be, too, and your parents wouldn't."

"No, but my brothers are – a couple of them." Wauh Oonae didn't seem to shy away at that, so maybe meeting his brothers wasn't as not-yet as meeting his parents. And here they were on neutral ground, so… "Lemme see, Donald is… Oh, Donald's busy jigging with Christy Matheson, they'll get tired eventually. But Aleck is…"

Hugh peered around and found Aleck standing in a nearby corner sipping a cup of punch and watching the festivities without joining in. Hugh called: "Aleck!" and waved him forward. When Aleck got up to them, Hugh said: "Aleck Sutherland, Nancy Prince."

Wauh Oonae said: "Pleased to meet you," and stuck out her hand. Aleck looked down at it, sidled a glance at Hugh, then stuck out his own hand and shook hers quickly, then let go. Nancy murmured: "Aleck…" as though trying to place something. "Oh! You're the smart one who pretends he ain't!"

Aleck's face went stony and he shot a look at Hugh that was betrayed, confused and angry at the same time. Then he turned and walked away. Hugh looked at Wauh Oonae, then at the ceiling, and said: "Damn! Jesus shit, I wish you hadn't said that."

"Why?" Her voice had gone metallic. "Isn't that just exactly what you told to me about your brother Aleck? Isn't that just what you and your family have said to him many times?"

"Yes, but –" But before Hugh could continue with *'...but we don't say it to him anymore, it don't do any good and just makes things worse,'* she cut him off:

"But I'm not one of you, am I? And never will be." She spun around and plunged into the mob of dancers.

Hugh cried: "Nancy!" and tried to follow her, but it was hard to negotiate a path through all the bouncing and weaving bodies and he lost her. He made his way to the staircase up to the second floor of the Gunns' big stone house, climbed halfway up and looked down at the swirling colours. He could see lots of black-haired heads, but no purply calico dresses. He hurried down to the front door and stepped outside. Through the wall of noise coming from behind him he thought he heard a horse galloping in the distance, galloping north toward St. Peters.

Hugh didn't dance that night, so drank too much and on the way home had to lean over the side rail of the cart-sled. In the morning he didn't feel very day-before-Christmasy and was just as glad that Kildonan people and St. Boniface people didn't make as big a fuss about Christmas as The Company's officers and Little Britain people. In most of Red River the big celebration was New Year's, but Hugh wondered if he'd have anything to celebrate this Hogmanay.

He was feeling a little bit less scoured, physically, by the time it came time for the family to get dressed in their best to join their neighbours at Midnight Mass, as they had every Christmas Eve Hugh could remember. This year, St. Boniface Cathedral was less crowded than other years, and there were many more women than men. It seemed the men of St. Boniface and St. Norbert and St. Vital had more pressing business than Heaven to attend to this Christmas. Excepting, of course, Louis Riel. After Mass, when the Point Douglas Sutherlands trailed out of the cathedral – Hugh carrying sound-asleep Mary Ann Bella – Louis Riel was standing on the snow-packed walkway surrounded by a gaggle of women. He called out: "Bon fête, Sutherlands!" and broke away from his admirers.

The Sutherlands called back the good wishes as Louis Riel approached. He stopped in front of Da and said: "It is very good of you to show your neighbourliness in these troubled times."

Da said: "Well, it's our tradition, and, um, in more ways than one. Tomorrow – well, today now, by the clock – is Hugh's twenty-first birthday. I think he was, um, eight or nine before he caught on that the... *reason* everyone stayed up late and went to a place where there was, um, singing and gold and bright colours, wasn't because it was his birthday."

"Congratulations, Hugh. A boy born on Christmas Day – that is very auspicious. And now you are a man. Monsieur Jean Sutherland, would you take a little walk with me?"

"Certainly. I'll meet you back at the sleighs, Mother."

Donald had driven one cart-sled to the cathedral and Da the other. Hugh chose to follow Mum up onto the one Da was going to drive home, partly because she was bound to ask Da what Louis Riel had wanted to say and partly so she'd be near if Mary Ann Bella woke up cranky. Not that he minded carrying his baby sister; she didn't weigh much and her slumbering warmth was a kind of comfort. Any kind of tidings of comfort and joy were a rare commodity after the night before. When Da climbed on board and clucked the pony into motion, Mum said: "Well?"

"Hm? Oh, he wanted to tell me, um... Seems John Bruce resigned today, as... *President* of the National Committee, or the Provisional Government, as it calls itself now. Well, it's no secret John Bruce hasn't been well – although he seemed to've... *recovered*, but I guess he had, um, a relapse. Anyway, he decided being President was, uh, too much of a strain on his health."

Mum said: "Hm. Yes, I can see how being President of the Provisional Government might be bad for a man's health."

Da didn't seem to hear her, just murmured: "Funny, he didn't correct me."

Mum said: "Pardon me?"

"Hm? Oh – Louis Riel, when I called him 'Monsieur Riel' this time, he didn't tell me he should always be 'Louis' to me."

Christmas Day for Hugh was an exercise in not glooming-over everyone else's delight at the miraculous dozen apples – not crabs, but real apples – that Da had somehow managed to procure from some freight shipment in the fall, and Mum had somehow managed to keep hidden and whole till Christmas. Since Mary Ann Bella's teeth and jaws weren't up to crunching apples yet, there was one for each child. Hugh said he'd save his for later.

Keeping a Christmas face on took even more work when Da singled him out with: "Now, everyone, there are now three men in the home of the Point Douglas Sutherlands, since John Hugh Sutherland turned twenty-one today." There was applause and cheers, along with shoulder punches from the boys and squeals of 'Purple Hugh!' from the girls and Roddy. "When Donald turned twenty-one last year, he was given his grandfather's pocket watch, as is only, um, fitting for the eldest son. But for Hugh...

"Hugh, you knew your grandmother well – as well as anybody – so it won't seem as, um, odd to you as it might to some others what she... *decreed*. You know the story that when, um, Sandy Sutherland and Catherine MacPherson were to be married – not long after they first... *arrived* here at the Selkirk Colony, as it was then – he cut the middle out of a silver shilling to make a wedding ring for her. Well, not long after your grandfather's funeral, when he, um, had no say in the matter, your grandmother – being the... *careful* person that she was – told your mother and I that it would be a sinful waste to, um, bury a silver ring. So she made us promise that when, um, the time came we would... *take* it off her finger, and save it to give to you to put on the finger of another woman some day. I have a feeling your grandmother had a feeling you had a feeling who that woman was going to be..."

That was pretty much the last thing Hugh wanted anybody to talk about just now, much less the good-natured teasery from his brothers and sisters about him blushing. He managed to not tell them that the red in his face wasn't exactly what they thought, and managed to make it through the supposedly red letter day without bursting into tears or shooting anybody. The only day that mattered to Hugh just now was in the next week. Not Hogmanay, but December 29th, which would be the first Wednesday and first Montrose 'exercising' day since the horrible surprise party at the Gunns'.

In the days between, a few things happened that seemed to matter to other people. For one thing, the Oak Point representative in the Provisional Government, who'd been in the National Committee since its first days, pulled out and went home. And two Commissioners arrived from Canada to do some horse-trading about what would make the people of Red River happy to become part of the Dominion. Well, *one* of them arrived, a Grand Vicar Thibault or Deveaux or something, but the other one, a Colonel Salisbury or something, was still waiting in Pembina for permission to pass the barricade at St. Norbert. And a third man had come from Canada, a plain Mr. Smith, but he wasn't *from* Canada. Smith was said to be an old-time Company officer who'd spent most of his career in the north-east of Rupert's Land, and now been dispatched to the north-west to help pick up the load Governor Mactavish couldn't carry from his sickbed.

Hugh didn't pay much attention to all that, he was fully occupied trying to keep his stomach from eating itself as the 26th, 27th and 28th crawled slowly by. The night before the 29th he didn't sleep much, even less than the nights before. He pushed his breakfast around his plate for just long enough to have a hint of sunrise when he went out to saddle Montrose. By the time he got to the little bridge over the frozen stream, there was enough light to see there were no footprints or hoofprints in the new snow on the left of the road. But that didn't necessarily mean disaster. What with the cold and the ice, he and Wauh Oonae hadn't actually gone down into the hollow since the day she came back from the autumn buffalo hunt, just spent their Montrose-exercising days riding up and down the road, with an occasional pause in a handy stand of evergreens.

He decided that if she didn't appear today riding south to meet him, he'd keep on riding north until he got to her home in St. Peters. What he would do when he got there was a matter of speculation. But he did know he wasn't going to let his life and hers just melt away, not without doing his damnedest to sort things out.

He was passing by Kildonan Kirk on the other side of the river when he saw another rider, coming south toward him. At first he could only see that it was an Indian pony, not a seventeen-hands-high like Montrose – but that would apply to most horses at Red River. Then he could see it was a light-coated horse with a dark-coated rider. Then he could see it was dappled Cheengwun, with Wauh Oonae in her blue capote. While still about thirty yards ahead of him, she reined in, jumped down and walked toward him leading her horse, so he followed suit. When almost up to him she stopped and stood still, so he did, too.

Hugh cracked his mouth open and said: "I'm sorry, I shouldn't've –" then stopped, because exactly the same words a half-octave higher were coming out in perfect harmony and rhythm. She stopped, too. He shrugged one shoulder and said: "Is there an echo around here?" She laughed. "Look, Nancy, if I didn't want you to say anything to Aleck about Aleck I should've told you back when – or not told you anything about Aleck at all. It's not your fault he's so twisted-up he takes offence at –"

"No, how could you know I was gonna say something like that? I was nervous and trying to be smart – if I didn't know I shouldn'ta said it as soon as I said it, I wouldn'ta tried to put the blame on you."

"You know, if you keep cutting off my apologies with your apologies we're not gonna get anywhere."

In other circumstances it might've been complicated getting their arms around each other and kissing while still holding their horses, but it came off without a hitch. When they stopped for breath, Nancy said: "I have a birthday present for you. Well, more'n just 'birthday' present, I had it a long while waiting, but it seems about time, you being now officially a man and all…"

She reached inside her coat and brought out what looked to be a chain-link necklace, except that the chain was woven black hair. He'd seen men from Little Britain sporting watch chains and the like made from their wives' or fiances' hair – apparently it had become a fashion in England and eventually made its way to Red River. The Indians found it funny, that the white men carried around scalps, too. Hugh rolled one of the links between the tips of his thumb and forefinger, feeling silky and thatchy at the same time. He said: "Yours?"

"Uh-huh. Brush harvest, over a long time. But that ain't the present, really."

Attached to the chain was a thumb-sized, smoked moosehide pouch with a tiny blue crown beaded onto it. He said: "Um… if it's a Medicine Bag, I shouldn't open it."

"It's not really a Medicine Bag, only sort of. My grandfather gave it to me in his last days, said I should give it to the man that smelled right to me, but only the one man and only the once."

Hugh gingerly pried open the tiny drawstring and dumped the contents of the pouch into his cupped left hand. There was only one item, a kind of shrivelled dark leathery mushroom. Hugh said: "Um… it's, um… What is it?"

"It's my grandfather's nose. Well, the part that got bit off and spat out. My grandfather smoked it – not in a pipe, I mean, over a fire – and kept it."

"Well, I, um – thank you. I'll put it around my neck when I next got my coat and scarf off. And," he had an inspiration, "my grand*mother* gave me something to give to you – though I didn't know she'd gave it to me till a few days ago." The silver shilling wedding ring, wrapped in a worn-thin piece of cotton handkerchief, was still in his trousers pocket where he'd tucked it after the presentation. He pulled it out, told Wauh Oonae the story, then took hold of her left hand and went to put it on the finger.

"No!" she pulled her hand back. "It's bad luck, before the day. But I'll keep it until then. Thank you, my dearest, darling man." She touched his cheek, then looked away and around, seeming a bit bashful. "Well, even though it's a pretty mild day it's still cold for standing around. We should give the horses a bit of a run."

Hugh looked around and realised it actually was a relatively mild day for late December, he hadn't noticed. He climbed back on Montrose and he and Nancy Prince cantered north for awhile. It gave him time to debate whether he should explain more to her about him and Aleck, or better to leave well enough alone. When they slowed to a walk, he said: "Um, you know, about Aleck and all that... I tend to bristle a bit about Aleck. I think why I got annoyed so quick about what you said to Aleck, wasn't really what you said, but 'cause I feel kinda guilty."

"Guilty?"

"Well, uh, without him really doing anything to deserve it, he can aggravate me, and embarrass me. I mean, the way he combs his hair like me, grew the same kinda mustache, talks like me... It's all so... clumsy, and phony. But I wonder, sometimes, if maybe why I get aggravated and embarrassed is 'cause he's like I'm looking at a mirror, and what I see is... clumsy and phony."

She didn't say anything. Hugh wondered if maybe he'd exposed too much of himself, or maybe she wasn't saying anything because she agreed with the last thing he'd said. Then she said: "Maybe you can be a bit clumsy sometimes – God knows *I* never am – but you couldn't be phony if somebody put a gun to your head. The way you do things, the way you talk, that's what comes natural to you. Maybe what's natural to you looks clumsy and embarrassing on somebody it's not natural to."

"Huh. Well. How about that." Just like that, that little worm that had been niggling at him was gone.

After the next gallop, Wauh Oonae said: "My father says my uncle the chief says things are looking good to get straightened out pretty soon, now that that Canadian commissioner's here."

"Which one? The Grand Vicar or the Colonel?"

"Not neither. They're both just for show, or so my father says his brother the chief says. The real horsetrader is Smith."

Hugh was confused, even more so than usual in the last month, which took some doing. "But... Da said, and everybody else says, this Smith fella is just a Company man that just came out here to help Governor Mactavish manage things while he's so sick."

"That's what Canada and London want people to think – or so my Uncle Henry says. So that this Smith can go around and talk to people unofficial-like, and find out what's really going on here." A sly smile crept onto her face and into her voice. "Because there's a fact about this Smith fella that'll make people around here trust him and talk to him straight."

When Wauh Oonae didn't go on to say what that 'fact' was, Hugh said: "Well... seems to me someone said this Smith's wife's Metis, or whatever they call that in east Rupert's Land..."

"Seems to me someone probably would said that to you, since her maiden name was Margaret *Sutherland*. There was a lot of Sutherlands in The Company in the old days. So, yeah, the fact Mrs. Smith's Metis will make a lot of people around here more inclined to be trusting of Mr. Smith. But that ain't it."

"Okay, I give up – what's the secret?"

"Oh, it ain't a secret, pretty soon everybody'll be talking about it." She smiled more widely and not slyly. "The fact is… Donald A. Smith is – *was*… cousin to Mr. Grant."

"No!"

"Yes. Well, not *close* cousins – just what they call Highland cousins – but close enough that the uncle that sponsored Donald Smith into The Company is the same uncle that was the executive of Mr. Grant's will. One of the first things Smith did when he got here was ride straight out to White Horse Plains to pay his respects to Mary Falcon, Mr. Grant's sister. But," Wauh Oonae interrupted herself with a giggle, "it turned out Mr. Smith couldn't hardly squeeze his respects in sideways, 'cause that little old lady kept pinching the cheeks of that full-growed, big-bearded man and squealing 'Little Donald, little Donald!'"

Nancy stopped her horse, so Hugh did, too. She reached up to squeeze his wool-padded shoulder with her mitten-buffered hand. Her eyes were glistening. "So you see, my Purple Hugh, all this mess is going to get sorted out. Just like you said at the surprise party. Next Christmas we'll be sitting cozy in Jean Claude MacGregor's house – *our* house – with our own fire in our own hearth."

CHAPTER 47

On the first day of the new year 1870, Schultz stood staring out the bars of his cage. He'd been shut into a room on the top floor of a Fort Garry warehouse for a week now. Christmas Eve had been the day Riel had decided Schultz should be locked up alone, instead of abiding with his wife in Dr. Cowan's house and allowed the freedom of the fort. It was obvious to Schultz that Riel had just been looking for an excuse to make his life as miserable as possible, and had hatched up the notion that Schultz was planning to take advantage of the holiday season to engineer a wholesale jailbreak while the guards were so befuddled with good cheer that by the time they caught on all the prisoners would be safely away to the Stone Fort. Of course that was exactly what Schultz had been planning, but that was beside the point.

It was clear now that 'The National Committee' was Riel, and always had been Riel – 'President' John Bruce was just a stalking horse. And 'Adjutant General' Ambroise Lépine was just a facilitator. Lépine had shown a humane reluctance to separate Schultz and his wife when Agnes clung screaming that she couldn't bear to be parted from her husband, especially on the eve of the anniversary of Our Saviour's birth. But Lépine had nonetheless followed Riel's bidding. Lépine was like a big dumb Newfoundland dog – with nothing to prove and always the last in the pack to lose his temper. Riel was a crossbred terrier, threatening and snarling when he didn't get his way. And no doubt somewhere in the background jerking Riel's chain was his sister, Attila the Nun.

The window of Schultz's cell was much higher than the walls of Fort Garry, so Schultz had a full view of the courthouse halfway between Fort Garry and his home. Some of the fifty or so prisoners – Riel had been arresting so many men it was hard to keep track – had been shifted from Fort Garry to the cells in the courthouse, but Schultz wasn't exactly sure which ones. He was pretty sure Charles Mair and James Stewart were still among those in the two big rooms three floors below him, the ones with barred windows. There were no actual bars on Schultz's window, just casement frame, and no need for them. It was a good fifty feet high with a sheer drop to the frozen courtyard. The only salubrious aspect of the window was that it was in a gable jutting out of the slope of the roof, and the width of the gable frame and Schultz's shoulders fit just right that he could shift from leaning against the left wall or the right just by shifting his weight, depending on which leg was getting tired.

There was some sort of activity going on along the snowfield between Fort Garry and the courthouse – men and horses milling around. Then two horsemen broke away from the pack and charged toward a lone tree out on the prairie, circled around it and came surging back. Schultz turned away from the window. New Year's Day horseraces were more frustrating than entertaining when you had no way of knowing who was racing and couldn't lay bets anyway. He did some pacing around his cell but couldn't do much, since although it was a fair-sized room it was still an attic room and much of the ceiling slanted below his height. Slanting so low at one end that there was nothing he could do in that part of the room but stretch out on the buffalo robes and blankets they'd given him for a bed.

When pacing back and forth wore out its welcome, Schultz tugged off his boots to do some push-ups. He was up to thirty, and beginning to work up a sweat, when he heard footsteps coming along the corridor. He put one ear to the floor and held his breath to hear them better. They were quick, sharp, hard-heeled footsteps, which could mean Agnes. Barely audible along with them were the softer, slower, heavier footfalls of a man in moccasins.

Schultz stood up as the iron bolt clanked and the door swung open. It was Agnes, with her crossed arms clutching a book to her breasts. Beside her was a Metis guard, holding a flintlock pistol his grandfather must've got in trade for his grandmother. Schultz and Agnes started toward each other, but the guard put up his arm between them and said: "Sorry, not touch. Orders. Too easy things be…" he flapped his free hand back and forth, "…smuggle."

Agnes said: "Are you well? Are they feeding you enough?"

"Enough to keep me alive. Edible if I work up an appetite."

"I brought you a book to read, from Dr. Cowan's library. Elizabeth Barret Browning, 'Sonnets From the Portugese'." She proffered him the Morocco-bound volume, but the guard took it from her hand and tucked his pistol under his armpit so he could inspect the book. It put the guard in a precarious position. For an instant, Schultz contemplated knocking him down and out and taking his pistol. But only for an instant: there would still be a fortful of well-armed Metis to cope with.

The guard riffled through the pages – Schultz doubted the man could read French let alone English – then turned the book upside down and shook it before nodding there was nothing 'smuggle' in it, and handed it to Schultz. Schultz had no doubt Agnes was clever enough to not try hiding anything inside any book she brought to him, until she'd seen how the guards inspected them. Schultz said: "Thank you, my dear."

"I'll bring you another when you're done perusing this one. Anything in particular you'd like, now that you have the enforced time to catch up on your reading?"

"Well, oddly enough, though Dr. Cowan may well not have it in his library… I've been thinking of Grimm's Fairytales. The story of Rapunzel has been running through my mind, but I'm not sure I might not be remembering it backwards." He sidled a glance at the buffalo robes and blankets laid out under the low end of the wall, and saw her eyes flick in that direction. He was quite sure the guard wouldn't know the story of the maiden locked in the tower, or put it together with the fact that if those blankets and buffalo robes were cut into strips they could be knotted into a very long rope – provided a prisoner was provided with something to cut with.

"I'll see what I can find."

"Thank you."

"Monsieur Riel paid me a visit this morning, at Dr. Cowan's."

"Oh, did he, now?" Riel seemed to have developed a habit of visiting Schultz's wife when Schultz wasn't there.

"He told me I was free to go now – now that you're in solitary confinement anyway, and since he would've let me stay at large to begin with if I hadn't insisted on staying with you."

"Ah."

"I haven't seen the inside of our home for three weeks now. I could go back there and make sure everything is kept in order."

"Yes, I suppose you could."

"But," she raised her chin bravely and blinked away the moisture glistening in her eyes, "once I've left the fort, there is no guarantee they will let me back in again to visit you. So I've decided to remain in Dr. Cowan's house."

Since he wasn't allowed to touch her, Schultz just tightened his mouth to contain his emotion, and nodded – at her bravery and devotion, and at her perspicacity in realising that if she stayed in Fort Garry she might be able to help him escape.

Agnes said: "Is there anything else I might bring you when next I come? That is, anything they will allow me to bring you…?"

"Um, a deck of cards would be good, might as well practise up on my solitaire in solitary. Oh, and some writing paper and pen and ink, or a pencil, if you could."

"And I'll bring you a change of clothes." She turned to the guard. "Surely that would be allowed."

The guard shrugged, "I will feel the pockets before hand on to him."

Two days later Agnes came again, apologising that they wouldn't let her visit him every day. She brought him a clean shirt and collar, fresh socks, a deck of cards, a thick volume of Gibbon's *Decline and Fall of The Roman Empire*, a blank notebook, two pencils and a penknife. The guard took the penknife from her and shook his head. She said: "For God's sake, the blade's barely an inch long! Do you think he's going to dig his way through the wall with it? He needs something to sharpen the pencils with!"

The amateur jailer wrinkled his beetled brows, then said ponderously, "Them pencils sharp now. When he need them re-sharp, he call me and I come re-sharp them," and he tucked the penknife in his ceinture flechée.

When the guard riffled through the pages of *Decline and Fall*, Agnes caught Schultz's eye and blinked twice. When she and the guard had gone, he turned through the book's pages one by one – after all, he had nothing but time. Page 274 turned to page 277. The pages between were glued together at the edges. Schultz carefully worked a fingernail along the seam and separated them. Pencilled into the margins of 275 and 276 was: *'The poet and friends are prevaricating chisellers at the taverns. In a week their tab comes due.'* So, Charlie Mair and some of his fellow prisoners were secretly chiselling away at the bars in their cell window. And they expected it would take another week to finish the job.

Schultz was elated for a moment, and then even more frustrated than he'd been before. Well enough for Mair and cohorts to slip out their first-floor window under cover of darkness, and scuttle over the fort walls and away; he'd still be stuck up in his Rapunzel tower without a rope. He decided to do some more push-ups and some upside-down bicycling legs, maybe work off enough steam to think clearly.

When next Agnes came, she brought a newspaper fresh off the press. Schultz had known that the proprietor of *The Pioneer* had decided that publishing a newspaper at Red River wasn't a healthy occupation these days, and that Enos Stutsman had offered to buy him out and publish a paper approved by the Provisional Government – no doubt with Stutsman's subtle advertisements for the U.S.A. salted throughout. But he hadn't known it was a done deal.

After the guard had flipped through the newspaper to make sure there wasn't a flying-machine inside, and handed it on to Schultz, Agnes said: "It's called *The New Nation.*" Schultz laughed at her joke, then laughed louder when he saw it actually was the name on the masthead. The guard looked miffed, but undoubtedly wasn't aware – just as well – that 'nation' was a printers-lingo adjective for anything useless, ridiculous or obstreperous, an abbreviation of 'damnation.'

Schultz handed Agnes his latest little bundle of laundry, after the jailer had taken a cursory glance through it. The jailer seemed not much concerned about anything that might pass *out* of Schultz's cell, provided it wasn't Schultz. Schultz said: "Do try and pay a bit more attention to the collar this time, my dear."

"I will, my dear, sorry if I didn't get it quite clean last time."

"No recriminations, my dear." He was quite sure the guard was too dim to suspect anything beyond a husband gently chiding his slipshod wife.

When Agnes was gone and Schultz locked alone again, he sat down on his blankets and buffalo robes to read *The New Nation.* There was an editorial declaring that the only hope for the future happiness of the people of Red River was to become a territory of the U.S.A. Apparently 'subtle' and Stutsman didn't feel they needed to be acquainted in the present circumstances.

A separate enclosed sheet was headlined *'ORDERS of THE PROVISIONAL GOVERNMENT OF RUPERT'S LAND'* and contained such gems as *'All the officers and employees of the old Government, who might pretend to exercise that old authority shall be punished for high treason...'* Funny that the phrase 'high treason' would be on the minds of the leaders of the Provisional Government.

Another of the *ORDERS* was actually quite encouraging: *'All Licenses for the Sale of intoxicating liquors must be...'* well, essentially *must be* approved by Louis Riel and his priest-kissing cronies. The encouraging aspect of that had to do with public opinion, and the annoyingly neutral stance of much of the local public so far. It was hard to imagine anything more odious to the people of Red River than being told what they could or couldn't drink, when there were still three or four months of winter staring them in the face.

Schultz tossed *The New Nation* aside and went and looked out of his window again. It was still a long drop, but nowhere near as long a drop as Louis Riel was going to take once John Christian Schultz got free again.

CHAPTER 48

Given Red River's longtime isolation from the rest of the world and its five- or six-month winters, one of its major forms of entertainment was gossip – or, to put it more politely, the exchange of news and opinions. Hugh had pleasant memories from back when he was a knee-high, when the Point Douglas Sutherlands still lived on Point Douglas, sitting with his grandmother in other people's kitchens while the click of knitting needles punctuated female voices saying things that often went straight over his head.

This winter there was more to talk about than all the winters Hugh could remember, and the Point Douglas Sutherlands' kitchen was a natural gravitational point for undercurrents from both sides of the river. So they were naturally among the first to hear, very early one morning, that a number of prisoners had escaped from Fort Garry the night before, and Metis horsemen were out scouring the countryside to find them. Da immediately told Hugh to saddle him a pony and took off across the river. A while later, Hugh and Aleck were heaving hay down from the loft to fill the mangers for the cattle and Montrose, and out the loft door to feed the ponies, when Donald called from the paddock, "Da's home!"

Hugh stuck his pitchfork upright in the hay pile, said: "This'll wait," and headed inside.

Da was thawing out his fingers around a mug of tea, and Mum was waiting for his tentative sips to thaw his mouth enough to tell her what was what. Eventually Da said: "There definitely was an escape. Some say a dozen, some half-a-dozen. A few have been recaptured already. Dr. Cowan is operating on one of them – feet so badly frostbit it'll be lucky if he only loses a few toes. Silly bast – um, silly fools, trying to foot it to Portage la Prairie in January. But a few are definitely still at large – Charles Mair, Thomas Scott, a few others whose names are uncertain or I can't remember."

Hugh said: "Dr. Schultz…?"

"No, if he'd escaped his name would've been at the top of the list. Funny you should ask, though, as it seems he was in on it, and planned to get away with the others. Yesterday, or the day before, his jailers intercepted a message he'd written on a shirt collar going to Mrs. Schultz to be laundered. Um, let me see if I can remember it rightly… yes: *'Get the usual – spit blood – and have me sent for.'* So, it seems clear Dr. Schultz had a plan for his wife to pull some trick that would have him brought out of his cell the night of the escape. Although no one can fathom what *'the usual'* is, or was, he wanted her to get for him."

Mum snorted, "*Men.* It's obvious." Hugh and the other males in the room looked to her for illumination. "'The usual' is 'deathly ill.' 'Get deathly ill, spit blood, and have me sent for.'"

Hugh had to laugh – if nothing else, the Schultzes were good for entertainment. Although by this point he would've been more than glad if they and the rest would stop the show, so he could get on with his life.

Da said: "Oh," then, "Well, maybe then, Mother, you can also explain to me something else as well. While I was talking with A.G.B. Bannatyne in his kitchen just now, one of his clerks came across from the store with something odd he'd found while sweeping out his office: bits of an empty envelope that had been torn up and dropped on the floor. When the bits were pieced together, the envelope was addressed to Louis Riel from someone in the United States."

Mum said: "Seems simple enough – Louis grew up used to his mother and sisters picking up after him."

"Ah, but..." Da pushed his emptied teacup toward Mum and the teapot, "Louis Riel hadn't come in yet to pick up the mail that came in this morning."

Mum pushed the teapot and still-empty cup toward Da and said: "Well then I don't understand what your riddle is supposed to mean."

"Neither do I exactly. But I do know this – Mr. W.B. O'Donoghue did come in to collect his own mail this morning, and any mail for the Grey Nuns' school in Winnipeg. Since Mrs. Bannatyne happened to've stepped out, he went behind the post office counter to pick it out himself. Then he borrowed the clerk's empty office to peruse *his* mail, then bought a blank envelope and borrowed a pen and ink. So there still is a letter addressed to Louis Riel, from someone in the United States, waiting for him at the post office counter at Bannatyne's."

Mum said: "Cheeky."

Donald said: "And about as illegal as you can get, under any jurisdiction in the world."

Da said while re-filling his teacup, "Well, that's the question of the year, isn't it – whether there is any jurisdiction here at all?"

Mum said: "What did it say?"

Da said: "Hm?"

"The letter."

"Well, I don't know, do I? But I can say for certain the Sisters of Charity do, or will soon, since O'Donoghue does."

Hugh said: "Well, the Grey Nuns'd know soon enough anyways, eh? I mean, if it was anything that mattered – and O'Donoghue musta figured it mattered enough to sneak into it – Louis Riel'd tell his sister, his sister the Sister."

Da rubbed the heels of his hands against the sides of his head and said: "I don't know, son, I don't know anymore who's on what side or where the sides are or who wants what or if anyone even knows what they want. It's all turned into an endless guessing game that changes its rules from one day to the next."

Hugh was inclined to agree with that, and went back to the barn and something he could make sense of: forking hay down to the creatures who knew exactly what they wanted. Through the whispering hiss and swish of the hay stocks on the wooden tines came an interior whisper telling him he hadn't noticed that he'd noticed something peculiar about the conversation that'd just happened in the kitchen. He realised that Da had hardly stammered and *uhm*ed at all, hadn't had a halt in his speech, hadn't hesitated in the middle and then barked out the next word. Hugh had got accustomed to the fact that Da's speech-tics disappeared when there was some immediate crisis to deal with. But now, thinking back over the last weeks, Hugh realised they hardly ever happened at all anymore.

Hugh wondered if maybe that was because every minute at Red River these days was an immediate crisis. Or maybe Da losing his stammer had something to do with the fact that, with Gran and Granda gone, he wasn't anybody's child anymore. Or maybe it was because Da had had to do more communicating in the last few weeks than most decades, what with public meetings and negotiating the surrender of Fort Schultz and all those serious conversations in the Bannatynes' kitchen and others. Well, whatever the actual reason, or probably reasons, John Hugh Sutherland certainly wasn't the boy to study it out. He told himself to let it go as 'maybe this, maybe that,' and let the fact speak for itself. The fact, though, did raise the strange and unsettling notion that parents could change, almost as though they were still growing themselves.

Encouragingly, the stories that passed through the Point Douglas Sutherlands' did seem to suggest that Wauh Oonae had been right about this Donald A. Smith fellow. It seemed that Smith had been given some papers by the Canadian government, spelling out what he was authorized to horsetrade with the people of Red River. But Smith was clever enough, or skittish enough, to realise that if he handed the papers over to Louis Riel or anybody else in the Provisional Government, he might have a little trouble getting them back. Then whoever kept the papers could keep them to himself, and cherrypick what he wanted the general public to know about what was in them.

So Smith had left the papers at Pembina before crossing the border, and he told the Provisional Government he would only present the papers to a full public meeting, to be read out in full. The Provisional Government agreed, but the next day Louis Riel and some friends rode south and intercepted the man Smith had sent to fetch the papers. What Louis Riel got instead of the papers was a close look down the barrel of Pierre Léveillé's revolver, and the unnegotiable message that the papers would be delivered as promised.

There was no building at Red River large enough to hold the thousands of people expected for the public meeting, so it was set for the Parade Ground in Fort Garry.

Hugh, Da, Donald and Aleck set off for it in a sleigh hitched to one of the ponies, after doing their morning chores and having breakfast. The day felt like it was going to be colder than yesterday, and yesterday had been fairly cold – Hugh guessed about twenty below.

As the snow-packed road down the middle of the river passed by the town of Winnipeg, Hugh looked up to see if the flag was still there. A week ago, the American flag had suddenly appeared on a flagpole on top of the Emmerling Hotel. It was flown at half-mast, because Dutch George's only excuse to be flying it at all was in honour of some famous and important American government man who'd just died. It was still there, but all the way up now. So the only flags flying over Red River these days were those of the Provisional Government and the United States of America.

The only parades Hugh had ever seen or heard of on the Parade Ground in Fort Garry were the cart trains and boat brigades loading or unloading. But those were enough to need a wide swath of open ground left permanently in the middle of the fort, with the buildings horseshoed around it. Hugh had never seen so many people in one place before: in buffalo coats and blanket coats, fur hats and toques, murmuring to each other in English, French, Bungee or a mixture of all three, and the windows of all the buildings were filled with faces – some of the faces cross-hatched with the iron bars in the windows where the forty-some prisoners of the Provisional Government were still shut in.

What with all the bodies crowded together, and the buildings to break the wind, the cold was almost tolerable, if you periodically flapped your arms against yourself and stomped your feet on the frozen ground. Some men occasionally pulled a bottle of warming liquid out of their coats and passed it around; Hugh wondered how many of them also had pistols or knives inside their coats.

There was a kind of raised, railed platform in front of the building at the head of the square, and standing on it were Louis Riel and several others. Hugh figured the largish man with the square-cut beard to be Donald A. Smith. In short order, the late Dr. Bunn's son Thomas was appointed chairman of the meeting, Judge Black Secretary and Louis Riel Interpreter. Oddly, or at least it seemed odd to Hugh, Louis Riel's motion to appoint Thomas Bunn was seconded by Pierre Léveillé, the same Pierre Léveillé that only yesterday had been tickling Riel's nose with his pistol barrel. Then again, Hugh reconsidered, maybe it wasn't so odd. Maybe it and all the other incomprehensible shiftings of who was on whose side were no different from the fact that Donald could infuriate the hell out of him one day and be his trusty big brother the next.

Mr. Bunn called the meeting to order, said a few words about this being the most important public meeting ever held at Red River, and then called on Mr. Smith to read out his papers. The first was an official letter to Donald A. Smith from Joseph Howe, the Dominion's Secretary of State for the Provinces, the same Joseph Howe who'd visited Red River in the fall and apparently'd had a lot of meetings, but no public ones. The letter had a lot of high-sounding language that Hugh let pass by him, but the gist was that Nancy's uncle the Chief had guessed right: Mr. Smith had indeed been appointed Special Commissioner to find out what had made the people of Red River unhappy about the transfer to Canada, and what would make them happier.

The second official letter was from the Governor General of Canada and all of British North America. There were cheers when Mr. Smith read out: *'The people may rely upon it that respect and protection will be extended to the different religious persuasions,'* and when that was followed by: *'titles to every description of property will be strictly guarded,'* Hugh burst out joining in the cheers.

What with all the drawn-out formalities in the letters Smith read out, and Louis Riel translating it all into French and occasionally raising quibbles about whether the formalities were formal enough to make the letters official, it was some while before the business was done. And then Mr. Donald A. Smith flicked a card out from the bottom of the deck.

His dispatch from the Governor General had made mention of three other dispatches the Governor General had dispatched at the same time: to the Protestant Bishop of Rupert's Land, to Vicar General Thibault – who was filling-in while Bishop Taché was away to Rome – and to Governor Mactavish. Mr. Smith wondered aloud what had happened to those dispatches.

Hugh didn't have any idea why such an innocent question should cause such a kerfuffle, but it certainly did. Agitated pronouncements burst out of the mouths of Chairman Bunn, Vicar General Thibault, Judge Black, President Riel, Bishop Machray, and a number of untitled men in the crowd. It eventually came out that all three letters had somehow come to be in the possession of Mr. W. B. O'Donoghue, even though his name hadn't figured on the address of any of them.

Mr. Smith expressed the opinion that since those three letters had been intended for the three men best-positioned to relay the Crown's intentions to all segments of the people of Rupert's Land, the letters should be read out to the public meeting of the people of Rupert's Land. The more the leaders of the Provisional Government protested that reading out the letters wouldn't be in order, the more it seemed to the crowd that it wasn't the letters that were out of order. Hugh found himself shouting along with everybody else: *"Let them be read!"* Even though the thrill wasn't the point, there was a thrill in the fact that he and several thousand other people were spontaneously shouting the same thing at the same time. Well, spontaneously once someone had shouted it first.

After some quibbling, and what Granda would've called rearguard-action, it was decided that the letters would be surrendered by Mr. O'Donoghue and read out publicly – tomorrow. The sun was edging its way down, and the day's crippling cold would soon be killing cold. Although nothing had been accomplished but talk, Hugh got the same feeling from the men around him as at a harvest-time sunset: it had been a good day's work. But just as the crowd was breaking up peaceably, someone with a very loud voice shouted: *"Free the prisoners!"*

A chorus of other voices took up the chant, but Hugh didn't join in this time. He was too busy noticing Ambroise Lépine's soldiers dodging into the buildings where they'd left their guns to stay warm, and other men skedaddling for the gate out of the fort, and wondering whether he'd been a fool to not've brought his revolver or would've been a fool to bring it. Louis Riel was shouting from the podium, "Not yet!" but Hugh wasn't sure whether that was a reply to the call to free the prisoners, or an order to Lépine to not start shooting yet. Donald and Aleck, standing on either side of Da, had automatically turned sideways. Hugh took a step backward and turned around, to make it a square of Point Douglas Sutherlands facing outward. Da was yelling – well, not yelling, there was no harshness in his voice – that everyone should calm down. And, remarkably, everyone did.

The next day's meeting began with the man who'd yelled *'Free the prisoners!'* making a public apology for agitating things yesterday. He said 'someone else' had convinced him he should agitate to have the prisoners freed immediately, but he now realised it would be too soon – that just when it looked like the people of Red River were finding a way to sort out their differences, it would be foolish to let-loose men known to dwell on and trade on those differences. Then Mr. Bunn called the meeting to order. Judge Black declined to serve as Secretary again, so Mr. Bannatyne was appointed in his place. Father Ritchot made a very cheering speech about how all the people of the settlement had been good friends up till today and would still be good friends tonight. And then Mr. Smith was called forward to read the letters that had been liberated from Mr. O'Donoghue.

The letters were about as official as you could get, short of an actual Queen's Proclamation, all signed by the Governor General, the Secretary of State for the Provinces, and the Secretary of State period. It sounded to Hugh like all three gentlemen weren't happy with the way the transfer had been handled, and genuinely wanted the people of Red River to be guaranteed their rights to their land titles and to a fair say in their government. Best of all, between letters Mr. Smith made a point of pointing out that he personally had only ever exchanged a few passing words with the Honourable Mr. Lieutenant Governor William McDougall, had never corresponded with the man, and had no connection whatsoever with any of the appointed carpetbaggers the Honourable McDougall had brought with him to take over Rupert's Land.

Well, Mr. Smith didn't actually say 'carpetbaggers,' but the impression was there that that was his impression. Mr. Smith also pointed out that, as Wauh Oonae had told Hugh, Donald A. Smith had more commonality with the people of Rupert's Land than with the people of Canada.

Hugh could hear all around him murmured, good-natured imitations of old-lady voices, *"Little Donald, little Donald..."* and he chuckled along with them. But then it struck him that maybe Smith's visit out to White Horse Plains hadn't had anything to do with family feeling at all, just clever politics. Hugh couldn't think of anything better-calculated to get Donald A. Smith accepted and respected by the people of Red

River than to be family-welcomed by the sister of Mr. Grant. Hugh could hear Nancy Prince's voice: *'Trust nobody, trust nothing... Everybody lies.'*

But what the hell kind of way was that for anybody to live, suspicious of everything? Hugh was intending to eventually convince Nancy that there was at least one person she could trust, and here he was sinking into suspiciousness. He decided that the sensible way to look at it was that Smith had known it was a smart political move *and* had wanted to visit his aging cousin – would've done so even if he'd just been passing through Red River on no official business. There, that seemed like a healthy balance between wide-eyed and slit-eyed.

By day's end, the public meeting reached agreement that a committee of five men – including Point Douglas John Sutherland – would wrangle out how to apportion twenty Representatives among the twelve parishes that hadn't decided to join the Provisional Government. Once those twenty Representatives were elected, they would sit down with twenty Representatives from the parishes already in on the Provisional Government, and the Convention of Forty would wrangle out what terms and conditions and guarantees from Ottawa would make them comfortable about becoming part of Canada.

As the crowd funnelled its way out the gates of Fort Garry, Hugh found himself feeling kind of drunk – though the feeling didn't have that sickish undercurrent of the few times he'd got truly drunk, and all he'd had to drink today was a few warming sips. The feeling seemed to be extremely mutual: people who barely knew each other were grinning at each other, slapping each other on the back and laughing for no reason. Jean Claude MacGregor appeared beside Hugh, bumped shoulders with him and said: "Well, Hugh Sutherland, from the looks of things, come spring – or once the spring mud dries out – me and my family'll be moving out and you'll be moving in. If we still got a deal."

"If you say we still got a deal, Monsieur MacGregor, we sure by God got a deal."

CHAPTER 49

Schultz sat on his bed on the floor, watching the cruciform shadow thrown by his prison window edge its way across the wall. There was an egg-shaped knothole in one of the wall planks, about an inch farther along the path of the sunlight through the window. He decided that when the shadow touched the knothole he'd get up and go look out the window.

Not that he expected there'd be much to see. There hadn't been yesterday. There'd been plenty to see the day before, and the day before that, but that had ended up being even more frustrating than nothing to see. His window had given him a view of half the platform that the chairman and so on of the public meeting had occupied, but only half, and only about one quarter of the crowd. And sometimes even cupping his ear against the glass hadn't allowed him to hear all that was being said, even though it was being said loud enough to carry across the parade ground at ground level.

He'd got the gist, though, and it wasn't a pleasant gist. Away in the backrooms of Ottawa, Joseph Howe and Donald Smith had maneuvered William McDougall out of his rightful position. And now Smith and Riel had inveigled the locals into believing they could demand conditions before they agreed to join the Dominion of Canada. *Conditions*, from the Imperial Government? What most likely would happen was that Ottawa and London would laugh in the face of their bloody conditions, and then the American Army garrisoned along the frontier would have an excuse to move north.

The other possible outcome, almost as bad, was that Joseph bloody Howe and his cabal might be able to make enough noise in Ottawa to get some of the conditions granted. Red River might even be granted the right to elect its own officials, trampling Schultz's hard-won campaign to convince Ottawa that would be a mistake until enough Canadians with experience of democracy had moved into the territory. The locals were likely to pass over a man of ability to elect some mouldy old fur trader, or worse, some priests' puppet. Any candidate blessed from the pulpit of St. Boniface Cathedral – even someone like Louis Riel – would automatically get the vote of all faithful Catholics. Schultz was all for religious tolerance, but 'tolerance' didn't include the Pope's fingers stuck into democratic government. And if the right to elections went so far as creating new seats in Parliament... Ontario was already having a hard enough time holding its own against

Quebec, without another batch of Church-manipulated MPs coming in from the west. Very few people at Red River could see the big picture that could be affected by this tiny corner of it, and they were mostly on the wrong side.

As for the Dominion guaranteeing all existing property rights, that would just be an invitation to every wandering halfbreed and his mongrel dog to claim the piece of riverfront they were squatting on had been the family home for generations. All the work Schultz and Snow and others had done – with extracurricular surveying, and mapping out properties, and listening to old fools yarn over free liquor – would go out the window. The new land titles would only last until someone came along with a bottle of whiskey and a piece of paper to mark an X on, but that someone was just as likely to be someone other than John Christian Schultz. And 'someone' was likely to be just an agent for some far-away land speculator with no knowledge of the country and no vision for its future.

But the game wasn't lost yet. From hints Agnes had managed to slide past his jailer, Schultz was quite sure Charles Mair and Tom Scott were still at large – he guessed probably in Portage la Prairie, where there were enough loyal Canadians to give Ambroise Lépine second thoughts about sending his horsemen after them. The galling part was that Schultz would've been out there with Mair and Scott, if the Metis had had an ounce of chivalry and allowed him to attend to his deathly ill wife the night of the escape. As it was, the enforced inactivity when there was so much to be done – or undone – was driving him a little batty, and he knew it.

He heard footsteps approaching along the hall and pushed himself to his feet and moved forward, crouching until he got out from under the sloped part of the wall. It was Agnes, looking dimpled and pink-cheeked, along with the frazzle-bearded guard who was the one most often on duty when she was allowed a visit. The guard stood by, keeping an eye on them, while Schultz and his wife talked of what each had had for dinner last night, whether they'd slept well and whether the weather seemed to be milder or harsher than previous days.

Agnes had brought another book with her, and handed it to the guard to do his riffling-through-the-pages routine. When the guard handed the book on to Schultz, Agnes said: "It's *Great Expectations*, by Charles Dickens. *Great Expectations*. Some people say the story is spineless, but I think you'll find it of interest."

When Agnes and the guard had gone, Schultz sat down on his bed and revolved the book in his hands, looking it over carefully. He could see no sign of tampering: the worn, green cloth cover showed no seam where it might've been cut to insert something, ditto the glued-paper facing of the inside covers. *Spineless*... He hooked a finger into the thin gap between the butts of the pages and the spine of the cover and pulled. It didn't want to give way at first, but with a little more pressure the cloth spine began to peel away from the cover leaves it was hinged to.

Glued to the spine of the pages was a knife-blade – just a one-piece bit of steel with a four-inch blade and its haft-spike not fitted into a handle. The clever darling had realised that any kind of handle would've belled out the book's spine and be feelable. But Schultz couldn't figure out how she'd got it glued in there without cutting the spine open and leaving a seam. After studying it a while longer, Schultz saw what his more-than-clever-darling must've done: pour a little glue down between the spine of the pages and the spine of the cover, push the knife blade in and wait for it to set. He pried the knife blade loose, chipped off as much glue residue as he could with his fingernails, and began to saw one of the buffalo robes into strips. Rapunzel was in business.

It was slow going. The short knife blade couldn't cut much length at a go, and gripping it by the haft pin meant he had to stop frequently to uncramp his fingers. He had to sit with his back toward the door, with a blanket heaped beside him ready to cover the evidence and his ears constantly on the alert, because the guards in their damned moccasins often gave him no warning till they unbolted the door. His bedding consisted of two buffalo robes and three HBC blankets, and he calculated it would take everything except one blanket to make a long enough rope to get him to the ground. It soon became clear that he wasn't going to finish it in time to escape tonight. But he could lay the strips out side-by-side to sleep on, and with a blanket on top the guards wouldn't know the buffalo robes weren't still whole.

Since winter daylight was so short, Schultz's jailers had allowed him candles and matches, trusting he had sense enough to know that if he tried to burn his way out he'd only immolate himself. So after an interruption for the inevitable supper of rubaboo, he worked on into the night. When his eyes and fingers started aching, he lay down to give them a rest and surprised himself by actually falling asleep.

By suppertime the next day he was almost ready. After the guard came to collect his bowl and spoon and leave him alone for the night, Schultz knotted the last few strips of blanket and buffalo hide together, then blew out his candle and went to the window. There was a bit of a moon – not dangerously bright, but enough to make out shapes once eyes adjusted. Fort Garry was tucking itself in for the night. Amber light showed in many of the windows and no doubt would for some hours to come, but in this bloody cold nobody was going to be loitering about outside unless they had to. The nightwatch guards would be snugged inside the gatehouse, and not poke their noses out unless somebody banged on the gate.

The window of Schultz's cell was a wooden latticework framing hand-sized squares of glass; importing full-sized panes all the way to Red River was a risky and expensive business. Schultz wrapped a corner of his one remaining blanket around his right fist, and punched the middle pane. Some shards flew out and some stayed in the frame. He held his breath and listened to hear if anyone had noticed. It seemed no one had, and with luck those few shards would be the only pieces of glass that fell outside. Now that he had a hole to get a grip through, he proceeded to pull the window apart frame by frame, carefully and quietly laying down the bits of wood and glass on the floor behind the corner of the gable.

The cold came in quickly, and his buffalo coat was locked away somewhere with all the other prisoners' coats and gloves and hats. But he expected to be running and hiking briskly very soon and not feel the cold. Once there was nothing left of the window but the outside frame, he knotted one end of his rope around a roof beam – one advantage to an attic cell – and uncoiled the other end out the window. Looking out and down, he guessed the rope ended about eight or ten feet above the ground, which wouldn't make for a long drop for a man his height.

It was tricky squeezing his shoulders through the window. The only way for it was headfirst and backward, one shoulder and then the other, holding onto the rope and contorting sideways. When he'd got himself perched on the windowledge, with the side of his face pressed against the cold wall above the window, he paused. His heart and lungs were hammering home the message that if he shifted his centre of gravity any farther backwards, he'd discover that the rope wouldn't hold his full weight and fifty feet was a long drop for a man of any height. He told his heart and lungs there was one way to find out, and crabwalked his thighs backward. The rope held.

Once his legs and feet were safely out and he was hanging by his hands, he blindly maneuvered his feet to wrap the rope around one leg and clamp it with the other, then started lowering himself gradually. He'd climbed up and down many a rope before, in his summers' employment on the lake boats, and was glad to discover that his body remembered automatically. But when he was a little more than halfway down, he heard a tearing sound above him, and then the rope was a snake in his hands and he was plummeting.

Schultz hit the ground and rolled, glad there was a good two feet of snow. But it was hard-packed snow, and when he stood up there was a jab of pain in his left ankle. He thought of sitting down to take a look at it, but someone might come out of one of the other buildings or around a corner any minute. So he just limped as quickly as he could to the nearest ladder up to the catwalk on the nearest fort wall. Once on the catwalk he leaned his midriff onto the top of the wall, squirmed around until his lower half was on the free half of the wall, gingerly lowered himself until he was dangling by the length of his arms, then let go and dropped the few feet remaining to the ground, trying to land with most of his weight on his right foot. A few steps brought him into the tangle of naked trees along the riverbank, where he wouldn't be silhouetted against the snow.

His left ankle hadn't stopped hurting. In his professional opinion it wasn't broken, just sprained, or maybe only twisted. But he couldn't follow what his professional advice would've been, to stay off it. His only hope was that the Metis wouldn't discover he was gone until morning, and that he'd have covered enough ground by then to be out of their reach. He wasn't going to run west as Mair and Scott and the others had done, but north toward the Stone Fort. He knew he couldn't make it all that way on foot overnight, but if he could get north of Kildonan into St. Paul's, or Middlechurch, he could find one of the several men from there he'd drilled with in Colonel Dennis's militia. Whichever one he found would surely lend him a horse – and maybe a coat. The cold was piercing, and he cursed himself for not throwing the one uncut blanket out the window before the rope. He could've wrapped it around him like an old Indian.

Schultz worked his way through the winter-brittle poplars and alders as quickly and silently as possible. The bush came to an end where The Company kept the riverbank cleared for the ferry traffic to Fort Garry. He paused and peered out to make sure there was nobody patrolling. At first he thought his eyes were playing tricks in the pale blue light. What should be a sloped expanse of snow was a *flat* expanse of snow, with amber windowlights beyond it. Then he realised he wasn't looking north along the riverbank, but east across the river. He'd got turned around in the woods and was on a heading straight toward St. Boniface. He turned left and limped back through the woods.

There was a rhythmic crunching sound up ahead. Schultz stopped dead and peered through the branches. He saw the vague shape of a man with a gun walking along in front of the east wall of the fort. It seemed Lépine had enough control over his 'soldiers' to send them out patrolling around the fort on a dead cold winter's night. If it weren't for the crunching snow Schultz wouldn't have heard the moccasined feet.

As the sentry rounded the south-east corner, Schultz took the chance that Lépine only sent them out one at a time to do a full circuit of the fort. Schultz broke out of the woods onto the frozen river and ran north as fast as he could run with a left ankle that was screaming at him and threatening to give way. After a couple of hundred yards he slowed to a brisk, lopsided walk, gauging that the high angle of the riverbank would mask him from anyone looking north from the fort. He could see the shape of his home and store up to his left. If it weren't for Riel and his disciples he'd be sitting in there now, with a toasty fire in front of him and his wife beside him.

Assuming that the night patrols of Winnipeg hadn't been discontinued, Schultz stuck close to the riverbank, where he couldn't be seen unless someone came right to the edge above and peered down. Once he reached Point Douglas he figured it was safe to move out into the middle of the river, where the lane of snow packed down by sleighs and horses made for easier and faster going. He still couldn't go all that fast, though, just the occasional spate of jogging until his ankle felt like it was grinding glass, and then limping along with his arms crossed and his hands in his armpits to try and keep his fingers and lungs from freezing. A soothing voice in his head kept suggesting that if he sat down to catch his breath and rest his ankle, he'd make better time when he got back up. But Schultz knew that if he sat down in the snow he'd never get up again. Farm dogs barked as he went by, but farm dogs always barked at something in the night.

As the eastern sky turned grey, Schultz looked around to get his bearings. He could just barely make out the silhouetted belltower of St. Paul's church about a quarter-mile ahead, the Middle Church where he used to take Miss Agnes Farquharson in his carriage on Sundays. But as the sky lightened, he saw it was the more pointed spire of Kildonan Kirk. He was still in Kildonan. Dawn meant they would soon know in Fort Garry that he was gone, if not already. Metis gallopers would be fanning out to look for him, and in daylight on the snow he would stand out like an exclamation mark on a blank page. He was half lame and shivering and couldn't run any longer, even if he had anywhere to run to.

He decided to take his chances with the only chance he had: climb the riverbank to the nearest farmhouse and knock on the door. He had no idea whose door he was knocking on, except that it was someone who lived in Kildonan. The door was opened by old Robert MacBeth, and Schultz muttered in his mind, *'Oh hell.'* He didn't know much about Robert MacBeth, except that he was an uncle-in-law of Point Douglas John Sutherland, was one of the few Kildonan 'Scotchmen' still living who'd actually been born in the Highlands, and was a fierce supporter of The Company. Schultz had heard it said that Auld Rab MacBeth would not allow a bad word about The Company to be uttered in his presence, so he wasn't likely to be fond of Dr. John Christian Shultz and his ilk. But there was something else Schultz had heard of, and fervently hoped had some truth to it, the immutable law of Highland Hospitality: friend or enemy, you never turn away a hunted man.

Old Robert MacBeth gaped, "Bless me, Doctor, is this really you?"

"I think so."

"Well, come in, man, come sit by the fire. Mother, fetch the man a cup of tea, and a dram to go in it."

CHAPTER 50

The first glimmer of dawnlight through Dr. Cowan's parlour window found Agnes sitting fully dressed and listening, as she had been the morning before. This time she heard what she'd been listening for: a great many running feet, and voices shouting in French. So, he'd done it. And now she had to do what *she* had to do, and do it quickly.

She threw on and fastened her heavy winter cloak on her way out the door. Back when she'd been congratulating herself for coming up with a clever way to help Christian escape his dilemma, she'd realised she'd created a dilemma of her own. If she were still in the fort after her husband escaped, Riel & Co. would no doubt hold her hostage. But if she left the fort before Christian escaped, after three weeks of not taking advantage of Riel's clearance to leave whenever she wished, it was bound to arouse suspicions. So what she had to do was try and slip through the very narrow gap between before and after.

She skirted around behind the buildings facing the parade square where all the shouting was erupting, to the little-used postern gate on the east wall. There was a lone guard there, warming his hands over an open fire. As Agnes approached, he picked up his gun and said: "Where you think you go, Madame Schultz?"

"To visit my father and sister. President Riel gave me permission to leave Fort Garry whenever I wish. If you don't believe me, you can ask him."

The guard didn't reply to that, just cocked his head to look past her toward the noise coming from the parade ground. Fortunately, from where they were standing the sound was just general tumult. If it had been possible to pick out individual words, undoubtedly one of them would be 'Schultz.' The gate guard jerked his beard in that direction and said: "What goes on?"

"Oh, I think there was a bit of a fire in one of the warehouses. I'm sure Monsieur Lépine has the situation under control."

"Ah. Well..." The gatekeeper thought for a moment, apparently an activity he hadn't often practised, then said: "Well then nobody gonna hear me if I call for someone to ask the President if he true did say you can come and go. I think you would not say he did if he did not." He swivelled up the bar across the gate and pulled it open for her.

Outside, there was a well-worn path through the snow, from the sentries circuiting the walls, and then a much wider path down to the winter road running along the middle of the Red. Agnes found it hard not to run and make herself conspicuous. Once on the river road it became a little easier. A little. With the hood of her cloak up and cowling her face, she was just another anonymous woman walking from the direction of St. Boniface in the direction of the Sisters of Charity auxiliary school in Winnipeg. Up ahead she could see and hear a horde of Metis gallopers disappearing around a bend in the river, and no doubt there were more charging north along Main Road and west along the Portage Road and the Assiniboine. She reassured herself that they would be looking for a very tall man, not a shortish woman.

Agnes had not the remotest intention of visiting her father and sister, although she was headed in that general direction. Since he'd turned Anglican again, they now lived in an old cabin near St. John's Church. But her father's home was one of the first places Lépine's men would come looking for her, once they started looking. Besides, if one wanted to be clandestine, one's first choice of accomplices wouldn't be a man whose main stocks-in-trade were bombast and bluster.

By the time Agnes reached the top of the riverbank path to the Grey Nuns' school, her legs were tired and achy. They weren't a length made for long walks in the snow, even beaten-down snow, and for the last seven weeks they'd had little opportunity for exercise. But she couldn't pause to rest them until she'd got where she was going, and got there as quickly as her legs could carry her.

There were several tramped-down paths through the snowdrifts around the Grey Nuns' school, and one of them angled off all the way to Bannatyne's store – even nuns and their students occasionally craved a bit of peppermint candy or a hair ribbon. Once she'd reached the road in front of Bannatyne's, Agnes did pause, to decide which route to take from there. She could go to her left along this little sideroad to Main Road, which would take her directly to her destination. Or she could go to her right along the sleigh path running to the Ross homes, James Ross's and his mother's, and hope there was a path from there to the place she needed to get to.

Maybe after Fort Schultz had surrendered, Riel had let Lépine let his men off the duty of guarding Main Road at the north edge of Winnipeg. Maybe not. If they were still there they would most probably let her pass, on her word of 'President' Riel's word. But they would note her passing, and would see where she'd gone. So Agnes turned right, toward the Ross property.

At the east end of the little sleigh road were two neat, thatched, whitewashed cabins, with a wide area of foot- and hoof-tamped snow around them and their outbuildings. But there was no beaten path leading north from there. Across the wind-waved sea of snow as high as her waist, Agnes could see the shingled roof of the place she was trying to get to, near the base of Point Douglas: the home of E.L. Barber.

Edmund Lorenzo Barber was American born and bred, but not part of the American annexionist party of McKenney & Emmerling et al. Mr. Barber, like the McDermots, had refrained from taking any part whatever in the turmoil of the last few months. His refrainment wasn't because he was a timid man; he liked to boast that he'd got his higher education by crewing on a freighter sailing from his New England home around Cape Horn to California. His aversion to politics hadn't made him averse to doing a fair bit of business with the local leader of the Canada party over the years. Last year he'd gone into partnership with Christian to develop Point Douglas. Point Douglas John Sutherland hadn't yet been informed of that, but that hadn't yet been necessary.

Agnes put one hand on top of the wall of snow in front of her and pressed down. It gave way easily; there was only a thin crust on top and then three feet of cold quicksand. The white field between her and the Barber house might as well have been the Red Sea, and there was no Moses handy. In her years at Red River she'd been snowshoeing more than a few times, for recreation, but she had no snowshoes to hand. She turned to the two cabins behind her, and considered knocking on one of their doors. But James Ross was unpredictable and Granny Sally Ross's native sympathies might well lie with the Metis.

Agnes turned again to the wall of snow. Well, there was nothing for it but to do it, or try. She cocked her elbows in front of her breasts, to bring her gloved hands up in front of her face, and fell forward. When she pushed herself upright again, sputtering and shaking snow out of her hair, she'd made a kind of ramp to walk up. It gave way beneath her buttoned boots as she walked up it, but at least it was better than walking straight into the wall. She ploughed ahead, half wading and half swimming, with each sinking step harder than the last one, and snow climbing under her skirt above her boots and stockings to her bare thighs. When she felt like her heart and lungs were about to burst through her ribs, she stopped. When her heartbeat and breathing settled down to only twice faster than normal, she considered the possibility that she was being an idiot. Now that she wasn't moving, she could feel bracelets of jabbing needles where snow had filled the gaps between the cuffs of her gloves and sleeves. If she fell, the snow was deep and powdery enough, and she exhausted enough, that she actually might suffocate. But when she looked back she saw she'd gone more than half way already. She pulled her right boot up out of the sucking snow and pushed another step forward.

When Agnes finally pushed out onto the hard-pack around the Barber house, she stayed hunched for awhile with her hands on her knees, breathing herself out like an over-driven pony, getting used to the feeling that there was nothing pressing against her except air. *There now, that wasn't so bad, was it?*

The Barbers' house, like most houses at Red River, had a sort of cubbyhole of an entranceway tacked on in front of the front door. Unlike most others, the Barber's entranceway opened from the side so the front wall would have room for two small windowpanes. Once inside the entranceway, Agnes thought of knocking, but decided this wasn't a time for niceties so just pushed open the door and stepped inside. She was in a small foyer. An open door to her left showed a parlour where Mr. Barber, in waistcoat and shirtsleeves, was sitting at a desk with his back to her. He started to rise and turn, practically shouting, "Again? I told you – Oh! Mrs. Schultz…" The stricken expression on his face told her, better than anything he might've said, that she looked in even worse repair than she felt. He called his wife and they bundled her into a chair beside the kitchen fire, got her boots off and her feet wrapped in a blanket. Various Barber children peered curiously from the kitchen doorway. While Agnes shakily sipped brandied tea, Mr. Barber explained, in the New England twang he'd probably never lose, that *'Again?'* had been because Lépine's hunters had already been there, looking for her husband.

Mrs. Barber said: "They'll be back sooner or later, looking for you."

Mr. Barber murmured: "Probably sooner," and sent one of the children to fetch Mr. Logan. The Logans were the Barbers' closest neighbours, in more ways than one: Mrs. Barber was Mr. Logan's younger sister. The Logan family business was the big windmill near the base of Point Douglas, and the Logans owned the portion of Point Douglas that wasn't owned by the Sutherlands. There was undoubtedly a well-worn footpath to the Logans' home from the Barbers' and, now that Agnes thought about it, probably another one from the Logans' to the Rosses'. If she'd thought to circle around behind the Ross houses, she would've found it. Oh well.

Mr. Logan came in stomping snow off his boots and took in the situation quickly. "Well, we'll have to get you out of here. Somewhere closest and safest..."

Mrs. Barber said: "Dr. Black's."

Mr. Barber said: "Perfect. But how to get her there? We could hitch up the cutter, but they'll be watching the roads."

Agnes said: "Why not a decoy?" The warmth of the fire and the tea had slowed her shivering enough that she could speak evenly, although something uncertain inside her made her voice still sound a bit jumpy to her. But one certainty was that both the Barbers and the Logans owned a cutter. "One sleigh could take one route, and the other another."

Mrs. Barber said: "Well... I could go in one and say I'm just taking the baby to my mother's for safety. I was half-thinking of doing that anyway. Dr. Black's is on the way."

Mr. Logan said: "I can always come up with a legitimate reason to be taking a sleigh ride in that direction."

An idea jumped into Agnes's head, and she jumped out with it. "And whichever cutter I'm actually in – if you have a big enough blanket to wrap me up in and still leave enough slack for a small child to wrap around its shoulders, I could curl up on the seat like a lump and the child could sit on top of me, just like any small child needs a bolster to see over the dashboard. A child like..." She looked at the faces clustered in the doorway. One of them was a girl about five years old. "That one. Can you keep a secret, dear?"

Mrs. Barber said drily, "Oh, Harriet can keep secrets."

Mr. Logan said: "I've got just the ticket. Back in a minute or two."

Once Mr. Logan had left the house, and Mrs. Barber left the room to fetch the baby and get herself and little Harriet dressed for outdoors, Agnes had time to absorb what the Barbers and the Logans had volunteered to do for her, or try to do. She had to tamp down the emotion to say relatively levelly to Mr. Barber, "It is very… well, 'generous' isn't a strong enough word, and there probably isn't one… but it is very good of you and your family, and Mr. Logan, to put yourself to all this trouble and in danger –"

"Oh, the only one in any real danger is you. And I'd guess if they do catch you the worst they'd do is take you back to Fort Garry and put a guard on you. But once Riel's got his hands on you, your husband'd be bound to give himself up right quick. But, probably the worst they'd do to your husband is lock him up again, but more securely. *Probably…*" Mr. Barber looked thoughtful. "I don't know… I really don't know… It may be Ambroise Lépine's about fed-up with Dr. John Christian Schultz."

The 'ticket' Mr. Logan brought back with him was a huge, black and white checkered quilt. The bottom half of it wrapped around Agnes completely, with enough slack at the edges to furl over her head and feet. Mr. Logan apologised in advance for the coming indignity, then picked up her cocooned self and carried her out to his waiting cutter. Once laid down sideways on the cutter seat, Agnes blindly curled herself up a bit so Mr. Logan would have room. The next thing she knew, little Harriet was sitting on top of her and the sleigh was moving.

The plan was that the Barbers' cutter, carrying Mrs. Barber and her youngest, would head north along Main Road, while the Logans', carrying Harriet and her bolster, would go along the river road. Agnes felt the seat beneath her slant forward as the cutter angled down the riverbank, then right itself and pick up speed. She could hear the swish of the runners and the drumming of the trotting hooves, but no sleighbells. Mr. Logan undoubtedly had harness with bells on, but had chosen not to use it this trip.

After a while, Harriet suddenly squealed: "Oh, sorry, Mrs. Schultz! I farted!" Mr. Logan must've cast a disapproving glance at his niece's vulgarity, because she protested: "Well, I did!"

Agnes anticipated with every breath that the cutter would be called upon to halt and she'd have to hold that breath as long as she could. But after what seemed like a long time, she could feel the cutter angling upward and then come to a halt without being ordered to. Mr. Logan said: "You don't have to worry about being seen now, Mrs. Schultz. If any of Lépine's men came kicking down Dr. Black's door, Ambroise'd skin 'em alive in public to show Kildonan he didn't approve."

Little Harriet's weight, which had grown less inconsiderable as the journey went on, lifted itself off Agnes's side. Agnes sat up, stretching cramped muscles and breathing-in air that didn't taste of old feathers. The glare of sunlight off the snow blinded her for a moment. When she could see again, she could see Mr. Logan standing beside the sleigh with his hand out to help her down, and Mrs. Black – Granny Sally Ross's daughter – coming out the door of the manse wrapping a shawl on. Mr. Logan pointed a thumb at Agnes and said to Mrs. Black: "All right?"

"Of course."

When she had her feet on the ground, Agnes said fervently to Mr. Logan, "I won't forget this."

"Please do. Come along, Harriet."

Mrs. Black ushered Agnes into the manse and said: "I fear you'll find things a bit crowded and lively here, what with my sister-in-law and her children, and my own children…"

"Just a blanket in a corner will be the safest place I've slept in months. Have you heard anything of my husband?"

"Well… we have, um, reason to believe, that he is in another house in Kildonan, a house much closer to Fort Garry than here. I've heard… rumours, that he plans to move to another house much further north in the settlement. But first he has to recover –"

"Recover?" Agnes felt a stab of ice through the soft bone at the bottom of her ribcage, colder than the snow she'd waded through. "Is he hurt?"

"Oh, not badly. Do forgive me, I didn't mean to alarm you. I'm told that he injured his leg, or his foot, but only very slightly. But he has to rest and recover some of his strength, and that may take a day or two."

An idea popped into Agnes's mind, and out of her mouth. "He could come here! Mr. Logan said the… Metis," she'd almost said 'halfbreeds,' but wasn't sure how Mrs. Black would take to that, "won't dare to barge in here."

"Oh, no. He can't come here. No, no, no, no, no." Mrs. Black shook her neatly-bunned head. "It's one thing, Mrs. Schultz, for the manse to give sanctuary to *you*, for a short time. But your husband? That would seem like Dr. Black were taking sides. And that would never do."

Agnes couldn't quite see why taking sides would never do, especially when one side was clearly the side of duly-constituted authority. But she was in no position to argue. She stayed in the manse for two days, and slept much of the first afternoon. Mrs. Black's children seemed generally well-behaved; her sister-in-law's less so, but James Ross seemed hardly the type to have a firm hand as a father. Dr. Black's saying of grace seemed to go on longer than the meals.

On the second night, after the children had gone to bed, Dr. Black said in a voice pitched to not carry upstairs, "Your husband is being moved tonight, to a house in St. Peters. A neighbour of ours has offered to take you there late tonight, when there will likely be no one patrolling the roads. But I'm afraid it will have to be *very* late tonight."

"Oh, I think I'll be able to stay awake."

Dr. and Mrs. Black stayed up with her, although it became obvious they'd gone long past their bedtime. When the neighbour did arrive, he proved to be a grizzle-stubbled man who smelled of whiskey. No introductions were made, and the Blacks made no comment on a man bringing the smell of alcohol into a Presbyterian manse. Dr. Black just said to him, "It's good of you to come out so late."

"T'ain't late for me. I keeps late hours since the wife died and the boys took over the farm. Well, lets get at 'er 'fore I gets too warm."

Agnes thanked the Blacks for their kindness, but not at length – they seemed as eager to get to sleep as she was to get going. In the neighbour's cutter there was a tartan travelling rug for her to drape across her legs. There were also two double-barrelled guns leaned against the seat, and Agnes saw that the driver's right hand wore a hunter's mitten, with the trigger finger separated from the rest. He seemed to notice her noticing the guns, and said: "I'm a wore-out old man and I'd rather go down shootin' than have some pissant tell me where I can or can't go in my own backyard. Hell, it'd be better'n the damned arthritis." Agnes somehow didn't find that reassuring.

They took the road along the river, and skimmed along at a bracing pace. There wasn't much conversation. A while after they'd passed the Stone Fort, the driver angled his horse to the right up the riverbank. They stopped in front of what looked to be several log cabins tacked together side by side. At one end, the moonlight showed what seemed to be the shape of an Indian tipi. In the tramped-snow yard was a hitched-up cart-sled, with a young man climbing onto it. Strangely, for this time of night, there were several children still up and about, clustered around the carthorse and the side of the sleigh. The children were happily shouting in some language, or languages, that were foreign to Agnes. But there were a few phrases in English, such as *'Bye-bye, Barney!'* and *'Come visit again, Barney!'*

The 'wore-out old man' halted the cutter and half-muttered: "Huh. That'd be the young fella that brung your husband. Thought they'd get here long before us, what with takin' Main Road 'stead of windin' along the river. Well, maybe they did and the young fella stopped in for a pot of tea. Well, come on…"

Agnes climbed out of her side of the cutter as the driver climbed out of his. As he escorted her past the cart-sled, she called out to the young man taking up the reins of the carthorse, "Thank you, Barney!" He looked at her perplexedly, so she explained, "For taking care of my husband." He looked even more perplexed, then looked away, shaking his head, and snapped the reins to start his sled in motion.

The older man escorting Agnes to the cabin door was sputtering with suppressed laughter. When he'd got control of it, he said: "Barney's the horse."

Beyond the cabin door was a dirt-floored room with a surprisingly well-crafted, almost elegant, dining table in the middle of it, lateral to the door. Sitting at the table, facing the door, was a medium-sized halfbreed or Indian young woman, perhaps twenty years old. On the table in front of her were two braces of old one-shot horse pistols, and she appeared to be loading them. There were several candles burning at both ends of the table, just close enough to light the pistols without lighting the gunpowder. The young woman looked up as Agnes and her escort came through the door. The escort said: "Signed, sealed and delivered," the young woman nodded, and he was closing the door behind him before Agnes realised he was gone.

Agnes looked around the room. There was no sign of her husband, but there were several blanket-curtained doorways in the side walls. The young woman said: "You'd be Mrs. Schultz."

"Yes, and you'd be Mrs. ...?"

"Miss. Prince. Around here, you call anybody 'Prince' and it's good odds you'd be right."

"Well, it's very good of you, Miss Prince, to allow my husband and I the shelter of your house."

"Ain't my house. It was the house of my grandfather, the Chief, now it's the widow's house and their ungrowed children's."

Agnes wasn't sure whether she'd said *widow's* or *widows'*, or whether *their children* meant the children of the deceased chief and his widow, or the children of his several widows. She decided not to ask.

"My uncle the Chief," Miss Prince continued, "couldn't take you into his house, it'd look too much like taking sides..."

Not taking sides seemed like an epidemic around Red River these days.

"... but the widows don't speak much English..."

This time it was definitely plural widows.

"... so he asked me to come translate." Miss Prince picked up one of the pistols and proceeded with what she'd been doing with them, which Agnes could see now wasn't loading them but unloading them. "Your husband had these on him when he got here, but he won't need to use 'em here, and with all the children running around... That Kildonan boy that brought him here – well, guess he's nearabouts a man now – the morning when your husband showed up outta nowhere at his family's door, that young man snuck into town and somehow got ahold of these to give your husband. Well, it ain't up to me to say that young man's name, or his family's."

"For fear of reprisals." Miss Prince cocked her head and one eyebrow, and it occurred to Agnes that the young woman's knowledge of English might not extend to words as sophisticated as 'reprisals.' "That is to say, the Metis might take revenge on whomever sheltered their enemy, if they knew who it was."

"They know already, or at least some of 'em do. There's been winters they'd've starved to death if they couldn't track a rabbit through the snow, you think they couldn't follow your man's big footprints?"

"Ah." Agnes smiled and nodded and pointed at the pistols. "But they were afraid to confront him."

Miss Prince's dark eyes went into a squint, and she peered at Agnes as though the distance between them was more like the width of the prairie than the width of a table. Miss Prince slowly shook her head and said: "You don't know shit, do you?"

"I don't much care for your language, young lady."

"I don't much give a shit, old lady." Miss Prince pointed at one of the blanket-curtained doorways and said flatly, "Your husband's in there, prob'ly asleep by now, take a candle," and went back to unloading the next pistol.

Agnes hesitated, debating whether she should put Miss Prince in her place. But then, they were in Miss Prince's place, or her family's place. Better to just file a mental picture of this Miss Prince's face, in case they ever met again after the world was put back in order.

Agnes picked up one of the candlesticks on the table, went through the doorway she'd been pointed to and let the curtain fall behind her. Half of the cramped little cubicle beyond was taken up by a crude bedstead made of rough-hewn planks, but at least it raised the mattress and bedclothes off the cold dirt floor. Lying on his back with his eyes closed, breathing slowly and deeply, was her Viking husband. His left foot was outside the covers, but had some insulation from a bandage wrapped around the instep and ankle. The bandage didn't look puffy enough for a wound dressing, more of a brace and a binding to hold in swelling. His face looked gaunt, maybe partly because a few days had passed since he'd last been able to shave down from his cheekbones to his jawline beard, so the stubble made a shadow on his cheeks. But that wasn't the only reason. He'd obviously been through an ordeal that would've killed a lesser man, and most men were.

Agnes pursed her lips and tightened the tendons under her jaw. Giving in to emotion wouldn't do. What was needed was pluck, and a jaunty sense of humour in the face of the worst their enemies could do. By the changing rhythm of her husband's breathing, and the twitching of his eyelids, she knew the candlelight was bringing him awake. She said loudly something she'd said to him before, on mornings when she'd been up and doing before him, one of the lines that had stuck in her mind from *Pilgrim's Progress*, "Go to the ant, thou sluggard; consider her ways, and be wise."

His eyelids fluttered open. He smiled. She went and perched on the edge of the bedstead. They talked awhile about his escape, and hers, but it was obvious he was too wrung-out to talk for long, and so was she. She took off her dress and boots and crawled in to lie down beside her husband for the first time in a month. Not that either of them were up for doing anything in bed besides sleeping. It was enough for her to snuggle in with her head pillowed on her husband's shoulder, and his great arm draped across her. She hadn't had an unfitful night's sleep since the day Riel decreed that Dr. Schultz would be removed from Dr. Cowan's house to solitary confinement.

It crossed Agnes's mind for an instant to worry whether this good night's sleep in this Indian bed weren't going to cost her an infestation of fleas or lice. But only for an instant. Whatever it cost her was worth the price, and could be sorted out in the not too distant future. As of tomorrow, a lot of nasty vermin around Red River were going to start getting fumigated.

CHAPTER 51

Oscar Malmros stepped into the Bannatyne general store, and immediately his spectacles fogged over with the sudden change from polar air to stove heat. He stood blind, leery of moving sideways for fear of knocking something over, struggling to get his heavy gloves off so he could get his glasses off, hoping some man larger than he wouldn't come barging through the door while he was standing there. Most men were larger than Oscar Malmros. With the operation safely accomplished, Malmros stepped aside of the doorway, pulled his breath-frost-crusted muffler down from over his mouth and nose, and squinted to see if there were any impediments between him and the post office counter.

There weren't any, but halfway there Malmros created an impediment of his own and swerved over to a display of shoes and boots in a corner. He wasn't in the market for footwear, but he'd decided to take one last look through the letter he was planning to send – he didn't need his spectacles to read. He was well aware that he must perform his function more than adequately; not many Danish immigrants got appointed official representatives of the United States Government. But back in the autumn, when things were becoming obviously unsettled at the Red River Settlement, Oscar Malmros had happened to be doing occasional government errands in St. Paul. Coincidence and geography made him suddenly appointed American Consul to Red River and the Town of Winnipeg, establishing official residence at the Emmerling Hotel.

His letter was to a Mr. J.W. Taylor in Pembina. J.W. Taylor was well-known to be a western representative of the U.S. Treasury regarding trade and reciprocity, and an advisor to railroad interests. So it was perfectly natural that the American Consul in Winnipeg would be corresponding with him. What wasn't well-known was that Mr. Taylor was also a Special Agent of the State Department in Washington. Although the mails between Red River and Pembina were still running more or less on schedule, it was rumoured that some envelopes got opened along the way, and their contents perused. So the most important part of the letter had to be the most innocuous, while still getting the message across to the right reader.

'Regarding that real estate deal...' Malmros was quite sure the average letter-snooper wouldn't realise the 'real estate deal' was Red River and the entire North-west Territories. *'... the scruple-free gentleman still can't be pinned-down, which may lead to a clash between the parties.'* Given that J.W. Taylor had once referred to Dr. John Christian Schultz in writing as 'entirely unscrupulous,' Agent Taylor would surely read that correctly as: *'Dr. Schultz is still at large, so there may yet be the all-out civil war at Red River that was avoided in December.'* Schultz was said to be somewhere in the vicinity of the Stone Fort, where Ambroise Lépine's roughriders couldn't go unless they wanted to start a shooting war. Oscar Malmros had heard many contradictory rumours of where Schultz had gone the night of his escape, and how he'd got there. All that mattered was that Dr. Schultz was still in the area, but out of reach of the Provisional Government for now.

Malmros carefully studied the next and most important paragraph of his letter, the one most difficult, and most necessary, to disguise as small business while still getting the big business across. *'So, the situation with that piece of property seems thusly: The Scotch drunkard reneged on the down payment, the reading of Granny's letter cancelled the old trader's claim, and the sick man is in no condition to rearrange matters. So, sad to say, at this point it is impossible to tell who owns clear title. Or if anyone does.'*

Malmros reassured himself that Special Agent Taylor would correctly translate that as: *'Sir John A. Macdonald, Prime Minister of the Dominion of Canada, has refused to pay the Hudson's Bay Company its three hundred thousand pounds until the transfer can be peaceably fulfilled. So, the Imperial Government has already transferred the HBC territories to Canada, but the Dominion has refused to take possession. The Honourable William McDougall's reading-out of the Queen's Proclamation effectively ended the HBC's rule in Rupert's Land – spurious proclamation or not, he was the duly-appointed representative of the Crown. And Governor Mactavish is too ill to take charge and sort it out, even if he wanted to. So, not so sad to say, legally Rupert's Land doesn't currently belong to anybody – not the Hudson's Bay Company, not the Dominion of Canada, and not the British Empire. The entire northern half of North America is up for grabs.'* That should catch their attention in the State Department.

The last sentence that mattered, before the letter closed with a few face-value facts about the English parishes' electing representatives to the Convention of Forty, was: *'I estimate the current caretakers could afford to remain in possession longer if you underwrote their expenses with 25 of our grand, old American dollars, or could be coaxed into a partnership with 100.'* Special Agent Taylor would surely interpret that as: *'Given twenty-five thousand dollars, all the buffalo hunters could afford to keep on holding the fort, instead of going on the summer buffalo hunt; a hundred thousand dollars would persuade the leaders of the Provisional Government that Washington is more friendly than Ottawa.'* Mr. Taylor had specifically requested that estimate, after hearing from reliable sources that Sir John A. Macdonald had already asked Canadian agents to find out how much it would cost to buy off the ringleaders.

Satisfied that he'd done as well as could be done, Oscar Malmros sealed the letter and re-donned his spectacles. They had now adjusted enough to the inside air to have only a thin halo of fog around the rims. Apple-cheeked Mrs. Bannatyne, behind the post office counter, exchanged some cheery remarks about the weather as she stamped his letter and made change for the postage.

Mission accomplished, Malmros headed back for the outdoors, adjusting his scarf and tugging on his gloves. He was almost at the door when it swung wide open and in marched a tall, straight-backed man with piercing eyes and bushy sidewhiskers. Captain J.E.N. Gay was a very recent arrival at Red River, and apparently had been until recently a soldier of France and was now a soldier of fortune. He'd been in Red River just long enough for Oscar Malmros and others to assume the N stood for Napoleon and then find out it was mundane Norbert.

Captain Gay claimed to be a correspondent for a Paris newspaper that thought its readers would be interested in a French-led Provisional Government cropping up in the wilds of North America, but there was something suspicious about him. But then, there was something suspicious about everybody at Red River these days. Malmros nodded politely at Captain Gay, Captain Gay nodded back and held the door for him.

Captain Joseph Ettiene Norbert Gay closed the door behind the American Consul and strode to the post office counter. "Bonjour, Madame Bannatyne – the brisk weather brings out the roses in your cheeks."

"Now, now, Captain Gay," she waggled a stubby finger, "your Paris flatteries don't cut ice at Red River," but her eyes twinkled.

"I have a dispatch – that is to say, a letter – to be posted to the telegraph in St. Paul, for cabling to my newspaper in Paris."

Mme. Bannatyne weighed the envelope in her hand. "My, my, Captain Gay, that's a lot of telegraph."

"Oh, my newspaper will pay the charges. It is the first of my articles on the situation at Red River. Well, that is to say, the raw material for an article, my newspaper will decide what is germane to our readers and where to edit it."

Actually, the newspaper would decide nothing except to forward it immediately to a certain government office, where de-coders would decipher certain information by extracting every seventh word. The key was in the first sentence, to cipher clerks familiar with the system. Sometimes it would be every sixth word, or eighth word, or etcetera.

Captain Gay wasn't an ex-soldier of the French Army, but still on active service, although a secret service. Emperor Napoleon III wished the French Empire to expand into North America. After all, much of North America had originally been colonized by France. The Emperor's first step had been the conquest of Mexico – Captain Gay's hussars had been among the troops that captured Mexico City – and the installation of a puppet Emperor Maximilian of Mexico. But that had ended ignominiously, with the French troops sailing home and Emperor Maximilian facing a Mexican firing squad. Lately, though, news had come to Emperor Napoleon III that an intrepid band of French-speaking North Americans had taken control of a significant portion of the continent, and might be able to keep possession of it with a little help from the Mother Country…

As Mme. Bannatyne counted out the change from Captain Gay's postage, she said: "I hope your article says nice things about us."

"Now, now, Madame Bannatyne," it was his turn to waggle a finger, "I would not be such a fool as to spread slander. I have been a soldier, but my courage has its limits. Do you still keep a horsewhip behind the counter?"

She blushed and ducked her head. "Oh, that was… I lost my temper. I shouldn't have."

"By all accounts, Madame Bannatyne, you *should* have, and I congratulate you. Now, I am afraid I must go back out into the cold. I wish you a pleasant afternoon."

"And you, Captain Gay."

Captain Gay stopped at the doorway and looked at his pocket watch before buttoning his coat. The watch told him he was more or less on schedule for starting to fulfill another part of the Emperor's orders: to determine whether the Metis 'soldiers' could be taught discipline and tactics, and thus be turned into proper soldiers and an effective military force.

Captain Gay mounted his borrowed horse – not a 'horse' by cavalry standards, but these scruffy ponies did seem to have stamina and zeal – and trotted back toward Fort Garry. When he neared the fort, he didn't carry on toward the front gates, but veered to the west along the north wall. The wooden north wall had a stone gatehouse set into it, but Captain Gay didn't attempt to go through it. For one thing, that part of the fort was the Governor's residence and gardens, separated from the rest of the fort by the stone wall that had been the north wall of the original Fort Garry. For another thing, Captain Gay's next appointment wasn't anywhere inside the fort, but on the snow plain beyond the west wall.

Ambroise Lépine and twenty of his 'soldiers' were waiting there, with their tethered ponies unconcernedly standing in a clump in the biting wind. They had set up targets as Captain Gay had requested, or the backwoods equivalent of same: ten rough-cut fenceposts with burlap sacks of straw fixed around them. The men seemed affable enough, and amenable to following his instructions. As far as they were concerned – as far as everybody at Red River was concerned, Captain Gay hoped – he was just an ex-military man who'd volunteered his coaching services.

He began by getting them to form two firing lines facing the targets. That turned out not as easy as it sounded. They tended to slouch against each others' shoulders, or lean sideways. Finally Captain Gay had to draw two straight lines in the snow, and get across to the front and rear ranks that they should stand with the toes of both moccasins on the appropriate line. Lépine had to translate his instructions, as it seemed some of the swarthier men couldn't understand French except in an archaic form mixed with Red Indian words.

The first exercise was simplicity itself: the front rank was to fire a volley at the targets, and then kneel and reload while the rear rank fired a volley over their heads. The first 'volley' came out as a ragged stutter of gunshots, and the second one was worse. Some of the men who'd knelt to reload were on one knee, some on two, some squatting on their heels, and some seemed unsure which end of their gun to start with. Captain Gay took out his pocket telescope and peered at the targets. He counted half-a-dozen black, smouldering holes, out of twenty shots. So much for the fabled master-marksmen of the plains.

Lépine shrugged abashedly at Captain Gay. "These are not rifles, monsieur, but smooth-bore muzzle-loaders – they have not the range."

So Captain Gay moved the lines ten paces forward and tried again. The result wasn't much better. It seemed sadly clear that all the travellers' accounts of the skills of the wild Metis huntsmen had been so much Munchausen. Most likely, most of their hunting was actually done up-close with shotguns.

Lépine said hesitantly, "Do you think, monsieur, we might – they might – try it once on horseback? You were a cavalry officer, yes?"

"Yes. Yes, well they might as well give it a try," though how they would aim better on horseback, juggling guns and reins, than standing upright, was beyond him. Any experienced cavalryman knew that the weapons for mounted warfare were sabres and lances. Cavalry carbines were only for situations where the troop dismounted and formed a skirmish line.

Lépine shouted: "Mount and charge!" and it seemed to take him an effort to stay standing there, instead of joining the whooping mob running for their horses. They were mounted in an instant and thundering past Captain Gay and Lépine toward the targets, all of the riders with both hands as free to deal with their guns as the centaur Sagittarius his bow, guiding their ponies with their knees or by osmosis. Through the stormcloud of gunsmoke and kicked-up snow, Captain Gay could see that some of them were crisscrossing each other to confuse enemy fire, some were firing from under their horses' necks, some reloading at full gallop by dumping in a charge from a powder horn and spitting out a musketball squirrelled in their cheeks, and some whipped out knives or hatchets to throw or hack as they passed the targets…

Then the whole demon crew were past the targets and were slowing and turning their horses, laughing and joking with each other about who had killed which straw-sacked fencepost how many times. Captain Gay didn't need his pocket telescope to see that there was nothing left of the targets but a few shards of burlap still smouldering from hot lead, and that the posts themselves were studded with hatchets, knives and bullet holes.

Captain Gay realised he hadn't yet let out the breath he'd breathed in when they started their charge. He expelled it with: "Holy Mother of Christ!" then heard a chuckling behind him, and turned to see a grinning death's head with blue eyes and a blonde goatee and black fur hat. W.B. O'Donoghue, the Secretary-Treasurer of the Provisional Government.

O'Donoghue said jauntily, "A bit surprised, Captain?"

"Aren't you? Or have you seen that before?"

"No, no, I've never been out on the plains with them – just a townboy, I am. But I'm not surprised. Well, I'd best get back to the council table and leave you to educate the benighted Metis in the science of battling on horseback."

William Bernard O'Donoghue was grinning to himself as he strode from Captain Gay to the gatehouse into Fort Garry, toward the stove-warmth of the Provisional Government's headquarters. What he'd just seen warmed him more than the stove would, for reasons no one else at Red River would understand, and he was more than happy to keep them to himself for now.

But he'd barely got through the gates when his grin was wrenched away by a coughing fit. He had to stop and hunker forward, with his left hand propping him against the nearest wall and his right hand holding today's handkerchief to his mouth. When he could breathe and stand upright again, he inspected the handkerchief. On the fresh white cotton, against the brighter white background of sun-glared snow, there was only the barest discernible fleck of pale pink. Still a few years left. He fully expected he'd end up like that poor bastard Mactavish, coughing his lungs out in a sickbed no different for a Governor of Rupert's Land than a Kilkenny beggar. But not yet. The more immediately important factor of that barely-discernible pink was that it meant he wasn't contagious yet. The minute he crossed that line, he would have to tell the Sisters of Charity that his mathematics-teaching days were done.

O'Donoghue stuffed his handkerchief back in his pocket and carried on toward the Provisional Government's provisional headquarters. He suspected he would have to spend the rest of the day talking with Louis Riel and Louis Schmidt and others about the latest compromise proposals from the Convention of Forty, but he was already composing the letter he would pen to his cousin in St. Paul tonight. Given that letters to and from Red River these days weren't entirely secure, it had to be composed in a way that any third party would find it perfectly natural that the letter-writer would chattily describe the demonstration of Metis military capabilities he'd happened to see that day.

Unbeknownst to any possible third party, O'Donoghue's cousin in St. Paul was in constant communication with the leaders of the Fenian Brotherhood in the eastern States, where thousands of well-armed Brothers were ready to entrain west at a moment's notice. O'Donoghue had no doubt they would be interested to know that if they launched an expedition to Red River, and convinced the Provisional Government to stand with them against the English Empire, they would have on their side several thousand of the deadliest light cavalry the world had ever seen.

CHAPTER 52

Since he'd first learned to comprehend the calendar, Hugh's opinion was that February was the evilest month of the year. Just when you started to congratulate yourself on making it through January, you realised you had another month of unbroken cold ahead of you. Everything became brittle and hard to work with, including people.

He came back into the house one morning from breaking last night's ice on the water hole and found his father sitting at the kitchen table with Gran's old shawl across his shoulders. Da had a pen in one hand and a wadded handkerchief in the other, and said: "Hugh, your mother says..." although it sounded more like *'door mudder zez...'* "I'm to stay indoors today. But, the Convention of Forty is convening again at Fort Garry today..." Point Douglas John Sutherland had been elected the Kildonan delegate to the convention, even though he lived on the other side of the river. No one was going to question the right of Sandy Sutherland's and Kate MacPherson's son to represent Kildonan.

No one had explained to Hugh why the Convention of Forty met in Fort Garry instead of just in the courthouse like the conventions a couple of months back, and he hadn't troubled to ask. It seemed pretty obvious to him that the siege of Fort Schultz, and a few other happenstances, had made some people inclined to have guarded gates and fortified walls around them when they sat down to talk.

"It'll be a Convention of Thirty-nine," Mum put in from stirring the hearth fire, "if you don't have the sense to stay inside and keep warm for a day or two."

"But," Da continued to Hugh, "at the meeting at the kirk last night I was charged to deliver a specific message to the leaders of the Provisional Government. I'd meant to get there early and deliver it verbally before the sitting started, but..." He glanced at Mum, who seemed to think she'd already delivered her message to him and there was nothing more to be said about that.

Da picked up the paper he'd been writing on and waved it in the air to help dry the ink. "So, Hugh, I want you to ride to Fort Garry now, please, and deliver this to either Louis Riel or Louis Schmidt. No one else."

"I don't mind, me whatever."

Da folded and sealed the paper in an envelope and handed it to him. Hugh tucked it in his coat and went back out to the barn. Since whichever horse he was going to ride likely wouldn't have to stand around waiting for him for long, and that would be within the wind-shelter of Fort Garry, he didn't see any reason not to take Montrose.

It was a pleasant ride. Fat snowflakes were drifting down from low clouds in a kind of grey-white haze, and the cold always eased off a bit when it snowed. The guard at the gate to Fort Garry called: "Bonjour, Point Douglas – Wait a minute, that's his horse but you ain't him!"

"I'm his son – John Hugh Sutherland. My father asked me to deliver a note to either Louis Riel or Louis Schmidt."

"I don't know about that. Ambroise!"

Ambroise Lépine came out of the guardhouse shrugging on his horse-sized blanket coat. "Bonjour, young Sutherland."

"Monsieur Lépine, my father's ill today –"

"Nothing bad, I hope."

"Just a cold, I think. But he can't come to the convention today, so he asked me to deliver a note to Louis Riel or Louis Schmidt before it started."

"Well, you give it to me and I'll give it to them."

"Um…" It was a quandary. "I can't do that. My father said either Louis Riel or Louis Schmidt, no one else. I'm sure if he'd known you'd be at the gatehouse, he would've said or you. But he didn't. So, you see, I can't give it to anyone but one of the Louix."

"Huh. I do see what you mean. Well, you don't have the look of an assassin about you, and if I make you ride back to ask your father can you give it to me, the convention will be started by the time you get back here… So," he waved one oak-slab hand toward the inside of the fort, "go on in. If anyone asks, tell 'em I passed you through."

"Thank you."

Hugh trotted on through the echo-y, squared-off cave inside the gatehouse – arched at both ends, but squared-off in that it was as wide as it was long and tall – and came out into the big open square where he and half Red River had crowded in to hear Donald A. Smith. One of the buildings facing the square was now the headquarters of the Provisional Government. Hugh looped Montrose's reins around the railing of its front steps, then wondered whether the appropriate thing was to knock on the front door and wait. But it wasn't like this was somebody's house, after all, and he might stand waiting till long after he was supposed to deliver Da's message, while the people inside went about their business oblivious to the distant tapping sound. So he decided to just open the door and step in.

As soon as he'd crossed the threshold, he decided he'd made a mistake. He was at the end of a long hallway, and in the middle of it was a small table where two tough-looking men dropped their playing cards, snatched up their guns and sprang out of their chairs. Hugh said: "Uh…" and showed his empty hands. "I have a note I'm s'posed to deliver to either Louis Riel or Louis Schmidt. Ambroise Lépine passed me through the gates."

One of the guards lowered his gun, but didn't put it down, and beckoned Hugh to follow him. Halfway down the hallway there was a closed door where the guard stopped, knocked lightly and called softly, "Monsieur le Président…?" A sort of affirmative syllable came from inside. The guard opened the door, moved aside and gestured Hugh to go in.

Hugh stepped into a large room with a long table islanded with stacks of papers. It was an elegant-looking table, fashioned from wood Hugh didn't recognise from any kind of tree he was acquainted with, as were the chairs around it. Word had it that the Provisional Government had furnished its headquarters with selections from what the Honourable William McDougall had shipped on ahead of him for his Lieutenant Governor residence, and from Dr. Schultz's home.

At the head of the table sat President Riel, with Louis Schmidt on his right and W.B. O'Donoghue on his left. Louis Riel looked dapper, but troubled. Although whatever was troubling him obviously hadn't put him off his feed, his face was still rounded and meaty. When Hugh came through the doorway he stood up, with one hand on the table and the other on his hip. Louis Schmidt and W.B. O'Donoghue stayed sitting and staring at Hugh: Louis Schmidt curiously and O'Donoghue coldly.

Hugh said: "Uh… Adjutant-General Lépine passed me through the gates. My father's got a bad cold and can't come to the convention today, so he asked me to deliver a note to either Louis Riel or Louis Schmidt, no one else."

Louis Riel sidled his eyes down at W. B. O'Donoghue, and a wry twist lifted one corner of his chestnut mustache, then looked back up at Hugh. "Your father is proven once again, John Hugh, to be a very wise man. You may deliver the letter to me." Hugh walked forward and did so. "Do please tell your father we will pray for his swift recovery. We have sore need of any man so honest and pacific, in our attempts to resolve the difficulties we are all in."

"Uh, thanks. Well, I better be getting back…" Hugh went back out to Montrose, and was hoisting his moccasin to the stirrup when he heard a cracking and thudding noise from somewhere behind him. He paused to look. Through the haze of gust-whirled snow, he could see two men at the far end of the square unloading cordwood from a sled and setting up sawhorses. One of them had the long back and shortish legs of Norbert Parisien. Hugh thought of calling hello, but remembered what happened the last time he'd called out to Norbert when Norbert and his father were shifting cordwood, so just climbed onto Montrose and headed straight toward the gatehouse. He was almost there when the sentry above the gates sang out, "A rider coming in! Or, maybe, I think…"

Hugh reined in Montrose to wait for the rider to come in before he went out. If there *was* a rider coming in. Ambroise Lépine came out of the gatehouse and called up, "You *think*…?"

Looking out through the dark, stubby tunnel of the gatehouse, Hugh could see only a grey and white swirl. Then the form of a horseman began to coalesce out of the haze, and Hugh could see why the sentry'd been confused. It was a pale horse and the rider wore a grey-white wolfskin coat and cowl, and his head was bent forward against the wind. Wolf fur was the best for winter, because it had long guard hairs that kept the underfur dry. But people usually only used it to trim cuffs and hoods, because the skin was so thin it had to be troublesomely sewn onto some kind of backing if you didn't want it to tear.

Cradled across the pommel of the horseman's saddle was a wolf fur rifle scabbard. Ambroise Lépine drew a pistol, planted himself in the horseman's path and called: "Halt!" The wolf man halted his horse and slowly raised his head. Between the black leather bill of the cowl and the black, frost-rimed beard, were battered-looking, jutting cheekbones and eyebrows. Between those ridges were two blazing coals – if coals could burn inside and still be black. Hugh saw Ambroise Lépine's head snap back as though one of the fort walls had jumped forward and smacked into his face. Then the Adjutant General stepped aside and the horseman trotted on into the fort, without a word passing between them.

As Hugh watched the horseman trot past, looking neither to left nor right, he tried to tell his eyes they weren't really seeing what they were seeing. But his eyes didn't listen. Instead, Hugh heard his dead Granda's voice whisper hoarsely, "*Oh my, and all the saints in hell.*" Hugh had only once heard his Granda say that, or whisper it, back when the Point Douglas Sutherlands were still living on Point Douglas, and they looked out their door one morning to see the Red River pouring over its banks.

As Hugh trotted Montrose into the mouth of the gatehouse, Ambroise Lépine shot a furl-browed glance at him, as though uncertain whether to tell Hugh he couldn't've seen what he thought he saw, or whether Hugh maybe didn't realise what he'd seen and it was best not to say anything. Either way, before anything got said Hugh was out of the fort. Once he'd got Montrose down onto the packed road along the river, he kicked him into a gallop. Once in the barn, he rushed to strip off Montrose's saddle and bridle, gave him a lick-and-a-promise rubdown and hustled into the house.

Da was still sitting at the kitchen table, but had the shawl draped up over his head now and was bent over a steaming pot that smelled of spruce and camomile. He looked up, blinking his streaming eyes, and said: "Did you deliver the note?"

"Yes, to Louis Riel, but…"

"But what? You put it into his hand, not O'Donoghue's, or anyone else's that got in between?"

"Yeah, straight into his hand – Louis Schmidt was there, too, but Louis Riel's hand came out first."

"Good. That's good, then. Thank you. And no buts about it."

"But…"

Da's eyes stopped blinking. He straightened his back, furled the shawl down from over his head to over his shoulders, and cocked his head. Funny how those blue eyes looking slightly sideways at Hugh seemed even more direct and serious than straight-on. "But what?"

"I saw someone. Someone riding into Fort Garry when I was riding out... It was Gabriel Dumont."

Da's head sank backward and his shoulders hunched upward. He whispered hoarsely, "Oh my, and all the saints in hell."

Mum said with certainty, "That's impossible, Hugh. You must've seen someone else. The whole Dumont clan moved west years ago, when things got too crowded and civilized here. They're all way out on the South Saskatchewan or somewhere. Nobody rides from there to here in the depths of winter."

Hugh started to open his mouth, but Mum jumped back in with: "Oh, sure, people go from fort to fort by dog team, but not from the Saskatchewan to here on horseback."

Da said, and he didn't sound happy about it, "It's been done. I remember my mother telling me there was a time, back in the Fur Trade War, Mr. Grant was wintering on the Qu'Appelle and got word that a friend of his here had been arrested and locked up by the Hudson's Bay Company. Mr. Grant rode here posthaste, on horseback, in the depths of winter, and sprung his friend free. Now, the Qu'Appelle isn't quite as far as the South Saskatchewan, but far enough. And Mr. Grant wasn't born to the plains like Gabriel Dumont." Da pushed the steaming pot away from him, as though reviving his health had become inconsequential. "I see now I've been wrong."

Hugh and Mum waited while Da wiped the steamed sweat off his face and beard with the shawl, and Mum didn't even complain that she was going to have to wash that now.

"It had seemed to me that Louis Riel and Ambroise Lépine were two halves of Mr. Grant – Riel with the elegant education, and Lépine the size and strength. But now I realise they were only two thirds. What was missing was the most dangerous part."

Hugh and Mum looked at each other, and it seemed Mum didn't have any better idea of what Da was getting at than he did. Hugh certainly knew Gabriel Dumont could be dangerous, everyone between Red River and the Rockies knew that, but he didn't see what that had to do with Mr. Grant. Da murmured, nodding to himself, "Volatility."

Hugh said: "Volley-what?"

The look Da turned on him wasn't '*you're ignorant*,' but apologetic for not explaining it right. It was the look Hugh'd once thought all older men turned on younger ones who got things mixed up, until he got out into the world outside his family and met more older men. Da said: "You remember, Hugh, back years ago when you had two fistfights with Tim Matheson in one week?"

Hugh squirmed a little. So much for Da being considerate. It wasn't fair for people to dredge up embarrassing memories of your boyhood when you were just getting used to being a man. "Well, I'd hardly call 'em fistfights, just boys scuffling..."

"Whatever you call them, in the first one you beat Tim Matheson immediately, and the second one was a long standoff, until you broke your knuckle. Why were they different?"

"Well, uh..." Hugh could feel himself blushing, and was suddenly conscious of the funny-looking finger that couldn't line up properly with the others. But, there was no way out but to bull on through and try to answer the question. "I sorta remember you saying something about that, on the way back from Dr. Schultz's. You said, uh, the first fight I got mad, and the second one I was just doing it cause I was s'posed to."

"That's right," Da nodded as though something was getting across. "In the first fight, one minute Tim Matheson was bullying Norbert Parisien, and the next minute you had Tim in a headlock and were pummelling him. If you think back to what you were thinking, or feeling – whatever you want to call it – your frame of mind that turned that one minute into the next one, I bet it was just like:" Da snapped his fingers.

"Well, uh, it was a long time ago, and I don't think 'thinking' was what I was doing – rarely is. But, yeah, I guess it was just like that. Snap."

"Now, try and imagine someone who's like that all the time. I'd bet you that within thirty seconds of deciding to ride from the South Saskatchewan to Red River, Gabriel Dumont was saddling his horse and stuffing his coat pockets with dried meat."

"But why," Mum put in, sounding less certain Hugh couldn't possibly have seen Gabriel Dumont today, "would he decide to come to Red River?"

Da said: "I don't know," although it sounded like he had some surmises he didn't like. "Maybe Riel and Lépine sent for him."

Hugh said: "No, Ambroise Lépine was surprised to see him. Surprised and then some." It felt better to be back talking about today, instead of back when he was a boy.

Da drummed his fingers on the table, as though deciding whether to say something. He started to say it, but was cut off by a fit of sneezing. He blew his nose in his big, red, polka-dotted handkerchief, caught his breath and said: "It may be, that some rumours have made their way farther west than here. The rumours are getting stronger that, come the spring..." Maybe Da didn't hardly 'um' and bark anymore, but he still paused to think through what he was going to say next. "... the Dominion and Imperial Governments will send an army here. The wilder Metis out west – what the priests call 'les sauvages' – and the Crees and Assiniboines they ride with... If Gabriel Dumont were to say: 'Come to Red River and help our brothers fight the white man,' a lot of them would."

Mum said: "They can't fight the British Army!"

Da said: "Oh, they could make a fight of it. A hell of a fight. If all the buffalo hunters and voyageurs stayed here into the summer, and if they did get help from out west... and help from..." Da's eyes sidled at Hugh. "Other places..."

It seemed to Hugh that Da was hinting at something he was supposed to know, but he couldn't imagine what. Da's eyes shifted off Hugh to down at the table. "An Expeditionary Force coming from Canada would either have to sail into Hudson's Bay and then boat south through Lake Winnipeg..." Da's forefinger drew an imaginary line on the table, "or come west through the Great Lakes and down the Winnipeg River..." another line joined the first one in a kind of crooked V. "Either way, they'd have to come up the Red to get here," another line made the V into a Y. "Now, I've heard it said lately that if an Expeditionary Force does come, Chief Henry Prince plans to send logs shooting down St. Andrew's Rapids and smash their boats." Da looked directly at Hugh. "Have you heard anything of that?"

Hugh found himself again sliding back into feeling like a boy in a grown-up world. "No, she, uh, she don't know much about what her Uncle Henry's thinking. She just says he'll do whatever seems the wind's blowing best for his tribe."

"And what *you're* going to do," Mum stood up and took hold of Da's shoulders to tug him to his feet, "is go up to bed and I'll bring you some rose hip tea. I'll tuck you in. You won't get better today by worrying yourself sick over what might happen tomorrow, or next summer."

But when Mum came back down, she said worriedly to Hugh, "Are you sure it was Gabriel Dumont? You couldn't have seen him all that often before, and not for years."

"Well, you couldn't've seen him all that often either, Mum, and not for years. But if you caught a glimpse, you think you'd know for sure it was Gabriel Dumont?"

Mum looked down at the floor and nodded.

Next morning Da was well enough to go to the Convention, and he came home in a jovial mood, before the scholars were back from school and college. So jovial that Hugh saw Mum sneak a close-in whiff to see if Da'd spent the day in the 'refreshment room' just out back of the meeting hall, where snowbanks made a handy home for bottles of stuff that wouldn't freeze.

Hugh, Donald and Aleck had pulled chairs close to the kitchen fire, to soak in some warmth before going back out to wrestle a tree. A maple limb had cracked with the cold and was threatening to claw off part of the barn thatch if it sagged much further. They all knew Da would've been in the thick of the wrestling if he didn't have to be wrestling with the predicament the whole settlement was in. When Da came in and got uncoated, they pulled their chairs back over to the table to hear what had made him so jovial.

"Well, the first part of the good news didn't come out of the formal meeting. A lot of what actually gets sorted out, or comes out, is in neighbours' kitchens –"

"Or the refreshment room?" Mum put in.

"The news is, Gabriel Dumont is gone. He only spent one night in Fort Garry and then started back west..." That didn't sound like necessarily good news to Hugh, more like ominous; it sounded like maybe Gabriel Dumont headed straight back west to start beating the war drums. "I have it on good authority that he offered to bring five hundred of les sauvages to help the Provisional Government fight its enemies..." That sounded to Hugh like exactly what Da was afraid of. "... and Louis Riel said: 'Thank you kindly, Monsieur Dumont, but no.'"

Mum exhaled: "Oh! Bless Louis Riel, for a change."

"As for the formal Convention meeting..." Da rubbed his palms together and inhaled through his teeth. "I think... I *think*... maybe we can see daylight. The final two clauses of the List of Rights have been agreed. And part of Donald A. Smith's commission is to ask Red River to send commissioners to Ottawa, so the Dominion does seem willing to talk treaty with us. There's still the big question of whether all the parishes will vote to join the Provisional Government –"

"Huh?" came out of Hugh, and everybody looked at him. "Oh, sorry, Da, but… I thought that'd already happened, like when Kildonan Parish voted you to be the representative…"

"No, I'm just the Kildonan representative in the Convention of Forty, which is a meeting between the parishes who've joined the Provisional Government and those who haven't, yet."

"Oh." It was still damned confusing.

"Everything happens in stages, son. If the next stage doesn't happen, our commissioners can still take the List of Rights to Ottawa, as representing the Convention of Forty. I don't think that'd be as strong as representing a united Provisional Government, but still, we've come a long way. You may think I'm being overly optimistic, Mother – well, maybe I do, too – about reaching an accommodation with Canada. But Sheriff Henry McKenney has started dismantling his sawmill works, just in case. The word is he's deep in debt to Canadian investors, and wants to have all his goods and chattels ready to move south into American jurisdiction. So, Sheriff McKenney obviously believes there's a good chance Canada will accommodate us."

Donald said, in his I'm-a-college-graduate way, "What form did those last two clauses take, in the Bill of Rights?"

"Well, Clause Nineteen is a compromise, about how long someone will have to be a resident here before he gets the right to vote – a compromise between those who say all Canadian citizens should automatically have the right to vote, and those who're afraid that a flood of Canadian immigrants would start deciding things here before they know what 'here' is…"

Hugh's mind wandered away from the details. But he could see that Aleck was interested: not committing himself to saying anything, but leaning forward to listen. That was good. Hugh stood up and said: "Well, this is all over my head. I won't need another pair of hands to get a rope around that branch so's it won't crash down when we cut it free."

But as Hugh was making his way to his coat and the door, he heard a chair scrape behind him, and Aleck saying: "Over my head, too. I'll give you a hand, Hugh." Hugh wanted to tell him: *'I said I don't need a hand – sit back down and be yourself for a change.'* But it had been decided that Aleck had to decide for himself who he wanted to be. Hugh wondered if maybe he'd just had a little more patience and waited a little longer before getting up, Aleck might've got hooked-in enough to the conversation to stay there. Things got damned complicated when you cared what somebody did, and thought you knew what they should do, but couldn't tell them. Then again, who was John Hugh Sutherland to know what anybody should do?

When next Da came home from the convention, he wasn't jovial. He growled at the cup of tea Mum set in front of him, "Damn fools."

"Who, dear?"

"The Provisional Government – or Riel, rather. It *is* Riel these days. Oh, some of them will argue with him after the fact, after he's gone ahead and done what he's decided to do, maybe egged on by O'Donoghue..."

"What's he done?"

"Arrested A.G.B. Bannatyne."

Hugh said: "*What?*" then realised Mum and Donald had said the exact same thing at the same time.

Mum said: "Why?"

"For trying to speak with Governor Mactavish – they've got a guard on the Governor's door, and nobody's supposed to talk to him without permission from the Provisional Government. A.G.B. says he was only trying to talk to *Mrs.* Mactavish, to see if she wanted to take a few days' feet-up rest with her father, his father-in-law. But Riel says A.G.B. was conspiring with The Company. Oh hell, what difference does it make why? Of all the bloody stupid things to do, just when we were getting so close..."

This was one thing in all the talk of politicking Hugh could understand, because the heart of it wasn't politics. He had no doubt that in every kitchen up and down Red River, people were saying the same thing he and Mum and Donald had, when they heard that Mr. Bannatyne had been arrested: "*What?*"

"Damn!" Da made a fist that vibrated, as though it wanted to hit somebody but didn't know who. "It always comes down to the bloody prisoners. The ones from Fort Schultz may have been damn fools, but they've been locked up two months now, some of them in irons... And since then, I'd have to look at a list to count – arrest one here, arrest two there, no trials, no sentences, just locked away. If they'll arrest A.G.B. Bannatyne they'll arrest anybody – any time, any place, any reason, or no reason at all."

Mum put her hands on Da's shoulders and said: "Well, one step forward, two steps back, but we'll get there." Da's shoulders came unhunched, but they didn't so much relax as slump. Hugh couldn't do anything about the worry in the air, and he felt a little guilty that what was mostly on his mind was that tomorrow was Wednesday.

When tomorrow kindly came, Hugh did his morning chores in the dark, saddled Montrose, grabbed a bit of breakfast and headed north. A chilly-looking full moon hung incongruously in a pale blue sky. The marks and shadows on the moon's face were the same blue as the sky, so looked like ragged holes punched through it. A few clouds were coming in from the west, but it was too cold to snow.

Nancy Prince met him more than halfway, and after they'd climbed down off their horses to say hello they climbed back on again and rode along side-by-side. She seemed closed-in, like she was thinking about but not talking about... something. When he told her about a few funny or semi-interesting things that had happened in his vicinity over the week, she didn't come back with any stories of her own. Questions about her family, or other people she usually liked to talk about, just brought out verbal shrugs – maybe physical ones as well, it was hard to tell in her puffy blanketcoat.

Finally, to try and get some kind of response out of her, Hugh said: "I heard your uncle the Chief is thinking of rolling logs into St. Andrew's rapids, to smash the boats of the Canadian army coming in, if the Canadian army comes in."

"I dunno, I dunno… I heard he's maybe thinking of joining up with Dr. Schultz."

"Dr. Schultz?" Chief Prince taking orders from Dr. Schultz seemed like an implausibility.

"Schultz was in St. Peters awhile, now he's down around the Stone Fort, shifting from one house to another every night – I don't know what houses. But in the days, he's going around trying to raise up enough men to attack Fort Garry and free the prisoners." Her voice had gone all tight, and her forehead was furrowed so hard it looked like it would crack in the cold. So maybe this was the 'something' that was chewing at her. "The moccasin telegraph still works, and it says there's a big war party coming here from the west."

"Oh, that's nothing to get worried about – it ain't gonna happen. We may not have the moccasin telegraph at our place, but we're a lot closer to Fort Garry than you. Louis Riel said no to Gabriel Dumont."

"Huh? What's Gabriel Dumont got to do with it?"

"The war party coming from the west. The five hundred of les sauvages Gabriel Dumont offered to bring here."

"I never heard nothing about that – and if it ain't gonna happen anyway… I'm talking about two hundred men coming from Portage la Prairie and Headingley, to help Dr. Schultz attack Fort Garry." She murmured, as if to herself, "*… a lot closer to Fort Garry…* " then flicked a glance at him, her dark eyes more like mirrors than windows. She was still closed-in, so what they'd just talked about wasn't the 'something' she was thinking about hard but wasn't saying. What she did say was: "We better get the horses running again, or all four of us are gonna freeze solid."

By the time they'd had a gallop and a trot, and slowed to a walk again, they'd passed Kildonan Kirk on the other side of the river and were in St. Pauls, or Middlechurch. The horses and riders had almost caught their breath when Nancy abruptly brought Cheengwun to a dead halt and looked around warily. Hugh looked to see what she was looking for. On the far side of the river, a miniature man stepped out of a miniature house and looked at them, then went back inside. But Hugh got the prickly feeling they were still being watched, through a window and maybe a spyglass.

Nancy said: "It's got worse. You can't go no further."

"Why?"

"Spies."

"Spies?"

"That's what they're afraid of. Oh, Hugh, you don't know what's been going on north of Kildonan –" Her words tumbled out in a rush, almost stumbling over each other, like someone on the edge of panic. " – men marching around with guns, going from house to house gathering everybody's gunpowder together into one war stock…

They even got a cannon dragged down from the Stone Fort through Little Britain, so far.

"But they're afraid of spies. They're stopping everybody, asking where you're going and what's your business, and you better have an answer they like. They're even stopping women, but they won't mess with a niece of Chief Prince, everybody wants him on their side. But you…"

The rush of words petered out. Even though Hugh'd been sure the day was too cold to snow, a few white lace snowflakes had settled onto Wauh Oonae's black velvet eyelashes. Hugh pulled his right hand out of its mitten to brush them off and incidentally brush his fingers down her cheek. He said: "Hey, things looked like they were gonna go real bad in December, didn't they? With Fort Schultz and Colonel Dennis's militia and all? But that ended without one gun getting fired, didn't it?"

Nancy gave a little nod, but stiffly and with her lips rolled-in tight together, as though she agreed that that was what had happened in December, but not that December had anything to do with February. She turned her head away from him. Then she nodded again, but a different kind of nod, as though she'd decided something. She turned in the saddle to look directly at him. "Hugh…" She blinked against tears and her face twisted up, then untwisted. "Monday is St. Valentine's Day. Even though it's not a Wednesday, I want you to come meet me again. Can you do that?"

"Well, sure, I guess, but –"

"But don't bring Montrose, bring a pony that can stand out in the cold awhile if needs be."

"Okay, but –"

"Well," she cut him off, no buts about it, "it's a damn cold day for standing around, and you can't go no further," she interrupted herself with an odd little self-contained laugh, "not today. First thing Monday morning I'll start riding south to meet you." Then she wheeled Cheengwun and was galloping away.

When Hugh got home he didn't check to see if Da was back from Fort Garry yet, just led Montrose straight into his stall, fed him some oats and stripped him down and rubbed him down. When Hugh was coming out of the barn he heard sleighbells, and looked down the path to the river. Da was climbing out of the cutter belonging to one of the other convention delegates. Hugh waited at the top of the path while Da climbed up, perhaps not quite as steadily as usual. When Da reached the top he clapped Hugh on the shoulder and beamed, "Come inside, Hugh, and call your brothers."

When Hugh and Da and Donald and Aleck were seated around the table, and Mum pouring tea, Da said: "I think a little regale is in order, Mother." Mum looked askance, but brought out the bottle of medicinal whiskey and added a dollop to each tea mug. Da said: "Well, today we came to the sticking point. All forty of the Convention of Forty were agreed on the List if Rights, and agreed that all the parishes should support the Provisional Government, *but…* some delegates were nervous that joining the Provisional Government might be illegal, since maybe The Company was still officially the legal government. So, a couple of us got deputized to go ask Governor Mactavish about it."

Da took a long sip of tea and smacked his lips until Mum said: "Well? What did Governor Mactavish say?"

"It's difficult for the poor man to say anything – it'd break your heart to see him, nothing left but bones and parchment and whiskers. First thing he said was that when The Company'd asked him to serve another term as Governor, he'd told them: 'I'd rather be a stoker in hell,' then realised they weren't *asking* him.

"After he'd said that, it took awhile for him to say anything more. Getting his breath back, I guess, and maybe he's grown unused to talking about government business, since the guards haven't been letting him see anyone outside his household. Then he said that when he'd been in Canada last spring, he'd offered to talk about Red River and so on to any Canadian official who would talk to him. But none of them would, because – how did he put it? – 'those gentlemen seemed to think they knew more about Rupert's Land than I did.'

"We had to wait a long while for Governor Mactavish to say anything else. Finally, he said: 'Form a government, for God's sake, any kind of government, and restore peace and order.' So, my fine lads and lasses, it's done – tomorrow we work out who takes which office in the Provisional Government, and then we work out a way to gradually release all the prisoners, probably over the next week or so. It's done."

"Oh, John!" Mum sprang out of her chair and flung her arms around Da's neck, spilling his tea.

The next day, the Provisional Government got finalised. A.G.B. Bannatyne was to be Postmaster, which he couldn't do in a lock-up. Point Douglas John Sutherland was to be Collector of Customs, which Hugh figured would have Granda spinning in his grave – given his tales of helping his uncles to pony little kegs by moonlight from glen to glen.

The night that followed was a celebration in Fort Garry and Winnipeg and all the houses up and down the river. There were even fireworks, which were all the more fun because the rockets and pinwheels and such were the ones Dr. Schultz had imported for the celebration of Lieutenant Governor McDougall's arrival at Red River. Hugh hoped that Nancy Prince could see the fireworks from St. Peters. Not at all the kind of fireworks she'd feared.

CHAPTER 53

Agnes was just getting ready for bed when she heard the click of the bedroom door-latch opening behind her. She snatched closed her dressing gown with both hands, and turned to set straight whomever thought it proper to enter a lady's chamber without knocking. The Company's people at the Stone Fort had been very kind to allow her one of the empty bedrooms in what was still called The Governor's House, but kindness wasn't a licence for rudeness.

The person in the doorway was her husband, looking rough-edged but cheerful. She hadn't seen him for two days; he'd been surreptitiously circulating through Middlechurch and Little Britain, and sleeping in the homes of various brave and loyal persons. She flew to him, unclenching her hands from her dressing gown. He wrapped his arms around her and she around him, as far around as her arms would go. After a moment, he said to the top of her head, "I'm afraid, my dear, you'll have to get dressed again, although I'd rather the opposite… And dress warmly."

She stepped back and cocked her head at him. His bright blue eyes were even brighter than usual, and the corners of his mouth kept twitching upward, as though he were suppressing a grin.

He said: "There's something I think you'd very much like to see, by moonlight," and obviously didn't want to say anything more about whatever the surprise was. She picked out a heavy wool dress that wasn't much too big for her. Some ladies in Little Britain had kindly leant her some clothing, including the dressing gown. Once she was dressed for outdoors, Christian escorted her out the door to a light, one-bench cutter harnessed to a swift-looking horse hitched to a ring on a porch post. When they were both seated aboard, Christian spread a buffalo robe as a lap rug for them both, then took up the reins. Agnes didn't have to look down to tell that the metallic object her heels bumped up against was the barrel of a rifle lying under the seat.

Christian turned the cutter south and snapped the reins to set the horse into its trot. Despite the tribulations of their overall situation, Agnes found it quite delightful to be skimming along under the stars with her husband by her side. He shifted the reins into one hand, stuck his other hand inside his coat and came out with a folded piece of paper. He said: "I thought you'd be interested in reading the latest decree from 'President' Riel.

A secret friend pencilled a copy and smuggled it to me. Oh, of course, the moon's not bright enough for reading pencil..."

Actually, the moon wasn't even bright enough for reading bold print. It was a little past full and had only just come up.

"Well, I've read it out to so many interested parties, I've probably got it word-for-word by now." Christian put on a pompously official voice. *"Dr. Schultz is an exile from this country and anybody finding him is at liberty to shoot him. His property is to be confiscated and sold to pay his debts – first his back customs duties, then debts due in this country and the balance to liquidate his liabilities elsewhere."*

Agnes only half-heard everything after *'at liberty to shoot him.'* She'd taken it as a given that if certain parties caught sight of her husband there would be shooting, unless he surrendered himself to them. But now there was no talk of surrender or arrest. And for Riel to give *permission* for murder... It wasn't a question of: 'Who does he think he is?' but: '*What* does he think he is – God?'

But railing against Riel was only going to make her feel more ineffectual, and that wasn't going to help her husband. So she just said: "'Confiscate' seems a little after the fact. From what I've heard, they've already pilfered everything except the floorboards, and maybe they'll get around to those, too."

"We'll get it all back, my dear, and more, don't you worry. As you said, something drastic has to happen at Red River, and happen soon." Agnes was touched and gratified that he would remember her exact words, and take them to heart. She'd said them the last time she'd seen him, when he'd told her that the Provisional Government had selected the three commissioners who would carry that precious List of Rights to Ottawa: Judge Black, Father Ritchot and Alfred Scott. Judge Black was a creature of The Company, Father Ritchot's interests obviously lay in filling the territory with French Catholics from Quebec, and Alfred Scott was the most worrisome of the three. Very little was known about Alfred Scott, definitely no relation to Thomas Scott, except that he'd arrived at Red River last spring and since then had worked for Hugh O'Lone as a bartender and for Henry McKenney as a store clerk: both American annexionists. Even though Henry was packing up his sawmill and his goods just in case, the Americans hadn't given up yet.

Even if the chosen three's private agendas weren't so questionable, just the fact of Ottawa officially welcoming commissioners from Red River would give the outside world the impression that the Provisional Government was legitimate, and truly represented the majority of the people. Something had to be done to correct that impression.

"There's even more reason now –" Christian began, then interrupted himself a moment to make the horse make the right choice about a split in the road. "There's even more reason now that something drastic needs to happen at Red River, and soon. Some of the prisoners are being released, about a dozen today. But only those who sign their parole not to cause any trouble – more or less an oath of loyalty to the Provisional Government. Two of the dozen today were men who'd stood with us behind the barricades at the White Store: Dr. O'Donnell..." That was disappointing, but didn't surprise Agnes unduly.

Dr. O'Donnell had been the first to sign the surrender of Fort Schultz. "… and James Stewart."

"*Stewart*? After all you've done for him? Breaking him out of jail, and giving him employment, and a home?"

"Well, it grates, I know, but Stewart has a wife and children, and Mrs. Stewart isn't the stalwart you are."

Agnes smiled and squeezed his arm, as much as she could squeeze through the thick duffle of his borrowed coat. They'd had a few good laughs together over the way that coat fit him, since the only coat at the Stone Fort even remotely big enough had been made for a very fat man.

"Stewart," Christian continued, "just goes to prove that there is an air of defeatism in the air." He didn't sound defeated, though, more like jaunty. "But we're going to change that tonight."

"How are we going to change that?"

"Ah, you'll see, my dear, you'll see. Here, in case you're starting to feel the cold…" He reached into one of the coat's voluminous pockets and came out with a silver flask. When she uncapped it and sniffed, brandy fumes went up her nose. She took a small sip and was gratified to see that Christian only took a small sip, too, before putting it away. She hadn't been feeling the cold all that much, since the buffalo robe held in the combined warmth of both their lower bodies. But even though it was a still night, the cutter speeding through the cold air had the same effect as an icy wind blowing into her face. Just that small sip of brandy sent warming blood coursing through her cheeks.

The horse was trotting at such a clip that they were already through Little Britain and halfway into Middlechurch. Christian said: "If you look to the right side of the road, my dear, you'll soon see something interesting."

Agnes turned her gaze to the right, but wasn't sure she'd be able to see anything but snowdrifts and shadows; the moon had risen a little higher and its light grown a little brighter, but not much. If she were going to actually see something in particular, it would have to be pretty big. It was: a cannon sitting on a wooden sledge. The cannon looked to be at least twice the size of the ones Ambroise Lépine had pointed at the White Store, maybe large enough to punch holes in stone walls.

Christian said cheerfully, "That's as far south as seemed safe to bring it so far. Tomorrow we'll haul it a good deal farther."

"And how much farther are *we* going to go tonight?" That came out somewhat more nervously than Agnes had intended to sound. *'At liberty to shoot him'* passed through her mind.

"Oh, a little ways yet, my dear." There was a chuckle in his voice, but also a certainty and resolve. "We'll have plenty of protection."

They travelled on southward for long enough for her cheeks to begin to feel the cold again after the effects of a second sip of brandy dissipated. Then Christian whoaed the horse, and the cutter slowed to a halt in the middle of the road. Agnes looked around.

The moonlight showed her the pointed spire of Kildonan church off to her left. Without the sounds of trotting hooves and gliding runners, the silence was eerie. So eerie that when she spoke she whispered, "Why do we stop here?"

Christian didn't whisper, but his voice was lower than when they'd been moving. "I expect you'll see why very soon." He shifted the reins into one hand and draped the other arm over her shoulders to snuggle her in beside him. She put her hands under the buffalo robe to warm them and settled one onto his thigh.

A sudden burst of sound made her jump. Christian chuckled, patted her reassuringly and said: "I expect they kept silence till they were through Winnipeg and well into Kildonan."

Agnes could hear now that the sound wasn't as near as she'd thought, it was just that the crystal stillness of the night made it seem like it was echoing off the horizons. It was many male voices singing, and getting gradually nearer. They weren't near enough yet, or choir-practised enough, for Agnes to make out the words distinctly, but she recognized the tune as an old song her father used to sing:

Ah then tell me, Sean O'Farrell, tell my why you hurry so.
"Hush, me boy, now hush and listen," and his eyes were all aglow.
"I bear orders from the captain, get ye ready quick and soon,
"For the pikes must be together by the rising of the moon."
By the rising of the moon, by the rising of the moon,
For the pikes must be together by the rising of the moon…

As the singing got closer, Agnes began to hear a rhythmic drumming under it: the sounds of horses' hooves and marching feet. Dark shapes began to appear on the white road ahead. Agnes stood up in the cutter to see over the horse's head. It was a column of armed men, some on horseback, some in cart-sleds or cutters, some on foot. The broad-chested, broad-mustached horseman in front was Captain Boulton. Standing in a front corner of the cart-sled directly behind him was Charles Mair. The tall man in the front rank of the squad of footmen following the sled had to be Thomas Scott.

Agnes could feel tears squeezing out of the corners of her eyes, and the corners of her mouth squeezing up to meet them. She was hard-pressed not to wave, or clap her hands. Christian, obviously delighted at her surprise and several other things, said: "Those are just the lads from Portage la Prairie and Headingley. Tomorrow, we'll be joined by the lads from St. Andrews and St. Pauls. And possibly even St. Peters."

"St. Peters?" The possibility seemed so impossible, it tore her eyes away from the approaching parade.

"Oh, I'm not expecting Chief Prince has committed himself to the cause of Canada First. But 'wily Indian' didn't get coined for nothing. I think Chief Prince may be thinking that if Rupert's Land does become part of Canada – I only say 'if' because I'm talking from his point of view – it will stand him and his tribe in good stead if they've helped us out. And if the United States or some other foreign power were to end up taking over here, he can say they only helped us out to free the prisoners, and that will still stand them in good stead. Well, we won't know for sure until tomorrow, or the next day."

Captain Boulton had wheeled the column to the right, where the feet and conveyances of churchgoers and schoolchildren had created a wide space of packed-down snow. The men were climbing down from their sleighs and horses, and unloading sledfuls of wood to build campfires. Somebody had thought out a lot of details in advance.

Christian turned the cutter in off the road, stepped out and offered her a hand down. She walked with him to where Captain Boulton had dismounted and was gazing about to make sure everything was proceeding in an orderly fashion. Christian tugged off his right glove and stuck his hand out, saying: "Good to see you, Captain."

Captain Boulton looked down at the proffered hand as though this wasn't exactly military procedure. Nonetheless, he shook hands and nodded politely at Agnes. Agnes was slightly acquainted with Captain Boulton from several social occasions. Although he'd come to Red River with Colonel Dennis's survey expedition, most of his activities had been west of Winnipeg, around Portage la Prairie. She did know he was the only man in Red River who'd served overseas as an officer in the British Army.

Christian stepped toward the bustle of men in front of them, and let-out in his fill-the-hall voice, "Welcome to Camp Justice, lads!" They stopped, or paused, what they were doing, to laugh and cheer. "Tomorrow there'll be twice as many again of you – of us! Glad to see you brought scaling ladders, we'll need them soon!" They laughed and cheered some more.

Agnes heard a kind of grim, unhappy grunt from beside her, and turned her head to look up at Captain Boulton. He wasn't looking at her, but at her husband's back, and the volunteers cheering *'Dr. Schultz!'* The captain muttered sourly, not particularly to her or to anybody, more as a For The Record, "Only reason I agreed to lead this bonehead-stupid expedition was to try and keep the stupidity to a minimum."

Agnes was disappointed in Captain Boulton. She'd expected more of him than schoolboy jealousy. He should've expected that of course he'd take second place as soon as the men were faced with that giant Viking who'd suffered the same torments as the prisoners they'd come to free, and had hazarded his life to escape and effect a rescue.

A voice like the wrath of God came from behind Agnes, "What is the meaning of this?" It was Dr. Black, stomping forward from the manse. He was wearing high boots and a long coat, and Agnes suspected only a nightshirt in between. His craggy face, naked between the jawbeard and dishevelled hairline, had the hue of an over-stoked stove with the flues wide open.

Christian intercepted him and said mildly, "Ah, Dr. Black, sorry we didn't give you any warning, but it had to be kept secret. For strategic and tactical reasons, this was the best spot to assemble the volunteers coming to free the prisoners. We don't plan to be here long. We were hoping to be able to use the kirk for temporary shelter – after all, it's Sunday night, you won't be needing it for a while."

Dr. Black looked past Christian at the hundred men in the light of their few feeble campfires. His head moved in jerky little sideways motions, as though taking in images from a panorama. Finally he growled, "What else am I supposed to do – let you sleep in the snow and freeze to death on my doorstep?"

"And perhaps the schoolhouse as well…?"

Dr. Black raised a fist toward Christian, but the fist had its forefinger extended. Dr. Black's finger and forearm and voice shook, "But you stay away from the manse. You hear me? Stay the hell away." As Dr. Black turned to go, his eyes touched across Agnes's, and she saw a flicker of: *'This is what I get for giving you sanctuary.'*

Christian announced to the volunteers, "Dr. Black has kindly offered to let us use the church and schoolhouse as temporary barracks. But treat everything with respect!"

As the men gathered up their jury-rigged packsacks and their weapons, Agnes saw that not all the weapons were guns. Some of the men were armed with just a pitchfork or an axe, or a scythe blade fixed to a pole. *'The pikes'* was supposed to be just a poetic anachronism.

CHAPTER 54

Hugh had only the vaguest notion of what St. Valentine's Day was supposed to signify. Saint's Days didn't figure in the Presbyterian calendar, but maybe Anglicans like Wauh Oonae were different. He could remember when printed Valentine cards had first started appearing at Red River, imported from the States or England, and he knew secondhand that they'd become all sorts of fashionable in Little Britain. Maybe St. Peters, next door to Little Britain, was the same. Maybe he was supposed to buy Nancy Prince one of those cards. But there wasn't much buying and selling of dainty items going on around Red River these days, barely even of necessities.

On the morning of St. Valentine's Day, Hugh gobbled a quick bit of breakfast and excused himself while the rest of the family was still digging in. Aleck had agreed to take Hugh's turn cleaning out the milking stalls if Hugh took Aleck's turn hauling water to the barn troughs tomorrow, so all Hugh had to do was saddle a pony and go. As Hugh was reaching down his coat, Da said: "You can take Montrose if you like, I won't be riding him today."

Mum said to Da, "Why's that?"

"Oh…" Da seemed a bit evasive, which didn't sit natural on him. "It's liable to be a long session today, and the stables in Fort Garry are so full already, Montrose might end up standing out in the cold all day. So, Louis Schmidt offered to detour this way in his cutter."

Hugh said: "Well, thanks, Da – wish I could take you up on it and take Montrose, but she said specific to take one of the ponies instead." Some of the younger children snickered like they were in on a secret, which Hugh knew damn well they weren't. They knew exactly and entirely as much as he did about Nancy Prince asking him to meet her on St. Valentine's Day, which was just that she had.

Out in the tack room corner of the barn, Hugh regretfully passed over Montrose's professional-crafted leather saddle and lifted down one of the homemades cobbled from wood and old blankets and buffalo pelt. When he plunked the saddle onto the paddock fence and stooped through the rails, the pony that came to him quickest was the spotted one called Spot. Hugh had Spot saddled and haltered and headed north before the scholars came out the door to head for school and college. He heard a jingle of sleighbells, and looked back to see Louis Schmidt's cutter coming up the road to pick up Da.

It actually wasn't all that unpleasant riding a shagganappi pony instead of Montrose. Spot was friskier, turned more quickly, and practically danced when Hugh let him break into a gallop. They didn't dance far; a little ways past the bridge over Hugh and Nancy's creek he saw Wauh Oonae riding down the road to meet him. When they met up, she didn't stop and get off her horse for a hello, just turned and fell in beside him. She said by way of explanation, "We got a ways to go."

"Where we goin'?"

"You'll see."

It took Hugh a moment to adjust to looking across at Nancy Prince riding on almost the same level as him, instead of looking downward from Montrose. Spot and Cheengwun didn't seem to need to adjust to each other; probably they were related. Hugh decided that it wasn't just the different angle that made Nancy look different today. She looked like she hadn't slept much. She wore an oddly complicated expression, like she was worried and afraid about something but also glad about it. She seemed to be there and not there, like part of her was somewhere else, or several somewhere elses. Hugh said: "What's got you spooked?"

"Oh… There's a lot of men moving around around the Stone Fort, and further this way. Lotsa rumours moving around, lotsa men, lotsa guns…" That sounded to Hugh like it wasn't entirely true – well, true in fact, but not truly the answer to his question. "The old people back home, the ones old enough to remember war times, say once the young men get their blood up you never know what may happen."

"Well, I'm a young man and *my* blood ain't up – except for you."

The look she tossed him was saucy and secretive and uncertain all at once. She was definitely being complicated today.

They came to another little bridge across another creek flowing into the Red from the east. Nancy turned Cheengwun to the right, off the road and down the creekbank. Hugh started to follow her, then stopped and looked to his left. Across the river, in the open compound of Kildonan Kirk – church and school and manse – there was a crowd of men milling around, and Hugh could see a dark line moving south on the road from Little Britain and the Stone Fort. He muttered: "What the hell…?"

Wauh Oonae called: "I told you – lotsa men moving around. Come on."

Hugh nudged Spot to angle down the bank and fall in walking east beside Cheengwun along the frozen, snow-covered creek. The snow would've made for hard slogging but had been packed down pretty good; several horses had come and gone this way recently, or maybe one horse several times. Hugh could see now at least one reason why Nancy hadn't wanted him to bring big Montrose. The bare willow boughs bending over the stream would've been more than a nuisance on a higher horse, and Montrose's long legs and big hooves weren't made for picking your way carefully along uneven ice and snow. Even on Spot, there were bends where the creek valley narrowed so much Hugh had to drop behind and follow Wauh Oonae Indian-file.

Down out of the wind, the creek path felt hushed and sheltered. Nancy seemed disinclined to break the silence. But once, out of nowhere, she let out a little trickle of a giggle. When Hugh asked her why – his voice naturally keeping itself soft in this enclosed world of snow-muffled hoof-falls and sighing branches – she just closed her mouth and shook her head. Her eyes had gone even brighter than usual and her cheeks flushed. Sometimes she smiled, sometimes looked solemn.

The sort-of path they were following took an angle up the creekbank and into a stand of old spruce and young poplar and twisted bur-oak. Hugh smelled woodsmoke and said: "Odd place to camp," barely a mile from the snug houses on the riverbank.

Wauh Oonae said: "Just enough to keep it smouldering."

"Huh?"

"You'll see."

They came into a small clearing. Hugh stopped his horse and gawked. There was a lean-to like the ones he'd made for winter hunting, but somewhat wider, and its evergreen thatch looked more thickly and carefully woven. There was a smouldering firepit in front of it, running almost the lean-to's length, with deadfall firewood and cut spruce boughs piled at either end. There was a kettle sitting on a flat rock near enough to the fire to keep warm, but not near enough to boil away.

Wauh Oonae slid down off Cheengwun and tied the end of his halter to a poplar tree with a mound of hay beneath it. She said: "There's enough for both of them, I don't think they'll fight," so Hugh tethered Spot beside Cheengwun.

Hugh managed to find enough of a voice to say: "You did all this?"

"Uh-huh, the last few days. First thing, we better get the fire built up again." She started layering spruce boughs on the coals, and cross-hatching bigger sticks on top of them. Hugh went to the other wood pile and started doing the same thing at the other end. The spruce needles exploded in smoky perfume.

Nancy said: "We'll see if that'll catch," moved the kettle in closer to the fire and sat down on the threshold of the lean-to. Hugh went and sat beside her. The floor of the lean-to was a bed of buffalo robes and wool blankets, and Hugh could feel and smell there were springy spruce boughs layered beneath them.

Hugh was consciously breathing very slowly and deeply through his nose, afraid if he opened his mouth to say anything he'd break the spell. Nancy took a smaller pouch out of her shoulder pouch and crumpled some tea into the kettle, then magicked two tin cups out of the snow beside the lean-to and set them to wait. The kindling was crackling nicely now, so Hugh got up and started shifting on larger pieces from the woodpile nearest to him. Wauh Oonae did the same with the other woodpile. When they sat back down, she half-filled the cups from the tea kettle, then took a leather bottle out of her shoulder bag and gurgled a dram into each cup.

Nancy handed one cup to Hugh, raised hers as though making a toast, and opened her mouth to say something, but seemed strangled by emotion. Hugh didn't know whether it was fear or sadness or happiness, just emotion. She bit her lip and blinked her eyes clear, then said to him, "Today is St. Valentine's Day. Who knows if there'll be a tomorrow?"

Hugh said hoarsely, "Nancy, you don't have to do this…"

"I want to."

Hugh didn't feel it necessary to say he did, too. He raised the cup to his mouth and could taste the whiskey vapours in the back of his nose before taking a sip. It wasn't enough whiskey to get drunk, but enough to spread warmth out to his fingers and toes.

Nancy set down her cup, said: "It's gettin' warm in here," loosed the lacing on her high-topped moccasins and kicked them off, shucked her coat, and slipped sideways in between the layers of blankets and buffalo robes. Hugh followed her, a bit more slowly – of course the knot on one of his moccasins had chosen to get frozen and he had to thaw it with his hand. Once in bed with Wauh Oonae, he kissed her and pressed her body to his, then leaned back to unbutton his shirt while pushing his right foot up and down his left ankle to try and get his thick wool socks off at the same time as his shirt. Nancy giggled and moved her feet between his, to help him and to try and get shut of her socks, too. It didn't work, but they did manage to get the tops of all four socks down around their ankles. Hugh bent under the covers to finish the job, resting his head on Nancy's still-clothed belly. When he straightened up again, she sat up with her arms above her head, and he knelt up to pull off her wool blouse and the cotton one underneath. The instant that was accomplished, they both burrowed down under the covers again. Even with the firepit sizzling in front of the lean-to, just that instant in the open air meant her breasts against his chest were cold. But not for long.

It wasn't the first time Hugh and Wauh Oonae had undressed together, but the first time in winter and in a bed. Since that glorious day in the pond two summers ago, Hugh had got fairly accustomed to his hands on her body and his on hers, and more often than not with some of their clothes still on. But it seemed to him that this time the proper thing was that they both be fully naked, even though it was a complex operation under the circumstances.

Once that was accomplished, and her skirt and his trousers and underwool pushed down to the bottom of the bed with the socks, Hugh lay the top half of his body across Nancy Prince's and kissed her mouth. He pulled back quickly and said: "You're trembling…"

"Just the cold. I'm getting warmer."

As his hand travelled across her body under the covers, he could see each part it touched: her left breast with her wet shift gauzed over it in the pond, her knee bared when her skirt hiked itself up across Cheengwun's saddle, the curve of her hip kissed golden with sunlight as she reclined on a moss couch by the stream… His fingers explored between her thighs to find the familiar but always different nest of crinkly, downy hair. Sometimes what he'd found there was a narrow slit he'd had to fumble for among the thatchy hairs, sometimes she'd already been open and warm and moist. Today she was more open than ever before. Her hand slid down across his stomach, reaching, and he edged away, pretending he was just shifting to get his head down low enough to kiss her breasts – he was afraid that if she touched him where he was already vibrating, he'd go off like a rocket and spoil everything.

Her hands wrapped around the tops of his arms and tugged him to move up and forward with his legs between hers. It seemed to him it was his job to get the two parts connected, so he worked one hand down between her belly and his, held her open with two fingers and pushed himself in. As soon as he was inside her, though only a little ways so far, his whole body felt wrapped in a soft warmth that had traces of holding the wires of the galvanic battery that big James McKay had surprised his guests with at that long ago surprise party when Hugh and Nancy had watched the electric dancers in the sky. This was only going to get better.

Hugh pushed in a little farther and encountered an obstacle. He'd heard about this; farmboys had many expert conversations about the resemblances and differences between animals' sex and humans'. Wauh Oonae whispered through gritted teeth: "Push. Hard!" He did, or thought he did, but didn't get any farther. "Do it!" He rammed his hips forward. She let out a scream, and then clutched his back to tell him not to stop. Soon he was all the way inside her and she had her legs wrapped around his and her arms around his back. The throaty, moaning sounds she was making and the feel of her body and the sensations inside his and the rhythm of their movements all blended together. Time disappeared. Then the sensations exploded and he was lying across her like he'd just swum across a spring-flood river and she was the shore. Her fingers were toying with the sweat-curled hair at the back of his neck, and her lips were brushing kisses on his cheek. It occurred to him that since a good sweat curled his hair up even more than it naturally was, shortening it as much as an inch or more, he could save Mum's haircut scissors some wear and tear if he did this every day.

After a moment, Hugh rolled onto his back so that Nancy could breathe without his weight pressing down on her ribcage. She shifted onto her side, and snuggled her shoulder up his side to stretch his left arm out and pillow her head on it. Her head and thick waves of hair kept his upper arm warm, and by crooking his elbow he could at least keep his hand and wrist under the covers. He propped one knee up slightly, to raise the weight of the blankets and buffalo robe off his mid-section. He was sore in a very tender part of his body, but she was probably feeling worse than sore, given that scream.

Hugh knew that other farmboys would've called it blasphemous, but it seemed to him this was the best part of all: he and she lying twined together peacefully, with no barriers between them, murmuring about this and that and nothing at all. It only lasted, though, until Wauh Oonae said: "If we don't feed that fire she's gonna die on us."

"Well… the day ain't quite so cold as it started out…" and indeed the biting cold of the morning seemed to've settled down to nibbling, or maybe it was just him. "And, you know, no matter how cold it is outside, when you step out the door you still got a little layer of indoor warmth on you, and a minute or two before that distipates and you start to feel the cold…"

Hugh threw back the covers, jumped upright, took two quick barefoot-in-the-snow steps to the nearest woodpile and started chucking sticks onto the bed of embers. He heard a noise and looked up. Wauh Oonae was at the other woodpile doing the same thing. He decided against pausing to admire her naked body against the white background. She called across the firepit: "You're all bloody!"

"Huh?" He looked down. His upper thighs and the pathetic little, cold-shrivelled tuber between them were rust-dappled with dried blood.

When he looked up again, Nancy was stepping toward him, looking concerned. She said: "Better wash you clean," and, before he saw what she was up to, she slapped-on the two handfuls of loose snow she'd scooped up while he wasn't looking. He bellowed and chased her around the firepit, scooping up snow of his own. She escaped into the lean-to and under the covers. He dropped his handful of snow before scooting in after her.

They lay there shivering for awhile, alternating between wanting to get close to share body warmth and pushing each other away when colder parts of one body touched warmer parts of the other. After awhile, though, even Hugh's fingers and toes felt human again. Nancy said: "I don't think it'll hurt this time." It didn't.

Partway through, though, something occurred to Hugh that puzzled him. The physical feeling of moving back and forth inside a woman – clinging folds of liquid silk – was exactly and entirely the same as what he'd imagined in the kinds of dreams that made him embarrassed about the next time his nightshirt got laundered. And the inside of a woman, at least this woman, felt like the inside of a seashell looked, which was what had made him so embarrassed when the exotic conch shell was passed around the class. How had he known? But the instant after the puzzlement crossed his mind he stopped thinking again.

After another while of lying happily wrung-out in each others' arms, Wauh Oonae said: "I think we better think about getting back before your people and my people start gettin' worried – lotta worryin' going on these days. I don't wanna, but I think we better."

It took some time, what with dragging their coats and moccasins in under the buffalo robe to warm them, retrieving the rest of their clothes from the bottom of the bed and squirming into them without raising the covers enough to let the cold in. When they were both dressed and standing, Hugh checked the firepit and decided it could be left to die on its own – already down to coals and surrounded by snow, with enough frozen ground below that it couldn't catch onto a tree root and travel. He waved his arm to indicate the bedding and kettle and all, and said: "Guess we should pack all this up."

"No need – too much and too awkward for Cheengwun to carry all of it and me. I'll come by another day with a packhorse."

"Maybe we both will – day after tomorrow's Wednesday."

"Maybe," but there was something forlorn in her voice.

The ride back down the creek was quiet and slow, with a delicious weariness to it. As they neared the road, Hugh began to hear singing – not close by, but a massed choir of male voices carried far on the wind in the frosty air. Not that they were anything like a practised choir, but together enough that Hugh could recognise the tune. He muttered: "Funny, that's *Johnny Cope*."

"Johnny who?"

"*Johnny Cope* – it's a song my grandparents used to sing when they were feeling jolly, about one of the times the Highland Clans kicked the… stuffing out of the English army."

When Spot carried Hugh up onto the road, Hugh reined him in and stared at what was across the river. There were a lot more men in the schoolyard and churchyard now, at least a couple of hundred. Some of them were moving in and out of the kirk, some marching back and forth in formation, some standing around a bonfire. Many of them were carrying guns, and the long, dark object sticking out the back of a sledge was unmistakably a cannon barrel. Without the muffling creek valley, Hugh could hear the singing more clearly, and it wasn't exactly *Johnny Cope*. They'd changed two or three of the words.

Hey Riel, are ye waking yet?
Or are yer drums a-beating yet?
If ye're nae waking, we'll nae wait,
For we'll take the fort in the morning.

What made it even stranger was that Hugh was sure there weren't many, if any, Kildonan men among those bellowing singers, and the Canadians were all proudly English British. But then, as Hugh's Granda used to say, if the English had had any war songs worth singing they wouldn't've needed Highland regiments.

One of the men at the bonfire broke away, ran to the riverbank, pointed a rifle at Hugh and Wauh Oonae and shouted: "Halt! Who goes there!"

Hugh thought it a bit silly to be ordered to halt when he was already halted, but thought better of pointing that out to a man pointing a rifle at him. Instead, he raised his empty mittens in the air and called back, "Hugh Sutherland, Point Douglas! And Nancy *Prince!*" He leaned on the 'Prince,' to let the man aiming the rifle know he was aiming it in the direction of a near relation of Chief Henry Prince.

A much taller man came forward, put his hand on the rifle barrel to lower it, and swept off his hat to show the red-gold crown of Dr. John Christian Schultz. It seemed Dr. Schultz wasn't in hiding anymore, nor confining himself to the safety of the Stone Fort and Little Britain. Dr. Schultz's voice boomed across the river, "A good day to you, Hugh Sutherland! Come join us," and he waved a beckoning arm.

"I can't now, Dr. Schultz, I have to be getting home!"

"Well, we'll still be here tomorrow, and a good deal more of us!"

Hugh turned to Wauh Ooonae. He could see she understood that it wouldn't be possible to make a fitting au revoir while they were pinned in plain sight of all those men across the river. She twitched her head in that direction and said: "See what I mean? And it's only gonna get worse. If some miracle don't sort this out by day-after-tomorrow, I'll stay home. And you will, too."

"Well…"

"Promise me you'll stay home, too."

"All right, I promise, but I'm sure this'll all get sorted out in a few days. If we miss this Wednesday I'll see you the next."

She took off her right hand mitten to raise her bare hand to his cheek. "You're my life, Hugh Sutherland. Please be careful with my life."

Hugh tugged off his right mitten to bring her hand to his mouth and kiss it. He said with stunning eloquence, "Well, um, yeah, goes both ways." Then she turned her horse and started north, so he turned his and started south. When he looked back over his shoulder, she was looking back over hers, but soon they both had to straighten their necks to see what was ahead of them.

Hugh felt a little guilty about feeling a bit relieved that he and Nancy had to ride in separate directions. Although he certainly didn't want it to be long before they were riding in the same direction again. But the fact was, he was just about talked-out for now, and it took a lot of energy to focus that much attention on someone without a pause. Maybe she felt the same way, too. But his wore-outness wasn't unpleasant, it was loose and comfortable and peaceful. Everything seemed a bit different than it had this morning. When he hummed a bit of *Johnny Cope* to himself, it sounded like his voice had dropped an octave. Now that he was noticing the rest of the world again, he could see that the day had turned lovely: a bit of cloudcover had drifted in and a hint of snow was sifting down –

"Arrèt!"

Hugh halted his horse. Half a dozen Metis horsemen came out of the woods, holding guns at the ready. One of them said: "Where you going?"

"Um, home – just going home…"

One of the others, who looked vaguely familiar, pointed at Hugh with his hunter's mitten – a mitten with one glove finger for the trigger – and said: "Point Douglas Sutherland, right?"

Hugh nodded.

The one who'd spoken first pointed his thumb north and said: "What were you doing up there with Dr. Schultz and all them others?"

"Nothing. I don't have anything to do with them."

"Then why're you coming back from that way?"

"Well, there's this girl…"

They all laughed, not unkindly. The leader said: "You go on home, and maybe best you stay there for awhile – girl or no girl. These are crazy days around Red River. Crazy days."

As Hugh neared home, he heard children happily squealing and shouting. What words he could pick out were English, not French or Bungee as the neighbours' children were most likely to use. And the voices did sound like some of his younger brothers and sisters. He looked at the sky. The sun was down to the tops of the riverside trees, which at this time of year meant it was still too early for school to be out and the scholars made their way home. But when he got into the yard, it was sure enough a gaggle of young Sutherlands taking turns sliding down the bank on a frozen buffalo hide to see who could get farthest out onto the river. They were too busy to notice him unsaddling Spot and putting him back in the paddock.

When Hugh went into the house, there was another clutch of young Sutherlands warming their toes in front of the fire, and Donald was sitting with Mary Ann Bella on his knee, reading to her from a book of Bible stories. Twelve year old Willy jumped up and crowed: "Hugh! No more school while Dr. Schultz's and Captain Boulton's army are there! They all got guns and they're gonna attack the fort, just like Ivanhoe and the castle! You gonna take your gun and join up with 'em?"

Hugh glanced at Donald, who glanced back the same expression Hugh was feeling: *No point telling a twelve year old boy he's thinking like a twelve year old boy.* Donald closed the book, slid Mary Ann Bella off his knee and said to Hugh, "I don't think Dr. Black's ecstatic about letting them use the kirk and the schoolhouse, but what's he gonna do, make them camp out in the snow?"

Hugh said: "Da's not back yet?"

"Not yet."

"Where's Mum?"

"Gone visiting."

That wasn't an eyebrow-raiser. Although visiting had always been a prime way to while away the winter at Red River, this winter had been even more so. Just about every afternoon that neighbours didn't drop by the Point Douglas Sutherlands' for tea, Hugh, Donald and Aleck had to take turns looking after Mary Ann Bella, because Mum was dropping by some neighbours' for tea.

Mum got home just before the odour of the big pot of beef stew she'd left to simmer became too much of a temptation. When she was told Da wasn't back yet, she just said: "Well, he did say it was going to be a long session. I'll set a small pot aside to keep warm for him." But it seemed to Hugh she wasn't feeling as matter-of-fact as she was trying to sound.

After the wondrously wearying day he'd had, Hugh would've been more than happy to curl up around his bellyful of supper and hibernate. But he kept drinking strong tea with maple sweetener to keep himself awake. Da still wasn't home by the younger children's bedtime, nor by the time Donald, Aleck, Morrison and Hector started yawning their way up the staircase. Aleck glanced back at Hugh from the foot of the stairs. Hugh indicated his not-quite-empty cup and said: "I'll be up directly."

When the last footfalls had faded up the staircase, Hugh methodically cleaned the ashes out of his pipe, reloaded it and relit it, waiting for Mum to look up from her agitated knitting and say something. She didn't, so eventually he said: "What's going on, Mum?"

"Oh..." then she cut herself off with a trace of a laugh that didn't sound rib-tickled. "Funny how I could always talk to you about things I couldn't talk about with the other children, even when you were little. I don't know why that is..."

"Maybe 'cause I got such a feeble memory you don't have to worry about anything you say coming back to haunt you."

This time there was some good humour in her laugh, but it didn't last. She set her knitting aside and warmed her cup with the dregs from the teapot, as though buying time to decide whether to talk about whatever it was or not. She sipped her tea, made a face and got up to move the kettle from the hearthstone to the stove, and scoop fresh tea leaves into the pot. She sat back down again, put her hand on her knitting sitting on the table, then put her hand back in her lap and said: "Well... There's something your father didn't tell me about that happened in Saturday's sitting of the Provisional Government, or maybe it was Friday's, but...

"One of the people I was visiting told me about it. It seems that President Riel was lecturing the parish representatives that it was their duty to vote unanimously for something-or-other. Your father, um, thumped his fist on the council table and said, a bit hotly, 'I have been giving my time all winter without fee or reward in efforts for the good of the country, I am here to speak for the people who sent me, and I do not propose to be taught my duty by Louis Riel.' Or, something more or less like that, was what you father... said."

"Good on Da." Hugh doubted that 'said' was exactly the word for the way Point Douglas John Sutherland had expressed himself. Da didn't lose his temper often, but when the dam burst you better head for high ground.

Mum didn't look like there was anything to be jolly about. She said: "And then... It seems that when Captain Boulton's men were making their night march from Headingley to Kildonan kirk, they passed by Henri Coutu's house, where Louis Riel sometimes spends the night. They surrounded the house, and Captain Boulton and Thomas Scott went in with drawn pistols, looking for Louis Riel. He wasn't there, but no doubt the story got back to him."

"Well, so...? I don't mean to flip it off, Mum, but anybody'll know Da didn't have anything to do with that."

"Hugh..." Mum shook her head at him like he was still just a child after all, or perhaps just male. "The world doesn't always follow in logical order, or at least not the kind that only happens here," she tapped a forefinger against the side of her forehead. "I would've thought, out of all my children, my wild child would be the first to know that.

"The Metis in Fort Garry are looking over their walls at an angry army that almost killed or kidnapped their president – only missed by mischance. Your father told President Riel in public to go stuff his high horse. I remember, way back when this house was still on Point Douglas, Madame Lagimodière clucking over tea with your grandmother that she didn't know what was to become of her grandson, little Louis, because he flew into a blind fury whenever anyone defied his wishes – anyone except his mother and father.

"Well, little Louis isn't little anymore, but he's still the same person. And your father most certainly defied him. And Ambroise Lépine and his soldiers take their cues from Louis Riel. For all I know…" Mum's voice got too thick for her throat, and she had to cough and breathe before carrying on. "For all I know, your father is now sitting in chains with the prisoners he'd been trying to get released."

Hugh leaned forward and tentatively touched his mother's hand. "Look, Mum, I'll just ride over to Fort Garry and ask –"

"No! I don't want you going anywhere near Fort Garry. Not you or any of your brothers and sisters. I don't want any of you leaving our property until your father comes home and things settle down."

"Well –"

"John Hugh, I know you've always gone your own way and you're a grown man now, but I want you to promise me you won't stray from here until I say so."

"Um, yeah, all right, Mum, I promise." There seemed to be a lot of women today making him promise to stay home.

Mum didn't seem inclined to go to bed anytime soon, so Hugh sat up with her drinking tea and out-loud remembering funny and wistful old happenings in and around the family – remembering some of them quite differently from each other. They would shush each other and strain to listen whenever there was a faint sound of sleighbells or hoofbeats, but invariably the sounds faded away.

Hugh had never had much chance to sit and talk with his mother, what with a dozen other children and the endless bustle the whole family had to keep up to keep themselves fed and clothed and sheltered on their little piece of Planet Earth. She was actually quite sparky and humorous and wide-thinking when you got to know her.

Nonetheless, Hugh dozed off in his chair and was wakened by the commotion of his brothers and sisters attacking the start of the day. Across the table from him, his mother was rubbing the sleep out of her eyes and rising stiffly from her own chair. The morning passed with no sounds of gunfire or signs of marching men on the other side of the river, despite *'We'll take the fort in the morning.'* But then again, Dr. Schultz had said: 'We'll still be here tomorrow.' Maybe they were waiting one more day for more volunteers to join them.

The morning also passed with no sign or sound of Point Douglas John Sutherland passing beyond the gates of Fort Garry.

CHAPTER 55

Norbert Parisien picked up another piece of wood from the pile of sawn stove-lengths and set it on the chopping block for his father to split. They'd been splitting firewood at Fort Garry all morning long, trading jobs when the axer's arms got tired. Norbert crouched down to make sure the round of wood was sitting square on the block and wouldn't wobble, and then something interesting crossed the corner of his eye. He looked. It was a dog, trotting across the tramped-down snow of the big open yard in the middle of the fort. You didn't see many dogs inside Fort Garry; the sled dogs were kept outside the walls where they couldn't hurt anybody except each other. Some of The Company's officers kept hunting dogs, but this was no hunting dog. It was small, with stubby legs that scooted along in a comical kind of a way and a blocky little head with a thick chunky mustache that bounced up and down as it –

"*Norbert!*"

The shout was very loud but very close. Norbert looked up. His father was standing with the splitting axe poised over his shoulder, but now started lowering it slowly sideways instead of swinging it straight down. "Dammit, Norbert, I coulda taken off your hands!"

Norbert looked down. His mittened hands were still clasped around the piece of wood on the chopping block. He realised he'd fallen out of the rhythm of two-steps-from-the-woodpile-to-the-chopping-block, set-the-piece-of-wood- down-straight, two-steps-*to*-the-woodpile, pick-up another-piece-of-wood, two-steps-*from*-the-woodpile... He liked the rhythm. But he'd also liked looking at the funny little dog.

Norbert's father let out a sigh, the kind of sigh Norbert had been hearing from him all his life – not exactly angry, more kind of sad. "You gone dreamy again, Norbert. Go walk around the fort awhile, find things to look at..."

"But I should help."

"You're no help to me when you're dreamy. It's all right, I split wood by myself before. Go wander around awhile, and then come back and help."

Norbert got up and wandered around. There were for sure things to look at. The twisted icicle sheets hanging from the eaves of one of the buildings looked like someone had turned the Northern Lights to glass. One of the Company ladies went by in a hoop-hooded purple cape. Norbert wanted to ask her if the little dog was hers. Maybe she was looking for it. But she looked in a hurry to get from one warm place to another, and maybe she only spoke English.

Back behind the big tall houses around the big open square were a bunch of sheds with just a spiderweb of narrow paths between the hip-high snowdrifts. But between the sheds and the stone wall of the fort was another stretch of tramped-down open space, and there some men had set up a wide plank with a red dot painted on it and were taking turns throwing a knife and betting. Some of the men looked like Paquins, a clan from farther up the Assiniboine who were some kind of cousins to Norbert's father; some of the men he half-recognized from around St. Boniface; some he didn't recognise at all.

Norbert stood and watched and listened to them for a while. It had always been a mystery to him how men betting against each other could sound like they were angry and having fun at the same time. One of the men Norbert half-recognized said: "Hey, Norbert, you want to take a try?"

One of the men Norbert didn't recognise at all snorted, "Him? Two-to-one he couldn't hit the board, much less the target."

The first man said: "Oh? What odds on a bullseye?"

"Ha! Ten to one!"

"Done. Here, Norbert, you take a try." The knife they'd been using was an odd sort of knife: all one piece of steel, the handle only slightly thicker than the blade, with a thin wrapping of shagganappi around the handle to keep it from freezing to your fingers. Norbert didn't cock the knife back over his shoulder like he'd seen the other men do. He held it by the tip between his right thumb and forefinger, let his right arm dangle loose and then flicked his wrist and elbow. The only trick to it was in snapping your hand back so hard and fast when you let go the knife you almost broke your wrist, like you were giving all the strength of your body into the body of the knife. Norbert could vaguely remember there'd been a time when his wrist wasn't strong enough to do that. That had been a frustrating time.

Norbert turned and started wandering again before the thunk of the knife biting into the wood. The red dot was where the knife was supposed to go, so that was where the knife would go. Hitting a mark that didn't move was nothing to hunting rabbits with a throwing knife.

Norbert left the crowing and cursing behind and wandered back among the maze of canyons between the big houses. He heard a squawky croak and looked up. He had to back up as far as the next building would let him before he could see what he'd heard. Way up on the peak of the tall building in front of him was a raven perched beside a chimney for warmth. Some people didn't like ravens, said they were raggedy and thieving, but Norbert did. Ravens didn't leave the people to face the winter alone like most other birds did. The raven looked down at him, let out another throaty grunt and then flew away. Well, not 'flew' in the way other birds might, just jumped off the roof, spread its wings and let the wind glide it, soaring lazily over the rooftops and out of sight.

Now that Norbert wasn't working, he began to feel the cold. He tugged his toque down lower over his ears and pulled his heavy-knit scarf up over his mouth and nose. He wondered what was inside the buildings around him, but knew better than to just open their doors and wander in. But the snow was piled up high enough he thought he might be able to see into the first floor windows, if he didn't sink in too deep.

He found he could just manage it, by standing on tiptoe and holding onto the bottom windowledge for balance. But the room he was looking into was so much darker than outside, he could only make out vague shapes of furniture. The next room he tried had a lamp burning on a desk, and a man sitting writing something. The name Louis Riel popped into Norbert's head. But that couldn't be right – Louis Riel was wider and older and had a big beard, not just a mustache. But then Norbert remembered that that Louis Riel was long gone to Heaven, and this was the other Louis Riel, the one everybody was talking about, who'd made himself boss of The Company or something.

The Louis Riel at the desk glanced up and saw Norbert seeing him. Louis Riel jumped up and ran out of the room, shouting something. Norbert couldn't make out the words through the glass, but they sounded angry. Norbert decided to go somewhere else, but before he could wade out of the snowdrift, two men with guns came running out of the building and told him to come with them. They walked along a path behind the buildings, not through the open square where his father was. When they got to the gatehouse, one of the men knocked on a door with his gun butt, and out stepped a tall, dangerous-faced man Norbert recognized: Ambroise Lépine.

The man who'd knocked on the door said: "President Riel caught this fellow spying through a window at him. He's a spy for Schultz." Norbert started to protest, but his tongue got all twisted-together like it usually did when he got over-excited.

Ambroise Lépine said in a calm, low voice, "Bonjour Norbert."

Norbert's tongue untwisted. "Bonjour, Monsieur Lépine."

Ambroise Lépine looked at the sky and said: "Norbert Parisien the spy… I don't think so. But there's no use trying to explain that to the President today. Everybody's jumpy these days. Best thing for today, Norbert, is you just go home."

"But –"

"It's all right, I'll tell your father." There was a normal-sized door set into one of the big gates. Ambroise Lépine patted Norbert's shoulder out the door. "You just go home for now, Norbert, and stay there till your father comes. But go carefully."

When the door closed behind him with the clanking of iron bolts, Norbert looked around at the world of white snow and black skeleton-finger brush, then climbed down to the beaten trail along the middle of the river and started walking north. It wouldn't be the first time he'd walked home from The Forks, or the other way around, but it was late in the day to start. But one good thing was it hadn't been very long since he and his father stopped for their noon-time meal, so he wouldn't be hungry for some while. And if he got too tired or cold or hungry, there were relatives just north of Kildonan where he could get something to eat and maybe borrow a horse or even stay overnight. Or maybe before he got that far, someone in a sleigh going north would come along and stop and offer him a ride.

Now that that possibility occurred to him, though, Norbert noticed something strange: there was no one on the river but him. Usually there would be riders and sleighs and dogsleds and people walking in all directions. When he passed by the Point Douglas Sutherlands' place he could hear children playing, but up in their yard beyond the trees, not on the riverbank. And when he got to the place where the Kildonan boys kept the ice clear for skating, it was still powdered-over with the snow from a couple of days ago. He hadn't noticed when he and his father passed by with their sledful of wood that morning.

The snow from a couple of days ago, though, wasn't so deep that Norbert couldn't get the soles of his moccasins down onto the ice and slide along, bending forward so he could keep his balance through long, gliding strides. It wasn't as good as skating, but more fun than walking. About halfway along, though, Norbert got a better idea. He climbed up onto the shoulder of snow rimming the rink, ran along it a few steps to pick up speed and then jumped down. His moccasins almost shot out from under him, but he windmilled his arms and kept upright till the slide petered out and he climbed back onto the shoulder to go again. But after three or four times of that game, he came to the end of the cleared ice and was back to trudging along in the snow.

Norbert's shadow was getting very long in front of him when he began to hear a low, burbling sound, like water running though one of the gorges on the Winnipeg River, but that couldn't be. A little farther on and the sound turned itself into men's voices, a lot of men's voices, talking and barking and singing. He saw the pointed tower of Kildonan church ahead and remembered there'd been a big crowd of men around the church and school that morning when he and his father went by on their way to Fort Garry. One of the men had shouted something in English from the riverbank and Norbert's father had just pointed at the firewood piled on the sled and kept on going. Norbert had wanted to stop and see what all those men were doing, but Norbert's father had shaken his head and snapped the pony's reins to make it go faster.

Well, Norbert's father wasn't there to tell him no now. When Norbert got near the church, he veered off the packed snow of the trail and climbed the riverbank, grabbing hibernating tree branches to help heave his legs in and out of the snowdrifts. When he got to the top, he stopped and peered out through the last fringe of brush, looking and listening for a hint of why all those men had flocked together in the cold. They didn't look to be building anything, just gabbling and laughing and showing each other their guns, although some of them didn't have guns, just hatchets or scythes. A lot of them were white and talking English, but some of them were darker and Norbert could pick out a bit of French or Bungee here and there. A couple of the men looked like they might be Paquins. It seemed odd that there would be Paquins here among these men while there were other Paquins at Fort Garry, although Norbert couldn't say exactly why it seemed odd.

After Norbert had been watching the men for a moment, they began to look very much like a flock of giant birds scratching in the snow, some with their shoulders hunched against the cold like folded wings, some flapping their arms…

Someone shouted. Norbert looked in that direction and saw a man pointing at him, then a bunch of men running at him. Norbert turned to run away – not that he thought he'd been doing anything wrong, but their faces were snarling. When he turned to run, though, his legs got mired in the snowdrift and he fell face-down. Many hands grabbed him and dragged him up the slope and stood him on his feet. There were men all around him shouting things he didn't understand, pushing and prodding him and slapping his face. He clumsily swung out his right fist and the face it connected with fell back, but then someone drove a gunbutt into his stomach and he doubled over.

When Norbert straightened up again, slowly, rubbing his stomach and gasping, the crowd of men in front of him was parting to let another man come forward. Through blurring tears, Norbert could make out that it was a very tall man with a short, red-gold beard. Norbert had never seen Dr. Schultz up close, but he was a hard man to mistake. Dr. Schultz said in a French that had a funny tang to it, but was still French, "So, spying for Riel, are you?"

"No! I was just…" But then Norbert's tongue got twisted-up again, and he couldn't think what to say even if he got it untwisted.

"You were just hiding in the bushes in the snow watching us for the fun of it…?"

Norbert nodded eagerly, happy to be understood. Some of the men around him laughed, but it wasn't a pleasant kind of laughter. Dr. Schultz said: "Well, after tomorrow it won't matter what you might tell Riel, but we'll keep you here till then," then trailed off into something in English that sounded a bit perplexed. One of the other men offered up something else in English that made Dr. Schultz nod. Several hands took tight hold of Norbert's arms and marched him toward Kildonan church.

Norbert had never been inside a Protestant church, and he didn't take in much of this one as his guards marched him quickly down the aisle. He did notice there were no crosses, and very few colours. Some of the pews had blankets on them, and slumbering men who sat up and called questions in English. At the head of the aisle wasn't a normal altar, but a square wooden tower that Norbert figured the Protestant priest must stand on to say his sermons. Set into the side of the tower was a narrow door that one of the men unbolted and held open while the others pushed Norbert inside.

It was very dark with the door closed and bolted again. The space inside wasn't quite tall enough for Norbert to stand up straight, and so narrow that when he sat down with his knees up his toes were pressed tight against one wall and his back against the other. But he became aware he wasn't alone in there. There was a puppy whimpering in the dark. Norbert gingerly fumbled his hands around what little open floor space there was, feeling for the puppy so he could pick it up and nestle it in his lap. Then he realised the sounds were coming from him.

Hugh was fishing from a dugout canoe, peacefully drifting downstream, when the sun burst open like a cracked egg, spreading its flaming yoke across the sky and searing his eyes. Then someone shook his shoulder and he blinkingly realised he was in his bed, and it was Donald with a candle. Donald said softly, "Your watch." After last night, Hugh and Donald, Aleck and Morrison had agreed to take turns sitting up with Mum, and longshot-hoping to convince her she could go to bed since one of them would be keeping watch for any signs or news of Da.

Hugh sat up and murmured: "She sleep at all?"

"A little, but I couldn't talk her into going up to bed. I did manage to get her to put a quilt on her chair and wrap it around herself."

Hugh tugged on his socks and trousers and carried Donald's candle downstairs. Mum was sitting bundled in a quilt, as Donald had said, with her feet up on another chair. But she wasn't sleeping, just sipping tea. She looked as scoured-out as she had when baby Mary Ann died, but at least that had been a finality, while this had the added torture of not knowing what was going to happen, or might've happened already. It occurred to him that his grandparents would've said Mum had turned *fey* – one foot in this world and the other in the next.

Hugh poured himself a half-cup of tea, all that was left in the pot, sat down across from her and said: "Why don't you go up to bed, Mum?"

"You're the last watch of the night, aren't you? So by the time I went up and changed into my nightgown and got into bed, I'd've barely closed my eyes when the little ones would start bouncing awake."

"You could stay in bed. Me and Donald could get 'em dressed and breakfasted."

She reached across to pat his hand. "Not in my kitchen you don't."

"Well, it was worth a try." Hugh got up to feed the stove and move the kettle onto it for another pot of tea. Somebody was definitely going to have to get another couple buckets of water at first light. He fed and fussed with the fire in the hearth, then angled his chair so he could either gaze into the flames or look at Mum. He said: "Well, at least we won't have to build a fire in the morning."

Mum said, in that languid way of exhausted-but-can't-sleep, "You remember when you were ten or twelve or so and learning bits and pieces of things in school, you made up a theory about fire…? You said fire was a living thing, because like all living things – like us – it needs food and air, and shelter from the rain and snow…"

"That warn't no theory, Mum, just fact."

"And you said geology says the whole world was fire once. And that's why, you said, although we need fire, we have to keep it in cages, keep it from breaking free, because it remembers that it once ruled the whole world and wants to again."

"Huh. You sure that wasn't Donald?"

"Oh no, dear," Mum laughed. "It certainly wasn't Donald." Her eyes drifted closed and Hugh thought maybe she was drifting off to sleep. But after a moment she said: "Maybe that's why I could always talk to you about things I couldn't talk to the other children about. You were a fanciful child, but always wise beyond your years."

"Mum, I don't know a damn thing about anything."

"Isn't that what I just said?"

They both laughed. Then Mum looked off into the distance and murmured: "What a world of trouble would be spared if people would just admit we don't think as good as we think we do. Ah, well..." She looked back at Hugh. "You know, I always felt a bit guilty about you."

"Me? Why?"

"Because of all my children, you were the one that always had to learn things the hard way."

"Huh. Well, but look at it this way, Mum – that way things stick. Well, the fourth or fifth time, anyway." They both laughed again, and Hugh got up to deal with the kettle and the teapot.

The watch passed, sometimes in conversation, sometimes dozing, sometimes just watching the fire dance. It was still dark when Hugh heard the thumping and squealing of his younger brothers and sisters greeting the day; it'd be another month or so before the sun started getting up before people. The fixing-breakfast bustle was in full commotion when Hugh thought he heard something outside and said: "Ssh!"

Mum said, much more loudly and to better effect, "Hush!" and cocked her head to listen. She nodded at Hugh that she heard it, too: sleighbells. There'd been more than a few times in the last thirty-six hours they'd heard sleighbells or hoofbeats approaching and getting louder, but the sounds had always got quieter and faded as they passed by the house. This time they didn't fade, just stopped. There was a sound of footsteps crunching through the snow and rounding the house. All eyes went to the door. It opened and in stepped Point Douglas John Sutherland, looking bone-weary but not dead or in chains.

The youngest children were on him in a bounce and a squeak. Da waded toward the table with Mary Ann Bella crooked in one arm, Roddy clinging to one leg and Christina the other, and Jamie clutching his free hand, and Mum protesting from her stance at the stove, "Children! Children! Your father's tired!"

Da slumped into his chair. Mum came and stood behind him and put her hand on his shoulder. Da sloped one hand up on top of hers, lolled his head back against her belly, and said as though it was something he had to get across quickly, "The prisoners are all being released. It took a lot of sawing back and forth – the hardest part was finding a wording for the oath of parole that would convince Riel and company that the prisoners were swearing not to take up arms against the Provisional Government, and convince the prisoners they weren't swearing to take up arms *for* the Provisional Government. Well, there were a lot more complications, but the point is it's done, all the prisoners have signed their parole – well, all but one. Riel and company told Dr. Schultz's father-in-law he's broken so many oaths there was no point wasting ink on another, so they just pushed him out of the fort and told him to go away..."

Da seemed to've lost his thread, befuddled with too much too tired. He shook his head and bore down, and looked across the table. "So, you farmboys go and saddle Montrose quickly, please, and one of you gallop to the kirk and tell Dr. Schultz and Captain Boulton the prisoners are all being set free. It's done, it's over. Everyone can go home."

'Farmboys' was Da's teasing term for Hugh, Donald and Aleck, as opposed to the 'scholars' who were still going to school. Hugh suspected it was also Da's way of telling Aleck he should still be going to school, too, without singling him out. Anyway, all three of them were out the door in a lick, buttoning their coats as they ran for the barn. None of them questioned why the cutter that had delivered Da hadn't just carried on to deliver the message to Dr. Schultz and Captain Boulton. Louis Schmidt was so identified with the National Committee and Provisional Government he was more likely to get shot at than listened to.

Norbert heard an iron tongue click beside his left shoulder, and looked in that direction. There was nothing to see but darkness, as the world had been for he didn't know how many hours. He didn't know whether he'd fallen asleep for parts of that time or not. For the last long while he'd been sitting with his wrists clamped between his thighs, and his elbows against his sides, trying to keep his bloated bladder from releasing itself. It had been years and years since the last time he'd wet himself, and he certainly didn't want it to happen again in this wooden cage with all those strangers around. It didn't seem possible that his body could be so full of liquid and his mouth so dry, but so it was. And it wasn't just liquid, there was pressure at the small of his back.

The door of his cage swung open and poured in light that burned Norbert's eyes. Blinking and blinded, he let hands on his arms tug him out and stand him up on cramped-stiff legs. His eyes got used to the light and he saw it was just lamplight, the windows of the church were still dark. The man on Norbert's right said, in a flattened-out attempt at French, "Va toilettes," and angled his head toward the door of the church. The man on Norbert's left handed him a tin cup of water. Norbert sipped just enough to wet his mouth, practically dancing to keep what was already in his body from gushing out. The other men in the church laughed; the two on either side of Norbert took hold of his arms and walked him toward the church door.

Once Norbert was walking, the pressure inside him wasn't quite so desperate. But there was another kind of desperation. He had no idea of what these men meant to do with him after they let him have a drink of water and relieve himself. He'd heard somewhere that spies got shot or hanged, and here there was no Ambroise Lépine to say he could just go home.

Outside, the sun had edged its rim up just high enough to show the general shapes of things. As the men holding his arms marched him around the corner of the church, Norbert could see the crescent-moon-doored shed set back in the bush. And he could see something else between him and the shed: an unhitched cutter standing in the snow. And lying slantwise across the seat of the cutter was a double-barrelled gun.

When Norbert got as near to the cutter as the path to the toilettes was going to take him, he flung his arms out and back with all the strength that years of hauling and splitting logs had given him. The hands gripping his arms tore loose, as both his guards squawked and fell backwards. Norbert grabbed the gun and ran.

Hugh paused a few seconds before buckling Montrose's saddle cinch – Montrose always took in and held a deep breath when the saddle went on him, hoping to fool the saddler into buckling him loose. When Montrose exhaled, Hugh tightened and fastened the cinch, then nodded at Donald and Aleck, who'd already finished with Montrose's bridle and reins. Donald and Aleck led Montrose out of the barn, and Hugh walked along with his hand on a warm and furry, rolling flank. When they got out of the barn, Hugh said: "Well, Da said one of us three should go, so who'll it be?"

Donald said: "Don't be ridiculous. Da was just being polite to me and Aleck. He said one of us should *gallop* – that means you."

Hugh took the reins and started to lift his foot for the stirrup, but two things made him hesitate. One was that the reins got twisted around his crooked little finger; most days he didn't even notice it anymore, but some days it kept getting in the way. The second thing was remembering that the day before yesterday Nancy Prince had made him promise to stay home 'day after tomorrow.' But she'd also said: *'If some miracle don't sort this out by day-after-tomorrow,'* and some miracle had. Maybe after delivering the message he'd just keep on riding north toward St. Peters, and Montrose could have his weekly romp with Cheengwun after all.

Montrose felt the weight swing up onto the saddle on his back, and snorted contentedly – it was the young one, not the heavier slower older one. The young one didn't ride on him, he rode with him. There was always a good stretch of galloping with the young one on board, and never a worry that the rider might bounce off or not swerve him from some crack in the road ahead. Sure enough, once they got down onto the frozen river the rider leaned forward to whisper in his ear: "Go get 'em, Montrose."

Halfway to Kildonan Kirk, with Montrose's muscles joyously churning beneath him and the wind whipping his face, Hugh began to hear another sound seeping in through the bass drum roll of galloping hooves on snowpacked ice: a kind of keening, or a baying of hounds, but chopped with squawking edges. Hugh straightened his back to peer over Montrose's surging head and mane; the dawn had come on just enough to brush a tinge of grey into the black and blue-white world. Up ahead, a ragged flock of ravens was swooping forward low along the river. But ravens didn't travel in flocks. It was a pack of running men, some with long coats flapping behind them, charging full-tilt behind a leader brandishing a sword or walking stick or something-like, pumping it up and down like a relay runner's baton.

If this was the morning Dr. Schultz's men were going to *'take the fort'* and this was the way they were going about it, they'd be out of breath by the time they got there, and there certainly wouldn't be any element of surprise. Anyway, the news that the prisoners were being released would stop them and let them pack up their shouts and guns and go home. Hugh shifted the reins to angle Montrose in that direction and intercept the leader.

But as Montrose altered course, Hugh's jouncing vision picked out that the man in front wasn't their leader, they were chasing him, and that the fleeing man's frantically churning legs were somewhat short for the length of his body – somewhat like Norbert Parisien. Well, that wasn't bloody right, and all the more reason to head them off.

Norbert could hear, between his own gasping breaths and thudding moccasins, that the howling wolfpack was gaining on him. He'd seen wolves catch up with a deer, tearing strips of its living flesh off as it kept on running. The weight of the gun pumping up and down in his right hand seemed to help move him forward. If he could just keep ahead of them till he rounded Point Douglas and got within sight of Fort Garry, he'd be safe. He could fire the gun in the air to draw the lookouts' attention. The men running after him would run in the other direction if they saw Ambroise Lépine and a pack of Metis horsemen galloping toward them.

He was beginning to believe he could maybe outrun them that far, so long as hoofbeats coming up behind didn't signal that some of the men back at the church had mounted up to run him down. But as soon as he started to believe that, he heard galloping hoofbeats. Not coming from behind him, though, but coming toward him. For a beautiful instant he thought it was Ambroise Lépine's men come to rescue him, that they'd somehow got wind of what was going on before he came in sight of Fort Garry. But then his ears told him it was only one horse. Out of the shadows ahead, silhouetted against the snow, came the figure of a man on a big dark horse, swerving to cut him off. Still running, Norbert threw the gun up to his shoulder and fired.

Hugh saw the silhouetted figure ahead of him change shape, the long baton shifting from vertical to horizontal. A tongue of orange flame spat out into the black, blue-white and dove-grey world and he felt a hot spike drive through his reins hand and into his chest. As it drove into his chest it changed from a spike into a fence maul that lifted him up and sideways off the saddle. His moccasined feet slid naturally out of the stirrups – so much for the people who'd teased him he should start wearing heeled boots instead of moccasins like an Indian child – but his crooked little finger wouldn't let him disentangle the reins on his way down. He thumped onto his back on the snow, head lolling, right arm jerking upwards as Montrose shied and reared. The thudding in his ears was maybe Montrose's panicked hoof-drumming or his own pulsing blood.

Norbert grabbed the reins of the plunging horse and yanked to free them from the rider's hand. Then he saw who it was that was lying there in the snow with blood pumping out of the hole Norbert had put in his chest. He saw who it was… Norbert barely felt the hands grabbing him from behind and hitting him. Not at first.

CHAPTER 56

John Sutherland sat at his kitchen table seeing the window turning a lighter grey, thinking that even though the day was beginning he just might lie down and have the first real sleep he'd had in forty-eight hours, or fifty-six or whatever it had been. He'd just planted his hands on the table to push himself up to his feet so his feet could carry him up to his lovely warm soft bed, when Aleck burst through the door with the barn shovel still in his hand, shouting: "Montrose's back!"

John shook his head to try and clear the cobwebs, and said: "What? He's back?"

"No, *his* back! Montrose's back! Well, he *is* back – came galloping up from the river alone and trotted into his stall. But his back – there's blood…"

John went out the door without reaching for his coat. Montrose was standing in his stall, quivering, still saddled and bridled. Several of the children were standing around uncertainly looking at Montrose and at each other. There was blood dappled across Montrose's back and flank, but no sign of a wound on him. John looked to see that Aleck had followed him out of the house. "Aleck, fetch my coat and Hugh's revolver."

"Hugh never told me where he –"

"*Fetch* it!" This was no time to be quibbling whether Hugh had told him or not, Aleck would know where it was. "Margaret, Catherine, fetch me some handfuls of snow."

Catherine, whom Purple Hugh had christened Her Royal Whyness, said: "What's happened, Father?"

John opened his mouth to answer, but nothing came out. Janet, who it seemed had charged out to the barn on his and Aleck's heels, said tightly, "Just do as your father told you, dear."

John looked around at the remaining children, and answered the question Catherine had asked, the question in all their eyes, "I don't know. I'm going to find out."

Donald said: "I will, too."

Morrison, Hector and Angus began to chime in with Donald, but Janet barked: "No!"

John said: "Your mother's right. I'm not going there to start any trouble, or expecting any, but if a whole gang of us rides in it'll look that way." Where 'there' might be was an open question, just somewhere along the path Hugh and Montrose would've taken toward the kirk. But there was no question that no more of John and Janet's sons were going to take that path this morning.

The girls came back with their mitt-scoops of snow and John rubbed it over the splatters on Montrose's back and saddle, to sluice away the blood and take the smell out of Montrose's nostrils. Donald and Morrison were at Montrose's head, rubbing his neck and whispering soothing things into his ears. The quivering in Montrose's flanks slowed down, but the quivering inside John's chest didn't. Just when Montrose looked like he might be rideable again, a shout came from the direction of the river.

John walked warily out of the barn, with the rest of his family trailing along behind. It was the junior of the two Kirk Elders who'd talked John into calling a public meeting in December. The junior elder was wheezing his way up the riverbank path. When he got to the top he paused and looked at the congregation of Point Douglas Sutherlands, then said: "It seems ye already ken something has happened."

John said: "What 'something'?"

"John Hugh Sutherland has been shot – wounded. They've carried him up to Dr. Black's house. I happened to be at the manse for – well, it makes nae difference why – but I happened to be there, and borrowed a cutter to come fetch ye."

Janet said: "I'll get my cloak. Donald, you're in charge of the house till your father and I get back."

On the ride to the kirk the elder more or less explained what had happened, as much as it could be explained. When they got to the manse John climbed down off the cutter and walked quickly along the path between the snowdrifts, with his wife's arm clamped in his. Before they reached the door Dr. Black opened it and ushered them in. Dr. Black said: "He's upstairs, in our bed," which John took to mean Dr. Black's and his wife Henrietta's. "I'll show you…"

But before they reached the foot of the staircase, Dr. Schultz stepped out of the parlour and said gravely, "He's been wounded twice – through the hand and in the chest. Unfortunately I don't have my medical instruments with me, thanks to Riel – as all of this is thanks to Riel – but my educated guess diagnosis is that one of his lungs has been punctured."

The front door flew open and blew in a gust of snow along with Henrietta Black and her mother, Granny Sally Ross, both of them looking hurried and harried. John hadn't seen Granny Ross for some while, but she didn't appear to have changed. Her head still looked too big and heavy for her body, like it was carved out of mahogany granite, and her eyes were still eerily pale, almost the same silvery grey as her hair. Mrs. Black put her hand on Janet's shoulder and said: "It will take a while to fetch Dr. Bird from Bird's Hill, and with the way things are today there's small hope of getting Dr. Cowan from Fort Garry, so I thought while we were waiting for Dr. Bird my mother might be able to help."

Before John could thank her, Dr. Schultz said: "Meaning no offence, but I don't believe Mrs. Ross has ever had any actual medical training."

Granny Sally Ross looked up at Dr. Schultz and said: "And how many gunshot wounds have you tended in your life?" Then she turned to John and Janet. "You haven't seen him yet?"

"No, we only just –"

"Well, come along then." They followed Granny Ross up into a room where Hugh was lying in a bed with his eyes closed and his right arm outside the covers and that hand wrapped in a bandage oozing blood. Granny Ross clucked: "That's no good," and gestured John to help her swing a dresser around to beside the bed, so they could prop Hugh's right hand up on top of it. "Damn fools'd let him bleed to death."

Hugh's eyes opened, then his mouth. A pale pink froth wreathed his lips as he breathed out. He said in a laboured whisper, "Sorry, Mum, I've gone and made a mess again."

Janet's hand gripping John's arm loosened and fell away and she knelt beside the bed, smoothing their son's sweat-plastered hair off his forehead. "No you haven't, my dear wee bairn – somebody's gone and hurt you. But you'll be right as rain again if you just hush now and rest."

"But I have to –" Hugh's voice cut off with a gasp from some corkscrew of pain deep inside him, and his head snapped sideways. His mother tried to shush and sooth him but he shook his head and went on. "I have to say… Norbert didn't mean to hurt me. He was scared and didn't know what… *Uh…* no blame on him, no guilty…" Hugh's misting-over, blue-green eyes shifted over Janet's shoulder to find John's eyes. "You have to tell people, make sure they don't hurt Norbert."

John swallowed and nodded and said: "I will do that, son. I will do that now, and be back directly."

On his way downstairs, John made an effort to keep his jaw firm and his eyes dry. When he stepped into the parlour, Dr. Black and Dr. Schultz and several other men stood up. John said: "My son has asked me to make sure that no blame or harm comes to the young man who shot him. Norbert Parisien was terrorised and mistook Hugh for part of the gang that was chasing him. He only fired because he was afraid his escape was being cut off, or perhaps to get the horse and get away. It was an accident."

Dr. Schultz said: "That is an extremely generous and Christian thing for your son to say, John. But the fact is, Norbert Parisien had a double-barrelled gun, and fired *two* shots into your son: one bullet that passed through Hugh's hand and knocked him off his horse, and then, once your son was down and lying wounded in the snow, Norbert Parisien fired the second barrel into his chest. It was no accident, it was deliberate murder – *attempted* murder."

John couldn't find words for the blatant idiocy of what he'd just heard. How much brains did it take for anyone even vaguely familiar with guns to know that a bullet that passed through a rider's hand wouldn't knock him off his horse? The impact comes when a bullet hits something it can't move through. But the only way John could think of to try and get that across was to hold up his right fist in front of his chest, to show the obvious fact that a rider holding his horse's reins could be shot once and wounded twice – through the hand and into the chest.

Dr. Schultz looked down at John's trembling fist and said: "Yes, I can see how that would make you want to get your hands on Norbert Parisien. But don't you worry, he's been well taken care of."

John gritted out through a throat filled with gravel, "What... do you... mean... *'well taken care of'*...?"

Dr. Schultz nodded assuringly. "Fists and boots and gunbutts, and Tom Scott had a hatchet but only used the blunt end. After we'd given Parisien a good thumping we got a rope to hang him, but Dr. Schultz and Captain Boulton intervened and insisted it be done by law. So he's been carted down to the Stone Fort, and if he lives long enough to stand trial –"

There was a roaring sound, and the next thing John saw was Dr. Schultz's head pressed back against a wall and John's hands around his throat, squeezing to pop the knuckles. A number of other hands grabbed John's arms and shoulders and pulled him back. Dr. Schultz shook his head dazedly, rubbed his throat and said: "No fault, he's not in his right mind, understandably. Still, it's lucky you pulled him off before I..."

John stared at what was in front of him. He saw a tall, broad-shouldered man with red-gold hair and beard framing a strong-boned face. And there was nothing there. Nothing at all.

John turned and went back upstairs. When he stepped into the room where his son was lying, Granny Sally Ross was bending over the bed, looking down and holding up one corner of the coverlet draped over Hugh. John glimpsed the edge of a blood-soaked bandage on Hugh's chest. Dr. and Mrs. Black's bed looked drenched in blood. The whispery sound of Hugh's laboured breathing seemed to fill the room.

Granny Ross turned her mahogany-driftwood face and polished-steel eyes toward John in the doorway and slowly shook her head. John nodded that he understood, and came on into the room. Hugh's eyes fluttered open and focused on him. Hugh said hoarsely, "You told them...?"

"I did. Norbert's fine, son. He's gone home."

Hugh smiled and nodded and let his eyes close again. Not long after, Dr. Bird arrived. He murmured with Granny Ross in the hallway first, then came in and inspected the patient, listening here and there with his wooden stethoscope. When Dr. Bird stood up and closed his medical bag, John and Janet left Hugh alone for a moment and went back out in the hallway with the doctor. Dr. Bird said softly, "Granny's opinion and mine are essentially the same, although we word it differently." Sally Ross nodded stiffly, lips clenched together. "Definitely one lung has been punctured, and there is other internal damage, a lot of internal haemorrhaging. I could try to cut out the bullet, but it would cause him a good deal of pain and only make a bigger wound. All I can do is..." he took a tiny bottle out of his black bag. "One drop in a few ounces of water will help with the pain, if you can get him to swallow."

John said: "How long?"

"A few hours. Maybe till tomorrow. I'm sorry. I'm so sorry."

Granny Ross said: "It's a damn shame. A damn, dirty, crying shame."

John and Janet went back into the room. Someone thoughtfully brought up two chairs so they could sit beside the bed, Janet holding Hugh's left hand and John holding hers. Every now and then she'd let go to dab away at the pink froth on Hugh's lips with her handkerchief, but what with that and her own tears the handkerchief was soon soaked through. Mrs. Black came in to see if she could get them anything, saw the problem immediately and took a stack of handkerchiefs out of a drawer in the dresser Hugh's right hand was propped on.

The bedroom window started turning dark. Janet said: "Oh, dear… I don't know what to… I don't want to…"

John said: "I know, you have other children to care for. And they'll be in a state. You go and I'll stay."

Janet leaned forward to kiss Hugh's forehead and whisper: "I'll be back as soon as I can." He barely-perceptibly smiled and nodded, but his eyes stayed closed. John couldn't tell how much Hugh was aware or if he was drifting in a daze.

Now it was John's turn to hold Hugh's hand and dab at the pink froth. Someone had brought in an oil lamp as the night came on. It seemed to John that the pink bubbles were growing darker and Hugh paler, but maybe it was just the light.

"Da?"

"Hm?" John had been doing a bit of drifting-dazing of his own. He saw that Hugh's eyes were open, and glistening as though sheened with glass.

Hugh said: "I ain't gonna make it, am I?"

"Oh, um, you're young and strong and…" John's voice trailed away as Hugh held his eyes on him and shook his head. "Well… people who know a lot more about these kinds of things than I do, say it's, um, maybe a few hours."

"Oh, hell…" Tears started in Hugh's eyes, and then his throat made a sound that might've been a laugh. "Well, let's hope that ain't where…"

"You know it isn't. You'll be with your Gran and Granda."

"Well…" Hugh coughed, then found the remnants of his voice again. "As Granda used to say to Gran… 'We'll all know for sure about all that sooner or later.' Looks like sooner for me. Um… the money I saved, that you been… banking for me. You know who to give it to."

"Yes."

"That's who it was for anyways. But don't… not right away, or she won't take it. Might not anyway, but… better chance if you wait awhile. Maybe till summer." A cloud passed over Hugh's eyes, then he focused again. He squeezed John's hand and gave him a smile. "Look, Da, you're like Donald… Fine fellas, but… I prob'ly had more fun in twenty years than both you will in eighty."

Hugh closed his eyes again. John sat holding his son's hand in both of his. He couldn't tell what time of night it was when the pink froth stopped coming out of Hugh's mouth.

CHAPTER 57

Janet Sutherland sat in her kitchen, looking through the parlour doorway at the sealed coffin resting on sawhorses. Last night she'd washed her dead son's body and dressed him in his Sunday clothes, with the help of his two oldest sisters. The first dead man's body she'd washed and dressed had been her grandfather's, helping her mother and grandmother. His skin had been wrinkled and saggy; Hugh's smooth and soft. Except for the pads of callus on the palms of Hugh's hands from working, and on the soles of his feet from wearing moccasins instead of thick-soled boots, and on the ball of his right thumb from tamping his smouldering pipe. Thin white scar lines had told part of the story of his life: across his right shin where he'd fallen out of a tree and limped home with his trouser leg soaked in blood, along his left forearm where he'd driven the bucksaw too hard and the blade had snapped and sprung back at him…

Janet's husband came into the house and said: "It's time, Mother – Dr. Black is coming up the path." Janet stood up and so did all her children, who'd been sitting silently around the table. They donned their coats and cloaks, and the rest waited while John, Donald, Aleck and Morrison lifted the coffin and carried it outside. Janet followed the coffin, and the rest of the children followed her. Dr. Black was waiting outside, with his clerical robe on over his coat, and he led the way toward the path down to the river.

When they'd cleared the farmyard and Janet caught her first glimpse of the river, she thought her eyes were playing tricks on her. The river was dark, but it should still be white with snow. It couldn't possibly have melted overnight. Then she saw that the river was still covered with ice and snow, but the ice and snow were covered with people, from bank to bank and all the way back around Point Douglas, waiting to walk in the funeral procession.

Not all of them would walk, though. There were a few cart-sleds filled with people too old or infirm to walk the miles to the kirk. But there was one very old- but very spry-looking woman standing leaning on a walking staff: the Widow Lagimodière, Hugh's grandmother's old friend, and grandmother to Louis Riel. Beside and behind Madame Lagimodière's black-cloaked figure was a swath of softer colour: the Grey Nuns.

The funeral procession had barely gone twenty paces when Dr. Black raised his staff and called: "Relief!" The four men walking beside John, Donald, Aleck and Morrison slid their shoulders in under the coffin, John and the boys stepped back, and four other men came forward as the next relief. *Relief* was called again about one minute later, and every minute or two all the way to the kirk; it was the only way that all the men who'd come to help carry the coffin could have their turn.

At the graveside, after Janet had crumbled her handful of frozen earth down onto the coffin, she noticed something beyond the crowd, something silhouetted against the vast white sweep of winter prairie and cloud-shrouded sky. It was a smallish figure on an Indian pony, and it might've been a statue except that the horse's mane and the rider's long hair were floating in the wind. The wind was blowing in that direction from the direction of the cemetery, so the rider had placed herself where the hymns and prayers of the burial would be carried to her.

Janet put her hand on John's shoulder and said: "Excuse me, I just have to… I'll be back." Janet stepped out of the crowd and started to walk out onto the prairie. But as soon as the rider saw someone coming toward her, she wheeled her pony and galloped away.

Dr. Black had offered to give Janet and John a ride home in his cutter, along with as many of their children as could be squeezed on. As the Point Douglas Sutherlands approached the cutter, Dr. Black was standing with his daughter Margaret – Catherine's schoolfriend – who was crying: "But why did it have to be one of *our* men?"

Dr. Black said gently, "If it had been the son of a family outside of Kildonan, dear, it would have brought grief to some hearts all the same."

When the cutter pulled into the Sutherlands' yard, Dr. Black said: "I'll go back for the rest of the children and Henrietta and then stay here for the day."

Janet said: "Thank you." The day was going to be a succession of people bringing biscuits and pies and condolences. Although the condolences were likely to be more felt than spoken. At the funeral, more than any of the many funerals Janet had attended, people had seemed to find it impossible to say anything, except to mutter something almost unintelligible, then shake their heads and look at the ground. The closest thing to coherent had been one of the Kirk Elders murmuring that the only blessing was that 'Kate and Sandy didnae live to see this.'

The first cargo of Sutherlands from Dr. Black's cutter had barely got in the door – Janet had barely got the youngest children's coats off, and John had barely got the fire built up – when other sleighbells came into the yard and the dogs started barking. John murmured: "I didn't think it'd start this soon…"

But it wasn't anybody from the funeral, it was A.G.B. Bannatyne and Vickie McVicar. Miss Victoria McVicar was the daughter of an aunt of Janet's who'd married an HBC man who'd spent most of his career in eastern Rupert's Land. Janet found it just a bit coincidental that Vickie McVicar had chosen this year to make her first visit to her many cousins at Red River, the same year Rupert's Land was due to be transferred to Canada. Her father's death had left the family poorly off, and she'd been supporting them by claiming and selling land around Thunder Bay. Whatever the reasons for her visit, in her short time at Red River Vickie McVicar had already established a reputation for being a bit… flamboyant.

Mr. Bannatyne said: "Mr. Sutherland, Mrs. Sutherland. My apologies for not being at the funeral. The only thing that could've prevented me was trying to prevent other killings."

Vickie McVicar blared tearfully, "He means to murder them!"

Janet rubbed her forehead and muttered: "What? Who?"

"Captain Boulton and Thomas Scott and two other Canadians! Riel means to stand them up in front of a firing squad! He calls it execution, but it's cold-blooded, heartless murder!"

Mr. Bannatyne rolled his eyes at the theatrical way it had been put, but nodded that it was true. Janet did have a vague awareness that the day after Hugh had been shot, the men from Portage la Prairie and Headingley were on their way back to their homes when Ambroise Lépine led a force out of Fort Garry and made them all prisoners. Some people said that the Provisional Government had broken its promise of safe passage, some said that if the Portage and Headingley men had travelled in twos and threes instead of an armed mass, and not passed threateningly near Fort Garry, they would've been allowed to go their way. Either way, it hadn't been the first thing on Janet's mind the past couple of days, or her heart.

Mr. Bannatyne said: "I've tried to talk Riel out of it, so has Donald A. Smith, so has the Bishop and several others… he won't listen to anybody. But he would at least *listen* to the mother and father of Hugh Sutherland." Janet looked at her husband, who was looking at her. "The executions might be carried out today."

Janet said wearily, "Margaret, I'm afraid you and Catherine will have to manage tea and such for any visitors for a while. But Mrs. Black will be here soon, and I'm sure she'll be willing to take charge till your father and I get back."

A.G.B. Bannatyne's cutter was naturally an illustrious affair, with both a front and a back seat, and a matched team instead of a one-horse sleigh. Normally the two men would've sat up front and talked business, but Janet and John had stayed as close as possible ever since Montrose galloped back into the yard alone. So Mr. Bannatyne explained the situation over his shoulder, keeping one eye on the reins, "It's not just Riel – although of course he's the decision-maker. There's more than a few in the Provisional Government who think Schultz and his ilk will keep on agitating trouble until the whole settlement goes up in flames, unless something drastic is done. And who's to say they're wrong? But this isn't the way to go about it. They hoped to get Schultz and Mair when they bagged the Portage men, but they'll settle for Boulton and Scott and a couple of others who've made themselves conspicuous."

Although Janet found it beyond unfair that she should be forced to think of any lives today except her dead son's and his devastated brothers' and sisters', part of her found it a relief that anything could drag her out of that place for even a moment. Mostly, though, she found it unfathomable that anyone could think of killing anyone.

As Dr. Black had said, 'it would have brought grief to some hearts just the same.'

The gates of Fort Garry were open, but a number of sentries were patrolling the opening. One of them stepped in front of the cutter and raised his arm, while the others raised their guns. The leader shouted: "Damn, I told you two! No come back today!" and then his eyes caught who was sitting behind the two in the front seat. He took off his hat and lowered his head, stepped aside and waved the cutter into the fort. As the sleigh passed through the gates, the other sentries took off their hats and made the sign of the cross or kissed their crucifixes. One of them murmured something in an Indian language Janet didn't understand but was quite sure Hugh would have.

When the cutter pulled up in front of the headquarters of the Provisional Government, Mr. Bannatyne said: "You two go in, Miss McVicar and I will wait here." Vickie McVicar started to protest, but Mr. Bannatyne said firmly, "We'll wait here."

Inside the foyer of what had been Dr. Cowan's house, there was now a table with two guards facing the door. The sheet of paper on the table was probably a list of who was allowed to pass today. When the guards saw who was approaching the table, they both stood up and neither of them looked at the list. John said: "We are here to see Monsieur Riel, if that's possible."

"But of course. Please come with me." He led them down the hallway and knocked on a door.

A voice from beyond the door said: "Not now."

The guard said to the door, "It is Monsieur and Madame Sutherland, of Point Douglas."

A moment later the door was opened by Louis Riel, who said: "Come in, come in, please. Do sit down." He pushed two chairs closer to the desk he'd been working at. "May I call for anything for you? Tea, sherry…?"

John said: "Thank you, but we can't stay long, we have people coming to our house…"

"Of course, of course. I wish… I pride myself on my facility with eloquent words, but I can only vainly wish I had words to say how very, very sorry I am for the tragedy that has befallen your family, and the loss of your fine son."

Janet said: "Thank you."

"He is with le bon dieu now. Regardless what the priests may tell us, He cares more for what is in a man's heart than what he wears around his neck. And John Hugh Sutherland had the best of hearts. I would have come to the funeral, but it would only have caused trouble."

John said: "We understand."

Janet said: "Your grandmother was there."

"Ah. So she would be." President Riel went and sat behind his desk and said: "So, what is it that brings you to come and see me on such a day?"

John said: "Captain Boulton, Thomas Scott and the other two condemned men. Hasn't there been enough killing?"

"Ah. I am… deeply touched," and it seemed he truly was, "that you two should care about the fates of strangers when you have just buried your son. But his has been the first blood shed in all the months since the National Committee took Fort Garry, and his death was caused by these men and others who are still at large. They must be stopped."

John said: "You have them imprisoned already, where they can do no harm."

"They have all escaped before – all but Captain Boulton, who has not been our prisoner before." Louis Riel stood up and planted one fist on his desk and the other on his hip. "As long as these men believe there are no consequences to their actions, they will continue to foment trouble, and more innocents will die. Because it is always the innocents who die, while those who set the catastrophe in motion continue to hide and plot and scheme and pursue their ends. And what are their ends? To convince Canada and the United States and France, and *all* those who covet our land, that we who live here are like a pack of wild dogs snapping and tearing at each others' throats, a pack yearning and clamouring for any foreign master to tame us and train us to his will."

Watching and listening to Louis Riel, Janet tried to remember all she could of him and his family, trying to think of a way to reach him. Although she didn't doubt the stories that he'd been devastated by his father's death, he had grown up as his mother's jewel, and the bond between mother and son was as sacred to him as Mary and Jesus.

Janet stood up out of her chair, then propped one hand on the desk to ease the bending of knees grown creaky from scrubbing too many floors. She knelt down in front of Louis Riel and said: "Please, give me those four men's lives in exchange for my son's."

He put his hand over his eyes, and she could see his dimpled chin trembling. When he reached his hand down to help her to her feet, it was wet with tears. He said with some difficulty, "Mrs. Sutherland, you have saved three lives today… But," his voice grew firmer, "Captain Boulton must die. He has caused the death of a son of this country and must pay for it."

Janet looked into the dark, moist eyes and didn't say what she was thinking: *"'Caused the death of'…? And who was it caused Norbert Parisien to be kicked-out of Fort Garry, and set the catastrophe in motion?"* There was no point in saying it. Either he'd said it to himself already, or he would never hear it. She had a feeling that, somewhere inside him, the grandson of Marie-Anne Lagimodière had counted back the steps that killed the grandson of Kate MacPherson.

John said: "We must be getting home." As Janet and her husband walked arm-in-arm back down the hallway, President Riel called out a name and one of the guards came running past them to the office doorway. Janet could only hear a general murmuring of the President's instructions, but thought she'd distinctly picked-out 'Smith.'

Back in the cutter, John announced: "All but Captain Boulton have been reprieved, thanks to my wife."

Vickie McVicar wailed: "But what of Captain Boulton?"

Mr. Bannatyne said: "Three lives in one day is miracle enough," and clucked the horses into motion.

Once the cutter was back skimming along the river, John said to Janet, in what she suspected was a quieter voice than he would've used if Mr. Bannatyne's had been the only ears in the front seat, "I think you may have saved four, my dear. I've become fairly well acquainted with Louis Riel fils over the winter. He doesn't like to give away his trumps for nothing, even when he's planning to give them away. And I could see he could see what you were thinking after he gave his speech about why Captain Boulton must die."

"Oh? What was I thinking?"

"The same thing I was."

The next day, the news shot through the whole settlement that Captain Boulton would not be shot after all. A few days later, when the Provisional Government had started sitting again, John came home from Fort Garry and told Janet: "As I said about *four* lives, and trumps… Apparently, immediately after you and I spoke to President Riel, he summoned Donald A. Smith and said he was considering giving a reprieve to Captain Boulton, but what would Smith give in return? Donald A. Smith pledged to do all he can to make the Dominion Government agree to the List of Rights the delegates will carry to Ottawa. Then, and only then, did President Riel announce that Captain Boulton would be spared."

Janet nodded and *'hm-ed'* but she had more important matters to deal with. Like getting the children adjusted to sitting at different places around the table. It had happened more than a few times before, but until now – except for the deaths of their grandmother and grandfather – places had only been shuffled when a new child grew big enough to sit at the table.

CHAPTER 58

The door to Schultz's borrowed bedroom crashed open and he bolted upright, blinking. He'd expected to be wakened early, but not this rudely. A certain halfbreed gentleman who'd done work for him in the past had agreed to take him east by dogsled via the old voyageur route, as far as Duluth on the nose of Lake Superior. Any direct route to St. Paul and the railhead would be watched by Ambroise Lépine's patrols. Even taking the back trails, Schultz and his guide would have to leave while it was still dark and be well away from Red River before sunrise.

Oddly, though, the room wasn't entirely dark, although the light didn't seem to be coming from anywhere in particular. And the man in the doorway was neither Schultz's eccentric old duffer of a host, nor the halfbreed gentleman Schultz was expecting. The man was definitely a halfbreed, though, and Schultz thought for a second he'd been trapped and should snatch the revolver from under his pillow and sell his life as dearly as possible. But this halfbreed wasn't one he'd ever seen before, and he definitely would've remembered seeing this one.

The man was as tall as Schultz, but wider and heavier, filling the doorway like Ambroise Lépine – but it wasn't Ambroise Lépine. This one's black hair was cut shorter than Lépine's, and his broad-boned, oval face was clean-shaven. He was wearing a fringed and quill-worked deerskin jacket cut in imitation of an old-style European coat. Underneath it was a white linen shirt and neckloth from the days before Victoria was Queen.

Oddly, standing in the upstairs hallway, behind the man in the doorway, was a horse. A white horse with red eyes – perhaps some kind of albino effect. Odder still, the man's eyes looked somewhat like a normal horse's: slightly slanted, big, dark and alien. The dark eyes stayed focused on Schultz in a disconcerting way, unblinking and unfathomable.

Schultz opened his mouth to say *'What do you want?'* but before he could get a word out the man had crossed the room in two strides and fastened his hand over Schultz's mouth and nose. Schultz tried to pull away, but the grip of thumb and fingers held him, digging cruelly into both sides of his face. He battered his fists against the arm beyond the hand, but it was like punching an oak tree. He was suffocating –

"Dr. Schultz?" There was a knocking at the door. "Dr. Schultz, are you all right?"

Schultz awoke to discover he'd somehow got the edge of the quilt stuck in his mouth and draped over his nose. He spat it out and laughed at himself.

"Dr. Schultz...?" The voice beyond the door was Joseph Monkman's, the halfbreed gentleman Schultz was expecting. Schultz called back that he'd be down directly, dressed himself quickly, tucked his revolver in the waistband of his trousers and went downstairs.

On his way downstairs, Schultz still clung to the faint hope that the murder of a Kildonan boy by a Metis had finally tipped the Kildonan men out of their torpor, and he wouldn't have to flee. The hope was based on sound principle. A Scotsman working on the lake boats had once explained to him how clan feuds could go on for centuries: *'Ye kill my parents, or my brothers, maybe someday I can forgive ye and we can hae peace. Ye kill my children, I never forgive ye.'*

Schultz's host was sitting at one end of the kitchen table in a velvet smoking jacket and a tasselled fez. Monkman was sitting at the other end, with his coat and dog whip waiting on the floor beside him. The dog whip meant nothing had changed overnight; the men of Kildonan couldn't even be roused by the murder of one of their children.

The host gestured at an empty chair and said: "You have enough time for a spot of breakfast and some strong tea and a noggin before you have to set off. Um, Monkman tells me you were sounding... agitated, when he went to wake you."

"Oh," Schultz chuckled it off, "just an agitating dream."

"Ah, then I see Queen Mab hath come to visit you."

"Who?"

"Shakespeare," his host elucidated. "Mischievous Queen Mab brings agitating dreams to people. Such as dreams of battles to a soldier, or of hefty fees to a lawyer, that sort of thing."

"Well, in this case it was Queen Quilt. I dreamt a man had his hand over my mouth and was suffocating me, and when I woke up I found I'd got the corner of the quilt stuck in my mouth." Schultz laughed and the others laughed with him. "Wonderful the impossibilities we take for granted when we're dreaming. The man had a white horse standing behind him in your upstairs hallway, and I didn't think twice about it."

The host said, in mock alarm, "Dear, dear, I'd best go get the stable scoop and see if the stairs need cleaning up."

Schultz laughed and his host laughed with him, but Joseph Monkman didn't this time. Monkman said in a quirkily thoughtful way, "A white horse...?"

"Yes, a white horse with red eyes. Well, what's a night-mare without a horse?"

"This man," Monkman said carefully, "what he look like?"

"Well..." Schultz was a bit surprised that Monkman seemed actually interested in hearing about it. Telling people about what one dreamt last night was usually the fastest way to bring on yawns. "He was a big man, as tall as me, but," Schultz basketed his right hand out around the end of his left shoulder to show the heft. "He was dressed half-Indian and half-civilized, but of a very old style."

"Strong man?" Monkman crooked-up his right arm and fist, as though making a muscle.

"Well, I guess people in dreams can be as strong as they like. This one was, well, physically strong, yes." Schultz didn't want to get into the embarrassing detail that he'd felt like a child in that grip on his face, and battering helplessly against that implacable dream-arm.

"This man, he was…" Monkman furled a hand around his own beard, "clean-shaved?"

Schultz nodded. Monkman and Schultz's host looked at each other, and Schultz got the feeling that if they'd both been Catholic they would've crossed themselves. Very odd behaviour. Odder still, the host lowered his head perplexedly and muttered to the tabletop, "There are more things in heaven and earth…"

Monkman turned back to Schultz. "This man have big, dark eyes?"

"Yes." That was no great leap of intuition, since he'd more-or-less said already that the man in the dream was a halfbreed.

"And them eyes, the face, the expression, when they look at you, you can't tell if he gonna offer you a cup of tea or stick a knife in you…"

"Why yes, something like that. I wouldn't necessarily have put it that way, but now that you do –"

Monkman stood up and said: "We go now."

"But –"

"Now. We go."

Schultz looked to his host, who was sitting far back in his chair looking distracted. His host said to the air, in Schultz's general direction, "Yes, I believe Mr. Monkman is right, best thing is for you to get away from here immediately."

Outside, the dogs were already hitched to the carriole and waiting. Schultz shoehorned his long legs and torso into the buffalo-robe-padded carriole. Which seemed appropriate, since the conveyance was shaped somewhat like a shoe. He wished he could've said good-bye to Agnes – for that matter, wished she could've come along. But he was sure she'd be safe alone at Red River, and he intended to return soon and not alone.

Monkman crouched in the snow, lashing on his snowshoes as though the hounds of hell were coming after his dog team. Schultz said: "There's no need to panic, we'll be far out of sight before sunrise."

Monkman said: "Sunrise ain't in it. We get as far away as we can as fast as we can. That was no Queen Mab come visit you, or King Mab or Prince Mab or any kind of Mab. That was Mister Grant."

CHAPTER 59

Two weeks after burying his son, John Sutherland rode to Fort Garry on a day when the Provisional Government wasn't sitting, and on an errand he didn't wish to take on but felt compelled to. He left Montrose in the fort stables and walked past Dr. Cowan's house – rather, the Headquarter of the Provisional Government – to the warehouse which had been housing prisoners since Fort Schultz fell.

John said to the Captain of Ten whose squad had pulled jail duty: "I've come to speak with one of the prisoners, if that's possible."

"Which one?"

"Thomas Scott."

"Oh, Monsieur Sutherland, I don't think you want to do that. He don't speak pleasant."

"He might to me. Anyway, I have to at least try to see if I can calm things down. If you'll allow me."

"Monsieur Sutherland, no one here can refuse you anything – nor should they."

Thomas Scott, like Dr. Schultz before him, was being held in a separate cell from all the other prisoners, but in Scott's case it was because he'd come down with dysentery. The Captain called two of his Ten to come along, shrugging at John, "You never know, if only one guard opens the door Scott might try to bolt, or give him a punch or a push – better to try and make Scott think twice."

When they got to the bolted door, the Captain knocked and called: "Monsieur Scott, you have a visitor."

A brassy shout came back from inside: "What – one of your Papist so-called-men in a black dress and necklace? Come to convert me?"

"It is Monsieur John Sutherland." The voice inside went quiet. "Please to stand away from the door."

The captain unbolted the door, and the two guards braced themselves for whatever might happen when he swung it open. Nothing did. John stepped inside and the door closed behind him.

It was a small room with a barred window and a foul smell. The only furnishings were a bed on the floor and a cloth-draped, footstool-sized object in one corner that John assumed to be a chamberpot. Thomas Scott was standing against the wall opposite the door. John's vague remembrance of him was of a very tall, raw-boned, sun-flushed young man, with even bigger hands than the rest of his size would suggest. Now he looked gaunt, but maybe that was just the scraggly, prisoner's beard.

Scott said: "My condolences, Mister Sutherland, on the loss of your son."

"Thank you."

"I knew him, you know, worked on the road gang with him."

"I know. He said you were the only foreman who worked harder than any man on his crew."

Scott tightened his mouth and ducked his head, then said hoarsely: "He was a good lad, never a word of complaint. But the damn Frogs'll pay for his death when an army from Canada comes calling – and I do mean *when*. I worked on the east end of the road, too, at Thunder Bay, so I know the territory and I know it can be done. It'll be hard slogging, but our boys can do it."

"Well, I'm hoping it needn't come to that. Things are peaceful here now, and our delegates will be on their way to Ottawa soon, so –"

Scott didn't seem to hear him, but cut in with: "Excuse me for not offering you a chair, but," he raised his voice to a blare, "those brave buffalo-hunters are afraid to let me have anything I might crush their skulls with!"

John took a step farther into the cell and said: "No matter, I don't expect to be here long." He started to take a deep breath before plunging to the point, but then, given the air in the cell, curtailed it to a medium-deep breath. "Mr. Scott –"

"Tom, sir."

"Tom… I came here to try and prevent another killing. I've had word that the Provisional Government, or rather the National Committee, is considering putting you on trial for insubordination, treason to the standing government… basically being an incorrigible troublemaker. The penalty is death."

Thomas Scott laughed and stepped forward to clap one hand on John's shoulder. "I appreciate your concern, Mr. Sutherland, I truly do. I don't doubt the Frogs've been making the kinds of noises you say, but it's just blowhard threats."

"Tom…" John pinched the bridge of his nose and squeezed his eyes shut, to focus himself on getting through a wall that was even thicker than he'd imagined. "These men don't make threats – if you're lucky you get a warning. Out on the buffalo hunt, one man who refuses to do as the Captain of the Hunt says can endanger the whole caravan. Out there, the rules of the hunt have to be as stark and merciless as the prairie. That's the kind of law they live by."

"Have you ever been out on the buffalo hunt?"

"No, but –"

"There, you see, you only have their word for how brave and tough and dangerous it all is. Just gas."

"Was it just gas when the National Committee issued permission for anyone to shoot Dr. Schultz on sight? Dr. Schultz is out of their reach now, but you're not."

"But nobody actually *did* shoot Dr. Schultz, did they?" Scott smiled and shook his head slowly. "I don't mean to argue with you, Mr. Sutherland, and I really am, uh, touched that you're worried about me – 'specially given your… circumstances. I'm just trying to tell you there's nothing to worry about."

John searched for another tack. "Tom, I'm told that a week or so ago, when you were still housed with the other prisoners, you so annoyed two of the guards that they dragged you outside. What do you think they meant to do with you?"

"Prob'ly lay a beating on me. But then they saw there was only two of 'em so they thought better of it."

"They meant to *kill* you, and then thought better of it. I'm told that the prisoners are constantly jostling the guards, insulting them – more or less spitting on them – and it's your lead the other prisoners are following. The Metis aren't used to taking that sort of thing meekly. It's amazing their patience has lasted this long. It may be that the only two choices Louis Riel has facing him, are an execution or a murder."

Thomas Scott grinned and cracked his knuckles. "I'd like to see them try. Even half-weak with the bloody shits, it'd be a mistake for any of 'em to try conclusions with me."

"Tom, with all respect, on the best day of your life, if Ambroise Lépine stepped through that door alone and barehanded, when he opened the door again there'd be nothing left of you but a sack of broken bones."

"With all respect, Mr. Sutherland, I doubt it." Scott went to the window, looked out and tugged on the bars. "Damn Frogs even make sure they take back the spoon after my bowl of swill, afraid I'll use it to chisel out the bars. That's how brave they are."

"Tom, my wife and I have already saved your life once, when you and Captain Boulton and two others were slated for execution –"

"I appreciate that, I truly do. But Riel and his gang wouldn't've actually gone through with it. They wouldn't dare."

John looked at the corners of the room for inspiration and didn't find any. He'd never been any good at convincing people to see things his way, he'd learned to just let them have theirs. But sometimes plain facts worked. He said: "I won't argue with you about what might or might not've happened then. But this situation is different. If things keep on going the way they're going, pretty soon some guard is going to stick a knife into some prisoner's guts, and once it's happened once… If you get executed, though, the other prisoners will think twice about aggravating their guards. And that would solve the problem.

"But you could solve the situation and still save your life. They don't mean to keep you locked up here forever. I'm sure all the prisoners will be released as soon as the Provisional Government's delegates reach Ottawa, and word comes back that talks are in progress. After all, that's what you and the other Canadians want, isn't it, for Rupert's Land to be part of the Dominion? So then there'd be nothing to fight about."

Thomas Scott looked sceptical.

"So if, for the short while till then, you just accepted the temporary fact of being a prisoner – because you're going to win out in the not-very-long-run anyway – and treated your guards with respect, the other prisoners would follow suit."

"I'm already treating those bastards with the respect they deserve. Oh, bloody hell!" Scott's face contorted and he sprang toward the chamberpot in the corner. John turned his head discreetly, but that didn't shut out the sounds and smells. A few moments later, Thomas Scott went to the door carrying the steaming chamberpot and bellowed: "Hey, shitmonkeys! The chamberpot's full! Better take it away and mix it with the swill you feed us!"

The door opened, and one of the guards waiting with the Captain reached in to take the chamberpot. John couldn't think of any more convincing words to say, so he decided to take advantage of the open door to leave. But he paused on the threshold and said to Thomas Scott: "By the way, Norbert Parisien died two days ago."

"Who?"

A few mornings later, word travelled through Red River that Thomas Scott was going to be executed by firing squad at noon, on the open ground in front of Fort Garry. John heard later, from the minister who'd attended the last hours, that Thomas Scott didn't believe they were actually going to do it until they put the blindfold over his eyes.

John shocked himself by realising that he didn't really much care whether somebody shot Thomas Scott or not. Except insofar as it might affect Red River's negotiations with Canada. He heard that when Donald A. Smith had made a last-chance attempt to get Scott a reprieve, Louis Riel had said: "We must make Canada respect us," which didn't make any sense that John could see. But then, in the last few weeks he'd given up hope of finding any sense in anything. Maybe in time he'd find it again.

CHAPTER 60

On a fine spring evening in the city of Toronto, Schultz stood on the steps of City Hall with Charles Mair, looking out over a crowd of some five thousand citizens. The meeting was originally to be held in St. Lawrence Hall, but by the time it had been due to start the hall was packed to the rafters, literally – some enterprising souls had climbed up to perch in the porticoes because there was no standing room left – and thousands more people waiting outside. So the meeting had been moved to the grounds in front of City Hall, where the Mayor was currently in the process of introducing the lions of the day.

The Mayor made stirring reference to Dr. Schultz's heroic snowshoe journey through hundreds of miles of trackless wilderness, on a leg injured in his escape from unlawful imprisonment. Schultz didn't demur. Although he'd spent most of the trip skimming along in the carriole, Monkman had been on snowshoes, so it had been a snowshoe journey. The germane point was that the arduous odyssey had been undertaken to bring the truth of the situation at Red River to the people of Ontario. Mair had garnered his own experience of dogsledding, taking a wide arc south-east from Portage la Prairie to St. Paul, and his guides had only got lost once along the way.

The Mayor was hitting his rhetorical stride: "Another reason I agreed to the requisition for this meeting, is the murder of Thomas Scott!" The crowd erupted. "Yes, I will call it by its right name, a foul and unnatural murder!" The crowd surged even louder with the appropriate emotions, and on that high note the Mayor introduced Charles Mair. Mair made rather a botch of it. He was a poet, not an orator, and he was under the impression that the crowd would be interested in hearing a general overview of the geography and population of Red River. It wasn't.

Mair did manage to get a stir out of the audience, but in an unfortunate way. "The French are drunk with power and bloodlust and stolen liquor. Jesuitical Fenianism rules at Red River today, and must be crushed! With the murder of Thomas Scott, the French have rung their own death knell!"

Schultz could perfectly understand how a man could get a bit bloodyminded after getting roughed-up, imprisoned and chased through the snow by a pack of French halfbreeds. But he wished Mair had kept in mind that this meeting would undoubtedly be reported in Quebec newspapers, where French voters elected Members of Parliament, and that many of the French at Red River could be very useful in the future.

Mair went back to geography, and Schultz could feel the crowd's attention drifting. As Mair trailed off, the Mayor stepped forward and proclaimed: "Citizens of The Great City of Toronto, I give you… Doctor… John… Christian… Schultz!"

The long and enthusiastic ovation gave Schultz time to look over the assemblage. It looked different from the front of the platform than the back. There were prosperous-looking men of business, ruddy-faced farmers and dockworkers, the well-tailored scions of old money… every segment of the city. It was by far the biggest audience he'd ever had to address, and definitely outnumbered the gathering in the courtyard of Fort Garry, when he'd watched from his window of frustration while Donald A. Smith and Louis Riel spoke uncontradicted. Well, it was his turn now.

As a lucky charm, Schultz conjured up the memory of Agnes telling him he underestimated the effect his height and gold hair and strong voice had on a crowd: *'You don't have to capture their attention, just use it.'* And he reminded himself he'd mentally rehearsed what he was going to say a hundred times, along the trail and on the train, leaving room for extemporizations.

He began with some gallows humour, about the forty pound reward Riel had offered for his capture, and the rope that had been prepared for his neck in Fort Garry. "But although I had serious apprehensions of catching a very sore throat then, there is no danger to it now – in fact, I never was in better voice in my life."

That brought laughter and applause. He definitely had them now, just a question of what to do with them.

"The current situation at Fort Garry is simply this: the Fenian flag floats from its flagstaff."

That brought hisses and curses and shouts of *"We'll tear it down!"*

"The rebels hold high revelry within Fort Garry's walls, while," Schultz's voice naturally dropped deeper into his chest with emotion, "Canadians lie in dungeons underneath." He raised his voice again, "It was to tell this to the people of Canada that I made a long and wearisome journey, and to ask you what you intend to do about the matter."

Someone shouted: *"We'll hang Riel!"* and a roar of approbation went up.

"But, in manifesting your very just wrath, and in speaking of the people of Red River, I caution you against falling into what seems to be a general error, of charging all the halfbreeds of Red River with this most atrocious crime. I would like to point out that it was not the halfbreeds, but a very mere section of that people, who by their utter want of energy in every walk of life had failed to draw notice to themselves. No one knew Riel or O'Donoghue eight months ago – they belong to this class. It must be distinctly understood that at least four hundred French halfbreeds today are loyal, and will join any force that will go to Red River to put down the rebellion."

The cheers were cut through by a very sharp voice demanding: *"But what did Mr. Mair say?"*

Charles Mair stepped forward for long enough to say: "Um, some of my remarks must have been misunderstood. There is a very considerable portion of the French people who are industrious and in comfortable circumstances, and that section has always been loyal. When I, um, spoke of the French in context of the rebellion, I of course, um, only referred entirely to those of Riel's party."

Schultz took back the floor to deal with the rumour that the Indian tribes would harass and attack any Canadian force marching from the head of Lake Superior to Red River. "Amongst the blackest of Riel's lies, this is the darkest. He cannot get one Indian to join him, for the simple fact that his interests and theirs are antagonistic. The halfbreeds claim a title to the lands. This is quite clearly understood by the Indians, and they see quite clearly that two parties cannot be paid for the same property." And Schultz had already paid for a considerable amount of property from said Indians, at least on paper.

"My reason for taking the route I did, from Red River to The Lakehead, was especially to find out this matter clearly. Although I already knew those Indians well, and have sent trappers among them, I wanted to go to their camps myself and find out their sentiments towards Canada. I went amongst them, ate with them, slept in their wigwams, and conversed with them..." There truthfully had been more than a few times along the trail when he and Monkman stumbled across a hunting camp that offered them food and shelter for the night. "... and I assure you that between Lake Superior and Red River, Riel cannot get a single Indian, but the Government of Canada can at any time, on asking them, obtain their aid in every possible way. In a hundred ways in which Indians must be employed, we can command their services."

There was a raft of cheers for the Noble Red Man, and the even nobler white man who'd gone among them.

"I could tell you many important things with respect to the origins of the insurrection, but it would involve very grave charges against certain parties –"

There were shouts of: *"Let us hear them!"*

"But, as I purpose to bring them up before the public, and maybe in the presence of those I now address, I will make no accusations against anybody."

A voice cried: *"What about Howe?"*

Schultz couldn't have planted it better; it was a phrase that would stick in people's minds. It was a well-known fact that the Secretary of State for the Provinces had kept Nova Scotia out of Confederation until the Dominion offered better terms; it was a well-known fact that Joseph Howe had visited Red River on the eve of the rebellion; and it was rumoured that Howe had encouraged the rebels-to-be to believe that Ottawa would only respect what it had to. Despite Agnes's high opinion of her husband's oratorical skills, Schultz wasn't about to try conclusions with Joseph Howe. But, the more credence given to the rumour, the more awkward it would be for Howe to push the government toward ratifying the rebels' ridiculous List of Rights.

Schultz responded to the salubrious interjection with: "I will enter into no accusation now, for nothing is to be gained by looking at the past, it is better to look forward to the future. If I know the Canadians right, the snow will not cover the ground next fall before they have possession of Red River. What Canadians can not do, I hold, cannot be done at all. We are told it is impossible to go from Superior to Red River Settlement by boat, and over the really good road the Government is making. Such a statement is a lie. What men have done, men can do, and especially Canadian men.

"Twenty years ago when the route was entirely unimproved, troops were taken over it by bark canoes…" Schultz was perfectly aware that the Royal Canadian Rifles had travelled to Red River by the other route, in The Company's York Boats after taking ship to York Factory on Hudson's Bay. But he doubted there were any veterans present, and if there were the crowd was in no mood for listening to quibbles. "… and now that the route is being improved and with the preparations that are being made by Government, troops can easily be transported to the territory, and once there, will put a speedy end to Riel's reign."

"What about coming back?"

"There is no need to think of that, for when people go to Red River and see the country they have no desire to return to Canada." Especially since the Dominion Government would provide desirable homestead land to any soldier of the Red River Expedition who chose to stay there, land that the government would first have to purchase from whoever currently held title, at least on paper.

"What about the climate?"

"I am a native of the western part of Canada," Amherstburg truly was as west as Canada went before now, "and all of you know what kind of climate we have there. The winter is a succession of snows and thaws and frosts and miserable changes, but in Red River there is nothing of the sort. The mercury sometimes falls to thirty or thirty-five degrees below zero, but it is not thought anything of, for it is a steady, dry cold, preferable to the climate at Toronto. With regard to agriculture I need only remark that the average of the wheat crop over the country is thirty-five bushels to the acre.

"I beg you to accept my hearty thanks for your kind attention –"

He was interrupted by cries of *"Go on!"* which could've been interpreted in different ways, but Schultz was quite sure it had gone off well and all that was left was the rousing finish:

"I will speak to you again on coming back from Ottawa. It was from Ontario this movement to add Red River to the Dominion commenced; it is in Ontario this expression of indignation is expressed; and it is to Ontario the Territory properly belongs. I only hope the day is not far distant when Ontario will have peaceable possession of it, and that I will meet many of you in Red River."

The waves of cheers near knocked the seagulls out of the sky.

CHAPTER 61

On a late summer late afternoon, Janet Sutherland sat in the shade behind her house, holding hands with her husband. They were expecting an official visit from an important personage. Since it was a clear day and the mosquitoes not so bad, Janet had set a small table outside with three chairs, and a pitcher of cranberry tea chilled with chips from the icehouse. She'd managed to persuade John to put on his Sunday suit, but he'd dug in his heels at a necktie and left his collar open. As for holding hands, that sort of thing had become a natural habit since the 16th of February. Whenever Janet and her husband happened to be near each other and didn't have to be working at something, one would rest a hand on the other's shoulder, or they'd sit shoulder-to-shoulder or knee-to-knee, or one of their hands would find the other's.

A week earlier Janet had been standing in the pelting rain on the same spot she now was sitting in the sun, and watched the Canadian and British troops beach their boats and form up on Point Douglas. It had taken them all summer to get to Red River through the granite and spruce country west of Superior, but they'd got there. Word had it that when the expedition's boats reached the mouth of the Red at the foot of Lake Winnipeg, Chief Henry Prince had been there to welcome them, hovering his canoe in mid-stream. From Point Douglas the troops had marched in battle order to Fort Garry and found the gates open and no one there but The Company's people. Louis Riel, Ambroise Lépine and W.B. O'Donoghue had scooted out the back door as Colonel Wolseley's soldiers approached the front. Word had it that all three of them were now south of the border.

Colonel Wolseley's army had certainly brought peace, order and good government to Red River. In their frustration at not being able to get their hands on Louis Riel, some of them had chased Elzéar Goulet through the streets of Winnipeg, throwing rocks at him, until he jumped into the river to try to get away from them and drowned. Elzéar was said to be a strong swimmer and likely would've made it, if the soldiers hadn't kept on practising their pitching after he was in the water.

Throwing rocks seemed to be the soldiers' favourite pastime. James Tanner, a half-Ojibway missionary, grandson of the White Indian who'd guided Lord Selkirk's German mercenaries to Red River after Seven Oaks, had picked the wrong day to bring his wagon to Red River for supplies. The soldiers had pelted his horse with stones until it bolted, the wagon overturned and Reverend Tanner was killed in the wreck. François Guillimette had been killed by persons unknown, or at least unidentified. André Nault had been beaten and left for dead, perhaps by the same persons. Bob O'Lone had been killed in a brawl in the Red Dog Saloon, and his brother Hugh had put the place up for sale so he could return to the safety of Hell's Kitchen, New York City. Janet had ordered her children to not go anywhere near Fort Garry as long as the troops were bivouacked there – at least not until the new Lieutenant Governor arrived and there was some sort of law again, maybe.

The dogs jumped up barking and Janet looked to the cart lane that came into the farmyard from the road. A carriage rounded the corner of the house. Janet recognized the carriage. It belonged to St. Boniface Cathedral, and when the priests weren't using it they were willing to rent it out to people from the west side of the river who had business on the east side. She didn't recognise the man driving the carriage, but had no doubt he was the gentleman they were expecting. He was not quite middle-aged, and wearing what someone in the east might think fitting for the west: a khaki safari jacket and a broad-brimmed hat that looked like it had just come out of the box. John got up to greet him, and the dogs went back to soaking up the sun.

After the visitor was sat down and poured a cup of iced cranberry tea and small-talked for a moment, the official personage said: "Unofficially, I've come to inform you of a few matters that will become official once the Lieutenant Governor arrives. By the way, you'll be glad to know that Lieutenant Governor Archibald is a very different kettle of fish from William McDougall. No matter how many titles get put in front of his name, he still wears the same size hat.

"Before I get to the other business, though, I'm surprised you haven't put in a claim for compensation. I would've thought you knew about the federal government's program to compensate losses suffered during the rebellion, since your business partner Dr. Schultz has already put in a claim."

Janet knew John knew that Dr. Schultz had already put in a claim. Everybody at Red River knew, and knew that the amount of business losses he was claiming meant he must've been selling gold bars out the back door of the White Store.

John said, in a measured voice, "I have done some business with Dr. Schultz in the past, but he was never my business partner. I haven't put in a claim for compensation because we suffered no material losses during what you call 'the rebellion.'"

Janet put her hand on top of her husband's resting on the table, official personages and public etiquette bedamned. She knew what John had left unsaid: *'And how could any government or anybody compensate us for what we've lost?'*

The visitor said: "Ah. Well, to the point then... Since Sheriff McKenney is no longer in evidence, the position is open. The Sheriff's office is as much clerical as active – he is authorized to deputise constables whenever a show of force is necessary. We would like the next sheriff to be Mr. John Sutherland."

The gentleman smiled broadly after presenting them with the news, then looked a little disjointed and disappointed, as though he'd expected them to turn cartwheels across the yard. Instead, Janet just turned her head to look at her husband. John looked at her and said: "Should I?"

She said: "I don't see why not. Donald and –" Something caught in her throat, and she had to pause and breathe deeply before continuing, "… the other boys are old enough to handle most of the farm chores now."

John said to the official: "I'll give it a try then, thank you."

"Well, the Sheriff's Office would in fact be only an interim position, for you. You see, since the area around Red River will be entering Confederation as the Province of Manitoba, not just a Territory, it will have several elected representatives to the federal House of Commons. And, two appointed representatives to the national Senate. Senate appointments are for life and carry a very handsome salary – *very* handsome. Senators must spend some time in Ottawa every year, or at least every two years. But it will only be a few years that the two Senators from Manitoba will have to make their way to the railhead in St. Paul, because the Canadian Pacific Railway is fast laying track in the direction of your doorstep.

"Senate appointments are very delicate matters. It must be a man who has the respect and trust of the local population he represents, but has sufficient political sophistication to see the national picture. Now, this is decidedly on the Q.T., Mr. and Mrs. Sutherland," he lined a finger along his nose, "but I'm in the confidence of the personages who will be making those two appointments, and I know they've already made a decision about one of them." He paused to beam. "What would you say to 'Senator John Sutherland'?"

There was a silence of sibilating poplar leaves, the murmur of the river and the distant lowing of pastured cattle. Then Janet's husband said flatly: "I would say to him, 'And what does Norbert Parisien's father get?'"

On the first day of the first school term since 'Canada' and 'Manitoba' became keywords in the curriculum of Kildonan school, Hector MacBeth was taking the roll. He'd listed his pupils' names in ink and would check off their attendance day-by-day in pencil. Halfway through the list, the children started giggling and stifling guffaws. He tapped his pencil against his desk for quiet and looked up to see what they'd been giggling at. At the back of one row, a full-grown, mustached young man was awkwardly squeezing himself into a child-sized desk. Hector MacBeth looked down again, then uncapped his ink bottle and added another name to his list. "Aleck Sutherland…?"

"Present."

Author's Note

It wouldn't be Miss Manners to foist this fat book of historical fiction upon you without touching on the question of how much of it is historical and how much is fiction, (a much more slippery question is how much of history is fiction, but anyway…) First off, the most outrageously theatrical characters in the story, the Schultzes, are the most thoroughly documented. Most of the things that I have them saying and doing in public are a matter of public record: court reports, newspapers, journals, firsthand accounts that can be checked against each other. Of course I had to invent their private moments, but there was a lot to extrapolate from.

What little is known about John Hugh Sutherland is centred around his death. He definitely was at least acquainted with Norbert Parisien, as every account of his deathbed plea for mercy on his killer contains a variation of: "the poor simple fellow was too frightened to know what he was doing." I based the whole notion of Hugh being the wild child of the family, the nature boy, on one tiny fact. Hugh wasn't the oldest son, yet he was the one sent to tell Schultz & Co. that the prisoners were being freed. Donald certainly would've been home with the rest of the worried family when their father finally emerged from Fort Garry. Usually the eldest son is the one entrusted with – saddled with – the important errands; it was certainly like that in my family. So why wasn't Donald sent on this vitally important errand? The likeliest explanation I can see is that Hugh was the roughrider in the family, and if there was any galloping to be done Hugh was the boy to do it.

There are a number of recorded events in the life of Hugh's immediate family that certainly were events in his life, although he isn't recorded as part of them: Alexander Sutherland being the jury foreman who shakily read out the verdict on the Reverend Griffith Owen Corbett; Kate MacPherson breaking her hip, and her too-arthritic-for-church husband building her a wheelchair; Mary Ann dying in infancy; 'Doctor' Schultz's extreme interest in the family property on Point Douglas; etc. etc.

But I must admit under oath that the most important event I've written into Hugh's life – Wauh Oonae Nancy Prince – was a complete invention, although Chief Peguis certainly had enough granddaughters to go around and was definitely acquainted with Hugh's grandparents from the old days, as were the Lagimodières and the fella who became known as simply 'Mr. Grant.' Hugh's brother Donald did marry Christy Matheson on December

21, 1871, once the dust of the 'rebellion' finally settled, so in the preceding years the Point Douglas Sutherland boys had definitely been up to something with some girls somewhere. Most Kildonan boys tended to marry Kildonan girls, but not all, and Red River truly was a place where Presbyterians attended Midnight Mass and the Governor's wife was proudly half Cree. Although Nancy was invented, a lot of her came from descriptions and accounts of Metis and Indian girls of the time.

But some details in this story that may seem fictional, because you'll find them contradicted in some history texts, aren't. A couple of For Instances: Long years ago, an eminent Canadian historian annotated Norbert Parisien as 'b. 1814, d. 1870,' and many later historians – though not all – have simply followed suit. Likewise, the authoritative editorial notes to *Alexander Begg's Red River Journal*, published years after Begg's death, make a point of instructing readers not to confuse Point Douglas John Sutherland with the John Sutherland who lived across the river from Point Douglas and became a senator.

I've never been accused of being a feminist or a soldier in the Herstory crusade, but I have to admit the only way those authoritative mispronouncements could've found their way into print is if the male writers couldn't or wouldn't hear female voices. You see, there's a book called *Women of Red River*, been around a long time, containing the reminiscences of old ladies who'd grown up in the Red River Settlement. One of them, Catherine Black nee Sutherland, clearly explains how her family came to be living across the river from their land on Point Douglas. In remembering her brother's killing (she was thirteen at the time) she refers to "the half-witted and badly frightened young Parisien," which doesn't sound like someone in his mid-fifties. She also says: "I remember Dr. Black (her father-in-law) saying how pitiable an object *young* Parisien was as he saw him lying half unconscious with the blood streaming from a wound in the side of his head which one of the men had given him with a hatchet."

But the worst distortion that's come from ignoring *Women of Red River* has been missing out the reason Hugh Sutherland was riding toward Kildonan kirk that morning. Even historians who aren't big on Sir John Christian Schultz wrote that Hugh just happened to be passing by, or maybe was just nosing around out of curiosity. Catherine's remembrance that her father had sent her brother to tell Schultz/Boulton that all the prisoners were going to be released, changes the whole story.

Now, I'm old enough and have waded through enough contradictory firsthand accounts of historical events to know that people's memories can be faulty. But Mrs. Catherine Black's memory would've had to be more than faulty to mis-recall her family anxiously waiting two or three days and nights while her father was disappeared into Fort Garry, and their jubilation when he reappeared with a whole skin and the good news that the prisoners-crisis was over. Even if Mrs. Black were pathological enough to invent those events, she'd lived out the intervening fifty years in close proximity to her many brothers and sisters, who surely would've called her on it. They also would've called her on her memory that the first thing Captain Boulton did when he was eventually released was come straight to their house and thank her mother for saving his life.

But I do believe Catherine Sutherland Black recollected incorrectly when she said that Norbert Parisien fired twice. Well, she was correctly recollecting what she'd been *told*. The only people who actually saw what happened were the men who chased down Norbert Parisien and beat him to death, or eventual death, and it was very much in their best interests to say that Norbert fired twice, so they were taking revenge for a deliberate murder. The notion that Norbert Parisien fired twice has been repeated so many times with so many variations that nobody's thought to butt it up against the hard fact that a bullet which passes *through* doesn't have the kind of impact that would knock a man off his horse; the impact comes when the bullet stops. The only scenario that makes any logical sense to me is the one I guessed John Sutherland would've guessed: Norbert Parisien fired once, and the bullet passed through Hugh Sutherland's reins-hand and into his chest.

The question of whether Norbert fired once or twice may seem a quibble, but it's emblematic of the way this story has been distorted and covered-over ever since it happened. The rousing speeches Schultz and Mair et al gave in Ontario dwelt heavily on the death of Thomas Scott and rarely, if ever, mentioned the deaths of John Hugh Sutherland and Norbert Parisien. There are still history books around that'll tell you Norbert Parisien just coincidentally happened to die of natural causes some while after being slightly roughed-up while being apprehended. Politically, the actuality of what happened was just too messily complicated and raised uncomfortable questions. And not just politically. The more I've lived with this story, the more it's seemed that the deaths of these two inconsequential young men raise questions of how much us human sapiens actually know about the side consequences of our self-interested actions. Or care.

But if this story were just the story of the sad and stupid deaths of two young guys long ago, I wouldn't've taken up lo these many pages. Their deaths, though, mark the end of the Red River Settlement, and so mark its existence. There are more than enough firsthand accounts by 19th century travellers, and by curmudgeonly locals disappointed that they didn't have much to be curmudgeonly about, to prove I haven't exaggerated the remarkable society that existed there. If anything, I've backpedalled it. There truly was a place where for almost half a century people of very different races, languages and religions lived together in relative harmony with virtually no laws or law enforcement. I am not by nature optimistic about human nature – after all, I'm one myself. So awhile ago I mentioned to my wife that, even after years of studying-up on the people of Red River, I still couldn't figure out how they managed to pull it off. She said: "They were grateful."

I didn't even remotely exaggerate the interest foreign powers took in what was going on at Red River in 1869-70. Paris, Washington and the Fenian Brotherhood were all watching for an opening to come in and take over, and there are plenty of documents to prove it. It truly was a close-run thing (as Wellington said of Waterloo) that the western half of Canada became part of Canada.

Schultz's and Riel's first arrival and re-arrival at Red River may or may not have happened in different years than this story has it. Most historical articles on Schultz (there is no full biography, and likely never will be) state that he had already spent a summer at Red River a year or two before he came to stay in 1861. But it did and does seem odd to me that someone who had a summer off between university terms (that's how the story goes) would jaunt off to a place that took at least six weeks to get there and the same to get back. It may be some confusion around the fact that another brother of Henry McKenney's, Eliza's father, was at Red River for a short time in early days; one of those grey areas. Anyway, I needed to start the story with someone seeing Red River for the first time, and it was a great, documented set-up that the 1861 steamboat ran aground and Schultz hitchhiked a horse, so…

As for Riel's first appearance in this story, there is a document in the Public Archives of Manitoba unequivocally stating that Louis Riel Jr. arrived back at Red River in the summer of 1868, not late in 1867 as I have it. But since the document also unequivocally states that he arrived by steamboat, and there were no steamboats on the Red from 1863 till definitely 1870…

I did a bit of fudging around the arrival of Agnes Campbell Farquharson at Red River. It seems that her father had already been in Rupert's Land for some years earlier, possibly, while the rest of the family (whatever 'the family' was) languished in Indiana or somewhere, maybe. It's all a bit murky. So I settled for the documented fact that James Farquharson and his two daughters showed up at Red River from St. Paul in the summer of 1864.

Lady Schultz in later years said that the reason they'd left British Guiana was her sister had consumption and a doctor said a northern climate would be better for her health. Which sounds much more genteel than 'heading for the goldfields,' but doesn't add up at all with the Farquharson family's material circumstances. In the decades after 1870, though, it wasn't politic to ask too many questions about the people who'd become the Ascendency, as I hope I suggested in the prologue through Colin Inkster. It wasn't until years after both Sir John and Lady Schultz were dead that anyone had the temerity to send a query to Queen's University about their alumni records of John Christian Schultz. There are hints in various old writings that the people who'd lived at Red River before it became Winnipeg had their doubts about 'Dr.' Schultz's medical degree, but as I said about 'politic'…

Various versions of Schultz's escape from Fort Garry say his wife baked either a knife or a knife and a gimlet into either a cake or a pudding. In those days hacksaw blades in cakes weren't a cartoon cliché from old prison movies, but they are today, so I thought I'd better come up with something else lest the Metis guards seem like total idiots. There are all kinds of contradictory second- and third-hand accounts of where Schultz went that night and how he got there, after he'd hobbled away from the walls of Fort Garry. I went with the firsthand account in a book by R.G. MacBeth, who was a schoolboy having breakfast when his father answered the door. And, yes, R.G.'s older brother's favourite horse was named Barney.

Now as I've patted myself on the back with all the evidentiary back-up for this book (well, not *all*, that'd take up more pages than the story, but enough to maybe give the general gist) I guess it's fess-up time. Those who look closely (please don't) will notice that the nine years the story covers actually happens in eight years, I did a little fudging and compressing in the middle. I also made John Black the Reverend Doctor Black some years before he actually got his DD, partly to help distinguish him from Judge John Black and partly because countryboy Jimmy Dean had a novelty hit in the 1960s with *The Reverend Mister Black* and I didn't want readers of a certain age with packrat memories to get confused. And the building John

Sutherland was putting up in Winnipeg wasn't exactly where I placed it; I initially misread some scrawled numbers on a very old map, and when I realised my mistake decided that if I re-placed it the things that needed to happen would have to happen in ways as convoluted as this sentence and a couple of hundred yards weren't that much difference.

Wrapping-up time. Lady Agnes Campbell Farquharson Schultz outlived her husband by more than thirty years and passed the time by polishing his legacy and financing charitable works. The large collection of documents titled *The Schultz Papers* she donated to the Public Archives of Manitoba contains virtually nothing of an even remotely personal nature, just business and legislative correspondence, texts of speeches, etc. It's as if Schultz and Agnes didn't exist except as their official personages and titles. Or maybe Lady Schultz culled the papers to make it appear that way, which I suppose amounts to the same thing. What little 'personal correspondence' she included serves a political posterity agenda, such as a letter from Schultz to an acquaintance saying essentially: "I wasn't at that riot – horse pulled up lame – but I have no doubt the French started it."

Lady Schultz also apparently wrote several wee books, sized for Victorian ladies' reticules. I say 'apparently' because I've only been able to get my hands on one: *On Providing Good Reading For Children*. It advises mothers that children under the age of twelve shouldn't read or hear any kinds of fairytales or adventure stories or such-like flights of fancy, because they're too young to know the difference between truth and fiction. Young children should only be exposed to Bible stories, which are just as exciting as any fiction but are true. I'm guessing that the rest of Lady Schultz's oeuvre are of the same ilk: a childless woman telling other women how to raise their children.

A long-time houseguest in Lady Schultz's Winnipeg mansion, in one of North America's first gated communities, was Dr. Walter Bown, ex-owner and -publisher of *The Nor'Wester*. He went through rather an embarrassing trial when his sister launched a court case that his inheritance should be put in the hands of trustees, because he was mentally incompetent. He won his court case, largely because of a star witness attesting he was perfectly rational: Lady Schultz. When Dr. Bown deceased, his will left his entire estate to... you guessed it: Lady Schultz.

John Sutherland sat in the Canadian Senate for twenty-five years as an Independent Conservative – meaning he'd been appointed by a Conservative government but had no intention of toeing the party line. In those days the only way a Senator could be removed from office, outside of dying, was if he failed to put in an appearance for two years running. When Senator Sutherland's two years were up, the official announcement was that he'd ceased attending because of ill health, and it is true he died a few years later – but all he'd had to do to keep his impressive title and his commodious salary was take a leisurely First Class train ride to Ottawa once every two years, sign the roll and head back home. Sounds suspiciously to me like he just got fed up.

It was said that Senator John Sutherland didn't often take the floor and when he did it was usually to offer a calming compromise when things were getting out of hand. The obituaries stated that the one subject that got Senator Sutherland's dander up was any proposal to separate public schools into French/Catholic and English/Protestant. He seemed to think it unhealthy for children to grow up thinking of each other as The Other. Oddly coincidentally, or maybe not so oddly, in Louis Riel's last speech to the jury trying him for Treason in 1885, he said his dearest hope was that someday 'my children's children will shake hands with the Protestants of the new world in a friendly manner.'

Oh, there's one more major character in the story I should do an 'and then' about: Point Douglas herself. Point Douglas did become the railway terminal, and made a lot of money for a lot of people. For some years in the early 20th century, Point Douglas was also a gold mine of another kind: the only legalized Red Light District in North America.

Closing time. I'd intended to write this book twenty years ago, as the second volume of what my publisher at the time christened The Red River Trilogy, which I'd always planned to be a tetralogy, even though my spell-checker tells me it doesn't exist. But my publisher convinced me to deal with other stories first – amazing how convincing people can be when they're signing the cheques – and then circumstances kept pushing other projects in my way. It may be that my then-publisher and circumstances were doing me a favour. I would've approached this story differently twenty years ago. For one thing, I would've villainized the Schultzes, when, after all, they were just hungry – and very entertaining, from a distance. For another thing, it wasn't until just a few years ago that an old friend who died too young put me in mind that Hugh Sutherland might've borne some resemblance to the boy I spent summers with chasing girls through the woods and falling out of canoes. I'm still treading water, Patrick.